Great Stories of
Mystery
and
Suspense

Great Stories of
Mystery
and
Suspense

Selected and condensed by the editors of
The Reader's Digest

The Reader's Digest Association
Pleasantville, New York
Montreal, Sydney, Cape Town, Hong Kong

CONTENTS

The Lady
in the Lake

A CONDENSATION OF
THE BOOK BY

Raymond
Chandler

ILLUSTRATED BY HOWARD ROGERS

It was the body of a woman that floated up from the bottom of the lake. Long submersion and the fish had made it impossible to identify her. The horror-struck man standing beside detective Philip Marlowe was certain it was his wife, but Marlowe had been sent up to the lake to find someone else. Who was the lady in the lake? The answer to this intriguing conundrum sends the tough, cynical private eye on a search that takes him high up into the California mountains and down into the back alleys and mean streets of Los Angeles.

Raymond Chandler, author of such highly acclaimed mystery classics as *Farewell, My Lovely* and *The Long Goodbye*, is at his best here in this unforgettable tale of terror.

Chapter 1

THE Treloar Building was, and is, on Olive Street, near Sixth, on the west side. The sidewalk in front of it had been built of black and white rubber blocks. They were taking them up now to give to the government, and a hatless pale man with a face like a building superintendent was watching the work and looking as if it was breaking his heart.

I went past him through an arcade of specialty shops into a vast black and gold lobby. The Gillerlain Company was on the seventh floor, behind swinging double plate-glass doors bound in platinum. Their reception room had a Chinese rug, dull silver walls, angular but elaborate furniture, sharp shiny bits of abstract sculpture on pedestals and a tall display in a triangular showcase in the corner. On tiers and steps and islands of shining mirror glass it seemed to contain every fancy bottle and box that had ever been designed. There were creams and powders and soaps and toilet waters for every season and occasion.

A neat little blonde sat off in a far corner at a small switchboard, behind a railing and well out of harm's way. At a flat desk in line with the doors was a tall, lean, dark-haired lovely whose name, according to the plaque on her desk, was Miss Adrienne Fromsett.

She wore a steel-gray business suit and under the jacket a dark blue shirt. On her wrist she wore a linked bracelet and no other jewelry. Her dark hair was parted and fell in loose but not unstudied waves. She had smooth ivory skin and rather severe eyebrows and large dark eyes that looked as if they might warm up at the right time and in the right place.

I put my plain card, the one without the tommy gun in the corner, on her desk and asked to see Mr. Derace Kingsley.

She looked at the card and said, "Have you an appointment?"

"No appointment."

"It's difficult to see Mr. Kingsley without an appointment."

That wasn't anything I could argue about.

"What is the nature of your business, Mr. Marlowe?"

"Personal."

"I see. Does Mr. Kingsley know you, Mr. Marlowe?"

"I don't think so. He may have heard my name. You might say I'm from Lieutenant M'Gee."

She put my card beside a pile of freshly typed letters. Then she leaned back and put one arm on the desk and tapped lightly with a small gold pencil.

"Mr. Kingsley is in conference. I'll send your card in when I have an opportunity."

I thanked her and went and sat in a chromium and leather chair that was a lot more comfortable than it looked. Time passed and silence descended on the scene. Nobody came in or went out. The minutes went by on tiptoe, with their fingers to their lips.

Half an hour and three or four cigarettes later a door opened behind Miss Fromsett's desk and two men came out laughing. A third man held the door for them and helped them laugh. They all shook hands heartily and the two men went across the office and out. The third man dropped the grin off his face and looked as if he had never grinned in his life. He was a tall bird in a gray suit and he didn't want any nonsense.

"Any calls?" he asked in a sharp bossy voice.

Miss Fromsett said softly, "A Mr. Marlowe to see you. From Lieutenant M'Gee. His business is personal."

"Never heard of him," the tall man barked. He took my card, didn't even glance at me, and went back into his office. His door closed on the pneumatic closer and made a sound like "phooey." I ate another cigarette and more time staggered by. Ten minutes later the same door opened again and the big shot came out with his hat on and sneered that he was going to get a haircut. He started off across the Chinese rug in a swinging athletic stride, made about half the distance to the door, and then did a sharp cutback and came over to where I was sitting.

"You want to see me?" he barked.

I stood up. "If you're Mr. Derace Kingsley."

He was about six feet two and not much of it soft. His eyes were stone gray with flecks of cold light in them. He filled a large size in smooth gray flannel with a narrow chalk stripe, and his manner said he was very tough to get along with.

"Who's M'Gee?" he snapped.

"He's just a fellow I know."

"I'm fascinated," he said, glancing back at Miss Fromsett. She liked it. She liked it very much. "Anything else you would care to let drop about him?"

"Well, they call him Violets M'Gee," I said. "On account of he chews little throat pastilles that smell of violets. He's a big man with soft silvery hair and a cute little mouth made to kiss babies with. When last seen he was wearing a neat blue suit, wide-toed brown shoes, gray homburg hat, and he was smoking opium in a short briar pipe."

"I don't like your manner," Kingsley said in a voice you could have cracked a Brazil nut on.

"That's all right," I said. "I'm not selling it."

He reared back as if I had hung a week-old mackerel under his nose. After a moment he turned his back on me and said over his shoulder, "I'll give you exactly three minutes. God knows why."

He burned the carpet back past Miss Fromsett's desk to his door, yanked it open, and let it swing to in my face. Miss Fromsett liked that too, but I thought there was a little sly laughter behind her eyes now.

THE PRIVATE OFFICE WAS everything a private office should be. It was long and dim and quiet and air-conditioned and its windows were shut and its gray venetian blinds half closed to keep out the July glare. Gray drapes matched the gray carpeting. There was a large black and silver safe in the corner and a row of low filing cases that exactly matched it.

Derace Kingsley marched briskly behind about eight hundred dollars' worth of executive desk and planted his backside in a tall leather chair. He reached himself a panatela out of a copper and mahogany box, then trimmed it and lit it with a fat copper desk lighter. He took his time about it. It didn't matter about my time. When he had finished this, he leaned back and blew a little smoke and said, "I'm a businessman. I don't fool around. You're a licensed detective your card says. Show me something to prove it."

I got my wallet out and handed him things to prove it. He looked at them and threw them back across the desk.

"I don't know M'Gee," he said. "I know Sheriff Petersen. I asked for the name of a reliable man to do a job. I suppose you are the man."

"M'Gee is in the Hollywood substation of the sheriff's office," I said. "You can check on that."

"Not necessary. I guess you might do, but don't get flip with me. And remember when I hire a man he's my man. He does exactly what I tell him and he keeps his mouth shut. Or he goes out fast. Is that clear? I hope I'm not too tough for you."

"Why not leave that an open question?" I said.

He frowned. He said sharply, "What do you charge?"

"Twenty-five a day and expenses. Plus eight cents a mile for my car."

"Absurd," he said. "Far too much. Fifteen a day flat. That's plenty. I'll pay the mileage, within reason. But no joyriding."

I blew a little gray cloud of cigarette smoke. He seemed surprised that I said nothing.

He leaned over the desk and pointed with his cigar. "I haven't hired you yet," he said, "but if I do, the job is confidential. No talking it over with your cop friends. Is that understood?"

"Just what do you want done, Mr. Kingsley?"

"What do you care? You handle all kinds of detective work, don't you?"

"Not all kinds," I said. "For one thing I don't do divorce business. And I get a hundred down as a retainer—from strangers."

"Well, well," he said, in a voice suddenly soft. "Well, well."

"And as for your being too tough for me, most of the clients start out either by weeping down my shirt or bawling me out to show who's boss. But usually they end up very reasonable—if they're still alive."

"Well, well," he said again, in the same soft voice. He stared at me level-eyed. "Do you lose very many of them?" he asked.

"Not if they treat me right," I said.

"Have a cigar," he said.

I took a cigar and put it in my pocket.

"I want you to find my wife," he said. "She's been missing for a month."

"Okay. I'll find your wife."

He patted his desk with both hands. He stared at me solidly. "I think you will at that," he said. Then he grinned. "I haven't been called down like that in years," he said.

I didn't say anything.

"Damn it all," he said, "I liked it. I liked it fine." He ran a hand through his thick dark hair. "She's been gone a whole month," he said. "From a cabin we have in the mountains. Near Puma Point. Do you know Puma Point?"

I said I knew Puma Point.

"Our place is three miles from the village," he went on. "It's on a private lake. Little Fawn Lake. There's a dam three of us put up to improve the property. I own the tract with two other men. My friends have cabins. I have a cabin and a man named Bill Chess lives with his wife in another cabin rent free and looks after the place. He's a disabled veteran with a pension. My wife went up the middle of May, came down twice for weekends, was due down the twelfth of June for a party and never showed up. I haven't seen her since."

"What have you done about it?" I asked.

"Nothing. Not a thing. I haven't even been up there."

I said, "Why?"

He pushed his chair back to get a locked drawer open. He took out a Postal Telegraph form and passed it over. The wire had been filed at El Paso on June 14 at 9:19 a.m. It was addressed to Derace Kingsley, 965 Carson Drive, Beverly Hills, and read:

AM CROSSING TO GET MEXICAN DIVORCE STOP WILL MARRY CHRIS STOP GOOD LUCK AND GOOD-BY CRYSTAL

I put this down on my side of the desk and he handed me a large and very clear snapshot on glazed paper which showed a man and a woman sitting on the sand under a beach umbrella. The man wore trunks and the woman something that looked like a very daring white sharkskin bathing suit. She was a slim blonde, young and shapely and smiling. The man was a hefty dark handsome lad with fine shoulders and legs, sleek dark hair and white teeth. Six feet of a standard type of home wrecker.

"That's Crystal," Kingsley said, "and that's Chris Lavery. She can have him and he can have her and to hell with them both."

I put the photo down on the telegram. "All right, what's the catch?" I asked him.

"There's no telephone up in the cabin," he said, "and there was nothing important about the affair she was coming down for. So the wire surprised me only mildly. Crystal and I have been washed up for years. She lives her life and I live mine. She has her own money and plenty of it. She plays around and I knew Lavery was one of her playmates. I might have been a little surprised that she would actually marry him, because the man is nothing but a professional chaser. But the picture looked all right so far, you understand?"

"And then?"

"Nothing for two weeks. Then the Prescott Hotel in San Bernardino got in touch with me and said a Packard Clipper registered to Crystal Grace Kingsley at my address was unclaimed in their garage and what about it. I told them to keep it and I sent them a check. The day before yesterday I met Lavery in front of the Athletic Club. He said he didn't know where Crystal was, that he hadn't gone away with her, hadn't seen her in two months, hadn't had any communication with her of any kind."

I said, "You believed him?"

"If I believed him," Kingsley said, "and I was probably wrong to do it—it wasn't because he's a fellow you have to believe. Far from it. It's because he's a no good son of a bitch who thinks it's smart to play around with his friends' wives and brag about it. I know this tomcat only too well. He rode a route for us for a while and he was in trouble all the time. He couldn't keep his hands off the office help. And apart from all that there was this wire from El Paso and I told him about it. Why would he think it worthwhile to lie about it?"

"She might have tossed him out on his can," I said. "That would have hurt him in his deep place—his Casanova complex."

Kingsley shook his head. "But there's another and very worrying angle. I have a good job here, but I can't stand scandal. I'd be out of here in a hurry if my wife got mixed up with the police."

"Police?"

"Among her other activities," Kingsley said grimly, "my wife occasionally finds time to lift things in department stores when she's been hitting the bottle too hard. We've had some pretty nasty scenes with store managers. So far I've been able to keep them from filing charges, but if something like that happened in a strange city where nobody knew her"—he lifted his hands and let them fall with a smack on the desk—"well, it might be a prison matter, mightn't it?"

"Has she ever been fingerprinted?"

"She's never been arrested," he said.

"That's not what I mean. Sometimes in large department stores they make it a condition of dropping shoplifting charges that you give them your prints. It scares the amateurs and builds up their file of kleptomaniacs. When the prints come in a certain number of times they call time on you."

"Nothing like that has happened to my knowledge," he said.

"Well, I think we might almost throw the shoplifting angle out of this for the time being," I said. I tapped the blue and white telegraph form. "And this is a month old. If what you are thinking about happened around that time, the case would have been settled by now. If it was a first offense, she would get off with a scolding and a suspended sentence."

Kingsley gave me a quick look and poured himself a drink to help him with his worrying. "You're making me feel a lot better," he said.

"There are too many other things that could have happened," I said. "That she did go away with Lavery and they split up. That she went with some other man and the wire is a gag. That she went away alone or with a woman. That she drank herself over the edge and is holed up in some private sanatorium taking a cure. That she got into some jam. That she met with foul play."

"Good God, don't say that!" Kingsley exclaimed.

"Why not? You've got to consider it. I get a very vague idea of Mrs. Kingsley—that she is young, pretty, reckless and wild. That she drinks and does dangerous things when she drinks. That she is a sucker for the men and might take up with a stranger who might turn out to be a crook. Does that fit?"

He nodded. "Every word of it."

"How much money would she have with her?"

"She liked to carry enough. She had her own bank and her own bank account. She could have any amount of money."

"Any children?"

"No children."

"Do you have the management of her affairs?"

He shook his head. "She hasn't any—except depositing checks and drawing out money and spending it. And her money certainly never does me any good, if that's what you are thinking."

I gathered my exhibits together and put them away in my pockets. "There are more angles to this than I can even see now," I said, "but I'll start by talking to Lavery and then taking a run up to Little Fawn Lake and asking questions there. I'll need Lavery's

18

address and a note to your man in charge at the mountain place."

He got a letterhead out of his desk and wrote and passed it over. I read:

Dear Bill: This will introduce Mr. Philip Marlowe who wishes to look over the property. Please show him my cabin and assist him in every way. Yours, Derace Kingsley.

I folded this up and put it in the envelope he had addressed while I was reading it. "How about the other cabins up there?" I asked.

"Nobody up this year so far. One man's in government service in Washington and the other is at Fort Leavenworth."

"Now Lavery's address," I said.

He looked at a point well above the top of my head. "In Bay City. I could find the house but I forget the address. Miss Fromsett can give it to you, I think. She needn't know why you want it. She probably will. And you want a hundred dollars, you said."

"That's all right," I said. "That's just something I said when you were tramping on me."

He grinned. I stood up and hesitated by the desk, looking at him. "You're not holding anything back, are you?"

"No. I'm not holding anything back. I'm worried and I want to know where she is. If you get anything at all, call me anytime, day or night."

I said I would do that. We shook hands and I went back out to where Miss Fromsett sat elegantly at her desk.

"Mr. Kingsley thinks you can give me Chris Lavery's address," I told her and watched her face.

She reached very slowly for a brown leather address book and turned the leaves. Her voice was tight and cold when she spoke.

"The address we have is 623 Altair Street, in Bay City. Telephone Bay City 12523. Mr. Lavery has not been with us for more than a year. He may have moved."

I thanked her and went on to the door. From there I glanced back at her. She was sitting very still, with her hands clasped on

19

her desk, staring into space. A couple of red spots burned in her cheeks. Her eyes were remote and bitter.

I got the impression that Mr. Chris Lavery was not a pleasant thought to her.

Chapter 2

ALTAIR Street lay on the edge of the V forming the inner end of a deep canyon. To the north was the cool blue sweep of the bay out to the point above Malibu. To the south the beach town of Bay City was spread out on a bluff above the coast highway.

The street was only three or four blocks long and ended in a tall iron fence enclosing a large estate. On the inland side of Altair Street the houses were well kept and fairly large, but the few scattered bungalows on the edge of the canyon were nothing much. In one short half block were only two houses, on opposite sides of the street and almost directly across from each other. The smaller was number 623.

The house was built downward, one of those clinging vine effects, with the front door a little below street level, the patio on the roof, the bedrooms in the basement, and a garage like the corner pocket on a pool table. The door was narrow, grilled and topped by a lancet arch. Below the grille there was an iron knocker. I hammered on it.

Nothing happened. I pushed the bell at the side of the door and heard it ring inside not very far off and waited and nothing happened. I went along to the garage and lifted the door far enough to see that a car with white sidewall tires was inside. I went back to the front door.

A neat black Cadillac coupe came out of the garage across the way, backed, turned, and came along past Lavery's house, slowed, and a thin man in dark glasses looked at me sharply, as if I hadn't any business being there. I glared back and he went on his way.

I did some more hammering on Lavery's knocker. This time I got results. The judas window opened and I was looking at a handsome bright-eyed number through the bars of the grille.

"You make a hell of a lot of noise," a voice called.

"Mr. Lavery?"

He said he was Mr. Lavery and what about it. I poked a card through the grille. A large brown hand took the card. The bright brown eyes came back and the voice said, "So sorry. Not needing any detectives today please."

"I'm working for Derace Kingsley."

"The hell with both of you," he said, and banged the judas window.

I leaned on the bell until the door was yanked open and a big guy in bathing trunks, beach sandals, and a white terry-cloth bathrobe started to come out at me.

I took my thumb off the bell and grinned at him. "What's the matter?" I asked him. "Scared?"

"Ring that bell again," he said, "and I'll throw you clear across the street."

"Don't be childish," I told him. "You know perfectly well I'm going to talk to you and you're going to talk to me."

I got the blue and white telegram out of my pocket and held it up in front of his bright brown eyes. He read it morosely, chewed his lip and growled, "Oh for God's sake, come on in then."

He held the door wide and I went in past him, into a dim pleasant room with an apricot rug that looked expensive, deep-sided chairs, a number of white drum lamps, a big Capehart in the corner, a long and very wide davenport in pale tan mohair with dark brown, and a fireplace with a copper screen and an overmantel in white wood. A fire was laid behind the screen and partly masked by a large spray of manzanita bloom. There was a bottle of Vat 69 and glasses on a tray and a copper ice bucket on a low round burl walnut table with a glass top.

Lavery swung the door shut and sat on the davenport. He grabbed a cigarette out of a hammered silver box and lit it and looked at me irritably.

I sat down opposite him and looked him over. He had everything in the way of good looks the snapshot had indicated. His eyes were chestnut brown and the whites of them slightly gray white. His hair was rather long and curled a little over his temples.

I could understand that women would think he was something to yell for.

"Why not tell us where Mrs. Kingsley is?" I said. "We'll find out eventually anyway and if you tell us now, we won't be bothering you."

"Look," he said, leaning forward and pointing his cigarette at me. "I know what that wire says, but it's the bunk. I didn't go to El Paso with Crystal Kingsley. I haven't seen her in a long time—long before the date of that wire. I told Kingsley that."

"He didn't have to believe you."

"Why would I lie to him?" He looked surprised.

"If you didn't go to El Paso with her," I said, "why did she send this telegram?"

"I haven't the faintest idea."

"You can do better than that," I said. I pointed to the manzanita in the fireplace. "You pick that up at Little Fawn Lake?"

"The hills around here are full of manzanita," he snapped.

"It doesn't bloom like that down here."

He laughed. "I was up there the third week in May. If you have to know. That's the last time I saw her."

"You didn't have any idea of marrying her?"

He blew smoke and said through it, "I've thought of it, yes. She has money. Money is always useful. But it would be too tough a way to make it."

"This wire has to mean something," I said stubbornly.

"It's probably just a gag. She's full of little tricks like that. All of them silly, and some of them vicious."

"I don't see any point in this one."

He flicked cigarette ash carelessly at the glass-top table, then gave me a quick glance and immediately looked away.

"I stood her up," he said slowly. "It might be her idea of a way to get back at me. I was supposed to run up there one weekend. I didn't go. I was—sick of her."

I said, "Uh-huh," and gave him a long steady stare. "I don't like that so well. I'd like it better if you did go to El Paso with her and had a fight and split up. Could you tell it that way?"

He flushed solidly behind the sunburn. "Damn it," he said, "I told you I didn't go anywhere with her. Not anywhere. Can't you remember that?"

"I'll remember it when I believe it."

He leaned over to snuff out his cigarette. He stood up with an easy movement, not hurried at all, pulled the belt of his robe tight, and moved out to the end of the davenport.

"All right," he said in a clear tight voice. "Out you go. Take the air. And don't bother coming back. I won't be at home."

I went over to the door and pulled it open. "I may have to come back," I said. "But it won't be just to swap gags. It'll be because I find out something that needs talking over."

"So you still think I'm lying," he said savagely.

"I think you have something on your mind. I've looked at too many faces not to know. It may not be any of my business. If it is, you're likely to have to throw me out again."

"A pleasure," he said. "And bring somebody to drive you home. In case you land on your fanny and knock your brains out."

"So long, beautiful hunk," I said, and left him standing there. I closed the door and went up the path to the street. I stood on the sidewalk looking at the house across the way.

It was a wide shallow house with rose stucco walls faded out to a pleasant pastel shade and trimmed with dull green at the window frames. The roof was of green tiles, round rough ones. Outside the wall to the left was the three-car garage, with a door opening inside the yard and a concrete path going from there to a side door of the house.

Set into the gatepost was a bronze tablet which read: ALBERT S. ALMORE, M.D.

While I was standing there staring across the street, the black Cadillac I had already seen came purring around the corner and then down the block. It went into the empty third of the garage across the way.

The thin man in sunglasses went along the sidewalk to the house, carrying a double-handled doctor's bag. Halfway along he slowed

23

down to stare across at me. I went along toward my car. At the house he used a key and as he opened the door he looked across at me again.

I got into the Chrysler and sat there smoking and trying to make up my mind whether it was worthwhile hiring somebody to put a tail on Lavery. I decided it wasn't, not the way things looked so far.

Curtains moved at a lower window close to the side door where Dr. Almore had gone in. A thin hand held them aside and I caught the glint of light on glasses. They were held aside for quite some time, before they fell together again.

I wondered idly if the doctor knew Lavery and how well. He probably knew him, since theirs were the only two houses in the block. But being a doctor, he wouldn't tell me anything about him. As I looked, the curtains which had been lifted apart were now completely drawn aside.

Behind the middle segment of the triple window Dr. Almore stood staring across my way, with a sharp frown on his thin face. I shook cigarette ash out of the window and he turned abruptly and sat down at a desk. His hand reached for the telephone, touched it and came away again. He lit a cigarette, shook the match violently, then strode to the window and stared out at me again.

I was reaching down to turn the ignition key when Lavery's front door opened. I took my hand away and leaned back again. Lavery came briskly up the walk of his house, shot a glance down the street, and turned to go into his garage. He had a rough towel and a steamer rug over his arm. I heard the garage door lift up, then the car door open and shut, then the grind and cough of the motor starting. It was a cute little blue convertible, with the top folded down and Lavery's sleek dark head rising just above it. He was wearing a natty pair of sun goggles with very wide white sidepieces. The convertible swooped off down the block and danced around the corner.

I gave my attention back to Dr. Almore. He was on the telephone now, not talking, holding it to his ear, smoking and waiting. Then he leaned forward as you do when the voice comes back, listened, hung up and wrote something on a pad in front of him. Then a heavy book with yellow sides appeared on his desk and he opened it just about in the middle. While he was doing this he gave one quick look out of the window, straight at the Chrysler.

He found his place in the book, wrote something else, put the book away, and grabbed for the telephone again. He dialed, waited, began to speak quickly, pushing his head down and making gestures in the air with his cigarette.

He finished his call and hung up. He leaned back and sat there brooding, staring down at his desk, but not forgetting to look out the window every half minute. He was waiting, and I waited with him, for no reason at all. Doctors make many phone calls, talk to many people. But there was something about his behavior that intrigued me. I looked at my watch, decided it was time to get something to eat, lit another cigarette and still didn't move.

It took about five minutes. Then a green sedan whisked around the corner and bore down the block. It coasted to a stop in front of Dr. Almore's house and its tall buggy-whip aerial quivered. A big man with dusty blond hair got out and went up to Dr. Almore's front door. He rang the bell.

The door opened and he went into the house. An invisible hand gathered the curtains at Dr. Almore's study window and blanked the room. I sat there and stared at the sun-darkened lining of the curtains. More time trickled by.

The front door opened again and the big man loafed casually down the steps and through the gate. He shrugged once and walked diagonally across the street. His steps in the quiet were leisurely and distinct. Dr. Almore's curtains moved apart again behind him. Dr. Almore stood in his window and watched.

A big freckled hand appeared on the sill of the car door at my elbow. A large deeply lined face hung above it. The man had eyes of metallic blue. He looked at me solidly and spoke in a deep harsh voice.

"Waiting for somebody?" he asked.

"I don't know," I said. "Am I?"

"I'll ask the questions."

25

"Well, I'll be damned," I said. "So that's the answer to the pantomime."

"What pantomime?" He gave me a hard level unfriendly stare.

I pointed across the street with my cigarette. "Nervous Nellie and the telephone. Calling the cops, after first getting my name from the auto club, probably, then looking it up in the city directory. What goes on?"

"Let me see your driver's license."

I leaned down and turned my ignition key and pressed the starter. The motor caught and idled down.

"Cut that motor," he said savagely, and put his foot on the running board.

I cut the motor and leaned back and looked at him.

"Damn it," he said, "do you want me to drag you out of there and bounce you on the pavement?"

I got my wallet out and handed it to him. He drew the celluloid pocket out and looked at my driver's license, then turned the pocket over and looked at the photostat of my other license on the back. He rammed it contemptuously back into the wallet and handed it to me. I put it away. His hand dipped and came up with a blue and gold police badge.

"Degarmo, detective lieutenant," he said in his brutal voice.

"Pleased to meet you, Lieutenant."

"Skip it. Now tell me why you're here casing Almore's place."

"I'm not casing Almore's place, as you put it, Lieutenant. I never heard of Dr. Almore and I don't know of any reason why I should want to case his house."

"Her folks hire you?" he asked suddenly.

I shook my head.

"The last boy that tried it ended up on the road gang."

"If only I could guess," I said. "Tried what?"

"Tried to put the bite on him," he said thinly.

"Too bad I don't know how," I said. "He looks like an easy man to bite."

"That line of talk don't buy you anything," he said.

"All right," I agreed. "Let's put it this way. I don't know Dr.

Almore, never heard of him, and I'm not interested in him. I'm down here visiting a friend and looking at the view. If I'm doing anything else, it doesn't happen to be any of your business. If you don't like that, the best thing to do is to take it down to headquarters and see the day captain."

He moved a foot heavily on the running board and looked doubtful. "Straight goods?" he asked slowly.

"Straight goods."

"Aw hell, the guy's screwy," he said suddenly and looked back over his shoulder at the house. "He ought to see a doctor." He laughed, without any amusement in the laugh. He took his foot off my running board and rumpled his wiry hair.

"Go on—beat it," he said. "Stay off our reservation, and you won't make any enemies."

I pressed the starter again, let the clutch in, and drove away. Back in Los Angeles I ate lunch and went up to my office in the Cahuenga Building to see what mail there was. I called Kingsley from there.

"I saw Lavery," I told him. "He told me just enough dirt to sound frank. I tried to needle him a little, but nothing came of it. I still like the idea that they quarreled and split up and that he hopes to fix it up with her yet."

"Then he must know where she is," Kingsley said.

"He might, but it doesn't follow. By the way, a rather curious thing happened to me on Lavery's street. There are only two houses. The other belongs to a Dr. Almore." I told him briefly about the rather curious thing.

He was silent for a moment at the end and then he said, "Is this Dr. Albert Almore?"

"Yes."

"He was Crystal's doctor for a time. He came to the house several times when she was—well, when she had been overdrinking. I thought him a little too quick with a hypodermic needle. His wife—let me see, there was something about his wife. Oh yes, she committed suicide."

I said, "When?"

27

"I don't remember. Quite a long time ago. I never knew them socially. What are you going to do now?"

I told him I was going up to Puma Lake, although it was a little late in the day to start.

He said I would have plenty of time and that they had an hour more of daylight in the mountains.

I said that was fine and we hung up.

Chapter 3

SAN Bernardino baked and shimmered in the afternoon heat. The air was hot enough to blister my tongue. I drove through it gasping, stopped long enough to buy a pint of liquor in case I fainted before I got to the mountains, and started up the long grade to Crestline. In fifteen miles the road climbed five thousand feet, but even then it was far from cool. Thirty miles of mountain driving brought me to the tall pines and a place called Bubbling Springs. It had a clapboard store and a gas pump, but it felt like paradise. From there on it was cool all the way.

The Puma Lake dam had an armed sentry at each end and one in the middle. The first one I came to had me close all the windows of the car before crossing over the dam. About a hundred yards from the dam a rope with cork floats barred the pleasure boats from coming any closer. Beyond these details World War II did not seem to have done anything much to Puma Lake.

Canoes paddled about on the blue water and rowboats with outboard motors put-putted and speedboats showing off like fresh kids made wide swaths of foam and turned on a dime and girls in them shrieked and dragged their hands in the water.

The road skimmed along a high granite outcrop and dropped to meadows of coarse grass in which grew what was left of the summer's wild flowers. Tall yellow pines probed at the clear blue sky. Then the road dropped again to lake level. People on bicycles wobbled cautiously over the highway and now and then an anxious-looking bird thumped past on a power scooter.

A mile from the village the highway was joined by a lesser road which curved back into the mountains. A rough wooden marker under the highway sign said: LITTLE FAWN LAKE 1¾ MILES. I took it. Presently another very narrow road debouched from this one and another rough wooden sign said: LITTLE FAWN LAKE. PRIVATE ROAD. NO TRESPASSING.

I turned the Chrysler into this and crawled carefully around huge bare granite rocks and past a little waterfall and through a maze of black oak trees and ironwood and manzanita and silence. I came to a five-barred gate and another sign.

Beyond the gate the road wound for a couple of hundred yards and then suddenly below me was a small oval lake deep in trees and rocks and wild grass, like a drop of dew caught in a curled leaf. At the near end of it was a rough concrete dam with a rope handrail across the top, and at the side stood a small cabin of native pine with the bark on it.

Across the lake, the long way by the road and the short way by the top of the dam, a large redwood cabin overhung the water and farther along, each well separated from the others, were two other cabins. All three were shut up and quiet, with drawn curtains. The big one had orange-yellow venetian blinds and a twelve-paned window facing on the lake. At the far end of the lake was what looked like a small pier.

I got out of the car and started down toward the nearest cabin. Somewhere behind it an axe thudded. I pounded on the cabin door. The axe stopped. A man's voice yelled from somewhere. I sat down on a rock and lit a cigarette. Steps came around the corner of the cabin, uneven steps. A man with a harsh face and a swarthy skin came into view carrying a double-bitted axe.

He was heavily built and not very tall and he limped as he walked, giving his right leg a little kick out with each step and swinging the foot in a shallow arc. He had a dark unshaven chin and steady blue eyes and grizzled hair that curled over his ears and needed cutting badly. He wore blue denim pants and a blue shirt open on a brown muscular neck. A cigarette hung from the corner of his mouth. He spoke in a tight tough city voice.

"Yeah?"

"Mr. Bill Chess?"

"That's me."

I stood up and got Kingsley's note out of my pocket and handed it to him. He squinted at it, then clumped into the cabin and came back with glasses. He read the note carefully and then again. He put it in his shirt pocket and buttoned the flap of the pocket.

He put his hand out. "Pleased to meet you, Mr. Marlowe."

We shook hands. He had a hand like a wood rasp.

"You want to see Kingsley's cabin, huh? Glad to show you. He ain't selling, is he?" He eyed me steadily and jerked a thumb across the lake.

"He might," I said. "Everything's for sale in California."

"Ain't that the truth! That's his—the redwood job. Lined with knotty pine, composition roof, stone foundations and porches, full bath and shower, venetian blinds all around, big fireplace, oil stove in the big bedroom—everything first class. And private reservoir in the hills for water."

"How about electric light and telephone?" I asked.

"Electric light, sure. No phone. You couldn't get one now with the war and all. If you could, it would cost plenty to string the lines out here."

He looked at me with steady blue eyes and I looked at him. In spite of his weathered appearance he looked like a drinker.

I said, "Anybody living there now?"

"Nope. Mrs. Kingsley was here a few weeks back. She went down the hill. Back any day, I guess. Didn't he say?"

I looked surprised. "Why? Does she go with the cabin?"

He scowled and then put his head back and burst out laughing.

"If that ain't a kick in the pants!" he gasped. "Does she go with the—" He put out another bellow and then his mouth shut tight as a trap.

"The beds in the cabin comfortable?" I asked.

He leaned forward. "Maybe you'd like a face full of knuckles," he snarled. "How would I know if the beds are comfortable?"

"I don't know why you wouldn't know," I said. "I won't press the point. I can find out for myself."

"Yeah," he said bitterly, "think I can't smell a dick when I meet one? Nuts to you, pal. And nuts to Kingsley. So he hires himself a dick to come up here and see am I wearing his pajamas, huh?"

I put a hand out, hoping he wouldn't pull it off and throw it in the lake.

"You're slipping your clutch," I told him. "I didn't come up here to inquire into your love life. I never saw Mrs. Kingsley. I never saw Mr. Kingsley until this morning. What the hell's the matter with you?"

He dropped his eyes and rubbed the back of his hand viciously across his mouth, as if he wanted to hurt himself.

"Sorry, Mr. Marlowe," he said slowly. "I was out on the roof last night and I've got a hangover like seven Swedes. I've been up here alone for a month and it's got me talking to myself. A thing happened to me."

"Anything a drink would help?"

His eyes focused sharply on me and glinted. "You got one?"

I pulled the pint of rye out of my pocket and held it so that he could see the green label over the cap.

"I don't deserve it," he said. "Damn it, I don't. Wait till I get a couple of glasses, or would you come into the cabin?"

"I like it out here. I'm enjoying the view."

He swung his stiff leg and went into his cabin and came back carrying a couple of small cheese glasses.

I tore the metal cap off the bottle and poured him a stiff drink and a light one for myself. We touched glasses and drank.

"Man that's from the right bottle," he said. "I wonder what made me sound off like that. I guess a guy gets the blues up here all alone. No company, no real friends, no wife." He paused and added with a sideways look, "Especially no wife."

I kept my eyes on the blue water of the tiny lake. Under an overhanging rock a fish surfaced in a lance of light and a circle of widening ripples.

"She left me," he said slowly. "She left me a month ago. Friday the twelfth of June. A day I'll remember."

I stiffened, but not too much to pour more whiskey into his

empty glass. Friday the twelfth of June was the day Mrs. Crystal Kingsley was supposed to have come into town for a party.

He drank and looked across the lake. "She was one swell kid," he said softly. "A little sharp in the tongue sometimes, but one swell kid. It was love at first sight with me and Muriel. I met her in a joint in Riverside, a year and three months ago. Not the kind of a joint where a guy would expect to meet a girl like Muriel, but that's how it happened. We got married. I loved her. And I was too much of a skunk to play ball with her."

I moved a little to show him I was still there, but I didn't say anything for fear of breaking the spell.

He went on sadly, "But you know how it is with marriage. After a while a guy like me wants to feel a leg. Some other leg. Maybe it's lousy, but that's the way it is."

He looked at me and I said I had heard the idea expressed.

He tossed his second drink off. I passed him the bottle.

"Yeah," Bill Chess said. "Here I am sitting pretty, no rent to pay, a pension check every month, half my bonus money in war bonds, I'm married to as neat a little blonde as ever you clapped an eye on, and all the time I'm nuts and I don't know it. I go for *that*." He pointed at the redwood cabin across the lake.

He drank his third drink and steadied the bottle on a rock. "Hell," he said, "you'd think if I had to jump off the dock, I'd go a little ways from home and pick me a change in types at least. But little roundheels over there ain't even that. She's a blonde like Muriel, same size and weight, same type, almost the same color eyes. But, brother, how different from then on in. Well, I'm over there burning trash that morning and minding my own business. And she comes to the back door of the cabin in peekaboo pajamas and says in her lazy, no-good voice, 'Have a drink, Bill. Don't work so hard on such a beautiful morning.' And me, I like a drink. So I go to the kitchen door and take it. And then I take another and another and then I'm in the house."

He paused and swept me with a hard level look.

"You asked me if the beds over there were comfortable and I got sore. You didn't mean a thing. I was just too full of remembering.

Yeah—the bed I was in was comfortable." He took a long savage drink out of the bottle and then screwed the cap on tightly, as if that meant something.

"I came back across the dam," he said slowly, in a voice already thick with alcohol. "I'm as smooth as a new pistonhead. I'm getting away with something. Us boys can be so wrong about those little things, can't we? I'm not getting away with anything at all. Not anything at all. I listen to Muriel telling me things about myself I didn't even imagine. Oh yeah, I'm getting away with it lovely."

"So she left you," I said, when he fell silent.

"That night. I wasn't even here. I felt too mean to stay even half sober. I hopped into my Ford and went over to the north side of the lake and holed up with a couple of no-goods like myself and got good and stinking. Along about four a.m. I got home and Muriel is gone, packed up and gone, nothing left but a note on the bureau and some cold cream on the pillow."

He pulled a dog-eared piece of paper out of a shabby old wallet and passed it over. It was written in pencil on blue-lined paper from a notebook. It read: "I'm sorry, Bill, but I'd rather be dead than live with you any longer. Muriel."

I handed it back. "What about over there?" I asked, pointing across the lake.

"Nothing over there," he said. "She packed up and went down the same night. I haven't heard a word from Muriel in the whole month, not a single word. I don't even have any idea where she's at."

He stood up and took keys out of his pocket and shook them. "So if you want to go across and look at Kingsley's cabin, there isn't a thing to stop you. And thanks for listening to the soap opera. And thanks for the liquor. Here." He picked the bottle up and handed me what was left of the pint.

WE WENT down the slope to the bank of the lake and the narrow top of the dam. Bill Chess swung his stiff leg in front of me, holding on to the rope handrail set in iron stanchions. At one point water washed over the concrete in a lazy swirl.

I followed him up a flight of heavy wooden steps to the porch of the Kingsley cabin. He unlocked the door and we went into hushed warmth. The living room was long and cheerful. It had Indian rugs, padded mountain furniture with metal-strapped joints, chintz curtains, a plain hardwood floor, plenty of lamps, and a little built-in bar with round stools in one corner. The room was neat and clean and had no look of having been left at short notice.

We went into the bedrooms. Two of them had twin beds and one a large double bed with a cream-colored spread having a design in plum-colored wool stitched over it. This was the master bedroom, Bill Chess said. On a dresser of varnished wood there were toilet articles and accessories. A couple of cold-cream jars had the wavy gold brand of the Gillerlain Company on them. One whole side of the room consisted of closets with sliding doors. I slid one open and peeked inside. It was full of women's clothes of the sort they wear at resorts. Bill Chess watched me sourly while I pawed over them. When I turned he was planted squarely in front of me, with his chin pushed out and his hard hands on his hips.

"So what did you want to look at the lady's clothes for?" he asked in an angry voice.

"Reasons," I said. "For instance Mrs. Kingsley didn't go home when she left here. Her husband hasn't seen her since. He doesn't know where she is."

He dropped his fists and twisted them slowly at his sides. "Dick it is," he snarled. "The first guess is always right. I had myself about talked out of it. Boy, did I open up to you."

"I can respect a confidence as well as the next fellow," I said, and walked around him into the kitchen.

There was a big combination range, an automatic water heater in the service porch, and opening off the other side of the kitchen a cheerful breakfast room with many windows and a plastic breakfast set. The shelves were gay with colored dishes and glasses and a set of pewter serving dishes.

Everything was in apple-pie order. There were no dirty cups or plates on the drainboard, no smeared glasses or empty liquor bottles hanging around.

34

I went back to the living room and out on the front porch again and waited for Bill Chess to lock up. When he had done that and turned back to me with his scowl well in place I said, "I didn't ask you to take your heart out and squeeze it for me. Kingsley doesn't have to know his wife made a pass at you, unless there's a lot more behind all this than I can see now."

"The hell with you," he said, and the scowl stayed right where it was.

"All right, the hell with me. Would there be any chance your wife and Kingsley's wife went away together?"

"I don't get it," he said.

"After you went to drown your troubles they could have had a fight and made up and cried on each other's shoulders. Then Mrs. Kingsley might have taken your wife down the hill. She had to have something to ride in, didn't she?"

"Nope. Muriel didn't cry on anyone's shoulder. They left the weeps out of Muriel. And as for transportation she has a Ford of her own. She couldn't drive mine easily on account of the way the controls are switched over for my stiff leg."

"It was just a passing thought," I said.

"If any more like it pass you, let them go right on," he said.

"Look, pal," I said, "I'm working hard to think you're a fundamentally good egg. Help me out a little, can't you?"

He breathed hard for a moment, then dropped his hands and spread them helplessly.

"Boy, can I brighten up anybody's afternoon." He sighed. "Want to walk back around the lake?"

"Sure, if your leg will stand it."

"Stood it plenty of times before."

We started off side by side, as friendly as puppies again. It would probably last all of fifty yards. The roadway, barely wide enough to pass a car, hung above the level of the lake and dodged between high rocks.

Bill Chess said after a minute or two, "That straight goods? Little roundheels lammed off?"

"So it seems."

"You a real dick or just a shamus?"

"Just a shamus."

"She go with some guy?"

"I should think it likely."

"Sure she did. It's a cinch. Kingsley ought to be able to guess that. She had plenty of friends."

"Up here?"

He didn't answer me.

"Was one of them named Lavery?"

"I wouldn't know," he said.

"There's no secret about this one," I said. "She sent a wire from El Paso saying she and Lavery were going to Mexico." I dug the wire out of my pocket and held it out. He fumbled his glasses loose from his shirt and stopped to read it.

"Lavery was up here once," he said slowly.

"He admits he saw her a couple of months ago, probably up here. Claims he hasn't seen her since. We don't know whether to believe him. No reason why we should and no reason why we shouldn't."

"She isn't with him now, then?"

"He says not."

"I wouldn't think she would fuss with little details like getting married," he said soberly. "A Florida honeymoon would be more in her line."

We had come to the end of the lake now. I walked out on the little pier and leaned on the wooden railing at the end of it. Bill Chess came and leaned on the railing at my side.

"Any fish in the lake?" I asked.

"Some smart old trout. No fresh stock. I don't go for fish much myself. I don't bother with them."

I stared down into the deep still water. Down below there was what looked like an underwater flooring. I couldn't see the sense of that. I asked him.

"Used to be a boat landing before the dam was raised. That lifted the water level so far the old landing was six feet under."

A flat-bottomed boat dangled from a frayed rope tied to a post of the pier. It lay in the water almost without motion, but not quite. The air was peaceful and calm and sunny and held a quiet you don't get in cities.

There was a hard movement at my side and Bill Chess said, "Look there!" in a voice that growled like mountain thunder.

He was bending far out over the railing, staring down like a loon, his hard fingers digging into the flesh of my arm. I looked down with him into the water at the edge of the submerged staging.

Languidly at the edge of this green and sunken shelf of wood something waved out from the darkness, hesitated, waved back again out of sight under the flooring.

The something had looked far too much like a human arm.

Bill Chess straightened his body rigidly. He turned without a sound and clumped back along the pier. He bent to a loose pile of stones and heaved. He got a big one free and lifted it breast-high and started back out on the pier with it. It must have weighed a hundred pounds. He reached the end of the pier and steadied himself and lifted the rock high. His mouth made a vague distressful sound and his body lurched forward hard against the quivering rail and the heavy stone smashed down into the water.

The splash it made went over both of us. The rock fell straight and true and struck on the edge of the submerged planking, almost exactly where we had seen the thing wave in and out.

For a moment the water was a confused boiling, then the ripples widened off into the distance and there was a dim sound as of wood breaking underwater. An ancient rotted plank popped suddenly through the surface, stuck out a full foot of its jagged end, and fell back with a flat slap and floated off.

The depths cleared again. Something moved in them that was not a board. It rose slowly, with an infinitely careless languor, and broke surface casually, lightly, without haste. I saw wool, sodden and black, a leather jerkin blacker than ink, a pair of slacks. I saw a wave of dark blond hair straighten out in the water and hold still for a brief instant as if with a calculated effect, and then swirl into a tangle again.

The thing rolled over once more and an arm flapped up barely

above the skin of the water and the arm ended in a bloated hand. Then the face came. A swollen pulpy gray-white mass without features, without eyes, without mouth. A blotch of gray dough, a nightmare with human hair on it.

A heavy necklace of green stones showed on what had been a neck, half imbedded, large rough green stones with something that glittered joining them together.

Bill Chess held the handrail and his knuckles were polished bones. "Muriel!" his voice said croakingly. "Good God, it's Muriel!"

Chapter 4

BEHIND the window of the board shack one end of a counter was piled with dusty folders. The glass upper half of the door was lettered in flaked black paint: CHIEF OF POLICE. FIRE CHIEF. TOWN CONSTABLE. CHAMBER OF COMMERCE. In the lower corners a USO card and a Red Cross emblem were fastened to the glass.

I went in. There was a potbellied stove in the corner and a rolltop desk in the other corner behind the counter. There was a large blueprint map of the district on the wall and beside that a board with four hooks on it, one of which supported a frayed and much mended mackinaw.

A man sat at the desk in a wooden armchair whose legs were anchored to flat boards, fore and aft, like skis. A spittoon big enough to coil a hose in was leaning against the man's right leg. He had a sweat-stained stetson on the back of his head and his large hairless hands were clasped comfortably over his stomach. His hair was mousy brown except at the temples, where it was the color of old snow. He sat more on his left hip than his right, because there was a hip holster down inside his right hip pocket, and a half foot of .45 gun reared up and bored into his solid back. The star on his left breast had a bent point.

He had large ears and friendly eyes and his jaws munched slowly. He looked as dangerous as a squirrel and much less nervous. I liked everything about him.

I lit a cigarette and looked around for an ashtray.

"Try the floor, son," the large friendly man said.

"Are you Sheriff Patton?"

"Constable and deputy sheriff. What law we got to have around here I'm it. Come election anyways. There's a couple of good boys running against me this time and I might get whupped."

"Nobody's going to whip you," I said. "You're going to get a lot of publicity."

"That so?" he asked indifferently and ruined the spittoon.

"That is, if your jurisdiction extends over to Little Fawn Lake."

"Kingsley's place. Sure. Something bothering over there?"

"There's a dead woman in the lake."

That shook him to the core. He unclasped his hands and scratched one ear. He got to his feet by grasping the arms of his chair and deftly kicking it back from under him. Standing up he was a big man and hard.

"Anybody I know?" he inquired uneasily.

"Muriel Chess. I guess you know her. Bill Chess's wife."

"Yep, I know Bill Chess." His voice hardened a little.

"Looks like suicide. She left a note which sounded as if she was just going away. But it could be a suicide note just as well. She's not nice to look at. Been in the water a long time, about a month, judging by the circumstances."

He scratched his other ear. "What circumstances would that be?"

"They had a fight a month ago. Bill went over to the north shore of the lake and was gone some hours. When he got home she was gone. He never saw her again."

"I see. Who are you, son?"

"My name is Philip Marlowe. I'm up from L.A. to look at the property. I had a note from Kingsley to Bill Chess. He took me around the lake and we went out on that little pier. We were leaning on the rail and looking down into the water when something that looked like an arm waved out under the old boat landing. Bill dropped a heavy rock in and the body popped up."

Patton looked at me without moving a muscle.

"Look, Sheriff, hadn't we better run over there? The man's half crazy with shock and he's there all alone."

"How much liquor has he got?"

"Very little when I left. I had a pint but we drank most of it talking."

He moved over to the rolltop desk and unlocked a drawer. He brought up three or four bottles and held them against the light.

"This baby's near full," he said, patting one of them. "Mount Vernon. That ought to hold him."

He put the bottle on his left hip, and locked the desk up and lifted the flap in the counter. He fixed a card against the inside of the glass door panel. I looked at the card as we went out. It read: BACK IN TWENTY MINUTES—MAYBE.

"I'll run down and get Doc Hollis," he said. "Be right back and pick you up. That your car?"

"Yes."

"You can follow along then, as I come back by."

He got into a car which had a siren on it, two red spotlights, two fog lights, a red and white fire plate, a new air-raid horn on top, and three axes and two heavy coils of rope in the back seat. Behind the right-hand lower corner of the windshield there was a white card printed in block capitals. It read:

VOTERS, ATTENTION! KEEP JIM PATTON CONSTABLE. HE IS TOO OLD TO GO TO WORK.

He turned the car and went off down the street in a swirl of white dust.

HE STOPPED in front of a white frame building across the road from the depot. He went into the white building and presently came out with the local doctor, who got into the back seat with the axes and the rope. The official car came back up the street and I fell in behind. Beyond the village we went up a dusty hill and stopped at a cabin. Patton touched the siren gently and a man in faded blue overalls opened the cabin door.

"Get in, Andy. Business."

The man in blue overalls nodded morosely and ducked back into his cabin. He came back out and got in under the wheel of Patton's car while Patton slid over. He was about thirty, dark, lithe, and had the slightly underfed look of the native.

We drove out to Little Fawn Lake with me eating enough dust to make a batch of mud pies. At the five-barred gate Patton got out and let us through and we went on down to the lake. Patton got out again and went to the edge of the water and looked along toward the little pier. Bill Chess was sitting naked on the floor of the pier with his head in his hands. Something was stretched out on the wet planks beside him.

"We can ride a ways more," Patton said.

The two cars went on to the end of the lake and then all four of us trooped down to the pier from behind Bill Chess's back.

The thing that had been a woman lay face down on the boards with a rope under the arms. Bill Chess's clothes lay to one side. His stiff leg, flat and scarred at the knee, was stretched out in front of him, the other leg bent up and his forehead resting against it. He didn't move or look up as we came down behind him.

Patton took the pint bottle of Mount Vernon off his hip and unscrewed the top and handed it to him.

"Drink hearty, Bill."

The man called Andy got a dusty brown blanket out of the car and threw it over the body. Then without a word he went and vomited under a pine tree.

Bill Chess drank a long drink and sat holding the bottle against his bare bent knee. He began to talk in a stiff wooden voice, not looking at anybody, not talking to anybody in particular. He told about the quarrel and what happened after it, but not why it had happened. He said that after I left he'd got a rope and stripped and gone down into the water and got the thing out.

Patton put a cut of tobacco into his mouth and chewed on it silently, his calm eyes full of nothing. Then he shut his teeth tight and leaned down to pull the blanket off the body. The late afternoon sun winked on the necklace of large green stones that were partly imbedded in the swollen neck. They were roughly carved and lusterless, like soapstone or false jade. A gilt chain with an eagle clasp set with small brilliants joined the ends. Patton straightened his broad back and blew his nose on a tan handkerchief.

"What you say, Doc, about cause and time of death?"

"Don't be a damn fool, Jim Patton."

"Can't tell nothing, huh?"

"By looking at that? Good God!"

Patton sighed. "Looks drowned all right," he admitted. "But you can't always tell. There's been cases where a victim would be knifed or poisoned or something, and they would soak him in the water to make things look different."

"Cop stuff," Bill Chess said disgustedly and put his pants on and sat down again to put on his shoes and shirt. When he had them on he stood up and thrust his hairy wrists out toward Patton.

"That's the way you guys feel about it, put the cuffs on and get it over," he said in a savage voice.

Patton ignored him and went over to the railing and looked down. "Funny place for a body to be," he said. "No current here to mention, but what there is would be toward the dam."

Bill Chess lowered his wrists and said quietly, "She did it herself, you darn fool. Muriel was a fine swimmer. She dived down in and swum under the boards there and just breathed water in. Had to. No other way."

"I wouldn't quite say that, Bill," Patton answered him mildly. He spat over the railing. "Something was said about a note," he went on absently.

Bill Chess rummaged in his wallet and drew the folded piece of ruled paper loose. Patton took it and read it slowly.

"Don't seem to have any date," he observed.

Bill Chess shook his head somberly. "No. She left a month ago. June twelfth."

"Left you once before, didn't she?"

"Yeah." Bill Chess stared at him fixedly. "I got drunk and stayed with a chippy. Just before the first snow last December. She was gone a week and came back all prettied up. Said she just had to get away for a while and had been staying with a girl she used to work with in L.A."

"This note here looks middling old," Patton said, holding it up.

"I carried it a month," Bill Chess growled. "Who told you she left me before?"

"I forget," Patton said. "You know how it is in a place like this. Not much folks don't notice. Except maybe in summertime when there's a lot of strangers about."

Nobody said anything for a while and then Patton said, "June twelfth you say she left? Or you thought she left? Did you say the folks across the lake were up here then?"

"Mrs. Kingsley was here," Chess said. "She went down the hill that same day. Nobody was in the other cabins. Perrys and Farquars ain't been up at all this year."

Patton nodded and was silent. A kind of charged emptiness hung in the air, as if something that had not been said was plain to all of them and didn't need saying.

Then Bill Chess said wildly, "Take me in, you sons of bitches! Sure I did it! I drowned her. She was my girl and I loved her. I'm a heel, always was a heel, always will be a heel, but just the same I loved her."

Patton said quietly, "Got to take you down the hill for questioning, Bill. You know that. We ain't accusing you of anything, but the folks down there have got to talk to you."

Bill Chess said heavily, "Can I change my clothes?"

"Sure. You go with him, Andy. And see what you can find to kind of wrap up what he got here."

Chapter 5

THE Indian Head Hotel was a brown building on a corner across from the dance hall. I parked in front of it and used its rest room to wash up before I went into the dining-drinking parlor that adjoined the lobby. The whole place was full to overflowing with males in leisure jackets and females with high-pitched laughs and oxblood fingernails. The manager of the joint, a low-budget tough guy in shirt sleeves, was prowling the room with watchful eyes. At Puma Point summer, that lovely season, was in full swing.

I gobbled what they called the regular dinner, drank a brandy to sit on its chest and hold it down, and went out onto the main street. It was still broad daylight but some of the neon signs had been turned on, and the evening reeled with the cheerful din of auto horns, children screaming, bowls rattling, Skee-Balls clunking, .22s snapping merrily in shooting galleries.

In my Chrysler a thin, serious-looking brown-haired girl in dark slacks was sitting smoking a cigarette and talking to a dude-ranch cowboy who sat on my running board. I walked around the car and got into it. The cowboy strolled away hitching his jeans up. The girl didn't move.

"I'm Birdie Keppel," she said cheerfully. "I'm the beautician here daytimes, and evenings I work as a reporter on the Puma Point *Banner*. Excuse me sitting in your car."

"That's all right," I said. "You want to just sit or you want me to drive you somewhere?"

"You can drive down the road a piece where it's quieter, Mr. Marlowe. If you're obliging enough to talk to me."

"Pretty good grapevine you've got up here," I said, and started the car.

I drove down past the post office to a corner where a blue and white arrow marked TELEPHONE pointed down a narrow road toward the lake. I turned down that, drove on past the telephone office, which was a log cabin with a tiny railed lawn in front of it, and pulled up in front of a huge oak tree that flung its branches all the way across the road.

"This do, Miss Keppel?"

"Mrs. But just call me Birdie. Everybody does. This is fine. Pleased to meet you, Mr. Marlowe."

She put a firm brown hand out and I shook it.

"I was talking to Doc Hollis," she said, "about poor Muriel Chess. I thought you could give me some details. I understand you found the body."

"Bill Chess found it really. I was just with him. What do you want to know?" I offered her a cigarette and lit it for her.

"You might just tell me the story."

"I came up here with a letter from Derace Kingsley to look at his property. Bill Chess showed me around, got talking to me, told me his wife had moved out on him, and showed me the note she left. I had a bottle along and he punished it. The liquor loosened him up, but he was lonely and aching to talk anyway. That's how it happened. I didn't know him. Coming back around the end of the lake we went out on the pier and Bill spotted an arm waving out from under the planking down in the water. It turned out to belong to what was left of Muriel Chess. I guess that's all."

"Any doubt about the suicide note, Mr. Marlowe?"

I looked at her sideways. Thoughtful dark eyes looked out at me under fluffed-out brown hair.

"I guess the police always have doubts in these cases," I said.

"How about you?"

"My opinion doesn't go for anything."

"But for what it's worth?"

"I only met Bill Chess this afternoon," I said. "He struck me as a quick-tempered lad and from his own account he's no saint. But he seems to have been in love with his wife. I can't see him hanging around there for a month knowing she was rotting down in the water under that pier, and knowing he put her there."

"No more can I," Birdie Keppel said softly. "No more could anybody. And yet we know in our minds that such things have happened and will happen again. Are you in the real estate business, Mr. Marlowe?"

"No."

"What line of business are you in, if I may ask?"

"I'd rather not say."

"That's almost as good as saying," she said. "Besides, Jim Patton told Doc Hollis your full name and where you came from. We have an L.A. city directory in our office and I looked you up, but I haven't mentioned it to anyone."

"Don't draw any wrong conclusions," I said. "I had no interest in Bill Chess whatever."

"No interest in Muriel Chess?"

"Why would I have any interest in Muriel Chess?"

She snuffed her cigarette out carefully into the ashtray under the dashboard. "Have it your own way," she said. "But here's a little item you might like to think about, if you don't know it already. There was a Los Angeles copper named De Soto up here about six weeks back, a big roughneck with damn poor manners. He had a photograph with him and he was looking for a woman called Mildred Haviland, he said. It was an enlarged snapshot, not a police photo. He said he had information the woman was staying up here. The photo looked a good deal like Muriel Chess."

I drummed on the door of the car and after a moment I said, "What did you tell him?"

"We didn't tell him anything. First off, we couldn't be sure. Second, we didn't like his manner. Third, even if we had been sure and had liked his manner, we likely would not have sicced him onto her."

"You might have got yourself a story," I said.

"Sure. But up here we're just people."

"Did this man De Soto see Jim Patton?"

"Sure, he must have. But Jim didn't mention it."

"Did anybody tell Muriel about this guy?"

She hesitated, looking quietly out through the windshield for a long moment before she turned her head and nodded.

"I did. Wasn't any of my damn business, was it?"

"What did she say?"

"She didn't say anything. She gave a funny little embarrassed laugh, as if I had been making a bad joke. Then she walked away. But I did get the impression that there was a queer look in her eyes, just for an instant. You still not interested in Muriel Chess, Mr. Marlowe?"

"Why should I be? I never heard of her until I came up here this afternoon. Honest. And I never heard of anybody named Mildred Haviland either. Drive you back to town?"

"Oh no, thanks. I'll walk. It's not far. Much obliged to you. I kind of hope Bill doesn't get into a jam. Especially a nasty jam like this."

I said good night and she walked off into the evening. I sat there watching her until she reached the main street and turned out of sight. Then I got out of the Chrysler and went over toward the telephone company's little rustic building.

IN THE telephone office a small girl in slacks sat at a small desk working on the books. She got me the rate to Beverly Hills and the change for the coin box. The booth was outside, against the front wall of the building.

I shut myself into the booth. For ninety cents I could talk to Derace Kingsley for five minutes. He was at home and the call came through quickly.

"Find anything up there?" he asked me in a three-highball voice. He sounded tough and confident again.

"I've found too much," I said. "And not at all what we want."

"Well, get on with it, whatever it is," he said.

"I had a long talk with Bill Chess. He was lonely. His wife had left him—a month ago. They had a fight and he went out and got drunk. When he came back she was gone. She left a note saying she would rather be dead than live with him anymore."

"I guess Bill drinks too much," Kingsley said.

"When he got back, both the women had gone. He has no idea where Mrs. Kingsley went. Lavery was up here in May, but not since. Lavery admitted that much himself. I thought that possibly Mrs. K. and Muriel Chess might have gone away together, only Muriel also had a car of her own. But that idea, little as it was worth, has been thrown out by another development. Muriel Chess didn't go away at all. She went down into your little private lake. She came back up today. I was there."

"Good God!" Kingsley sounded properly horrified. "You mean she drowned herself?"

"Perhaps. The note she left could be a suicide note. The body was stuck down under that old submerged landing below the pier. Bill was the one who spotted an arm moving down there while we were standing on the pier looking down into the water. He got her out. They've arrested him. The poor guy's pretty badly broken up."

"Good God!" Kingsley said again. "I should think he would be. Does it look as if he—" He paused as the operator came in on the line and demanded another forty-five cents. I put in two quarters and the line cleared.

"Look as if he what?"

Suddenly very clear, Kingsley's voice said, "Does it look as if he murdered her?"

I said, "Very much. Jim Patton, the constable up here, doesn't like the note not being dated. It seems she left him once before over some woman. Patton sort of suspects Bill might have saved up an old note. Anyhow they've taken Bill to San Bernardino for questioning and they've taken the body down to be postmortemed."

"And what do you think?" Kingsley asked slowly.

"Well, Bill found the body himself. He didn't have to take me around by that pier. She might have stayed down in the water very much longer, or forever. The note could be old because Bill had carried it in his wallet and handled it from time to time, brooding over it. It could just as easily be undated this time as another time. I'd say notes like that are undated more often than not. The people who write them are apt to be in a hurry and not concerned with dates."

"The body must be pretty far gone. What can they find out now?"

"I don't know how well equipped they are. They can find out if she died by drowning, I guess. They could tell if she had been shot or stabbed. If the hyoid bone in the throat was broken, they could assume she was throttled. The main thing is that I'll have to tell why I came up here. I'll have to testify at an inquest."

"That's bad," Kingsley growled. "What do you plan to do now?"

"On my way home I'll stop at the Prescott Hotel and see if I can pick up anything there. Were your wife and Muriel Chess friendly?"

"I guess so. Crystal's easy enough to get along with most of the time. I hardly knew Muriel Chess."

"Did you ever know anybody named Mildred Haviland?"

"Who?"

I repeated the name.

"No," he said. "Is there any reason why I should?"

"No, there isn't any reason why you should know Mildred Haviland. Especially if you hardly knew Muriel Chess. I'll call you in the morning."

"Do that," he said, and hesitated. "I'm sorry you had to walk into such a mess," he added, and then hesitated again, said good night and hung up.

I stepped out of the booth and gathered some air into my lungs. It was getting dark and a single bright star glowed low in the northeast. I climbed into the Chrysler and started back in the direction of Little Fawn Lake.

THE gate across the private road was padlocked. I put the Chrysler between two pine trees and climbed the gate and pussyfooted along the side of the road until the glimmer of the little lake bloomed suddenly at my feet. Bill Chess's cabin was dark. The three cabins on the other side were abrupt shadows against the pale granite outcrop. I listened, and heard no sound at all.

The front door of the Chess cabin was locked. I padded along to the back door and found a brute of a padlock hanging on that. I went along the walls feeling window screens. They were all fastened. One window higher up was screenless, a small double cottage window halfway down the north wall. This was locked too.

I tried a knife blade between the two halves of the small window. No soap. The catch refused to budge. I leaned against the wall and thought. Then suddenly I picked up a large stone and smacked it against the place where the two frames met in the middle. The catch pulled out of dry wood with a tearing noise. The window swung back into darkness. I heaved up on the sill, wangled a cramped leg over, and edged through the opening. Then I rolled and let myself down into the room.

A blazing flash beam hit me square in the eyes.

A very calm voice said, "I'd rest right there, son. You must be all tuckered out."

The flash pinned me against the wall like a squashed fly. Then a light switch clicked and a table lamp glowed. The flash went out. Jim Patton was sitting in an old brown morris chair beside the table. His hands were empty except for the flash. His eyes were empty. His jaws moved in gentle rhythm.

"What's on your mind, son—besides breaking and entering?"

I poked a chair out and straddled it and leaned my arms on the back and looked around the cabin.

"I had an idea," I said. "It looked pretty good for a while, but I guess I can learn to forget it."

Patton nodded and his eyes studied me without rancor. "I heard a car coming," he said. "I knew it had to be coming here. You walk right nice though. I didn't hear you walk worth a darn. I've been a mite curious about you, son."

I said nothing.

He grinned. "There's a mess of detectives in the L.A. phone book," he said. "But only one of them is called Marlowe. Bill Chess told me you was some sort of dick. You didn't bother to tell me yourself."

"I'd have got around to it," I said. "I'm sorry it bothered you."

"I guess you was aiming to search the cabin."

"Yeah."

He scratched his ear. "You telling who hired you?"

"Derace Kingsley. To trace his wife. She skipped out on him a month ago. She started from here. So I started from here. She's supposed to have gone away with a man. The man denies it. I thought maybe something up here might give me a lead."

"You didn't have no interest in Bill Chess at all?"

"None whatever."

"None of what you've been saying don't hardly explain your wanting to search Bill's cabin," he said judiciously.

"I'm just a great guy to poke around."

"Hell," he said, "you can do better than that."

"Say I'm interested in Bill Chess then. But only because he's in trouble and rather a pathetic case. If he murdered his wife, there's something here to point that way. If he didn't, there's something to point that way too."

He held his head sideways, like a watchful bird. "As for instance what kind of thing?"

"Clothes, personal jewelry, toilet articles, whatever a woman takes with her when she goes away, not intending to come back."

He leaned back slowly. "But she didn't go away, son."

"Then the stuff should still be here. But if it was still here, Bill would have noticed she hadn't taken it. He would know she hadn't gone away."

"By gum, I don't like it either way," he said.

"But if he murdered her," I said, "then he would have to get rid of the things she ought to have taken with her, if she had gone away."

"And how do you figure he would do that, son?" The yellow lamplight made bronze of one side of his face.

"I understand she had a Ford car of her own. Except for that I'd expect him to burn what he could burn and bury what he could not burn out in the woods. But he couldn't burn or bury her car. Could he drive it?"

Patton looked surprised. "Sure. He can't bend his right leg at the knee, so he couldn't use the foot brake very handy. But he could get by with the hand brake."

"Wherever he took the car he would have to get back," I said. "He would rather not be seen coming back. So the chances are he hid it in the woods within walking distance of here. And walking distance for him would not be very far."

"For a fellow that claims not to be interested, you're doing some pretty close figuring on all this," Patton said dryly. "What next?"

"He has to consider the possibility of the car's being found. The woods are lonely, but rangers and woodcutters get around in them from time to time. If the car is found, it would be better for Muriel's stuff to be found in it. That would give him a couple of outs—neither one very brilliant but both at least possible. One, that she was murdered by some unknown party who fixed things to implicate Bill when and if the murder was discovered. Two, that Muriel did actually commit suicide, but fixed things so that he would be blamed. A revenge suicide."

Patton shook his head. He said, "Killing yourself and fixing things so as somebody else would get accused of murdering you don't fit in with my simple ideas of human nature at all. What I like is that she did plan to go away and did write the note, but he caught her before she got clear and saw red and finished her off."

"I never met her," I said. "So I wouldn't have any idea what she would be likely to do. Bill said he met her in a place in Riverside something over a year ago. She may have had a long and complicated history before that. What kind of girl was she?"

"A mighty cute little blonde when she fixed herself up. She kind of let herself go with Bill. A quiet girl, with a face that kept its secrets. Bill says she had a temper, but I never seen any of it. I seen plenty of nasty temper in him."

"And did you think she looked like the photo of somebody called Mildred Haviland?"

"Where did you get that information?"

"A nice little girl called Birdie Keppel told me. She was interviewing me in the course of her spare-time newspaper job. She happened to mention that an L.A. cop named De Soto was showing the photo around."

Patton smacked his thick knee and hunched his shoulders forward. "I done wrong there," he said soberly, "I made one of my mistakes. This big bruiser showed his picture to darn near everybody in town before he showed it to me. That made me kind of sore. It looked some like Muriel, but not enough to be sure by any manner of means. I asked him what she was wanted for. He said it was police business. I said I was in that way of business myself, in an ignorant countrified kind of way. He said his instructions were to locate the lady and that was all he knew. Maybe he did wrong to take me up short like that. So I guess I done wrong to tell him I didn't know anybody that looked like his little picture."

The big calm man smiled vaguely at the corner of the ceiling, then brought his eyes down and looked at me steadily.

"I'll thank you to respect this confidence, Mr. Marlowe. You done right nicely in your figuring too. You ever happen to go over to Coon Lake?"

"Never heard of it."

"Back about a mile," he said, pointing over his shoulder with a thumb, "there's a little narrow wood road turns over west. It climbs about five hundred feet in another mile and comes out by Coon Lake. Pretty little place. Folks go up there to picnic now and then, but not often. It's hard on tires. There's a bunch of old hand-hewn log cabins that's been falling down ever since I recall, and there's a big broken-down frame building that Montclair University used to use for a summer camp maybe ten years back. This building sits back from the lake in heavy timber. Round at the back of it there's a big woodshed with a sliding door hung on rollers. It was built for a garage but they kept their wood in it and they locked it up out of season. I guess you know what I found in that woodshed."

"I thought you went down to San Bernardino."

"Changed my mind. I sent Andy down with Bill. I figured I kind of ought to look around a little more before I put things up to the sheriff and the coroner."

"Muriel's car was in the woodshed?"

"Yep. And two unlocked suitcases in the car. Packed with clothes and packed kind of hasty, I thought. Women's clothes. The point is, son, no stranger would have known about that place."

I agreed with him. He put his hand into the slanting side pocket of his jerkin and brought out a small twist of tissue paper. He opened it up on his palm and held the hand out flat.

"Take a look at this."

I went over and looked. What lay on the tissue was a thin gold chain with a tiny lock hardly larger than a link of the chain. The gold had been snipped through, leaving the lock intact. The chain seemed to be about seven inches long. There was white powder sticking to both chain and paper.

"Where would you guess I found that?" Patton asked.

I picked the chain up and tried to fit the cut ends together. They didn't fit. I made no comment on that, but moistened a finger and touched the powder and tasted it.

"In a can or box of confectioner's sugar," I said. "The chain is an anklet. Some women never take them off, like wedding rings. Whoever took this one off didn't have the key."

"What do you make of it?"

"Nothing much," I said. "There wouldn't be any point in Bill cutting it off Muriel's ankle and leaving that green necklace on her neck. There wouldn't be any point in Muriel cutting it off herself—assuming she had lost the key—and hiding it to be found. A search thorough enough to find it wouldn't be made unless her body was found first. If Bill cut it off, he would have thrown it into the lake. But if Muriel wanted to keep it and yet hide it from Bill, there's some sense in the place where it was hidden."

Patton looked puzzled this time. "Why is that?"

"Because it's a woman's hiding place. Confectioner's sugar is used to make cake icing. A man would never look there. Pretty clever of you to find it, Sheriff."

He grinned a little sheepishly. "Hell, I knocked the box over and some of the sugar spilled. Without that I don't guess I ever would have found it." He rolled the paper up and slipped it back into his pocket. He stood up with an air of finality.

"You staying up here or going back to town, Mr. Marlowe?"

"Back to town. Until you want me for the inquest. I suppose you will."

"That's up to the coroner, of course. If you'll kind of shut that window you bust in, I'll put this lamp out and lock up."

I did what he said and he snapped his flash on and put out the lamp. We went out and he felt the cabin door to make sure the lock had caught. He closed the screen softly and stood looking across the moonlit lake.

"I don't figure Bill meant to kill her," he said sadly. "He could choke a girl to death without meaning to at all. He has mighty strong hands."

I said, "I should think he would have run away. I don't see how he could stand it to stay here."

Patton spat into the black velvet shadow of a manzanita bush. He said slowly, "He had a government pension and he would have to run away from that too. And most men can stand what they've got to stand, when it steps up and looks them straight in the eye. Well, good night to you. I'm going to walk down to that little pier again and stand there awhile in the moonlight and feel bad. A night like this, and we got to think about murders."

He moved quietly off into the shadows and became one of them himself. I stood there until he was out of sight and then went back to the locked gate and climbed over it. I got into the car and drove back down the road looking for a place to hide.

THREE hundred yards from the gate a narrow track, sifted over with brown oak leaves from last fall, curved around a granite boulder and disappeared. I followed it for fifty or sixty feet, then swung the car around a tree and set it pointing back the way it had come. I cut the lights and switched off the motor and sat there waiting.

Half an hour passed. Then far off I heard a car motor start up and grow louder and the white beam of headlights passed below me on the road. When the sound faded into the distance I got out of my car and walked back to the gate and to the Chess cabin. A hard push opened the sprung window this time. I climbed in again and let myself down to the floor. I switched the lamp on and listened a moment, heard nothing, and went out to the kitchen. A door opened from the kitchen into the bedroom, and from that a very narrow door led into a tiny bathroom. The bathroom told me nothing.

The bedroom contained a double bed, a pinewood dresser with a round mirror on the wall above it, a bureau, two straight chairs and a tin wastebasket.

I poked around in the drawers. An imitation-leather trinket box with an assortment of gaudy costume jewelry had not been taken away. The bureau contained both men's and women's clothes, not a great deal of either. Underneath a sheet of blue tissue paper in one corner I found something I didn't like. A seemingly brand-new peach-colored silk slip trimmed with lace. Silk slips were not being left behind that year, not by any woman in her senses.

This looked bad for Bill Chess. I wondered what Patton had thought of it.

I went back to the kitchen and prowled the open shelves above and beside the sink. They were thick with cans and jars of household staples. The confectioner's sugar was in a square brown box with a torn corner. Patton had made an attempt to clean up what was spilled. Near the sugar were salt, borax, baking soda, cornstarch, brown sugar and so on. Something might be hidden in any of them.

Something that had been clipped from a chain anklet whose cut ends did not fit together.

I got a newspaper from the back of the woodbox and spread it out and dumped the baking soda out of the box. I stirred it around with a spoon. There seemed to be an indecent lot of baking soda, but that was all there was. I funneled it back into the box and tried the borax. Nothing but borax. I tried the cornstarch. It made too much fine dust, and there was nothing but cornstarch.

I went back to the box of confectioner's sugar and emptied it on the newspaper.

Patton hadn't gone deep enough. Having found one thing by accident he had assumed that was all there was.

Another twist of white tissue showed in the fine white powdered sugar. I shook it clean and unwound it. It contained a tiny gold heart, no larger than a woman's little fingernail.

I spooned the sugar back into the box and put the box back on the shelf and crumpled the piece of newspaper into the stove. Then I went back to the living room and turned the table lamp on. Under that brighter light the tiny engraving on the back of the little gold heart could just be read without a magnifying glass.

It was in script. It read: *Al to Mildred. June 28th 1938. With all my love.*

Al to Mildred. Al somebody to Mildred Haviland. Mildred Haviland was Muriel Chess. Muriel Chess was dead—two weeks after a cop named De Soto had been looking for her.

I wrapped it up again and left the cabin and drove back to the village.

Patton was in his office telephoning when I got around there. The door was locked. I had to wait while he talked. After a while he hung up and came to unlock the door.

I walked in past him and put the twist of tissue paper on his counter and opened it up.

"You didn't go deep enough into the powdered sugar," I said.

He looked at the little gold heart, looked at me, went around behind the counter, and got a cheap magnifying glass off his desk. He studied the back of the heart. He put the glass down and frowned.

"Might have known if you wanted to search that cabin, you was going to do it," he said gruffly. "I ain't going to have trouble with you, am I, son?"

"You ought to have noticed that the cut ends of the chain didn't fit," I told him.

He looked at me sadly. "Son, I don't have your eyes." He pushed the little heart around with his square blunt finger.

I said, "If you were thinking that anklet meant something Bill could have been jealous about, so was I—provided he ever saw it. But strictly on the cuff I'm willing to bet he never did see it and that he never heard of Mildred Haviland."

Patton said slowly, "Looks like maybe I owe this De Soto party an apology, don't it?"

"If you ever see him," I said.

He gave me another long empty stare and I gave it right back to him. "Don't tell me, son," he said. "Let me guess all for myself that you got a brand-new idea about it."

"Yeah. Bill didn't murder his wife."

"No?"

"No. She was murdered by somebody out of her past. Somebody who had lost track of her and then found it again and found her married to another man and didn't like it. Somebody who knew the country up here and knew a good place to hide the car and the clothes. Somebody who hated and could lie. Who persuaded her to go away with him and when everything was ready and the note was written, took her around the throat and gave her what he thought was coming to her and put her in the lake and went his way. Like it?"

"Well," he said judiciously, "it does make things kind of complicated. But there ain't anything impossible about it."

"When you get tired of it, let me know. I'll have something else," I said.

"I'll just be doggone sure you will," he said, and for the first time since I had met him he laughed.

I said good night again and went out, leaving him there.

Chapter 6

SOMEWHERE around eleven I got down to San Bernardino and parked in one of the diagonal slots at the side of the Prescott Hotel. I pulled an overnight bag out of the trunk and had taken three steps with it when a bellhop in braided pants and a white shirt and black bow tie yanked it out of my hand.

The clerk on duty was an egg-headed man with no interest in me or in anything else. He yawned as he handed me the desk pen and looked off into the distance as if remembering his childhood.

The hop and I rode a four-by-four elevator to the second floor and walked a couple of blocks around corners. As we walked it got hotter and hotter. The hop unlocked a door into a boy's-size room with one window on an air shaft. The air-conditioner inlet up in the corner of the ceiling was about the size of a woman's handkerchief. The bit of ribbon tied to it fluttered weakly, just to show that something was moving.

The hop was tall and thin and cool as a slice of chicken in aspic. He put my bag on a chair and then stood looking at me.

"Maybe I ought to have asked for one of the dollar rooms," I said. "This one seems a mite close-fitting."

"I reckon you're lucky to get one at all. This town's fair bulgin' at the seams."

"Bring us up some ginger ale and glasses and ice," I said.

"Us?"

"That is, if you happen to be a drinking man."

"I reckon I might take a chance this late."

He went out. I took off my coat, tie, shirt and undershirt and walked around in the warm draft from the open door. I was breathing a little more freely when the tall languid hop returned with a tray. He shut the door and I brought out a bottle of rye. He mixed a couple of drinks and we made the usual insincere smiles over them and drank.

"How long can you stay?"

"Doin' what?"

"Remembering."

"I ain't a damn bit of use at it," he said.

"I have money to spend," I said, "in my own peculiar way." I got my wallet unstuck from the lower part of my back and spread tired-looking dollar bills along the bed.

"I beg yore pardon," the hop said. "I reckon you're a dick."

"Don't be silly," I said. "You never saw a dick playing solitaire with his own money. You might call me an investigator."

"I'm interested," he said. "The likker makes my mind work."

I gave him a dollar bill. "Try that on your mind," I said.

He grinned and tucked the folded dollar neatly into the watch pocket of his pants.

"What were you doing on June twelfth?" I asked him. "Late afternoon or evening. It was a Friday."

He sipped his drink and thought, shaking the ice around gently. "I was right here, six-to-twelve shift."

"A woman, a slim, pretty blonde, checked in here and stayed until time for the night train to El Paso. I think she must have taken that because she was in El Paso Sunday morning. She came here driving a Packard Clipper registered to Crystal Grace Kingsley, 965 Carson Drive, Beverly Hills. She may have registered as that, or under some other name, and she may not have registered at all. Her car is still in the hotel garage. Thinking about that wins another dollar."

I separated another dollar from my exhibit and it went into his pocket with a sound like caterpillars fighting.

"She never checked in at the desk," he said. "But I remember the Packard. She gave me a dollar to put it away for her and to look after her stuff until traintime. She ate dinner here. A dollar gets you remembered in this town. And there's been talk about the car bein' left so long."

"What was she like to look at?"

"She wore a black and white outfit, mostly white, and a panama hat with a black and white band. She was a neat blond lady like you said. Later on she took a hack to the station. I put her bags into it for her."

I dug in my coat for the snapshot of Crystal and Lavery on the beach and handed it to him.

He held it away from his eyes, then close.

"You won't have to swear to it in court," I said.

He nodded. "I wouldn't want to. These small blondes are so much of a pattern that a change of clothes or light or makeup makes them all alike or all different." He stared at the snapshot.

"What's worrying you?" I asked.

"I'm thinking about the gent in this snap. He enter into it?"

"Go on with that," I said.

"I think this fellow spoke to her in the lobby, and had dinner with her. A tall good-lookin' jasper, built like a fast light heavy. He went in the hack with her too." He picked the snapshot up again and looked at me over it.

"This gent takes a solid photo," he said. "Much more so than the lady."

"You've helped a lot," I said. "Thanks very much."

I gave him a five to keep his two dollars company. He thanked me, finished his drink, and left softly. I finished mine and decided I would rather drive home than sleep in that hole. I put my shirt and coat on again and went downstairs with my bag.

The egg-headed clerk separated me from two dollars without even looking at me.

I wiped the back of my neck and staggered out to the car. Even the seat of the car was hot, at midnight.

I got home about two forty-five and Hollywood was an icebox.

I WENT to bed and slept until nine o'clock. When I woke up, the sun was on my face. The room was hot. I showered and shaved, partly dressed, and made the morning toast and eggs and coffee in the dinette.

When I had finished breakfast I dialed police headquarters down-town and asked for the detective bureau and then for De Soto.

"Who?"

I repeated the name.

"What's his rank and department?"

"Plainclothes something or other."

"Hold the line."

I waited. The burring male voice came back after a while and said, "What's the gag? We don't have a De Soto on the roster. Who's this talking?"

I hung up and dialed the number of Derace Kingsley's office. The smooth and cool Miss Fromsett said he had just come in and put me through without a murmur.

"Well," he said, loud and forceful at the beginning of a fresh day, "what did you find out at the hotel?"

"She was there all right. And Lavery met her there. The hop who gave me the dope brought Lavery into it himself, without any prompting from me. Lavery had dinner with her and went with her in a cab to the railroad station."

"Well, I ought to have known he was lying," Kingsley said slowly. "I got the impression he was surprised when I told him about the telegram from El Paso. I was just letting my impressions get too sharp. By the way, why were you asking me last night about Mildred something or other?"

I told him, making it brief. I told him about Muriel Chess's car and clothes being found and where.

"That looks bad for Bill," he said. "It not only looks bad, it looks premeditated."

"I disagree with that. Assuming he knew the country well enough it wouldn't take him any time to search his mind for a likely hiding place. He was very restricted as to distance."

"Maybe. What do you plan to do now?" he asked.

"Go up against Lavery again, of course."

He agreed that that was the thing to do. He added, "This other, tragic as it is, is really no business of ours, is it?"

"Not unless your wife knew something about it."

His voice sounded sharp, saying, "Look here, Marlowe, I think I can understand your detective instinct to tie everything that happens into one compact knot, but don't let it run away with you. Better leave the affairs of the Chess family to the police and keep your brains working on the Kingsley family. I'll be at the Athletic Club later if you want to reach me."

"Okay," I said.

"I don't mean to be domineering," he said.

I laughed heartily, said good-by, and hung up. I finished dressing and went down to the basement for the Chrysler. I started for Bay City again.

I DROVE past the intersection of Altair Street to where the cross street continued to the edge of the canyon and ended in a semicircular parking place with a sidewalk and a white wooden guard fence around it. I sat there in the car a little while, thinking, looking out to sea and admiring the blue-gray fall of the foothills toward the ocean. I was trying to make up my mind whether to try handling Lavery with a feather or go on using the back of my hand and the edge of my tongue. I decided I could lose nothing by the soft approach. If that didn't produce for me, nature could take its course and we could bust up the furniture.

I left the car where it was and walked along Altair Street to number 623. The venetian blinds were down across the front windows and the place had a sleepy look. I punched the bell and saw that the door was not quite shut. I gave it a little push and it moved inward with a light click. The room beyond was dim, but there was some light from the west windows. Nobody answered my ring. I didn't ring again. I pushed the door a little wider and stepped inside.

The room had a hushed warm smell, the smell of late morning in a house not yet opened up. The bottle of Vat 69 on the round table by the davenport was almost empty and another full bottle waited beside it. The copper ice bucket had a little water in the bottom. Two glasses had been used, and half a syphon of carbonated water.

I went farther into the room and stood peering around, listening and hearing nothing. I started along the rug toward an archway at the back.

A hand in a glove appeared on the slope of a white metal railing, at the edge of the archway, where the stairs went down. It appeared and stopped.

It moved and a woman's hat showed, then her head. The woman came quietly up the stairs. She came all the way up, turned through the arch and still didn't seem to see me. She was a slender woman of uncertain age, with untidy brown hair, a scarlet mess of a mouth, too much rouge on her cheekbones, shadowed eyes. She wore a blue tweed suit that looked like the dickens with the purple hat that was doing its best to hang on to the side of her head.

She saw me and didn't stop or change expression in the slightest degree. She came slowly on into the room, holding her right hand away from her body. Her left hand wore the brown glove I had seen on the railing. The right-hand glove that matched it was wrapped around the butt of a small automatic.

She stopped then and her body arched back and a quick distressful sound came out of her mouth. Then she giggled, a high nervous giggle. She pointed the gun at me, and came steadily on.

I kept on looking at the gun.

The woman came closer. When she was close enough to be confidential she pointed the gun at my stomach and said, "All I wanted was my rent. The place seems well taken care of. Nothing broken. He has always been a good tidy careful tenant. I just didn't want him to get too far behind in the rent."

I heard my strained unhappy voice ask politely, "How far behind is he?"

"Three months," she said. "I've had a little trouble collecting before, but it always came out very well. He promised me a check this morning. Over the telephone. I mean he promised to give it to me this morning."

I shuffled around a bit in an inconspicuous sort of way with the idea of getting close enough to make a sideswipe at the gun, knock it outward, and then jump in fast before she could bring it back in line. I made about six inches, but not nearly enough for a first down. I said, "And you're the owner?" I didn't look at the gun directly. I had a faint, a very faint hope that she didn't know she was pointing it at me.

"Why, certainly. I'm Mrs. Fallbrook. Who did you think I was?"

"Well, I thought you might be the owner," I said. "You talking about the rent and all. But I didn't know your name." Another eight inches.

"And who are you, if I may inquire?"

"I just came about the car payment," I said. "The door was open just a teensy-weensy bit and I kind of shoved in."

"You mean Mr. Lavery is behind in his car payments?" she asked, looking worried.

"A little. Not a great deal," I said soothingly.

I was all set now. I had the reach and I ought to have the speed. All it needed was a clean sharp sweep inside the gun and outward.

"You know," she said, "it's funny about this gun. I found it on the stairs. Nasty oily things, aren't they? And the stair carpet is a very nice gray chenille. Quite expensive."

And she handed me the gun.

My hand went out for it, as stiff as an eggshell, almost as brittle. I took the gun. She sniffed with distaste at the glove which had been wrapped around the butt and went on talking in exactly the same tone of cockeyed reasonableness. My knees cracked, relaxing.

"Well of course it's much easier for you," she said. "About the car, I mean. You can just take it away, if you have to. But taking a house with nice furniture in it isn't so easy. It takes time and money to evict a tenant. There is apt to be bitterness and things get damaged, sometimes on purpose."

I hardly heard what she said. The gun had my interest.

I broke the magazine out. It was empty. I looked into the breech. That was empty too. I sniffed the muzzle. It reeked.

I dropped the gun into my pocket. A six-shot .25-caliber automatic. Emptied out. Shot empty, and not too long ago. But not in the last half hour either.

THE LADY IN THE LAKE

"Has it been fired?" Mrs. Fallbrook inquired pleasantly. "I certainly hope not."

"Any reason why it should have been fired?" I asked her. The voice was steady, but the brain was still bouncing.

"Well, it was lying on the stairs," she said. "After all, people do fire them."

"How true that is," I said. "But Mr. Lavery probably had a hole in his pocket. He isn't home, is he?"

"Oh no." She shook her head and looked disappointed. "And I don't think it's very nice of him. He promised me the check and I walked over—"

"When was it you phoned him?" I asked.

"Why, yesterday evening." She frowned, not liking so many questions.

"He must have been called away," I said.

She stared at a spot between my big brown eyes.

"Look, Mrs. Fallbrook," I said. "Let's not kid around anymore. Not that I don't love it. And not that I like to say this. But you didn't shoot him, on account of he owed you three months' rent?"

She sat down very slowly on the edge of a chair and worked the tip of her tongue along the scarlet slash of her mouth.

"Why, what a perfectly horrid suggestion," she said angrily. "I don't think you are nice at all."

"Okay, my idea was wrong. Just a gag anyway. Mr. Lavery was out and you went through the house. Being the owner, you have a key. Is that correct?"

"I didn't mean to be interfering," she said, biting a finger. "But I have a right to see how things are kept."

"Well, you looked. And you're sure he's not here?"

"I didn't look under the beds or in the refrigerator," she said coldly. "I called out from the top of the stairs when he didn't answer my ring. Then I went down to the lower hall and called out again. I even peeped into the bedroom."

"Well, that's that," I said.

She nodded brightly. "Yes, that's that. And what company did you say you are employed with?"

"I'm out of work right now," I said. "Until the police commissioner gets in a jam again."

She looked startled. "But you said you came about a car payment."

"That's just a fill-in job," I said.

She rose to her feet and looked at me steadily. Her voice was cold. "Then in that case I think you'd better leave."

I said, "I thought I might take a look around first, if you don't mind. There might be something you missed. This gun, you know, is kind of queer."

"But I told you I found it lying on the stairs," she said angrily.

"That's your story," I said. "I don't have to get stuck with it."

She stamped her foot. "Why, you perfectly loathsome man," she squawked. "How *dare* you be so insulting? I won't stay in this house another minute with you."

She put her head down, purple hat and all, and ran for the door. As she passed me she put a hand out as if to stiff-arm me, but she wasn't near enough and I didn't move. She jerked the door wide and charged out through it and up the walk to the street. The door came slowly shut and I heard her rapid steps above the sound of its closing.

The house seemed now to be abnormally still. I went along the apricot rug and through the archway to the head of the stairs. I stood there for another moment and listened again.

I shrugged and went quietly down the stairs.

THE lower hall had a door at each end and two in the middle side by side. One of these was a linen closet and the other was locked. I went along to the end and looked in at a spare bedroom with drawn blinds and no sign of being used. I went back to the other end of the hall and stepped into a second bedroom with a wide bed, angular furniture in light wood, a box mirror over the dressing table and a long fluorescent lamp over the mirror.

Face powder was spilled around on the dressing table. There was a smear of dark lipstick on a towel hanging over the wastebasket. On the bed were pillows side by side, with depressions in them that could have been made by heads. A woman's handkerchief peeped from under one pillow. A pair of sheer black pajamas lay across the foot of the bed. A rather too emphatic trace of chypre hung in the air.

I wondered what Mrs. Fallbrook had thought of all this.

I turned around and looked at myself in the long mirror of a closet door. I turned the knob in my handkerchief and looked inside. The cedar-lined closet was fairly full of men's clothes. There was a nice friendly smell of tweed. But the closet contained not only men's clothes.

There was also a woman's black and white tailored suit, black and white shoes under it, a panama with a black and white rolled band on a shelf above it. There were other women's clothes too, but I didn't examine them.

I shut the closet door and went out of the bedroom, holding my handkerchief ready for more doorknobs.

The door next the linen closet, the locked door, had to be the bathroom. I bent down and saw there was a short, slit-shaped opening in the middle of the knob. I knew then that the door was fastened by pushing a button in the middle of the knob inside, and that the slitlike opening was for a metal key without wards that would spring the lock open in case somebody fainted in the bathroom, or the kids locked themselves in and got sassy. I went back to the bedroom and got a flat nail file off the dresser. It worked. I opened the bathroom door.

A man's sand-colored pajamas were tossed over a painted hamper. A pair of heelless green slippers lay on the floor. There was a safety razor on the edge of the washbowl and a tube of cream with the cap off. The window was shut, and there was a pungent smell in the air that was not quite like any other smell.

Three empty shells lay bright and coppery on the nile-green tiles of the bathroom floor, and there was a nice clean hole in the frosted pane of the window. To the left and a little above the window were two scarred places where something, such as a bullet, had gone in. I slid aside the shower curtain and felt my neck creak a little as I bent down. He was there all right—there wasn't anywhere else for him to be. He was huddled in the corner under the two shining faucets, and water dripped slowly on his chest, from the chromium showerhead.

His knees were drawn up but slack. The two holes in his naked chest were dark blue and both of them were close enough to his heart to have killed him.

Nice efficient work. You've just finished shaving and stripped for the shower and you're leaning in against the shower curtain and adjusting the temperature of the water. The door opens behind you and somebody comes in. The somebody appears to have been a woman. She has a gun. You look at the gun and she shoots it.

She misses with three shots. It seems impossible, at such short range, but there it is. Maybe it happens all the time. I've been around so little.

You haven't anywhere to go except into the shower.

That is where you go. Then there are two more shots, possibly three, and you slide down the wall, and your eyes are not even frightened anymore now. They're just the empty eyes of the dead.

She reaches in and turns the shower off. She sets the lock of the bathroom door. On her way out of the house she throws the empty gun on the stair carpet. She should worry. It's probably your gun.

Is that right? It had better be right.

I went into the bedroom and pulled the handkerchief out from under the pillow. It was a minute piece of linen rag with a scalloped edge embroidered in red. Two small initials were stitched in the corner, in red. A.F.

"Adrienne Fromsett," I said. I laughed—a rather ghoulish laugh.

I shook the handkerchief to get some of the chypre out of it and folded it up in a tissue and put it in my pocket. I went back upstairs to the living room and poked around in the desk against the wall. It contained no interesting letters, phone numbers or provocative match folders.

I went to the door and set the lock so I could come in again, and shut the door tight, pulling it hard over the sill until the lock clicked. I went up the walk and stood in the sunlight looking across the street at Dr. Almore's house.

Nobody yelled or ran out of the door. Nobody blew a police whistle. Everything was quiet and sunny and calm.

I walked back to the intersection and got into my car and started it and backed it and drove away from there.

Chapter 7

THE bellhop at the Athletic Club was back in three minutes with a nod for me to come with him. We rode up to the fourth floor and went around a corner and he showed me a half-open door.

"Around to the left, sir. As quietly as you can."

I went into the club library. It contained books behind glass doors and magazines on a long central table and a lighted portrait of the club's founder. But its real business seemed to be sleeping. Outward-jutting bookcases cut the room into a number of small alcoves and in the alcoves were high-backed leather chairs of an incredible size and softness. In a number of the chairs old boys were snoozing peacefully.

I climbed over a few feet and stole around to the left. Derace Kingsley was in the very last alcove in the far end of the room. He had two chairs arranged side by side, facing into the corner. His big dark head just showed over the top of one of them. I slipped into the empty one and gave him a quick nod.

"Keep your voice down," he said. "Now what is it? You made me break an important engagement."

I put my face close to his. "She shot him," I said.

His eyebrows jumped and his face got that stony look.

"Go on," he said, in a voice the size of a marble.

"No answer at Lavery's place," I said. "Door slightly open. Room dark, two glasses with drinks having been in them. House very still. In a moment a slim dark woman calling herself Mrs. Fallbrook, landlady, came up the stairs with her glove wrapped around a gun. Said she had found it on the stairs. Said she came to collect her three months' back rent. Inference is she used her key to get in and snooped around looking the house over. Took the gun from her and found it had been fired recently, but didn't tell her so.

She said Lavery was not home. Got rid of her by making her mad and she departed in high dudgeon."

I paused. Kingsley's head was turned toward me and his eyes looked sick.

"I went downstairs. Signs of a woman having spent the night. Pajamas, face powder, perfume and so on. Bathroom locked, but got it open. Three empty shells on the floor, two shots in the wall, one in the window. Lavery in the shower stall, naked and dead."

"My God!" Kingsley whispered. "Do you mean to say he had a woman with him last night and she shot him this morning in the bathroom?"

"Why not in the bathroom? Could you think of a place where a man would be more completely off guard?"

He said, "You don't know that a woman shot him. I mean, you're not sure, are you?"

"No," I said. "That's true. It might have been somebody who used a small gun and emptied it carelessly to look like a woman's work. The woman who spent the night might have left—or there need not have been any woman at all. The appearances could have been faked. Does your wife own a gun?"

He turned a drawn miserable face to me and said hollowly, "Good God, man, you can't really think that!"

"Well does she?"

He got the words out in small gritty pieces. "Yes—she does. A small automatic."

"Could you recognize this gun?"

I reached in my pocket and put the gun on Kingsley's hand. He stared down at it miserably.

"I don't know," he said slowly. "It's like it, but I can't tell."

"There's a serial number on the side," I said.

"Nobody remembers the serial numbers of guns."

"I was hoping you wouldn't," I said. "It would have worried me very much if you did."

His hand closed around the gun and he put it down beside him in the chair.

"We can't let the police have this gun," he said. "Crystal had a permit and the gun was registered. So they will know the serial number, even if I don't."

"The gun will have to go back," I said. "I can't cover up a murder, even for a ten-dollar bonus."

"I was thinking of five hundred dollars," he said quietly.

"Just what did you expect to buy with it?"

He leaned close to me. His eyes were serious and bleak, but not hard. "Is there anything in Lavery's place, apart from the gun, that might indicate Crystal has been there lately?"

"A black and white dress and a hat like the bellhop in Bernardino described on her. There may be a dozen things I don't know about. There almost certainly will be fingerprints. You say she was never printed, but that doesn't mean they won't get her prints to check. Her bedroom at home will be full of them. So will the cabin at Little Fawn Lake. What kind of perfume does she use?"

He looked blank for an instant. "Oh—Gillerlain Regal, the Champagne of Perfumes," he said woodenly.

"What's this stuff of yours like?"

"A kind of chypre. Sandalwood chypre."

"The bedroom reeks with it," I said. "It smelled like cheap stuff to me. But I'm no judge."

"Cheap?" he said, stung to the quick. "My God, cheap? We get thirty dollars an ounce for it."

"Well, this stuff smelled more like three dollars a gallon."

He put his hands down hard on his knees and shook his head. "I hired you to protect me from scandal," he said gravely, "and of course to protect my wife, if she needed it. Through no fault of yours the chance to avoid scandal is pretty well shot. It's a question of my wife's neck now. I don't believe she shot Lavery. I have no reason for that belief. None at all. I just feel the conviction. She may even have been there last night, this gun may even be her gun. It doesn't prove she killed him. She would be as careless with the gun as with anything else. Anybody could have got hold of it."

"The cops down there won't work very hard to believe that," I said. "If the one I met is a fair specimen, they'll just pick the first head they see and start swinging with their blackjacks. And hers will certainly be the first head they see when they look the situation over."

He ground the heels of his hands together. His misery had a theatrical flavor, as real misery so often has.

"I'll go along with you up to a point," I went on. "The setup is almost too good, at first sight. She leaves clothes there she has been seen wearing and which can probably be traced. She leaves the gun on the stairs. It's hard to think she would be as dumb as that."

"You give me a little heart," Kingsley said wearily.

"Here's the only thing I can do," I said. "Go back and replace the gun and call the law. The story will have to come out. What I was doing down there and why. At the worst they'll find her and prove she killed him. At the best they'll find her a lot quicker than I can and let me use my energies proving that she didn't kill him, which means, in effect, proving that somebody else did. Are you game for that?"

He nodded slowly and said, "Yes. And the five hundred stands. For showing Crystal didn't kill him."

"I don't expect to earn it," I said. "You may as well understand that now. By the way, how well did Miss Fromsett know Lavery? Out of office hours?"

His face tightened up like a charley horse. He said nothing.

"She looked kind of queer when I asked her for his address yesterday morning," I said.

He let a breath out slowly.

"Like a bad taste in the mouth," I said. "Like a romance that fouled out. Am I too blunt?"

His nostrils quivered a little and his breath made noise in them for a moment. Then he relaxed and said quietly, "She—she knew him rather well—at one time. She's a girl who would do just about what she pleased in that way. Lavery was, I guess, a fascinating bird—to women."

"I'll have to talk to her," I said.

"Talk to her then," he said tightly. "As a matter of fact she knew the Almores. She knew Almore's wife, the one who killed herself. Lavery knew her too. Could that have any possible connection with this business?"

"I don't know. You're in love with Miss Fromsett, aren't you?"

"I'd marry her tomorrow, if I could," he said stiffly.

I nodded and stood up. "There's just one thing," I said, looking down at Kingsley. "Cops get very hostile when there is a delay in calling them after a murder. There's been delay this time and there will be more. I'd like to go down there as if it was the first visit today. I think I can make it that way, if I leave the Fallbrook woman out."

"Fallbrook?" He hardly knew what I was talking about. "Who the hell—oh yes, I remember."

"Well, don't remember. I'm almost certain they'll never hear a peep from her. She's not the kind to have anything to do with the police of her own free will."

"I understand," he said.

"Be sure you handle it right then. Questions will be asked you *before* you are told Lavery is dead, before I'm allowed to get in touch with you—so far as they know. Don't fall into any traps. If you do, I won't be able to find anything out. I'll be in the clink."

"I understand," he said again. "You can trust me to handle it."

We shook hands and I left him standing there.

In the Gillerlain Company's reception room the same fluffy little blonde sat behind the switchboard in the corner. I pointed to Miss Fromsett's empty desk and the little blonde nodded and pushed a plug in and spoke. A door opened and Miss Fromsett swayed elegantly out to her desk and sat down and gave me her cool expectant eyes.

"Yes, Mr. Marlowe? Mr. Kingsley is not in, I'm afraid."

"I just came from him. Where do we talk?"

"Talk?"

"Business," I said. "Mr. Kingsley's business."

She stood up and opened the gate in the railing. "We may as well go into his office then."

THE LADY IN THE LAKE

We went into the long dim office and she took a chair at the end of the desk. She was wearing tan today, with a ruffled jabot at her throat.

I offered her a cigarette. She took it, took a light from Kingsley's lighter, and leaned back.

"We needn't waste time being cagey," I said. "You know by now who I am and what I am doing. If you didn't know yesterday morning, it's only because he loves to play big shot."

She looked down at the hand that lay on her knee, then lifted her eyes and smiled almost shyly.

"He's a great guy," she said. "In spite of the heavy executive act he likes to put on. And if you only knew what he has stood from that little tramp—" She waved her cigarette. "Well, perhaps I'd better leave that out. What was it you wanted to see me about?"

"Kingsley said you knew the Almores."

"I knew Mrs. Almore. That is, I met her a couple of times."

"Where?"

"At a friend's house. Why?"

"At Lavery's house?"

She nodded slightly. "At Chris Lavery's house, yes. I used to go there—once in a while. He had cocktail parties."

"Then Lavery knew the Almores—or Mrs. Almore."

She flushed very slightly. "Yes. Quite well."

"Did Mrs. Kingsley know her too?"

"Yes, better than I did. Mrs. Almore is dead, you know. She committed suicide, about a year and a half ago."

"Any doubt about that?"

She raised her eyebrows, but the expression looked artificial to me, as if it just went with the question I asked, as a matter of form. She said, "Have you any particular reason for asking that question in that particular way? I mean, has it anything to do with—with what you are doing?"

"I didn't think so. I still don't know that it has. But yesterday Dr. Almore called a cop just because I looked at his house. Now why would he think it necessary to call a cop? And why would the cop think it smart to say that the last fellow who tried to

76

put the bite on Almore ended up on the road gang? And why would the cop ask me if her folks—meaning Mrs. Almore's folks, I suppose—had hired me? If you can answer any of those questions, I might know whether it's any of my business."

She thought about it for a moment, giving me one quick glance while she was thinking, and then looking away again.

"I only met Mrs. Almore twice," she said slowly. "But I think I can answer your questions—all of them. The last time I met her was at Lavery's place, as I said, and there were quite a lot of people there. There was a lot of drinking and loud talk. There was a man there named Brownwell who was very tight. He was ribbing Mrs. Almore about her husband's practice. The idea seemed to be that he was one of those doctors who run around all night with a case of loaded hypodermic needles, keeping the local fast set from having pink elephants for breakfast. Florence Almore said she didn't care how her husband got his money as long as he got plenty of it and she had the spending of it. Well, Brownwell told her not to worry, it would always be a good racket. But one thing bothered him, he said, how a doctor could get hold of so much dope without underworld contacts. He asked Mrs. Almore if they had many nice gangsters to dinner at their house. She threw a glass of liquor in his face."

"Fair enough," I said. "Who wouldn't, unless he had a large hard fist to throw?"

"Yes. A few weeks later Florence Almore was found dead in the garage late at night. The door of the garage was shut and the car motor was running." She stopped and moistened her lips slightly. "It was Chris Lavery who found her. Coming home at God knows what o'clock in the morning, he heard the motor and went over to investigate. She was lying on the concrete floor in pajamas, with her head under a blanket which was also over the exhaust pipe of the car. Dr. Almore was out. There was nothing about the affair in the papers, except that she had died suddenly. It was well hushed up."

She lifted her clasped hands a little and then let them fall slowly into her lap again.

I said, "Was something wrong with it then?"

"People thought so, but they always do. Some time later I heard what purported to be the lowdown. I met this man Brownwell on Vine Street and he asked me to have a drink with him. We sat at the back of Levy's bar and he asked me if I remembered the babe who threw the drink in his face. I said I did. The conversation then went something very much like this.

"Brownwell said, 'Our pal Chris Lavery is sitting pretty, if he ever runs out of girl friends he can touch for dough.'

"I said, 'I don't think I understand.'

"He said, 'Hell, maybe you don't want to. The night the Almore woman died she was over at Lou Condy's place losing her shirt at roulette. She got into a tantrum and said the wheels were crooked and made a scene. Condy practically had to drag her into his office. He got hold of Dr. Almore and after a while the doc came over. He shot her with one of his busy little needles. Then he went away, leaving Condy to get her home. So Condy took her home and the doc's office nurse showed up, having been called by the doc, and Condy carried her upstairs and the nurse put her to bed. Condy went back to his chips. So she had to be carried to bed and yet the same night she got up and walked down to the family garage and finished herself off with monoxide. What do you think of that?' Brownwell was asking me.

"I said, 'I don't know anything about it. How do you?'

"He said, 'I know a reporter on the rag they call a newspaper down there. There was no inquest and no autopsy. It's easy to fix a thing like that in a small town, if anybody with any pull wants it fixed. And Condy had plenty at that time. He didn't want the publicity of an investigation and neither did the doctor.' "

Miss Fromsett stopped talking and waited for me to say something. When I didn't, she went on, "I suppose you know what all this meant to Brownwell."

"Sure. Almore finished her off and then he and Condy between them bought a fix. It has been done in cleaner little cities than Bay City ever tried to be. But that isn't all the story, is it?"

"No. It seems Mrs. Almore's parents hired a private detective as soon as they heard their daughter was dead. He was a man who ran a night-watchman service down there and he was the second man on the scene that night, after Chris. Brownwell said he must have gotten something in the way of information but he never had a chance to use it. They arrested him for drunk driving and he got a jail sentence."

I said, "Is that all?"

Miss Fromsett said, "I think that's all I can tell you, Mr. Marlowe. And I ought to be outside."

She started to get up. I said, "It's not quite all. I have something to show you."

I got the little perfumed rag that had been under Lavery's pillow out of my pocket and leaned over to drop it on the desk in front of her.

SHE looked at the handkerchief, looked at me, picked up a pencil and pushed the little piece of linen around with the eraser end.

"What's on it?" she asked. "Fly spray?"

"Some kind of sandalwood, I thought."

"A cheap synthetic. Repulsive is a mild word for it. And why did you want me to look at this handkerchief, Mr. Marlowe?" she asked.

"I found it in Chris Lavery's house, under the pillow on his bed. It has initials on it."

She unfolded the handkerchief without touching it by using the rubber tip of the pencil. Her face got a little grim and taut.

"It has two letters embroidered on it," she said in a cold angry voice. "They happen to be the same letters as my initials. Is that what you mean?"

"Right," I said. "He probably knows half a dozen women with the same initials. Is it your handkerchief—or isn't it?"

She hesitated. She reached out to the desk and very quietly got herself another cigarette and lit it with a match.

"Yes, it's mine," she said. "I must have dropped it there. It's a long time ago. And I assure you I didn't put it under a pillow on his bed."

"Chris Lavery is dead," I said. "He was shot in his shower and it looks as if it was done by some woman who spent the night there. He had just been shaving. The woman left a gun on the stairs and this handkerchief on the bed."

For a moment she just sat there and looked at me as if I hadn't said anything and she was waiting for me to say something. Then a slow shudder started at her throat and passed over her whole body. Her hands clenched and the cigarette bent into a crook. She looked down at it and threw it into the ashtray with a quick jerk of her arm.

"And did you expect me to be able to give you information about that?" she asked me bitterly. Her eyes were perfectly empty now. Her face was as cold as a carving.

"Look, Miss Fromsett, I'd like to be smooth and distant and subtle too. I'd like to play this sort of game just once the way somebody like you would like it to be played. But nobody will let me—not the clients, nor the cops, nor the people I play against. However hard I try to be nice I always end up with my nose in the dirt and my thumb feeling for somebody's eye."

She nodded as if she had only just barely heard me. "When was he shot?" she asked, and then shuddered slightly again.

"This morning, I suppose. Not long after he got up. I said he had just shaved and was going to take a shower."

"That," she said, "would probably have been quite late. I've been here since eight thirty."

"I didn't think you shot him."

"Awfully kind of you," she said. "But it is my handkerchief, isn't it? Although not my perfume. God," and she put the back of her hand hard against her mouth.

"He was shot at five or six times," I said. "And missed all but twice. He was cornered in the shower stall. It was a pretty grim scene. There was a lot of hate on one side of it, I should think. Or a pretty cold-blooded mind."

"He was quite easy to hate," she said emptily. "And poisonously easy to love. Women—even decent women—make such ghastly mistakes about men."

"All you're telling me is that you once thought you loved him, but not anymore, and that you didn't shoot him."

"Yes?" Her voice was light now. "Dead," she said. "The poor, egotistical, cheap, nasty, handsome, treacherous guy. Dead and cold and done with. No, Mr. Marlowe, I didn't shoot him."

I waited, letting her work it out of her. After a moment she said quietly, "Does Mr. Kingsley know?"

I nodded.

"And the police, of course."

"Not yet. At least not from me. I found him. The house door wasn't quite shut. I went in and there he was."

She picked the pencil up and poked at the handkerchief again. "Does Mr. Kingsley know about this scented rag?"

"Nobody knows about that, except you and I, and whoever put it there."

"Nice of you," she said dryly. Then, "Have you any idea who did it?"

"Ideas, but that's all they are. I'm afraid the police are going to find it simple. Some of Mrs. Kingsley's clothes are hanging in Lavery's closet. And when they know the whole story—including what happened at Little Fawn Lake yesterday—I'm afraid they'll just reach for the handcuffs. They have to find her first. But that won't be so hard for them."

"Crystal Kingsley," she said emptily. "So he couldn't be spared even that."

I said, "It doesn't have to be. It could be an entirely different motivation, something we know nothing about." I stood up and tapped on the edge of the desk, looking down at her. She had a lovely neck. She pointed to the handkerchief.

"What about that?" she asked dully. "It has to mean something, doesn't it? It might mean a lot."

I laughed. "I don't think it means anything at all. Women are always leaving their handkerchiefs around. A fellow like Lavery would collect them and keep them in a drawer with a sandalwood sachet. Somebody would find the stock and take one out to use. Or he would lend them, enjoying the reactions to the other girls' initials. I'd say he was that kind of a heel. Good-by, Miss Fromsett, and thanks for talking to me."

I started to go, then I stopped and asked her, "Did you hear the name of the reporter down there who gave Brownwell all his information?"

She shook her head.

"Or the name of Mrs. Almore's parents?"

"Not that either. But I could probably find that out for you. I'd be glad to try."

"That would be very nice of you," I said. I ran a finger along the edge of the desk and looked at her sideways. Pale ivory skin, dark and lovely eyes, hair as fine as hair can be.

I walked back down the room and out.

Chapter 8

No POLICE cars stood in front of Lavery's house, nobody hung around on the sidewalk, and when I pushed the front door open there was no smell of cigar or cigarette smoke inside. I went down to the end and hung over the railing that led downstairs. Nothing moved in Mr. Lavery's house. Nothing made sound except very faintly down below in the bathroom the quiet trickle of water dripping on a dead man's shoulder.

I went to the telephone and looked up the number of the police department in the directory. I dialed and while I was waiting for an answer, I took the little automatic out of my pocket and laid it on the table beside the telephone.

When the male voice said, "Bay City police—Smoot talking," I said, "There's been a shooting at 623 Altair Street. Man named Lavery lives there. He's dead."

"Six two three Altair. Who are you?"

"The name is Marlowe."

"You there in the house?"

"Right."

"Don't touch anything at all."

I hung up, sat down on the davenport, and waited.

Not very long. A siren whined far off, growing louder with great surges of sound. Tires screamed at a corner, and the siren wail died to a metallic growl, then to silence. Steps hit the sidewalk and I went over to the front door and opened it.

Two uniformed cops barged into the room. They were the usual large size and they had the usual weathered faces and suspicious eyes. They stood and looked at me warily, then the older one said briefly, "All right, where is it?"

"Downstairs in the bathroom, behind the shower curtain."

"You stay here with him, Eddie."

He went rapidly along the room and disappeared. The cop called Eddie looked at me steadily and said out of the corner of his mouth, "Don't make any false moves, buddy."

I sat down on the davenport again. There were sounds below-stairs, feet walking. The cop with me suddenly spotted the gun lying on the telephone table. He charged at it violently, like a downfield blocker.

"This the death gun?" he almost shouted.

"I should imagine so. It's been fired."

"Ha!" He leaned over the gun, baring his teeth at me, and put his hand to his holster.

His eyes were being careful of me. "What you shoot him for?" he growled.

"Let's just sit down and wait for the homicide boys," I said. "I'm reserving my defense."

"Don't give me none of that," he said.

"I'm not giving you any of anything. If I had shot him, I wouldn't be here. I wouldn't have called up. You wouldn't have found the gun. Don't work so hard on the case. You won't be on it more than ten minutes."

The other cop came back up the stairs, looking grave. He stood in the middle of the floor and looked at his wristwatch and made a note in a notebook and then looked out of a front window, holding the venetian blind aside.

The one who had stayed with me said, "Can I look now?"

"Let it lie, Eddie. Nothing in it for us. You call the coroner?"

"I thought homicide would do that."

"Yeah, that's right. Captain Webber will be on it and he likes to do everything himself." He looked at me and said, "You're a man named Marlowe?"

I said I was a man named Marlowe.

"What's your line, mister? Friend of his?" He made a thumb toward the floor.

"Saw him yesterday for the first time. I'm a private operative from L.A."

"Oh." He looked at me sharply. Then he looked out of the front window again. "That's the Almore place across the street, Eddie," he said.

Eddie went and looked with him. "Sure is," he said. "You can read the plate. Say, this guy downstairs might be the guy—"

"Shut up," the other one said and dropped the venetian blind. They both turned around and stared at me woodenly.

A car came down the block and stopped and a door slammed and more steps came down the walk. The older of the prowl-car boys opened the door to two men in plain clothes, one of whom I already knew.

THE one who came first was a small man for a cop, middle-aged, thin-faced, with a permanently tired expression. His nose was sharp and bent a little to one side, as if somebody had given it the elbow one time when it was into something. His porkpie hat was set square on his head and chalk-white hair showed under it. The man behind him was Degarmo, the big cop with the dusty blond hair and the metallic-blue eyes and the savage lined face who had not liked my being in front of Dr. Almore's house.

The two uniformed men looked at the small man and touched their caps.

"The body's in the basement, Captain Webber. Been shot twice after a couple of misses, looks like. Dead quite some time. This party's name is Marlowe. He's a private eye from Los Angeles. I didn't question him beyond that."

"Quite right," Webber said sharply. He passed a suspicious eye over my face and nodded briefly. "I'm Captain Webber," he said. "This is Lieutenant Degarmo. We'll look at the body first."

He went along the room. Degarmo looked at me as if he had never seen me before and followed him. They went downstairs, the older of the two prowl-car men with them. Eddie and I stared each other down for a while.

I said, "This is right across the street from Dr. Almore's place, isn't it?"

"Yeah. So what?"

"So nothing," I said.

He was silent. The voices came up from below, blurred and indistinct. Eddie cocked his ear and said in a more friendly tone, "You remember that one?"

"A little."

He laughed. "They killed that case pretty," he said. "They wrapped it up and hid it in back of the shelf. The top shelf in the bathroom closet."

"So they did," I said. "I wonder why."

The cop looked at me sternly. "There was good reasons, pal. Don't think there wasn't. You know this Lavery well?"

"Not well."

"On to him for something?"

"Working on him a little," I said. "You knew him?"

Eddie shook his head. "Nope. I just remembered it was a guy from this house found Almore's wife in the garage that night." He scratched his ear and listened. Steps were coming back up the stairs. Eddie's face went blank and he moved away from me and straightened up.

Captain Webber hurried over to the telephone and dialed a number and spoke, then held the phone away from his ear and looked back over his shoulder.

"Who's deputy coroner this week, Al?"

"Ed Garland," the big lieutenant said woodenly.

"Call Ed Garland," Webber said into the phone. "Have him come over right away. And tell the flash squad to step on it."

He put the phone down and barked, "Who handled this gun?"

I said, "I did."

He came over and teetered on his heels in front of me and pushed his small sharp chin up at me.

"Don't you know enough not to handle a weapon found at the scene of a crime?"

"Certainly," I said. "But when I handled it I didn't know there had been a crime. I didn't know the gun had been fired. It was lying on the stairs and I thought it had been dropped."

"A likely story," Webber said bitterly.

I didn't say anything to that. Webber swiveled sharply and said to the two uniformed men, "You boys can get back to your car and check in with the dispatcher."

They saluted and went out. Webber listened until their car went away. Then he put his bleak and callous eye on me once more.

"Let me see your identification."

I handed him my wallet and he rooted in it. Degarmo sat in a chair and crossed his legs and stared up blankly at the ceiling. Webber gave me back my wallet. I put it away.

"People in your line make a lot of trouble," he said.

"Not necessarily," I said.

He raised his voice. "I said they make a lot of trouble, and a lot of trouble is what I meant. But get this straight. You're not going to make any in Bay City. We don't have any political tug-of-war down here. We work on the straight line and we work fast. Don't worry about us, mister."

"I'm not worrying," I said. "I don't have anything to worry about. I'm just trying to make a nice clean dollar."

Degarmo brought his eyes down from the ceiling and curled a forefinger to stare at the nail. He spoke in a heavy bored voice.

"Look, Chief, the fellow downstairs is called Lavery. He's dead. I knew him a little. He was a chaser."

"What of it?" Webber snapped, not looking away from me.

"The whole setup indicates a dame," Degarmo said. "You know what these private eyes work at. Divorce stuff. Suppose we'd let him tie into it, instead of just trying to scare him dumb."

Webber poked a thin hard finger at me and said, "Talk."

I said, "I'm working for a Los Angeles businessman who can't take a lot of loud publicity. A month ago his wife ran off and later a telegram came which indicated she had gone with Lavery. But my client met Lavery in town a couple of days ago and he denied it. The client believed him enough to get worried. It seems the lady is pretty reckless. She might have taken up with some bad company and gotten into a jam. Anyhow I came down to see Lavery and he denied again that he had gone with her. I half believed him but later I got reasonable proof that he had been with her in a San Bernardino hotel the night she was supposed to have left the mountain cabin where she had been staying. So I came down to tackle Lavery again. No answer to the bell, the door was slightly open. I came inside, looked around, found the gun, and searched the house. I found him. Just the way he is now."

"The name of this man you're working for?"

"Kingsley." I gave him the Beverly Hills address. "He manages a cosmetic company in the Treloar Building on Olive. The Gillerlain Company."

Webber looked at Degarmo. Degarmo wrote lazily on an envelope. Webber looked back at me and said, "What else?"

"I went up to this mountain cabin where the lady had been staying. It's at a place called Little Fawn Lake, near Puma Point, forty-six miles into the mountains from San Bernardino."

I looked at Degarmo. He was writing slowly. His hand stopped a moment and seemed to hang in the air stiffly, then it dropped to the envelope and wrote again. I went on, "About a month ago the wife of the caretaker at Kingsley's place up there had a fight with him and left, or so everybody thought. Yesterday she was found drowned in the lake."

Webber almost closed his eyes and rocked on his heels. Almost softly he asked, "Why are you telling me this? Are you implying a connection?"

"There is a connection in time. Lavery was up there. I don't know of any other connection, but I thought I'd better mention it."

Degarmo was sitting very still, looking at the floor in front of him. His face was tight and he looked even more savage than usual.

Webber said, "This woman that was drowned. Suicide?"

"Suicide or murder. She left a good-by note. But her husband has been arrested on suspicion. The name is Chess. Bill and Muriel Chess, his wife."

"I don't want any part of that," Webber said sharply. "Let's confine ourselves to what went on here. I'm going to ask you a question and I want an honest answer. You know I'll get it eventually. You have looked through the house and I imagine pretty thoroughly. Have you seen anything that suggests to you that this Kingsley woman has been here?"

"The answer is yes," I said. "There are women's clothes hanging in a closet downstairs that have been described to me as being worn by Mrs. Kingsley at San Bernardino the night she met Lavery there. The description was not exact though. A black and white suit, mostly white, and a panama hat with a black and white band."

Webber was staring at me fixedly, with little or no expression on his face but a kind of tight watchfulness.

"Anything else?" he asked quietly.

Before I could answer, a car stopped outside the house, and then another. Webber skipped over to open the door. Three men came in, a short curly-haired man and a large oxlike man, both carrying heavy black leather cases. Behind them a tall thin man in a dark gray suit and black tie. He had very bright eyes and a poker face.

Webber pointed a finger at the curly-haired man and said, "Downstairs in the bathroom, Busoni. I want a lot of prints from all over the house, particularly any that seem to be made by a woman."

"I do all the work," Busoni grunted. He and the oxlike man went along the room and down the stairs.

"We have a corpse for you, Garland," Webber said to the third man. "Let's go down and look at him. You've ordered the wagon?"

The bright-eyed man nodded briefly and he and Webber went downstairs after the other two.

Degarmo put the envelope and pencil away. He stared at me. I said, "I'd like to know more about the Almore case."

He flushed slowly and his eyes got mean. "You said you didn't know Almore."

"I didn't yesterday. I still don't know anything about him. But since then I've learned that Lavery knew Mrs. Almore, that she committed suicide, that Lavery found her dead, and that Lavery has at least been suspected of blackmailing Almore—or of being in a position to blackmail him. Also both your prowl-car boys seemed interested in the fact that Almore's house was across the street from here. And one of them remarked that the case had been killed pretty, or words to that effect."

Degarmo said in a slow deadly tone, "I'll have the badge off the son of a bitch. All they do is flap their mouths."

"Then there's nothing in it," I said.

He looked at his cigarette. "Nothing in what?"

"Nothing in the idea that Almore murdered his wife, and had enough pull to get it fixed."

Degarmo came to his feet and walked over to lean down at me. "Say that again," he said softly.

I said it again.

He hit me across the face with his open hand. It jerked my head around hard. My face felt hot and large.

"Say it again," he said softly.

I said it again. His hand knocked my head to one side again.

"Say it again."

"Nope. Third time lucky. You might miss." I put a hand up and rubbed my cheek.

He stood leaning down, his lips drawn back over his teeth, a hard animal glare in his very blue eyes.

"Anytime you talk like that to a cop," he said, "you know what you got coming. Try it on again and it won't be the flat of a hand I'll use on you."

I bit hard on my lips and rubbed my cheek.

"Poke your big nose into our business and you'll wake up in an alley with the cats looking at you," he said.

I didn't say anything. He sat down again, breathing hard. I stopped rubbing my face and held my hand out and worked the fingers slowly, to get the hard clench out of them.

"I'll remember that," I said. "Both ways."

IT WAS EARLY EVENING when I got back to Los Angeles and up to my office. I unlocked the door and picked up an envelope that lay in front of the mail slot and dropped it on the desk without looking at it. I ran the windows up and leaned out, looking at the first neon lights glowing, smelling the warm, foody air that drifted up from the alley ventilator of the coffee shop next door.

I peeled off my coat and sat down at the desk and tore open the envelope. The note read:

Mr. Marlowe: Florence Almore's parents are a Mr. and Mrs. Eustace Grayson, presently residing at the Rossmore Arms, 640 South Oxford Avenue. I checked this by calling the listed phone number. Yours, Adrienne Fromsett.

I ran a finger across the corner of the desk and looked at the streak made by the wiping off of the dust. I looked at the dust on my finger and wiped that off. I looked at my watch. I looked at the wall. I looked at nothing.

I went over to the washbowl and washed my hands and bathed my face in cold water and looked at it. The flush was gone from the left cheek, but it looked a little swollen. Not very much, but enough to make me tighten up again. I brushed my hair. There was getting to be plenty of gray in it. The face under the hair had a sick look. I didn't like the face at all.

I went back to the desk and read Miss Fromsett's note again. I smoothed it out and folded it and put it in my coat pocket.

I sat very still and listened to the evening grow quiet outside the open windows. And very slowly I grew quiet with it.

Chapter 9

THE Rossmore Arms was a gloomy pile of dark red brick built around a huge forecourt. It had a plush-lined lobby containing silence, tubbed plants, a bored canary in a cage as big as a doghouse, a smell of old carpet dust and the cloying fragrance of gardenias long ago.

The Graysons were on the fifth floor in front, in the north wing. They were sitting together in a room which seemed to be deliberately twenty years out of date. It had fat overstuffed furniture and dark red plush side drapes by the windows. It smelled of tobacco smoke and behind that the air was telling me they had had lamb chops and broccoli for dinner.

Grayson's wife was a plump woman who might once have had big baby-blue eyes. They were faded out now and dimmed by glasses and slightly protuberant. She had kinky white hair. She sat darning socks with her thick ankles crossed, her feet just reaching the floor, and a big wicker sewing basket in her lap.

Grayson was a long stooped yellow-faced man with high shoulders, bristly eyebrows and almost no chin. The upper part of his face meant business. The lower part was just saying good-by. He had been gnawing fretfully at the evening paper. I had looked him up in the city directory. He was a CPA and looked it. He even had ink on his fingers and there were four pencils in the pocket of his open vest.

He read my card carefully for the seventh time and looked me up and down and said slowly, "What is it you want to see us about, Mr. Marlowe?"

"I'm interested in a man named Lavery. He lives across the street from Dr. Almore. Your daughter was the wife of Dr. Almore. Lavery is the man who found your daughter the night she—died."

They pointed like bird dogs when I deliberately hesitated on the last word. Grayson looked at his wife and she shook her head.

"We don't care to talk about that," Grayson said promptly. "It is much too painful to us."

I waited a moment and looked gloomy with them. Then I said, "I don't blame you. I don't want to make you. I'd like to get in touch with the man you hired to look into it, though."

Grayson asked, "Why?"

"I'd better tell you a little of my story." I told them what I had been hired to do, not mentioning Kingsley by name. I told them of the incident with Degarmo outside Almore's house.

Grayson said sharply, "Am I to understand that you were unknown to Dr. Almore, had not approached him in any way, and that he nevertheless called a police officer because you were outside his house?"

I said, "That's right."

"That's very queer," Grayson said.

"I'd say that was one very nervous man," I said. "And Degarmo asked me if her folks—meaning your daughter's folks—had hired me. You've always thought Almore murdered her, haven't you? That's why you hired this detective."

Mrs. Grayson looked up with quick eyes and ducked her head down and rolled up another pair of mended socks.

Grayson said nothing.

I said, "Was there any evidence, or was it just that you didn't like Almore?"

"There was evidence," Grayson said bitterly, and with a sudden clearness of voice, as if he had decided to talk about it after all. "There must have been. We were told there was. But we never got it. The police took care of that."

"I heard they had this fellow arrested and sent up for drunk driving."

"You heard right."

"But he never told you what he had to go on?"

"No."

"I don't like that," I said. "That sounds a little as if this fellow hadn't made up his mind whether to use his information for your benefit or keep it and put the squeeze on the doctor."

Grayson looked at his wife again. She said quietly, "Mr. Talley didn't impress me that way. He was a quiet unassuming little man. But you can't always judge, I know."

I said, "So Talley was his name. That was one of the things I hoped you would tell me."

"And what were the others?" Grayson asked.

"How I can find Talley—and what it was that laid the groundwork of suspicion in your minds."

Mrs. Grayson said, "Dope."

"She means that literally," Grayson said at once, as if the single word had been a green light. "Almore was, and no doubt is, a dope doctor. Our daughter made that clear to us."

"Just what do you mean by a dope doctor, Mr. Grayson?"

"I mean a doctor whose practice is largely with people who are living on the raw edge of nervous collapse, from drink and dissipation. People who have to be given sedatives and narcotics all the time. A lucrative practice," he said primly, "and I imagine a dangerous one to the doctor."

"No doubt of that," I said. "But there's a lot of money in it. Did you know a man named Condy?"

"No. We know who he was. Florence suspected he was a source of Almore's narcotic supply."

I said, "Could be. He probably wouldn't want to write himself too many prescriptions. Did you know Lavery?"

"We never saw him. We knew who he was."

"Ever occur to you that Lavery might have been blackmailing Almore?"

He shook his head. "No, why should it?"

"He was first to the body," I said. "Whatever looked wrong to Talley must have been equally visible to Lavery."

"It's an idea," Grayson said.

I looked at Mrs. Grayson. Her hands had never stopped working. She had a dozen pairs of darned socks finished.

"What's happened to Talley? Was he framed?" I asked.

"I don't think there's any doubt about it. His wife was very bitter. She said he had been given a doped drink in a bar and he had been drinking with a policeman. She said a police car was waiting across the street for him to start driving and that he was picked up at once. Also that he was given only the most perfunctory examination at the jail."

"That doesn't mean too much. That's what he told her after he was arrested. He'd tell her something like that automatically."

"Well, I hate to think the police are not honest," Grayson said. "But these things are done, and everybody knows it."

I said, "If they made an honest mistake about your daughter's death, they would hate to have Talley show them up. It might mean several lost jobs. If they thought what he was really after was blackmail, they wouldn't be too fussy how they took care of him. Where is Talley now? What it all boils down to is that if there was any solid clue, he either had it or was on the track of it and knew what he was looking for."

Grayson said, "We don't know where he is. He got six months, but that expired long ago."

"How about his wife?"

He looked at his own wife. She said briefly, "At 1618½ Westmore Street, Bay City. Eustace and I sent her a little money. She was left bad off."

I made a note of the address and leaned back in my chair and said, "Somebody shot Lavery this morning in his bathroom."

Mrs. Grayson's pudgy hands became still on the edges of the basket. Grayson sat with his mouth open, holding his pipe in front of it. "Of course it would be too much to expect," he said, "that Dr. Almore had any connection with that."

"I'd like to think he had," I said. "He certainly lives at a handy distance. The police think my client's wife shot him. They have a good case too, when they find her. But if Almore had anything to do with it, it must surely arise out of your daughter's death. That's why I'm trying to find out something about that."

Grayson said, "A man who has done one murder wouldn't have much hesitation in doing another." He spoke as if he had given the matter considerable study.

I said, "Yeah, maybe. What was supposed to be the motive for the first one?"

"Florence was wild," he said sadly. "A wild and difficult girl. She was wasteful and extravagant, always picking up new and rather doubtful friends, talking too much and too loudly, and generally acting the fool. A wife like that can be very dangerous to a man like Albert S. Almore. But I don't believe that was the prime motive, was it, Lettie?"

He looked at his wife, but she didn't look at him. She jabbed a darning needle into a round ball of wool and said nothing.

Grayson sighed and went on, "We had reason to believe he was carrying on with his office nurse and that Florence had threatened him with a public scandal. He couldn't have anything like that, could he? One kind of scandal might too easily lead to another."

I said, "How did he do the murder?"

"With morphine, of course. He always had it. He was an expert in the use of it. Then when she was in a deep coma he would have placed her in the garage and started the car motor. There was no autopsy, you know. But it was known that she had been given a hypodermic injection that night."

I nodded and he leaned back satisfied and ran his hand over his head and down his face and let it fall slowly to his bony knee.

I looked at them. A couple of elderly people sitting there quietly, poisoning their minds with hate, a year and a half after it had happened. They would like it if Almore had shot Lavery. They would love it. It would warm them clear down to their ankles.

I said, "You're believing a lot of this because you want to. It's always possible that she committed suicide, and that the cover-up was partly to protect Condy's gambling club and partly to prevent Almore from being questioned at a public hearing."

"I think you have taken up enough of our time," Grayson said.

I stood up and started for the door. Grayson hoisted himself out of his chair and dragged across the room after me. There was a flush on his yellow face.

"I didn't mean to be rude," he said. "I guess Lettie and I oughtn't to brood about this business the way we do."

"I think you've both been very patient," I said. "Was there anybody else involved that we haven't mentioned by name?"

He shook his head, then looked back at his wife.

I said, "The way I got the story, Dr. Almore's office nurse put Mrs. Almore to bed that night. Would that be the one he was supposed to be playing around with?"

Mrs. Grayson said sharply, "Wait a minute. We never saw the girl. But she had a pretty name. Just give me a minute."

We gave her a minute. "Mildred something," she said.

I took a deep breath. "Would it be Mildred Haviland, Mrs. Grayson?"

She smiled brightly and nodded. "Of course, Mildred Haviland. Don't you remember, Eustace?"

He didn't remember. He looked at us like a horse that has got into the wrong stable. "What does it matter?" He opened the door. "If you get him," he said and clamped his mouth hard on his pipe-stem, "call back with a bill. If you get Almore, I mean."

I said I knew he meant Almore, but there wouldn't be any bill.

I went back along the silent hallway. The self-operating elevator was carpeted in red plush. It had an elderly perfume in it, like three widows drinking tea.

THE house on Westmore Street was a small frame bungalow behind a larger house. A narrow concrete path led to the house at the back. It had a tiny porch with a single chair on it. I stepped up on the porch and rang the bell.

It buzzed not very far off. The front door was open behind the screen but there was no light. From the darkness a querulous voice said, "What is it?"

I spoke into the darkness. "Mr. Talley in?"

The voice became flat and without tone. "Who wants him?"

"A friend."

The woman sitting inside the darkness made a vague sound in her throat.

"All right," she said. "How much is this one?"

"It's not a bill, Mrs. Talley. I suppose you are Mrs. Talley?"

"Oh, go away and let me alone," the voice said. "Mr. Talley isn't here. He hasn't been here. He won't be here."

I put my nose against the screen. I could see the vague outlines of a couch. A woman was lying on it. She seemed to be lying quite motionless on her back and looking up at the ceiling.

"I'm sick," the voice said. "I've had enough trouble. Go away and leave me be."

I said, "I've just come from talking to the Graysons."

There was a little silence, but no movement, then a sigh. "I never heard of them."

I leaned against the frame of the screen door and looked back along the narrow walk to the street. There was a car across the way with parking lights burning.

I said, "Yes, you have. I'm working for them. They're still in there pitching. How about you? Don't you want something back?"

The voice said, "I want to be let alone."

"I want information," I said. "I'm going to get it. Quietly if I can. Loud, if it can't be quiet."

The voice said, "Another copper, eh?"

"You know I'm not a copper, Mrs. Talley. The Graysons wouldn't talk to a copper. Call them up and ask them."

"I never heard of them," the voice said. "I don't have a phone, even if I knew them. Go away, copper. I'm sick."

"My name is Philip Marlowe," I said. "I'm a private eye in Los Angeles. I've got something, but I want to talk to your husband."

The woman on the couch let out a dim laugh which barely reached across the room. "You've got something," she said. "That sounds familiar. My God it does! You've got something. George Talley had something too—once."

"He can have it again," I said, "if he plays his cards right."

"If that's what it takes," she said, "you can scratch him off right now." The pale blur of face on the couch moved and disappeared. The woman had turned her face to the wall.

"I'm tired," she said, her voice now muffled by talking at the wall. "I'm so damn tired. Beat it, mister. Be nice and go away."

"Would a little money help any?"

"Can't you smell the cigar smoke?"

I sniffed. I didn't smell any cigar smoke. I said, "No."

"They've been here. They were here two hours. God, I'm tired of it all. Go away."

"Look, Mrs. Talley—"

She rolled on the couch and the blur of her face showed again.

"Look yourself," she said. "I don't know you. I don't want to know you. I have nothing to tell you. I wouldn't tell it, if I had. Now you get out and leave me alone."

"Let me in the house," I said. "We can talk this over. I think I can show you—"

She rolled suddenly on the couch again and feet struck the floor. A tight anger came into her voice.

"If you don't get out," she said, "I'm going to start yelling my head off. Right now. Now!"

"Okay," I said quickly. "I'll stick my card in the door. So you won't forget my name. You might change your mind."

I got the card out and wedged it into the crack of the screen door. I said, "Well good night, Mrs. Talley."

No answer. Her eyes were looking across the room at me, faintly luminous in the dark. I went down off the porch and back along the narrow walk to the street.

Across the way a motor purred gently in the car with the parking lights on.

I got into the Chrysler and started it up, driving north on Westmore. At the next corner I bumped over disused interurban tracks and on into a block of junkyards full of the decomposing carcasses of old automobiles. Headlights glowed in my rearview mirror. They got larger. I stepped on the gas and reached keys out of my pocket and unlocked the glove compartment. I took a .38 out and laid it on the car seat close to my leg.

Beyond the junkyards there was a brick field. The tall chimney of the kiln was smokeless, far off over wasteland. Piles of dark bricks, a low wooden building, no one moving, no light.

The car behind me gained. The low whine of a lightly touched siren growled through the night. The sound loafed over the fringes of a neglected golf course to the east, across the brickyard to the west. I speeded up, but the car behind me came up fast and a huge red spotlight suddenly glared all over the road.

The car came up level and started to cut in. I stood the Chrysler on its nose, swung out behind the police car, and made a U-turn with half an inch to spare. I gunned the motor the other way. Behind me sounded the rough clashing of gears and the howl of an infuriated motor.

It wasn't any use. They were behind me again. I didn't have any idea of getting away. I wanted to get back where there were houses and people to come out and watch and perhaps to remember.

I didn't make it. The police car heaved up alongside again and a hard voice yelled, "Pull over, or we'll blast a hole in you!"

I pulled over to the curb and set the brake. I put the gun back in the glove compartment and snapped it shut. The police car jumped on its springs just in front of my left front fender. A fat man slammed out of it roaring.

"Don't you know a police siren when you hear one? Get out of that car!"

I got out of the car and stood beside it in the moonlight. The fat man had a gun in his hand.

"Gimme your license!" he barked in a voice as hard as the blade of a shovel.

I took it out and offered it to him. The other cop in the car slid out from under the wheel and came around beside me and took what I was holding out. He put a flash on it and read.

"Name of Marlowe," he said. "Hell, the guy's a shamus. Just think of that, Cooney."

Cooney said, "Is that all? Guess I won't need this." He tucked the gun back in his holster and buttoned the leather flap down over it. "Guess I can handle this with my little flippers."

The other one said, "Doing fifty-five. Been drinking, I wouldn't wonder."

"Smell the bastard's breath," Cooney said.

The other one leaned forward with a polite leer. "Could I smell the breath, shamus?"

I let him smell the breath.

"Well," he said, "he ain't staggering. I got to admit that."

" 'S a cold night for summer. Buy the boy a drink, Officer Dobbs."

"Now that's a sweet idea," Dobbs said. He went to the car and got a half-pint bottle out of it. He held it up. It was a third full. "No really solid drinking here," he said. He held the bottle out. "With our compliments, pal."

"Suppose I don't want a drink," I said.

"Don't say that," Cooney whined. "We might get the idea you wanted footprints on your stomach."

I tilted the bottle, locked my throat, and filled my mouth with whiskey. Cooney lunged forward and sank a fist in my stomach. I sprayed the whiskey and bent over choking. I dropped the bottle.

I bent to get it and saw Cooney's fat knee rising at my face. I stepped to one side and straightened and slammed him on the nose with everything I had. His left hand wènt to his face and his voice howled and his right hand jumped to his gun holster. Dobbs ran at me from the side and his arm swung low. The blackjack hit me behind the left knee, the leg went dead, and I sat down hard on the ground, gritting my teeth and spitting whiskey.

Cooney took his hand away from his face full of blood.

"Damn it," he cracked in a thick horrible voice. "This is blood. My blood." He let out a wild roar and swung his foot at my face.

I rolled far enough to catch it on my shoulder. It was bad enough taking it there.

Dobbs pushed between us and said, "We got enough, Charlie. Better not get it all gummed up."

Cooney turned and moved heavily away to the police car. He leaned against it muttering through his handkerchief.

Dobbs said to me, "Up on the feet, boy friend."

I got up and rubbed behind my knee. The nerve of the leg was jumping like an angry monkey.

"Get in the car," Dobbs said. "Our car."

I went over and climbed into the police car.

Dobbs said, "You drive the other heap, Charlie."

"I'll tear every lousy fender off'n it," Cooney roared.

Dobbs picked the bottle off the ground, threw it over the fence, and slid into the car beside me. He pressed the starter.

Cooney slammed into the Chrysler and started it and clashed the gears as if he was trying to strip them. Dobbs tooled the police car smoothly around and started north again along the brickyard.

"You'll like our new jail," he said.

"What will the charge be?"

He thought for a moment, guiding the car with a gentle hand and watching in the mirror to see that Cooney followed.

"Speeding," he said. "Resisting arrest. HBD." HBD is police slang for "had been drinking."

Chapter 10

THE jail was on the twelfth floor of the new city hall. It was a nice jail and the cellblock was almost brand-new. The battleship-gray paint on the steel walls and door still had the fresh gloss of newness disfigured in two or three places by squirted tobacco juice. I sat on the lower bunk and rubbed the hot swelling behind my knee. The pain radiated all the way to the ankle.

I looked at my watch. Nine fifty-four. Time to go home and get your slippers on and play over a game of chess. Time for a tall cool drink and a long quiet pipe. Time to sit with your feet up and think of nothing. Time to start yawning over your magazine. Time to be a human being, a householder, a man with nothing to do but rest and suck in the night air and rebuild the brain for tomorrow.

A man in the blue-gray jail uniform came along between the cells reading numbers. He stopped in front of mine and unlocked the door and gave me the hard stare they think they have to wear on their pans forever and ever.

"Out," he said.

I stepped out of the cell and he relocked the door and jerked his thumb and we went along to a wide steel gate and he unlocked that and we went through and he relocked it and the keys tinkled pleasantly on the big steel ring and after a while we went through a steel door that was painted like wood on the outside and battleship gray on the inside.

Degarmo was standing there by the counter talking to the desk sergeant. He turned his metallic-blue eyes on me and said, "How you doing?"

"Fine."

"Captain Webber wants to talk to you."

"That's fine," I said.

"You're limping a little," he said. "You trip over something?"

"Yeah," I said. "I tripped over a blackjack. It jumped up and bit me behind the left knee."

"That's too bad," Degarmo said, blank-eyed.

The desk sergeant lifted his shaggy head and gave us both a long stare. "You ought to see Cooney's little Irish nose," he said. "If you want to see something fine. It's spread over his face like syrup on a waffle."

Degarmo said absently, "What's the matter? He get in a fight?"

"I wouldn't know," the desk sergeant said. "Maybe it was the same blackjack that jumped up and bit him."

"For a desk sergeant you talk too damn much," Degarmo said.

"A desk sergeant always talks too damn much," the desk sergeant said. "Maybe that's why he isn't a lieutenant on homicide."

"You see how we are here," Degarmo said. "Just one great big happy family."

"With beaming smiles on our faces," the desk sergeant said, "and our arms spread wide and welcome, and a rock in each hand."

Degarmo jerked his head at me and we went out.

CAPTAIN Webber pushed his sharp bent nose across the desk at me and said, "Sit down."

I sat down in a round-backed wooden armchair and eased my left leg away from the sharp edge of the seat. It was a large neat corner office. Degarmo sat at the end of the desk and crossed his legs and rubbed his ankle thoughtfully, looking out of a window.

Webber went on, "You asked for trouble, and you got it. You were doing fifty-five miles an hour in a residential zone and you attempted to get away from a police car that signaled you to stop with its siren and red spotlight. You were abusive when stopped and you struck an officer in the face."

I said nothing. Webber picked a match off his desk and broke it in half and threw the pieces over his shoulder.

"Or are they lying—as usual?" he asked.

"I didn't see their report," I said. "I was probably doing fifty-five in a residential district. I went a little fast, but all I was trying to do was get to a better-lighted part of town."

Degarmo moved his eyes to give me a bleak meaningless stare. Webber snapped his teeth impatiently.

I said, "These cops that picked me up were parked in front of the house where George Talley's wife lives. They were there before I got there. George Talley is the man who used to be a private detective down here. I wanted to see him. Degarmo knows why I wanted to see him."

Degarmo picked a match out of his pocket and chewed on the soft end of it quietly. He nodded, without expression. Webber didn't look at him.

I said, "You are a stupid man, Degarmo. Everything you do is stupid, and done in a stupid way. When you went up against me yesterday in front of Almore's house you had to get tough when there was nothing to get tough about. You had to make me curious when I didn't even know Almore and had nothing to be curious about. You even had to drop hints which showed me how I could satisfy that curiosity, if it became important."

Webber said, "What the devil has all this got to do with your being arrested in the twelve-hundred block on Westmore Street?"

"It has to do with the Almore case," I said. "George Talley worked on the Almore case—until he was pinched for drunk driving."

"Well, I never worked on the Almore case," Webber snapped. "Stick to the point, can't you?"

"I am sticking to the point. Degarmo knows about the Almore case and he doesn't like it talked about. Even your prowl-car boys know about it. Cooney and Dobbs had no reason to follow me unless it was because I visited the wife of a man who had worked on the Almore case. I wasn't doing fifty-five miles an hour when they started to follow me. I tried to get away from them because I had a good idea I might get beaten up for going there. Degarmo had given me that idea."

Webber looked quickly at Degarmo. Degarmo's hard blue eyes looked across the room at the wall in front of him.

I said, "And I didn't bust Cooney in the nose until after he had forced me to drink whiskey and then hit me in the stomach when I drank it, so that I would spill it down my coat front and smell of it. This can't be the first time you have heard of that trick, Captain."

Webber broke another match. He leaned back and looked at his small tight knuckles. He looked again at Degarmo and said, "If you got made chief of police today, you might let me in on it."

Degarmo said, "Hell, the shamus just got a couple of playful taps. Kind of kidding. If a guy can't take a joke—"

Webber said, "You put Cooney and Dobbs over there?"

"Well—yes, I did," Degarmo said. "I don't see where we have to put up with these snoopers coming into our town and stirring up a lot of dead leaves just to promote themselves a job and work a couple of old suckers for a big fee. Guys like that need a good sharp lesson."

"Is that how it looks to you?" Webber asked.

"That's exactly how it looks to me," Degarmo said.

"I wonder what fellows like you need," Webber said. "Right now I think you need a little air. Would you please take it, Lieutenant?"

Degarmo opened his mouth slowly. "You mean you want me to breeze on out?"

Webber leaned forward and his sharp little chin seemed to cut the air like the forefoot of a cruiser. "Would you be so kind?"

Degarmo stood up slowly, a dark flush staining his cheekbones. He walked to the door and out. Webber waited for the door to close before he spoke.

"Is it your line that you can tie this Almore business a year and a half ago to the shooting in Lavery's place today? Or is it just a smoke screen you're laying down because you know damn well Kingsley's wife shot Lavery?"

I said, "It was tied to Lavery before he was shot. In a rough sort of way, but enough to make a man think."

"I've been into this matter a little more thoroughly than you might think," Webber said coldly. "Although I never had anything personally to do with the death of Almore's wife and I wasn't chief of detectives at that time. If you didn't even know Almore yesterday morning, you must have heard a lot about him since."

I told him exactly what I had heard, both from Miss Fromsett and from the Graysons.

"Then it's your theory that Lavery may have blackmailed Dr. Almore?" he asked at the end. "And that that may have something to do with the murder?"

"It's not a theory. It's no more than a possibility. But if there was nothing funny about the Almore case, why get so tough with anybody who shows an interest in it? It could be coincidence that George Talley was hooked for drunk driving just when he was working on it. It could be coincidence that Almore called a cop because I stared at his house. But it's no coincidence that two of your men were watching Talley's home tonight, ready, willing and able to make trouble for me, if I went there."

"I grant you that," Webber said. "And as I understand you weren't even booked, you're free to go home anytime you want to. And if I were you, I'd leave Captain Webber to deal with the Lavery case and with any remote connection it might turn out to have with the Almore case."

I said, "And with any remote connection it might have with a woman named Muriel Chess being found drowned in a mountain lake near Puma Point yesterday?"

He raised his eyebrows. "You think that?"

"Only you might not know her as Muriel Chess. Supposing that you knew her at all you might have known her as Mildred Haviland, who used to be Dr. Almore's office nurse. Who put Mrs. Almore to bed the night she was found dead in the garage, and who, if there was any hanky-panky about that, might know what it was, and be bribed or scared into leaving town shortly thereafter."

Webber picked up two matches and broke them. His small bleak eyes were fixed on my face. He said nothing.

"And at that point," I said, "you run into a real basic coincidence, the only one I'm willing to admit in the whole picture. For this Mildred Haviland met a man named Bill Chess in a Riverside beer parlor and for reasons of her own married him and went to live with him at Little Fawn Lake. And Little Fawn Lake was the property of a man whose wife was intimate with Lavery, who had found Mrs. Almore's body. That's what I call a real coincidence. It can't be anything else, but it's basic, fundamental."

Webber got up from his desk and went over to the water cooler and drank two paper cups of water. He crushed the cup slowly in his hand and dropped it into a brown metal wastebasket by the cooler. He walked to the windows and stood looking out over the bay. He came slowly back to his desk and sat down. He was making up his mind about something. Then he said slowly, "I can't see what the hell sense there is in trying to mix that up with something that happened a year and a half later."

"Okay," I said, "and thanks for giving me so much of your time." I got up to go.

"Your leg feel pretty bad?" he asked, as I leaned down to rub it.

"Bad enough, but it's getting better."

"Police business," he said almost gently, "is a hell of a problem. It's a good deal like politics. It asks for the highest type of men, and there's nothing in it to attract the highest type of men. So we have to work with what we get—and we get things like this."

"I know," I said. "I've always known that. I'm not bitter about it. Good night, Captain Webber."

"Wait a minute," he said. "Sit down a minute. If we've got to have the Almore case in this, let's drag it out into the open and look at it."

"It's about time somebody did that," I said. I sat down again.

WEBBER said quietly, "What did you want to see Talley about when you went to his house tonight?"

"He had some line on Florence Almore's death. Her parents hired him to follow it up, but he never told them what it was."

"And you thought he would tell you?" Webber asked sarcastically.

"All I could do was try."

"Talley was a petty blackmailer," Webber said contemptuously. "On more than one occasion. Any way to get rid of him was good enough. So I'll tell you what it was he had. He had a slipper he had stolen from Florence Almore's foot."

"A slipper?"

He smiled faintly. "Just a slipper. It was later found hidden in his house. It was a green velvet dancing pump with some little stones set into the heel. Now ask me what was important about this slipper."

"What was important about it, Captain?"

"She had two pair of them, exactly alike, custom-made on the same order. That's not unusual. In case one of them gets scuffed or some drunken ox tries to walk up a lady's leg." He paused and smiled thinly. "It seems that one pair had never been worn."

"I think I'm beginning to get it," I said.

He leaned back and tapped the arms of his chair. He waited.

"The walk from the side door of the house to the garage is rough concrete," I said. "Fairly rough. Suppose she didn't walk it, but was carried. And suppose whoever carried her put her slippers on—and got one that had not been worn."

"Yes?"

"And suppose Talley noticed this while Lavery was telephoning to the doctor, who was out on his rounds. So he took the unworn slipper, regarding it as evidence that Florence Almore had been murdered."

Webber nodded his head. "It was evidence if he left it where it was, for the police to find it. After he took it, it was just evidence that he was a rat."

"Was a monoxide test made of her blood?"

He put his hands flat on his desk and looked down at them. "Yes," he said. "And there was monoxide all right. Also the investigating officers were satisfied with appearances. There was no sign of violence. They were satisfied that Dr. Almore had not murdered his wife. Perhaps they were wrong. I think the investigation was a little superficial."

"And who was in charge of it?" I asked.

"I think you know the answer to that."

We sat there and looked at each other, thinking about it.

"Unless," Webber said slowly, "we can suppose that this nurse of Almore's was involved with Talley in a scheme to put the bite on Almore. It's possible. There are things in favor of it. There are more things against it. What reason have you for claiming that the girl drowned up in the mountains was this nurse?"

"Two reasons, neither one conclusive separately, but pretty powerful taken together. A tough guy who looked and acted like Degarmo was up there a few weeks ago showing a photograph of Mildred Haviland that looked something like Muriel Chess. Nobody helped him much. He called himself De Soto and said he was a Los Angeles cop. There isn't any Los Angeles cop named De Soto. When Muriel Chess heard about it, she looked scared. If it was Degarmo, that's easily established. The other reason is that a golden anklet with a heart on it was hidden in a box of powdered sugar in the Chess cabin. It was found after her death, after her husband had been arrested. On the back of the heart was engraved: *Al to Mildred. June 28th 1938. With all my love.*"

Webber leaned forward. "What do you want to make of all this?"

"I want to make it that Kingsley's wife didn't shoot Lavery. That his death had something to do with the Almore business. And with Mildred Haviland. I want to make it that Kingsley's wife disappeared because something happened that gave her a bad fright, that she may or may not have guilty knowledge, but that she hasn't murdered anybody. There's five hundred dollars in it for me, if I can determine that. It's legitimate to try."

He nodded. "Certainly it is. And I'm the man that would help you, if I could see any grounds for it. But I can't help you put something on one of my boys."

I said, "I heard you call Degarmo Al. But I was thinking of Almore. His name's Albert."

Webber looked at his thumb. "But he was never married to the girl," he said quietly. "Degarmo was. I can tell you she led him a pretty dance. A lot of what seems bad in him is the result of it."

I sat very still. After a moment I said, "I'm beginning to see things I didn't know existed. What kind of a girl was she?"

"Smart, smooth and no good. She had a way with men. She could make them crawl over her shoes. The big boob would tear your head off right now, if you said anything against her. She divorced him, but that didn't end it for him. If you think Degarmo went up there looking for her because he wanted to hurt her, you're as wet as a bar towel."

"I never quite thought that," I said. "It would be possible, provided Degarmo knew the country up there pretty well. Whoever murdered the girl did."

"This is all between us," he said. "I'd like to keep it that way."

I nodded, but I didn't promise him. I said good night again and left. He looked after me as I went down the room.

THE Chrysler was in the police lot at the side of the building with the keys in the ignition and none of the fenders smashed. Cooney hadn't made good on his threat. I drove back to Hollywood and went up to my apartment in the Bristol. It was almost midnight.

The green and ivory hallway was empty of all sound except that a telephone bell was ringing in one of the apartments. It rang insistently and got louder as I came near to my door and unlocked it. It was my telephone.

I walked across the room in darkness to where the phone stood on the ledge of an oak desk against the side wall. It must have rung at least ten times before I got to it.

I lifted it out of the cradle and answered, and it was Derace Kingsley on the line.

His voice sounded tight and brittle and strained. "Good Lord, where in hell have you been?" he snapped. "I've been trying to reach you for hours."

"All right. I'm here now," I said. "What is it?"

"I've heard from her."

I held the telephone very tight and drew my breath in slowly and let it out slowly. "Go ahead," I said.

"I'm not far away. I'll be over there in five or six minutes. Be prepared to move."

He hung up.

Chapter 11

THE discreet midnight tapping sounded on the door and I went over and opened it. Kingsley looked as big as a horse in a creamy shetland sport coat with a green and yellow scarf around the neck inside the loosely turned up collar. A dark reddish brown snap-brim hat was pulled low on his forehead. Miss Fromsett was with him. She was wearing slacks and sandals and a dark green coat and no hat and her hair had a wicked luster.

I shut the door and indicated the furniture and said, "A drink will probably help."

Miss Fromsett sat in an armchair and crossed her legs and looked around for cigarettes. She found one and lit it with a long casual flourish and smiled bleakly at a corner of the ceiling.

Kingsley stood in the middle of the floor trying to bite his chin. I went out to the dinette and mixed three drinks and brought them in and handed them. I went over to the chair by the chess table with mine.

Kingsley said, "What have you been doing and what's the matter with the leg?"

I said, "A cop kicked me. A present from the Bay City Police Department. As to where I've been—in jail for drunk driving."

"This is no time to kid around," he said shortly.

"All right," I said. "What did you hear and where is she?"

He sat down with his drink and flexed the fingers of his right hand and put it inside his coat. It came out with an envelope.

"You have to take this to her," he said. "Five hundred dollars. She wanted more, but this is all I could raise. I cashed a check at a nightclub. She has to get out of town."

I said, "Out of what town?"

"Bay City somewhere. I don't know where. She'll meet you at a place called the Peacock Lounge, on Arguello Boulevard, at Eighth Street, or near it."

He tossed the envelope across and it fell on the chess table.

I said, "What's the matter with her drawing her own money? Any hotel would clear a check for her. Most of them would cash one. Has her bank account got lockjaw or something?"

"That's no way to talk," Kingsley said heavily. "She's in trouble. She won't risk cashing a check now. It was all right before. But not now." He lifted his eyes slowly and gave me one of the emptiest stares I had ever seen.

111

"All right, we can't make sense where there isn't any," I said. "So she's in Bay City. Did you talk to her?"

"No. Miss Fromsett talked to her. She called the office. It was just after hours but that cop from the beach, Captain Webber, was with me. Miss Fromsett naturally didn't want her to talk at all then. She told her to call back. She wouldn't give any number we could call."

"So she called back later," I said. "And then?"

"It was almost half past six," Kingsley said. "We had to sit there in the office and wait for her to call. You tell him." He turned his head to Miss Fromsett.

She said, "I took the call in Mr. Kingsley's office. He was sitting right beside me, but he didn't speak. She said to send the money down to the Peacock Lounge and asked who would bring it."

"Did she sound scared?"

"Not in the least. Completely calm. I might say, icily calm. She had it all worked out. She realized somebody she might not know might have to bring the money. She seemed to know Derry—Mr. Kingsley wouldn't bring it."

"Call him Derry," I said. "I'll be able to guess who you mean."

She smiled faintly. "She will go into this Peacock Lounge every hour about fifteen minutes past the hour. I—I guess I assumed you would be the one to go. I described you to her. And you're to wear Derry's scarf. I described that. It's distinctive enough."

It certainly was that. It was a pattern of fat green kidneys laid down on an egg-yolk background. It would be almost as distinctive as if I went in there wheeling a red, white and blue wheelbarrow.

"For a blimp brain she's doing all right," I said.

"This is no time to fool around," Kingsley put in sharply.

"You said that before," I told him. "You've got a hell of a crust assuming I'll go down there and take a getaway stake to somebody I know the police are looking for."

He twisted a hand on his knee and his face twisted into a crooked grin. "I admit it's a bit thick," he said. "But I'm going to make it worth your while. And we wouldn't be accessories, if she hasn't done anything."

"I'm willing to suppose it," I said. "Otherwise I wouldn't be talking to you. And in addition to that, if I decide she did commit a murder, I'm going to turn her over to the police."

"She won't talk to you," he said.

I reached for the envelope and put it in my pocket. "She will, if she wants this." I looked at my strap watch. "If I start right away, I might make the one-fifteen deadline."

"She's dyed her hair dark brown," Miss Fromsett said.

Kingsley stood up and got the scarf off his neck and handed it to me. As I put it on I asked, "You two want to wait here?"

Kingsley shook his head. "We'll go to my place and wait for a call from you."

Miss Fromsett stood up and yawned. "No. I'm tired, Derry. I'm going home to bed."

"Where do you live, Miss Fromsett?" I asked.

"Bryson Tower on Sunset Place. Apartment 716. Why?" She gave me a speculative look.

"I might want to reach you sometime."

Kingsley's face looked bleakly irritated, but his eyes were the eyes of a sick animal. I went out to the dinette to switch off the light. When I came back they were both standing by the door. Kingsley had his arm around her shoulders.

"Well, I certainly hope—" he started to say, then took a quick step and put his hand out. "You're a pretty level guy, Marlowe."

"Go on, beat it," I said. "Go away. Go far away."

He gave a queer look and they went out.

I waited until I heard the elevator come up and stop, and the doors open and close again, and the elevator start down. Then I went out myself and took the stairs down to the basement garage and got the Chrysler awake again.

THE Peacock Lounge was a narrow front next to a gift shop in whose window a tray of small crystal animals shimmered in the streetlight. I went in around a Chinese screen and looked along the bar and then sat at the outer edge of a small booth.

A wizened waiter with evil eyes and a face like a gnawed bone gave me a Bacardi cocktail. I sipped it and looked at the amber face of the bar clock. It was just past one fifteen.

A tiny white-faced Mexican boy with enormous black eyes came in with morning papers and scuttled along the booths trying to make a few sales before the barman threw him out. I bought a paper and looked through it to see if there were any interesting murders. There were not.

I folded it and looked up as a slim brown-haired girl in coal-black slacks and a yellow shirt and a long gray coat came out of somewhere and passed the booth without looking at me. I tried to make up my mind whether her face was familiar or just such a standard type of lean, rather hard prettiness that I must have seen it ten thousand times. She went out of the street door around the screen. Two minutes later the little Mexican boy came back in and scuttled over to stand in front of me.

"Mister," he said, his great big eyes shining with mischief. Then he made a beckoning sign and scuttled out again.

I finished my drink and went after him. The girl in the gray coat and yellow shirt and black slacks was standing in front of the gift shop, looking in at the window. Her eyes moved as I went out. I went and stood beside her.

She looked at me again. Her face was white and tired. Her hair looked darker than dark brown. She looked away and spoke to the window. "Give me the money, please." A little mist formed on the plate glass from her breath.

I said, "I'd have to know who you are."

"You know who I am," she said. "How much did you bring?"

"Five hundred."

"It's not nearly enough," she said. "Give it to me quickly. I've been waiting half of eternity for somebody to get here."

"Where can we talk?"

"Damn you," she said acidly, "I don't want to talk. I want to get away as soon as I can."

"But you've got to talk to me," I said. "I'm a private detective and I have to have some protection too."

"What do you want to talk about?"

114

"You, and what you've been doing and where you've been and what you expect to do. Little things, but important."

"I think it would be much better," she said in the same cool empty voice, "for you to give me the money and let me work things out for myself."

"No."

She shrugged the shoulders of the gray coat impatiently. "Very well, if it has to be that way. I'm at the Granada, two blocks north on Eighth. Apartment 618. Give me ten minutes. I'd rather go in alone." She turned quickly and walked away.

I went and sat in the Chrysler and gave her her ten minutes before I started it.

The Granada was an ugly gray building on a corner. I drove around the corner and saw a milky globe with GARAGE painted on it. The entrance to the garage was down a ramp into the hard rubber-smelling silence of parked cars in rows. A lanky Negro came out of a glassed-in office and looked the Chrysler over.

"I want to leave this here a short time," I said. "I'm going upstairs."

He gave me a ticket and I got out. Without my asking him he said the elevator was in back of the office, by the men's room.

I rode up to the sixth floor and looked at numbers on doors and listened to stillness and smelled beach air coming in at the ends of corridors. I came to the door of apartment 618 and stood outside it a moment and then knocked softly.

SHE still had the gray coat on. She stood back from the door and I went past her into a square room with twin wall beds and a minimum of uninteresting furniture. A small lamp on a window table made a dim yellowish light. The window behind it was open.

The girl said, "Sit down and talk then."

She closed the door and went to sit in a gloomy Boston rocker across the room. I sat down on a thick green davenport. There was a dull green curtain hanging across an open door space at the end of the davenport.

The girl crossed her ankles and leaned her head back against the chair and looked at me under long lashes. It was a quiet, secret

115

face. It didn't look like the face of a woman who would waste a lot of motion.

"I got a rather different idea of you," I said, "from Kingsley."

Her lips twisted a little. She said nothing.

"From Lavery too," I said. "It just goes to show that we talk different languages to different people."

"I haven't time for this sort of talk," she said. "What is it you have to know?"

"Kingsley hired me to find you. I've been working on it. I supposed you would know that."

"Yes. His office sweetie told me that over the phone. She told me your name was Marlowe. She told me about the scarf."

I took the scarf off my neck and folded it up and slipped it into a pocket. I said, "So I know a little about your movements. Not very much. I know you left your car at the Prescott Hotel in San Bernardino and that you met Lavery there. I know you sent a wire from El Paso. What did you do then?"

"Well, we went to El Paso," she said, in a tired voice. "I thought of marrying him then. So I sent that wire. Then I changed my mind. I asked him to go home and leave me. He made a scene, but he left."

"What did you do then?"

"I went to Santa Barbara and stayed there a few days. Over a week, in fact. Then to Pasadena. Same thing. Then to Hollywood. Then I came down here. That's all."

"What was the idea?"

"Idea of what?" Her voice was a little sharp.

"Idea of going to these places and not sending any word. Didn't you know he would be very anxious?"

"Oh, you mean my husband," she said coolly. "I don't think I worried much about him. He'd think I was in Mexico, wouldn't he? As for the idea of it all—well, I just had to think things out. My life had got to be a hopeless tangle. I had to be somewhere quite alone and try to straighten myself out."

"Before that," I said, "you spent a month at Little Fawn Lake trying to straighten it out and not getting anywhere. Is that it?"

"I seemed to need a new place," she said. "Without associations. A place where I would be very much alone. Like a hotel."

"Why did you come down here, to the town where Lavery was?"

She bit a knuckle and looked at me over her hand.

"I wanted to see him again. He's all mixed up in my mind. I'm not in love with him, and yet—well, I suppose in a way I am. But I don't think I want to marry him. Does that make sense?"

"That part of it makes sense. But staying away from home in a lot of crummy hotels doesn't."

"I had to be alone, to—to think things out," she said a little desperately and bit the knuckle again, hard. "Won't you please give me the money and go away?"

"Sure. Right away. But wasn't there any other reason for your going away from Little Fawn Lake just then? Anything connected with Muriel Chess, for instance?"

She looked surprised. "Good heavens, what would there be? That frozen-faced little drip—what is she to me?"

"I thought you might have had a fight with her—about Bill."

"Bill? Bill Chess?" She seemed even more surprised. Almost too surprised.

"Bill claims you made a pass at him."

She put her head back and let out a tinny and unreal laugh. "Good heavens, that muddy-faced boozer?" Her face sobered suddenly. "What's happened? Why all the mystery?"

"He might be a muddy-faced boozer," I said. "The police think he's a murderer too. Of his wife. She's been found drowned in the lake. After a month."

She moistened her lips and held her head on one side, staring at me fixedly.

"I'm not too surprised," she said slowly. "So it came to that in the end. They fought terribly at times."

"Muriel's dead," I said. "Drowned in the lake. You don't get much of a boot out of that, do you?"

"I hardly knew the girl," she said. "Really. She kept to herself. After all—"

"Did you know she had once worked in Dr. Almore's office?"

117

She looked completely puzzled now. "I was never in Dr. Almore's office," she said slowly. "He made a few house calls a long time ago. I—what are you talking about?"

"Muriel Chess was really a girl called Mildred Haviland, who had been Dr. Almore's office nurse."

"That's a queer coincidence," she said wonderingly.

I said, "I guess it's a genuine coincidence. They do happen. But you see why I had to talk to you. Muriel being found drowned and you having gone away and Muriel being Mildred Haviland who was connected with Dr. Almore at one time—as Lavery was also, in a different way. And of course Lavery lives across the street from Dr. Almore."

"I don't think Chris had anything to do with Dr. Almore," she said. "He knew Dr. Almore's wife. I don't think he knew the doctor at all, or Dr. Almore's office nurse."

"Well, I guess there's nothing in all this to help me," I said. "But you can see why I had to talk to you. I guess I can give you the money now."

I got the envelope out and stood up to drop it on her knee. She let it lie there. I sat down again.

"You do this character very well," I said. "This confused innocence with an undertone of hardness and bitterness. People have made a bad mistake about you. They have been thinking of you as a reckless little idiot with no brains and no control. They have been very wrong."

She said nothing. Then a small smile lifted the corners of her mouth. She reached for the envelope, tapped it on her knee, and laid it aside on the table.

"You did the Fallbrook character very well too," I said. "Looking back on it, I think it was a shade overdone. But at the time it had me going all right. That purple hat that would have been all right on blond hair but looked like hell on straggly brown, that messed-up makeup that looked as if it had been put on in the dark by somebody with a sprained wrist, the jittery screwball manner. All very good. And when you put the gun in my hand like that—I fell like a brick."

She snickered and put her hands in the deep pockets of her coat. Her heels tapped on the floor.

"But why did you go back at all?" I asked. "Why take such a risk in broad daylight, in the middle of the morning?"

"So you think I shot Chris Lavery?" she said quietly.

"I don't think it. I know it."

"Why did I go back? Is that what you want to know?"

"I don't really care," I said.

She laughed. A sharp cold laugh. "He had all my money," she said. "He had stripped my purse. He had it all, even silver. That's why I went back. There wasn't any risk at all. I know how he lived. It was really safer to go back. To take in the milk and the newspaper for instance. People lose their heads in these situations. I don't. It's so very much safer not to."

"I see," I said. "Then of course you shot him the night before. I ought to have thought of that. He had been shaving, but guys sometimes do shave the last thing at night, don't they?"

"It has been heard of," she said. "And just what are you going to do about it?"

"You're a cold-blooded little bitch if ever I saw one," I said. "Do about it? Turn you over to the police naturally. It will be a pleasure."

"I don't think so." She threw the words out, almost with a lilt. "You wondered why I gave you the empty gun. Why not? I had another one in my bag. Like this."

Her right hand came up from her coat pocket and she pointed it at me.

I grinned. It may not have been the heartiest grin in the world, but it was a grin.

She got up and moved toward me softly across the carpet. "You don't seem to be afraid," she said, and slowly licked her lips, coming toward me very gently without any sound of footfalls on the carpet.

"I'm not afraid," I lied. "It's too late at night, too still, and the window is open and the gun would make too much noise. It's too long a journey down to the street and you're not good with guns. You'd probably miss me. You missed Lavery three times."

"Stand up," she said.

I stood up.

"I'm going to be too close to miss," she said. She pushed the gun against my chest. "Like this. I really can't miss now, can I? Now be very still. Hold your hands up by your shoulders and then don't move. If you move at all, the gun will go off."

I put my hands up beside my shoulders. I looked down at the gun. My tongue felt a little thick, but I could still wave it.

Her left hand didn't find a gun on me. It dropped and she bit her lip. The gun bored into my chest. "You'll have to turn around now," she said, polite as a tailor at a fitting.

"There's something a little off-key about everything you do," I said. "You're definitely not good with guns. You're much too close to me, and I hate to bring this up—but there's that old business of the safety catch not being off. You've overlooked that."

So she started to do two things at once. To take a long step backward and to feel with her thumb for the safety catch, without taking her eyes off my face. Two very simple things, needing only a second to do. But she didn't like my telling her. The slight confusion of it jarred her.

She let out a small choked sound and I dropped my right hand and yanked her face hard against my chest. My left hand smashed down on her right wrist. The gun jerked out of her hand to the floor. Her face writhed against my chest and I think she was trying to scream.

She tried to kick me and lost what little balance she had left. Her hands came up to claw at me. I caught her wrist and began to twist it behind her back. She was very strong, but I was stronger. She started to go down and I had to bend down with her.

I thought a curtain ring checked sharply on a rod. I wasn't sure and I had no time to consider the question. A figure loomed up suddenly on my left, just behind, and out of range of clear vision. I knew there was a man there and that he was a big man.

That was all I knew. The scene exploded into fire and darkness. I didn't even remember being slugged. Fire and darkness and just before the darkness a sharp flash of nausea.

Chapter 12

I SMELLED of gin. Not just casually, as if I had taken four or five drinks of a winter morning to get out of bed on, but as if the Pacific Ocean was pure gin and I had nose-dived off the boat deck. The gin was in my hair and eyebrows, on my chin and under my chin. It was on my shirt. I smelled like dead toads.

My coat was off and I was lying flat on my back on somebody's carpet. I reached up wearily and felt the back of my head. It felt pulpy. A stabbing pain from the touch went clear to the soles of my feet. I groaned, and made a grunt out of the groan. I rolled over slowly and carefully and looked at the foot of a pulled-down wall bed; one twin, the other being still up in the wall. When I rolled, a square gin bottle rolled off my chest and hit the floor. It was water-white, and empty. It didn't seem possible there could be so much gin in one bottle.

I got my knees under me and stayed on all fours for a while, sniffing like a dog who can't finish his dinner, but hates to leave it. I moved my head around on my neck. It hurt. I moved it around some more and it still hurt, so I climbed up on my feet.

"It will all come back to you," I said. "Someday it will all come back to you. And you won't like it."

There was the lamp on the table by the open window. There was the fat green davenport. There was the doorway with the green curtain across it. Never sit with your back to a green curtain. It always turns out badly. Something always happens. A girl with a gun. A girl with a clear empty face and dark brown hair that had been blond.

I looked around for her. She was still there. She was lying on the pulled-down twin bed.

She was wearing a pair of tan stockings and nothing else. Her hair was tumbled. There were dark bruises on her throat.

Across her naked belly four angry scratches leered crimson red against the whiteness of flesh. Deep angry scratches, gouged out by four bitter fingernails.

On the davenport there were tumbled clothes, mostly hers. My coat was there also. I disentangled it and put it on. Something crackled under my hand in the tumbled clothes. I drew out a long envelope with money still in it. I put it in my pocket.

I stepped on the balls of my feet softly, as if walking on very thin ice. I bent down to rub behind my knee and wondered which hurt most, my knee, or my head when I bent down to rub the knee.

Heavy feet came along the hallway and there was a hard mutter of voices. The feet stopped. A hard fist knocked on the door. The steps went away. I wondered how long it would take to get the manager with a passkey. Not very long. I went to the green curtain and brushed it aside and looked down a short dark hallway into a bathroom. Two wash rugs on the floor, a bath mat folded over the edge of the tub, a pebbled-glass window at the corner of the tub. I shut the bathroom door and stood on the edge of the tub and eased the window up. This was the sixth floor. There was no screen. I put my head out and looked into darkness and a narrow glimpse of a street with trees. I looked sideways and saw that the bathroom window of the next apartment was not more than three feet away. A well-nourished mountain goat could make it without any trouble at all. The question was whether a battered private detective could make it, and if so, what the harvest would be.

Behind me a rather remote and muffled voice seemed to be chanting the policeman's litany: "Open it up or we'll kick it in." I grabbed a towel off the rack and pulled the two halves of the window down and eased out on the sill. I swung half of me over to the next sill, holding on to the frame of the open window. I could just reach to push the next window down, if it was unlocked. It wasn't. I got my foot over there and kicked the glass over the catch. Then I wrapped the towel around my left hand and reached in to turn the catch. I pushed the broken window down and climbed across to the other sill. The towel fell and fluttered down into the darkness. I climbed in at the window of the other bathroom.

I CLIMBED down and groped through darkness to a door and opened it and listened. Filtered moonlight coming through north windows showed a bedroom with twin beds, made up and empty.

I moved past the beds to another door and into a living room. I felt my way to a lamp and switched it on. This room contained a library dining table, an armchair radio, a big bookcase full of novels with their jackets still on them, a dark wood highboy, with a syphon and a cut-glass bottle of liquor and four striped glasses upside down on an Indian brass tray. Beside this, paired photographs in a double silver frame, a youngish middle-aged man and woman, with round healthy faces and cheerful eyes. They looked out at me as if they didn't mind my being there at all.

I sniffed the liquor, which was Scotch, and used some of it. It made my head feel worse but it made the rest of me feel better. I put a light on in the bedroom and poked into closets. One of them had a man's clothes, tailor-made. The tailor's label inside a coat pocket declared the owner's name to be H. G. Talbot. I went to the bureau and poked around and found a soft blue shirt that looked a little small for me. I carried it into the bathroom and stripped mine off and washed my face and chest and wiped my hair off with a wet towel and put the blue shirt on. I got my coat back on and looked at myself in the mirror. I looked slightly too neat for that hour of the night, even for as careful a man as Mr. Talbot's clothes indicated him to be. I went to the living-room door, the one giving on the hallway, and opened it and leaned in the opening smoking. I didn't think it was going to work. But I didn't think waiting there for them to follow my trail through the window was going to work any better.

A man coughed a little way down the hall and I poked my head out farther and he was looking at me. He came toward me briskly, a small sharp man in a neatly pressed police uniform.

I yawned and said languidly, "What goes on, Officer?"

He stared at me. "Little trouble next door to you. Hear anything?"

"I thought I heard knocking. I just got home a little while ago."

"Little late," he said.

"That's a matter of opinion," I said. "Trouble next door, ah?"

"A dame," he said. "Know her?"

"I think I've seen her."

"Yeah," he said. "You ought to see her now...." He put his

hands to his throat and bulged his eyes out and gurgled unpleasantly. "Like that," he said. "You didn't hear nothing, huh?"

"Nothing I noticed—except the knocking."

"Yeah. What was the name?"

"Talbot."

"Just a minute, Mr. Talbot. Wait there just a minute."

He went along the hallway and leaned into an open doorway through which light streamed out. "Oh, Lieutenant," he said. "The man next door is on deck."

A tall man came out of the doorway and stood looking along the hall straight at me. A tall man with blond hair and very blue, blue eyes. Degarmo. That made it perfect.

"Here's the guy lives next door," the small neat cop said helpfully. "His name's Talbot."

Degarmo looked straight at me, but nothing in his acid blue eyes showed that he had ever seen me before. He came quietly along the hall and put a hard hand against my chest and pushed me back into the room. When he had me inside he said over his shoulder, "Come in here and shut the door, Shorty."

The small cop came in and shut the door.

"Quite a gag," Degarmo said lazily. "Put a gun on him, Shorty."

Shorty flicked his black belt holster open and had his .38 in his hand like a flash. "Oh boy," he said. "A sex killer. He pulled the girl's clothes off and choked her, Lieutenant. How'd you know he was the killer?"

Degarmo didn't answer him. He just stood there, rocking a little on his heels, his face empty and granite hard.

"Yah, he's the killer, sure," Shorty said suddenly. "Sniff the air in here, Lieutenant. The place ain't been aired out for days. And look at the dust on those bookshelves. And the clock on the mantel's stopped, Lieutenant. He come in through the— Lemme look a minute, can I, Lieutenant?"

He ran out of the room into the bedroom. I heard him fumbling around. Degarmo stood woodenly.

Shorty came back. "Come in at the bathroom window. There's broken glass in the tub. And here's a shirt, Lieutenant. Smells like it was washed in gin. You remember how that apartment smelled of gin when we went in?"

Degarmo looked at the shirt vaguely and then stepped forward and yanked my coat open and looked at the shirt I was wearing.

"I know what he done," Shorty said. "He stole one of the guy's shirts that lives here. You see what he done, Lieutenant?"

"Yeah." Degarmo held his hand against my chest and let it fall slowly. "Frisk him, Shorty."

Shorty ran around me feeling here and there for a gun. "Nothing on him," he said.

"Let's get him out the back way," Degarmo said. "It's our pinch, if we make it before Webber gets here. That lug Reed couldn't find a moth in a shoe box."

"But you ain't detailed on the case," Shorty said doubtfully. "Didn't I hear you was suspended or something?"

"What can I lose," Degarmo asked, "if I'm suspended?"

"I can lose this here uniform," Shorty said.

Degarmo looked at him wearily. "Okay, Shorty, go and tell Reed."

The small cop's eyes were anxious. He licked his lip. "You say the word, Lieutenant. I'm with you. I don't have to know you got suspended."

"We'll take him down ourselves, just the two of us," Degarmo said with finality.

"Yeah, sure."

Degarmo put his finger against my chin. "A sex killer," he said quietly. "Well, I'll be damned." He smiled at me thinly, moving only the extreme corners of his wide brutal mouth.

WE WENT out of the apartment and along the hall to the fire door beyond the elevator and then down echoing concrete steps, floor after floor. At the lobby floor Degarmo stopped and held his hand on the doorknob and listened. He looked back over his shoulder.

"You got a car?" he asked me.

"In the basement garage."

"That's an idea."

We went on down the steps and came out into the shadowy basement. The lanky Negro came out of the little office and I gave him my car check. He said nothing. He pointed to the Chrysler.

Degarmo climbed in under the wheel. I got in beside him and Shorty got into the back seat. We went up the ramp and out into the damp cool night air. A big car with twin red spotlights was charging toward us from a couple of blocks away.

Degarmo spat out of the car window and yanked the Chrysler the other way. "That will be Webber," he said. "Late for the funeral again. We sure skinned his nose on that one, Shorty."

Degarmo drove the car hard for ten blocks and then slowed a little.

Shorty said uneasily, "I guess you know what you're doing, Lieutenant, but this ain't the way to the hall."

"That's right," Degarmo said. "It never was, was it?"

He let the car slow down to a crawl and then turned into a residential street of small exact houses squatting behind small exact lawns. He braked the car gently and coasted over to the curb and stopped about the middle of the block. Then he threw an arm over the back of the seat and turned his head to look at Shorty.

"Who reported it, Shorty?"

"How the hell would I know? A guy called up and said a woman had been murdered in 618 Granada Apartments on Eighth. Reed was still looking for a cameraman when you come in. The desk said a guy with a thick voice, likely disguised. Didn't give any name at all."

"All right then," Degarmo said. "If you had murdered the girl, how would you get out of there?"

"I'd walk out," Shorty said. "Why not? Hey," he barked at me suddenly, "why didn't you?"

I didn't answer him. Degarmo said tonelessly, "You wouldn't climb out of a bathroom window six floors up and then bust in another bathroom window into a strange apartment where people would likely be sleeping, would you? You wouldn't pretend to be the guy that lived there and you wouldn't throw away a lot of your time by calling the police, would you?" Hell, that girl could have

127

laid there for a week. You wouldn't throw away the chance of a start like that, would you, Shorty?"

"I don't guess I would," Shorty said cautiously. "But you know these sex fiends do funny things, Lieutenant. And this guy could have had help and the other guy could have knocked him out to put him in the middle."

"Don't tell me you thought that last bit up all by yourself," Degarmo grunted. "So here we sit, and the fellow that knows all the answers is sitting here with us and not saying a word." He turned his big head and stared at me. "What were you doing there?"

"I can't remember," I said. "The crack on the head seems to have blanked me out."

"We'll help you to remember," Degarmo said. "We'll take you up back in the hills a few miles where you can be quiet and look at the stars and remember. You'll remember all right."

Shorty said, "That ain't no way to talk, Lieutenant. Why don't we just go back to the hall and play this the way it says in the rule book?"

"To hell with the rule book," Degarmo said. "I like this guy. I want to have one long sweet talk with him. He just needs a little coaxing, Shorty."

"I don't want any part of it," Shorty said.

"What you want to do, Shorty?"

"I want to go back to the hall."

"Nobody's stopping you, kid. You want to walk?"

Shorty was silent for a moment. "That's right," he said at last, quietly. "I want to walk." He opened the car door and stepped out onto the curbing. "And I guess you know I have to report all this, Lieutenant?"

"Right," Degarmo said. "Tell Webber I was asking for him."

The small cop slammed the car door shut. Degarmo let the clutch in and gunned the motor and hit forty in the first block and a half. After a little while we passed the city limits and Degarmo spoke. "Let's hear you talk," he said quietly. "Maybe we can work this out."

The car topped a long rise and dipped down to where the boulevard wound through the parklike grounds of the veterans hospital. I began to talk.

"Kingsley came over to my apartment tonight and said he had heard from his wife over the phone. She wanted some money quick. The idea was for me to take it to her and get her out of whatever trouble she was in. She was told how to identify me and I was to be at the Peacock Lounge at Eighth and Arguello at fifteen minutes past the hour. Any hour."

Degarmo said slowly, "She had to breeze and that meant she had something to breeze from, such as murder."

"I went down there, hours after she had called. I had been told her hair was dyed brown. She passed me going out of the bar, but I didn't know her. I had never seen her in the flesh. She sent a Mexican kid in to call me out. She wanted the money and no conversation. I wanted her story. Finally she saw she would have to talk a little and told me she was at the Granada. She made me wait ten minutes before I followed her over."

Degarmo said, "Time to fix up a plant."

"There was a plant all right, but I'm not sure she was in on it. She didn't want me to come up there, didn't want to talk. Anyhow I went and we talked. Nothing she said made very much sense until we talked about Lavery getting shot. Then she made too much sense too quick. I told her I was going to turn her over to the police."

Westwood Village, dark except for one all-night service station and a few distant windows in apartment houses, slid away to the north of us.

"So she pulled a gun," I said. "I think she meant to use it, but she got too close to me and I got a headlock on her. While we were wrestling, somebody came out from behind a green curtain and slugged me. When I came out of that the murder was done."

Degarmo said slowly, "You get a look at who slugged you?"

"No. I felt or half saw he was a man and a big one. And I found this lying on the davenport, mixed in with clothes." I pulled Kingsley's yellow and green scarf out of my pocket. "I saw Kingsley wearing this earlier this evening," I said.

Degarmo looked down at the scarf. "You wouldn't forget that too quick," he said. "It steps right up and smacks you in the eye. Kingsley, huh? Well, I'm damned. What happened then?"

"Knocking on the door. Me still woozy in the head, not too bright and a bit panicked. I had been flooded with gin and maybe I looked and smelled a little like somebody who would yank a woman's clothes off and strangle her. So I got out through the bathroom window, cleaned myself up as well as I could, and the rest you know."

"What's your idea of the motivation here?" Degarmo asked.

"Why did Kingsley kill her—if he did? That's not too hard. She had been cheating on him, making him a lot of trouble, endangering his job, and now she had killed a man. Also Kingsley wanted to marry another woman. Also he saw a chance to make me the goat. It wouldn't stick, but it would make confusion and delay."

Degarmo said, "All the same it could be somebody else, somebody who isn't in the picture at all. Even if he went down there to see her, it could still be somebody else. Somebody else could have killed Lavery too."

"If you like it that way."

He turned his head. "I don't like it any way at all. But if I crack the case, I'll get by with a reprimand from the police board for butting into it. If I don't crack it, I'll be thumbing a ride out of town for not taking you in. You said I was dumb. Okay, I'm dumb. Where does Kingsley live? One thing I know is how to make people talk."

"Nine sixty-five Carson Drive, Beverly Hills. About five blocks on, you turn north to the foothills."

He handed me the green and yellow scarf. "Tuck that back into your pocket until we want to spring it on him."

Chapter 13

IT WAS a two-storied white house with a dark roof. Bright moonlight lay against its wall like a fresh coat of paint. All the visible windows were dark.

Degarmo moved down the driveway and I heard the sound of a garage door going up, then the thud as it was lowered. He reappeared and walked to the front door and leaned his thumb on the bell and juggled a cigarette out of his pocket with one hand and put it between his lips.

After a while there was light on the fan over the door. The peephole in the door swung back. From where I sat in the car I could see Degarmo holding up his shield. Slowly and as if unwillingly the door was opened. He went in.

He was gone four or five minutes. Light went on behind various windows, then off again. Then he came out of the house and while he was walking back to the car the light went off in the fan and the whole house was again as dark as we had found it.

He stood beside the car smoking and looking off down the curve of the street.

"No car in the garage," he said. "No sign of Kingsley. The cook says she hasn't seen him since this morning. I looked in all the rooms. I guess she told the truth. Where would he be—Kingsley?"

"Anywhere," I said. "On the road, in a hotel, in a Turkish bath getting the kinks out of his nerves. But we'll have to try his girl friend first. Her name is Fromsett and she has apartment 716 at the Bryson Tower on Sunset Place."

"She does what?" Degarmo asked, getting in under the wheel.

"She holds the fort in his office and holds his hand out of office hours. She's no office cutie, though. She has brains and style."

"This situation is going to need all she has," Degarmo said. He drove down to Wilshire Boulevard and we turned east.

Twenty-five minutes brought us to the Bryson Tower, a white stucco palace with fretted lanterns in the forecourt and tall date palms. The lobby was too big and had a carpet that was too blue. There was a desk and a night clerk.

Degarmo lunged past the desk toward an open elevator. The clerk snapped at Degarmo's back like a terrier.

"One moment, please. Whom did you wish to see?"

"Look, buddy," Degarmo said to the clerk, "we want up to 716. Any objection?"

"Certainly I have," the clerk said coldly. "We don't announce guests at twenty-three minutes past four in the morning."

"That's what I thought," Degarmo said. "So I wasn't going to bother you. You get the idea?" He took his shield out of his pocket and held it so the light glinted on the gold and the blue enamel. "I'm a police lieutenant."

The clerk shrugged. "Very well. I hope there isn't going to be any trouble. I'd better announce you then. What names?"

"Lieutenant Degarmo and Mr. Marlowe."

"Apartment 716. That will be Miss Fromsett. One moment."

He went behind a glass screen and we heard him talking on the phone after a longish pause. He came back and nodded.

"Miss Fromsett is in. She will receive you."

The clerk gave a small cold smile and we got into the elevator.

The seventh floor was cool and quiet. There was an ivory button beside the door of 716. Degarmo pushed it and chimes rang inside the door and it was opened.

Miss Fromsett wore a quilted blue robe over her pajamas. On her feet were small tufted slippers with high heels.

We went past her into a rather narrow room with several handsome oval mirrors and gray period furniture upholstered in blue damask. She sat down on a slender love seat and leaned back and waited calmly for somebody to say something.

I said, "This is Lieutenant Degarmo of the Bay City police. We're looking for Kingsley. He's not at his house. We thought you might be able to give us an idea where to find him."

The girl looked at him with a complete absence of expression. She looked at me and said, "I think you had better tell me what this is all about, Mr. Marlowe."

"I went down there with the money," I said. "I met Mrs. Kingsley as arranged. I went to her apartment to talk to her. While there I was slugged by a man who was hidden behind a curtain. I didn't see the man. When I came out of it she had been murdered."

"Murdered?"

I said, "Murdered."

She closed her fine eyes and the corners of her lovely mouth drew in. Then she stood up with a quick shrug and went over to a small marble-topped table with spindly legs. She took a cigarette out of a small embossed silver box and lit it, staring emptily down at the table.

"I suppose I ought to scream or something," she said. "I don't seem to have any feeling about it at all."

Degarmo said, "We're not too interested in your feelings right now. What we want to know is where Kingsley is. You can tell us or not tell us. Either way you can skip the attitudes."

I said, "Miss Fromsett, if you know where he is, or where he started to go, please tell us. You can understand that he has to be found."

She said calmly, "Why?"

Degarmo put his head back and laughed. "This babe is good," he said. "Maybe she thinks we should keep it a secret from him that his wife has been knocked off."

She said, "Is it just because he has to be told?"

I took the yellow and green scarf out of my pocket and shook it out loose and held it in front of her. "This was found in the apartment where she was murdered. I think you've seen it."

She looked at the scarf and she looked at me, and in neither of the glances was there any meaning. "How was she murdered?" she asked.

"She was strangled and stripped naked and scratched up."

"Derry wouldn't have done anything like that," she said quietly.

Degarmo made a noise with his lips. "Nobody ever knows what anybody else will do, sister. A cop knows that much."

She didn't look at him. In the same level tone she asked, "Do you want to know where we went after we left your apartment and whether he brought me home—things like that?"

"Yes."

"He didn't bring me home," she said slowly. "I took a taxi on Hollywood Boulevard, not more than five minutes after we left your place. I didn't see him again. I supposed he went home."

"So he did have time," I said.

She shook her head. "I don't know. I don't know how much

time was needed. I don't know how he could have known where to go. He didn't know where she was living."

I folded the scarf up and put it back in my pocket. "We want to know where he is now."

"I can't tell you because I have no idea." Her eyes had followed the scarf down to my pocket. "You say you were slugged."

"Yes. By somebody who was hidden out behind a curtain. She had pulled a gun on me and I was busy trying to take it away from her. There's no doubt she shot Lavery."

"You're making yourself a nice smooth scene, fellow, but you're not getting anywhere," Degarmo growled. "Let's blow."

I said, "Wait a minute. Suppose he had something on his mind, Miss Fromsett, something that was eating pretty deep into him. He would want to go somewhere quietly and try to figure out what to do. Don't you think he might?"

After a moment the girl said tonelessly, "He wouldn't run away or hide, because it wasn't anything he could run away and hide from. But he might want a time to himself to think."

"In a strange place, in a hotel," I said, thinking of the story that had been told me in the Granada. "Or in a much quieter place than that." I looked around for the telephone.

"It's in my bedroom," Miss Fromsett said, knowing at once what I was looking for.

I went down the room and through the door at the end. Degarmo was right behind me. The bedroom was ivory and rose. The phone was on a night table by the bed.

I sat down on the edge of the bed and lifted the phone and dialed long distance. When the operator answered I asked for Constable Jim Patton at Puma Point, person-to-person, very urgent. I put the phone back in the cradle and lit a cigarette. Degarmo glowered down at me, standing with his legs apart, tough and tireless and ready to be nasty. The phone rang in a moment.

"Ready with your Puma Point call."

Patton's sleepy voice came on the line. "Yes? This is Patton at Puma Point."

"This is Marlowe in Los Angeles," I said. "Remember me?"

"Sure I remember you, son. I ain't only half awake though."

"Do me a favor," I said. "Go or send over to Little Fawn Lake and see if Kingsley is there. Don't let him see you. You can spot his car outside the cabin or maybe see lights. And see that he stays put. Call me back as soon as you know. I'm coming up. Can you do that?"

Patton said, "I got no reason to hold him if he wants to leave."

"I'll have a Bay City police officer with me who wants to question him about a murder. Not your murder, another one, and call me back at Tunbridge 2722."

"Should likely take me half an hour," he said.

I hung up. Degarmo was grinning now. "This babe flash you a signal I couldn't read?"

I stood up off the bed. "No. I'm just trying to read his mind. He's no cold killer. I thought he might go to the quietest and most remote place he knows—just to get a grip on himself. In a few hours he'll probably turn himself in. It would look better for you if you got to him before he did that."

"Unless he puts a slug in his head," Degarmo said coldly. "Guys like him are very apt to do that."

"You can't stop him until you find him."

"That's right."

We went back into the living room. Miss Fromsett poked her head out of her kitchenette and said she was making coffee, and did we want any. We had some coffee and sat around looking like people seeing friends off at the railroad station.

Patton's call came through in about twenty-five minutes. There was light in the Kingsley cabin and a car was parked beside it.

WE ATE some breakfast at Alhambra and I had the tank filled. We drove out Highway 70 and started moving past the trucks into the rolling ranch country. I was driving. Degarmo sat moodily in the corner, his hands deep in his pockets.

I watched the fat straight rows of orange trees spin by like the spokes of a wheel. I listened to the whine of the tires on the pavement and I felt tired and stale from lack of sleep and too much emotion.

We reached the long slope south of San Dimas that goes up to a ridge and drops down into Pomona, then we came to the center of town and turned north on Euclid, along the splendid parkway.

After a while Degarmo said, "That was my girl that drowned in the lake up there. I haven't been right in the head since I heard about it. All I can see is red. If I could get my hands on that guy Chess—"

"You made enough trouble," I said, "letting her get away with murdering Almore's wife."

I stared straight ahead through the windshield. After a long time his words came. They came through tight teeth and edgeways, and they scraped a little as they came out.

"You a little crazy or something?"

"No," I said. "Neither are you. You know as well as anybody could know anything that Florence Almore didn't get up out of bed and walk down to that garage. You know she was carried. You know that was why Talley stole her slipper, the slipper that had never walked on a concrete path. You knew that Almore gave his wife a shot in the arm at Condy's place and that it was just enough and not any too much. You know that Almore didn't murder his wife with morphine, and that if he wanted to murder her, morphine would be the last thing in the world he would use. But you know that somebody else did, and that Almore carried her down to the garage and put her there—technically still alive to breathe in some monoxide, but medically just as dead as though she had stopped breathing. You know all that."

Degarmo said softly, "Brother, how did you ever manage to live so long?" He laughed. It was a grating unpleasant laugh, not only mirthless, but meaningless.

I said, "The girl, Mildred Haviland, was playing house with Almore and his wife knew it. She had threatened him. I got that from her parents. The girl, Mildred Haviland, knew all about morphine and where to get all of it she needed and how much to use. She was alone in the house with Florence Almore, after she put her to bed. She was in a perfect spot to load a needle with four or five grains and shoot it into an unconscious woman through the same puncture Almore had already made. Nobody would believe anybody else had drugged his wife to death. Nobody that didn't know all the circumstances. But you knew. I'd have to think you much more of a damn fool than I think you are to believe you didn't know. You covered the girl up. You were in love with her still. You scared her out of town, out of danger, out of reach, but you covered up for her. You let the murder ride. She had you that way. Why did you go up to the mountains looking for her?"

"And how did I know where to look?" he said harshly. "It wouldn't bother you to explain that, would it?"

"Not at all," I said. "She got sick of Bill Chess and his boozing and his tempers and his down-at-heels living. But she had to have money to make a break. She thought she was safe now, that she had something on Almore that was safe to use. So she wrote him for money. He sent you up to talk to her. She didn't tell Almore what her present name was or any details or where or how she was living. A letter addressed to Mildred Haviland at Puma Point would reach her. All she had to do was ask for it. But no letter came and nobody connected her with Mildred Haviland. All you had was an old photo and your usual bad manners, and they didn't get you anywhere with those people."

Degarmo said gratingly, "Who told you she tried to get money from Almore?"

"Nobody. I had to think of something to fit what happened. If Lavery or Mrs. Kingsley had known who Muriel Chess had been, and had tipped it off, you would have known where to find her and what name she was using. You didn't know those things. Therefore the lead had to come from the only person up there who knew who she was . . . herself. So I assume she wrote to Almore."

"Okay," he said at last. "Let's forget it. It doesn't make any difference anymore now. If I'm in a jam, that's my business. I'd do it again, in the same circumstances."

"That's all right," I said. "I'm not planning to put the bite on anybody. Not even you. I'm telling you this mostly so you won't try to hang any murders on Kingsley that don't belong on him."

"Is that why you're telling me?" he asked.

"Yeah."

"I thought maybe it was because you hated my guts," he said.

"I'm all done with hating you," I said. "It's all washed out of me. I hate people hard, but I don't hate them very long."

Chapter 14

AT CRESTLINE, elevation five thousand feet, it had not yet started to warm up. We stopped for a beer. When we got back into the car, Degarmo took the gun from his underarm holster and looked it over. It was a .38 Smith & Wesson on a .44 frame, a wicked weapon with a kick like a .45 and a much greater effective range.

"You won't need that," I said. "He's big and strong, but he's not that kind of tough."

He put the gun back under his arm and grunted. We didn't talk anymore now. We had no more to talk about. We climbed through the tall oaks and on up to the altitudes where the oaks are not so tall and the pines are taller and taller. We came at last to the dam at the end of Puma Lake.

I stopped the car and the sentry threw his rifle across his body and stepped up to the window.

"Close all the windows of your car before proceeding across the dam, please."

I reached back to wind up the rear window on my side. Degarmo held his shield up. "Forget it, buddy. I'm a police officer," he said with his usual tact.

The sentry gave him a solid expressionless stare. "Close all windows, please," he repeated.

"Nuts to you," Degarmo said. "Nuts to you, soldier boy."

"It's an order," the sentry said.

"Suppose I told you to go jump in the lake," Degarmo sneered.

The sentry said, "I might do it. I scare easily." He patted the breech of his rifle with a leathery hand.

Degarmo turned and closed the windows on his side. We drove across the dam. There was a sentry in the middle and one at the far end. The first one must have flashed them some kind of signal. They looked at us with steady watchful eyes, without friendliness.

I turned off on the road to Little Fawn Lake and wound around the huge rocks and past the little waterfall. The gate into Kingsley's property was open and Patton's car was standing in the road pointing toward the lake, which was invisible from there.

Close to it and pointed the other way was a small battered coupe. Inside the coupe a lion hunter's hat. I stopped my car behind Patton's and locked it and got out. Andy got out of the coupe and stood staring at us woodenly.

I said, "This is Lieutenant Degarmo of the Bay City police."

Andy said, "Jim's just over the ridge. He's waiting for you."

We walked up the road to the ridge as Andy got back into his coupe. Beyond it the road dropped to the tiny blue lake. Kingsley's cabin across the water seemed to be without life.

Degarmo looked down at the lake. "Let's go get the bastard," was all he said.

We went on and Patton stood up from behind a rock. He was wearing the same old sweat-stained stetson.

"Nice to see you again," he said, not looking at me, but at Degarmo. He put his hand out and shook Degarmo's hard paw. "Last time I seen you, Lieutenant, you were wearing another name. Kind of undercover. I guess I didn't treat you right neither. I apologize. Guess I knew who that photo of yours was all the time."

Degarmo nodded and said nothing.

"Likely if I'd of been on my toes and played the game right, a lot of trouble would have been saved," Patton said. "Maybe a life would have been saved. I feel kind of bad about it, but then again I ain't a fellow that feels too bad about anything very long. Suppose we sit down here and you tell me what it is we're supposed to be doing now."

Degarmo said, "Kingsley's wife was murdered in Bay City last night. I have to talk to him about it."

"You mean you suspect him?" Patton asked.

"And how," Degarmo grunted.

Patton rubbed his thick neck and looked across the lake. "He ain't showed outside the cabin at all. Likely he's still asleep. Early this morning I snuck around the cabin. There was a radio goin' then and I heard sounds like a man would make playing with a bottle and a glass. I stayed away from him."

"We'll go over there now," Degarmo said.

"You got a gun, Lieutenant?"

Degarmo patted under his left arm. Patton looked at me. I shook my head, no gun.

"Kingsley might have one too," Patton said. "I don't hanker after no fast shooting around here, Lieutenant. It wouldn't do me no good to have a gunfight. You look to me like a fellow who would jack his gun out kind of fast."

"I've got plenty of swift, if that's what you mean," Degarmo said. "But I want this guy talking."

Patton looked at Degarmo, looked at me, looked back at Degarmo, and spat tobacco juice in a long stream to one side.

"I ain't heard enough to even approach him," he said stubbornly.

So we sat down on the ground and told him the story. He listened silently, not blinking an eye. At the end he said to me, "You got a funny way of working for people, seems to me. Personally I think you boys are plumb misinformed. We'll go over and see."

We stood up off the ground and started around the lake the long way. When we came to the little pier I said, "Did they autopsy her yet, Sheriff?"

Patton nodded. "She drowned all right. They say they're satisfied that's how she died. She wasn't knifed or shot or had her head cracked in or anything. There's marks on the body, but too many to mean anything. And it ain't a very nice body to work with."

Degarmo looked white and angry.

"I guess I oughtn't to have said that, Lieutenant," Patton added mildly. "Kind of tough to take. Seeing as how you knew the lady pretty well."

Degarmo said, "Let's get it over and do what we have to do."

We went on along the shore of the lake and came to Kingsley's cabin. We went up the heavy steps. Patton went quietly across the porch to the door. He tried the screen. It was not hooked.

He opened it and tried the door. That was unlocked also. Patton opened the door and we walked into the room.

Derace Kingsley lay back in a deep chair by the cold fireplace with his eyes closed. There was an empty glass and an almost empty whiskey bottle on the table beside him. The room smelled of whiskey. A dish near the bottle was choked with cigarette stubs. Two crushed empty packs lay on top of the stubs.

Patton moved to within a few feet of him and stood looking silently down at him for a long moment before he spoke.

"Mr. Kingsley," he said then, in a calm steady voice, "we got to talk to you a little."

KINGSLEY moved with a kind of jerk, and opened his eyes and moved them without moving his head. He sat up slowly in the chair and rubbed his hands up and down the sides of his face.

"I was asleep," he said. "Fell asleep a couple of hours ago. I was as drunk as a skunk, I guess."

Patton said, "This is Lieutenant Degarmo of the Bay City police. He has to talk to you."

Kingsley looked briefly at Degarmo and his eyes came around to stare at me. His voice when he spoke again sounded sober and quiet and tired to death. "So you let them get her?" he said.

I said, "I would have, but I didn't."

Patton sat in a chair and clasped his hands over his stomach. Degarmo stood glowering down at Kingsley.

"Your wife is dead, Kingsley," he said brutally. "If it's any news to you."

Kingsley stared at him and moistened his lips.

"Takes it easy, don't he?" Degarmo said. "Show him the scarf."

I took the green and yellow scarf out and dangled it. Degarmo jerked a thumb. "Yours?"

Kingsley nodded. He moistened his lips again.

"Careless of you to leave it behind you," Degarmo said. He was breathing a little hard.

Kingsley said very quietly, "Leave it behind me where?" He had barely glanced at the scarf. He hadn't looked at all at me.

141

"In the Granada Apartments, on Eighth Street, in Bay City. Apartment 618. Am I telling you something?"

Kingsley now very slowly lifted his eyes to meet mine. "Is that where she was?" he breathed.

I nodded. "She didn't want me to go there. I wouldn't give her the money until she talked to me. She admitted she killed Lavery. She pulled a gun and planned to give me the same treatment. Somebody came from behind the curtain and knocked me out without letting me see him. When I came to she was dead." I told him how she was dead and how she looked. I told him what I had done and what had been done to me.

He listened without moving a muscle of his face. When I had done talking he made a vague gesture toward the scarf. "What has that got to do with it?"

"The lieutenant regards it as evidence that you were the party hidden out in the apartment."

Kingsley thought that over. "Go on," he said at length. "I suppose you know what you're talking about. I'm quite sure I don't."

Degarmo said, "All right, play dumb. See what it gets you. You could begin by accounting for your time last night after you dropped your girl friend at her apartment house."

Kingsley said evenly, "If you mean Miss Fromsett, I didn't. She went home in a taxi. I was going home myself, but I didn't. I came up here instead. I thought the trip and the night air and the quiet might help me to get straightened out."

Degarmo jabbed his finger at Kingsley. "I suppose you didn't go down to Bay City at all," he said harshly.

"No. Why should I? Marlowe was taking care of that. And I don't see why you are making a point of the scarf. Marlowe was wearing it."

Degarmo stood rooted and savage. He turned very slowly and gave me his bleak angry stare.

"I don't get this," he said. "It wouldn't be that somebody is kidding me, would it? Somebody like you?"

I said, "All I told you about the scarf was that it was in the apartment and that I had seen Kingsley wearing it earlier this evening.

That seemed to be all you wanted. I might have added that I had later worn the scarf myself, so the girl I was to meet could identify me. I told you all I had ever seen of Mrs. Kingsley was a snapshot. One of us had to be sure of being able to identify the other. The scarf seemed obvious enough for identification. As a matter of fact I had seen her once before, although I didn't know it when I went to meet her. But I didn't recognize her at once." I turned to Kingsley. "Mrs. Fallbrook," I said.

"I thought you said Mrs. Fallbrook was the owner of the house," he answered slowly.

"That's what she said at the time. That's what I believed at the time. Why wouldn't I?"

Degarmo made a sound in his throat. His eyes were a little crazy. I told him about Mrs. Fallbrook and her purple hat and her fluttery manner and the empty gun she had been holding and how she gave it to me.

When I stopped, he said very carefully, "I didn't hear you tell Webber any of that."

"I didn't tell him. I didn't want to admit I'd already been in the house three hours before. That I had gone to talk the murder over with Kingsley before I reported it to the police."

"That's something we're going to love you for," Degarmo said with a cold grin. "God, what a sucker I've been. How much you paying this shamus to cover up your murders for you, Kingsley?"

"His usual rates," Kingsley told him emptily. "And a five-hundred-dollar bonus if he can prove my wife didn't murder Lavery."

"Too bad he can't earn that," Degarmo sneered.

"Don't be silly," I said. "I've already earned it."

There was a silence in the room, which remained, hung heavy and solid, like a wall. Kingsley moved a little in his chair, and after a long moment, he nodded his head.

"Nobody could possibly know that better than you know it, Degarmo," I said.

Patton had as much expression on his face as a chunk of wood. He watched Degarmo quietly. He didn't look at Kingsley at all.

After what seemed a very long time, Degarmo said quietly, "I don't see why. I don't know anything about Kingsley's wife. To the best of my knowledge I never laid eyes on her—until last night."

He lowered his eyelids a little and watched me broodingly. He knew perfectly well what I was going to say. I said it anyway.

"And you never saw her last night. Because she had already been dead for over a month. Because she had been drowned in Little Fawn Lake. Because the woman you saw dead in the Granada Apartments was Mildred Haviland, and Mildred Haviland was Muriel Chess. And since Mrs. Kingsley was dead long before Lavery was shot, it follows that Mrs. Kingsley did not shoot him."

Kingsley clenched his fists on the arms of his chair, but he made no sound, no sound at all.

THERE was another heavy silence. Patton broke it by saying in his careful slow voice, "That's kind of a wild statement, ain't it? Don't you kind of think Bill Chess would know his own wife?"

I said, "After a month in the water? With his wife's clothes on her and some of his wife's trinkets? With water-soaked blond hair like his wife's hair and almost no recognizable face? Why would he even have a doubt about it? She left a note that might be a suicide note. She was gone away. Her clothes and car were gone. For a month he had heard nothing from her. And then this corpse comes up out of the water with Muriel's clothes on it. A blond woman about his wife's size. Of course there would be differences and if any substitution had been suspected, they would have been found and checked. But there was no reason to suspect any such thing. Crystal Kingsley was still alive. She had gone off with Lavery. She had left her car in San Bernardino. She had sent a wire to her husband from El Paso. She didn't enter the picture so far as Bill Chess was concerned. Why should she?"

Patton said, "I ought to of thought of it myself. But if I had, it would be one of those ideas a fellow would throw away almost as quick as he thought of it. It would look too kind of farfetched."

"Superficially yes," I said. "But only superficially. Suppose the body had not come up out of the lake for a year, or not at all, unless the lake was dragged for it. Muriel Chess was gone and nobody was going to spend much time looking for her. We might never have heard of her again. Mrs. Kingsley on the other hand had money and connections and an anxious husband. She would be searched for eventually, but it might have been a matter of months. Even if the lake had been dragged and the body was found, there was better than an even chance that it would not be correctly identified. Bill Chess was arrested for his wife's murder. If he had been convicted that would have been that as far as the body in the lake was concerned. Crystal Kingsley would still be missing, and it would be an unsolved mystery if it hadn't been for Lavery.

"Lavery is the key to the whole thing. He was in the Prescott Hotel in San Bernardino the night Crystal Kingsley was supposed to have left here. He saw a woman there who had Crystal Kingsley's car, who was wearing Crystal Kingsley's clothes, and of course he knew who she was. But he didn't have to know there was anything wrong. He didn't have to know they were Crystal Kingsley's clothes or that the woman had put Crystal Kingsley's car in the hotel garage. All he had to know was that he met Muriel Chess. Muriel took care of the rest."

I stopped and waited for somebody to say something. Nobody did. Degarmo leaned against the wall by the fireplace, taut and white-faced and cold, a big hard solemn man whose thoughts were deeply hidden.

I went on talking.

"If Muriel Chess impersonated Crystal Kingsley, she murdered her. That's elementary. We know who she was and what kind of woman she was. She had already murdered someone before she met and married Bill Chess. She had been Dr. Almore's office nurse and his little pal and she had murdered Dr. Almore's wife in such a neat way that Almore had to cover up for her. And she had been married to a man in the Bay City police who also was sucker enough to cover up for her. She got the men that way, she could make them jump through hoops. Her record proves it. What she was able to do with Lavery proves it. Very well, she killed people who got in her way, and Kingsley's wife got in her way too. Crystal Kingsley could make the men do a little jumping through hoops too. She made Bill Chess jump and Bill Chess's wife wasn't the girl to take that and smile. Also she was sick to death of her life up here and she wanted to get away. But she needed money. She had tried to get it from Almore, and that sent Degarmo up here looking for her. That scared her a little. Degarmo is the sort of fellow you are never quite sure of. She was right not to be sure of him, wasn't she, Degarmo?"

Degarmo moved his foot on the ground. "The sands are running out on you, fellow," he said grimly. "Speak your little piece while you can."

"Mildred didn't have to have Crystal Kingsley's car and clothes and credentials, but they helped. What cash Crystal had must have helped for a while. Also she must have had jewelry that eventually could be turned into more money. All this made killing her a rational as well as an agreeable thing to do. That disposes of motive, and now we come to means and opportunity.

"The opportunity was made to order for her. She had quarreled with Bill and he had gone off to get drunk. She knew her Bill and how drunk he could get and how long he would stay away. Time was of the essence. Otherwise the whole thing flopped. She had to pack her own clothes and take them in her car to Coon Lake and hide them. She had to murder Crystal Kingsley and dress her in Muriel's clothes and get her down in the lake. As to the murder itself, I imagine she got Crystal drunk or knocked her on the head and drowned her in the bathtub in this cabin. She was a nurse, she knew how to handle things like bodies. She knew how to swim—we have it from Bill that she was a fine swimmer. And a drowned body will sink. All she had to do was guide it down into the deep water where she wanted it. She did it, she dressed in Crystal Kingsley's clothes, packed what else of hers she wanted, got into Crystal Kingsley's car and departed. And at San Bernardino she ran into her first snag, Lavery.

"Lavery knew her as Muriel Chess. He had been up here and seen her and he would probably come up here again. All he would find would be a locked-up cabin but he might get talking to Bill and it was part of her plan that Bill should not know positively that she had ever left Little Fawn Lake. So she put her hooks into Lavery at once, and that wouldn't be too hard. If there is one thing we know for certain about Lavery, it is that he couldn't keep his hands off the women. He would be easy for a smart girl like Mildred Haviland. So she played him and took him away with her. She took him to El Paso and there sent a wire he knew nothing about. Finally she played him back to Bay City. She probably couldn't help that. He wanted to go home and she couldn't let him get too far from her. Because Lavery was dangerous to her. Lavery alone could destroy all the indications that Crystal Kingsley had ever gone to El Paso. When the search for Crystal Kingsley eventually began, it had to come to Lavery, and at that moment Lavery's life wasn't worth a plugged nickel. So Lavery was shot dead in his bathroom, the very night after I went down to talk to him. That's about all there is to it, except why Mildred went back to the house the next morning. That's just one of those things that murderers seem to do. She went back and I found her there and she put on an act that left me with both feet in my mouth."

Patton said, "Who killed her, son? I gather you don't like Kingsley for that little job."

I looked at Kingsley. "You didn't talk to her on the phone, you said. What about Miss Fromsett? Did she think she was talking to your wife?"

Kingsley shook his head. "All she said was that she seemed very changed and subdued. I had no suspicion then. I didn't have any until I got up here. When I walked into this cabin last night, I felt there was something wrong. It was too clean and neat and orderly. Crystal didn't leave things that way. There would have been clothes all over the bedroom, cigarette stubs all over the house, bottles and glasses all over the kitchen. I thought Bill's wife might have cleaned up, and then I remembered that Bill's wife wouldn't have, not on that particular day. She had been too busy quarreling with Bill and being murdered, or committing suicide, whichever it was. I thought about all this in a confused sort of way, but I don't claim I actually made anything of it."

Patton got up from his chair and went out on the porch. He

came back wiping his lips with his tan handkerchief. He sat down again, and eased himself over on his left hip, on account of the hip holster on the other side. He looked thoughtfully at Degarmo. Degarmo stood against the wall, hard and rigid, a stone man. His right hand hung down at his side, with the fingers curled.

Patton said, "I still ain't heard who killed Muriel. Is that part of the show or is that something that still has to be worked out?"

I said, "Somebody who thought she needed killing, somebody who had loved her and hated her, somebody who was too much of a cop to let her get away with any more murders, but not enough of a cop to pull her in and let the whole story come out. Somebody like Degarmo."

DEGARMO straightened away from the wall and smiled bleakly. His right hand made a hard clean movement and was holding a gun. He held it with a lax wrist, so that it pointed down at the floor in front of him. He spoke to me without looking at me.

"I don't think you have a gun," he said. "Patton has a gun but I don't think he can get it out fast enough to do him any good. Maybe you have a little evidence to go with that last guess. Or wouldn't that be important enough for you to bother with?"

"A little evidence," I said. "Not very much. But it'll grow. Somebody stood behind that green curtain in the Granada for more than half an hour and stood as silently as only a cop on a stakeout knows how to stand. Somebody who had a blackjack. Somebody who stripped the girl and raked her body with scratches in the kind of sadistic hate a man like you might feel for a woman who had made a small private hell for him. Somebody who has blood and cuticle under his fingernails right now, plenty enough for a chemist to work on. I bet you won't let Patton look at the fingernails of your right hand, Degarmo."

Degarmo stood silent for a moment, thinking. His face was grim, but his metallic-blue eyes held a light that was almost amusement. The room was hot and heavy with a disaster that could no longer be mended. He seemed to feel it less than any of us.

"I want to get out of here," he said at last. "Not very far maybe, but no hick cop is going to put the arm on me. Any objections?"

Patton said quietly, "Can't be done, son. You know I got to take you. None of this ain't proved yet, but I can't just let you walk out."

"You have a nice big belly, Patton. I'm a good shot. How do you figure to take me?"

"I been trying to figure," Patton said and rumpled his hair under his pushed-back hat. "I ain't got very far with it. I don't want no holes in my belly. But I can't let you make a monkey of me in my own territory either."

"Let him go," I said. "He can't get out of these mountains. That's why I brought him up here."

Patton said soberly, "Somebody might get hurt taking him. That wouldn't be right. If it's anybody, it's got to be me."

Degarmo grinned. "You're a nice boy, Patton," he said. "Look, I'll put the gun back under my arm and we'll start from scratch. I'm good enough for that too."

He tucked the gun under his arm. He stood with his arms hanging, his chin pushed forward a little, watching. Patton chewed softly, with his pale eyes on Degarmo's vivid eyes.

"I'm sitting down," Patton complained. "I ain't as fast as you anyways. I just don't like to look yellow." He looked at me. "Why the hell did you have to bring this up here? It ain't any part of my troubles. Now look at the jam I'm in."

Degarmo put his head back a little and laughed. While he was still laughing, his right hand jumped for his gun again.

I didn't see Patton move at all. The room throbbed with the roar of his frontier Colt.

Degarmo's arm shot straight out to one side and the heavy Smith & Wesson was torn out of his hand and thudded against the knotty-pine wall behind him. He shook his numbed right hand and looked down at it with wonder in his eyes.

Patton stood up slowly. He walked slowly across the room and kicked the revolver under a chair. He looked at Degarmo sadly. Degarmo was sucking a little blood off his knuckles.

"You give me a break," Patton said. "You hadn't ought ever

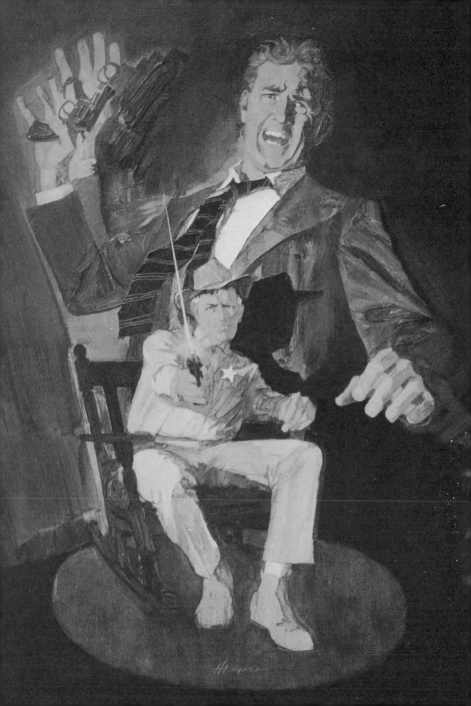

to give a man like me a break. I been a shooter more years than you been alive, son."

Degarmo nodded to him and straightened his back and started for the door.

"Don't do that," Patton told him calmly.

Degarmo kept on going. He reached the door and pushed on the screen. He looked back at Patton and his face was very white.

"I'm going out of here," he said. "There's only one way you can stop me. So long, fatty."

Patton didn't move a muscle.

Degarmo went out through the door. His feet made heavy sounds on the porch and then on the steps. I went to the front window and looked out. Patton still hadn't moved. Degarmo came down off the steps and started across the top of the little dam.

"He's crossing the dam," I said. "Has Andy got a gun?"

"I don't figure he'd use one if he had," Patton said calmly. "He don't know any reason why he should."

"Well, I'll be damned," I said.

Patton sighed. "He hadn't ought to have given me a break like that," he said. "Had me cold. I got to give it back to him. Won't do him a lot of good. You lock your car?"

I nodded. "Andy's coming down to the other end of the dam," I said. "Degarmo has stopped him. He's speaking to him."

"He'll take Andy's car maybe," Patton said sadly.

"Well, I'll be damned," I said again. Degarmo was out of sight beyond the rise. Andy was halfway across the dam, coming slowly, looking back over his shoulder now and then. The sound of a starting car came distantly. Andy looked up at the cabin, then turned and started to run back along the dam.

The sound of the motor died away. When it was quite gone, Patton said, "Well, I guess we better go back to the office and do some telephoning."

Kingsley got up suddenly and went out to the kitchen and came back with a bottle of whiskey. He poured himself a stiff drink and drank it standing.

Patton and I went quietly out of the cabin.

PATTON HAD JUST FINISHED putting his calls through to block the highways when a call came from the sergeant in charge of the guard detail at Puma Lake dam.

We went out and got into Patton's car and Andy drove very fast along the lake road through the village and along the lakeshore back to the big dam at the end. We were waved across the dam to where the sergeant was waiting in a jeep beside the headquarters hut.

The sergeant waved his arm and started the jeep and we followed him a couple of hundred feet along the highway to where a few soldiers stood on the edge of the canyon looking down. The sergeant got out of the jeep and Patton and Andy and I climbed out of the official car and went over by the sergeant.

"Guy didn't stop for the sentry," the sergeant said, and there was bitterness in his voice. "Damn near knocked him off the road. The sentry in the middle of the bridge had to jump fast to get missed. The one at this end had enough. He called the guy to halt. Guy kept going."

The sergeant chewed his gum and looked down into the canyon.

"Orders are to shoot in a case like that," he said. "The sentry shot." He pointed down to the grooves in the shoulder at the edge of the drop. "This is where he went off."

A hundred feet down in the canyon a small coupe was smashed against the side of a huge granite boulder. It was almost upside down, leaning a little. There were three men down there. They had moved the car enough to lift something out.

Something that had been a man.

Rogue Male

Rogue Male

A CONDENSATION OF
THE BOOK BY

Geoffrey
Household

ILLUSTRATED BY JIM SHARPE

Pursued by implacable Nazi assassins and the
British police as well, the tall Englishman had
nowhere to turn for safety. Who would believe
that he had trained his telescopic rifle sight on the
Führer with nothing more in mind than a sporting
stalk, or the incredible events that had followed?
So he fled—across Europe, across the Channel,
across England, to the lonely southern downs he
knew so well. There he went to earth like an
animal, and in his burrow he waited, his stalkers
hot on the trail.

Rogue Male stands by itself as a classic of
suspense, and along with other tales such as
Watcher in the Shadows has earned for Geoffrey
Household a distinguished and permanent
reputation as a master storyteller.

Part I

I CANNOT blame them. After all, one doesn't need a telescopic sight to shoot boar and bear; so that when they came on me watching the terrace at a range of five hundred and fifty yards, it was natural enough that they should jump to conclusions. And they behaved, I think, with discretion. I am not an obvious anarchist or fanatic, and I don't look as if I took any interest in politics; I might perhaps have sat for an agricultural constituency in the South of England, but that hardly counts as politics. I carried a British passport, and if I had been caught walking up to the house instead of watching it, I should probably have been asked to lunch. It was a difficult problem for angry men to solve in an afternoon.

They must have wondered whether I had been employed on, as it were, an official mission; but I think they turned that suspicion down. No government—least of all ours—encourages assassination. Or was I a free lance? That must have seemed very unlikely; anyone can see that I am not the type of avenging angel. Was I, then, innocent of any criminal intent, and exactly what I claimed to be—a sportsman who couldn't resist the temptation to stalk the impossible?

After two or three hours of their questions I could see I had

159

them shaken. They didn't believe me, though they were beginning to understand that a bored and wealthy Englishman who had hunted all commoner game might well find a perverse pleasure in a purely formal stalk of the biggest game on earth. But even if my explanation were true, it made no difference. I couldn't be allowed to live.

By that time I had, of course, been knocked about very considerably. Only now are my nails growing back, and my left eye is still pretty useless. I wasn't a case you could turn loose with apologies. They would probably have given me a picturesque funeral, with huntsmen firing volleys and sounding horns, with all the bigwigs present in fancy dress, and put up a stone obelisk to the memory of a brother sportsman. They do those things well. As it was, they bungled the job.

They took me to the edge of a cliff and put me over, all but my hands. That was cunning. Scrabbling at the rough rock would have accounted for the state of my fingers when I was found. I did hang on, of course; for how long I don't know. I cannot see why I wasn't glad to die, seeing that I hadn't a hope of living and the quicker the end the less the suffering. But one always hopes—if a clinging to life can be called hope. And so I hung on till I dropped.

I have always believed that consciousness remains for a while after physical death, so I thought I was probably dead. I had been such a hell of a long time falling; it didn't seem reasonable that I could be alive. And there had been a terrifying instant of pain. I felt as if the back of my thighs and rump had been shorn off, pulled off, scraped off—off, however done. I had parted, obviously and irrevocably, with a lot of my living matter.

My second thought was a longing for death, for it was revolting to imagine myself still alive and of the consistency of mud. All around me there was a pulped substance, and I supposed that this bog was me; it tasted of blood. Then it occurred to me that this soft substance might really be bog, and that anything into which I fell would taste of blood.

I had crashed into a patch of deep marsh. Now I thought that I was alive—for the moment, at least—for in the darkness I couldn't see how much damage had been dealt, and I felt quite numb. I hauled myself out by the tussocks of grass, a creature of mud, bandaged in mud.

A rocky slope rose sharply from the marsh. I had evidently grazed it in my fall. I didn't feel the pain any longer, so I could persuade myself that I was no more seriously hurt than when they had put me over the cliff. I therefore determined to move off before they came to find my body.

I had, though I didn't know it then, a good deal of time to play with; they hadn't any intention of finding my body until there were independent witnesses with them. Then the corpse of the unfortunate brother sportsman would be accidentally discovered, and the whole history of his fate perfectly plain on the nasty sloping rock from which he had slipped.

The country at the foot of the cliff was wooded. I walked through it about a mile before choosing a thick darkness to faint in. Several times during the night I came to a sort of consciousness, but let it slide away. I wasn't returning to this difficult world till dawn.

When it was light I tried to stand on my feet, but of course I couldn't. Any movement interfered with my nice cake of mud. Whenever a crust fell off I started to bleed. No, I certainly wasn't interfering with the mud.

I knew where there was water. I had never seen that stream, and my certainty of its direction may have been due to a subconscious memory of the map. I made for it on my belly, using my elbows for legs and leaving a track like that of a wounded crocodile, all slime and blood.

I crawled to the edge of the water and drank, turning myself around in a shallow about two inches deep, where the signs of my wallowing would be washed out. I wasn't going into the stream, but I made the trail look as if I had. They could track me to the cover where I had lain up for the night, and from there to the water. Where I had gone when I left the water they would have to guess.

I had no doubt where I was going, and the decision must be credited to my ancestors. A deer would trot upstream or downstream

161

and leave the water at some point that the hunter's nose or eyes could determine. A monkey would do nothing of the sort; he would confuse his tracks and vanish into a third dimension.

When I had turned around in the shallows, I wriggled back again along the damned crocodile track I had made. It was easy to follow; indeed it looked as definite as a country lane, for my face was only six inches above the ground. Thinking about it now, I wonder that they didn't notice, when they followed me to the stream, that some of the grass was bent the wrong way and that I must have gone back on my tracks. But on such a monster of a trail there was no apparent need to look for details.

The outward journey had taken me under a stand of larch, where the earth was soft and free of undergrowth. I had brushed past the trunk of one tree, which I now meant to climb. The lowest branch was within two feet of the ground; above that the sweet-smelling sooty branches were as close together as the rungs of a ladder. The muscles of my hands were intact; I had gone beyond worrying about the state of surfaces.

Until I was well above the level of a man's eyes I did not dare rest boots on branch; they would have left caked prints that no one could miss. I went up the first ten feet in a single burst, knowing that the longer I held on to a branch the less strength remained to reach the next. My arms were two pistons shooting alternately from heaven knows what cylinder of force. Friends have sometimes accused me of taking pride in the maceration of my flesh. They are right. But I did not know that I could persuade myself to such agony as that climb.

The rest was easier, for I could let my feet bear my weight and could pause as long as I wished before each hoist. When I climbed into the narrowing of the cone and the boughs were thicker and smaller and greener, I got jammed. That suited me; I couldn't fall, wedged in as I was, so I fainted again. It was a luxury.

When I became conscious, the tree was swaying in the light wind and smelling of peace. I felt deliciously secure, as if I were a parasite on the tree, grown to it. I was not in pain, not hungry, not thirsty, and I was safe. There was nothing in each passing moment of the present that could hurt me. I was dealing exclusively with the present. If I had looked forward, I should have known despair, but for a hunted, resting mammal it is no more possible to experience despair than hope.

It must have been the early afternoon when I saw the search party working down the wooded slope to the north of my tree. The sun was in their eyes, and there was no risk of their spotting my face among the soft green feathers of the larch. Three uniformed police were trampling down the hillside: heavy, stolid fellows good-humoredly following a plainclothesman who was ranging about on my trail like a dog they had taken for a walk. I recognized him. He was the detective from the house who had conducted my interrogation. He had proposed a really obscene method of dragging the truth out of me and had actually started it when his colleagues protested. They had no objection to his technique, but they had the sense to see that it might be necessary for my corpse to be found and that it must not be found unreasonably mutilated.

When they came nearer I could hear scraps of their conversation. The policemen knew nothing of the truth. They had been notified, I gathered, that a cry or a fall was heard in the night. They were in doubt whether I had been man or woman and whether the case had been an accident or attempted suicide. Unobtrusively guided by the detective, they had found my knapsack and the disturbance in the patch of marsh.

Seeing my reptilian trail disappear into the stand of larch, the detective perked up and took command. He seemed certain that I should be found under the trees. He shouted to his three companions to run around to the other side in case I should escape, and himself crawled under the low boughs. He wanted to find me himself and alone. If I was alive, it was necessary to finish me off discreetly.

He passed rapidly beneath my tree and on into the open. I heard him curse when he did not find me in the wood. Then I heard their faint voices as they shouted to one another up and down the stream. Their closeness surprised me. I had thought of the stream, naturally, as a morning's march away.

I saw no more of the hunt. A few hours later there was a lot

of splashing and excitement down by the water. They must have been dragging the pools for my body. The stream was a shallow mountain torrent, but quite fast enough to roll a man along with it until he was caught by rock or eddy.

In the evening I heard dogs and felt really frightened. I started to tremble, and knew pain again, aches and stabs and throbbings, all the symphony of pain. I had come back to life, thanks to that healing tree. The dogs might have found me, but their master, whoever he was, never gave them a chance. He was casting up and down the stream, searching for a trail that he could not follow himself. When night fell I came down from my tree. I could stand, and with the aid of two sticks I could shuffle slowly forward, flat-footed and stiff-legged.

I MUST try to make my behavior intelligible. This confession—shall I call it that?—is written to keep myself from brooding, to get down what happened in the order in which it happened. I am not content with myself. With this pencil and exercise book I hope to find some clarity. I create a second self, a man of the past by whom the man of the present may be measured. Lest what I write should ever, by accident or intention, become public property, I will not mention who I am. My name is widely known. I have been frequently and unavoidably dishonored by the headlines and praises of the penny press.

This shooting trip of mine started, I believe, innocently enough. Like most Englishmen, I am not accustomed to inquire very deeply into motives. I dislike cold-blooded planning. I remember asking myself when I packed the telescopic sight what the devil I wanted it for; but I just felt that it might come in handy.

It is undoubtedly true that I had been speculating upon the methods of guarding the head of a nation, and how they might be circumvented. I had a fortnight's sport in Poland, and then crossed the frontier for more. I began moving rather aimlessly from place to place, and as I found myself getting a little nearer to the great man's house with each night's lodging, I became obsessed by this idea of a sporting stalk. I have asked myself, once or twice

since, why I didn't leave the rifle behind. I think the answer is
that it wouldn't have been cricket. Now, I argued, here am I with
a rifle and telescopic sight, with a permit to carry it, with an
excuse for possessing it. Let us see whether, as an academic point,
such a stalk and such a bag are possible. I went no further than
that. I planned nothing. It has always been my habit to let things
take their course.

I sent my baggage home by train and covered the last hundred
miles or so on foot, traveling only with a knapsack, my rifle, my
maps, and my field glasses. I marched by night. During daylight
I lay up in timber or heath. I have never enjoyed anything so
much. Whoever has stalked a beast for a couple of miles would
understand what a superbly exciting enterprise it was to stalk over
a hundred miles, passing unseen through the main herds of human
beings, the outliers, the young males walking unexpectedly upon
hillsides.

I arrived on the grounds at dawn and spent the whole day in
reconnaissance. It was an alarming day, for the forest surrounding
the house was most efficiently patrolled. From tree to tree and
gully to gully I prowled over most of the circuit, but only flat
on the earth was I really safe. Often I hid my rifle and glasses,
thinking that I was certain to be challenged and questioned. I never
was. I might have been transparent.

At all points commanding the terrace and the gardens surrounding
the house, clearings had been cut; nobody, even at extreme ranges,
could shoot from cover. Open spaces, constantly crossed by guards,
there were in plenty. I chose the narrowest of them; about fifty
feet broad, it ran straight through the woods and sloped to the
edge of a low cliff. From the grass slope the terrace and the doors
leading onto it were in full sight. I worked out the range as five
hundred and fifty yards.

I spent the night on a couch of pine needles, well hidden under
a tree, finished my provisions, and slept undisturbed. A little before
dawn I climbed a few feet down the cliff and squatted on a ledge
where the overhang protected me from anyone who might peer
from above. A stunted elder, clawing at the gravel with the tips

of its top-heavy roots, was safe enough cover from distant eyes looking upward. In that cramped position my rifle was useless, but I could, and very clearly, see the great man were he to come out and play with the dog or smell a rose.

A path ran across the slope just above my head, and continued along the lower edge of the woods. I timed the intervals at which I heard the guard's footsteps, and discovered that he passed about every fourteen minutes. When at last the great man came out to the terrace, the guard had just passed. I had ten minutes to play with. I was up at once onto the slope.

I made myself comfortable, and got the three pointers of the telescopic sight steady on the V of his waistcoat. He was facing me and winding up his watch. He would never have known what shattered him—if I had meant to fire, that is. Just at that moment I felt a slight breeze on my cheek. It had been dead calm till then. I had to pause to allow for the wind. The next thing I knew, I was coming around from a severe blow on the back of the head, and the guard was covering me with his revolver. He had hurled a stone at me and himself after it—immediate, instinctive action far swifter than fiddling with his holster.

We stared at each other. He was a young guard of splendid physique, loyalty written all over him, with one of those fleshy open faces and the right instincts—a boy worth teaching. I remember complaining incoherently that he was seven minutes early. He looked at me as if I had been the devil in person. Together with his commanding officer he took me down to the house, and there, as I have already written, I was questioned by professionals. My young captor left the room after disgracing his manhood—or so he thought—by being violently sick. I myself was resigned.

I suspect that resignation was a lot easier for me than for a real assassin, since I had nothing at all to give away—no confederates, no motive. I couldn't save myself by telling them anything interesting. So I kept on automatically repeating the truth without the slightest hope that it would be believed.

At last someone recognized my name, and my story of a sporting stalk became faintly possible; but, whether it were true or not, it was now more than ever essential that I be discreetly murdered. And that was easy. I had admitted that I had not spent a night under a roof for five days, and that nobody knew where I was. They put all my papers and possessions back into my pockets, drove me fifty miles to the north, and staged the accident.

WHEN I came down from that blessed larch and found that my legs would carry me, I began to look forward. If I could walk, if I had new breeches, and if I could pass the danger zone without calling attention to myself, my chance of getting clear out of the country was not negligible. The police in neighboring villages would be warned to look out for a moribund stranger, but it was most unlikely that any description of me would have been circularized to other districts. I had my passport, my maps, and my money. I spoke the language well enough to deceive anyone but a highly educated man. Dear old "Holy George"—my private nickname for their ambassador in London—insists that I speak a dialect, but to him polished grammar is more important than accent.

I wish I could apologize to Holy George. He had certainly spent some hours of those last twenty-four in answering very confidential cables about me—wiring as respectfully as possible that the body-guards of his revered master were a pack of bloody fools, and following up with a strong letter to the effect that I was a member of his club and that it was unthinkable I should be mixed up in any such business as was, he could hardly believe seriously, suggested. I fear he must have been reprimanded by his superiors. The body-guards were, on the face of it, right.

It was now, I think, Sunday night; it was a Saturday when I was caught, but I am not sure of the lapse of time thereafter. I missed a day somewhere; whether it was in my tree or later I cannot tell. I knew roughly where I was, and that to escape from this tumbled world of rock and forest I should follow any path which ran parallel to the stream. My journey would not have been difficult if I had had crutches, but I just couldn't find pieces of wood of the right height and shape, and I couldn't make my hands use enough pressure to break pieces of wood that would serve the purpose. I was angry with myself, angry to the point where I wept childish tears of impotence. Then I raged and cursed at myself. I thought my spirit had altogether broken.

Finally, of course, I had to make myself progress without crutches. With a rough staff in each hand I managed about four miles, shuffling over even ground and crawling whenever my legs became unbearably painful. I remember that common experience of carrying a heavy suitcase; one changes it from arm to arm at shorter and shorter intervals until one can no longer decide whether to continue the pain in the right or the left. So it was with me in my changes from crawling to walking and back again.

I thanked God for the dawn, for it meant that I need not drive myself any farther. Until I knew exactly where I was, and upon what paths men came and went, I had to hide. I collapsed into a dry ditch and lay there for hours. I heard no sounds except a lark and the crunch of cows chewing on the long grass in a neighboring field.

At last I stood up and had a look at my surroundings. I was near the top of a ridge. Below me and to the left was the wooded valley along which I had come. I had not noticed in the night that I was climbing. Part of my exhaustion had been due to the rising ground. I shuffled upward to the skyline. The long curve of a river was spread out at my feet, the near bank clothed in low bushes through which ran a footpath, appearing and disappearing until it crossed the mouth of my stream by an iron bridge. On the farther bank, a mile upstream, was a country town with a few small factories. Downstream there were pastures on both banks and a small islet in the center of the river. It was tranquil and safe.

I got out the map and checked my position. I was looking at a tributary which, after a course of thirty miles, ran into one of the main rivers of Europe. From this town, a provincial capital, the search for me would be directed, and to it the police, my would-be rescuers, presumably belonged. Nevertheless I had to go there. It was the center of communications: road, river, and railway. And since I could not walk I had to find some transport to carry me to the frontier.

At intervals the breeze bore to me the faint sound of cries and splashing, the collective voice of several women bathing in the stream. It occurred to me that men might come to swim at the same place at lunchtime, and I could lay my hands on a pair of trousers.

I waited until I saw the girls cross the iron footbridge on their way back to town, and then hobbled down the ridge. The bathing place was plain enough, a semicircle of grass with a clean drop of three feet into the river. Above and below it the bank was covered with a dense growth of willow and alder. I took to my elbows and belly again, and crawled into the thicket.

There was a path running through it; and my necessary males were not long in coming—five hefty lads. There were two pairs of shorts, two of nondescript trousers, and an old pair of riding breeches. For my build all had the waistbands too roomy and the legs too short, and I couldn't guess which pair would best fit me. It was that, I think, which gave me the brilliant idea of taking them all. To steal one pair of trousers would obviously direct attention to some passing tramp or fugitive; but if all disappeared, the theft would be put down as the practical joke of a comrade. I remember chuckling crazily as I worked my way back to the edge of the bushes.

The lads dived in within a few seconds of each other. Instantly I was out of the thicket and hunching myself across the grass. I got four pairs; the fifth was too far away. Only one had a wallet, and that, since it stuck out from a hip pocket, I managed to place on top of the rest of his clothes. I just had time to slip behind a bramble bush before a swimmer pulled himself up the bank. He didn't look at the clothes—why should he?—and I crawled downstream with the trousers, made for the bank, and slid under the willows into a patch of still water full of scum and brushwood. Two of them were swimming quite close, but the boughs trailing in the water protected me from casual glances.

I needn't have taken so much trouble. When they found their trousers missing, they dashed up the path yelling for one Willy. When Willy was not to be found, they draped towels around the tails of their shirts and took the path for home. I hope they didn't believe Willy's denials till he was thoroughly punished. The sort of man whom one instantly accuses of any practical joke that has been played deserves whatever is coming to him.

Together with the trousers I let myself float down to the islet which I had seen from the top of the ridge. I could use only my arms for swimming. However, I managed to keep myself and my soggy raft of trousers well out into the river, and the current did the rest.

The islet was bare, but with enough low vegetation on its shores to cover me from observation by anyone on the high ground where I had lain that morning. I spread out myself, my clothes, and the breeches to dry in the sun. I did not even attempt to examine my body. It was enough that the soaking had separated textile from flesh with no worse result than a gentle oozing of matter.

I remained on the islet for the Monday night and all the following day. Probably I was there for the Tuesday night too. I do not know; as I say, I lost a day somewhere. It was marvelous, for I lay on the sand naked and undisturbed, and allowed the sun to start the work of healing. I was barely conscious most of the time. I would hunch myself into the half-shade of the weeds and rushes and sleep till I grew cold, then I would hunch myself back again and roast, permitting my wounds to scar. I did not want food. I was, I suppose, running a fever, so my lack of appetite was natural. I had all the various garments to cover me, and at any other time I should have thought the weather too hot for easy sleep.

At the false dawn of what turned out to be Wednesday, I awoke feeling clearheaded and ravenously hungry. I chose the riding breeches—as I held them against my body they seemed roomy enough not to rub my hide—and threw shorts and trousers into the river. I tied two bits of driftwood together with my belt, and put all my possessions on this improvised raft. I found that I could splash now with more ease—though the regular motions of swimming were still beyond me—and reached the farther bank without being carried more than a hundred yards downstream.

On dry land and within a stone's throw of a main road, I had to take stock of my appearance. So far my looks had not mattered; but now I proposed to reenter the world of men, and the impression I made was vitally important. Only my shoes and stockings were respectable. I couldn't bend to take them off, so the river had cleaned them.

Item: I had to shave off a four days' beard. That was not the mere prejudice of an Englishman against appearing in public with his bristles. If a man is clean-shaven and has a well-fitting collar and tie, he can get away with a multitude of suspicious circumstances.

Item: Gloves. The ends of my fingers had to be shown while paying money and taking goods, and they were not human.

Item: An eye patch. My left eye was in a condition that could not be verified without a mirror. The eyelid had stuck to a mess of what I hoped was only blood.

Item: A clothes brush. My tweed coat had no elbows, but it might pass provided I brushed off the mud and did not turn away from anyone I spoke to.

I had to have these things. I had not the will to crawl and hobble night after night to the frontier, nor the agility to steal enough to eat; but if I entered a village shop as I was, the proprietor would promptly escort me to the police or a hospital.

The putting on of the breeches was an interminable agony. When at last I had them up, I could manage only three of the blasted buttons and had to forgo the rest for fear of leaving bloodstains all over the cloth.

I crossed a field and stood for a moment on the empty main road. It was the hour before dawn, the sky an imperial awning fringed with gold. At my disposal, as the map had told me, were river, road, and railway. I was inclined to favor escape by river. A man drifting down the current in a boat doesn't have to answer questions or fill in forms. But, again, there was the insuperable handicap of my appearance. I couldn't present myself as I was to buy a boat, and if I stole one, my arrest was likely at the next village downriver.

On the far side of the road was a farm cart, backed against the edge of a field of wheat. I knelt behind it to watch the passersby.

Men were already stirring—a few peasants in the fields, a few walkers on the road. From the latter I hoped to obtain help or at least, by observing them, an inspiration as to how to help myself.

There was a workman to whom I nearly spoke. He had an honest, kindly face—but so had most of them. Two aimless passing wanderers looked to be persons who would sympathize, but their faces were those of scared rabbits. Then there were several peasants on their way to the fields. I could only pray that they wouldn't enter mine. They would have had some sport with me before handing me over to the police; they seemed that sort. Then came a tall, stooping man with a fishing rod. He cut across to the river and began to fish not far from where I had landed. He had a melancholy, intellectual face with a great deal of strength in it, and, purely on intuition, I decided to approach him.

There was no cover on the farther side of the road and precious little on the bank, so that I had to make up my mind about the fisherman as I slowly and silently crossed the fields toward him. He was paying more attention to his thoughts than to his rod. By the angle of his float I could see that he had hooked the bottom, but he was quite unaware of it. I walked up behind him, wished him good morning, and asked if he had had any luck. He jumped to his feet with the butt of the rod pointed toward me as if to keep me off. I expect he hadn't seen a creature like me in a long time; this country has no tramps. He apologized for his fishing and said he didn't think there was anything wrong in it. He did his best to look servile, but his eyes burned with courage.

I held out my mutilated hands to him and asked if he knew how that was done. He didn't answer a word, just waited for further information.

"Look here!" I said to him. "I swear there isn't a soul in this country who knows I am alive except yourself. I want gloves, shaving tackle, a mirror, and a clothes brush. Don't buy them. Give me old things that have no mark on them by which they could be traced back to you if I am caught. And if you don't mind putting your hand in my inside coat pocket, you will find money."

"I don't want money," he said.

His face was absolutely expressionless. He might have meant that he wouldn't help a fugitive for all the money in the world, or that he wouldn't take money for helping a fugitive. The next move was up to me.

"Do you speak English?" I asked.

I saw a flicker of interest in his eyes, but he made no sign that he had understood me. I carried on in English. I was completely in his power, so there was no point in hiding my nationality. I hoped that the foreign tongue might break down his reserve.

"I won't tell you who I am or what I have done," I said, "because it is wiser that you shouldn't know. But so long as no one sees us talking together, I don't think you run the slightest risk in helping me a bit."

"I'll help you," he answered in perfect English. "What was it you wanted?"

I repeated my requirements and asked him to throw in an eye patch and some food if he could manage it. I also told him that I was a rich man and he shouldn't hesitate to take any money he might need. He refused—with a very sweet, melancholy smile— but gave me an address in England to which I was to pay what I thought fit if ever I got home.

"Where shall I put the things?" he asked.

"Under the cart over there," I answered. "And don't worry. I shall be in the wheat, and I'll take care not to be seen." He said good-by and moved off abruptly.

The traffic on the road was increasing, and I had to wait some minutes before I could safely cross into the shelter of the wheat. The sun rose and the landscape was soon thriving with men and business—barges on the river, a battalion out for a route march on the road, and damned, silent bicycles sneaking up every time I raised my head.

The fisherman was back in an hour, but the road was too busy for him to drop a parcel under the cart unseen. He solved the problem by sitting on the cart while he took his rod apart and packed it away. When he got up he accidentally left the parcel behind.

174

To get possession of it was the devil of a job, for I could not see what was about to pass until the traffic was nearly opposite me. At last I plucked up courage and reached the cart. I kept my back to the road and pretended to be tinkering with the axle. A woman wished me good morning, and that was the worst fright I had had since they pushed me over the cliff. I answered her surlily and she passed on.

Back in the wheat, I knelt in peace and unpacked the parcel which that blessed fisherman had left for me. There were a bottle of milk well laced with brandy, bread, and the best part of a cold chicken. He had thought of everything, even hot shaving water in a thermos flask.

When I had eaten I felt equal to looking in the small mirror. I was cleaner than I expected; the morning swim was responsible for that. But I didn't recognize myself. It was not the smashed eye which surprised me—that was merely closed, swollen, and ugly. It was the other eye. Glaring back at me from the mirror, deep and enormous, it seemed to belong to someone intensely alive, so much more alive than I felt. My face was all pallor and angles and bristles, like that of a Christian martyr in a medieval painting.

I put on my gloves—limp leather, God reward him, and several sizes too large!—then shaved, brushed my clothes, and dressed myself more tidily. My coat and shirt were patterned in shades of brown, and the bloodstains, weakened by my swim to the island, hardly showed. When I had cleaned up and adjusted the eye patch, I came to the conclusion that I aroused pity rather than suspicion. I looked like a poor but educated man, a clerk or schoolmaster, convalescent after some nasty accident. As soon as I was ready I left the wheat. Limping along as best I could and stopping frequently to rest, I covered the mile into town. When necessary I could walk very slowly and correctly, hanging on each foot as if waiting for somebody.

When first I entered the town I was desperately nervous. There seemed to be so many windows observing me, such crowds on the streets. Looking back on it, I cannot think that I passed more than a score of people. The streets were really no more full than those of my own country town, and normally I should not have been affected; but I seemed to have been out of human society for years.

I cut down to the river by the first turning, where I could stroll at my artificial pace without making myself conspicuous. Ahead, under the bridge, were moored a dozen boats. When I came abreast of them I saw the notice BOATS FOR HIRE on a prettily painted cottage.

There was a man leaning on the fence. I wished him good day and asked if I could hire a boat. He looked at me suspiciously. I explained that I was a schoolmaster recovering from a motor accident and had been ordered by my doctor to spend a week in the open air. He took his pipe out of his mouth and said that he didn't hire boats to strangers. Well, had he one for sale? No, he had not. He evidently didn't like the look of me.

A shrill yell came from an upstairs window. "Sell him the punt, idiot!"

I looked up. A red face and formidable bust were hanging over the sill, both quivering with exasperation. I bowed to her with the formality of a village teacher, and she came down.

"Sell him what he wants," she ordered.

Her small, screaming voice came most oddly from so huge a bulk. I imagine he had driven her voice higher and higher with impatience until it stuck permanently on its top note.

"I don't know who he is," insisted her husband with stupid surliness.

That set the old girl off again. "He's a proper man, not a shameless idler. And he shall have his boat!"

She stamped down to the waterfront and showed me the punt. It was far too long and clumsy to be handled by a man who couldn't sit to paddle. But there was a twelve-foot dinghy with a red sail, and I inquired about it. She said it was too expensive for me.

"I shall sell it again wherever I finish the trip," I answered. "And I have a little money—compensation for my accident."

She made her husband step the mast and hoist the sail. That boat was exactly what I wanted. The sail was hardly more than a toy, but it would be a considerable help with the wind astern, and was not large enough to be a hindrance if I were to let go the sheet and drift with the current. I knew that some days must pass before I felt equal to the effort of tacking.

While she raved at her husband, I got out my wallet. I didn't want them to see how much I had, or to wonder at my fumbling with gloved hands.

"There!" I said, holding out to her a sheaf of notes. "That's all I can afford. Tell me yes or no."

I don't know whether the money I offered was less or more than she intended to ask, but it was a sight more than the little tub was worth to anyone but me. She looked astonished at my rural simplicity, then she took it and gave me a receipt. In five minutes I was out on the river, and they were wondering, I suppose, why the crazy schoolmaster should kneel on the bottom boards instead of sitting on a thwart, and why he didn't have his coat decently mended.

OF THE days and nights that passed on the tributary and the main river there is little to write. I was out of any immediate danger and content—far more content than I am now. I recovered my strength as peacefully as if I had been the convalescent I pretended; indeed, thinking myself into the part actually helped me to recover. I nearly believed in my accident, my school, and my favorite pupils, about whom I prattled when I fell in with other users of the river, or when I took a meal in a riverside tavern.

From nightfall to dawn I moored my boat in silent reaches of the river, choosing high or marshy or thickly wooded banks where no one could burst in upon me with questions. At first I had taken to the ditches and backwaters, but the danger of that was impressed on me when a farmer led his horses down to drink in my temporary harbor, and insisted on regarding me as a suspicious character.

Rain was the greatest hardship. After a night's soaking I managed at last to buy a tarpaulin. It kept me dry and uncomfortably warm, but it was heavy, and hard for my hands to fold and unfold.

I made but sixty miles in the first week. My object was to heal myself rather than hurry. In the second week I tried to increase my speed by buying an outboard motor. I only just got out of the deal in time when I found that I had to sign enough papers to assure my arrest. At one town, however, there was a boatyard where I bought a businesslike lugsail and had a small foresail fitted into the bargain. Thereafter I carried my own supplies, and never put in to town or village. With my new canvas and the aid of the current I could sometimes do forty miles a day, and could keep out of the way of the barges and tugs that were now treating the river as their own.

All the way downriver I had considered the problem of my final escape from the country, but was still undecided as I neared the port. My voyage crept into its third week, and it seemed probable that the search for my body would have been abandoned, that it would be assumed I was alive, and that every blessed official would be praying for a sight of me and promotion. After arrival at the port I would not be permitted to sleep in a hotel without being invited to show my papers, or in the open without showing them to a policeman. But as soon as I came in sight of the wharves, I saw British ships and realized that I had merely to tell a good enough story to the right man to be taken aboard.

I moored my boat to a public landing stage and went ashore. At the first secondhand shop I came to I bought myself a nondescript outfit of blue serge, and changed in a public lavatory. My old clothes I sold in another secondhand shop—that seeming the best way to get rid of them without a trace.

Strolling along the quays, I got into conversation with two British seamen by means of the old introduction—"Got a match?" We had a drink together. Neither seaman was bound for England, but they had a pal who was in a ship that was sailing for London the next day.

The pal, haled from the bar to join us, was a bit wary; he was inclined to think that I was a parson from the seamen's mission masquerading as an honest worker. I calmed his suspicions with two double whiskeys and my most engaging dirty story, whereupon he declared that I was a "bit of orl right" and consented to talk about his officers. The captain, it seemed, was a stickler. But Mr.

Vaner, the first officer, was a "fair caution"; I gathered from his wry smile that pal found the mate a hard taskmaster, while admiring his flamboyant character. Mr. Vaner was obviously the man for me. And, yes, I might catch him still on board if I hurried, because he had been out late the night before.

She was a little ship, hardly more than a coaster, lying alongside an endless ribbon of wharf. Two dock policemen were standing nearby. I kept my back to them while I hailed the deck importantly.

"Mr. Vaner on board?"

The cook, who was peeling potatoes on a hatch cover, looked up from the bucket between his knees.

"I'll see, sir."

That "sir" was curious and comforting, given my shabby clothing and filthy shoes. The cook would undoubtedly describe me as a gent, and the first officer would feel he ought to see me.

Indeed I had only a brief wait before Mr. Vaner received me in his cabin. He was a dashing young man in his early twenties, with his cap on the back of a head of brown curls.

As soon as we had shaken hands, he said, "Haven't met you before, have I?"

"No. I got your name from one of the hands. I hear you're sailing tomorrow."

"Well?" he asked guardedly.

I handed him my passport.

"Before we go any further, I want you to satisfy yourself that I am British and really the person I pretend to be."

Mr. Vaner looked at my passport, then up at my face and eye patch. "That's all right," he said. "Take a seat, won't you? You seem to have been in trouble, sir."

"I have, by God! And I want to get out of it."

"A passage?" he asked cautiously. "If it depended on me—but I'm afraid the old man—"

I told him that I didn't want a passage, that I wouldn't put so much responsibility on either him or the captain; all I wanted was a safe place to stow away.

He shook his head and advised me to try a liner.

"I daren't risk it," I answered. "But show me where to hide, and I give you my word of honor that no one shall see me during the voyage or when I go ashore."

"You had better tell me a little more," he said.

He threw himself back in his chair and cocked one leg over the other. His face assumed a serious and judicial air, but his delightfully swaggering pose showed that he was enjoying himself.

I spun him a yarn which, so far as it went, was true. I told him that I was in deadly trouble with the authorities, that I had come down the river in a boat, and that an appeal to our consul was quite useless.

"I might put you in the storeroom," he said doubtfully. "We're going home in ballast, and there's nowhere in the hold for you to hide."

I suggested that the storeroom was too dangerous, that I didn't want to take the remotest chance of being seen and getting the ship into trouble. That seemed to impress him.

"Well," he replied, "if you can stand it, there's an empty freshwater tank which we never use, and I could prop up the cover so that you'd get some air. But I expect that you've slept in worse places, sir, now that I come to think of it."

"You recognized my name?"

"Of course. I wouldn't do this for everyone. I don't know who's down in the engine room, but there's nobody on deck except the cook. I'll just deal with the cops!"

He waited till the police had walked up the wharf, and then started waving and shouting good-by as if someone had just gone away between the warehouses. The two policemen looked around and continued their stroll; they had no reason to doubt that a visitor left the ship while they had their backs to her.

Mr. Vaner sent the cook ashore to buy a bottle of whiskey.

"You'll need something to mix with your water"—he chuckled, immensely pleased that he had now committed himself to the adventure—"and I don't want the cook around while I open up the tank. You wait here and make yourself comfortable." He settled his cap over one ear and marched out of the cabin.

He was back in ten minutes.

"Hurry!" he said. "The cops have just gone round the corner."

The manhole was on a level with and in full view of the wharf, being set into the quarterdeck between the after wall of the chart room and a lifeboat slung athwartships. We took a hasty look around, and I pushed myself through into a space about the size of half a dozen coffins.

"I'll make you comfortable later on," he said. "It will be slack water in about two hours."

I was comfortable enough, more relaxed than I had been since the first week on the river. The darkness and the cold iron walls gave me an immediate sense of safety.

At the bottom of the ebb, when the quarterdeck had sunk well below the edge of the wharf, Mr. Vaner turned up with blankets, the cushion of a settee, water, whiskey, biscuits, and a covered bucket for my personal needs.

"Snug as a bug in a rug!" he declared cheerfully. "And what's more, I've given you a safety valve."

"How's that?"

"I've disconnected the outflow. Can you see light?"

I looked down a small pipe at the bottom of the tank and did see light.

"Where do you dock?" I asked.

"We're going right up the Thames to Wandsworth. I'll tell you when it's safe to slip ashore."

I heard steps, and Mr. Vaner disappeared. I never saw him again. Then I dozed uneasily until all the noises on deck ceased; the crew, I suppose, had come on board and settled down for the night. Then I slept in good earnest, and awoke to the sound of heavy boots; it was morning, for I could see light at the end of my pipe. The manhole was screwed down tight.

When we sailed, there was a jangle of sounds like a hundred iron monkeys playing tag in a squash court. Some hours later my manhole was opened and propped, and a cold mutton chop with a note attached to it descended. I ate the chop and knelt below the crack of light to read the message.

Sorry I had to screw you down. The cops found a boat and traced it to you. They turned us inside out this morning and all other ships at the wharf. Caught four stowaways, I hear. We are outside territorial waters, so you're OK. They know all about your eye patch. If you're likely to run into any trouble in London, take it off. I'll slip you a pair of dark glasses when it's time to go. Dock police reported that a chap of your build had come on board and left. I said I had been asked for a passage, and refused. If you have any papers you want to get rid of, leave them in the tank and I'll deliver them wherever you direct.

Only within the last day or two, I expect, did the police give up their exhaustive search for my corpse and extend inquiries to road, rail, and river, finally learning about the boating schoolmaster who had an eye patch and always kept his gloves on. They hadn't picked me up, I should guess, for the simple reason that they had just begun to look for a boat with red sails and happened to miss the little yard where I changed them; but when some official noticed an unfamiliar dinghy moored where I probably had no right to moor her, she was at once identified.

Vaner's suggestion that my troubles might by no means be over when I reached London was disturbing. I hadn't given the matter any thought. One's instinct is against looking too far forward when the present demands all available resource.

I began to speculate on what would happen if I reappeared quite openly in England. I was perfectly certain that my pursuers would not appeal to the Foreign Office or to Scotland Yard. Whatever I might have done or intended, their treatment of me wouldn't stand publicity.

Would they, then, follow me up themselves? I had assumed that once I was over the frontier, bygones would be bygones. I now saw that this was a foolishly optimistic view. They couldn't go to the police, true, but neither could I. I had committed an extraditable offense; if I complained of being molested, I might force them into telling why I was molested.

It came to this: I was an outlaw in my own country as in theirs, and if my death were required, it could easily be accomplished.

Even assuming they couldn't fake an accident or suicide, no motive would be discovered for the crime, and no murderer would be arrested.

But why on earth, I argued, should they take the unnecessary risk of removing me in my own country? Did they imagine that I was likely to try another of these sporting expeditions? I reluctantly admitted that they might very well think so. They knew that I was an elusive person who could quite possibly return, if he chose, and upset the great man's nerves once more.

The manhole was never screwed down again, and I lay on my cushion, passing the voyage in sleep and nightmarish meditation.

THE boom and thump of the diesels, resonant and regular as distant tribal drums, indicated to me our progress up the Thames—through the Pool and the City, through Westminster and Chelsea, until the wheelhouse bell signaled "finished with engines." There were bangings and tramplings, and then silence.

Another note was dropped through the manhole, accompanied by a pair of dark glasses wrapped in brown paper.

> Don't go out through the gates. There's a chap watching I don't like the look of. The dinghy is under the starboard quarter. As soon as she floats I'll give you a knock, and you beat it quick. Row across to the public steps by Hurlingham east wall. I'll take the boat back later. Best of luck.

Vaner rapped on the manhole an hour or so later, and I pushed out my arms and shoulders by merely standing up. There was a light in his cabin, and a loud noise of conversation; he was assuring my privacy by entertaining the night watchman. I dropped into the dinghy, and pulled quietly across the river through the pink band of water that reflected the glare of London into the black band of water beneath the trees. My arrival was noticed only by the inevitable boy and girl to be found in every dark corner of a great city.

It was nearly ten o'clock. I walked to the King's Road and found a grillroom, where I ordered about all the meat they had. After my supper I took a bus to Cromwell Road and put up at one of those hotels designed for gentlewomen in moderately distressed circumstances. The porter didn't much care about taking me in, but fortunately I had a couple of pound notes and they had a room with a private bath. I gave them a false name and told them that I had just arrived from abroad and had my luggage stolen.

Their water, thank God, was hot! I had the most pleasurable bath that I ever remember. I have spent a large part of my life out of reach of hot baths; yet, when I enjoy a tub at leisure, I wonder why any man voluntarily deprives himself of so cheap and satisfying a delight. I had slept so much on the ship that my bath and my thoughts while lying in it had the flavor of morning.

There was no lack of mirrors in the bathroom, and I made a thorough examination of my body. My legs and backside were an ugly mess—I shall carry some extraordinary scars for life—but the wounds had healed. My fingers still appeared to have been squashed in a door and then sharpened with a penknife, but they were in fact serviceable for all but very rough or very sensitive work. The eye was the only part of me that needed attention. I dared not give up my freedom of movement for the sake of regular treatment, but I wanted a medical opinion and whatever lotions would do my eye the most good.

In the morning I changed all the foreign money in my possession, and bought myself a passable suit off the peg, and a hat. Then I got a list of eye specialists and taxied around Harley Street until I found a man who would see me at once. When he had opened the lid he was honest enough to say that he could do nothing, that I'd be lucky if I ever perceived more than light and darkness, and that, on the whole, for the sake of appearance, he recommended changing the real for a glass eye. He was wrong. My eye isn't pretty, but it functions better every day. He wouldn't hear of my going about in dark glasses with no bandage, so I had him extend the bandages over the whole head. My object was to give the impression of a man who had smashed his head rather than a man with a damaged eye. He was convinced that my face was familiar, and I allowed him to decide that we had once met in Vienna.

The next job was to see my solicitors in Lincoln's Inn Fields. Saul, the partner who has the entire handling of my estate, is a man of about my own age and an intimate friend who finds a vicarious pleasure in my travels and outlandish hobbies.

He greeted me with concern rather than surprise; it was as if he had expected me to turn up in a hurry and the worse for wear. He locked the door and told his office manager we were not to be disturbed. I assured him that I was all right and that the bandage was four times as long as was necessary. I asked what he knew and who had inquired for me.

He said that there had been a pointedly casual inquiry from my friend and their ambassador, Holy George, and that a few days later a fellow had come in to consult him about some inconceivable tangle under the Married Women's Property Act.

"He was so perfectly the retired British military man," said Saul, "that I felt he couldn't be real. He claimed to be a friend and neighbor of yours and was continually referring to you. When I cross-examined him a bit, it looked as if he had mugged up his case out of a lawbook. Major Quive-Smith, he called himself. Ever heard of him?"

"Never," I replied. "He certainly isn't a neighbor of mine. Was he really English?"

"I thought so. Did you expect him not to be?"

I said I wasn't answering any of his innocent questions, that he was, after all, an officer of the court, and that I didn't wish to involve him.

"Tell me this much," he said. "Have you been abroad in the employ of our government?"

"No, on my own business. But I have to disappear."

"You shouldn't think of the police as tactless," he reminded me gently. "A man in your position is protected without question. You've been abroad so much that I don't think you have ever realized the power of your name. You're automatically trusted, you see."

I told him that I knew as much of my own people as he did—

perhaps more, since I had been an exile long enough to see them from the outside. But I had to vanish. There was a risk that I might be disgraced.

"Can I vanish? Financially, I mean?" I asked him. "You have my power of attorney and you know more of my affairs than I do myself. Can you go on handling my estate if I am never heard of again?"

"So long as I know you are alive."

"What do you mean by that?"

"A postcard this time next year will do. Quite sufficient if in your own handwriting. You needn't even sign it."

"Mightn't you be asked for proof?" I inquired.

"No. If I say you are alive, why the devil should it ever be questioned? But don't leave me without a postcard from time to time. You mustn't put me in the position of maintaining what might be a lie."

I told him that if he ever got one postcard, he'd probably get a lot more; it was my ever living to write the first that was doubtful.

He blew up and told me I was absurd. He mingled abuse with affection in a way I hadn't heard since my father died. He begged me again to let him talk to the police. I had no idea, he insisted, of the number of strings that could be pulled.

I could only say I was awfully sorry, and after a silence I told him I wanted five thousand pounds in cash.

He produced my deedbox and accounts. I had a balance of three thousand at the bank; he wrote his own check for the other two—no nonsense about waiting for sales of stock or arranging an overdraft.

"Shall we go out and lunch while the boy is at the bank?" he suggested.

"I think I'll leave here only once," I said.

"You might be watched? Well, we'll soon settle that."

He sent for Peale, a gray little man in a gray little suit whom I had only seen emptying the wastepaper baskets or fetching cups of tea.

"Anybody taking an interest in us, Peale?"

"There is a person in the gardens between Remnant Street and here feeding the pigeons. He is not very successful with them, sir"—Peale permitted himself a dry chuckle—"in spite of the fact that he has been there for the past week during office hours. And I understand from Pruce and Fothergill that there are two other persons in Newman's Row. One of them is waiting for a lady to come out of their offices—a matrimonial case, I believe. The other is not known to us, and was observed to be in communication with the pigeon man, sir, as soon as this gentleman emerged from his taxi."

Saul thanked Peale and sent him out to fetch us some beer and a cold bird.

I asked where Peale watched from, having a vague picture of him hanging over the parapet of the roof when he had nothing to do.

"Good God, he doesn't watch!" exclaimed Saul, as if I had suggested a major impropriety. "He just knows all the private detectives who are likely to be hanging around Lincoln's Inn Fields—on very good terms with them, I believe. They have to have a drink occasionally, and then they ask Peale or his counterpart in some other firm to keep his eyes open. When they see anyone who is not a member of their trades union, so to speak, they all know it."

When Peale came back he had a packet of information straight from the counter of the saloon bar. The pigeon man had been showing great interest in our windows and had twice telephoned. The chap in Newman's Row had hailed my taxi as it drove away after dropping me. He would therefore be able to trace me back to Harley Street and to the clothes shop, where, by a little adroit questioning, he could make an excuse to see the suit I discarded; my identification would be complete. It didn't much matter, since the watchers already had a strong suspicion that I was their man.

Peale couldn't tell us whether another watcher had been posted in Newman's Row or whether the other exits from Lincoln's Inn Fields were watched. I was certain that they were, and that I shouldn't be allowed to escape too easily. I decided to throw off the hunt in my own way.

When I kept my gloves on to eat, Saul forgot his official discretion and became an anxious friend. I think he suspected what had happened to me, though not why it had happened. I had to beg him to leave the whole subject alone.

After lunch I signed a number of documents to tidy up loose ends, and we blocked out a plan I had often discussed with Saul for forming a sort of tenants' cooperative society at my estate. Since I never make a penny out of the land, I thought my tenants might as well pay rent to themselves, do their own repairs, and advance their own loans, with the right to purchase their own land by installments at a price fixed by the committee. I hope it works. At any rate Saul and my land agent will keep them from quarreling among themselves. I have no other dependents.

Then I told him something of the fisherman who had supplied my wants and passed on the address in London that he had given me. We arranged for an income to be paid where it would do the most good—a discreet trust that would appear to come from the estate of a recently defunct old lady who had left the bulk of her money to an institution for inoculating parrots. There was nothing further to be done but arrange my cash in a body belt, and say good-by. I asked him if at any time a coroner brought in a verdict of suicide on me, not to believe it but to make no attempt to reopen the case.

PEALE walked with me across the square and into Kingsway by Gate Street. I observed that we were followed by a tall, inoffensive fellow in a dirty mackintosh and shabby felt hat, who was the pigeon man. He looked the part. We also caught sight of a cheerful military man in Remnant Street, wearing a riding coat and trousers narrower than were fashionable, whom Peale at once recognized as Major Quive-Smith. So I knew two at least whom I must throw off my track.

We parted at Holborn underground station and I took a shilling ticket, with which I could travel to the remotest end of London. The pigeon man had gotten ahead of me. I passed him on the middle level and went down the escalator to the westbound Piccadilly tube. Ten seconds after I reached the platform Major Quive-

Smith also appeared upon it. He was gazing at the advertisements and grinning at the comic ones, as if he hadn't been in London for a year.

I pretended I had forgotten something, shot up the stairs, and then back down a ramp to the northbound platform. No train was in. Even if there had been a train, the major was too close behind for me to catch it and leave him standing.

I noticed that the shuttle train to the Aldwych station left from the opposite side of the same platform. This offered a way of escape if ever there were two trains in at the same time.

The escalator took me back to the middle level. There the pigeon man was talking to the ticket collector. I took the second escalator to the surface, and promptly dashed down again.

The pigeon man followed me, but a bit late. We passed each other about midway, he going up and I going down and both running like hell. I thought I had him, that I could reach a Central London train before he could, but he vaulted over the division onto the stationary staircase. We reached the bottom separated only by about ten yards. The ticket collector came to life and said, "'Ere! You can't do that, you know!" There the pigeon man had to remain and discuss his antisocial action. I had already turned to the right to go down to the Piccadilly line and onto Major Quive-Smith's preserves.

At the bottom of the Piccadilly escalator I ran over to the northbound platform. An Aldwych shuttle was just pulling in. I shot under the Aldwych line, down to the westbound platform, into the general exit, jamming the major in a stream of outcoming passengers, then ran back to the northbound Piccadilly. There was a train standing, and the Aldwych shuttle had not left. I jumped into the Piccadilly train, with the major so far behind that he had to enter another coach just as the doors were closing and just as I stepped out again. Having thus dispatched the major, I got into the Aldwych shuttle, which at once left on its half-mile journey.

This was all done at such a pace that I hadn't had time to think. After half a minute in the Aldwych shuttle I realized that I should have gone to the westbound Piccadilly and taken a train into the blue. When we arrived at the Aldwych station and I was strolling to the lifts, I saw that it was not yet too late to return to Holborn to catch a Piccadilly train. The pigeon man would still be on the middle level, for he might lose me if he left it for a moment.

I turned back and reentered the shuttle. The passengers were already seated in the single coach, and the platform clear, when a man in a black hat and blue flannel suit got in after me. I had noticed him on the shuttle as it approached Aldwych. That meant that he had turned back to Holborn when I had turned back.

At Holborn I remained seated to prove whether my suspicions of him were correct. They were. Black Hat got out, sauntered around the platform, and got in again just before the doors closed. They had been far too clever for me! They had evidently ordered Black Hat to travel back and forth between Holborn and Aldwych, and to go on traveling until either I entered that cursed coach or they gave him the signal that I had left by some other route. All I had done was to send Quive-Smith to Bloomsbury, whence no doubt he had already taken a taxi to some central clearing point to which all news of my movements was telephoned.

As we left again for Aldwych, Black Hat was at the back of the coach and I was in the front.

The Aldwych station is the end of the line, and a passenger cannot leave it except by the lift or the emergency spiral staircase. Its working is very simple. After the shuttle pulls in, the lift comes down. The departing passengers get into the train; the arriving passengers get into the lift. When the lift goes up and the train leaves, Aldwych station is deserted as an ancient mine. Nevertheless, down there I thought I had a wild chance of getting away from Black Hat.

When the doors of the train opened, I dashed onto and off the platform and went around a corner toward the lift. But instead of going into the lift, I hopped into a little dead-end alley that I had noticed on my earlier walk.

Black Hat came racing around the corner, pushing through the passengers with his eyes fixed straight ahead, and entered the lift.

In the time it took him to get there and to glance over the passengers I was out of my alley and back on the platform.

The train was still in, but if I could catch it, so could Black Hat. He couldn't be more than five seconds behind me. I jumped off the platform onto the track and flattened myself against the wall in the darkest section of the tunnel. There wasn't anyone to see me except the train driver, and he was in his compartment at the front of the coach. The platform, of course, was empty.

The lift descended to the platform again, disgorging Black Hat along with the passengers for Holborn. He looked through the coach and saw that I wasn't in it. The train pulled out, and when its roar had died away there was absolute silence. Black Hat and I were left alone a hundred feet beneath London. The station was so quiet that you could hear the drip of water and the beat of your heart.

I can still hear them—and the sound of steps and his scream and the hideous sound of sizzling. It was self-defense. He had a flashlight and a pistol. I don't know if he meant to use the pistol. Perhaps he was just as frightened of me as I was of him. I crawled right to his feet and sprang at him. By God, I want to die in the open! If ever I have land again, I swear I'll never kill a creature belowground.

I lifted the bandages from my head and put them in my pocket; that expanse of white below my hat attracted too much attention. Then I hoisted myself onto the platform, and as soon as the lift came down again I mingled with the passengers and waited for the train. When it came in, I went up in the lift with the new arrivals. A short time later I left the station, free, unwatched, unhurried, and took a bus back to the respectable squares of Kensington. I dined at leisure and then went to a cinema to think.

IN THESE days of visas and identification cards it is impossible to travel without leaving a trail that can, with patience, bribery, and access to public records, be picked up. Unless a traveler has some organization—subversive or benevolent—to help him, frontiers are an efficient bar to those who find it inconvenient or impossible

to show their papers; and even if a frontier be crossed without record, there isn't the remotest village where a man can live without having to justify himself. Thus Europe, for me, was a trap.

Where, then, could I go? I thought at once of a job on a ship, but it wasn't worth visiting shipping offices with my hands in the state they were. Rule out a long voyage as a stowaway. Rule out a discreet passage on a cargo ship. I could easily have gotten such a passage, but only by revealing my presence in England to some friend. That I wanted to avoid at all costs. Only Saul, Peale, Vaner, and the admirable secret service which was tracking me down knew that I wasn't on a hunting trip in Poland. None of them would talk. Of that I was sure.

There remained a voyage on a passenger vessel. I could certainly get onto the ship without showing my passport; I might be able to get off it. But passenger lists are open to inspection, and my hunters would be watching them.

Then I needed a false passport. In normal circumstances I have no doubt that Saul or my friends in the Foreign Office could have arranged some tactful documentation for me, but, as it was, I could not involve any of them. It was unthinkable, just as police protection was unthinkable. I could not risk embarrassing the officials of my country. If the extraordinary man I had looked at through a telescopic sight were moved by his daemon to poison international relations more than they already were, a very pretty case could be built up against a British government that helped me to escape.

As I sat back in that cheap cinema seat, with my eyes closed, the meaningless noises and music forcing my mind from plan to plan, I saw that I could disappear only by not leaving England at all. I must bury myself in some farm or country pub until the search had slackened.

When the film was at its most dramatic and the lavatory most likely to be empty, I left my seat, bathed my eye with the lotion the doctor had given me, and put on my bandages again. Then I wandered westward through the quiet squares, which smelled of a London August night—that perfume of dust and heavy flowers hovering in the warm ravines between the houses.

I decided against sleeping at a hotel; a porter might compel me into some act or lie that was unnecessary. I took a bus to Wimbledon Common, a considerable stretch of country that was open to the public at night. I slept there, in a grove of silver birch. The fine soil—silver too, it seemed to me, but the cause was probably the half-moon—held the heat of the day. There is, for me, no better resting place than the temperate forest of Europe. Can one reasonably speak of forest at half an hour from Piccadilly Circus? I think so. The trees and heath are there, and at night one sees no paper bags.

In the morning I brushed off the leaves and bought a paper in a hurry from the local tobacconist as if I were briskly on my way to the City. In my new and too smart clothes I looked the part. ALDWYCH MYSTERY occupied half a column of the center page. I retired to a seat on the common before committing myself to further dealings with the public.

The body had been discovered almost as soon as I was clear of the station. Foul play was suspected. In other words, the police were wondering how a man who had fallen on his back across the live rail could have suffered a smashing blow in the solar plexus.

The deceased had been identified. He was a Mr. Johns, who lived in a furnished room. His age, his friends, his background were unknown, but the paper carried an interview with his landlady. Though knowing nothing whatever about the man under her roof, she had said, "He was a real gentleman and I'm sure I don't know why anyone should have done him harm. His poor old mother will be brokenhearted."

But it appeared that nobody had discovered the address of the poor old mother. The only evidence of her existence was the landlady's statement that the mother would often telephone Mr. Johns, who thereupon rushed out in a great hurry to see her. When the aged mother was not mentioned at all in the evening papers, my conscience was easier.

The police were anxious to interview a well-dressed, clean-shaven man in his early forties, with a bruised and blackened eye, who was observed to leave the Aldwych station shortly before the body was discovered. I am not yet forty and I was not well dressed, but the description was accurate enough to be unpleasant reading.

It might have been worse. If they had wanted a man with a bandaged head, one of Saul's clerks or the taxi driver might have let information leak. As it was, the public were left with the impression that the man's eye had been injured in the struggle belowground.

That confounded eye finished any chance I might have had of living in some obscure farm or inn. A wanted man with any well-marked peculiarity cannot hide in an English village. The local bobby has nothing to do but see that the pubs observe a decent discretion, if not the law, and that farmers do not too flagrantly ignore the mass of official notices. He pushes his bicycle up the hills, dreaming of catching a real criminal, and when the usual chap with a scar or with a finger missing is wanted by the metropolitan police, he visits on the most improbable errands every person of small means who has recently retired to a village cottage.

There was nothing for it but to live in the open. I sat on my bench on Wimbledon Common and considered what part of England to choose. The North was the wilder, but since I might have to endure a winter, the rigor of the climate was not inviting. My own west county, though I carried the ordnance map in my eye and knew a dozen spots where I could go to ground, had to be avoided. I wonder what my tenants made of the gentleman who, at that very moment, was doubtless staying at the Red Lion near my estate, describing himself as a hiker who had fallen in love with the village, and asking questions.

I chose southern England, with a strong preference for Dorset. It is a remote county, lying as it does between Hampshire, which is becoming an outer suburb, and Devon, which is a playground. I knew one part of the county very well indeed, and, better still, there was no reason for anyone to suppose that I knew it. The business that had taken me to Dorset was so precious that I kept it to myself.

There are times when I am no more self-conscious than a chimpanzee. I had chosen my destination to within ten yards, as I realized later. Yet, that day, I couldn't have told even Saul exactly where I was going. This habit of thinking about myself and my motives has only grown upon me recently. In this confession I have forced myself to be analytical. At the time of the action, however, my reasons were insistent but frequently obscure.

Though the precise spot where I was going was no more or less present in my consciousness than the dark shadows which floated before my left eye, I knew I had to have a fleece-lined, waterproof sleeping bag. I dared not return to the center of London, so I decided to telephone and have the thing sent COD to Wimbledon station by messenger.

I spoke to my sporting-goods shop in what I believed to be a fine disguised bass voice, but the senior partner recognized me almost at once. Either I gave myself away by showing too much knowledge of his stock, or my sentence rhythm is unmistakable.

"Another trip, sir, I suppose?"

I could imagine him rubbing his hands with satisfaction at my continued custom.

He mentioned my name six times, burbling like a fatherly butler receiving the prodigal son.

I had to think quickly. To deny my identity could cause a greater mystery than to admit it. I felt pretty safe with him. He was one of the few dozen black-coated, archbishoplike tradesmen of the West End—tailors, gunsmiths, bootmakers, hatters—who would die of shame rather than betray the confidence of a customer, to whom neither the law nor the certainty of a bad debt is as anything compared to the pride of serving the aristocracy. These ecclesiasts of Savile Row and Jermyn Street are about the only dyed-in-the-wool snobs that are left.

I explained to him that I wished no one to know I was in England and that I trusted him to keep my name off his lips and out of his books. I gave him a full list of my requirements: a boy's slingshot, billhook, and the best knife he had; toilet requisites and a rubber basin; a Primus stove and a pan; flannel shirts, heavy trousers and underclothes, and a windproof jacket. Within an hour he was at Wimbledon station in person, with the whole lot neatly strapped into the sleeping bag. I should have liked a firearm of some sort, but it was laying unfair weight on his discretion to ask him not to register or report the sale.

I took a train to Guildford, and thence by slow stages to Dorchester, where I arrived about five in the afternoon. I changed clothes after Salisbury, where a friendly porter heaved my roll into an empty carriage on a train without any corridor. By the time we reached the next station I had become a holidaymaker, wearing Mr. Vaner's dark sunglasses.

I left my kit at Dorchester station. What transport to take into the green depths of Dorset I hadn't the faintest notion. I couldn't buy a motor vehicle or a horse because of the difficulty of getting rid of them. A derelict car or a wandering horse at once arouses inquiry. To walk with my unwieldy roll was nearly impossible. To take a bus merely put off the moment when I would have to find more private conveyance.

Strolling as far as the Roman amphitheater, I lay on the outer grass slope to watch the traffic on the Weymouth road and hope for an idea. The troops of cyclists interested me. I hadn't ridden a cycle since I was a boy, and had forgotten its possibilities. These holidaymakers carried enough gear on their backs and mudguards to last a week or two, but I didn't see how I could balance my own camping outfit on a bike.

I waited for an hour, and along came the very vehicle I wanted. I have since noticed that they are quite common on the roads, but this was the first I had seen. A tandem bicycle it was, with Pa and Ma riding and the baby slung alongside in a little sidecar.

I stood up and yelled to them, gesturing frantically. They dismounted and looked at me with surprise.

"Sorry to stop you," I said. "But might I ask where you bought that thing? Just what I want for me and the missus and the young un!" I thought that struck the right note.

"I made it," said Pa proudly.

He was a boy of about twenty-three or -four. He had the perfect self-possession and merry eyes of a craftsman. One can usually spot them, this new generation of craftsmen. They know the world is theirs. The wife was a sturdy wench in corduroy shorts—not my taste at all. But my taste is far from eugenic.

"Are you in the cycle trade?" I asked Pa.

"Aircraft!" he answered, with marked scorn for his present method of transport.

I should have guessed it. The aluminum plating and the curved, beautifully tooled ribs had the professional touch.

"You wouldn't like to sell it, I suppose?" I asked, handing him a cigarette.

"I might when we get home," he answered cautiously. "But my home's Leicester."

I said I was ready to make him an offer for bicycle and sidecar then and there.

"And give up my holiday?" he laughed. "Not likely, mister!"

"Well, what would it cost?"

"I wouldn't let it go a penny under fifteen quid!"

"I might go to twelve pound ten," I offered—I'd have gladly offered him fifty for it, but I had to avoid suspicion. "I expect I could buy the whole thing new for that, but I like your sidecar and the way it's fixed. My wife is a bit nervous, you see, and she'd never put the nipper in anything that didn't look strong."

"It is strong," he said. "And fifteen quid would be my last word. But I can't sell it, because what would we do?"

He hesitated and seemed to be summing up both me and the bargain. A fine, quick-witted mind he had. Most people would be far too conservative to consider changing a holiday in the middle.

"Haven't anything you'd like to swap?" he asked. "An old car or rooms at the seaside? We'd like a bit of beach to sit on."

"I've got a beach hut near Weymouth," I said. "I'll let you have it free for a fortnight, and ten quid for the tandem and sidecar."

The missus gave a squeal of joy, and was sternly frowned upon by her husband.

"I don't know as I want a beach hut," he said, "and it would be twelve quid. We're going to Weymouth tonight. Now suppose we did a swap, could we move in right away?"

I told him he certainly could, so long as I could get there ahead of him and have the place ready. I said I would see if there was a train.

"Oh, ask for a lift!" he said, as if it were the obvious way of traveling any short distance. "I'll soon get you one."

That chap must have had some private countersign to the freemasonry of the road. He let half a dozen cars go by, remarking "Toffs!" and then stopped one unerringly. It was a battered Morris, occupied by a sporty-looking gent who might have been a bookmaker or a pubkeeper. He turned out to be an employee of the county council, whose job it was to inspect the steamrollers.

"Hey, mister! Can you give my pal a lift to Weymouth?"

"Look sharp, then!" answered the driver cheerily.

I arranged to meet the family at the Weymouth station at seven thirty, and got in. I explained to the driver that I was hopping ahead to get rooms for the rest of our cycling party, and asked him if he knew of any beach huts for rent. He said there weren't any beach huts, and, what was more, we should find it difficult to get rooms. "A wonderful season!" he said. "People are sleeping on the beach."

This was depressing. I told him that I personally intended to stay some time in Weymouth, and what about a tent or a bungalow or even one of those caravans the steamroller men slept in?

"Ho!" he said. "They're county property, they are! They wouldn't let you have one of them things. But I tell you what"—he lowered his voice confidentially—"I know a trailer you could buy cheap, if you were thinking of buying, that is."

In Weymouth he drove me to a garage kept by some in-law of his, where there was a whacking great trailer standing in the yard. The in-law and the steamroller man showed me over it as if they were a couple of estate agents selling a mansion. It was a little home away from home, they said. And it was! I accepted their price on condition that they threw in the bedding and a cot for the baby, and towed me then and there to a campsite. They drove me a couple of miles to an open field with a dozen tents and trailers. I rented a site for six months from the landowner, then told him that friends would be occupying the trailer for the moment and that I myself hoped to get down for many weekends in the autumn. He showed no curiosity; after collecting five bob a week from campers in advance, he never went near them again.

When we got back to the town I had a quick drink with my saviors and vanished. It was nearly eight before I could reach the Weymouth station. Pa and Ma were leaning disconsolately against the railings. Pa was a little peeved at my being late. Evidently he had been thinking the luck too good to be true, and that he wouldn't see me again.

We then walked the two miles out to the campsite, rolling the tandem and sidecar along. The trailer was quite enchanting in the gathering dusk, and I damn near gave it to them. I said that I should probably be back before the end of his fortnight, but that if I was not, he should give the key to the landowner. I didn't think the trailer could be the object of any inquiry until the six months were up, and by that time I hoped to be out of England.

I rode the beastly combination back to Weymouth, spilling myself into the ditch at the first left-hand corner, for it wasn't easy to get the hang of it. Then I had a meal and, finding that the snack bars and tea shops were still open, filled up the sidecar with a stock of biscuits and a ham, plenty of canned foods and fruits, tobacco, and a few bottles of beer and whiskey.

At the third shop I entered, a dry-faced spinster gazed into my glasses suspiciously and remarked, " 'Urt your eye, 'ave you?"

I answered that it was an affliction from birth, and that I feared it was the Lord's will to take from me the sight of the other eye. She became most sympathetic, but I had had my warning.

I cycled through the darkness to Dorchester, arriving there dead beat about midnight. I picked up my kit and strapped it on the sidecar. Then I pedaled a few miles north into the silence of a valley, where the only moving thing was the Frome gurgling and gleaming over the pebbles. I wheeled my combination off the road and into a copse, unpacked, and slept.

The sleeping bag was delicious. In a month I had spent only half a night in bed. I slept and slept, brought up to consciousness at intervals by the stirring of leaves or insects, but then seizing upon sleep again as effortlessly as pulling a blanket over one's ears.

It was after ten when I awoke. I lay in my fleece till noon, looking up through the oak leaves to a windy sky and trying to decide whether it was less risky to travel by day or night. If by day, my vehicle was so odd that dozens of people would remember having seen it; if by night, anyone who saw me would talk about me for days. But between midnight and three nothing stirs in farm or village. I was prepared to gamble that nobody would see me.

I ADMITTED to myself now where I was going. The road I meant to take was a narrow track along the downs, a remnant of the old Roman road from Dorchester to Exeter, used only by farmers' carts. My meeting with any human being in the darkness was most improbable.

My temporary camp was fairly safe, though close to a road. All day I saw no one but a most human billy goat belonging to a herd of cows in the neighboring field.

At midnight I started. The first three miles were on a well-used byroad, but I met only one car. I had time to lean my bicycle against a hedge and get over into a field. The Roman road was teeming with life: sheep and cows lying on it, rabbits dancing in and out of ancient pits, owls gliding and hooting over the thorn. I carried no light and was continually upsetting in the ruts. Eventually I dismounted and walked.

With the slow going, the hedges were beginning to take shape in the half-light when I slipped silently through the sleeping village of Powerstock. It was time to leave the road. In the neighboring fields there was little cover. When I came upon a derelict cottage, I laid the tandem in the nettles that covered the old floor and detached the sidecar, which I half hid under debris. I made no attempt to conceal myself, lying down in the long grass beside a stream. It was a warm, silent day, beginning with a September mist that hung low over the meadows. If anyone saw me, I was merely sleeping with my head on my arms—a common enough sight by any stream in holiday time.

At dusk I reassembled my vehicle, and started out at eleven.

The dogs barked at me as I passed solitary farms and cottages. But before the householders could look out of their windows I had ridden by swiftly, for there was much to be done that night.

At half past twelve I was on the ridge of a half-moon of low hills, both horns of which rested upon the sea, enclosing between them a small, lush valley. The lanes, worn down by the packhorses of a hundred generations plodding up from the sea onto the dry, hard going of the ridges, were fifteen feet or more below the level of the fields. These trade-worn canyons of red and green upon the flanks of the hills are very dear to me.

I pushed my combination along the ridge until I came to a lane that dived down into the valley. In the dark I could hardly recognize it. I remembered it as a path, deep indeed, but dappled with sunlight. It looked to me now a cleft eroded in desert country, for its bottom was only a cart's width across, and its banks, with the hedges above them and young oaks leaping up from the hedge, seemed to rise as fifty feet of solid blackness.

I followed it down until another lane crossed at a right angle; this led northward back to the ridge, where it came up to the surface and branched into two farm tracks. These two tracks appear to be the end and aim of the ancient little highroad, but if you ignore them and walk across an acre of pasture, you come to a thick hedge running downhill. In the heart of this hedge, which I had been seeking all the way from London, the original lane reappears. It is not marked on the map. It had not been used, I imagine, for a hundred years.

The deep sandstone cutting, its hedges grown together across the top, is still there; anyone who wishes can dive under the sentinel thorns at the entrance and push his way through and come out in a cross hedge that runs along the foot of the hills. But who would wish? Where there is light, the nettles grow as high as a man's shoulder; where there is not, the lane is choked by deadwood. The interior of the double hedge is of no conceivable use to the two farmers whose boundary fence it is, and nobody but an adventurous child would want to explore it.

That, indeed, was the manner of its finding. In love one becomes a child again. This lane had been our discovery, a perilous passage made for us to force. It was only the spring of this year that I took her to England, choosing the Dorset downs to give her the first sight and feeling of the land that was to be her home. It was her last sight too. I cannot say that we had any sense of premonition, unless the tenseness of our love—that desperate sweetness between man and woman when the wings of the Four Horsemen drone inward from the corners of their world.

It was now my job to prevent children or lovers from pushing through that lane again. I worked the sidecar into the thicket and deposited it in the first bare stretch of lane, where the foliage overhead was so thick that nothing grew but ferns. Then I unpacked the billhook and slashed at the deadwood on the inside of the hedges. I jammed the bicycle crosswise between the banks and piled over it a hedge of thorn that would have stopped a lion. At the lower end of the lane the trailing brambles were sufficient defense, and I reinforced them with a dead holly bush. That was all I dared do for the moment. The light was growing, and the strokes of my billhook echoed down the hillside.

I cut steps up the western bank and up the inner side of a young elm; it had a top-heavy branch hanging low over the hedge and within reach of the ground beyond. This elm became my way in and out. I spent most of the day up the tree, whence I had a clear view to the north and west. I wanted to watch the routine of the neighboring farms and to see if I had overlooked any danger.

The field on the east of the lane was rough pasture. An hour after dawn the cows came wandering into it over the skyline, having been driven through a gate which I could not see. Farther to the east was a down where the short turf was good only for sheep. To the west, immediately below my tree, was a forty-acre field of wheat stubble, falling away sharply to a great gray prosperous farmhouse with generous barns and a duck pond.

It was as quiet a hillside as any in England. The activities of the farm below me were chiefly in the vale beyond the wheat field. Of the inhabitants of the farm to the east I saw none, only heard the boy who called the cows home in the evening—which he did without entering the pasture. In the other lanes there was little traffic. I saw the postman with his motorbike and red sidecar. I saw the school bus and an occasional car, and a couple of milk trucks bobbing among the trees to collect the cans set out on wooden platforms by the road.

The section of lane that I had chosen was so damp and dark that in the evening I moved my possessions farther down, into a tiny glade of bracken where the sun shone for three hours a day. It was protected by the high banks, topped by untrimmed hedges of ash, and buttressed on the east by bushes of blackberry and wild plum extending far out into the pasture. I cut the bracken and scraped out a channel for the stream that ran down the lane after every shower.

On this same night I began the work which has provided me with shelter from the rain and with a hearth. The eastern bank was full of rabbit holes which ran into the heavy layer of topsoil that covered sandstone. I slung ash poles from bank to bank—a bare six feet across. This platform of poles I covered with twigs and bracken. A day or two later, when I stole some bricks from a tumbledown barn and propped up my poles in the middle, it was as strong and dry as any floor.

Crouching on the platform, I made a hollow in the topsoil about two feet in height and width, and deep enough into the bank to receive my body. The roof and sides were of earth and the floor of sandstone. Burrowing into the sandstone, soft though it was, proved an interminable job; but I found that it was easy to scrape away the surface, and thus lower the floor inside the small entrance inch by inch.

In a week I had a shelter to be proud of. The roof had a high vault, packed with clay. The drip which trickled down the sides was caught on two projecting ledges that ran the length of the burrow and were channeled to lead the water into the lane. For air I had a narrow ventilation passage curving down from the bank to the side of the den. The floor was three feet below the level of the ledges and was crossed by sticks which kept my sleeping bag from resting on damp stone. The hole was very much the size and shape of two large bathtubs, one inverted upon the other.

As soon as my beard had grown I walked to Beaminster and came back with a knapsack full of groceries, a grill, iron spits, and a short pick, one blade of which was shaped like a battle-axe. It seemed admirably fitted for working sandstone in a confined space. I aroused no particular interest in Beaminster—a mere untidy holidaymaker with dark glasses—and gave out that I was camping on the hills just across the Somerset border. I had a meal in an inn and read the papers. There was only a passing reference to the Aldwych mystery. The verdict had been murder by a person or persons unknown. When I climbed down the elm into the lane I felt that I had come home—a half-melancholy sense of slippered relaxation.

I began a routine of sleeping by day and working on the burrow at night. Working by day was too dangerous; someone might walk past the hedge while I was underground and hear the noise of the pick.

I ran the hole a good ten feet back into the bank and then drove a gallery to the right, intending only to make a hearth; but I found the stone split by tree roots and so easily worked that I ended the gallery with a beehive grotto in which I could comfortably squat. After some difficult surface measurements (by sticking a pole through the hedge and climbing out to see where the tip had gotten to) I drove a chimney straight upward from the grotto into the center of a blackberry bush. I could then risk a fire at night and cook fresh food.

All this while I had wondered why it was that I had no trouble with dogs. I was prepared so to frighten any dogs which investigated me that they would never come back, but it appeared that something had already scared them; dogs gave the lane a wide berth. The cause was Asmodeus.

I observed him first as two ears and two eyes apparently attached to a black branch. When I moved my head, the ears vanished, and when I stood up, the rest of him had vanished. I put out some scraps of bully beef behind the branch, and an hour later they too had vanished.

One morning, when I had just gone to bed, he slunk onto my platform and watched me, rear end gripping the ground, head savage and expectant. He was a thin and powerful tomcat, black, but with many of his hairs ending in a streak of silver. I threw him a biscuit; he was out of sight while it was still in the air. It had gone, of course, when I woke up, and so had half a can of bully beef.

He began to consider me as a curious show for his leisure hours, sitting motionless at a safe distance of ten feet. In a few more days he would snatch food from my hand, hissing and bristling if I dared advance the hand to touch him. It was then that I named him Asmodeus—for the king of the demons—for he could make himself appear the very spirit of hatred and malignity.

I won his friendship with a pheasant's head attached to the end of a string. I have noticed that what cats most appreciate in a human being is not the ability to produce food—which they take for granted—but his or her entertainment value. Asmodeus took to his toy enthusiastically. In another week he permitted me to stroke him, producing a raucous purr but, in order to save face, pretending to be asleep. Soon afterward he started a habit of sleeping in the burrow with me during the day, and hunting while I worked at night. But bully beef was the meat he preferred; no doubt it gave him the maximum nourishment for the minimum effort.

I made two more journeys to Beaminster, walking there and back at night and spending the intervening day—after my shopping— hidden on a hillside of gorse. From the first expedition I returned with food and kerosene for the Primus; from the second with a glue pot and a small door which I had ordered from the local carpenter.

This door or lid fitted exactly into the entrance to my burrow. On the inside was a stout handle by which I could lift and jam it into position; on the outside was camouflage. I sprinkled over a coating of glue a rough layer of sandstone dust, and on that stuck an arrangement of twigs and dead plants, some of which trailed over the edges of the door so that they masked the outline when it was in place.

As soon as I was satisfied with the door I practiced a drill for removing myself completely from the lane. The platform was dismantled, the bricks scattered, and the poles thrust into the hedge; my latrine and rubbish pit were covered by a dead thorn, and I myself was inside the burrow, all in ten minutes. Anyone forcing his way into the lane might or might not notice that some gypsy had been camping there, but could not guess that the place was inhabited at the moment. The only sign was an apparent rabbit hole, a bit artificial in spite of the droppings I scattered around its entrance, which was really my air passage.

The tandem bicycle I took apart, propped the pieces against the bank, and covered them with a mass of dead vegetation. The sidecar was a nuisance. I couldn't bury it or take it to bits, and the bright aluminum shone through the brushwood I heaped on it. It was so new and strong that no one could be deceived into thinking it innocently abandoned. Wherever I put it, it might be found, and the more remote the place, the more the question as to how it came there. Finally I chucked it into a muddy little stream, with hawthorn arching overhead, hoping that the action of water would destroy it.

I am now prepared to spend the first half of the winter here. If the bottom of the lane is still invisible when the leaves have fallen, I won't be seen and, if I am careful, I won't be heard. I avoid chopping wood and risk the noise of my billhook only on one night a week, when I fill the smaller chamber with brushwood and burn it. This dries out the whole den and gives me a layer of hot ashes on which I can grill whatever store of meat I have.

My dry and canned food is sufficient, for I have been largely living on the country. There are nuts, wild plums, and blackberries at my door, and from time to time I extract a bowl of milk from a red cow; she has a great liking for salt, and can be tempted to stand quietly among the blackberry bushes that flank the eastern hedge along the lane.

My slingshot keeps me supplied with the rabbits I want. It's an inefficient weapon. As one whose hobby is the craft of ballistics, ancient and modern, I ought to be ashamed of myself for depending on rubber when a far better weapon could be made from twisted hair or cord. But I have a distaste for the whole business, though it is perfectly justifiable to kill for food.

I am not content, in spite of the fact that this Robinson Crusoe existence ought to suit my temperament pretty well. There is not, any longer, enough to do. I am not affected by loneliness or by the memories of this place. Asmodeus helps there. He is a ridiculous outlet for a lot of sentimentality. But I am uncertain of myself. Even this journal, which I was sure would exorcise my misgivings, has settled nothing.

Part II

I START on this exercise book again, for I dare not leave my thoughts uncontrolled. Sitting below the ventilation hole, I have just enough light. It is good to hold the white page before it. My eyes as well as my mind long for some object on which to concentrate.

A month ago I wrote that I did not feel lonely. It was true, and it accounts for my folly. The essence of safety for a hunted man is that he should feel lonely; then he becomes swift to imagine, sensitive as an animal to danger. But I was sunk in a moody preoccupation with my cat and my conscience. I committed the supreme folly of writing to Saul to send me books. I had too much leisure and no use for it. Besides all my other incoherent dissatisfactions, questions of sex were worrying me.

For me, sex has never been a problem. Like most normal people, I have been able to suppress my desires without difficulty when opportunity was lacking. When there was no need to suppress them, my appreciation has been keen, but my emotions not deeply involved. Indeed I begin to think that I have never known truly passionate love. I have no doubt that, say, an Italian would consider me the perfect type of frigid Anglo-Saxon.

Why, then, my strong resistance to coming to this lane? I take it that I showed a resistance, since I refused to admit to myself that this excellent hiding place was my destination until I was within twenty miles of it. Well, I suppose I wished to save myself pain. But I cannot even remember her face, except that her eyes appeared violet against the tawny skin. I repeat, I was never in love. The proof of it is that I so calmly accepted the destruction of my happiness. I was prepared for it. I had begged her to stay in England, or at least, if she felt it her duty to return, to temper her politics with discretion. But when I heard that she was dead, I really suffered very little.

I WROTE to Saul for books: meaty stuff which I could reread throughout the winter, penetrating with each reading a little further into what the author meant rather than what he said. I did not, of course, sign the letter, but wrote in block capitals, asking him to send the books to Professor Foulsham at a small post office in Lyme Regis.

I did not wish to use Beaminster anymore. A man who claimed to be still camping on the downs in the gathering gales of October would start any amount of gossip about where he was and why. Lyme Regis, a little town about a two-hour walk from my lane, had a winter colony of visitors, and there was nothing in my appearance of a harmless and rather dirty eccentric to arouse the curiosity of the police. I had a straggly beard, and my eye, as a result of continual washing in dew and lotion, was no longer swollen. It just looked odd, like a bad glass eye. I no longer needed the dark glasses. As for my other enemies, they had then no more reason to search Dorset than Kamchatka.

One evening a few days later I called at the post office, introduced myself as Professor Foulsham, and asked if a parcel of books had come for me. It was in one of those small shops that sell stationery and tobacco and have a back room with the inevitable pot of tea by the fire.

"Sorry! There is no parcel in that name," said the postmistress. She stared at me as if her eyes had stuck—shoe-button eyes they were, sharp and nervous.

I asked if there was a letter.

"I think there may be," she said archly, and reached under the counter for some letters. "There—there's more in the back room," she stammered, and edged through the door into the parlor.

I heard frantic whispering, and a girl's voice say, "Oo, Ma, I couldn't do that!"—followed by a resounding slap.

A schoolgirl of about twelve dashed out, dived under the flap of the counter, and with one terrified glance at me bolted down the road. The postmistress remained at the threshold of her room, still fascinated by my appearance.

It was no time for respecting His Majesty's mails. She had dropped the letters behind the wire enclosure which protected her cash and stamps. I reached over and took an envelope addressed to Professor Foulsham.

"Kindly satisfy yourself, madam," I said, seeing that she was mustering courage to scream, "that this letter is actually addressed to me. I regret that it will be my duty to report your extraordinary behavior. Good afternoon."

This pomposity, delivered in a most professorial tone, held her with her mouth open long enough for me to move with dignity out of the shop. I jumped on a bus that was running uphill out of the town, and got off it ten minutes later at a crossroads on the Devon and Dorset border. Safe for the moment in the thick cover of a wood, I opened my letter, hoping it would tell me why a description of me had been circulated to Dorset post offices. It was typewritten and unsigned. Saul wrote:

The parrots paid the fisherman. I must not send you books in case they are traced to the buyer. If you know nothing of a caravan trailer, write to me again and I will risk it.

About two weeks ago the Weymouth police tried to find the owner of the trailer. It was a routine inquiry. The trailer was deserted, and the landlord did not wish to be held responsible for damage done by children.

The police established that the owner had bought and leased the caravan on the same evening, that this was the evening after a man had been found killed in the Aldwych station, and that the owner wore dark glasses.

From a family at Leicester who had rented the thing they learned that the owner had taken, in exchange, a tandem bicycle and baby's sidecar, and that he had told a lot of complicated untruths. A woman in Weymouth from whom he bought food is sure that under his glasses one eye was worse than the other.

The owner of the trailer is wanted for murder. He is certain to be found, for he is known to be camping or living in the open on the downs near Beaminster. A person who had grown a beard but otherwise answered his description was seen three times at Beaminster before any police inquiries had begun.

Let me very urgently impress it on you that if the man was a person of good character, if he pleaded self-defense and gave good reason for the attack made upon him, the case would never go to court. I earnestly advise this course. The dead man was a thoroughly undesirable fellow, suspected of being in the pay of a foreign power.

You can take it as certain that the police know as much as I have told you and no more.

Saul ended with a request to me to burn the letter immediately, which I did.

My first reaction was to thank heaven that I now knew the worst and had been warned in time. But then I perceived the full extent of my folly; a desultory search which had spread over the whole of Dorset, and especially over the Dorset downs miles to the northeast of where I really was, would now be concentrated much nearer to me on the limited patch of country between Beaminster and Lyme Regis.

I seriously considered taking Saul's advice and telling the police my real name and enough of my trip abroad to account for my disappearance and for the attack upon me in the Aldwych tunnel. I forgot that I had worse enemies than the police. But the knowledge that one pack was on my trail had only temporarily excluded fear of the other.

If I resumed my identity, the story of my stalk would be exposed. Death or disgrace was certain. And if some unbalanced idiots chose to regard me as a martyr and take up my cause, there were the makings of a first-class international incident. It was my duty to kill myself—or, easier, arrange for myself to be killed incognito— rather than seek protection.

The police were at the crossroads ten minutes after I got off the bus. Neither they nor the postmistress' daughter had wasted any time. They switched the headlights of two cars into the woods where I was, and crashed into the undergrowth.

This didn't worry me. It was already dusk, and I knew that in the dark I could pass through a multitude of policemen and possibly take their boots off as well. For the time being I decided to stay in contact with this lot of police—about ten of them there were—so I jumped onto a stone wall that bounded the woods and pretended to remain there indecisively. At last one of them saw me and gave a hollo. I broke away into Devonshire—away from my own country—down a long, barren slope, with the police close behind.

I was magnificently fit as a result of my life in the open, and I remember how easily my muscles answered the call I made on them. By God, in all this immobility it does me good to think of the man I was!

I intended to lie still wherever there was a scrap of not too obvious cover and to let the hunt pass me. However, I didn't reckon on a young and active inspector who shed his overcoat and seemed able to do the quarter mile in well under sixty seconds.

At the bottom of the slope I saw a muddy farm path with water faintly gleaming in the deep hoofmarks. I pounded along the path, spattering as much mud as a horse over myself and the hedges. The inspector was not twenty yards behind, and wasting his breath by yelling at me to stop and come quietly.

While he was still in the wet clay, and the rest of the police had just entered it, I pulled out onto a hard surface. The wall of a farmhouse loomed up ahead; it was built in the usual shape of an E without the center bar, the house at the back, the barns forming the two wings. It seemed an excellent place for the police to surround and search; they would be kept busy for the next few hours, and the cordon between Lyme Regis and Beaminster, through which I had to pass, would be relaxed.

I looked back. The inspector had withdrawn a little; the rest of the hunt I could hear plunging and cursing in the mud. I put on a spurt and dashed around the lower bar of the E. Knowing the general layout of English farms, I was sure that my wanted patch of not too obvious cover would be right at the corner, and it was. I dropped flat on my face in a pattern of mounds and shadows, my elbow on an old millstone.

The inspector raced around the corner and into the open barn, flashing his light on the carts, the piles of fodder, and the cider barrels. He was shouting that he had the beggar cornered. As soon as he passed, I shot out of the yard, crouching and silent, and dropped against the outer wall of the barn.

As the other policemen rushed into the barn, the farm and its dogs woke up, and I left the police to their search; it was probably long and exhausting, for there was not, from their point of view, the remotest possibility of my escaping from the three-sided trap into which I had run.

I HAD no intention of going home. There could be no peace for me in the lane until I had laid a false scent and knew that the police were following it to the exclusion of all others. I had to make a false hiding place and satisfy them that I had lived there. Then I must persuade the police that I had left the district for good.

I followed the main road, along which I had come in the bus, back toward Lyme Regis. I say I followed it—I had to, since I wasn't sure of my direction in the dark—but I didn't walk on it. I moved parallel, climbing a fence or forcing a hedge about every two hundred yards for three solid miles. It's a major feat to follow a main road without ever setting foot on it, and I began to feel infernally tired.

The high ground to the east of Beaminster, where a new den had to be faked, was twenty miles away. I decided to jump a lorry on the steep hill outside Lyme Regis, where heavy vehicles had to slow to walking pace and I could be pretty sure of getting a lift unknown to the driver. I thought this ingenious, but the police had thought of it already. At the steepest part of the road there was a sergeant with a bicycle, keeping careful watch.

I cursed him heartily, for now I had to go down again to the bottom of the valley, draw him off, and return to the road. My knees were very weary, but there was nothing else for it. I stood in a little copse at the bottom of the hill and started yelling bloody murder in a terrified soprano—"Help!" and "Let me go!"—and then a succession of hysterical screams that were horrible to hear.

I heard the whine of brakes hastily applied, and several dim figures ran down into the valley as I ran up. I peered over the hedge. The sergeant had gone. A grocer's van and a sports car stood empty by the side of the road. I gave up my original idea of boarding a lorry and took the sports car. I reckoned that I should have the safe use of it for at least twenty-five minutes—ten minutes before the party gave up their search of the wooded bottom, five minutes before they could reach a telephone, and ten more minutes before patrols and police cars could be warned.

Over my head and around my beard I wrapped my muffler. Then I pulled out in front of a noisy milk truck that was banging up the hill, in case the owner should recognize the engine of his own car.

Twenty minutes later, near Dorchester, I abandoned the car in a neglected footpath between high hedges. I stuck ten pounds in the owner's license with penciled apologies (written in block capitals with my left hand) and my sincere hope that the notes would cover his night's lodging and any incidental loss.

It was now midnight. I crossed the down and entered the Sydling valley, which, by the map, appeared to be as remote a dead end as any in Dorset. I spent the rest of the night in a covered stack, sleeping warmly and soundly between the hay and the corrugated iron. The chances of the police finding the car till daylight were negligible.

After a breakfast of blackberries I struck north along the watershed. There was a main road a quarter of a mile to the west. I watched the posting of constables at two crossings. Down in the valley a police car was racing toward Sydling. They made no attempt to watch the grass paths, being convinced, I think, that criminals from London never go far from roads. My theft of a car had put me into the proper gangster pigeonhole.

The downs on both sides of the valley were country after my

own heart: patches of gorse and patches of woodland, connected by straggling hedges which gave me cover from the occasional shepherd or farmer. The valley ended in a great bowl of turf and hazelwood, crossed by no road and two miles from any village. The only signs of humanity were two ruined cottages.

On the green track that led to them, tall thistles grew unbroken, showing that few ever passed that way. The cottages were roofless, but in one was a hearth that ran two feet back into the thick masonry. I built a rough wall of fallen stone around it and succeeded in making a fairly convincing nest for a fugitive, drier and more airy than my own but not so safe. While I was working I saw no one but a farmer riding through the bracken on the opposite ridge. I knew what he was looking for—a cow that had just calved. I had run across her earlier in the day, and had been encouraged by this sure sign that the farm was large and full of cover.

It was hard to make the cottage look as if I had lived there for weeks. I distributed messily the corpse of a rabbit that was polluting the atmosphere a little way up the valley. I fouled and trampled the floor, stripped an apple tree, and strewed apple cores and nutshells over the ground. A pile of feathers from a wood pigeon and a rook provided further evidence of my diet. Plucking the ancient remains of a hawk's dinner was the nastiest job of all.

When night fell I lit a fire, piling it up fiercely so that the ashes and soot would appear the result of many fires. While it burned I lay in the hazelwood, in case anyone should be attracted by the light and smoke. Then I sat over the ashes dozing and shivering till dawn.

I spent the day sitting in the bracken and waiting for the police, but they refused to find me. I put the night to good use, going down to sleeping Sydling and doing a smash-and-grab raid on the village shop. My objects were to draw the attention of those obstinate police and to get hold of some dried fish. In this sporting country some damned fool was sure to try bloodhounds on my scent.

In the few seconds at my disposal I couldn't find any kippers but did get four cans of sardines and a small bag of fertilizer. Then I raced for the downs while the whole village squawked and slammed its doors. It was probably the first time in all the history of Sydling that a sudden noise had been heard at night.

As soon as I was back in my cottage I pounded the sardines and fertilizer together, tied up the mixture in the bag, and rubbed the corner of the hearth where I had sat. Trailing the bag on the end of a string, I laid a drag through the hazels, over the heather on the hilltop, around some oak trees, and into the bracken overlooking the cottage. There I remained, and got some sleep.

In spite of all the assistance I had given them, it was nearly midday before the police discovered the cottages. They moved around in them respectfully, dusting all surfaces for fingerprints. There weren't any. I had never taken off my gloves. They must have thought they were dealing with an experienced criminal.

The couple of bloodhounds that I had expected turned up, towing a bloodthirsty maiden lady in their wake. She was encouraging them with yawps and had feet so massive that I could see them clearly at two hundred yards—great, brogued boats navigating a green sea. She was followed by half the village of Sydling and a sprinkling of local gentry. Two fellows had turned out on horseback. I felt they should have paid me the compliment of pink coats.

Away went the bloodhounds on the trail of the fertilized sardines, and away I went too; I had a good half hour while they followed my bag through the hazels and heather. I crossed the main road—a hasty dash from ditch to ditch—and slid along the hedges into a great headland of gorse. After weaving a complicated pattern there, I waded into the Frome and paddled upstream for a mile or so, taking cover in the rushes whenever there was anyone to see me. Then I buried the sardines in the gravel at the bottom of the river and proceeded under my own scent. It was half past five and the dusk was falling.

I moved slowly westward, following the lanes but taking no risks—slowly, deliberately slowly, in the technique that I have developed since I became an outlaw. It was nearly four in the morning when I swung myself onto the elm branch that served as my front door, and climbed down into the lane. I felt Asmodeus brush against my legs, but I could not see him in that safe pit of blackness. That I consider darkness to be safety in itself sets me apart from my fellows. But darkness is safety only on condition that all one's enemies are human. I ate a tremendous breakfast of beef and oatmeal, and set aside my town suit to be made into bags and lashings—all it was now good for. I was relieved to be done with it; it reminded me too forcibly of the newspapers' "well-dressed man." Then I slipped into my bag, unwearing, dampproof citadel of luxury, and slept till nightfall.

When I awoke I felt sufficiently strong and rested to attempt the second feint: to convince the police that I had left the country for good. This was rash, but necessary. I still think it was necessary. If I hadn't gone, the bicycle would be in the lane, and the evidence of my presence here a deal stronger than it is.

By the light of two candles I turned to the unholy job of reassembling the tandem bicycle. It was after midnight before I had the machine, entire and unpunctured, clear of the lane, and the thorns replaced.

I dressed myself in the warmest of my working clothes, put a flask of whiskey in my inside breast pocket, and took plenty of food. I could be away for days without worrying. Cautiously I pedaled through the lanes of the Marshwood Vale and up into the hills beyond. The byroads were empty. Before crossing any main road I put the bicycle in the hedge and reconnoitered on foot and belly. By dawn I was well into Somerset. It was now time to let myself be seen and to put the police on a trail that obviously led north to Bristol or some little port on the Bristol Channel.

I shot through two scattered villages, then on into the Fosse Way, speeding along the arrow-straight road to Bristol and drawing cheers and laughter from the passing lorry drivers. I was too incredible a sight to be thought a criminal—muddy, bearded, and riding alone a bicycle for two.

After showing myself over a mile of main road I was more than ready to hide the bicycle for good and myself till nightfall. I pedaled on in the hope of reaching a wood or a quarry. It was all flat land with well-trimmed hedges and shallow drains. Finally I came to a field of cabbages by the side of the road—one of those melancholy

217

fields with a cinder path leading in and a tumbledown hut leaning against a pile of refuse. Close to the hut and at a stone's throw from the road was a derelict car.

When the only traffic was a cluster of black dots a mile or two away, I lifted the tandem to avoid leaving a track, and staggered into the shelter of the hut. I removed the pedals and twisted the two sets of handlebars so that the bicycle would lie flat on the ground, then shoved it under the car, afterward restoring the trampled weeds to a fairly upright position. It will not be found until the car molders away above it, and then will be indistinguishable from the other rusty debris.

I now had to take cover myself. The hut was too obvious a place. The hedges were inadequate. I dared not risk so much as a quarter-mile walk. There was nothing for it but to lie among those blasted cabbages. In the middle of the field I was perfectly safe, though it was exasperating to lie still on a clay soil in a gentle drizzle.

I was so bored that I was thankful when in the early afternoon a car stopped and three policemen crunched up the cinder path. I had been expecting them for hours. They looked into the hut and into that decaying car. I kept my face well down between my arms, so I don't know whether they even glanced at the cabbage field. Probably not. It was so open and innocent.

After they drove away I shivered and grumbled for an eternity in that repellent field. At last dusk fell and I stood up. I drank a quarter of my flask and struck straight across country, climbing or wading over whatever obstacles were in my way. This was sheer obstinacy. I was wet to the armpits; I was leaving a track like a hippopotamus; and, since I didn't know where I was heading, it was all objectless.

When the slow autumn dawn turned night to mist, I drank at the piped spring which fed a cattle trough and took refuge in the heart of a wild half acre of gorse and heather. Here I startled an old dog fox, and startled myself as well, when I came to consider it, a deal more. I flatter myself I am able to get as near to game as any civilized man and most savages; yet I should certainly not have backed myself to approach within three yards of a fox, even knowing where he was and deliberately stalking him. Oddly enough, it worried me that I had come to move with such instinctive quietness. I was already on the lookout for all signs of demoralization—morbidly anxious to assure myself that I was losing none of my humanity.

I chose a south bank where short heather was gradually overcoming the turf. The rising sun promised a mild heat, and I spread out my coat and leather jacket to dry. I dozed sweetly, awakening whenever a rabbit scuttered through the runways, but instantly and easily falling asleep again.

A little after midday I woke up for good. There was nothing immediately visible to account for the sudden clarity of my senses, so I peered over the gorse. Upwind were two men strolling along the crest of the hill. One was a sergeant of the Dorset constabulary; the other appeared to be a farmer. They passed within ten yards, and they were discussing me. The farmer had remarked, apropos of nothing, "'Tis my belief he was over to Zumerset all the time." I decided to follow these two solemn wanderers and hear what they had to say.

It's curious how much cover there is on the apparently bare chalk downs. There are prehistoric pits and trenches, lonely barns, and thickets of thorn. It was easy to catch them up. They went at an easy pace, stopping every now and then to exchange a few words. At last they leaned over a gate, contemplating twenty acres of steely green beets which sloped down to the vale. I crawled the length of a dry ditch and came within earshot.

The sergeant finished a long mumble with the word "foreigners," pronounced loudly and aggressively.

"Err, they bastards!" said the farmer.

Then he denied that any foreigners ever came to Dorset. The suggestion that they did was almost a criticism on his county.

"I tell 'ee there's been furr'ners askin' for 'm," said the sergeant after a deal more conversation which I couldn't hear.

"Mrs. Maydoone says 'e were a proper gent," chuckled the farmer.

Mrs. Maydoone was the respectably eager widow who owned the inn in Beaminster where I had lunched.

The sergeant showed offended dignity. "Told me she couldn't 'ardly call 'im to mind, she did! 'Don't 'ee come asking questions,' she says, 'as if the Bull were a nasty common public 'ouse.'"

My two friends marched off across the downs while I remained in the ditch digesting the scraps of news. I was perturbed, but not surprised. It was natural enough that my enemies should get possession of Scotland Yard's clues to my whereabouts. If their ambassador, dear old Holy George, couldn't manage it, then one of their newspaper correspondents in London could. It wasn't confidential information.

At dusk I ate the last of my provisions and drank again at the spring. By good fortune I left untouched the half flask of whiskey that remained. Moving now with utmost caution, I kept to the hilltops, following the ridgeways southward. I was suddenly terrified of the sleeping towns and villages that lay at my feet. Guilt was on me. I had killed without object, and my fellows all around me were waiting lest I should kill again. I stumbled down to the valley, compelling myself to move slowly. I was obsessed by this sense of all southern England crowding in upon the hill.

As I dodged and darted home from lane to lane and farmhouse to farmhouse, I couldn't get the sidecar out of my head. I wanted to know if it had been disturbed. Should the police have found it and taken it from the stream for identification, they might disbelieve the evidence of the cottages and search the country where I really was.

Although it was only a field away from a well-frequented byroad, the sidecar was in a safe place: a muddy little stream flowing between deep banks. It would remain unseen, I thought, for years, unless some yokel took it into his head to wade up the bed of the stream or a cow rubbed her way through the bushes.

I entered the stream at a cattle wallow, plunging up to my knees in mire, and forced my way under the hawthorn that hung overhead. I couldn't see the sidecar. I was sure of the place, but it wasn't there. I didn't allow myself to worry yet, but I felt, as a stab of pain, the cold of the water. I pushed on downstream, hoping that the sidecar had been shifted by the force of the current, and knowing very well, as I now remember, that nothing but a winter flood would shift it.

At last I saw it, a faint white bulk in the darkness canted up against a bank of rushes where the stream widened. I was so glad to find it that I didn't hesitate, didn't listen to the intuition that was clamoring to be heard.

I was leaning over the sidecar when a voice quite softly called my name. I straightened up, so astounded and fascinated that for a second I couldn't move. A thin beam of light flashed on my face and dropped to my heart with a roar and a smashing blow. I was knocked backward across the sidecar, pitching with my right side on the mud and my head half underwater. I have no memory of falling, only of the light and the simultaneous explosion. I must have been unconscious while I hit the mud for only so long as my heart took to recover its habit of beating.

I remained collapsed, trying to pick up the continuity of life. It seemed so very extraordinary to have a beam of light thrust through one's heart and be still alive. I heard my assassin give his ridiculous party war cry in a low, fervent voice, as if praising God for the slaughter of the infidel. Then a car cruised quietly up the road, and I heard a door slam as someone got out. I lay still, uncertain whether the gunman had gone to meet the newcomer or not. He had, for I heard their voices a moment later as they approached the stream, presumably to collect my body. I crawled off through the grass and rushes on the far bank, and bolted for home. I am not ashamed to remember that I was frightened, shocked, careless. To be shot from ambush is horribly unnerving.

I jumped into my tree and down into my burrow, despite the darting pain whenever I moved my right arm. Then I shut the door of the den behind me and lay down to collect myself. When I had regained a more graceful mastery of my spirit, I lit a candle and explored the damage.

The bullet—from a .45 revolver—had turned on the nickel of the flask in my breast pocket, plowed sideways through my leather jacket, and come to rest (point foremost, thank God!) in the fleshy part of my right shoulder. It was so near the surface that I squeezed

it out with my fingers. The skin was bruised and broken right across my chest, and I felt as if I had been knocked down by a railway engine, but no serious damage had been done.

I understood why the hunter had not even taken the trouble to examine his kill. He had shot along the beam of a flashlight, seen the bullet strike, and watched the stain of whiskey, which he couldn't distinguish from blood, leap to the breast of my coat and spread. It wasn't necessary to pay me any further attention for the moment.

I patched myself up and lit a pipe, thinking of the fellow who had shot me. He had used a revolver because a rifle couldn't be handled in such thick cover and at so close a range, but his technique showed that he had experience of big game. The enemy had dispatched a redoubtable emissary, and he had got into my mind. He knew that sooner or later I should have a look at that sidecar. And his gentle calling of my name to make me turn my head was perfect. He knew too, as the police did not, who I was and what sort of man I was. He guessed the plain facts: that I had committed a folly in going to Lyme Regis, and that my elaborate false trails thereafter were evidence of nothing but my anxiety. Therefore I had some secure hiding place not far from Lyme Regis and almost certainly on the Beaminster side of it. His private search for the sidecar, which he may have been carrying on for weeks, was then concentrated on the right spot. That he had found it was due to imagination rather than luck. It had to be near a path or lane; it was probably in wood or water.

Well, he had found the sidecar, but he had missed killing me. I think I have written somewhere that the Almighty looks after the rogue male. Nevertheless this sportsman (I allow him the title, for he must have waited up two or three nights over his bait) would be content. He had discovered the bit of country where I had been hiding and he could even be pretty sure whereabouts my lair was. My panic-stricken dash showed that I was bolting south. I wouldn't be camping in the marshland; therefore the only place for me was on or just over the semicircle of low hills beyond. All that he had to do was to go into the long grass, as it were, after his wounded beast. The hunt had narrowed from all England to Dorset, from Dorset to the western corner of the county, and from that to four square miles.

I had known that this fate, whether delayed for months or years, was on the way to me; so I clung, and cling, to what I have—this lane. I might have escaped and lived on the country, but sooner or later one pack or the other would run me to earth, and no earth could be so deep and well disguised as this.

It was obvious that if I stayed where I was, I must completely reverse my policy of keeping the lane closed. The camouflage must go and the place be wide open to inspection, while I myself lived underground.

A southwest gale was sweeping down the hillside, carrying along with it a driving, stinging rain. I welcomed it, for it helped me to obliterate all traces of myself and would discourage the two men in the car from attempting to follow me until visibility was better.

The eastern hedge, beneath which my burrow ran, was as wide as a cottage and promised to be as impenetrable in winter as in summer. The western hedge, however, formed a thinner screen. I built up the weak stretches, thus getting rid of the poles from my platform and a lot of loose brushwood. The holly bush and the larger branches of thorn I shoved into the eastern hedge, hiding the cut ends. I stamped the earth hard down over my rubbish pit, and the water that was now rushing along the bottom of the lane covered pit and floor with a smooth expanse of dead fern and red sand. I then retired indoors, leaving it to the rain to wash out my footprints.

Since the whole lane was filled with the dying debris of autumn, the traces of my presence were not very plain, though there was a faint but definite smell. Worst of all, there were the steps cut up the inside of the elm, which could not be disguised. My adversary had an observant eye. He was bound to consider the lane suspicious, but I hoped he would conclude that, whether or not I had once lived between the hedges, I had taken to the open and died of my wound.

The door was a faultless piece of camouflage; I had planted around it the same weeds as were over it, and no one could tell which had died with their roots in earth and which with their roots in glue. A few trails of living ivy hung over the door from the hedge above.

Thenceforth my way out of the burrow was the chimney. The diameter of its course through the solid sandstone was already sufficient to receive my body; only the last ten feet of broken stone and earth had to be widened. I completed the job that afternoon—a nightmarish job, for my shoulder was painful and I was continually knocking off to rest. For the first time I experienced a dazed and earthy dreaming; it has since become very common. Then I would get up again and go to work, half naked and foul with the red earth, a creature inhuman in mind and body.

A queer tunnel it seemed to me when I examined it after a night's sleep. I hadn't attempted to cut through any roots that were thicker than a thumb; I had gone around them. This was all to the good. Though the curve demanded odd contortions to get in and out, the roots acted as the rungs of a ladder, and the slope as a sump for water. The mouth was still well hidden under the blackberry bush. The only disaster was that my inner chamber was now full of wet earth, and I had no means of dumping it elsewhere.

I stared at my face today, hoping to see those spiritual attributes which surprised me when I first looked in the fisherman's mirror. I wanted comfort from my face, wanted to know that this torture, like the last, had refined it. I saw my eyes fouled with earth, my hair and beard dripping with red earth, my skin gray and puffed as that of a crushed earthworm. It was the mask of a beast in its den, terrified, waiting.

God! When I look back upon them, those blind hours of work seem to have been happy in spite of all their muddy horror. I had something to do. Something to do.

To PRESERVE my sanity it is necessary that I take things in their order. That is the object of this confession: to tell things in their order, reasonably, precisely; to recall my adversary with his insolence, his irony, his ingenuity. By writing of him I become him for the time being.

By now I had arrived at the identity of my assailant that night by the stream. It was Major Quive-Smith, who as a retired military man had nearly, but not quite, convinced Saul that he was a friend and neighbor of mine and whom Peale had identified before the major followed me into the underground that fateful day. I am sure of it because his subsequent behavior and his character, which I now know as an old fox knows the idiosyncrasies of the huntsman, correspond to those of the man who waited patiently over the sidecar, who called my name to make me turn my head.

Two days I spent recovering from the wound, light in itself but aggravated by all that sudden toil. On the third I emerged from my chimney and crawled from bush to bush along the edge of the eastern pasture until I reached an ivy-covered oak at the bottom of the lane. It was nearly dead, and a paradise of wood pigeons. From the top of the tree I could see the valley spread out as on a map, and I overlooked the courtyard of Patachon's farm.

Pat and Patachon are the names I have given to my two neighbors. Pat, the farmer to whom the cows and the eastern hedge belong, is a tall, thin youth with a lined brown face, a habit of muttering to himself, and a soul embittered by bad homemade cider. His little dairy farm can barely pay its way, but he has an active wife with a lot of healthy poultry which probably produce all the ready cash. On the other hand, she is prolific as her hens. They have six children with expensive tastes. I judge the kids by the fact that they suck sweets at the same time as eating blackberries.

Patachon, who owns the western hedge and the great gray farm, is a chunky red-faced old rascal, always with a tall ash walking stick in his hand when he hasn't a gun. His land runs past the lower end of the lane and around over the top of the hill, so that Pat's pasture is an enclave in the middle of it.

All morning I saw nothing of interest from the tree, but in the afternoon two men in a car drove into the yard of Patachon's farm and dropped a bag and a gun case. Then they bumped along the lower edge of the stubble, following the farm path which joined the serviceable portion of my lane. I guessed that they must be bound for Pat's farm; if they had been going beyond it, they would have taken a better road. I couldn't keep them under observation, for the southern slopes were much too dangerous in daylight. There were deep lanes which had to be crossed or entered, with no possibility of avoiding other pedestrians.

In half an hour they were back at Patachon's. One of the men got out and went indoors. The other drove the car away. Someone, then, had come to stay at the farm. I remained on watch in the tree, for I didn't like the look of things.

In the evening Patachon and his visitor emerged from the farmhouse with their guns under their arms. They started toward the low-lying thickets at the western end of the farm, and I didn't see them again for an hour. I heard a few shots. A flight of three ducks shot northward and vanished in the dusk. When I caught sight of the two guns again, the men were stealing along the edge of the lane, separated from me only by the width of the two hedges. Patachon's visitor was Major Quive-Smith.

The farmer picked up a stone and flung it smack into the tree, just missing my feet. "And if a pigeon had a bin there," said Patachon bitterly, " 'e'd a flewed t'other way."

"He would," agreed Major Quive-Smith. "By Jove! I can't think why that fellow wouldn't allow a little bit of shooting!"

That explained why he had gone to see Pat. And Pat, I am sure, refused his request rudely and finally.

"Sour man, 'e is!" said Patachon. "Sour!"

"What's that?" asked Quive-Smith.

I could see the swift, suspicious turn of his head, evidently in the direction of a noise he had heard in the hedge.

"A perishin' cat! Can't trap un. Can't shoot un."

"Very shy of man, I suppose?"

"Knows as well as we what us would do to un if us could catch un," Patachon agreed.

They strolled down to the farm. I observed that the major carried one of those awkward German weapons with a rifled barrel below the two gun barrels. As a rifle, it is inaccurate at two hundred yards; as a gun, unnecessarily heavy. But the three barrels were admirably adapted to his purpose of ostensibly shooting rabbits while actually expecting bigger game.

I don't yet know Quive-Smith's true nationality or name. In his present part, a nondescript gentleman amusing himself with some cheap shooting, there was no fault to be found. Tall, fair, slim, and a clever actor, he could pass as a member of half a dozen different nations, according to the way he cut his hair and mustache. His cheekbones are too high to be typically English, but so are my own. He might have been a Hungarian or Swede, and I have seen faces and figures like his among fair-haired Arabs. I think he is not of pure European origin; his hands, feet, and bone structure are too delicate.

To rent the shooting over three-quarters of the country where I was likely to be was a superb conception. He had every right to walk about with a gun and to fire it. If he bagged me, the chances were a thousand to one against the murder ever being discovered. In a year or two Saul would have to assume that I was dead. Where was my body? At the bottom of the sea or in a pit of quicklime, anywhere between Poland and Lyme Regis.

I was glad of my two unconscious protectors: Asmodeus, whose presence in the lane made my own rather improbable, and Pat, who wouldn't have trespassers on his land and wouldn't allow shooting. I know that type of dyspeptic John Bull. When he has forbidden a person to enter his ground, he is ready to desert the most urgent jobs merely to watch his boundary fence. Quive-Smith couldn't be prevented from exploring Pat's side of the hedge, but he would have to do it with discretion and preferably at night.

I returned to my burrow, now no larger than it had been in the first few weeks, and much damper. I cursed myself for not having widened the chimney before I cleaned up the lane; I could then have thrown out the earth and allowed the rain to distribute it. The inner chamber was uninhabitable and so remains.

I stayed in my sleeping bag for two wretched days. Twice Asmodeus came home with a rush through the ventilation hole and crouched at the back of the den, untouchable and malignant—a sure sign that somebody was in the lane. I lay still underground. Desperate I was, and am, but I want no further violence.

On the third afternoon I found the immobility and dirt no longer endurable and decided to reconnoiter. Asmodeus was out, so I knew that there was no human being in the immediate vicinity. I hoped that Quive-Smith was already paying attention to some other part of the county, or at least to some other farm, but I warned myself not to underestimate his patience. I poked my filthy head and shoulders out into the heart of the blackberry bush and remained there listening. It was a long and intricate process to leave the bush. I had to lie flat on the ground, separating the trailing thorny stems with gloved hands and pushing myself forward with my toes.

I sat among my green fortifications, enjoying the open air and watching Pat's field and the sheep down beyond. About five o'clock Pat came into the field to drive the cows home himself—the task that hitherto he had always left to the boy—and remained for some time staring about him truculently and swinging a stick. At sunset Major Quive-Smith detached himself from a rabbit warren on the hillside and put his field glasses back in their case. I had not had the remotest notion that he was there, but, since I had been assuming he was everywhere, I knew he had not seen me. To let me see him I thought obliging.

He struck down the hillside into the lane leading to Patachon's farm. As soon as he was out of range I crawled to the corner of the hedge to have a look at him when he passed beneath me. A clump of gorse covered me from observation from the pasture as I crouched there waiting. But he didn't come. Then it occurred to me that he must hate those deep lanes almost as much as I did; a man walking along them was completely at the mercy of anyone above him. So he was possibly behind the opposite hedge, working his way back to the farm across the fields. It seemed odd that he should take all that trouble when he could have gone home by the vale; it seemed so odd that I suddenly realized I had been outmaneuvered. He had shown himself deliberately. If I was haunting the lane, which he suspected, and out for revenge, then I would have waited for him just in that corner where I was.

I turned around and peered through the shrubs. He was racing silently down the slope toward me. He had decoyed me into a hiding place from which there was no escape.

But he hadn't seen me. He didn't know I was there; he could only hope I was. I tried a desperate bluff.

"Git off my land!" I yelled. "Git off ut, I tell 'ee, or I'll 'ave the law on 'ee!"

It was intended as an imitation of Pat's Dorset dialect. The major stopped in his stride. It was quite possible that Pat was standing in the lane and looking at him through the hedge, and he didn't want to quarrel more than could be helped.

"Go round by t' ga-ate, and git off my land!" I shouted.

"I say, I'm very sorry!" said Quive-Smith in a loud and embarrassed military voice—he was acting his part every bit as well as I was acting mine. "Thought I'd be late for supper, you know. Just taking a shortcut!"

"Well, cut oop ba-ack, damn 'ee!" I yelled.

He turned and strolled back up the field with offended dignity. I did not even wait for him to reach the skyline, for he might have lain down and continued observation. I sprinted along the twenty yards of straight hedge between the shrubbery and my own bramble patch, wriggled under the blackberry bush, and popped into my burrow. I remained till nightfall with my head and shoulders aboveground, but heard no more of him.

I have a reasonable certainty that Quive-Smith will never discover the deception. Pat is sure to be rude and taciturn in any conversation. If the major apologizes when they next meet, Pat will just accept the apologies with a grunt. My presence in the lane is still only suspected.

How much did Quive-Smith know? He had decided, obviously, that I had not been badly wounded; I had, after all, left the stream at a pace that defied pursuit, and there had not been a spot of blood. Then where was I? He had, I presumed, explored all the cover on Patachon's farm and on the two or three others over which he was shooting. He may have found traces of my presence in the lane and believed that at some time it had been my headquarters. Was I still there? No, but I might return; the lane was well worth watching until the police or the public reported me elsewhere.

His general routine was more or less predictable. If he made a habit of scouting around Pat's pasture in daylight, he ran a real risk of being assaulted or sued for trespass, and he had at all costs to avoid drawing attention to himself by a large local row. By day, then, he might be on the high ground or in the lane itself or on Patachon's side of it. After dusk he would explore or lie up in the pasture.

I was confident that, under these circumstances, he would not find the entrance of my chimney; but on one condition—that I cleaned it up and never used it again. There must not be a stem of the bush out of place, nor a blade of grass bent, nor any loose earth scraped from my clothes.

I resigned myself to remaining in the burrow, however unendurable. I have determined not to give way to impatience. I have now been underground for nine days. I dare not smoke or cook, but I have plenty of food: a large store of nuts and most of the canned meat and groceries that I brought back from my last trips to Beaminster. Of water I have far more than I need. It collects in the sandstone channels that run like wainscoting along the sides of the den, and slops over onto the floor. Lest it should undermine the door, I have drilled two holes, half an inch in diameter, through to the lane, using a can opener attached to the end of a stick. I keep them plugged during the day for fear that Quive-Smith might notice such unnatural springs.

Space I have none. The inner chamber is a morass of wet earth which I am compelled to use as a latrine. I am confined to my original excavation, the size of three large dog kennels, where I lie on or inside my sleeping bag.

I spend a part of each day wedged in the enlarged chimney, with my head just out of the top; but that is more for change of position than for fresh air. The bush is so thick and so shadowed by its companions and by the hedge that I can be sure it is day only when the sun is in the east.

Asmodeus, as always, is my comfort. It is seldom that one can give to and receive from an animal close, silent, and continuous attention. We live in the same space and on the same food, except that Asmodeus has no use for oatmeal, nor I for field mice.

Up until now I have been able to account for the march of events by conscious planning or by my own instinctive or animal reactions under stress. But now all initiative is at an end. All luck is at an end. Movement, wisdom, and folly have all stopped. Even time has stopped, for I have no space. That, I think, is the reason why I have again taken refuge in this confession. Through it I retain a sense of time, of the continuity of a stream of facts. I exist only in my own time, as one does in a nightmare, forcing myself to a fanaticism of endurance. Without a God, without a love, without a hate—yet a fanatic! An embodiment of that myth of foreigners, the English gentleman, the gentle Englishman. I will not kill; to hide I am ashamed. So I endure without object.

Part III

I HAVE a use for this record, so I finish it. This will not, I think, be a pleasant task, or dispassionate. But I can and must be frank.

I remained in my burrow for eleven days. That seemed ample to persuade Quive-Smith that I had either died in cover or left the district. Now I was entitled to find out whether he had gone. Asmodeus' behavior suggested that he had, and for the last three days I had not seen the cat at all. His delicate movements made the reason clear; he could not endure the dirt any longer.

At nightfall I emerged from the blackberry bush and crawled away on my stomach. It was cold and very dark, a foul November night, but it was a joy to be out on the grass and breathing. A blazing summer noon couldn't have given me more pleasure.

I could see the lights in Patachon's farmhouse and smell the sweet woodsmoke from his chimneys. I made my way there along the edge of the open road, coming to the back of the north wing across an orchard. Here there was a high wall with the sloping roof of a farm building above it. From the top of the gable I should have the yard and the whole front of the house under observation. I didn't dare to enter the yard itself. Even if the dogs neither heard nor saw me, the southwest wind would have carried my scent to them.

The wall was built of flints and easily climbed, but there was a gap of two feet between the top of the wall and the lower edge of the slates which gave me trouble. A rotten iron gutter ran below the slates, and it was difficult to reach the roof without momentarily putting some weight on this gutter. Eventually I got up by way of a stout iron bracket and the gable end.

I lay on the slated gable with my head over the coping. I could see right into the living room of the farmhouse—a peaceful and depressing sight. Quive-Smith was playing chess with Patachon's small daughter. I was surprised to see him sitting so carelessly before a lighted window with the blind up; but then I understood that, as always, I had underrated him. The clever devil knew that he was safe with his head nearly touching that of the child across the board. He was teaching her the game. I saw him laugh and show her some move she should have made.

It was a bitter shock to find him still there. The eleven days had seemed an eternity to me. To him they were just eleven days; it was even possible, I thought, that he had been enjoying himself. My disappointment turned to fury. It was the first time in the whole of this business that I lost my temper. I lay on that roof picking at the moss on the stone coping and cursing Quive-Smith, his country, his party, and his boss in a white-hot silence.

I watched the living room until the child went to bed. Then the major joined Patachon in front of the fire, and Patachon's wife entered with two huge china mugs of cider. All three settled down to newspapers. There was nothing more to be learned.

Quive-Smith might stay for weeks. I couldn't bear the thought of returning to the burrow. I determined to take to open country again. I meant to go on the run, desperate though my chances were. Considering my appearance, to live and move at all would be a hundred times harder than my original escape. Then I was believed to be dead and nobody was looking for me; now the police would be on me at the first rumor of my presence. But I wasn't going back. I intended to skulk around the downs, hiding in barns and shrubbery, and living, if there were no other food, upon the raw meat of sheep. I could keep Quive-Smith under observation until such time as he returned to London or wherever else his ability to increase the rottenness in a rotten world should be required.

I sidled toward the gable end, the weight of my body taken on shoulder and thigh, left hand on the coping. A few feet from the end the slates sagged beneath me, suddenly became brittle, and crashed to the floor of the barn. For an instant I swung from the coping and then that too gave way. Five feet of stone tile, a solid expanse of slate, and I myself roared down onto a pile of iron drinking troughs. It sounded like the collapse of a foundry.

I found later that I had reopened the wound in my shoulder and suffered various cuts and bruises, but at the time I was only shaken. I picked myself up and dashed to the open door of the barn. Quive-Smith had his long legs already over the living-room windowsill. My only thought was that he mustn't know I was still in this part of the country. The dogs started barking and jumping against their chains. Patachon opened the front door and stumped over the threshold, flashlight in hand.

I retreated into the barn and dived under the drinking troughs. They were ranged side by side, so that there was room for me to lie down between any two of them, and covered by the slates and rubble from the roof. Quive-Smith and the farmer entered immediately afterward.

"Damn un," stormed Patachon, observing the damage, " 'tis that beggarin' murderer after my cheeses! Over t' barn and down to dairy! I knew 'e was a stealin' of 'em. Over t' barn and down to dairy!"

I don't suppose he had lost an ounce, but farmers always suspect something is being stolen from them; there are so many things to steal.

Quive-Smith obligingly agreed with me. "Oh, I don't think there was anybody on the roof," he said. "Look at that!"

I knew what he was pointing at—a broken beam. It hadn't even broken with a crack. It had just simply given way like a sponge of wood dust.

"Deathwatch beetle," said the major. "I met the same thing in the East Riding, by Jove! Tithe barn it was. Poor chap broke his bloody neck!"

It didn't ring quite true, but it was a gallant attempt at the right manner.

"Rotted!" agreed Patachon in a disgusted tone. "Damn un, 'e's rotted!"

I heard them leave the barn, straining my ears to analyze their individual treads, making absolutely certain that one of them did not remain behind or return. I heard the front door of the farmhouse shut and bolted, and waited till the silence of the night was restored. Then I crawled to the door and out, creeping like a nocturnal caterpillar along the angle between the wall and the filthy courtyard.

For what I then did I have no excuse. I had begun to think as an animal; instinct, saving instinct, had preserved me time and again. I accepted its power complacently, never warning myself that instinct might be deadly wrong. Gone was my disgust with my burrow; gone my determination to take to open country. I didn't think, didn't reason. I was no longer the man who had challenged and nearly beaten all the cunning and loyalty of a first-class power. Living as a beast, I had become as a beast. I had had a bad fright. I was hurt and shaken. So I went without thinking to safety. And that meant my burrow—darkness, rest, freedom from pursuit. I hadn't a thought—any more than, I suppose, the fox has such a thought—that the earth might mean death.

I took, of course, the most cunning route; the animal could be trusted to perform that futility to perfection. I went through water and through sheep. I waited in cover to be sure there was no pursuit. I knew finally and definitely that there was none; that I was alone on the down above my lane. Then I covered the last lap with extreme caution and entered my burrow with attention to every dead leaf and every blade of grass.

All the next day I remained underground, congratulating myself on my good fortune. The stench and dirt were revolting, but I persuaded myself that in three or four days I could open my door and cleanse and dry the den. Then Asmodeus would come back and we could live peacefully until it was safe for me to hang around the ports and get out of the country.

AFTER nightfall I heard some activity in the lane, and sat with my ear to the ventilator. I couldn't translate the noises. There were two men, but they did not speak to each other. I expect they whispered, but owing to the curve of the little tunnel I could not hear so slight a sound. Something heavy was being moved, and once I heard a thud against the door. My thoughts played with the idea of a mantrap, a log perhaps that would fall on my head; they were certainly building something in the lane. Since I used it no longer, I felt very clever and secure. I told myself that I was disappointed, merely disappointed, for they would wait another week or two for the result of their trap and I should have to stay underground.

All the time, as I now see, I was conscious of extreme terror, and my heart was beating as if I had been running for my life. Only by an effort did I stop myself from talking aloud. I am very clever, I said to myself over and over again. And then the terror came up in my throat, for there was silence in the lane and little bits of earth were falling down my chimney into the inner chamber.

I lay between the two dens, watching the trickle of earth and listening to the quick strokes of a chopper. A man, as I thought, jumped or fell into the hole, and a wave of rubble rolled down to the bottom. I reached for my knife and waited. He's at my mercy, I said, I can make what terms I like. I was obsessed with the idea of talking, not killing. A reasonable man, I told myself. He'll see sense. He plays chess.

There was no further sound, none at all. The man had stuck in the hole or died. I crept up the slope of foul earth and lay on my back, poking an ash pole up the chimney as far as the twist. It didn't meet the body I expected; it met a hard obstruction. I withdrew myself as far as I could, for fear of some trap or explosive, and poked harder. The thing felt solid, with a smooth undersurface.

I lit a candle and examined it. It was the sawed-off end of a tree trunk.

I crawled to the door and pushed against it; nothing moved. Then I felt a sense of panic, with which was mingled relief that the end had come at last. I intended to rush out and let them shoot. A quick death, merited. I took the axe that had hollowed out the sandstone and drove it between the planks of the door. It turned. I ripped off the planks. On the far side of them was an iron plate. It rang hollow except in the center. They must have jammed it in place with a beam of timber, the other end of which rested against the opposite bank of the lane.

I don't know what happened to me then. When I heard Quive-Smith's voice I was lying on the bag with my head on my arms, pretending to myself that I was thinking things out. I was controlled, but my ears were drumming and my skin oozing cold sweat. I suppose that if one sits on hysteria long enough and hard enough, one loses consciousness. Something has to give way, and if the mind won't, the body must.

Quive-Smith was saying, "Can you hear me?"

I pulled myself together and sloshed a handful of water over my head. There was no point in keeping silence; he must have heard me battering on the iron. The only thing to do was to answer him and play for time.

"Yes," I said. "I can hear you."

"Are you badly wounded?"

Damn him for asking that question then! I should have found it very useful later if I could have persuaded him that I was suffering from a neglected wound, and incapacitated.

As it was, I answered the truth. "Nothing much. You hit a whiskey flask with a leather jacket behind it."

He muttered something that I could not hear. He was speaking with his mouth close to the ventilation hole. If he jerked his head, the voice was lost.

I asked him how he had found me. He explained that he had gone straight from the barn to the lane on the off chance that I had been responsible for the broken roof and that somewhere

in or near the lane he might see me returning to my mysterious hiding place and discover its exact location.

"Simple," he said. "So simple that I was very much afraid that it was what you meant me to do."

I told him that he hadn't run any risk, that I had never attempted to kill him, though I could have done it a dozen times if I had wished.

"I supposed so," he replied. "But I counted on your leaving me alone. You would only have exchanged me for the police, and it was obviously wiser to persuade me that you had gone. You did, as a matter of fact."

His voice had a weary harshness. He must have been in fear of his life all the time that he was at the farm. A braver man and cleverer than I am, but without—I was going to write "ethics." But God knows what right I have to claim any!

"Couldn't you give me a cleaner death than this?" I asked.

"My dear fellow, I don't want you to die at all," he said. "Not now. I am so glad you had the sense not to break out while I was sealing you up. This position has taken me by surprise as well as you. I can't promise you anything, but your death seems wholly unnecessary."

"The only alternative is the zoo," I answered.

He laughed at this for a nervous, uncontrollable moment. Lord, he must have been relieved to know where I was!

"Nothing so drastic," he said. "I'm afraid you wouldn't survive in captivity. No, if they take my advice, I shall be ordered to return you to your position and friends."

"On what condition?"

"Trifling—but we needn't go into that yet. Now, how are you off for food?"

I nearly lost my temper at this. For the cat-and-mouse act to be subtle enough to please his taste, it had to be hardly distinguishable from genuine kindness.

"Look here!" I said. "You won't get any more out of me than your police did, and you can't stay here indefinitely. So why not get it over?"

"I can stay here for months," he answered quietly. "I and my friend are going to study the habits and diet of the badger. The large beam of timber which is holding your door is for us to sit on. The bush placed in front of your door is a hide for the camera, and there will shortly be a camera in it. I'm afraid all these preparations are wasted, since nobody ever comes into the lane. But if anyone should—well, all he will see is my friend or myself engaged in harmless study."

I called him a damned fool and told him that the whole countryside would be consumed with curiosity—that all their doings would be public property in twenty-four hours.

"I doubt it," he answered. "Nobody at the farm pays any attention to my innocent rambles. Sometimes I go out with a gun, sometimes not. Sometimes on foot, sometimes in the car. Why should they guess I am always in this lane? They have never seen you. They won't see me. As for my assistant, he has no connection with me at all. He is staying in Chideock and his landlady thinks he is a night watchman at Bridport. He isn't as careful in making his way here as I should like. But we can't expect a paid agent to have our experience, can we, my dear fellow?"

This "dear fellow" of his infuriated me. I am ashamed to remember that I rammed my axe against the door in anger.

"How about that?" I asked.

"It makes surprisingly little noise," he said coolly.

It did, even in my closed space. He explained that there were felt and plywood over the iron.

"And if you think it out," he added, "what would happen if anyone did hear you? That disagreeable peasant who owns the field over your head, for example? You would compel me to remove the pair of you, and to arrange the bodies to show murder and suicide."

My mind cowered. I was at his mercy.

"We must stop talking now," he said. "No conversation in daylight will be our rule. I shall be on duty from ten a.m. to eight p.m., and we shall talk during the last couple of hours. My assistant will be on duty the rest of the time. Now, let me make the position perfectly clear. I cannot, I expect, prevent you from forcing your way out over the top of the door. But if you do, you'll be shot before you can shoot, and closed up again in your cozy home. Your back door is very thoroughly blocked, and if we hear you working, we shall cut off your air. So be careful, my dear fellow, and don't lose heart! Quite calm—that's the watchword. Your release is certain."

I SAT for hours with my ear to the ventilator. I didn't expect to learn anything, but hearing was the only one of my senses which could keep in touch with my captors. So long as I heard them, I had the illusion that I was not wholly defenseless, that I was planning, gathering data for an escape.

I heard the twittering of birds at dawn. I heard a crackle as Quive-Smith adjusted the screen of dead thorn outside my door. Then I heard a low mutter of voices, which I translated as the sound of Quive-Smith's colleague taking over the watch from him. They couldn't, of course, keep to their schedule on that first day. The major had presumably to telegraph a report.

All the time that I crouched at the ventilator my mind had been drifting over the wildest images of escape, enveloping them, rejecting them, concentrating finally upon the two practical schemes. The first, as Quive-Smith had suggested, was to cut a passage over the top of the door. I took one of my long spits and drove it through the red earth. It passed over the top of their plate, but the knowledge was useless. As he had said, if I stuck my head out, I should be shot—and by the tone of his voice I knew he did not mean killed, but deliberately crippled.

The second and far more likely way of escape was by the chimney. They hadn't caged me so neatly as they thought. Their tree trunk had not blocked the whole length of my tunnel; only its vertical section between the surface and the twist. The passage quarried through the sandstone was open. All I had to do was to cut a new passage through the earth, and surely I could work at that so silently that not a sound would be heard outside.

I crawled into the choked inner chamber and began to dig with my knife. There was no room to use the axe; I was kneeling on the pile of muck and earth, with my body filling the tunnel. Very silently and carefully, catching earth and stones in my hand, I dug a tunnel parallel to the tree trunk. My breath, thumping and gasping, was by far the loudest sound. God knows what I was breathing in that muck heap!

For short intervals, separated by lengthy halts to breathe at the ventilator, I worked at the old chimney. There was no space to swing or thrust, nowhere to put the earth that fell. It was like trying to burrow through a sand hill, impossible to breathe, impossible to remove the debris. The one strength of my position was that they could never see what I was doing. The ventilator was some four feet long. It had a diameter large enough for Asmodeus to go in and out, but so small and curved that I was always amazed he could.

THE day passed quickly. Time drags only when one is thinking fast, and all my mental processes were slowed down. I was lying by the ventilator when night fell and Quive-Smith wished me a cheerful good-evening.

"Everything has gone splendidly," he said. "Splendidly! We'll have you out of there in an hour. Free to go home, free to live on that lovely estate of yours, free to do anything you like. I'm very glad, my dear fellow. I have a great respect for you, you know."

I replied that I doubted his respect, that I knew him to be a good party man.

"I am," he agreed. "But I can admire such an individualist as you. What I respect in you is that you have no need of any law but your own. You're prepared to rule, or be suppressed, but you won't obey. A man in your position to commit what you described as a sporting stalk! And then calmly pitching a spy on the live rail at the Aldwych! I'm not blaming you in the least for defending yourself. The man was worthless and got in your way. I should be disappointed—really—to find a lot of sloppy scruples in such an anarchical aristocrat as you."

242

"That's your morality rather than mine," I answered.

"My dear fellow!" he protested. "It's the mass that we are out to discipline and educate. If an individual interferes, certainly we crush him; but for the sake of the mass—of the state, shall I say? You, you don't give a damn for the state. You obey your own taste and your own laws."

"That's true enough," I admitted. "But I have respect for the rights of other individuals."

"Of course. But none at all for the nation. Admit it now, my dear fellow—you could get along perfectly well without any state!"

"Yes, damn you!" I answered angrily—I hated his pseudo-Socratic cross-examination. "Without the shameless politicians who run this country or your blasted spotlight Caesars."

"There's no point in being rude." He laughed. "But I'm glad you have grown out of these rather childish allegiances, because we shan't have any difficulty in coming to terms."

I asked him what his terms were. He pushed a paper down the ventilator with a stick.

"Just sign that and you are free," he said. "There is only one serious restriction. You must undertake not to leave England. If you attempt to reach the Continent, this will begin all over again, and we shall show no mercy. I think you'll admit that, after what you did, it's a reasonable condition."

I asked him for a light. I wasn't going to use up candles and oxygen. He poked his flashlight down the hole without hesitation. He knew by this time that he could force me to give it back.

The form they wished me to sign was lengthy but simple. It was a confession that I had attempted to assassinate the great man, that I had undertaken this with the knowledge (they didn't quite dare to write approval) of the British government, and that I had been released without any punishment on condition that I remained in England. The document was signed by their chief of police, by witnesses, and by a London notary public attesting my signature, although it did not then exist.

I used the flashlight for the next quarter of an hour getting order into my excavations. Then I gave it back to him, together with his paper, unsigned, of course. There was no object in showing indignation.

"I wouldn't try to persuade you," he said, "if you had the usual bourgeois nationalism. But since you don't believe in anything but yourself, why not sign?"

I told him that I cared for public opinion.

"Public opinion? Well, we shouldn't publish this document unless there was imminent danger of war, and your government was acting its usual morality play. And from what I know of the English public's temper in time of crisis, they would probably make you a popular hero."

"They possibly would," I answered. "But I don't sign lies."

"Now, now, no heroics!" he begged me in his blasted patronizing manner. "You're a good Englishman, and you know very well that truth is always relative. Sincerity is what matters. I think that it would make it a lot easier for both of us if you told me why you attempted assassination."

"I told your people long ago," I retorted impatiently. "I wanted to see whether it was possible, and his death would be no great loss to the world."

"You did then intend to shoot," he said, accepting my statement quite naturally. "I couldn't really help you, you see, till you had admitted that."

I perceived that I had given myself away to him and to myself. "Yes," I admitted. "Of course I intended to shoot."

"But why? Surely political assassination settles nothing?"

"It has settled a good deal in history," I said.

"I see. A matter of high policy, then?"

"If you wish."

"Then you must have talked it over with someone?"

"No, I went alone, on my own responsibility."

"For the sake of your country?"

"Mine and others."

"Then even though your government knew nothing about you, you were acting in a sense on their behalf?"

"I don't admit that," I said, seeing where he was heading.

"My dear fellow!" he sighed. "Now you say you don't sign lies. Let me make your mind a little clearer. You have a number of friends in the Foreign Office, haven't you?"

"Yes."

"You sometimes give them an informal report on your return from trips abroad. I don't mean that you are an agent. But if you had any interesting impressions, you would pass them to the right man over the lunch table?"

"I have done so," I admitted.

"Then suppose you had succeeded and we had hushed the assassination up, would you have informed your friends that he was dead?"

"Yes, I expect so."

"You do, you see, consider yourself a servant of the state."

"Not in this matter."

"Oh dear, oh dear!" complained Quive-Smith patiently. "It is precisely and only in a matter of such importance that you consider yourself a servant of the state. In your daily routine you do not. You are an individualist obeying his own laws. Yet you admit that in this matter you acted for reasons of state and that you intended to inform the state."

I see now that he was destroying a great deal of nonsense in my mind. It was possibly that, more than anything else, which gave me the sense of wriggling at the end of a hook.

"But I did not act at the orders of the state," I said.

"I haven't asked you to sign your name to that. 'With the knowledge of the British government' is the phrase. That wouldn't be a lie at all. We needn't even stick to those words. 'With the knowledge of my friends'—how would that be?"

"It isn't true."

"I'm not suggesting you were paid. But a sporting assassination! Now, really, you wouldn't believe it yourself, you know."

"Why not?" I asked furiously.

"Because it is incredible. I want to know why you hate us to such a degree that you were ready to murder the head of the state. What were your motives?"

"Political."

"But you have admitted that you care nothing for politics, and I believe you implicitly. Perhaps we mean the same thing. Shall we say that your motives were patriotic?"

"They were not," I answered.

"My dear fellow!" he protested. "But they were certainly not personal!"

Not personal! But what else could they be? He had made me see myself. No man would do what I did unless he were consumed by grief and rage, consecrated by his own anger to do justice where no other hand could reach.

I left the ventilator and lay down with my head at the entrance to the inner chamber; it was the most privacy I could attain. His voice murmured on, grew angry. I didn't care. I was fighting against the self-knowledge he had forced upon me. At last he was silent, and I surrendered to misery.

I will try to write of this calmly. I think that now I can. I am a man who has only loved once, and did not know it till she was dead. Perhaps that is not quite correct. I loved with all my heart, but had little self-consciousness about it—not, at any rate, compared with the ecstasy and glory which love meant to her. I was too disciplined, too civilized.

When I heard of her death I did not weep. I grieved that so exquisite a work of nature had been destroyed. I grieved, in my conscious mind, with that same sorrow that I would have felt had my house, in which fifteen generations have lived, been burned—an irreparable, terrible sense of loss, transcending any injury, but no hot, human grief.

That, I say, is what I thought I felt. He who has learned not to intrude his emotions upon his fellows has also learned not to intrude them upon himself.

Yet at her death I was mad with grief and hatred. I describe myself as then mad because I did not know it. The tepidity of my sorrow was not indifference; it was the blankness which descends upon me when I dare not know what I am thinking. I know that I was consumed by anger. I remember the venomous thoughts, yet at the time I was utterly unaware of them. I suppressed them as fast as they came up into my conscious mind. I would have nothing to do with them, nothing to do with grief or hatred or revenge.

She was so alert and sensitive. She could do no other than make a generous cause her own. Impulsive, spiritual, intelligent, all at such an energy that she seemed to glow. She knew, I suppose, that in our mixture of impulse and intelligence we were alike. Her emotions governed her brain; though she would support her side with devastating logic, logic had nothing to do with her devotion. I should never have suspected that of myself, yet it is true. I am ruled by my emotions, though I murder them at birth.

They caught her and shot her. Shot her. Reasons of state. Yes, I know, but surely the preservation of such an individual is why we suffer, why we fight, why we endure this life. Causes? Politics? Religion? But the object of them is to produce such a woman—or man, if you will. To put her, her, against a wall—there is no cause that justifies an act so satanic.

When I went to Poland I considered that I was taking quite a conventional course: to go out and kill something in rough country in order to forget my troubles. I had not admitted what I meant to kill. I did not admit it till Quive-Smith destroyed all possible self-deception.

What I had done, then, was to declare war upon the men who could commit such sacrilege, and above all upon the man who has given them their creed. How ridiculous that one person should declare war upon a nation! That was another reason why I hid from myself what I was doing. My war was a futile cause to me, to be smiled at sympathetically just as I used to smile at her enthusiasm. Yet, in fact, my war is anything but futile. Its cost in lives and human suffering is low, and I should have destroyed the main body of the enemy but for a change of wind.

I realized that since the day I was caught I had been defeated only by the loneliness and uncertainty. How could I admit to myself that I, the unfeeling lover, had been so moved by the death of my beloved?

All that, as I lay in the silence of my temporary grave, was at last admitted. I was buoyed up by a feeling of lightheartedness, much the same, I suppose, as that of a penitent after confession. I knew why I was in my burrow. I felt that what I had done had been worthwhile. And so I passed to the offensive.

The offensive! How ridiculous for a man who hadn't the room to stand up to feel on the offensive! But now that I knew the cause for which I suffered—my God, I remembered that there were men at Ypres in 1915 whose dugouts were smaller and damper than mine!

I do not know how long I lay there as I passed in thought over all the movement of my attack and retreat, but there was no activity in myself or the outer world by which time could be measured. At last I was roused by the perceptible rising of the water.

I thought at first that there must be heavy rain outside, and thrust a stick down my two drains to clear them. It met hard obstructions. Of course they had found and plugged the holes. That added to my discomfort but put me in no danger. The water would leak out under the door when it rose to the height of the sill.

I spoke through the ventilator almost with gaiety. "Anyone there?"

Quive-Smith answered me. The night had passed, and the other man had come and gone.

"You will merely succeed in giving me pneumonia, my dear fellow," I said.

"Delirium," he replied, "won't change your handwriting."

It was the first time that I had annoyed him; he let me hear the cruelty in his voice.

I started to burrow up the chimney again, hoping with my new courage to get to the surface sometime after nightfall. But it was not courage that needed multiplying; it was oxygen. I had to leave the work at shorter and shorter intervals, and to allow a greater margin of safety than before. If I fainted with my head in the sea of mud on which my sleeping bag was floating, it would be all over.

When I could do no more, I rolled up the useless bag and spread a layer of cans on top of the bundle. On them I sat, crouched forward with the nape of my neck against the roof and my elbows on my knees. It was uncomfortable, but the only alternative was to lie full length in the water. That would have made me no wetter than I was, but a lot colder. I shivered continuously.

In the evening, the third since my imprisonment, Quive-Smith tried to make me talk, but I would not. At last I heard his colleague take over from him. The major wished me good night, and regretted that I should force him to increase my discomfort. I didn't understand what he meant.

The night dragged on and on. I began to suffer from hallucinations. I remember wondering how she had gotten in, and begging her to be careful. It was the growing effort of breathing which drove the dreams away. I was desperate for air. I couldn't make the man hear me when I spoke, so I hammered lightly on the door. A shaft of light showed at the angle of the ventilator. Quive-Smith had blocked it before he left.

"Stop that!" ordered a low voice.

"I thought it was still night," I answered idiotically.

"I have orders to break in and shoot if you make a noise."

He had the flat voice of a policeman in the witness box. From that, and from the major's description of him, I was pretty sure of his type. He wasn't in this service from ambition and love of the game itself, both of which undoubtedly counted with Quive-Smith; he was a paid hand.

I told him that I was a wealthy man and that if I escaped I could make him independent for life. I thought of pushing a fat bank note up the ventilator, but it was too dangerous to let him know I had money. He would have been in a position to force unlimited sums from me and give nothing in return.

"All right," I said. "I won't talk anymore. But I want you to know that when they let me out, I won't forget any little favors you can show me."

He made no answer, but he left the ventilator open.

I sat on my rolled bag, with my face pressed to it. The sun was shining outside. I could not see it, but in the curve of that imitation rabbit hole the deep orange crystals of the sandstone were glowing with light. There was an illusion of warmth and space.

My watch had stopped, but I think it must have been nearly midday before Quive-Smith came on duty. The first I heard of him was a shot—so close that I was sure he had potted something in the lane—and then the laughter of both men.

When dusk fell, Quive-Smith began to examine me for the fourth time. His approach was cordial and ingenious. He gave me a précis of the news in the morning paper, then talked of football, and so came around to his boyhood.

He had been educated in England. His mother had been an English governess. She felt socially inferior and morally superior to his father—a horrid combination—and had tried to make her son a good little Briton by waving the Union Jack and driving in patriotism with the back of a hairbrush. He gave away nothing about his father; I gathered that he was some obscure baron. When, later, I came to know Quive-Smith's real name, I remembered that his restless family had a habit of marrying odd foreign women and had consequently been cold-shouldered by their peers.

He led me on to talk of my own boyhood, but as soon as I felt myself affected by the confidential atmosphere that he was creating I dried up.

He threatened to block the ventilator again if I did not talk to him. I retorted that if he stuffed up that hole I should die; and, in case that should encourage him, I added that asphyxiation appeared to be a pleasanter death than any I could give myself.

I had not, in fact, the least thought of committing suicide now that I knew the object of my existence. Even during the first hopeless days suicide had only been a possibility, to which I gave as much consideration as to each of a dozen other plans.

He laughed and said he would give me all the air I wanted through the sort of filter that was fit for me. He dropped his English manner completely. It cheered me enormously to know that I was getting on his nerves. I heard him push some bulky object into the ventilator and ram it well down toward the curve. I didn't much care. I knew that there was enough air stored in the burrow and leaking under the door to keep me going for many hours.

I remained quiet, considering whether or not to pull the obstruction down into the burrow. I could get at it. But the risk was serious. If he caught my left arm as it groped upward, he would not thereafter be so dainty in his methods of cross-examination.

I poked with a stick, and found the thing to be soft and stiff. I advanced my fingers inch by inch until they brushed against it and then snatched my hand back. I had touched, as I thought, an arrangement of wires and teeth, but before my arm was fairly out of the tunnel I realized what it was. The simultaneous mixture of terror and relief and anger made me violently sick.

Taking Asmodeus' head in my hand, I drew his remains into the den. Poor old boy, he had been shot at close quarters full in the chest. It was my fault. People who sat quietly in the lane were, in his experience, friendly and fed him bully beef. He had been shot as he confidently sat up to watch them.

I was choking with sorrow and rage. Yes, I know that it was idiotic—the love of an Anglo-Saxon for his animal. But Asmodeus' affection had been earned at a much steeper price than that of a creature which one has fed and brought up from birth. Our companionship had a stern quality, as of the deep love between two people who have met in middle age, each looking back to an utterly unshared and independent life.

Quive-Smith cackled with laughter and told me that, really, I had only myself to blame; that he hoped I wouldn't be too proud to talk to him on the following evening. He couldn't, of course, have known that Asmodeus was my cat, but he had quite correctly calculated that I should draw his obstruction into the den and that I could never push it back. By God, if he had known the atmosphere I lived in, he would never have thought that a dead cat could make it any worse!

It seems ridiculous to say that by shooting Asmodeus, Quive-Smith condemned himself to death. Patachon would have shot the old poacher without hesitation. I should have grieved for him no less, but admitted Patachon's right. I can neither defend nor explain the effect that the shooting of this cat had upon me. It released me. I was at last able to admit that all my schemes for escaping

251

without violence were impossible. The only practical method was to kill the man on duty before, not after, I started digging.

The ventilator was my only means of physical contact with him. I contemplated a number of ingenious decoys to persuade the major to thrust his arm down the hole. This idea of a trap had not, apparently, occurred to him, and it might work. But it would do me no good, I decided, even if I caught Quive-Smith. You can't kill a man quickly with only his arm to work on.

To kill him through the ventilator? Well, there was only one way, and that was to straighten the curve so that I could shoot a missile up the tunnel. It was useless to poke at him with some improvised spear; to give instantaneous death I had to deliver a heavy weapon at a high initial velocity.

My iron cooking spit at once suggested itself as the weapon. And to propel it powerfully I had to have something in the nature of a bow. There was no room to handle a pole of such length that its bending would have the necessary force. A bow proper, or any method of propulsion by the resiliency of wood, was excluded. Bent steel or twisted rope might have done, but I had neither.

I looked over my full and empty cans in the hope of finding another source of power. Some were on my rolled sleeping bag; some under Asmodeus. I had laid his carcass on a platform of cans. A last tribute of sentimentality. He could never have endured the mud. When I laid my hand on him I realized that in his body was power. He could take his own revenge.

I skinned Asmodeus and cut his hide into strips. I have always been interested in the mechanics of obsolete weapons, and guilty of boring my friends by maintaining the supremacy of the Roman artillery over any other up to the Napoleonic Wars. The weapon that I now contrived was an extremely crude model of a hand-drawn ballista.

I made a square frame, of which the two uprights were bricks, and the horizontal bars at top and bottom stout logs of ash fitted into roughly scraped grooves in the bricks. On the inner side of each brick I stretched, from top to bottom bar, a twisted column of rawhide. Through the center of each rawhide column was driven a long peg, which projected three or four inches beyond the brick. A wide thong was attached to the tips of the two pegs, as a bowstring joins the ends of a bow. The twisting and shrinkage of the strips of hide held the whole frame rigid and forced the other ends of the pegs hard back against the bricks.

Lashed across the farther side of the frame was a strip of wood from a packing case, in the center of which I cut a semicircular aperture. In order to fire the ballista I would lie on my back with my feet outside the bricks, on the outer edges of this wooden strip. The point of my cooking spit passed through, and was supported by, the aperture; the ring of the spit would be gripped in the center of the thong by the thumb and forefinger of my right hand. Thus, by the pull between hand and feet, the pegs would be drawn toward my chest against the torsion of the columns of hide. When the thong was released, the pegs would thud back on the bricks, which were padded with cloth at the point of contact, and the spit would be discharged.

By the time I had made the machine it was morning, or later, and Quive-Smith was on duty again. I dared not practice for fear of noise, so I slept as best I could and waited for the evening examination. I intended to be polite, for I wanted information about the major's assistant. I hadn't the faintest idea what to do with him, but I had a feeling that he might be more useful to me alive than dead.

At the hour when Pat, Patachon, and their laborers had all retired to their respective firesides, Quive-Smith opened the conversation. After we had exchanged a few guarded commonplaces he said, "You're unreasonable, really unreasonable. I'm surprised at a man of your sense enduring such conditions!"

I noticed a touch of impatience in his voice. He must have begun to realize that watching badgers in a damp lane on November evenings was not an amusement that anyone would want to carry on for long, and wished that he had never thought of that invaluable confession.

"I can endure them," I answered. "You're the man who is suffering for nothing. I've come to the conclusion that if I sign that document of yours, you'll never have occasion to publish it. There isn't going to be any war. So it doesn't matter whether I sign or not."

I thought that would appeal to him as a piece of British casuistry: to deny that I was uncomfortable, but to produce a hypocritical justification for getting more comfort. It was a textbook illustration good enough to take in the foreigner.

"You're perfectly right, my dear fellow," said Quive-Smith. "Your signature is a mere necessary formality. The thing will probably stay at the bottom of the archives till the end of time."

"Yes, but look here!" I answered. "I trust you not to talk. I don't know who you are, but you must be pretty high up in your service and have a sense of responsibility. But what about this other fellow? I may lay myself open to blackmail, or he may change sides."

"He doesn't know who you are," replied Quive-Smith.

"How can I be sure of that?"

"Oh, use your head, man!" he answered contemptuously—I was pleased that his voice no longer had its usual note of ironical but genuine respect. "Is it likely? He doesn't even know who I am, let alone you. This morning he did his best to find out. I expect you tried to bribe him."

"Is he English?" I asked.

"No, Swiss. A people, my dear fellow, of quite extraordinary stupidity and immorality. A very rare combination, which only a long experience of democratic government could have produced."

I wanted to keep him talking, so that he wouldn't insist on my signing his document immediately.

I asked him what was the matter with democracy.

He read me a long lecture, which degenerated into a philippic against the British Empire. I slipped in a provocative word here and there to encourage him. He hated us like hell, considered us (he said it himself) as the Goths must have considered the Roman Empire, a corrupt bunch of moralizing luxury lovers. He even had the effrontery to invite me to join the winning side. He said that they needed in all countries natural leaders like myself; I had only to sign, and bygones would be bygones, and I should be given every chance to satisfy my will to power. I didn't tell him that natural leaders don't have any will to power. He wouldn't have understood what I meant.

I daresay he was sincere. I should have been a very useful tool, completely in their power.

"I'll sign in the morning," I said.

"Why not now?" he answered. "Why suffer another night?"

I asked him where on earth I could go. I told him that before I could be let loose on the public he would have to bring me clothes and, when I was decently dressed, take me to his farm to wash. All that couldn't be done at a moment's notice without arousing a lot of curiosity.

"I see your point," he said. "Yes, I'll bring you clothes in the morning."

"And get that Swiss of yours away before we talk! I don't trust him a yard."

"My dear fellow," he protested, "I wish you would give me credit for some discretion."

When the Swiss had come on duty and settled down for the night, I started to practice with the ballista, stuffing a coat into my end of the ventilator so that the thud of the pegs could not be heard. The strips of hide had shrunk into even tighter coils. It was a more powerful weapon than I needed, and the devil to pull; I had to use both hands, my left on the shaft of the spit, my right gripping the ring, held horizontally so that it did not catch as it flew through the aperture. At a range of four feet the spit drilled clean through two cans of tomatoes and buried itself six inches in the earth. I shot it off fewer than a dozen times, for the construction was none too strong.

I unstopped the ventilator and fanned for an hour to try to change the air. My next task was to persuade the Swiss to shut up his end of the ventilator, and keep it shut while I straightened the ventilator shaft. I began moaning and mumbling to shake his nerves a bit. When he ordered me to stop it, I said I would if he told me the time.

"Half past two," he answered sulkily.

I stayed quiet for another hour, and then went off my head again—sobs and maniacal laughter and appeals to let me out. He endured my noises with annoying patience, and compelled me to such a show of hysteria before he plugged the hole that I managed to get on my own nerves into the bargain. My acting was good enough to be a genuine release for my feelings.

The straightening of the shaft was easy and quite silent. I dug with my knife and gathered the earth handful by handful. At intervals I let off some moans to discourage him from removing the plug. The curve vanished and in its place was an empty hollow, like a rabbit's nest, with two mouths. The Swiss had plugged the outer mouth with a piece of sacking. I opened out its folds on my side without disturbing its position. I could breathe without difficulty and hear every sound in the lane.

I arranged my rolled sleeping bag under my shoulder blades, and lay on my back in the mud with the weapon ready at the ventilator. I had to fire the moment that a man's head appeared at the hole. The removal of the sacking would give me time to draw, and if anyone looked into the hole and noticed that its shape had been altered, that would be the last thing he ever noticed.

I hoped that the Swiss would leave the sacking alone. I felt no compunction in killing him, but if he removed the plug immediately before Quive-Smith's arrival, I might not be able to cut my way out in time to surprise the major. I kept up enough muttering to prove that I was a nuisance and alive, but not so much that he would be tempted to pull out the sacking and curse me.

The light of morning gleamed through the folds. I waited. I waited, it seemed to me, till long after midday before Quive-Smith arrived. As a matter of fact, he was early—if, that is, he usually came at ten.

For the first time I could hear all their conversation. At that hour in the morning they spoke in low voices and as little as possible.

"He has gone mad, sir," reported the Swiss stolidly.

"Oh, I don't expect so," answered Quive-Smith. "He's just avoiding the crisis. He'll soon be calm."

"Usual time tonight, sir?"

"If not, I will let you know. Your landlady has been warned that you may be leaving?"

"Yes, sir."

I heard his heavy steps sloshing off through the mud. All this time I was lying on my back and staring at the hole.

I cannot remember the slightest effort in drawing the ballista. There was a flash of light as Quive-Smith withdrew the plug. I started, and that slight jerk of my muscles seemed to pull the thong. Immediately afterward his head appeared. I noticed the surprise in his eyes, but by that time I think he was dead. The spit took him square above the nose. He looked, when he vanished, as if someone had screwed a ring into his forehead.

I hacked at my end of the ventilator until it was large enough to receive my body, then crawled through and burst into the lane with a drive of head and shoulders. Quive-Smith was lying on his back watching me. I had my thumbs on his windpipe before I realized what had happened. The foot of spit that projected behind his skull was holding up his head in a most lifelike manner. He hadn't brought any spare clothes. Perhaps he didn't intend me to live after he had my signature; perhaps he didn't believe that I would sign. The latter is the more charitable thought. He had a loaded revolver in his pocket, but that is no proof one way or the other.

I BURNED that scandalous document, then stretched myself and peered through the hedge over the once familiar fields. Pat was nowhere in sight, and his cows were grazing peacefully. Patachon was talking to his shepherd on the down. It was a damp November day, windless, sunless. Coming to it straight from interment, I couldn't tell whether the temperature was ten or thirty degrees above freezing point. By Quive-Smith's watch it was only eleven. I ate his lunch.

I destroyed his screen of bushes, buried his camera, and folded up the heavy lap robe which kept him warm. Then I shifted the log that was jammed between both banks of the lane, and opened the door of the burrow. The stench was appalling. I had been out only half an hour, but that was enough to notice, as if it had been created by another person, the atmosphere in which I had been living.

Boiling some muddy water on the Primus, I sponged my body—a gesture rather than a wash. It was heaven to feel dry and warm when I had changed into his clothes. He had heavy whipcord riding breeches, a short, fur-lined shooting coat—Central European rather than English—over his tweeds, and a fleece-lined trench coat over the lot.

When I was dressed I went through his papers. He had the party and identity documents of his own nation, with his real name on them. He also had a British passport. It was not in the name of Quive-Smith. He had put on that name and character for this particular job. His occupation was given as company director, almost as noncommittal as author.

In a belt around his waist I found two hundred pounds in gold and a second passport. It had twice been extended by obscure consulates, but had neither stamps nor visas on it, showing that it had never yet been used for travel. The photograph showed his face and hair darkened with stain, and without a mustache. If I were in Quive-Smith's game, I should take care to have a similar passport; should he have a difference of opinion with his employers, he could disappear completely and find a home in a very pleasant little Latin country.

I held up any definite plans until after I should have interviewed the Swiss, but when I cut my hair and shaved, I left myself a mustache exactly like the major's and brushed my hair, as his, straight back from the forehead. The name and identity of the company director might suit me very well.

I removed what was left of Asmodeus and buried him in the lane where he had lived and hunted, with a can of beef to carry him through until he learned the movements of game over his new ground. With my old clothes, my bedding, and earth, I plugged the ragged hole made by my escape, and took from the den my money and the exercise book that contained the two first parts of this journal. Then I replaced the original door and laid the iron plate against the bank of the lane, covering it with earth and debris. When the nettles and bracken grow up in the spring—and thick they will grow on that turned earth—there will be no trace of any of us.

I propped up Quive-Smith's body against a bush, where it was out of the way. Not a pretty act, but his siege had destroyed my sensibility. I had room for no feeling but immense relief. After dusk I walked around Pat's pasture to accustom my legs to exercise. I was very weak and probably a bit light-headed. It didn't matter. Since all that remained was to take crazy risks, to be a little crazy was no disadvantage.

The tracks in the mud told me that the Swiss always entered and left by the top of the lane. I squatted in the darkest section of the lane and waited. I heard the fellow a quarter of a mile away. He was moving quietly where the lanes were dry, but he had no patience with mud. When he was a few paces from me I beamed Quive-Smith's flashlight on his face and ordered him to put his hands up. I have never seen such a badly frightened man. I made him keep his face to the hedge while I removed his documents, his pistol, and his belt and trouser buttons. I had read of that trick, but never seen it done. A man with his trousers around his ankles is not only hindered; his morale is destroyed.

He carried a passport. A glance showed me that his name was Müller, that he was naturalized English, and that he was a hotel porter. He was a big man, fair-haired, with a fair mustache waxed to points.

"Is he dead?" Müller stammered.

I told him to turn around and look, keeping him covered while I flashed the light on Quive-Smith's naked body. Then I put him back with his face to the hedge. He was shaking with fear and cold. He kept on saying, "What . . . what . . . what . . ."

He meant, I think, to ask what I was going to do to him.

I placed the cold flat of my knife against his naked thighs. He collapsed on the ground, whimpering. I wanted him to keep his clothes reasonably clean, so I picked him up by one ear and propped him against the hawthorn alongside Quive-Smith.

"Who am I?" I asked.

"The Aldwych . . . police wanted you . . ."

"And who is the dead man?" I asked.

"Number forty-three. I never met him before this job. I know him as Major Quive-Smith."

"Why didn't Major Quive-Smith hand me over to the police?"

"He said you were one of his agents, and you knew too much."

That sounded a true piece of Quive-Smith ingenuity; it explained to Müller's simple intelligence why it was necessary to put me out of the way, and why they were working independently of the police.

"How many years have you worked in hotels?"

"Ten years. Two as night porter."

"From whom do you take your orders?" I asked.

"The hotel manager."

"No one else?"

"Nobody else, I swear!"

"What crime did you commit?" I asked.

It was obvious that they had some hold on him in order to make of him so obedient and unquestioning a tool.

"Sexual assault," he muttered, evidently ashamed of himself. "She invited me to her room—at least I thought she did. And then—then I went for her a bit roughlike. I thought she'd been leading me on, you see. And she screamed, and the manager and her father came in. The manager made me sign a confession."

"Why didn't you get another job?"

"They wouldn't give me any references, sir, and I don't blame them, really."

He was genuinely ashamed. They had a double grip on the poor devil. They had not only ensured his obedience, but shattered his self-respect.

"Don't you see that they framed you?" I asked.

"I'd like to believe it, sir," he said, shaking his head.

No wonder Quive-Smith was exasperated by him!

I myself became a human being again. I was almost as relieved as he when I could lay brutality aside. I told him to pull up his pants, and gave him a bit of string to hold them, and a cigarette.

I kept the revolver in sight, of course, just to remind him that all in the garden was not yet roses.

"They know you at the farm?" I asked.

"Yes. I drove the major over there. He told them I was his servant and was taking my own holiday on the coast."

"Have you been at the farm since?"

"Once. I had lunch there the day that—"

"That you buried me alive."

"Oh, sir! If only I had known!" he cried. "I thought you were one of them—honest, I did! I didn't care if they murdered each other. For my part it was a case of the more the merrier, if you see what I mean."

"You seem to be pretty sure now that I'm not one of them," I said.

"I know you're not. A gentleman like you wouldn't be against his own country."

"Wouldn't he? I don't know. I distrust patriotism."

I explained to him that he might consider himself out of danger so long as his nerve did not fail; he was going down to the farm to tell Patachon that Quive-Smith had been called back to London on urgent business, to pack up the major's things, and to take them away in the car.

Quive-Smith had almost certainly warned his hosts that he might be off any day, so the plan was not outrageously daring. The chief risk was that Müller, when he found himself in the farmhouse, would decide that his late employers were more to be feared than I. That point I put to him with utmost frankness. I told him that if he wasn't out of the house in a quarter of an hour, I should come and fetch him and claim to be the major's brother. I also told him that he was useful to me just so long as nobody knew the major was dead, and that the moment when his usefulness ceased would be his last.

"But if you are loyal to me for the next few days," I added, "you can forget that matter of criminal assault. I'll give you money to go abroad. You're of no further use to your late employers, and you don't know enough to be worth following. So there you are! Give me away, and I'll kill you! Play straight with me, and there's a new life open to you wherever you want to lead it!"

There were a good many holes in the argument, but he was in no state for analytical thinking. He was deeply impressed and became maudlin with relief.

He took the major's shoulders while I took his heels, and we moved cautiously down into the road that ran along the foot of the hill. There, thankfully and immediately, we dropped our burden in the ditch. I saw the sweat burst out on the back of Müller's thick neck as soon as he was convinced that we had not been observed by anyone.

At the gate to Patachon's farm we stopped. I told Müller that I should wait for him there, and should enter the car when he got out to open the gate. I handed him Quive-Smith's keys and gave him a story to tell. The major was dining with friends in Bridport. He had learned that he had to go abroad at once. His address for forwarding letters was Barclays Bank, Cairo. I knew from a letter in his pocket that he kept an account with a branch of Barclays—and Cairo is a complicated town through which to trace a man's passage.

I gave him a pound to tip the girl who had made the major's bed—if there was such a girl—and another which he was to hand to Mrs. Patachon for her daughter's savings bank.

"Give the little girl a message from Major Quive-Smith: that she must remember not to bring her queen out too soon. Explain to her that you don't understand what it means. But she will, and she'll laugh. Tell her not to bring her queen out too soon." It was perfectly safe advice to give a beginner at chess, and it would establish Müller's bona fides.

As he went around the corner of the barns into the yard, I squatted behind a tree whence I could see the front door. Mrs. Patachon received the caller with surprise but no hesitation. Soon an oil lamp was lit in an upper room, and I saw Müller pass back and forth across the window. He came out with a suitcase in his hand, followed by Patachon with a gun case and Mrs. Patachon with a packet of sandwiches. The whole party was chattering gaily and sending messages to the major. When they entered the stable to watch Müller load and start the car, I ran back to the gate.

We picked up Quive-Smith and put him in the back of the car under a rug.

"Where to, sir?" asked Müller.

I told him to drive to Liverpool and to go easy with the traffic laws. Southampton was too close, and London too full of eyes.

My plans were straightening out. I was sure that nobody would call at the farm until letters and telegrams had remained a week or more without reply. Anxiety would have to be very strong before any of the major's subordinates or superiors ventured to intrude upon his discreet movements. When they did they could take their choice of three theories: that I had gotten away, with Quive-Smith and Müller hard on my heels; that I had bribed the pair of them to let me go; or that they had killed me and in some way aroused the curiosity of the police.

We stopped for gas at Bristol and Shrewsbury. On the way I wired an assortment of ironmongery to Quive-Smith and dropped him into the Severn. I have no regrets. Reluctantly, belatedly, but finally, I have taken on the mentality of war; and I risk for myself a death as violent and unpleasant as any he could wish for me.

We reached Liverpool early in the morning. The town was in its vilest mood, and I was glad that the major had dressed himself for exposure to the elements. A northeast wind gathered the soot, dust, and paper from the empty streets, iced them, and flung them into the Mersey River. Putting up at a hotel, we breakfasted in our room. While Müller dropped off to sleep in front of the fire, I spent a couple of hours practicing the signature on Quive-Smith's passport. For convenience I still write of him and think of him as Quive-Smith, though the signature I practiced and the identity I had taken were those of his normal British self—the nondescript company director.

My forgery wouldn't have taken in a bank manager, but it was good enough for an embarkation form or a customs declaration—especially since it would be written on cheap paper with an office pen. The passport photograph was not very like me, but near enough.

263

No shipping clerk would question it. The common type of Quive-Smith and myself is manifestly respectable and responsible.

I woke up Müller and took him with me to the bathroom. While I washed off the accumulated filth of weeks (keeping the revolver handy on the soap dish) I made him sit on the lavatory seat and read me the shipping news.

We had ships sailing that afternoon for New York, for the West Indies, for Gibraltar and Mediterranean ports, for Madeira and South America, for Tangier and the East. All countries for which I needed a visa were excluded, and all voyages longer than a week. Gibraltar, Madeira, and Tangier remained—and Madeira was a dead end, to be avoided if possible.

How to lose Müller was a difficult problem. I had promised him his life and freedom, but it was going to be a hard promise to keep. He had only one set of documents; he hadn't the sense or presence to bluff. Whatever port he entered and left would be sure to have full particulars on him. I was sure that his employers would take no further interest in him after he had answered their questions, but I wanted to put off that questioning as long as possible.

I wondered what Quive-Smith would have done had he found himself saddled with Müller as the only witness to murder or bribery. The answer was not far to seek. He would have pushed Müller overboard on the night before reaching port, and concealed his absence. That seemed an admirable solution. This, then, was my plan; but instead of doing it wherever was convenient, I had to push him overboard within reach of land and with the means of landing. There were two places off the coast of Portugal where that could be done—the point near the mouth of the Tagus River where the Sintra hills come down to the sea, and Cape St. Vincent.

I sent for a barber to give me a decent haircut and, as soon as we left the hotel, bought a monocle, which disguised, or rather emphasized and accounted for, the glassy stare of my left eye. Then I led Müller around the shipping offices—prepared to pose as an eccentric holidaymaker with his secretary-valet. I asked silly questions, such as the times when various ships passed close to land; I hoped, I said, to be able to wave to an old friend who lived in Portugal. The clerks explained to me patiently that it depended where my friend lived, that Portugal had a long seaboard, and that in any case the largest of handkerchiefs could not be seen at a couple of miles.

I found out what I wanted to know. The Gibraltar ship wouldn't do; it passed the Tagus in the morning and Cape St. Vincent shortly after sunset. The Tangier ship, a slow old tub, was more suitable. It passed the Tagus between nine p.m. and midnight.

We booked two adjoining staterooms with a bath between, and then did our shopping. I provided Müller and myself with bags and necessaries for the voyage. Then I bought a collapsible rubber boat with a bicycle pump to inflate it, a pair of strong paddles—each in two pieces—and a hundred feet of light rope, all packed in a large suitcase. Müller, naturally, thought the boat was for my own escape; I didn't disillusion him. Then I put the car into storage for a year, and we went on board.

Down St. George's Channel and across the bay I had no need to trouble myself about Müller's whereabouts. He had never made an ocean voyage. The sea was very rough. I was free to spend my time eating, drinking, and washing; I needed as much of the three pleasures as the ship provided.

On the third night out from Liverpool we passed Cape Finisterre and awoke to a pale blue world with a rapidly falling swell; the gray-green hills of Portugal lay along the eastern horizon. I routed Müller out of bed and fed him breakfast. Then we occupied two deck chairs at the stern. I spread out my lap robes and legs as awkwardly as possible, and through my monocle stared offensively at anyone who dared to pick his way over them. None of the passengers showed the slightest desire to join us.

Müller was a teetotaler, so in the late afternoon I gave him a couple of lemonades to brace his courage. Then I explained to him the plan: he and the rubber boat were to be thrown overboard when we were a couple of miles from shore, and I would give him five hundred pounds with which to start a new life. He brightened up a bit at the thought of money, but was appalled by the difficulties facing him when he reached the shore. He seemed to think that he was a person of importance, and that his employers would ransack the world to find him.

"I know too much," he protested.

"You don't know a damn thing," I answered. "I doubt if you even know what country you were working for."

"I do, sir," he said, and mentioned it.

By God, it was the wrong one! I suppose it's a commonplace that the underlings of a secret service should not even know the nationality of their employers, but it seemed to me remarkably clever. I told him he was wrong, and proved it by the major's papers. After that I had no more trouble.

There was one thing Müller could be trusted to do: to follow orders. So I gave them.

"Your clothes will be in the boat," I said. "When you land, put them on. Rip the boat to pieces and hide them under a rock. Walk to Cascais and take the electric train to Lisbon. Don't go to a hotel. Spend the night where you do not have to register. In the morning, go to the docks to meet an imaginary friend who is arriving by ship. Pass back again through the customs as if you came off the boat, and get your passport stamped. Then buy yourself a visa and a ticket for any country you want to visit, and leave at once by another ship."

We were a little ahead of schedule, and the Sintra hills were in sight at sunset. That suited me well enough; we could get the job over while the passengers were at dinner. So that no one should be sent in search of us, I told the chief steward that I wasn't feeling well, and that my secretary would be looking after me.

Müller undressed in the cabin, and I tied the money around his neck in a fold of oilskin. As soon as the alleyways were clear, we unpacked and inflated the boat in the shelter of the deckhouse. We could see lights onshore, so he knew in which direction to row. I made Müller repeat his orders. Then I lashed his clothes and the paddles to the bottom of the boat, and looped the other end of the long line around his wrist.

The wash of a ship isn't inviting. The poor devil sat on the rail shivering with cold and panic. I didn't give him time to think, but hurled the boat over and snapped at him that he would drown if he let the line tauten. I saw the boat, a dark patch bobbing on the white wash, and I saw him come to the surface. A second later, the only sign that he had ever existed was a dressing gown lying on the deck. Good luck to him!

The next day was abominably long. There was some doubt whether we should arrive at Tangier in time for passengers to land that night; if we didn't, I had no hope of keeping Müller's disappearance secret. I missed breakfast and passed the morning in concealment, acting on the general principle that nobody would think of us if neither was seen, but that, if one were seen, there might be inquiries about the other. At lunchtime I entered the saloon to tip my table steward, but refused to eat. I told him that both I and my secretary had been badly upset by our food, and that I had prescribed for us a short period of starvation. There was nothing like starvation, I boomed pompously, for putting the stomach right.

While the cabin steward was off duty between two and four, I packed the bags and took them on deck. Tangier was in sight. The purser confirmed that we should certainly be able to leave the ship before the customs closed. I collected the two landing cards. Then again I went into hiding until we dropped anchor. As soon as the tender arrived and the baggage had been carried off the ship, I visited and tipped the cabin steward in a great hurry. He was not exactly suspicious, but he felt it his duty to ask a question.

"Is Mr. Müller all right, sir? I haven't seen him all day."

"Good heavens, yes!" I answered. "He packed up for me and took everything on deck. He's on the tender now with the baggage."

"I hadn't seen him all day, sir," he explained.

"I haven't seen much of him myself," I replied testily. "I understand he found an old friend in the engineers' department."

He let it go at that. Müller was my servant. I was eminently respectable. If I saw nothing wrong, nothing could be wrong.

The worst danger was before me now. Lest the tally should be wrong, I had to surrender two landing cards while appearing to surrender only one. I dashed into the smoking room and stuck the two landing cards lightly together with the gum from a penny stamp; they were of thin cardboard, and I hoped that the assistant purser who was collecting them wouldn't notice that I had shoved two into his hand. If he did notice, I proposed to say that Müller was already on the tender and that he must have gone down the gangway without surrendering his card. If someone then had a look at the tender and found he wasn't there, I could only show amazement and pray that I didn't find myself in the dock on a capital charge.

When I walked down the gangway the assistant purser received my two cards without a glance. Ten minutes later I was on the Tangier dock, surrounded by a yelling mob of coffee-colored porters draped in burnooses of sacking.

Passing through customs, I had my entry carefully noted. I took pains to see that the French immigration official wrote down the company director's name correctly. From then on there could be no shadow of doubt that the man who had called himself Major Quive-Smith had duly entered Tangier, and alone.

As for Müller, his late employers' discreet inquiries at the offices of the line would be duly passed on to the ship. The stewards would remember that Müller had not been seen for twenty-four hours. The assistant purser would remember that when he checked the landing cards he found two suspiciously stuck together. And it would be reported back to Liverpool that there was indeed grave reason to fear that something had happened to Mr. Müller. Whoever had put the inquiry on foot, having found out what he wanted to know, would then laugh and explain that Mr. Müller was perfectly safe and sound, and that—well, any yarn would do.

I drove to a hotel, deposited my baggage, and booked a room for a week, telling the proprietor that I had a little friend in Tangier, and that, if I didn't turn up for two or three nights, he was not to be surprised. Then I put a razor, a bottle of hair dye, and another of stain into my pocket, and walked off into the deserted hills. Besides money and the passports, the only thing I carried out of my past life was this confession, for I began to see in what manner it might be useful.

I do not think that in all my life I have known such relief and certainty as in the valley between those sun-dried hills, where the water trickled down the irrigation channels from one well-loved terrace to another, and no light showed but the blazing stars. My escape was over; my purpose decided; my conscience limpid. I was at war—and no one is so aware of the tranquillity of nature as a soldier resting between one action and the next.

I buried that company director's passport and my own, with which I have probably finished forever. I shaved off my mustache, bronzed my face and body with stain, and dyed my hair. Then I slept till dawn, my face in the short grass by the water's edge, my body drawing strength from that warm and ancient earth.

In the morning I strolled to the upper town, where I had not been the night before, and completed my change of identity. I bought a thoroughly Latin suit, spats, and some beastly pointed shoes, posting my other clothes in a parcel addressed to the Public Assistance Committee, Rangoon. I trust there is such a committee. I went to a barber, who duly doused me with eau de cologne and brushed my luscious black hair straight back from my forehead. When this was over, my resemblance to the photograph on Quive-Smith's second passport was a lot closer than my resemblance to the company director.

The regular packet was leaving that day for Marseilles. I got a French visa on my passport and bought a ticket in my new name. Since I had no baggage, it was easy to bluff my way onto the ship without passing the control. Thus there was no record for inquisitive eyes that this courteous and scented gentleman had either entered or left Tangier, and no means of connecting him with Quive-Smith. I think they will be looking for their vanished agent between Atlas and the Niger.

Extract from the letter which accompanied this manuscript:

My dear Saul,

I write this from a pleasant inn where I am accustoming myself to a new incarnation. I must not, of course, give you any clue to it; nor would the trail of the gentleman I describe

269

as Latin—even assuming it could be followed—lead to where or what I am.

I want these papers I'm sending you published. If necessary, have them brushed up by some competent hack and marketed under his name. You won't, of course, mention mine, or the name of the country to which I went from Poland and to which I am about to return. Let the public take its choice!

My reason for publishing is twofold. First, I have committed two murders, and the facts must be placed on record in case the police ever get hold of the wrong man. Second, if I am caught, there can never again be any possible question of the complicity of His Majesty's government. Every statement of mine can, at need, be checked, amplified, and documented. The three parts of the journal (two written accidentally and the last deliberately) form an absolute answer to any accusation from any quarter that I have involved my own nation.

Forgive me for never telling you of my engagement or of the happy weeks we lived in Dorset. I first met her in Spain a couple of years ago. We hadn't reached the point of an announcement in *The Times* and we didn't give a damn about it anyway.

The ethics of revenge? The same as the ethics of war, old boy! Unless you are a conscientious objector, you cannot condemn me. Unsporting? Not at all. It is one of the two or three most difficult shots in the world.

I begin to see where I went wrong the first time. It was a mistake to make use of my skill over the sort of country I understood. One should always hunt an animal in its natural habitat; and the natural habitat of man is—in these days—a town. Chimney pots should be the cover, and the method, snap shots at two hundred yards. My plans are far advanced. I shall not get away alive, but I shall not miss; and that is really all that matters to me any longer.

Psycho

Psycho

A CONDENSATION OF
THE BOOK BY

Robert Bloch

ILLUSTRATED BY ROBERT HEINDEL

She had made a bad mistake and now
she was on the run. All that money in her
purse—forty thousand dollars' worth—
and the police, no doubt, already on her trail.
Now it was night, she was on a lonely
country road, and it was raining.
The seedy little motel was the only refuge
for miles about. The big old house looming
up there just behind it seemed strangely
foreboding, but she was tired and she had
to get off the road. So she pulled in where
the little sign said: MOTEL—VACANCY.

So begins Robert Bloch's scalp-tingling tale
of horror, the unforgettable suspense
thriller upon which the classic
Alfred Hitchcock film was based.

Chapter 1

Norman Bates heard the noise and a shock went through him.

It sounded as though somebody was tapping on the windowpane.

He looked up hastily, half prepared to rise, and the book slid from his hands to his ample lap. Then he realized that the sound was merely rain. Late afternoon rain, striking the parlor window.

Norman hadn't noticed the coming of the rain, nor the twilight. It was quite dim in the parlor now, and he reached over to switch on the table lamp before resuming his reading.

It was one of the old-fashioned kind, with an ornate glass shade and crystal fringe. Mother had refused to get rid of it. Norman didn't really object; he had lived in this house for all of the forty years of his life, and there was something pleasant and reassuring about being surrounded by familiar things. Here everything was orderly and ordained; it was only outside that threatening changes took place. Suppose he had spent the afternoon walking? He might have been soaked to the skin and caught his death of cold. Besides, who wanted to be out in the dark? It was much nicer here in the parlor, with a good book for company.

The light shone down on his plump face, reflected from his rimless glasses, bathed the pinkness of his scalp beneath the thinning sandy hair as he bent his head to resume reading. It was really a fascinating book—no wonder he hadn't noticed how fast the time had passed. It was *Realm of the Incas*, by Victor W. von Hagen. Norman had never before encountered such a wealth of curious information. For example, this description of the *cachua*, or victory dance, where the warriors formed a great circle, moving and writhing like a snake. He read:

> The drum beat for this was usually performed on what had been the body of an enemy: the skin had been flayed and the belly stretched to form a drum, and the whole body acted as a sound box while throbbings came out of the open mouth—grotesque but effective.

Norman smiled, then allowed himself the luxury of a comfortable shiver. Imagine flaying a man alive and then stretching his belly to use it as a drum! How did they go about doing that, curing and preserving the flesh of the corpse to prevent decay? And what kind of a mentality did it take to conceive of such an idea in the first place?

When Norman half closed his eyes he could almost see the painted warriors wriggling in unison under a sun-drenched, savage sky, the old crone throbbing out a relentless rhythm from the contorted mouth of the corpse, probably fixed in a gaping grimace by clamps of bone.

For a moment he could almost hear it, and then he remembered that rain has its rhythm, too, and footsteps—

Actually, he was aware of footsteps without even hearing them. Mother was coming into the room. Not even looking up, he pretended to continue his reading. Mother had been sleeping, and he knew how crabby she could get when just awakened. So it was best to keep quiet and hope that she wasn't in one of her bad moods.

"Norman, do you know what time it is?"

He sighed and closed the book. He could tell now that she was going to be difficult. Norman glanced down at his wristwatch. "A little after five," he said. "I actually didn't realize it was so late. I've been reading—"

"Don't you think I have eyes? I can see what you've been doing." She was over at the window now, staring out at the rain. "And I can see what you haven't been doing, too. Why didn't you turn the sign on when it got dark? And why aren't you down at the office?"

"Well, it started to rain so hard, and I didn't expect there'd be any traffic in this kind of weather."

"Nonsense! That's just the time you're likely to get some business. Lots of folks don't care to drive when it's raining."

"But it isn't likely anybody would be coming this way. Everyone takes the new highway." Norman heard the bitterness creeping into his voice, felt it welling up into his throat until he could taste it, and tried to hold it back. But too late now; he had to vomit it out. "I told you how it would be when we got that advance tip that they were moving the highway. You could have sold the motel then. We could have bought all kinds of land over there for a song, closer to Fairvale, too. We'd have had a new motel, a new house, made some money. But you wouldn't listen. You never listen to me, do you? You make me sick!"

"Do I, boy?" Forty years old, and Mother called him boy; that's how she treated him, too. "Do I, boy?" she repeated softly. "I make you sick, eh? Well, I think not. No, boy, *I* don't make you sick. You make *yourself* sick. That's the real reason you're still sitting over here on this side road, isn't it, Norman? Because the truth is that you haven't any gumption. Never had the gumption to leave home, or go out and get yourself a job, or even find yourself a girl—"

"You wouldn't let me!"

"That's right, Norman. I wouldn't let you. But if you were half a man, you'd have gone your own way."

It was true. She'd always laid down the law to him, but that didn't mean he always had to obey. The things she was saying were the things he had told himself, over and over again, all through the years. There had been other widows, other only sons, and not all of them became enmeshed in this sort of relationship. It was really his fault as much as hers.

"You could have gone out and found us a new location," she was saying, "then put the place here up for sale. But all you did was whine. And I know why. You never fooled me for an instant. It's because you really didn't *want* to move. You've never wanted to leave this place, and you never will, ever. You *can't* leave, can you? Any more than you can grow up."

The beaded lamp, the heavy old overstuffed furniture, all the familiar objects in the room, suddenly became like the furnishings of a prison cell. He stared out of the window at the wind and the rain and the darkness. He knew there was no escape for him out *there*. No escape anywhere, from the voice that drummed into his ears like that of the Inca corpse in the book: the drum of the dead.

He clutched at the book now and tried to focus his eyes on it. Maybe if he ignored her, and pretended to be calm—

But it didn't work.

"Look at yourself!" Mother went on (*the drum going boom-boom-boom, and the sound reverberating from the mangled mouth*). "I know why you didn't bother to switch on the sign. You didn't really forget. It's just that you don't *want* anyone to come. You hope they *don't* come."

"All right!" he muttered. "I admit it. I hate running a motel, always have."

"It's more than that, boy." (*There it was again, "Boy, boy, boy!" drumming away out of the jaws of death.*) "You hate *people*. Because you're *afraid* of them, aren't you? Ever since you were a little tyke, you'd rather snuggle up in a chair under the lamp and read. And you're still hiding away under the covers of a book. You don't fool me, boy, not for a minute. It isn't as if you were reading the Bible, or even trying to get an education. I know the sort of thing *you* read. Trash. And worse than trash!"

"This happens to be a history of the Inca civilization—"

"And I'll just bet it's crammed full with nasty bits about those dirty savages, like that filthy thing you had about the South Seas. Hiding it up in your room—"

"Psychology isn't filthy, Mother!"

"Psychology, he calls it! I'll never forget that time you talked so dirty to me!"

"But I was only trying to explain something they call the Oedipus situation. I thought if both of us could try to understand the problem, maybe things would change for the better."

"Change, boy? Nothing's going to change. You can read all the books in the world and you'll still be the same. I don't need to listen to a lot of vile rigmarole to know what you are. Why, even an eight-year-old child could recognize it. They *did*, too, all your little playmates way back. Mama's boy. That's what they called you, and that's what you were, are, and always will be. A big, fat, overgrown mama's boy!"

It was deafening him, the drumbeat of her words. In a moment he'd have to cry. To think that she could still do this to him, even now! But she could, and she *would*, over and over again, unless—

"Unless what?"

God, could she read his *mind?*

"I know what you're thinking, boy. You're thinking that you'd like to kill me, aren't you, Norman? But you can't. Because you haven't the gumption. That's why you'll never get rid of me. And deep down, you don't want to. You need me, boy."

Norman stood up, slowly. He didn't dare trust himself to turn and face her, not yet. Be very, very calm, he told himself. Try to remember. *She's an old woman, and not quite right in the head. If you keep on listening to her, you'll end up not quite right in the head, too. Tell her to go back to her room and lie down. That's where she belongs.*

And she'd better go there fast, because if she doesn't, this time you're going to strangle her—

He started to swing around, his mouth working, framing the phrases, when the buzzer sounded.

That was the signal; it meant somebody had driven up to the motel and was ringing for service. Without a word Norman walked into the hall, took his raincoat from the hanger, and went out into the darkness.

Chapter 2

THE rain had been falling steadily for several minutes before Mary noticed it and switched on the windshield wiper. At the same time she put on the headlights; it had gotten dark quite suddenly, and the road ahead was only a blur between the towering trees.

Trees? She couldn't recall a stretch of trees along here the last time she'd driven up from Texas. Of course then she'd come into Fairvale in broad daylight. Now she was tired out from eighteen hours of steady driving, but she could sense that something was wrong. She could remember how she'd hesitated back there a half hour ago at the fork in the road. That was it; she'd taken the wrong turn. And here she was, God knows where, with everything pitch-black outside—

Get a grip on yourself, now. You can't afford to be panicky. The worst part of it is over.

It was true, she told herself. The worst part was over. The worst part had come yesterday afternoon, when she stole the money.

She had been standing in Mr. Lowery's office when old Tommy Cassidy hauled out that big green bundle of bills and put them down on the desk. Thirty-six thousand-dollar bills and eight five-hundreds. Tommy Cassidy put them down just like *that*, fanning forty thousand dollars casually as he announced he was closing the deal and buying a house as his daughter's wedding present.

Mr. Lowery pretended to be just as casual as he signed the final papers. But after old Cassidy went away, Mr. Lowery got a little bit excited. He scooped up the money and put it into a big manila envelope, and sealed the flap. Mary noticed how his hands were trembling.

"Here," he said, handing her the money. "Take it over to the bank. It's almost four o'clock, but I'm sure Gilbert will let you make a deposit." He paused, staring at her. "What's the matter, Miss Crane—don't you feel well?"

Maybe he had noticed the way *her* hands trembled, now that she was holding the envelope. She knew what she was going to say, even though she was surprised when she found herself actually saying it.

"I seem to have one of my headaches, Mr. Lowery. As a matter of fact, I was just going to ask if it was all right if I took the rest of the afternoon off."

Mr. Lowery was in good humor, and why shouldn't he be? Five percent of forty thousand was two thousand dollars. He could afford to be generous.

"Of course, Miss Crane. You just make this deposit and then run along home. See you Monday, then. Take it easy, that's what I always say."

In a pig's ear that's what *he* always said; Lowery would be perfectly willing to kill any of his employees for fifty cents. Mary had smiled at him sweetly, then walked out of his office and out of his life. Taking the forty thousand dollars with her.

You don't get that kind of an opportunity every day. In fact, when you come right down to it, some people don't seem to get *any* opportunities. Mary Crane had waited over twenty-seven years for hers.

The opportunity to go to college had vanished at seventeen, when Daddy was hit by a car. Mary went to business school for a year, instead, and then settled down to support Mom and her kid sister, Lila. The opportunity to marry disappeared at twenty-two, when Dale Belter was called up to serve his hitch in the army. Before long he began mentioning this girl in his letters from Hawaii, and then the letters stopped coming. When she finally got the wedding announcement she didn't care anymore.

Mom was pretty sick by then. It took her three years to die, while Lila was off at college. Mary had insisted Lila get to college, come what may, but between holding down a job all day and sitting up with Mom half the night, Mary was carrying the whole load, and there was no time for anything else.

Then Mom had the final stroke, and there was the business of the funeral, and Lila coming back from school, and all at once there was Mary looking in the big mirror and seeing this drawn, contorted face peering back at her. She'd thrown something at the mirror, and when the mirror broke into a thousand pieces she knew that *she* was breaking into a thousand pieces, too.

Lila had been wonderful, and even Mr. Lowery helped out by seeing to it that the house was sold right away. By the time the estate was settled they had about two thousand dollars in cash left over. Lila got a job in a record shop downtown, and they moved into a small apartment.

"Now you're going to take a real vacation," Lila told her. "You've kept this family going for eight years. I want you to take a trip. A cruise, maybe."

So Mary took the SS *Caledonia,* and after a week or so in Caribbean waters the drawn, contorted face had disappeared from the mirror of her stateroom. She looked like a young girl again. What was more important still, a young girl in love.

It wasn't the wild, surging thing it had been when she met Dale. Sam Loomis was a good ten years older and pretty much on the quiet side, but she loved him. It looked like the first real opportunity until Sam explained a few things.

"I'm sailing under false pretenses, you might say. There's this hardware store, you see. . . ."

Then Sam's story had come out.

There was this hardware store, in a little town called Fairvale, up north. Sam had worked there for his father. A year ago his father had died and Sam had inherited the business, plus about twenty thousand in debts. Sam's father had never told him about his little side investments in the market—or the racetrack. There were only two choices: go into bankruptcy or try to work off the obligations.

Sam Loomis chose to work. "It's a good business," he explained. "I'll never make a fortune, but with any kind of decent management, there's a steady eight or ten thousand a year to be made. Got over four thousand paid off already. I figure another couple of years and I'll be clear."

"But I don't understand—if you're in debt, how can you afford to take a trip like this?"

Sam grinned. "I won it in a contest—a dealer's sales contest.

I tried to settle for cash instead, but they wouldn't go for it. Well, this is a slack month, and I've got an honest clerk working for me. I figured I might as well take a free vacation. So here I am. And here *you* are." He grinned, then sighed. "I wish it was our honeymoon."

"Sam, why *couldn't* it be? I mean—"

But he shook his head. "We'll have to wait until everything is paid off."

"I don't want to wait! I don't care about the money. I could work in your store—"

"And sleep in it, too, the way I do?" He managed a grin again, but it was no more cheerful than the sigh. "That's right. Rigged up a place for myself in the back room. I'm living on baked beans most of the time. Folks say I'm tighter than the town banker, but long as I'm in there pitching, I've got their respect. They go out of their way to trade with me—they appreciate I'm trying to do my best, and I want to keep that reputation. Now that's important for us in the future. Don't you see?"

Mary sighed. "Two years, you said."

"I'm sorry. It isn't easy and it isn't pleasant. But you'll just have to be patient, darling."

So she was patient. But not until she learned that no amount of further persuasion would sway him.

There the situation stood when the cruise ended, and there it had remained for well over a year. Mary had driven up to visit him last summer; she saw the town, the store, the fresh figures in the ledger which showed that Sam had paid off an additional five thousand dollars. "Only eleven thousand to go," he told her proudly. "Another two years, maybe even less."

Two years. She'd be twenty-nine. She couldn't afford to pull a bluff and walk out on him like some girl of twenty. She knew there wouldn't be many more Sam Loomises in her life. So she smiled and went back home to the Lowery Agency and watched old man Lowery buy up shaky mortgages, watched him make quick, cutthroat cash offers to desperate sellers and then turn around and take a fat profit on a fast resale. It wouldn't take *him* two years to sweat out an eleven-thousand-dollar debt. He could sometimes make as much in two months.

Mary hated him, and she hated a lot of the buyers and sellers he did business with, because they were rich, too. This Tommy Cassidy was one of the worst—a big operator, loaded with money from oil leases. He was always dabbling in real estate, bidding low and selling high. He thought nothing of laying down forty thousand dollars in cash to buy his daughter a home for a wedding present. Any more than he thought anything about laying down a hundred-dollar bill on Mary Crane's desk one afternoon about six months ago and suggesting she take a "little trip" with him down to Dallas for the weekend.

It had been done with such a bland and casual smirk that she didn't have time to get angry. Then Mr. Lowery came in, and the matter ended. But she didn't forget. Forty thousand to a daughter for a wedding gift; a hundred dollars tossed carelessly on a desk for three days' rental privileges of the body of Mary Crane.

So I took the forty thousand dollars—

Subconsciously she must have been daydreaming about just such an opportunity for a long time. Because when it came, everything seemed to fall into place, as though part of a preconceived plan. It was Friday afternoon; the banks would be closed for the weekend and that meant Lowery wouldn't get around to checking on her activities until Monday, when she didn't show up at the office.

Better still, Lila had departed early in the morning for Dallas—she did all the buying for the record shop now. And she wouldn't be back until Monday, either.

Mary had driven right to the apartment and packed; just her best clothes in the suitcase and the small overnight bag. She and Lila had three hundred and sixty dollars hidden away in an empty cold-cream jar, but she didn't touch that. Lila would need it when she had to keep up the apartment alone. Mary wished that she could write her sister a note, but she didn't dare. It would be hard for Lila in the days ahead; still there was no help for it now. Maybe later on.

Mary had left the apartment around seven; an hour later she

drove in under an OK USED CARS sign and traded her sedan for a coupe. She lost money on the transaction; lost still more when she repeated the performance in a town four hundred miles north around noon the next morning. This time she found herself in possession of a battered old heap with a crumpled left-front fender, but the important thing was to make fast switches and cover her trail to Fairvale. Once there, how would the authorities trace down the whereabouts of a Mrs. Sam Loomis?

Because she intended to become Mrs. Sam Loomis, and quickly. She'd walk in on Sam with this story about coming into an inheritance. Not forty thousand dollars—that would be too large a sum, and might require too much explanation—maybe she'd say it was fifteen. And she'd tell him Lila had received an equal amount, quit her job, and gone off to Europe. That would explain why there was no sense inviting her to the wedding.

Maybe Sam would balk about taking the money, and certainly there'd be a lot of awkward questions to answer, but she'd get around him. They'd be married at once; that was the important thing. She'd have his name, be Mrs. Sam Loomis, wife of the proprietor of a hardware store in a town eight hundred miles away from the Lowery Agency.

The Lowery Agency didn't even know of Sam's existence. Of course they'd come to Lila, and she'd probably guess right away. But Lila wouldn't say anything—not until she contacted Mary first.

Mary would have to be prepared to handle her sister, keep her quiet in front of Sam and the authorities. It shouldn't be too difficult—Lila owed her that much.

The first step was to reach Fairvale. But it had taken her eighteen hours of cramped contortion, of peering and squinting, of fighting the road and the wheel to get this far. Now she had missed her turn and it was raining; the night had come down and she was lost on a strange road.

Mary glanced into the rearview mirror and caught a dim reflection of her face. Where had she seen that drawn, contorted countenance before?

In the mirror after Mom died, when you went to pieces—

And here, all along, she'd thought of herself as being so cool, so composed. There had been no consciousness of fear, of regret, of guilt. But the mirror told her the truth.

It told her, wordlessly, to stop. *You can't stumble into Sam's arms looking like this, with your face and clothing giving away the story of hasty flight. Sure, your story is that you wanted to surprise him with the good news, but you'll have to look as though you're so happy you couldn't wait.*

The thing to do was to stay over somewhere tonight, get a decent rest, and arrive in Fairvale tomorrow morning, alert and refreshed.

Mary scanned the side of the road through the blur of rainswept darkness, and then jerked erect. She had seen the unlit sign, set beside the driveway which led to the small building on the side of the road: MOTEL—VACANCY.

She drove in, noting that the entire motel was dark, including the glass-front cubicle on the end, which undoubtedly served as an office. She felt her tires roll over one of those electric signal cables. Now she could see the house on the hillside behind the motel; its front windows were lighted. Probably the proprietor, having heard the signal, would come down in a moment.

She switched off the ignition and waited, hearing the sullen patter of the rain on the roof and the sigh of the wind behind it. It had rained like that the day Mom was buried, she remembered, the day they lowered her into that little rectangle of darkness. And now the darkness was here, rising all around Mary. She'd taken the wrong turn and she was on a strange road. No help for it—she'd made her grave and now she must lie in it.

Why did she think that? It wasn't *grave*, it was *bed*.

She was still trying to puzzle it out when the big shadow emerged out of the other shadows and opened her car door.

"LOOKING for a room?"

Mary made up her mind very quickly, once she saw the fat, be-spectacled face and heard the soft, hesitant voice. There wouldn't be any trouble.

She nodded and climbed out of the car. He unlocked the door

of the office, stepped inside the cubicle, and switched on the light and the sign outside.

"Sorry I didn't get down sooner. I've been up at the house—Mother isn't very well."

The office was warm and bright. Mary shivered gratefully and smiled at the fat man. He bent over the ledger on the counter.

"Our rooms are seven dollars, single. Would you like to take a look, first?"

"That won't be necessary." She opened her purse and extracted a five and two singles as he pushed the register forward and held out a pen.

For a moment she hesitated, then wrote a name, "Jane Wilson," and an address, "San Antonio, Texas." She couldn't very well do anything about the Texas plates on the car.

"I'll get your bags," he said. She followed him outside again. The money was in the glove compartment, still in the big envelope. The best thing to do was to lock the car and leave it there.

He carried the bags over to the door of the room next to the office. "Nasty weather," he said, standing aside as she entered. "Have you been driving long?"

"All day."

When he pressed a switch the bedside lamp sent forth yellow petals of light. The room was plainly but adequately furnished; she noted the shower stall in the bathroom beyond. Actually she would have preferred a tub, but this would do.

"Everything all right?"

"Yes, but is there anywhere around here where I can get a bite to eat?"

"There used to be a hamburger stand up the road, but I guess it's closed now. Your best bet would be Fairvale."

"How far away is that?"

"About seventeen, eighteen miles from here." He stood in the doorway, pursing his lips. When she looked up to meet his stare he dropped his eyes and cleared his throat apologetically. "Uh—Miss—I was thinking. Maybe you don't feel like driving all the way to Fairvale and back in this rain. I was just going to fix a little snack for myself up at the house. You'd be perfectly welcome to join me."

"Oh, I couldn't do that."

"Why not? No trouble at all. Mother's gone to bed—I was only going to set out some cold cuts and make some coffee."

"Well . . . thank you very much, Mr.—"

"Bates. Norman Bates." He backed against the door, bumping his shoulder. "Look, I'll leave you this flashlight. You probably want to get out of those wet things first."

He turned away, but not before she caught a glimpse of his reddened face. Why, he was actually *embarrassed!*

For the first time in almost twenty hours Mary Crane smiled. She opened her overnight bag on the bed and took out a dress. Just time to freshen up a bit now, but when she came back she promised herself a good hot shower. First a little food. Let's see—her makeup was in her purse.

Fifteen minutes later she was knocking on the door of the big frame house on the hillside. A single lamp shone from the unshaded parlor window, but a brighter reflection blazed from upstairs. If his mother was ill, that's where she'd be. Maybe he was upstairs, too. She rapped again.

Waiting for a response, she peered through the parlor window. At first glance she couldn't believe what she saw: the floral wallpaper, the dark, heavy, ornately scrolled mahogany woodwork, the Turkey-red carpet, and the high-backed, overstuffed furniture were straight out of the Gay Nineties. There was even an old windup gramophone on an end table.

Now she could detect a low murmur of voices coming from upstairs. Mary knocked again, using the end of the flashlight. The sound ceased abruptly, and a moment later she saw Mr. Bates descending the stairs. He opened the door, gesturing her forward.

"Sorry," he said. "I was just tucking Mother in for the night. Sometimes she's apt to be a bit difficult." Mr. Bates glanced over his shoulder, then lowered his voice. "Actually, she's not *physically* sick. But sometimes she gets these spells. Let me take your coat and hang it up. Now, if you'll come this way . . ."

She followed him down a hallway which extended from under the stairs. "I hope you don't mind eating in the kitchen," he said. "Everything's all ready for us. Sit right down and I'll pour the coffee."

The kitchen was lined with ceiling-high glassed-in cupboards grouped about an old-fashioned sink with a hand pump. The big wood stove squatted in one corner, giving off a grateful warmth, and the round wooden table bore a welcome display of sausage, cheese, and homemade pickles in glass dishes scattered about on the red-and-white checkered cloth. Mary was not inclined to smile at the quaintness of it all, and even the inevitable hand-crocheted motto on the wall seemed appropriate enough.

GOD BLESS OUR HOME.

Mr. Bates helped her fill her plate. "Go right ahead, don't wait for me! You must be hungry."

She ate heartily, with such absorption that she scarcely noticed how little he was eating. When she became aware of it, she was faintly embarrassed.

"But you haven't touched a thing! I'll bet you really had your own supper earlier."

"No, I didn't. It's just that Mother gets me a little upset sometimes." The apologetic note returned. "I guess it's my fault. I'm not too good at taking care of her."

"You live here all alone, the two of you?"

"Yes. There's never been anybody else." He adjusted the rimless spectacles. "My father went away when I was still a baby. There was enough money on Mother's side of the family to keep us going until I grew up. Then she mortgaged the house, sold the farmland, and built this motel. We ran it together, and it was a good thing—until the new highway cut us off. Actually she started failing long before that. And then it was my turn to take care of her. Sometimes it isn't so easy."

"There are no other relatives?"

"None. Not anymore."

"And you've never married?"

His face reddened.

Mary bit her lip. "I didn't mean to ask personal questions."

"That's all right." His voice was faint. "I've never married. Mother was—funny—about those things. I—I've never even sat at a table with a girl like this before. But that's the way it has to be. I tell myself Mother would be lost without me now, but maybe the real truth is that I'd be even more lost without her."

Mary finished her coffee, fished in her purse for cigarettes, and offered one to Mr. Bates.

"No, thank you. I don't smoke." He hesitated. "I'd like to offer you a drink, but—you see—Mother doesn't approve of liquor in the house."

Mary leaned back, inhaling. Suddenly she felt expansive. An hour ago she'd been lonely, wretched, and fearfully unsure of herself. Now everything had changed. Perhaps it was listening to Mr. Bates that had altered her mood. *He* was the lonely, wretched, and fearful one. In contrast, she felt seven feet tall. It was this realization that prompted her to speak.

"You aren't allowed to smoke. You aren't allowed to drink. You aren't allowed to see any girls. Just what *do* you do, Mr. Bates, besides run the motel and attend to your mother?" she asked.

Apparently he was unconscious of her tone of voice. "Oh, I read quite a bit, and then I've got lots of hobbies." He glanced up at a wall shelf and she followed his gaze. A stuffed squirrel peered down at them.

"Hunting?"

"Well, no. Just taxidermy. George Blount gave me that squirrel to stuff. He shot it. Mother doesn't want me to handle firearms."

"Mr. Bates, you'll pardon me for saying this, but how long do you intend to go on this way? You must realize that you can't be expected to act like a little boy all your life."

"I understand. I know what the psychologists say about such things. But I have a duty toward my mother."

"Wouldn't you be fulfilling that duty to her, and to yourself as well, if you arranged to put her in an—institution?"

"She's not crazy!"

Suddenly his voice was high and shrill, and he was on his feet, his hands sweeping a cup from the table. It shattered on the floor, but Mary could only stare into the shattered face.

"She's not crazy," he repeated. "Those doctors out at the asylum would certify her in a hurry and lock her away. All I'd have to do is give them the word. But I wouldn't, because I *know* and they don't. They don't know how she took care of me all those years, how she worked for me and suffered because of me, the sacrifices she made. If she's a little odd now, I'm responsible. When she told me she wanted to get married again, I stopped her. Yes, I was to blame for that! You don't have to tell me about jealousy, possessiveness—I was worse than she could ever be. Ten times crazier, if that's the word you want to use. They'd have locked *me* up in a minute, if they knew the way I carried on. Who are you to say a person should be put away? I think perhaps all of us go a little crazy at times."

He stopped, not because he was out of words but because he was out of breath. His face was very red, and his lips were beginning to tremble.

Mary stood up. "I'm—I'm sorry," she said softly. "I had no right to say what I did."

"It doesn't matter. It's just that I'm not used to talking about these things. You live alone like this, and everything gets bottled up, or stuffed, like that squirrel there." He attempted a smile. "Cute little fellow, isn't he?"

Mary picked up her purse. "It's getting late."

"Please don't go. I was going to tell you about my hobbies. I've got a sort of a workshop down in the basement—"

"I'd like to stay, but I simply must get some rest."

"I'll walk down with you. I've got to close up the office. It doesn't look as if there'll be any more business tonight."

He helped her on with her coat. He was clumsy about it, and she realized the cause. He was afraid to touch her. The poor guy was actually afraid to get near a woman!

He held the flashlight and she followed him down to the gravel drive curving around the motel. The rain had stopped, but the night was dark and starless. Mary glanced back over her shoulder at the house. The upstairs light still burned, and she wondered if the old woman had listened to their conversation, heard the final outburst.

Mr. Bates halted before her door, waited until she opened it. "Good night," he said. "Sleep well."

"Thank you. And thanks for the hospitality." She closed her door and locked it. She could hear his retreating footsteps, the telltale click as he entered the office next door.

She didn't hear him leave; her attention had been immediately occupied with unpacking and rummaging through the big suitcase for the dress she planned to wear tomorrow, when she saw Sam. That would have to be put up, to hang out the wrinkles. Nothing must be out of place tomorrow.

Nothing must be out of place—

All at once she didn't feel seven feet tall anymore. Or was the change really so sudden? Hadn't it started with what Mr. Bates had said when he got so hysterical?

I think perhaps all of us go a little crazy at times.

Yes. It was true. All of us do go a little crazy at times. Just as she'd gone crazy yesterday afternoon, when she saw that money on the desk. She *must* have been crazy, to think she could get away with what she planned. Maybe she could manage to throw off the police. But Sam would ask questions. *Who* was this relative she'd inherited the money from? How was it that she brought the money along in cash?

And then there was Lila. Suppose she reacted as Mary anticipated and kept silent from a sense of obligation. The fact remained that Lila would *know*. And sooner or later Sam would want to meet her. She could never explain to Sam why she wouldn't go back to Texas even for a visit.

No, the whole thing was crazy. And it was too late to do anything about it now.

Or—*was it?*

Suppose she got herself a good long ten hours of sleep. Tomorrow was Sunday; if she left here about nine and drove straight through, she could be back in town Monday morning, before the bank opened.

She could deposit the money and go on to work. There was the matter of the car, of course. Maybe she could tell Lila that she'd started out for Fairvale, intending to surprise Sam over the weekend. The car broke down and she had to have it towed away—the dealer said it would need a new engine, so she decided to junk it, take this old heap instead, and come back home. Yes, that would sound reasonable.

Mary stood up.

She'd do it.

And all at once she was seven feet tall again. It was *that* simple.

She had a curious sense that everything that had happened was somehow *fated* to be. Her turning off on the wrong road, coming here, meeting that pathetic man, listening to his outburst, hearing that final sentence which brought her to her senses.

She giggled. It was nice to be seven feet tall, but right now she was going to take a nice hot shower. Get the dirt off her hide. *Come clean, Mary. Come clean as snow.*

She kicked off her shoes, stepped into the bathroom, pulled the dress over her head. She unhooked her bra and let it sail into the next room.

For a moment she stood before the mirror set in the door and took stock of herself. She had a good figure. Sam would like it. It was going to be hell to wait another two years. But she'd make up for lost time.

Mary giggled again and tossed her image a kiss. Then she stepped into the shower stall, turned both faucets on full force and let the warmth gush over her. The roar was deafening, and the room was beginning to steam up.

With the water running, she didn't hear the door open or note the sound of footsteps. And at first, when the shower curtains parted, the steam obscured the face.

Then she *did* see it there—hanging in midair like a mask. A head scarf concealed the hair, and the glassy eyes stared inhumanly, but it wasn't a mask, it couldn't be. The skin had been powdered dead white, and two hectic spots of rouge centered on the cheekbones. It wasn't a mask. It was the face of a crazy old woman.

As Mary started to scream the curtains parted further and a hand appeared, holding a butcher knife. It was the knife that, a moment later, cut off her scream.

And her head.

Chapter 3

THE minute Norman left Mary at her door and got inside the office he started to tremble. Too much had happened too quickly. He couldn't bottle it up any longer.

Bottle. That's what he needed—a drink. Mother wouldn't allow liquor in the house, but he kept a bottle here at the office. There were times when you had to drink, even if a few ounces were enough to make you dizzy, make you pass out. There were times when you *wanted* to pass out.

Norman remembered to pull down the venetian blinds and switch off the sign outside. Closed for the night. Now that the blinds were down, nobody could look in and see him opening the desk drawer and pulling out the bottle, his hands trembling like a baby's. *Baby needs his bottle.*

He tilted the pint back and drank. The warmth crept down his throat, exploded in his stomach. Maybe another drink would burn away the taste of fear.

It had been a mistake to invite the girl up to the house. He never would have dared, except that he'd been so angry with Mother. But he had done something far worse when he'd marched right up to the bedroom and told Mother he was having company, as much as to say, "I dare you to do something about it!"

She practically had hysterics. The things she said! "If you bring her here, I'll kill her! I'll kill the bitch!" The way she carried on—Mother was sick, very sick.

The whiskey burned. His third drink, but he needed it. Just getting through the meal had been an ordeal. He'd been afraid Mother would make a scene. After he locked the door to her room and left her up there he was afraid she'd start screaming and pounding. But she had kept very quiet, almost too quiet, as though she was listening. You could lock Mother up, but you couldn't keep her from listening.

Norman hoped she'd gone to sleep by now. Tomorrow she might forget the whole episode. Then he heard a sound, and he shifted quickly in his chair. Was Mother coming? No, she couldn't be. It must be that girl, in the next room, getting ready for bed. Yes, he could hear her now.

Norman took another drink. And this time it worked. His hand wasn't trembling anymore. He wasn't afraid. Not if he thought about the girl.

Funny, when he actually saw her he had this terrible feeling of—what was the word? *Im*-something. *Im*portance. No, he didn't feel important when he was with a woman. He felt—*im*possible? That wasn't right, either. He knew the word he was looking for, he'd read it a hundred times in the kind of books Mother didn't even know he owned.

Well, it didn't matter. When he was with the girl he felt that way, but not now. Now he could do anything.

And there were so many things he wanted to do with a girl so young, pretty, intelligent. He wished she would have stayed and talked more. As it was, tomorrow she'd be gone forever. He could fall in love with a girl like that, just seeing her a single time. But she'd laugh, probably. That's the way girls were—they always laughed.

Mother was right about them. But you *had* to see this girl again. If you were any kind of a man, you'd have told her so when you were in her room. You'd have brought in the bottle and drunk with her, and then you'd carry her over to the bed and—

No, you wouldn't. Not *you*. Because you *couldn't*, and that's why the girls always laughed.

Norman took another drink, just a sip. *Impotent*. That was the word he couldn't remember! Impotent, was he? Well, that didn't mean he couldn't see her again.

He was going to see her, right now.

Then he bent forward across the desk, his head almost touching the wall. He'd heard more sounds. And from long experience he knew how to interpret them. The girl had kicked off her shoes. Now she was in the bathroom.

He reached out his hand. It was trembling, but this time not with fear. This was anticipation; he was going to tilt the framed license on the wall to one side and peek through the little hole he'd drilled so long ago. Nobody else knew about the little hole, not even Mother. Most certainly not Mother.

The little hole was just a crack in the plaster on the other side, but he could see through it into the lighted bathroom. Sometimes he'd catch a person standing right in front of it. Sometimes he'd catch their reflection on the door mirror beyond. It was hard for Norman to focus his eyes. He felt hot and dizzy. He must be drunk. But most of it was due to her. She *was* in the bathroom, facing the wall. Now she was standing before the mirror, swaying back and forth, back and forth.

He couldn't stand it, he wanted to pound on the wall, he wanted to scream at the bitch to stop.

Then suddenly she was gone, and there was only the roaring. It welled up, shaking the wall, drowning out the words and the thoughts. It was coming from inside his head, and he fell back in the chair. *I'm drunk,* he told himself. *I'm passing out.*

But that was not entirely so. The roaring continued, and somewhere inside it he heard another sound. The office door was opening. How could that be? He'd locked it, and he still had the key. If only he'd open his eyes, he could find it. But he didn't dare. Because now he knew.

Mother had a key, too.

She had a key to her room. She had a key to the house. She had a key to the office.

And she was standing there now, looking down at him. He hoped she would think he had just fallen asleep. What was she doing here, anyway? Had she heard him leave with the girl, come down to spy on him?

Norman slumped back, not daring to move, not wanting to move. Every instant it was getting harder and harder to move, even if he *had* wanted to. The roaring had become steady now, and the vibration was rocking him to sleep. That was nice. To be rocked to sleep, with Mother standing over you . . .

Then she was gone. She'd turned around without saying anything and gone out. There was nothing to be afraid of. She'd come to protect him. Whenever he needed her, Mother was there to protect him. And now he could sleep. There was no trick to it at all. You merely went into the roaring, and then *past* the roaring. Then everything was silent.

NORMAN came to with a start, jerking his head back. God, it ached! He'd actually passed out there in the chair. No wonder everything was pounding, roaring. *Roaring.* He'd heard the same sound before.

Now he recognized it. The shower was going next door. But that had been so long ago—an hour, two hours? The girl couldn't *still* be in there, could she?

He reached forward, tilting the framed license on the wall. His eyes squinted, then focused on the brightly lit bathroom beyond. It was empty. He couldn't see into the shower stall on the side. The curtains were closed.

Maybe she'd forgotten about the shower and gone to bed, leaving it turned on. It seemed odd that she'd be able to sleep with the water running full force, but anyway, there didn't seem to be anything wrong. The bathroom was in order. Norman scanned it again, then noticed the floor.

Water from the shower was trickling across the tiles. Or was it water? Water isn't *pink.* Water doesn't have tiny threads of red in it, tiny threads of red like veins.

She must have slipped and hurt herself, Norman decided. The panic was rising in him, but he knew what he must do. He grabbed up his keys from the desk and hurried out of the office. Quickly he found the right one for the adjoining unit and opened the door. The bedroom was empty, but the open suitcase still rested on the bed itself. So he'd guessed correctly; there had been an accident in the shower. He'd have to go in there.

It wasn't until he actually entered the bathroom that he remembered something else, and then it was too late. The panic in him burst loose.

Mother had keys to the motel, too.

As he ripped back the shower curtains and stared down at the hacked and twisted thing sprawled on the floor of the stall, he realized that Mother had used her keys.

NORMAN locked the door behind him and went up to the house. His clothes were a mess. Blood on them, and water, and then he'd been sick all over the bathroom floor.

But that wasn't important now. There were other things which must be cleaned up first. This time he was going to put Mother where she belonged. All the panic, all the fear, all the horror and nausea and revulsion, gave way to this overriding resolve. What had happened was dreadful beyond words, but it would never happen again. He felt like a new man—his own man.

Norman hurried up the steps and tried the front door. It was unlocked. He gave a quick glance around the empty parlor, then mounted the stairs.

The door to Mother's room stood open, and lamplight fanned forth into the hall. He stepped in, not bothering to knock. She couldn't get away with this.

But she had.

The bedroom was empty.

He could see the rumpled indentation where she had lain, see the covers flung back on the big four-poster; smell the faint, musty scent still in the room. The rocker stood in the corner, the ornaments were arranged on the dresser just as always. Nothing had changed in Mother's room; nothing ever changed. But Mother was gone.

He stepped over to the closet, ruffling the clothing on the hangers. Here the musty scent was so strong he almost choked, but there was another odor, too. It wasn't until his foot slipped that he looked down and realized where it was coming from. A dress and a head scarf were balled up on the floor. He stooped to retrieve them, then shivered in revulsion as he noted the dark, reddish stains of clotted blood.

She'd come back here, then; come back, changed her clothes, and gone off once more.

He couldn't call the police.

That was the thing he had to remember. He mustn't call the police. Not even now, knowing what she had done. Because she wasn't really responsible. You aren't really a murderer when you're sick in the head. Anybody knows that. Only sometimes the courts didn't agree. And even if they did recognize what was wrong with her, they'd still put her away. Not in a rest home, but in one of those awful holes. A state hospital. No matter what she'd done, she didn't deserve *that*.

Norman stared at the neat, old-fashioned room with its wallpaper pattern of rambler roses. He couldn't take Mother away from this and see her locked up in a bare cell. Right now he was safe—the police didn't even know about Mother. She stayed here, in the house, and *nobody* knew. It had been all right to tell the girl, because she'd never see him again.

And he was pretty certain, now, that he could keep anyone from knowing. All he had to do was think over the events of the evening carefully.

The girl had driven in alone, said she'd been on the road all day. That meant she wasn't visiting *en route*. And she didn't seem to know where Fairvale was, didn't mention any other towns nearby, so the chances were whoever expected her—if anyone *was* expecting her—must live some distance farther north. She had signed the register, of course, but if anybody ever asked, he'd just say that she had spent the night and driven on.

All he had to do was get rid of the body and the car, and make sure that everything was cleaned up afterward. That part would be easy. He knew just how to do it. And it would save him from going to the police. It would save Mother.

Oh, he still intended to have things out with her—he wasn't backing down on that part of it—but this could wait until afterward. The big thing now was to dispose of the evidence.

Norman took Mother's wadded dress and scarf and carried them downstairs. He grabbed an old shirt and a pair of coveralls from the hook in the back hallway, then shed his bloodstained clothing in the kitchen, and donned the others. No sense stopping to wash up now—that could wait until the rest of the messy business was completed.

But Mother had remembered to wash when she came back. He could see more of the pink stains here at the kitchen sink, telltale traces of rouge and powder. He made a mental note to clean everything thoroughly when he got back. Norman went down into the basement and opened the door of the old fruit cellar. He found what he was looking for—a discarded clothes hamper with a sprung cover. It would do nicely.

Nicely—God, how can you think like that about what you're proposing to do?

He winced at the realization, then took a deep breath. This was no time to be self-conscious or self-critical. One had to be very careful, very calm.

Calmly, he tossed his clothes into the hamper. Calmly, he took an old oilcloth from the table near the cellar stairs. Calmly, he went back upstairs, snapped off the kitchen light, snapped off the hall light, and let himself out of the house in darkness, carrying the hamper with the oilcloth on top.

It was harder to be calm here in the dark. Harder not to think about a hundred and one things that might go wrong.

Mother had wandered off—where? Was she out on the highway, ready to be picked up by anyone who might come driving by? Would the shock of what she had done cause her to blurt out the truth? Had she actually run away, or was she merely in a daze? Maybe she'd gone down past the woods back of the house, along the narrow ten-acre strip of their land which stretched off into the swamp. Wouldn't it be better to search for her first?

No, he couldn't afford the risk. Not while that thing still sprawled in the shower stall. Leaving it there was even more risky. He'd turned off all the lights, but every once in a while some night owl would ring the buzzer at one or two o'clock in the morning, looking for accommodations.

He stumbled along in the pitch-blackness of moonless midnight.

If only it weren't so dark! He was very grateful when he finally opened the door of the girl's room, eased the hamper inside, and switched on the light. The soft glow reassured him for a moment, until he remembered what the light would reveal when he went into the bathroom. He began to tremble.

No, I can't do it. I can't look at her. I won't go in there. I won't!

But you have to. There's no other way. And stop talking to yourself!

He had to get back that calm feeling again. He had to face reality.

And what was reality? The girl his mother had killed. Walking away wouldn't bring the girl back to life again. Turning Mother in to the police wouldn't help alter the situation. The best thing to do under the circumstances, the *only* thing to do, was to get rid of her. He needn't feel guilty about it.

But he couldn't hold back his nausea, his dizziness, when it came to actually going into the shower stall and doing what must be done there. He found the butcher knife almost at once. He dropped *that* into the hamper immediately. There was an old pair of gloves in his coverall pockets; he had to put them on before he could bring himself to touch the rest. The head was the worst. Nothing else was severed, only slashed, and he had to fold the limbs before he could wrap the body in the oilcloth, crowd it down into the hamper, and slam the lid shut. Now he had to lug the hamper out into the bedroom, then put it down while he found the girl's purse and car keys.

He opened the door slowly, scanning the road for passing headlights. He could only pray that nothing would come now.

Sweating with fear, he managed to unlock the trunk of the car and place the hamper inside. Then, back in the room again, he picked up the girl's clothing and shoved it into the overnight bag and the big suitcase on the bed. Now what? Kleenex, hairpins, all the little things a woman leaves scattered around the room. He wanted to get rid of everything fast, while luck still held.

He put the two bags in the car, on the front seat. Then he closed and locked the door of the room. Again he scanned the roadway in both directions. All clear.

Norman started the motor and switched on the car lights. That was the dangerous part, using the lights. But he'd never be able to make it otherwise through the field. He drove slowly, up the slope behind the motel and along the gravel leading to the driveway and the house. Another stretch of gravel went to the rear of the house and terminated at the old shed which served as a garage for his Chevy.

He shifted gears and eased off into the field, bumping along. There was a rutted road here, worn by tire tracks. Every few months Norman took his car along this route, hitching up the trailer and going into the woods bordering the swamp to collect firewood for the kitchen.

That's what he'd do tomorrow, he decided. First thing in the morning. Then his own tire marks would cover up the marks he was making now. And if he left footprints in the mud, there'd be an explanation. If he *needed* an explanation. But maybe his luck would hold.

It held long enough for him to reach the edge of the swamp and do what he had to do. Starting the motor and shifting into reverse, he jumped out and let it back down the slope into the muddy quagmire. The slope would show tire tracks, too, and he must remember to smooth away the traces.

He could see the muck bubbling and rising up over the wheels. God, it had to keep sinking now; if it didn't, he could never pull it out again. It *had* to sink!

Now the fenders were going under very slowly. How long had he been standing here? It seemed like hours, and still the car was visible. But the ooze had reached the door handles; it was coming up over the side glass and the windshield. There wasn't a sound to be heard. The car kept descending, inch by silent inch. At last only the top was visible. Suddenly there was a sort of sucking noise, a nasty and abrupt *plop!* And the car was gone. It had settled beneath the surface of the swamp.

He turned away with a grimace. Well, that part of it was finished. The car was in the swamp. And the hamper was in the trunk. And the twisted torso and the bloody head—

But he couldn't think about *that*. He *mustn't*. There were other things to do.

He did them almost mechanically. There was soap and detergent in the office, a brush and a pail. He went over the bathroom inch by inch, then the shower stall. As long as he concentrated on scrubbing, it wasn't so bad.

Then he inspected the bedroom once more. Luck was still with him; just under the bed he found an earring. The other one would be around somewhere. Norman was bleary-eyed and weary, but he searched. It wasn't anywhere in the room, so it must either be in her baggage or still attached to her ear. In either case, it wouldn't matter. Just as long as he threw this one in the swamp tomorrow.

Now there was only the kitchen sink to scrub out.

It was almost two o'clock by the grandfather clock in the hall when he went back to the house. He could scarcely keep his eyes open long enough to wash the stains from the sink top. Then he stepped out of his muddy shoes and coveralls, stripped himself, and washed. The water was cold as ice, but it didn't revive him. His body was numb.

There now. No blood on his clothes, no blood on his body, no blood on his hands. He had even scoured the kitchen sink. He could fall into bed and sleep. With clean hands.

It wasn't until he was actually donning his pajamas that he remembered.

Mother hadn't come back! She was still wandering around, God knows where, in the middle of the night.

He had to get dressed again and go out, he had to find her. Or—did he?

The thought came stealing over his senses there in the silken silence. Why should *he* concern himself about Mother? Maybe she had been picked up. Maybe she'd even babble out what she'd done. But who'd believe it? There was no evidence anymore. All he'd need to do was deny everything. Maybe he wouldn't even have to do that much—anyone who saw Mother, listened to her wild story, would know she was crazy. And then they'd lock her up in a place where she didn't have a key and couldn't get out again, and that would be the end.

He hadn't felt like that earlier this evening, he remembered. But that was before he had to go into the shower stall and see those—*things*.

Mother had done that to the poor, helpless girl. She had taken a butcher knife and she had hacked and ripped—nobody but a maniac could have committed such an atrocity. He had to face facts. She was a maniac. She *deserved* to be put away, for her own safety as well as the safety of others.

If they did pick her up, he'd see that it happened.

But the chances were, actually, that she didn't go anywhere near the highway. Most likely she had stayed right around the house, or the yard. Maybe she had even followed him down into the swamp; she could have been watching him all the time. If she *had* gone to the swamp, perhaps she'd slipped into the quicksand. It was quite possible, there in the dark. He remembered the way the car had gone down.

Norman knew he wasn't thinking clearly anymore. He was faintly aware of the fact that he had been lying on the bed for a long time now. And he wasn't really deciding what to do or wondering where Mother was. Instead, he was *watching* her. He could *see* her now, even though his eyelids were closed.

He could see Mother, and she *was* in the swamp. That's where she was, in the swamp, and she couldn't get out again. The muck was bubbling up around her knees, she was trying to grab a branch, pull herself out again, but it was no use. Her hips were sinking under, her dress was pressed tight across her thighs.

He *wanted* to see her go down, down into the wet, slimy darkness. She deserved to go down, to join that poor, innocent girl. Now the scum had reached her breasts; he could see her gasping for breath, and it made him gasp, too; he felt as if he were choking with her, and then (*it was a dream, it had to be a dream!*) Mother was suddenly standing on the firm ground at the edge of the swamp and it was *he* who was sinking in filth up to his neck and who had nothing to hang on to unless Mother held out her arms. *She* could save him, she was the only one! He didn't want to go down the way the girl had gone down.

And then he remembered why the girl was there; it was because she had been killed, and she had been killed because she was evil. She had flaunted herself before him; she had deliberately tempted him. Why, he'd wanted to kill her himself when she did that, because Mother had taught him about evil and the ways of evil. So what Mother had done was to protect *him*, and even if she was crazy she wouldn't let him go under now. She *couldn't*.

Now the foul mud was sucking against his throat, and he was screaming, "*Mother, Mother—save me!*"

And then he was out of the swamp, back here in bed where he belonged, and his body was wet only with perspiration. It had been a dream, after all.

"It's all right, son," Mother was saying. "I'm here. Everything's all right." He could feel her hand on his forehead. He wanted to open his eyes, but she said, "Just go back to sleep, son."

"But I have to tell you—"

"I know. I was watching. You didn't think I'd go away and leave you, did you? You did right, Norman."

Yes. That was the way it should be. She was there to protect him. He was there to protect her. They wouldn't talk about what had happened tonight—not ever. And he wouldn't think about sending her away. Maybe she was crazy, but she was all he had. All he wanted. All he needed. Just knowing she was here, beside him, as he went to sleep.

Norman stirred, turned, and then fell into a darkness deeper and more engulfing than the swamp.

Chapter 4

AT SIX o'clock on the following Friday evening Ottorino Respighi's "Brazilian Impressions" was coming over the FM radio in the back room of Fairvale's only hardware store. For a moment Sam Loomis wished that he weren't alone. Music is meant to be shared. But there was no one in Fairvale who would recognize either the music itself or the miracle of its coming. In Fairvale music was just something you got when you put a nickel in the jukebox.

Sam Loomis shrugged, then grinned. Maybe small-town people didn't dig his sort of music, but at least they left him the freedom to enjoy it for himself.

Sam pulled out the big ledger and carried it over to the kitchen table. It looked very much as if he might be able to pay off another thousand this month. That would bring the total up to three thousand for the half-year mark. And this was the off-season, too. Sam scribbled a hasty figure-check on a sheet of scratch paper. Yes, he could probably swing it. Made him feel pretty good. And it ought to make Mary feel pretty good, too.

Mary hadn't been too cheerful, lately. At least her letters sounded as if she were depressed. Well, he didn't blame her. She'd been sweating things out for a long time. Come to think of it, she owed him several letters now. Maybe he ought to take a few days off next week, leave his clerk, Bob Summerfield, in charge here, and drop in and surprise her, cheer her up. Why not? Things were slack at the moment, and Bob could handle the store alone.

The music was spiraling to a minor key. Sam sighed. Chances were, Mary didn't like this kind of music. Sometimes he almost wondered if they hadn't made a mistake when they planned ahead. After all, what did they really know about each other? Aside from the cruise and the two days Mary had spent here last year, they'd never been together.

There were the letters, of course. But in her letters Sam had begun to find another Mary—a moody, almost petulant personality, given to emphatic likes and dislikes.

He shrugged. What had come over him? Was it the morbidity of the music? All at once he felt tension in the muscles at the back of his neck. He listened intently. Something was wrong. Something he could almost hear.

Sam rose. He could hear it now. As he pushed back his chair a faint rattling noise came from the front of the store. Somebody was turning the knob of the front door.

The store was closed for the night and the shades drawn. Maybe it was some tourist—if folks in town wanted anything after regular hours, they'd phone first.

Sam went hurrying down the dim aisle. He could hear the agitated rattling of the doorknob very plainly now. This must be an emergency. "All right," he called. "I'm coming."

He unlocked the door and swung it back. She stood there, silhouetted against the streetlamp's glow. For a moment the shock of recognition held him immobile; then he stepped forward and his arms closed around her.

"Mary!" he murmured. His mouth found hers greedily; but she was stiffening, her hands pushing against his chest.

"I'm not Mary!" she gasped. "I'm Lila."

"Lila?" He stepped back once more. "Mary's sister?"

She nodded and he caught a glimpse of her profile against the streetlight. Now he could see the difference in the shape of the snub nose, the higher angle of the broad cheekbones. She was a trifle shorter, too, and her shoulders seemed slimmer.

"I'm sorry," he murmured. "It's this light."

"That's all right." Her voice was different, too; softer and lower than Mary's.

"Come inside, won't you?" Sam scooped up her small suitcase. "My room is in back," he told her. "Follow me."

Respighi's tone poem still resounded from the radio when they entered Sam's makeshift living quarters. As he went toward the radio she lifted her hand. "Don't switch it off," she told him. "I'm trying to recognize that music." She nodded. "Villa-Lobos?"

"Respighi. Something called 'Brazilian Impressions.'" He remembered that Lila worked in a record shop.

"Now turn it off. We'd better talk."

He nodded, bent over the set, then faced her. "Please sit down," he invited her. "Take off your coat. You're here on a visit?"

"Just overnight. And it isn't exactly a visit. I'm looking for Mary."

"Looking for—" Sam stared at her. "But what would she be doing here?"

"I was hoping you could tell me that."

"But how could I? Mary isn't here."

"*Was* she here? Earlier this week, I mean?"

"I haven't seen her since she drove up last summer." Sam sat down on the sofa bed. "What's this all about?"

"I wish I knew."

She avoided his gaze, lowering her lashes and staring at her hands. In the brighter light Sam noticed that her hair was almost blond. She didn't resemble Mary at all now. She was quite another girl. A nervous, unhappy girl.

"Please," he said. "Tell me what's happened."

Lila looked up, her wide hazel eyes searching his. "You weren't lying when you said Mary hasn't been here?"

"No, it's the truth. I haven't even heard from her these last few weeks. I was beginning to get worried. Then you come bursting in here and—" His voice broke. "Tell me!"

She took a deep breath. "I haven't seen Mary since a week ago last night, at the apartment. That's the night I left for Dallas. I do the buying for the record shop. I got back early Monday morning. Mary wasn't at the apartment. At first I wasn't concerned; I decided to call her at the office around noon. Mr. Lowery answered the phone. He said he was just getting ready to call me and see what was wrong. Mary hadn't come in that morning. He hadn't seen or heard from her since the middle of Friday afternoon."

"Wait a minute. Let me get this straight. Today's Friday. Are you trying to tell me that Mary has been missing for an entire week?" Sam said slowly.

"I'm afraid so."

"Then why didn't you get in touch with me?" He stood up, feeling the tension in his throat. "What about the police?"

"Sam, I—"

"Why did you wait all this time? It doesn't make sense!"

"After what Mr. Lowery told me, I agreed not to call the police. And Mr. Lowery doesn't know about *you*. But I was so worried that I had to find out for myself. That's why I decided to drive up here. I thought maybe the two of you might have planned it together."

"Planned what?" Sam shouted.

"That's what I'd like to know." The voice of the man standing in the doorway was soft, but there was nothing soft about his face. He was tall, thin, and deeply tanned; a gray stetson shadowed his forehead. The eyes were ice-blue and ice-hard.

"Who are you?" Sam demanded. "How did you get in?"

"Front door was unlocked. I came here to get a little information about Mary Crane, but I see that her sister has beat me to it." The tall man moved forward, one hand dipping into the pocket of his gray jacket, extending an open wallet. "Milton Arbogast. Licensed investigator, representing Parity Mutual. We carry a bonding policy on the Lowery Agency your girl friend worked for. I'm here to find out what you two did with the forty thousand dollars."

THE gray stetson was on the table now, and the gray jacket was draped over the back of one of Sam's chairs. Arbogast snubbed out his third cigarette in the ashtray.

"All right," he said. "So you didn't leave Fairvale any time during the past week. I'll buy that, Loomis. You'd know better than to lie. Of course, that doesn't prove Mary Crane hasn't been to see *you*. She could have sneaked in some evening after your store closed, just like her sister did tonight."

Sam sighed. "But she didn't. I haven't even heard from Mary for weeks. I wrote her a letter last Friday, the very day she's supposed to have disappeared. Why would I do a thing like that, if I knew she was going to come here?"

"To cover up, of course. Very smart move."

Sam rubbed the back of his neck. "I'm not that smart. I didn't know about the money. The way you've explained it, not even Mr. Lowery knew in advance that somebody was going to bring him forty thousand dollars in cash on Friday afternoon. How could we possibly have planned anything together?"

"She could have phoned you from a pay station *after* she took the money, on Friday night, and told you to write her."

"Check with the phone company," Sam answered. "You'll find I haven't had any long-distance calls for a month."

Arbogast nodded. "So she drove straight up, told you what had

313

happened, and made a date to meet you later, when things cooled down a bit."

Lila bit her lip. "My sister's not a criminal. You have no right to talk about her that way. You have no proof that my sister took the money. Maybe Mr. Lowery took it himself and cooked up this whole story, just to cover up—"

"Sorry," Arbogast murmured. "You can't make him your patsy. Unless we discover what happened to the money, our company doesn't pay off—and Lowery is out forty grand. So he couldn't profit from the deal in any way. And Mary Crane has been missing ever since the afternoon she received that money. She didn't take it to the bank. She didn't hide it in the apartment. Her car is gone. And she's gone. It all adds up."

Lila began to sob softly. "No, it doesn't! I let you and Mr. Lowery talk me out of calling the police. Because you said maybe if we waited, Mary would decide to bring the money back. But Mary didn't take that money. Somebody must have kidnapped her. Somebody who knew about it . . ."

Arbogast rose wearily, walked over to the girl, patted her shoulder. "Listen, Miss Crane, we've been through this before. Your sister wasn't kidnapped. She went home and packed her bags, then drove off alone in her own car. Didn't your landlady see her go off? Be reasonable."

"I *am* reasonable! You're the one who doesn't make sense! Following me up here to see Mr. Loomis . . ."

The investigator shook his head. "What makes you think I followed you?" he asked quietly.

"How else did you happen to come here tonight? You didn't know that Mary and Sam Loomis were engaged. Outside of me, no one else knew."

Arbogast shook his head. "I knew. When I looked through your sister's desk I came across this envelope." He flourished it.

"Why, it's addressed to me." Sam rose to reach for it.

Arbogast drew his hand away. "There's no letter inside, just the envelope with your name and address. But I can use it, because it's in her handwriting." He paused. "As a matter of fact, I *have* been using it, ever since Wednesday morning when I started out for Fairvale."

"You started out for here—on *Wednesday?*" Lila dabbed at her eyes with a handkerchief.

"That's right. I wasn't following you. The envelope gave me a lead. That, plus Loomis' picture in the frame next to your sister's bed. 'With all my love—Sam.' Easy enough to figure out the connection. So I put myself in your sister's place. I've just laid my hands on forty thousand dollars in cash. I've got to get out of town, fast. Where do I go? Canada, Mexico? Too risky. Besides, I haven't had time to make long-range plans. My natural impulse would be to come straight to lover boy, here."

Sam hit the kitchen table hard. "That's about enough! You haven't offered one word of proof to back up any of this."

Arbogast fumbled for another cigarette. "You want proof, eh? Wednesday morning I found the car."

"You found my sister's car?" Lila was on her feet.

"Sure. I had a hunch that she'd ditch it, so I called around town, to all the used-car lots, giving a description and the license number. It paid off. I found the place. The dealer talked fast—guess he thought the car was hot. Turned out that Mary Crane made a fast trade with him on Friday night, just before closing time. Took a beating on the deal, too. I got a full description of the car she drove out with. Heading north.

"So I headed north, too. I was playing one hunch—that she'd stick to the highway, because she was coming here. I spent a lot of time around Oklahoma City, checking motels and used-car places along the way. I figured she might switch again, just to be on the safe side.

"But no dice. Thursday I got up as far as Tulsa. Same results. It wasn't until this morning when the needle turned up in the haystack. Another dealer, just north of there. She made the second trade last Saturday morning—took a shellacking—and ended up with a blue 1953 Plymouth, with a bad front fender."

He took a notebook from his pocket. "It's all down here in black and white," he said. "Title dope, engine number. And this is the place Mary Crane was heading for. Unless the car broke down or there was an accident, she should have arrived here late last Saturday night."

"But she didn't," Sam said. "Last Saturday night I was over at the Legion Hall, playing cards. Plenty of witnesses. Sunday morning I went to church. Sunday noon I had dinner at—"

Arbogast raised a hand. "Okay, you didn't see her. So something must have happened. I'll start checking back."

"What about the police?" Lila asked. "Suppose there *was* an accident—you couldn't stop at every hospital between here and Tulsa. Why, for all we know, Mary may be lying unconscious somewhere right now. . . ."

Sam patted her shoulder. "Nonsense. Mary's all right. If anything like that had happened, you'd have been notified." But he glared over Lila's head at the investigator. "You can't do a thorough job all alone," he said. "Report Mary missing; see if the police can locate her."

Arbogast picked up the gray stetson. "If we could locate her without dragging in the authorities, we might save Mr. Lowery a lot of bad publicity. We could save Mary Crane some grief, too, if we picked her up ourselves and recovered the money. Maybe there wouldn't be any charges that way. Wait another twenty-four hours," Arbogast suggested.

"What do you have in mind?"

"I'd like to nose around this territory a bit; visit the highway restaurants, filling stations, car dealers, motels. Maybe somebody saw her. Perhaps she did come here, changed her mind after she arrived, and went on."

Sam glanced at Lila. "What do you think?" he asked.

"I don't know. I'm so worried now, I *can't* think." She sighed. "Sam, you decide."

Sam nodded at Arbogast. "All right. But I'm warning you. If nothing happens by tomorrow night, and you don't notify the police, I will."

Arbogast put on his jacket. "Guess I'll get a room over at the hotel. How about you, Miss Crane?"

Lila looked at Sam. "I'll take her over in a little while," Sam said. "First I thought we'd go and eat. But we'll both be here tomorrow. Waiting."

For the first time that evening, Arbogast smiled. "I believe you," he said. "Sorry about the pressure act, but I had to make sure." He nodded at Lila. "We're going to find your sister for you. Don't you worry."

Long before the front door closed behind him, Lila was sobbing against Sam's shoulder. "Sam, I'm scared—something's happened to Mary, I know it!"

"It's all right," Sam said. "What you need right now is food and rest. Things won't look so black tomorrow."

"Do you really think so, Sam?"

"Yes, I do."

It was the first time he'd ever lied to a woman.

Chapter 5

TOMORROW became today, Saturday, and for Sam it was a time of waiting. He phoned Lila from the store around ten. Arbogast had gotten an early start and had left a note for Lila saying that he would call in sometime during the day.

"Why don't you come over here and keep me company?" Sam suggested. "No sense sitting around in your room. We can have lunch together. I'll ask the hotel operator to transfer any calls to the store."

Lila agreed, and Sam felt better. He didn't want her to be alone today, to start brooding about Mary. He'd done enough of it himself, all night.

He'd done his best to resist the idea, but he had to admit that Arbogast's theory made sense. Mary must have planned to come here after she took the money. If she had taken it, that is.

That was the worst part: accepting Mary in the role of a thief. Mary wasn't that kind of person.

And yet, how much did he really know about her? Just last night he'd acknowledged to himself how little. Perhaps Mary did steal the money. Perhaps she was tired of waiting for him to pay off his debts, and the sudden temptation was just too much. Maybe she thought she'd bring it here, cook up some story, get him to accept it. Maybe she'd planned for them to run away together. He had to be honest about this possibility.

And if he granted that much, then he had to face the next question. Why hadn't she arrived? Once you admitted to yourself that you didn't really know another person's mind, then you came up against the ultimate admission—anything was possible. A decision to take a wild fling out in Las Vegas; a sudden impulse to drop out of sight completely and start a whole new life under another name; a traumatic access of guilt, resulting from amnesia . . .

But he was beginning to make a federal case out of it, Sam told himself wryly. Or a clinical case. If he was going off on such farfetched speculations, he'd have to admit a thousand and one alternatives. That she had been in an accident, or picked up some hitchhiker who—

Sam closed off the thought. He couldn't bear to carry it any further. His job today was to cheer Lila up.

But Lila seemed in better spirits this morning. When she came into the store her step was buoyant.

Sam took her out to lunch. Inevitably, she began speculating about Mary and about what Arbogast might be doing today. Sam tried to keep his replies casual. Afterward he stopped at the hotel and arranged to have a transfer made on any calls which might come in for Lila during the afternoon.

Then they went back to the store. It was a light day, for Saturday, and much of the time Sam was able to sit in the back room while Bob Summerfield handled the customers. Lila seemed relaxed. She switched on the radio, picked up a symphonic program, and listened with apparent absorption.

"Bartok's Concerto for Orchestra, isn't it?" Sam asked.

She looked up, smiling. "That's right. Funny, your knowing so much about music."

"Just because a person lives in a small town doesn't mean he can't be interested in music, books, art."

"Maybe I've got things backward, then," she said. "Maybe the funny thing is that you're in the hardware business. It seems, well, so—trivial."

Sam stooped and picked up a small, shiny, pointed object from the floor.

"Trivial," he echoed. "Maybe it's all in the way you look at it. What's this in my hand?"

"A nail, isn't it?"

"That's right. Just a nail. I sell hundreds of pounds a year. Dad used to sell them, too. I'll bet we've probably sold ten tons of nails out of this store since it opened for business. But there's nothing trivial about a single one of them. Maybe half the houses here in Fairvale are held together by nails we've sold. Sometimes when I walk down the street I get the feeling that I helped build the town. The tools I sold shaped the boards and finished them. I've provided the paint that covers the houses, the brushes which applied it, the storm doors and screens, the glass for the windows—" He broke off with a self-conscious grin. "Listen to the master builder, will you? But I mean it. This business serves a real purpose. Drive even a single nail into a crucial place, and you can depend on it to keep on doing a job for a hundred years to come. Long after we're dead and gone."

The moment he said the words he regretted them. He watched the smile fade from her lips.

"Sam, it's almost four now, and Arbogast hasn't called—"

"He will. Just be patient; give him time."

"Sam, you aren't fooling me for one minute with all this routine about nails. You're just as nervous as I am."

"Yes, I guess so." He stood up, swinging his arms. "But I said I'd give Arbogast twenty-four hours. There aren't that many places in this area to check, not if he stopped at every highway hamburger joint and motel in the county! If he doesn't get in touch with us by eight o'clock, I'll go over to Jud Chambers myself. He's the sheriff here."

The phone rang, out in the store. Bob Summerfield called to Sam, "It's for you."

PSYCHO

As Sam rose to go to the phone, Lila followed him out. Picking up the receiver, he heard, "Arbogast here. Thought you might be worried about me."

"We were. What did you find out?"

There was a short pause. Then, "No dice, so far. I've covered this area from one end to another. Right now I'm in Parnassus."

"That's way down at the edge of the county, isn't it? What about the highway between?"

"I came out on it. But I understand I can come back another way, on an alternate."

"Yes, that's right. The old highway. But there's nothing along that route."

"Fellow in the restaurant here tells me there's a motel."

"Come to think of it, I guess there is. The old Bates place."

"Well, it's the last on the list, so I might as well stop in. How are you and the girl holding up?"

"Lila wants to notify the authorities immediately, and I think she's right. How long is this going to take?"

"An hour, maybe. Unless I run into something. Look, all I'm asking is for you to wait until I come back to town. Let me go with you to the police. It'll be a lot easier to get cooperation that way."

"We'll give you an hour," Sam said. "You can find us here at the store."

It wasn't a pleasant hour. Sam was grateful when the late Saturday afternoon crowd came in and he had an excuse to go out front and help wait on the overflow. He couldn't pretend to be cheerful any longer. Because he was beginning to feel it now.

Something had happened.

Something had happened to Mary.

Something—

"Sam!"

Lila had come out from the back room and was pointing at her wristwatch. "Sam, the hour's up!"

"Yes, but let's give him a few more minutes, shall we? I've got to close the store first, anyway."

"All right. But only a few minutes. *Please!* If you knew how I felt—"

"I do know." He squeezed her arm. "Don't worry, he'll be here any second."

Sam and Summerfield shooed out the last straggler at five thirty. But Arbogast didn't come. Sam checked the register. Still Arbogast didn't appear. Summerfield spread the dustcovers and departed. Sam got ready to lock the door. No Arbogast.

"Now," Lila said. "Let's go now. If you don't—"

"There's the phone," Sam said. And, seconds later, "Hello?"

"Arbogast."

"Where are you? You promised to—"

"Never mind what I promised." The investigator's voice was low, his words hurried. "I'm out at the motel, and I've only got a minute. Listen, I've found a lead. Mary Crane was here, all right. Last Saturday night."

"Mary? You're sure?"

"I checked the register, got a chance to compare handwriting. Of course she used another name—Jane Wilson—and gave a phony address. The car description tallies, and so does the description of the girl. The proprietor filled me in."

"How'd you manage that?"

"I pulled my badge and gave him the stolen-car routine. He got all excited. A real oddball, this guy. Name's Norman Bates. You know him?"

"No, can't say that I do."

"He says the girl drove in Saturday night, around six. Paid in advance. It was raining, and she was the only customer. Claims she pulled out early the next morning, before he came down to open up. He lives in a house behind the motel with his mother."

"Do you think he's telling the truth?"

"I don't know, yet. When I put a little heat on him, about the car and all, he let it slip that he'd invited the girl up to the house for supper. Said that was all there was to it, his mother could verify it."

"Did you talk to her?"

"No, but I'm going to. She's up at the house. He tried to hand me a line that she's too sick to see anyone, but I noticed her sitting at the bedroom window when I drove in. So I told him I was going to have a little chat with his old lady whether he liked it or not."

"But you have no authority—"

"Look, you want to find out about your girl friend, don't you? And he doesn't seem to know anything about search warrants. Anyway, he hotfooted it off to the house to tell his mother to get dressed. I thought I'd sneak through a call. So you stick around until I'm finished here. Oh-oh, he's coming back."

The receiver clicked and the line went dead. Sam hung up. He turned to Lila and reported the conversation.

"Feel better, now?"

"Yes. But I wish I knew—"

"We will know, in just a little while."

Chapter 6

SATURDAY afternoon Norman shaved. He shaved only once a week, and always on a Saturday.

Norman didn't like to shave, because of the mirror. It had those wavy lines in it that hurt his eyes.

Maybe the real trouble was that his eyes were bad. Yes, that was it, because he remembered how he used to enjoy looking in the mirror as a boy. He liked to stand in front of the glass without any clothes on. One time Mother caught him at it and hit him hard on the side of the head with the big silver-handled hairbrush. Mother said that was a nasty thing to do.

He could still remember how it hurt, and how his head ached afterward. Mother finally took him to the doctor, and the doctor said he needed glasses. The glasses helped, but he still had trouble seeing properly when he gazed into a mirror. So after a while he just didn't, except when he couldn't help it. And Mother was right. It *was* nasty to stare at yourself, all naked; to peek at the blubbery fat, the short hairless arms, the big belly . . .

When you did, you wished you were somebody else. Somebody who was tall and lean and handsome, like Uncle Joe Considine. "Isn't he the best-looking figure of a man you ever saw?" Mother used to remark.

Norman hated Uncle Joe Considine, even if he *was* handsome. And he wished Mother wouldn't insist on calling him Uncle Joe. Because he wasn't any real relation at all—just a friend who came around to visit Mother. And he got her to build the motel, too, after she sold the farm acreage.

That was strange. Mother always talked against men, and about your-father-who-ran-off-and-deserted-me, and yet Uncle Joe Considine could wrap her around his little finger. He could do anything he wanted with Mother. It would be nice to be like that, and to look the way Uncle Joe Considine looked.

Oh, no, it wouldn't! Because Uncle Joe was dead.

Norman blinked at his reflection as he shaved. Funny how it had slipped his mind. Why it must be almost twenty years now. Time is relative, of course. Einstein said so, and the ancients knew it, too; so did some of those modern mystics. Norman had read them all, and he even owned some of the books. Mother didn't approve; she claimed these things were against religion, but that wasn't the real reason. It was because when he read the books he wasn't her little boy anymore. He was a man who mastered the secrets of dimension and being.

It was like being two people, really—the child and the adult. Whenever he thought about Mother, he became a child again, with a child's vocabulary, frames of reference, and emotional reactions. But when he was by himself—not actually by himself, but off in a book—he was a mature individual. Mature enough to understand that he might even be the victim of a mild form of schizophrenia, or some borderline neurosis.

Granted, it wasn't the healthiest situation in the world, being Mother's little boy. On the other hand, as long as he recognized the dangers he could cope with them, and with Mother. It was just lucky for her that he knew when to be a man, that he *did* know a few things about psychology.

It had been lucky when Uncle Joe Considine died, and it was lucky again when that girl came along. If he hadn't acted as an adult, Mother would be in real trouble.

Norman fingered the razor. It was sharp, very sharp. He had to be careful to lock it up where Mother couldn't get hold of it. He couldn't trust Mother with anything that sharp. That's why he did most of the cooking, and the dishes, too. Not that he had said anything to her outright; he just took over.

Things had gone along for a whole week since that girl had come last Saturday, and they hadn't discussed the affair at all. It would have been awkward and embarrassing for both of them; Mother must have sensed it, for it seemed as if she deliberately avoided him—she spent a lot of time just resting in her room. Probably her conscience bothered her.

That was as it should be. Even if you're not quite right in the head, you can realize that murder is a terrible thing. Mother must be suffering quite a bit.

Norman was glad she hadn't spoken about it, though, because *he* was suffering, too. It wasn't conscience that plagued him—it was fear.

All week long he'd waited for something to go wrong. Every time a car drove up to the motel, he just about jumped out of his skin.

Last Sunday he'd taken his own car and loaded the trailer with wood, and by the time he'd finished, back there at the edge of the swamp, there wasn't anything left that would look suspicious. The girl's earring had gone into the swamp, too. And the other one hadn't shown up. So he felt reasonably secure.

But on Thursday night, when the State Highway Patrol car turned into the driveway, he almost passed out. The officer had just wanted to use the phone. Afterward Norman was able to laugh at himself, yet at the time it wasn't a joke to him at all.

Mother had been sitting at her window in the bedroom, and it was just as well the officer hadn't seen her. Norman tried to tell her to stay out of sight, but he couldn't bring himself to explain why, any more than he could discuss with her why he wouldn't permit her to come down to the motel and help out. You couldn't trust Mother around strangers, not anymore. And the less they knew about her, the better.

Norman finished shaving and washed his hands again. He'd noticed this compulsion in himself, particularly during the past week. A regular Lady Macbeth.

But there was no time to think about that now. He had to get down to the motel and open up.

There'd been some business during the week, not very much. Norman never had more than three or four units occupied on a given night, and that meant he didn't need to rent out number six. Number six had been the girl's room.

He hoped he'd never have to rent it out again. He was done with that sort of thing—the peeking, the drinking. That was what caused all the trouble in the first place. If he hadn't peeked, if he hadn't been drinking . . .

Norman wiped his hands, turning away from the mirror. Forget the past, let the dead bury the dead. Mother was behaving herself, he was behaving himself, they were together as they always had been. A whole week had gone by without any trouble, and there wouldn't *be* any trouble from now on. Particularly if he behaved like an adult instead of a mama's boy.

He tightened his tie and left the bathroom. Mother was in her room, looking out of the window again. Norman wondered if he ought to say anything to her. No, better not. Let her look, if she liked. Poor, sick old lady, chained to the house here. Let her watch the world go by. As long as he locked the downstairs doors when he went out.

Locking the doors all week long gave him a new sense of security. He'd taken her keys away from her, too—the keys to the house and the keys to the motel. Once he left, there was no way she could get out. There could be no repetition of what had happened last week as long as he observed the precaution. It was for her own good. Better the house than an asylum.

Norman came around the corner of the motel just as the laundry-service truck drove up to deliver a week's supply of clean sheets and towels and to take away the dirty linen. After the truck departed Norman went in and cleaned up number four—some traveling salesman from Illinois had pulled out earlier in the day, leaving the usual mess. Cigarette butts on the edge of the washbowl and one of those science fiction magazines on the floor. Norman chuckled as he picked it up. Science fiction! If they only *knew!*

Norman walked back to the office and put the sheets and towels away. Now he was ready for today's business—if any.

But nothing happened until around four o'clock. Sitting there watching the roadway outside, he got bored and fidgety. He was almost tempted to take a drink, until he remembered what he'd promised himself. No more drinking. That was part of the trouble, when there was trouble. Drinking had killed Uncle Joe Considine. Drinking had led to the killing of the girl, indirectly. Still, he could use a drink right now. Just one—

Norman was still hesitating when the car pulled in. Alabama plates. A middle-aged couple. Norman showed them to number one, way at the other end. They were just tourists.

After he sat down again, another car rolled up, with a lone man behind the wheel. Probably another salesman. Red Buick, Texas license.

Texas license! That girl, that Jane Wilson, had come from Texas!

Norman stood up and stepped behind the counter. He saw the man leave the car, heard the crunch of his approaching footsteps on the gravel, matched the rhythm with the muffled thumping of his own heart.

It's just coincidence, he told himself. *People drive up from Texas every day.*

The man entered. He was tall and thin, and he wore one of those gray stetson hats with a broad brim that shadowed the upper portion of his face. His chin showed tan under the heavy stubble of beard. "Good evening," he said, without much of a drawl.

"Good evening," Norman said, shifting his feet uneasily.

"You the proprietor here?"

"That's right. Would you like a room?"

"Not exactly. I'm looking for a little information."

"What is it you wanted to know?"

"I'm trying to locate a girl."

Norman's hands twitched. He couldn't feel them, because they were numb. He was numb all over. His heart wasn't pounding anymore—it didn't even seem to be beating. Everything was very quiet. It would be terrible if he screamed.

"Her name is Crane, Mary Crane," the man said. "From Fort Worth. I was wondering if she might have registered here."

Norman didn't want to scream now. He wanted to laugh. It was easy to reply. "There hasn't been anybody by that name here," he said.

"You sure?"

"Positive. We don't get too much business these days. I'm pretty good at remembering my customers."

"This girl would have stopped over about a week ago. Last Saturday night, say."

"I didn't have anyone here over the weekend. Weather was bad in these parts."

"Are you sure? This girl—woman, I should say—is about twenty-seven. Five feet five, weight around one twenty, dark hair, blue eyes. She drives a 1953 Plymouth sedan, a blue two-door model with a stove-in front fender on the left side. The license number is . . ."

Norman stopped listening. Why had he said there hadn't been anyone here? The man was describing that girl all right. Well, he still couldn't prove the girl had come, if Norman denied it. And he'd have to keep on denying it now. "No, I don't think I can help you."

"Doesn't the description fit anyone who's been here during the past week?" the man went on. "It's quite likely she would have registered under another name. If you'd let me look over your register—"

Norman put his hand on the ledger and shook his head. "Sorry, mister," he said. "I couldn't let you do that."

"Maybe this will help you change your mind."

The man reached into his inside coat pocket, flipped the wallet open, and laid it on the counter so Norman could read the card.

"Milton Arbogast," the man said. "Investigator for Parity Mutual."

"You're a detective?"

He nodded. "I'm here on business, Mr.—"

"Norman Bates."

"Mr. Bates, my company wants me to locate this girl. If you refuse to let me inspect your register, I can always get in touch with the local authorities."

Norman was sure of one thing. There mustn't be any local authorities to come snooping around. He hesitated, his hand still covering the ledger. "What did this girl do?" he asked.

"Stolen car," Mr. Arbogast told him.

"Oh." Norman was relieved. For a moment he'd been afraid it was something serious. But a missing car, particularly an old beat-up heap—

"All right," he said. "Help yourself. I just wanted to make sure you had a legitimate reason." He removed his hand.

First Mr. Arbogast took an envelope out of his pocket and laid it on the counter. Then he turned the ledger around and thumbed down the list of signatures.

Norman watched his blunt thumb move, saw it stop suddenly and decisively.

"Jane Wilson, San Antonio," he read. "I thought you said you didn't have any customers last Saturday?"

"Oh—come to think of it, we might have had one or two." The pounding had started up in Norman's chest again, and he knew he'd made a mistake when he pretended not to recognize the girl's description. How could he possibly explain in such a way that the detective wouldn't be suspicious?

The detective had picked up the envelope and laid it alongside the ledger page, comparing the handwriting. It was in *her* handwriting! Now he'd know. He *did* know!

Norman could tell, when the detective raised his head and stared at him. He could see the cold eyes, the eyes that *knew*.

"Jane Wilson—it's the girl, all right. This handwriting is identical. I'm going to get a photostat made, even if it takes a court order.

And that isn't all I can do, if you won't start talking. Why did you lie about not seeing this girl?"

"I didn't lie. I just forgot—"

"You said you had a good memory."

"Well, yes, generally I do. Only—"

"Prove it." Mr. Arbogast lit a cigarette. "This girl stole a car. In case you don't know, car theft is a federal offense. You wouldn't want to be involved as an accessory, would you?"

"Involved? A girl spends the night and drives away again. How can I possibly be involved?"

"By withholding information. You saw the girl. What did she look like?"

"Just as you described her, I guess. I didn't take a second look. She came alone, I let her sign in, gave her a key, and that was that. She seemed like just another tourist to me."

"Good enough." Mr. Arbogast ground his cigarette butt into the ashtray. "There was nothing to cause you to suspect anything was wrong with her. And on the other hand, she didn't particularly arouse your sympathies, either. You felt no emotion toward this girl at all."

"Certainly not."

Mr. Arbogast leaned forward casually. "Then why did you try to shield her by pretending you never remembered that she had come here?"

"I just forgot, I tell you." Norman knew he'd walked into a trap. "What are you trying to insinuate—do you think *I* helped her steal the car?"

Mr. Arbogast smiled. "Let's take it just a little slower, shall we? Maybe you can remember something. She left alone the next morning, is that it? About what time would you say?"

"I don't know. I was asleep up at the house Sunday morning."

"Then you don't actually know she was *alone* when she left?"

"I can't prove it, if that's what you mean."

"How about during the evening? Did she have any visitors?"

"No."

"You're positive?"

"Quite positive."

"She stayed in her room all evening?"

"Yes."

"Didn't even make a phone call?"

"No."

"Did anyone else happen to see her that night?"

"No. She was the only customer."

"What about the old lady—did *she* see her?"

"What old lady?"

"The one up at the house, in back of here. I noticed her staring out of the window when I drove in. Who is she?"

Norman's heart was going to beat its way right through his chest. He started to say, "There is no old lady," but there was no way out. He had to admit it. "That's my mother. She's pretty feeble, she never comes down here anymore."

"Then she didn't see the girl?"

"No. She's sick. She stayed in her room when we ate sup—"

It slipped out, just like that.

Mr. Arbogast wasn't casual anymore. "You had supper with Mary Crane, up at your house?"

"Just coffee and sandwiches. I thought I told you, but I guess it slipped my mind. You see, she asked where she could eat, and the nearest place is Fairvale, and that's almost twenty miles away, and it was raining, so I took her up to the house with me."

"What did you talk about?"

"We didn't talk about anything much. I told you Mother's sick, and I didn't want to disturb her. That's what's been upsetting me, making me forget things."

"Is there anything else that might have slipped your mind? Like you and this girl coming back here and having a little party—"

"No! Nothing like that! What right have you got to say such a thing? I've told you all you wanted to know. I won't even talk to you anymore. Now, get out of here!"

Mr. Arbogast pulled down the brim of his stetson. "First I'd like to have a word with your mother. Maybe she might have noticed something you've forgotten."

"I tell you she didn't even *see* the girl!" Norman came around the counter. "You can't talk to her. She's very ill." He could hear his heart pounding and he had to shout above it. "I forbid you to see her."

"In that case, I'll come back with a search warrant."

He was bluffing, Norman knew it now. "That's ridiculous. Who'd believe I'd want to steal an old car?"

Mr. Arbogast lit another cigarette. "I'm afraid you don't understand," he said, almost gently. "It isn't really the car at all. You might as well have the whole story. This girl—Mary Crane—stole forty thousand dollars in cash from a real estate firm in Fort Worth. It's a serious business. That's why I insist on talking to your mother, with or without your permission."

"But I've just told you she's not well at all."

"I won't say anything to upset her. Of course, if you want me to come back with the sheriff . . ."

Forty thousand dollars! No wonder Arbogast had asked so many questions. Of course he could get a warrant, no use making a scene. No way out, no way at all.

"All right, you can talk to her," Norman said. "But let me go up to the house first and tell her you're coming. I don't want you busting in and getting her all excited." He moved toward the door. "Give me ten minutes to explain things to her."

"Okay." Arbogast nodded, and Norman hurried out.

It wasn't much of a climb up the hill, but he thought he'd never make it. It was just like the other night now. Nothing had changed. No matter what you did, you couldn't get away from it. Nothing helped, because he was what he was, and that wasn't enough. Not enough to save him.

If there was going to be any help at all now, it would have to come from Mother.

He unlocked the front door and climbed the stairs and went into her room. He intended to speak to her very calmly, but when he saw her just sitting there by the window he began to shake and the sobs came tearing up out of his chest, the terrible sobs, and he put his head down against her skirt and told her.

"All right," Mother said. She didn't seem surprised at all. "We'll take care of this. Just leave everything to me."

"Mother—if you just talked to him for a minute, told him you don't know anything—he'd go away."

"But he'd come back. Forty thousand dollars, that's a lot of money. He probably thinks we're all in on it together. Or that we did something to the girl, because of the money. Don't you see how it is?"

"Mother—" He closed his eyes, he couldn't look at her. "What are you going to do?"

"I'm going to get dressed. We want to be all ready for your visitor, don't we? I'll just take some things into the bathroom. You can tell Mr. Arbogast to come up now."

"No, I won't bring him up here, not if you're going to—"

He wanted to faint, but even that wouldn't stop what was going to happen. In just a few minutes Mr. Arbogast would get tired of waiting. He'd walk up to the house, he'd knock on the door, and come in. And when he did—

"Mother, please, *listen* to me!"

But she was in the bathroom, she was getting dressed, she was putting on makeup, she was getting ready. *Getting ready.*

And all at once she came gliding out, wearing the nice dress with the ruffles. Her face was freshly powdered and rouged, and she smiled as she started down the stairs.

Before she was halfway down, the knocking came. Mr. Arbogast was here. Norman wanted to call out and warn him, but something was stuck in his throat. He could only listen as Mother cried gaily, "I'm coming! I'm coming! Just a moment, now!"

Mother opened the door and Mr. Arbogast walked in. He looked at her and then he opened his mouth to say something. As he did so he raised his head, and that was all Mother had been waiting for. Her arm went out and something bright and glittering flashed back and forth, back and forth—

It hurt Norman's eyes and he didn't want to look. He didn't have to look, either, because he already knew.

Mother had found his razor. . . .

Chapter 7

NORMAN smiled at the elderly couple from Illinois and said, "Here's your key. That'll be ten dollars for the two of you, please."

The wife opened her purse. "I've got the money here, Homer." She placed a bill on the counter, nodding at Norman. Then her eyes narrowed. "What's the matter, don't you feel good?"

"I'm—just a little tired, I guess. Going to close up now, it's almost ten."

Almost ten. Nearly four hours. Oh, my God.

The couple were going out now, and he could switch off the sign and close the office. But first he was going to take a drink, a big drink. Nothing mattered now; it was all over. All over, or just beginning.

Norman had already taken several drinks—the first as soon as he had returned to the motel, around six. If he hadn't, he would never have been able to stand here, knowing what was lying up at the house underneath the hall rug. He had just pulled up the sides of the rug and tossed them over to cover it. There was quite a bit of blood, but it wouldn't soak through. There was nothing else he *could* do, then. Not in broad daylight.

He'd given Mother strict orders not to touch anything, and he knew she'd obey. Funny, how she had collapsed again. It seemed as if she'd nerve herself up to almost anything—the manic phase, wasn't that what they called it?—but once it was over, she just wilted, and he had to take over. He told her to go back to her room, and *not* to show herself at the window, just lie down until he got there. And he had locked the door.

But he'd have to unlock it now.

Norman went outside. There was Mr. Arbogast's Buick, still parked just where he had left it.

Wouldn't it be wonderful if he could just climb into that car and drive away? Drive far away and never come back at all? Drive away from the motel, away from Mother, away from that thing lying under the rug in the hall?

For a moment the temptation welled up, but then it subsided

and Norman shrugged. He could never get far enough away to be safe. That thing was waiting for him.

So he glanced up and down the highway and looked at number one and number three to see if their blinds were drawn, and then he took out the keys he'd found in Mr. Arbogast's pocket. And he drove up to the house, very slowly.

All the lights were out. Mother was asleep in her room, or maybe she was only pretending to be asleep—Norman didn't care. Just so she stayed out of his way while he took care of this. He didn't want Mother around to make him feel like a little boy. He had a grown man's job to do.

It took a grown man just to bundle the rug together and lift what was in it. He lugged it down the steps and into the back seat of the car. There was no leaking. These old shag rugs were absorbent.

When he got through the field and down to the swamp, he drove along the edge a way until he came to an open space. Wouldn't do to sink the car in the same place he'd put the other one. But he used the same method. It was really very easy. *Practice makes perfect.*

Except that there was nothing to joke about; not while he sat there on the tree stump and waited. It was worse than the other time—you'd think because the Buick was a heavier car that it would sink faster. But it took a million years. Until at last, *plop!*

There. It was gone forever. Like that girl, and the forty thousand dollars. Where had it been? Not in her purse, certainly, and not in the suitcase. He should have looked, except that he'd been in no condition to search. And if he *had* found it, no telling what might have happened. Most probably he would have given himself away when the detective came around. You always gave yourself away if you had a guilty conscience.

Norman walked back through the field slowly. Tomorrow he'd have to return with the car and the trailer to cover his tracks. But that wasn't half as important as attending to other matters.

The facts just had to be faced. Somebody was going to come here and inquire about that detective. The company that employed him wasn't going to let him disappear without an investigation. And certainly the real estate firm would be interested. Everybody was interested in forty thousand dollars.

So sooner or later there'd be questions to answer. But he knew what was coming. And this time he was going to be prepared.

Nobody was going to get him excited or confused; not if he knew in advance what to expect. Already he was planning just what to say when the time came.

The girl had stayed at the motel, yes. He'd admit that right away, but of course he hadn't suspected anything while she was here—not until Mr. Arbogast came, a week later. The girl had spent the night and driven away. There'd be nothing about eating together at the house.

What he *would* say, though, is that he'd told everything to Mr. Arbogast, and the only part which seemed to interest him was that the girl had asked him how far it was from here to Chicago, and could she make it in a single day?

That's what had interested Mr. Arbogast. And he'd thanked him very much and climbed back into his car and driven off. Period. No, he had no idea where he was headed for. Mr. Arbogast hadn't said. What time had it been? A little after suppertime, Saturday. Sorry, mister, that's all I know about it.

Norman knew he could tell it that way, tell it calmly and easily, because he wouldn't have to worry about Mother.

She wasn't going to be looking out of the window. In fact, she wasn't going to be in the house at all. Even if they came with one of those search warrants, they weren't going to find Mother.

This wasn't like the other time, when he'd gone to pieces and needed to know Mother was there. Now he needed to know she was *not* there.

So he marched upstairs, in the dark, and went straight to her room. He switched on the light. She was in bed, of course, but she hadn't been sleeping at all, just playing possum.

"Norman, where on earth have you been?"

"You know where I've been, Mother. Don't pretend."

"Is everything all right?"

"Certainly." He took a deep breath. "Mother, I'm going to ask you to give up sleeping in your room for the next week or so."

"Are you out of your mind? This is my room."

"Mother, please listen and try to understand. We had a visitor here today."

"Must you talk about that?"

"I must." He gulped a breath, then rushed on. "It's for your own protection. I can't afford to let anyone see you, like that detective did today. Sooner or later somebody will be around to inquire after him. I don't want anyone to start asking you questions—you know why as well as I do."

"What are you going to do—bury me in the swamp?" She started to laugh. It was more like a cackle, and he knew that once she really got started she wouldn't stop. The only way to stop her was to outshout her. A week ago Norman would never have dared. But this wasn't a week ago, it was *now*, and he had to face the truth. Mother was more than sick, she was psychotic, dangerously so. He had to control her, and he would.

"Shut up!" he said, and the cackling ceased. "You must listen to me. I've got it all figured out. You're going down into the fruit cellar."

"I *won't!*"

"I'm not asking you, Mother. I'm telling you. You're going to stay in the fruit cellar until I think it's safe for you to come upstairs again. And I'll hang that old Indian blanket on the wall, so that it covers up the door."

"Norman, I'm not going to budge from this room!"

"Then I'll have to carry you."

"Norman, you wouldn't *dare*—"

But he did. He picked her up right off the bed, and she was light as a feather compared to Mr. Arbogast. She was too astonished to put up a fight, just whimpered a little. Norman was startled at how easy it was. Why, she was only a sick old lady, a frail, feeble thing! He didn't have to be afraid of her, not really. *She* was afraid of *him*, now. Yes, she must be. Not once, all through this, had she called him boy.

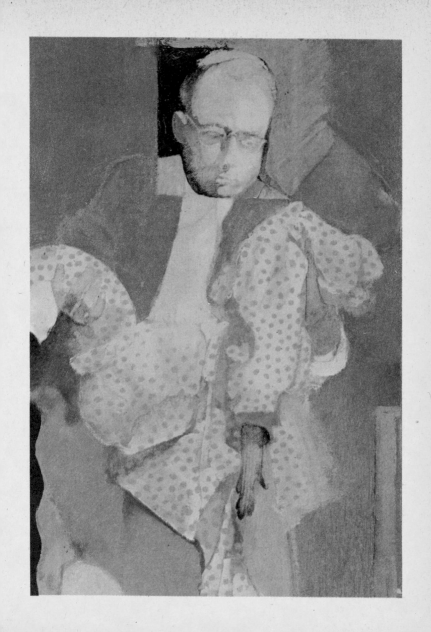

"I'll fix the cot for you," he told her. "And there's a pot, too—"

"Norman, *must* you talk that way?" For just an instant she flared up in the old way, then subsided. He bustled around, bringing blankets, arranging the curtains on the small window so that there'd be sufficient ventilation. She began muttering under her breath. "It's a prison cell; you're trying to make a prisoner out of me. You don't love me anymore, Norman, or else you wouldn't treat me like this."

"If I didn't love you, do you know where you'd be today?" He didn't want to say it, but he had to. "The State Hospital for the Criminal Insane. That's where you'd be."

He snapped out the light, wondering if she'd heard him. Apparently he had gotten through to her, because just as he closed the door she answered. Her voice was deceptively soft in the darkness, but somehow the words cut into him more deeply than the straight razor had cut into Mr. Arbogast's throat.

"Yes, Norman, I suppose you're right. That's where I'd probably be. But I wouldn't be there alone."

Norman slammed the door, locked it, and turned away. As he ran up the cellar steps he thought he could still hear her chuckling gently in the dark.

Chapter 8

SAM and Lila sat in the back room of the store, waiting for Arbogast to arrive.

"You can tell when it's Saturday night in a town like this," Sam commented. "The noises are different. All that rattling and squealing you hear—that's farm families in their old jalopies, coming in to see the show. Hired hands, in a hurry to head for the taverns. Hear that running? The kids are loose. Saturday's the night they stay up late. No homework."

"Sam, why doesn't Arbogast get here?" Lila said. "It's almost nine."

"Maybe he's tied up. Maybe he found out something important."

"I'm sick of waiting! He could call. He knows how worried we are." Lila stood up, began to pace back and forth across the narrow room. "How can you stand it? Why don't you *do* something?" She grasped her purse and pushed past him.

"Where are you going?" Sam asked.

"To see that sheriff of yours, right now."

Sam took her arm. "I'll phone the sheriff," he said.

She made no attempt to follow him into the store.

After Sam asked for Sheriff Chambers, Lila heard him say, "He's where? Fulton? When do you suppose he'll be back? Look, if he gets in anytime before midnight, would you ask him to call Sam Loomis here at the hardware store in Fairvale? Thanks, I'd appreciate that." Then Sam hung up.

He walked back into the rear room and reported. "Seems somebody robbed the bank over at Fulton around suppertime this evening. Chambers and the whole State Highway Patrol are out setting up roadblocks. I talked to old Peterson; he's the only one left in the sheriff's office. There's two cops walking the beat here in town, but they wouldn't be any use to us."

"So now what are you going to do?"

"Why, wait."

"But don't you even care what happens to—"

He cut in on her sharply. "Of course I care. Would it ease your mind if I called the motel and found out what's going on with Arbogast?"

Lila nodded. Again he went back into the store. This time she accompanied him and stood waiting while he asked the operator for information. She finally located the name—Norman Bates—and put the call through.

"Funny," Sam said, hanging up. "Nobody answers."

"Then I'm going out there."

"No, you're not. I'm going. You wait here, in case Arbogast comes in. Just relax. It shouldn't take me more than three-quarters of an hour."

And it didn't. Sam drove fast. In exactly forty-two minutes he unlocked the front door and came back into the store again.

Lila was waiting for him. "Well?" she asked.

"Funny. The place was closed up. No lights in the office. No lights in the house behind the motel. I banged on the door up there for five minutes straight. The garage next to the house was empty. Looks like this Bates went away for the evening."

"What about Mr. Arbogast?"

"His car wasn't there. Just two parked down at the motel—I looked at the licenses. Alabama and Illinois."

"But where could—"

"The way I figure it," Sam said, "is that Arbogast *did* find out something. Something important. It could be that he and Bates both went off together. And that's why we haven't had any word."

"Sam, I can't take much more of this. I've got to know!"

"You've got to eat, too." He displayed a bulging paper bag. "Stopped in at the drive-in and brought us some hamburgers and coffee."

By the time they finished eating it was after eleven.

"Look," Sam said. "Why don't you go back to the hotel and get some rest? Worrying isn't going to help. Chances are, I've figured it right. Arbogast *has* located Mary and we'll get good news by morning."

But there was no good news on Sunday morning.

By nine o'clock Lila was rattling the front door of the store.

"Hear anything?" she asked. And when Sam shook his head she frowned. "Well, I found out something," she continued. "Arbogast checked out over at the hotel yesterday morning—*before* he even started to look around."

Without a word Sam picked up his hat and walked out of the store with her.

Fairvale's courthouse was set back in a square on Main Street, surrounded by lawn on all four sides. One side contained a statue of a Civil War veteran. The other three sides displayed, respectively, a Spanish-American War trench mortar, a World War I cannon, and a granite shaft bearing the names of fourteen Fairvale citizens who had died in World War II. Vacant benches lined the sidewalks all around the square.

The courthouse itself was closed, but the sheriff's office was over in the annex, and the side door was open. They entered, climbed the stairs, walked down the hall to the office.

Old Peterson was doing duty at the outer desk, all alone.

"Good morning, Mr. Peterson. Sheriff around?"

"Nope. Hear about them bank robbers? Busted right through the roadblock down at Parnassus. FBI's after 'em now."

"Did you give him my message?"

The old man hesitated. "I—I guess I forgot. All this excitement around here." He wiped his mouth. " 'Course I intend to, today, when he comes in."

"What time will that be?"

"After lunch. Sunday mornings he's over to the church."

"What church?"

"First Baptist."

"Thanks."

Sam swung away. Lila's high heels clattered hollowly beside him in the hall. When they reached the street she turned to him. "Where are we going now?"

"First Baptist Church, of course."

The services had just ended; people were beginning to emerge from the steepled structure.

"There he is," Sam muttered. "Come on."

He led her over to a couple who stood near the curb. The woman was short, gray-haired, in a mail-order print dress; the man was tall, broad across the shoulders, and paunchily protruding at the waistline. He wore a blue serge suit, and his red, seamed neck twisted in rebellion against the restraint of a white, starched collar. He had graying hair and curly black eyebrows.

"How are you, Sam?" Sheriff Chambers held out a large red hand. "Ma, you know Sam Loomis, here."

"I'd like you to meet Lila Crane. Miss Crane is visiting here from Fort Worth."

"Pleased to meet you. Say, you aren't the one Sam keeps talking about, are you? Never let on you were so pretty—"

"It's my sister you're thinking of," Lila told him. "That's why we're here to see—"

"I wonder if we could go over to your office for a minute," Sam broke in.

"Sure, why not?" Jud Chambers turned to his wife. "Ma, I'll be home soon's I'm finished with these folks."

Once settled in Sheriff Chambers' office, Sam told his story. The sheriff interrupted frequently.

"Now let me get this straight," he said at the conclusion. "This fella who came to you, this Arbogast. Why didn't he check everything with me?"

"He was hoping to find Miss Crane and recover the money without any embarrassment to the Lowery Agency."

"You say he showed you his credentials?" the sheriff asked Lila.

"Yes." Lila nodded. "He was a licensed investigator for the insurance firm."

"But he wasn't at the motel when you drove out there?"

"There was nobody there at all, Sheriff," Sam answered.

"That's damned funny. I know this fella Bates who runs it. Scarcely even leaves for an hour to come into town. Why don't you let me try calling him now? Probably turn out he was sound asleep when you got there last night."

The big red hand picked up the phone.

"Don't tell him anything about the money," Sam said. "Just ask for Arbogast and see what he has to say."

Sheriff Chambers nodded. He put through the call, and they waited.

"Hello . . . Bates? This is Sheriff Chambers. I'm looking for a little information. Party here in town is trying to locate a fella name of Milton Arbogast, from Fort Worth. He's a special investigator for a firm called Parity Mutual.

"He what? When was that? I see. Did he say where he was going? Oh, you think so? No, there's no trouble. Just that I thought he might check in here. Say, while I've got you, you don't think he might have stopped back later on in the evening, do you? What time you generally go to bed out there? I see. Thanks for the information, Bates."

He hung up and swiveled around to face them.

"Looks like your man headed for Chicago," he said. "That's where the girl said she was going. Your friend Arbogast sounds like a pretty smooth operator."

"What do you mean? What did this man Bates tell you just now?" Lila leaned forward.

"The same thing Arbogast told you yesterday evening when he called in from there. Your sister stayed at the motel last Saturday, but she registered under the name of Jane Wilson, from San Antonio. Let it slip that she was on her way to Chicago."

"It couldn't have been Mary, then. Why she doesn't know anyone in Chicago; she's never been there in her life!"

"According to Bates, Arbogast was certain this was the girl. Even checked her handwriting. Her description, the car, everything fitted. Once Arbogast heard about Chicago, Bates says, he took off from there like a bat out of hell."

"But that's ridiculous! She has a week's start—*if* she was going there at all, that is. And he'd never find her in Chicago."

"Maybe he knew where to look. Maybe he didn't tell you two *all* he'd found out about your sister and her plans. Never can tell about these smart operators. Could be he had some idea of just what your sister was up to. If he could get to her and lay his hands on that money, he might not be so interested in reporting back to his insurance company again."

"Are you trying to say that Mr. Arbogast was a crook?"

"All I'm saying is that forty thousand in cash is a lot of money. And if Arbogast didn't show up here again, it means he had something figured out."

"Now wait a minute, Sheriff," Sam said. "You're jumping to conclusions. You've got nothing to go by except what this man Bates said over the phone just now. Couldn't he be lying?"

"Why should he? He told a straight story. Said the girl had been there, said Arbogast was there."

"Where was he last night when I came, then?"

"Fast asleep in bed, just like I thought," the sheriff answered. "I know this fella Bates. He's kind of an odd one, not too bright. But he certainly isn't the type who'd ever pull any fast ones. Why shouldn't I believe him? Particularly when I *know* your friend Arbogast was lying."

"Lying? About what?"

"You told me what he said when he called you from the motel last night. About going up to see Norman Bates's mother. Norman Bates's mother has been dead for the last twenty years." Sheriff Chambers nodded. "Quite a scandal around these parts. She built this motel with a fella name of Joe Considine. She was a widow, and the talk was that she and Considine were—"

The sheriff stared at Lila, then broke off with an aimless wave of the hand. "Anyways, they never did get married. Something must of went wrong; maybe she was in a family way; maybe Considine had a wife back where he came from. One night they both took strychnine together. Her son, this Norman Bates, he found them both. Guess it was pretty much of a shock. He was laid up in the hospital for a couple of months, after. Didn't even go to the funeral. But I went. That's how I'm sure his mother is dead. Hell, I was one of the pallbearers!"

Sam and Lila had dinner over at the hotel.

It was not an enjoyable meal for either of them.

"I still can't believe Mr. Arbogast would go off without a word to us," Lila said as she finished her coffee. "And I can't believe Mary would go to Chicago, either. As for Mr. Arbogast, he didn't know any more about Mary than what we could tell him."

Sam set his cup down. "I'm beginning to wonder how much any of us really knows about Mary," he said. "I'm engaged to her. You lived with her. Neither of us could believe she'd take that money. And yet there's no other answer. She did take it."

"Yes." Lila's voice was low. "I believe that, now. But she wouldn't do it for herself. Maybe she thought she could help you, maybe pay off your debts."

"Then why didn't she come to me?"

"She did. At least, she got as far as that motel." Lila crumpled her napkin, held it wadded tightly in her hand. "And just because Arbogast lied about seeing Bates's mother, there's no reason why this man Bates can't be lying, too. Why doesn't the sheriff go out there and take a look around for himself?"

"You can't go breaking in on people for no reason," Sam told her. "Besides, in a small town everybody knows everybody else, nobody wants to cause hard feelings. There's nothing to make anyone suspect Bates. Chambers has known him all his life."

"Yes, and I've known Mary all my life. But there were some things about her I didn't suspect, either. He admitted Bates was a little peculiar."

"He didn't go that far. He said he was sort of a recluse. That's understandable, when you think of what a shock it must have been to him when his mother died."

"If Arbogast *was* planning to run off to Chicago, then why did he bother to call up at all? Wouldn't it have been simpler to just leave, without our knowing he'd been to that motel? And why would he lie about seeing the mother?" Lila let go of the napkin and stared at Sam. "I—I'm beginning to get an idea."

"What?"

"Sam, just what *did* Arbogast say there at the last, when he called you? About seeing Bates's mother?"

"He said that he'd noticed her sitting at the bedroom window when he drove in."

"Maybe he wasn't lying."

"But he had to be. Mrs. Bates is dead."

"Maybe it was Bates who lied. Perhaps Arbogast merely assumed that the woman was Bates's mother, and when he spoke of it, Bates said yes, but that she was sick and nobody could see her."

"But I still don't see—"

"The point is, Arbogast did. He saw *somebody* sitting in the window when he drove in. And maybe that somebody was—Mary."

"Lila, you don't think that—"

"Why not? The trail ends there at the motel. Two people are missing. Isn't that enough? Isn't that enough for me, as Mary's sister, to go to the sheriff and insist that he make a thorough investigation?"

"Come on," said Sam. "Let's get going."

THEY FOUND SHERIFF CHAMBERS at his house, finishing dinner. He chewed on a toothpick while he listened to Lila's story.

"I dunno," he said. "Couldn't it wait? You'd have to be the one to sign the complaint—"

"I'll sign anything you want."

"Sheriff," Sam said, "this is a serious business. This girl's sister has been missing for over a week now. It isn't just a matter of money anymore. For all we know, her life could be in danger. She could even be—"

"All right, all right! Let's go over to the office and I'll let her sign. But if you ask me, it's a waste of time. Norman Bates is no murderer."

The word emerged, just like any other word, and died away. But its echo lingered. It stayed with Sam and Lila as they drove over to the courthouse with Sheriff Chambers. It stayed with them after the sheriff drove away, out to the motel. He'd refused to take either of them along, so they waited in the office. The two of them—and the word.

It was late afternoon when the sheriff returned. He came in alone, giving them a look in which disgust and relief were equally compounded.

"Just what I told you," he said. "False alarm. Went straight out there and didn't run into any trouble at all. Bates, he was down in the woods behind the house, getting himself some kindling. I never even had to show the warrant—he was nice as pie. Told me to go look around for myself, even gave me the keys to the motel."

"And did you look?"

"I went into every unit of the motel, and I covered that house of his from top to bottom. Didn't find a soul, except Bates. He's lived there alone all these years."

"What about the bedroom?"

"There's a bedroom up front on the second floor, all right, and it used to be his mother's, when she was alive. In fact, he's even kept it the way it was. Guess he's kind of an odd one, that Bates, but who wouldn't be, living alone like that?"

"Did you ask him about what Arbogast told me?" Sam asked. "About seeing his mother at the window when he drove in?"

"Sure, right away. He says it's a lie—Arbogast never even mentioned seeing anyone. I talked kind of rough to him at first, on purpose, just to see if there was something he was holding back, but his story makes sense. I still think that this Chicago business is the real answer."

"I can't believe it," Lila said. "Why would Mr. Arbogast make up that unnecessary excuse about seeing Bates's mother? You're *sure* she is dead?"

"I've already told you I was there, at the funeral. I saw the note she left for Bates when she and this Considine fella killed themselves. Do I have to dig her up and show her to you?" Chambers sighed. "I'm sorry, miss. But I've done all I can. I searched the house. Your sister isn't there; this man Arbogast isn't there. Seems to me the answer's pretty plain."

"What would you advise me to do now?"

"Why, check with this fella Arbogast's home office. Maybe they've got some lead on this Chicago angle. Don't suppose you can contact anyone until tomorrow morning, though."

"I guess you're right." Lila stood up. "Well, thank you for all your trouble. I'm sorry to be such a bother."

"That's what I'm here for. Right, Sam?"

"Right," Sam answered.

"I know how you feel about all this, miss," Sheriff Chambers said. "I wish I could have been more of a help to you. But there's just nothing solid for me to go on. If you had some kind of real evidence, then maybe—"

"We understand," Sam said. "And we both appreciate your cooperation." He turned to Lila. "Shall we go now?"

Then they were on the sidewalk. The late afternoon sun cast slanting shadows. As they stood there in the square the black tip of the Civil War veteran's bayonet grazed Lila's throat.

"Want to come back to my place?" Sam suggested.

The girl shook her head.

"Where would you like to go, then?"

"I don't know about you," Lila told him. "But I'm going out to that motel."

She raised her face defiantly, and the sharp shadow line slashed across her neck. For a moment it looked as though somebody had just cut off Lila's head. . . .

Chapter 9

NORMAN knew they were coming, even before he saw them driving in. He didn't know *who* they'd be, or how many of them would come, but he knew they were coming.

He'd known it ever since last night when he lay in bed and listened to the stranger pound on the door. He had stayed very quiet; in fact, he'd even put his head under the covers while he waited for the stranger to go away. Finally he *did* leave. It was lucky that Mother was locked in the fruit cellar. Lucky for him, lucky for her, lucky for the stranger.

But he'd known, then, that this wouldn't be the end of it. And this afternoon, when he was down at the swamp again, cleaning up, Sheriff Chambers had driven in.

It gave Norman quite a start, seeing the sheriff again after all these years. He remembered him very well from the time of the nightmare. That's the way Norman always thought about Uncle Joe Considine and the poison and everything—it had been a long, long nightmare from the moment he phoned the sheriff until months afterward, when they let him out of the hospital.

Seeing Sheriff Chambers now was like having the same nightmare all over, but people *do* have the same nightmare again and again. And the important thing to remember was that Norman had fooled the sheriff the first time, when everything had been much harder. This time it should be easier, if he just remembered to be calm.

How he'd fooled him the first time! Yes, and he fooled him just as easily this time. It was even funny, in a way—letting the sheriff go up to the house and search while Norman stayed down at the edge of the swamp and finished smoothing out all the footprints. It was funny, that is, as long as Mother kept quiet behind the

door of the fruit cellar. But Mother had been warned; and besides, the sheriff wasn't looking for Mother.

The sheriff came back and asked Norman some questions about the girl and Arbogast and going to Chicago. Norman was tempted to invent a little more, but he realized it was better to just stick to what he'd already made up. The sheriff believed that. He almost apologized before he went away.

But Norman knew there'd be more. Sheriff Chambers hadn't come out here on his own initiative. His phone call yesterday meant somebody else knew about Arbogast and the girl. They sent the stranger out here last night, to snoop. They sent the sheriff out today. And the next step would be to come out themselves. It was inevitable. Inevitable.

When Norman thought about that he wanted to do all sorts of crazy things—run away, go down into the fruit cellar and put his head in Mother's lap, go upstairs and pull the covers back over his head. But he couldn't run away and leave Mother, and he couldn't risk taking her with him in her condition. He couldn't go to her for comfort. He couldn't trust her after what had happened. And pulling the covers over his head wouldn't help. He'd just have to face them, stick to his story, and nothing would happen.

He sat in the office alone. Alabama had pulled out early in the morning, and Illinois had left right after lunch. There were no new customers. It was beginning to cloud up, and if the storm came, he needn't expect any business this evening. So one drink wouldn't hurt. Not if it made him calm down again.

Norman found a bottle in the cubbyhole under the counter. It was the second bottle of the three he'd put there over a month ago. That wasn't bad; just the second bottle. Drinking the first one had gotten him into all this trouble, but it wouldn't happen that way again. Not now, when he could be sure Mother was safely out of the way.

In a little while, when it got dark, he'd see about fixing Mother some dinner. Maybe tonight they could talk. Right now, he needed this drink. These drinks. The first didn't really help, but the second did the trick. He was quite relaxed now. He could even take another one if he wanted to. And then he wanted to very much, because he saw the car drive in.

Norman knew right away that *they* were here. When you're a psychic sensitive, you can *feel* the vibrations. And you can feel your heart pound, so you gulp the drink and watch them get out of the car. The man was ordinary-looking, and for a moment Norman wondered if he hadn't made a mistake. But then he saw the girl.

He saw the girl, and he tilted the bottle up—tilted it up to take a hasty swallow and to hide her face at the same time—because it was *the* girl.

She'd come back, out of the swamp!

No. No, she couldn't. That wasn't the answer, it couldn't be. Look at her again. Her hair wasn't the same color, really; it was brownish blond. And she was slimmer. But she looked enough like the girl to be her sister.

Yes, of course. That must be who she was. This Jane Wilson or whatever her name was had run away with that money. The detective came after her, and now her sister. That was the answer. That explained everything.

He knew what Mother would do in a case like this. But thank God he'd never have to run *that* risk again. All he had to do was stick to his story and they'd go away. Just remember nobody could find anything; nobody could prove anything. There was nothing to worry about, now that he knew what to expect.

The liquor had helped. It helped him to stand patiently behind the counter while he waited for them to come in, watching the dark clouds coming on out of the west. He saw the sky darken as the sun surrendered its splendor. *The sun surrendered its splendor*—why, it was like poetry; he was a poet! Norman smiled. He was many things. If they only knew . . .

But they didn't know, and they wouldn't know; right now he was just a fat, middle-aged motel proprietor who blinked up at the pair of them as they came in and said, "Can I help you?"

The man came up to the counter. Norman braced himself for the first question, then blinked again when the man didn't ask it. Instead he was saying, "Could we have a room, please?"

Norman nodded, unable to answer. Had he made a mistake? But no, the girl *was* the sister, no doubt about it. Norman smiled. "It's ten dollars, double. If you'll just sign here—"

He pushed the register forward. The man hesitated for a moment, then scribbled. Norman could read it upside down. "Mr. and Mrs. Sam Wright, Independence, Mo."

Filthy, stupid liars! Wright was wrong. They thought they were so clever, trying to pull their tricks on him. Well, they'd see!

The girl was staring at the register. At a name up on top of the page. At her sister's name. *Jane Wilson.*

"I'll give you number one," Norman said.

"How about number six?" the girl asked.

Number six. Norman had written it down, as he always did after each signature. The room he'd given the sister, of course. She'd noticed that.

"Number six is up at this end," he said. "But you wouldn't want that. The fan's broken."

"Oh, we won't need a fan. Storm's coming up, it'll cool off in a hurry." *Liar.* "Besides, six is our lucky number. We were married on the sixth of this month." *Dirty, filthy liar.*

Norman shrugged. "All right," he said.

And it *was* all right. It was even *better* than all right. If they were going to just sneak around, number six was ideal. He didn't have to worry about them finding anything in there. And he could keep an eye on them. Perfect!

So he took the key and escorted them next door to number six. It was only a few steps, but already the wind had come up, and it felt chilly there in the twilight. He unlocked the unit while the man brought out a bag. Then he opened the door, and they stepped in. "Will there be anything else?"

"No, we're all right now, thank you."

Norman went back to the office and took a congratulatory drink. This was going to be easy as pie, even easier than he'd dreamed. He tilted the license in its frame and stared through the crack into the bathroom of number six.

They weren't occupying it, of course; they were in the bedroom beyond. Once in a while he caught muffled phrases of their conversation. The two of them were searching for something.

The girl's voice. ". . . anything happened, there'd be something he overlooked. . . . Always little clues . . ."

Man's voice. "I still think . . . better to come right out, frighten him into admitting . . ."

Her voice, coming closer. "If we *could* find something . . . able to scare him . . ."

She was walking into the bathroom now, and he was following her. "With any kind of evidence we could make the sheriff come out again."

He was standing in the doorway of the bathroom, watching her as she examined the sink. "Look how clean everything is! We'd better talk to him. It's our only chance."

She had stepped out of Norman's field of vision. She was looking into the shower stall now, he could hear the curtains swishing back. The little bitch, she was just like her sister, she had to go into the shower!

Norman waited for her to step out of the shower stall, but she didn't reappear. Instead he heard the man ask, "What are you doing?"

Norman echoed the question. What *was* she doing?

"Just reaching around in back here. You never know . . . Sam. Look! I've found something!"

She was standing in front of the mirror again, holding something in her hand.

"Sam, it's an earring. One of Mary's earrings!"

"Are you sure?"

No, it couldn't be the other earring. It couldn't be.

"Of course it's one of hers. I ought to know. I gave them to her myself, for her birthday. There's a custom jeweler who runs a little hole-in-the-wall shop in Dallas. I had him make these for her. She thought it was terribly extravagant of me, but she loved them. She must have knocked one off when she was taking a shower. Unless something else hap—"

"Something else did happen, Lila."

The man's voice was excited now. He was holding the earring under the light.

"Sam, what's the matter?"

"Lila, do you see this? Looks to me like dried blood."

"Oh—*no!* Sam, we've got to get into that house. We've *got* to."

That girl. Listen to her, now.

"That's a job for the sheriff."

"He'd say she fell, bumped her head in the shower, something like that."

"Maybe she did."

"Do you really believe that, Sam? Do you?"

"No. But it's up to the sheriff to find out more."

"But I know he won't do anything! We'd have to have something that would really convince him, something from the house. I know we could find something there."

"No. Too dangerous. The smartest thing to do is to go after the sheriff right now."

"What if Bates is suspicious? If he sees us leave, he might run away."

"We could put through a call—"

"The phone is in the office. He'd hear us." Lila paused for a moment. "Listen, Sam. Let *me* go after the sheriff. You stay here and talk to Bates. Tell him I'm running into town to go to the drugstore, just so he doesn't get alarmed."

"Well—"

"Give me the earring, Sam."

The voices faded, but the words remained. The man was staying here while *she* went and got the sheriff. And he couldn't stop her. If Mother was here, she'd stop her. But Mother was locked up in the fruit cellar.

Yes, and if that little bitch showed the sheriff the bloody earring, he'd come back and look for Mother. For twenty years he hadn't even dreamed the truth, but now he might do the one thing Norman had always been afraid he'd do. He might find out what really happened the night Uncle Joe Considine died.

There were more sounds coming from next door. Norman could

hear the door slam. They were coming out of number six; she was going to the car and he was walking in here. Norman adjusted the license frame hastily.

He turned to face the man, wondering what he was going to say. But even more, he was wondering what the sheriff would do. *The sheriff could go up to Fairvale Cemetery and open Mother's grave. And when he opened it, when he saw the empty coffin, then he'd know the real secret.*

He'd know that Mother was alive.

There was a pounding in Norman's chest, a pounding that was drowned out by the first rumble of thunder as the man opened the door and came in.

"MIND if I come in for a few minutes?" Sam asked. "Wife's taking a little ride into town. She's fresh out of cigarettes."

Bates peered over Sam's shoulder, gazing off into the dusk, and Sam knew he was watching the car move onto the highway. "Too bad she has to go all that way. Looks as if it's going to be raining pretty hard in a few minutes," Bates said.

"Get much rain around here?" Sam sat down on the arm of a battered sofa.

"Quite a bit." Bates nodded vaguely. "We get all kinds of things around here."

What did he mean by that remark? The eyes behind the fat man's glasses seemed vacant. Suddenly Sam caught the telltale whiff of alcohol, and at the same moment he noticed the bottle standing at the edge of the counter. That was the answer; Bates was a little bit drunk.

Bates caught Sam looking at the whiskey bottle. "Care for a drink?" he asked.

Sam hesitated. "Well—"

"Find you a glass. There's one under here someplace." He bent behind the counter, emerged holding a shot glass. "Don't generally take a drink when I'm on duty. But with the damp coming on, a little something helps, particularly if you have rheumatism the way I do."

355

He filled the shot glass, pushed it forward on the counter. Sam rose and walked over to it.

It was raining hard now; he couldn't see more than a few feet up the road in the downpour. It was getting quite dark, too, but Bates made no movement to switch on any lights.

Sam returned to the sofa with the drink. He glanced at his watch. Lila had been gone about eight minutes. Even in this rain she'd get to Fairvale in less than twenty—then ten minutes to find the sheriff—twenty minutes more to return. Three-quarters of an hour was a long time to stall. What could he talk about?

Sam lifted his glass. Bates was taking a swig out of the bottle.

"Must get pretty lonesome out here sometimes," Sam said.

"That's right." The bottle thumped down on the counter.

"I'll bet you get to see all kinds of people in a spot like this," Sam said.

"They come and go. I don't pay much attention."

"Been here a long time?"

"All my life."

"And you run the whole place by yourself?"

"That's right." Bates moved around the counter, carrying the bottle. "Here, let me fill up your glass. I don't like to drink alone."

"I really shouldn't."

"Won't hurt you. I'm not going to tell your wife." Bates chuckled.

He poured, then retreated behind the counter.

Sam sat back. Looking at this man's face, only a gray blur in the growing darkness, listening to him, Sam was beginning to feel slightly ashamed. He sounded so damned *ordinary!* It was hard to imagine him being mixed up in something like this.

And just what was he mixed up in, anyway? Mary had stolen some money, Mary had been here overnight, she had lost an earring in the shower. But she could have cut her ear when the earring came off. Yes, and she could have gone on to Chicago, too, just the way the sheriff seemed to think.

Lila was a nice girl, but too hair-triggered, too impulsive. Always making snap judgments and decisions. Like wanting to run straight up and search Bates's house. Good thing he'd talked her out of that one. Maybe even bringing the sheriff was a mistake. The way Bates was acting now, he didn't seem like a man who had anything on his conscience.

Sam remembered that he was supposed to be talking. "It is raining pretty hard," he murmured.

"I like the way the rain comes down hard," Bates said. "It's exciting."

"Never thought of it that way. Guess you can use a little excitement around here."

"I don't know. We get our share."

"We? I thought you said you lived here alone."

"I said I operated the motel alone. But it belongs to both of us. My mother and me."

Sam almost choked on the whiskey. He lowered the glass, clenching it tightly in his fist. "I didn't know—"

"Of course not, how could you? Nobody does. That's because she always stays in the house. She has to stay there. You see, most people think she's dead."

The voice was calm. Sam couldn't see Bates's face in the dimness now, but he knew it was calm, too.

"Actually, there *is* excitement around here. Like there was twenty years ago, when Mother and Uncle Joe Considine drank the poison. I called the sheriff and he came out and found them. Mother left a note, explaining everything. Then they had an inquest, but I didn't go to it. I was very sick. They took me to the hospital. I was in the hospital a long time. Almost too long to do any good when I got out. But I managed."

"Managed?"

Bates didn't reply at once. Sam heard a gurgle and then the bottle's thump.

"Oh, yes." He was coming around the counter now, and his shadowy bulk loomed over Sam. "I brought Mother back home with me. That was the exciting part, you see—going out to the cemetery at night and digging up the grave. She'd been shut up in that coffin for such a long time that at first I thought she really *was* dead. But she wasn't, of course. Or else she wouldn't have been able to communicate with me when I was in the hospital all that while. It was only a trance state; what we call suspended animation. I knew how to revive her. There *are* ways, you know, even if some folks call it magic. It wasn't so very long ago that people were saying that electricity was magic. Actually, it's a force which can be harnessed, if you know the secret. Life is a force, too, a vital force. And like electricity, you can turn it off and on, off and on. I'd turned it off, and I knew how to turn it on again. Do you understand me?"

"Yes—it's very interesting. But Mr. Bates, are you quite sure you're all right? I mean—"

"I know what you mean. You think I'm drunk, don't you? But I wasn't drunk when you came here. I wasn't drunk when you found that earring and told the young lady to go to the sheriff. She isn't really your wife, is she?"

"I—"

"You see, I know more than you think I know. Sit still, now. Don't be alarmed. I'm not alarmed, am I? You don't think I'd tell you all this if there was anything wrong?" The fat man paused. "No, I waited until you came in. I waited until I saw her drive up the road. I waited until I saw her stop."

"Stop?" Sam tried to find the face in the darkness, but all he could hear was the voice.

"You didn't know that she stopped the car, did you? You thought she went on to get the sheriff, the way you agreed to. But she has a mind of her own. She wanted to take a look at the house. And that's where she is, now."

"Let me out of here—"

"Of course. I'm not hindering you. It's just that I thought you might like another drink, while I told you the rest about Mother. The reason I thought you might like to know is because of the girl. She'll be meeting Mother, now."

"Get out of my way!"

Sam rose swiftly, going toward the door.

"You don't want another drink, then?" Bates's voice sounded petulant. "Very well. Have it your own—"

The end of his sentence was lost in the thunder, and the thunder was lost in the darkness as Sam felt the bottle explode against the roof of his skull. Then voice, thunder, explosion, and Sam himself all disappeared into the night. . . .

IT WAS still night, but somebody was shaking him up out of the night and into this room where the light burned, hurting his eyes and making him blink. Sam could feel now, and somebody's arms were lifting him, so that at first he felt as if his head would drop off. Then it was only throbbing, throbbing, and he could open his eyes and look at Sheriff Chambers.

Sam was sitting on the floor next to the sofa and Chambers was gazing down at him. Sam opened his mouth.

"Thank God," he said. "He was lying about Lila, then. She did get to you."

The sheriff didn't seem to be listening. "Got a call from the hotel about half an hour ago. They were trying to locate your friend Arbogast. Seems he checked out, but he never took his bags with him. Left 'em downstairs Saturday morning, said he'd be back, but he never showed. Got to thinking it over, and then I tried to find you. Had a hunch you might have come out here on your own—lucky I followed through."

"Then Lila didn't reach you?" Sam tried to stand up. His head was splitting.

"Take it easy there." The sheriff pushed him back. "No, I haven't seen her at all. Wait—"

This time Sam managed to stand on his feet, swaying.

"What happened here?" the sheriff muttered. "Where's Bates?"

"He must have gone up to the house after he slugged me," Sam said. "They're up there now, he and his mother."

"But she's dead—"

"No, she isn't," Sam told him. "She's alive, the two of them are up at the house with Lila!"

"Come on." The big man plowed out into the rain. Sam followed him, scrambling, panting as they began the steep ascent to the house beyond.

"Are you sure?" Chambers called over his shoulder. "Everything's dark up there."

"I'm sure," Sam wheezed. But he might have saved his breath.

The sound came suddenly, shrilly. Both of them recognized it.

Lila was screaming.

Chapter 10

LILA reached the porch just before the rain came. The boards creaked under her feet, and she could hear the wind rattling the casements of the upstairs windows. She rapped on the front door angrily, not expecting any answer from within. She didn't expect anyone to do anything anymore.

The truth was that nobody else really *cared*. They didn't care about Mary at all, not a one of them. Mr. Lowery just wanted his money back, and Arbogast was only doing a job. As for the sheriff, all he was interested in was avoiding trouble. But it was Sam's reaction that really upset her.

Lila knocked again, and the house groaned a hollow echo.

All right, she *was* angry—and why shouldn't she be? A whole week of listening to *take it easy, be calm, relax, just be patient.* If they had their way, she'd still be back there in Fort Worth. At least she'd counted on Sam to help her, but she might have known better. Oh, he seemed nice enough, even attractive in a way, but he had that slow, cautious, conservative small-town outlook. He and the sheriff made a good pair. *Don't take any chances,* that was their whole idea.

Well, it wasn't hers. Not after she'd found the earring. How could Sam shrug it off and tell her to go get the sheriff again? Why didn't he just grab Bates and beat the truth out of him? That's what she would have done, if she were a man. One thing was certain, she was through depending on others—others who didn't care, who just wanted to keep out of trouble. She didn't trust Sam to stick his neck out anymore, and she certainly didn't trust the sheriff.

If she hadn't gotten so angry, she wouldn't be doing this, but she was sick of their caution, sick of their theories. There are times when you must stop analyzing and depend on your emotions. It was sheer frustration which prompted her to keep on with the hopeless task of rummaging around until she found Mary's earring. She was going to see for herself. There'd be something else here in the house. There *had* to be.

Just thinking about their smugness made Lila rattle the doorknob. That wouldn't do any good. There was nobody inside the house to answer her; she already knew that.

Lila dipped into her purse. Somewhere in there was a metal nail file. Yes, here it was. The lock was simple and old-fashioned. The nail file might just work. She inserted it in the lock and turned it partway. The lock resisted, and again anger came to her aid. She twisted the file sharply. It snapped with a brittle click, but not before the lock had given. She felt the door move away from her hand. It was open.

Lila stood in the hall. It was darker inside the house than out there on the porch. But there must be a light switch somewhere. She found one, snapped it on. The unshaded overhead bulb gave off a feeble, sickly glare against the background of peeling, shredded wallpaper. What was the design—bunches of grapes, or were they violets? Hideous.

The rooms on this floor could wait until later. Arbogast had said he saw someone looking out of a window upstairs. That would be the place to begin. There was no light switch for the stairway. Lila went up slowly, groping along the banister. As she reached the landing the thunder came. The whole house seemed to shake with it. Lila gave an involuntary shudder. It *was* involuntary, she told herself. Certainly there was nothing about an empty house like this to frighten anybody. And now she could turn on the light here in the upstairs hall.

She had her choice of three doors to enter. The first led to the bathroom. Lila had never seen such a place—an upright bathtub on legs, and dangling from the high ceiling next to the toilet, a metal pull chain. There was a small, flawed mirror over the washbowl. Here was the linen closet, stacked with neatly folded towels and perfectly ironed sheets. She rummaged through the shelves hastily; their contents told her nothing, except that Bates probably had his laundry sent out.

Lila entered the second door and switched on the light. Another weak and naked overhead bulb, but its illumination was sufficient to reveal the room for what it was. Bates's bedroom—singularly small, singularly cramped, with a low cot more suitable for a little boy than a grown man. Probably he'd always slept here, ever since he was a child. The bed itself was rumpled and showed signs of recent occupancy. There was a bureau over in the corner, next to the closet—one of those antique horrors with a dark oak finish and corroded drawer pulls. She had no compunctions about searching the drawers.

The top one contained neckties and handkerchiefs, most of them soiled. The neckties were wide and old-fashioned. The second drawer contained shirts, the third held socks and underwear. The bottom drawer was filled with shapeless garments which she finally—and almost incredulously—identified as nightgowns. Maybe he wore a bedcap, too!

It was odd that there were no personal mementos, though; no papers, no photographs. Lila turned her attention to the pictures on the walls. The first showed a small boy sitting on a pony, and the second showed the same child standing in front of a rural schoolhouse with five other children, all girls. It took Lila several moments before she identified the youngster as Norman Bates. He had been quite thin as a child.

Nothing remained, except the closet and the two bookshelves in the corner. The closet contained two suits on hangers, a jacket, an overcoat, a pair of soiled and paint-spotted trousers, two pairs of shoes, and a pair of bedroom slippers. There was nothing in the pockets of the garments.

The bookshelves now.

Lila found herself peering in perplexity at the contents of Norman Bates's library. *The Extension of Consciousness, The Witch-Cult in Western Europe, Dimension and Being.* These were not the books of a small boy, and they were equally out of place in the home of a rural motel proprietor. She scanned the shelves rapidly. Abnormal psychology, occultism, theosophy. And here, on the bottom shelf, an assortment of untitled volumes, poorly bound. Lila pulled one out and opened it. The illustration that leaped out at her was almost pathologically pornographic.

She replaced the volume hastily. As she did so the initial shock of revulsion ebbed away, giving place to a stronger reaction. There *was* something here, there must be. What she could not read in Norman Bates's dull, fat, commonplace face was all too vividly revealed in this library.

Frowning, she retreated to the hall. The rain clattered harshly on the roof as she opened the dark, paneled door leading to the third room. For a moment she stood staring into the dimness, inhaling a musty, mingled odor of stale perfume and—what?

She pressed the light switch, then gasped.

This was the front bedroom, no doubt of it. The sheriff had said something about how Bates had kept it unchanged since his mother's death. But Lila wasn't prepared to step bodily into another era. For the décor of this room had been outmoded many years before Bates's mother died. The room belonged in a world of gilt clocks, Dresden figurines, sachet-scented pincushions, tasseled draperies, and overstuffed chairs covered with antimacassars.

And it was still alive.

That was what gave Lila the feeling of dislocation in space and time. Downstairs were remnants of the past ravaged by decay, and upstairs all was shabbiness and neglect. But this room was composed, consistent, coherent. It was spotlessly clean and perfectly ordered. And yet, aside from the musty odor, there was no feeling of being in a showplace or a museum. The room *did* seem alive, as does any room that is lived in for a long time. Furnished more than fifty years ago, untenanted and untouched since the death of its occupant twenty years ago, it was still the room of a living person. A room where, just yesterday, a woman had sat and peered out of the window—

There are no ghosts, Lila told herself, and yet here in this room she could feel a living presence.

She turned to the closet. The short skirts, coats, and dresses of a quarter of a century ago still hung in a neat row, though sagging and wrinkled through long lack of pressing. Up on the shelf were hats, head scarves, shawls such as an older woman might wear in a rural community. And nothing more.

Lila started over to examine the dresser and vanity, then halted beside the bed. The hand-embroidered bedspread was very lovely; she put out a hand to feel the texture, then drew it back hastily.

The spread was tucked in tightly at the bottom and hung perfectly over the sides. But the top was out of line, so that an inch of the double pillow showed; the way a spread is tucked in when a bed has been made in a hurry—

She ripped back the covers. The sheets were a smudgy gray and covered with little brown flecks. The bed itself and the pillow above it bore the unmistakable indentation made by a recent occupant. She could almost trace the outline of the body by the way the under sheet sagged, and there was a deep depression in the center of the pillow, where the brown flecks were thickest.

There are no ghosts, Lila told herself again. This room has been used. Bates didn't sleep here—his own rumpled bed offered sufficient evidence of that. But somebody had been sleeping here, somebody had been staring out of the window. *And if it had been Mary, where was she now?*

Then she knew.

What was it Sheriff Chambers had said? That he found Norman Bates in the woods behind the house, gathering firewood? Firewood for the furnace. Yes, that was it. *The furnace in the basement—*

Angry, Lila turned and fled down the stairs. She knew why she had been so angry, too, ever since finding the earring. She had been angry because she was afraid, and the anger helped to hide the fear. The fear of what had happened to Mary, what she *knew* had happened to Mary, down in the cellar. He had kept her here all week, maybe he'd tortured her, maybe he'd done to her what that man was doing in that filthy book; he'd tortured her until he found out about the money, and then—

The cellar. She had to find the cellar.

Lila groped her way along the downstairs hall into the kitchen. She found the light, then gasped as the tiny furry creature crouched on the shelf before her, ready to spring. But it was only a stuffed squirrel, its button eyes idiotically alive in the reflection of the overhead light.

The basement stairs were just ahead. Her hand brushed over another switch. The light went on below, a faint and faltering glow in the darkened depths. Then she descended. Thunder growled in counterpoint to the clatter of her heels.

The bare bulb dangled from a cord directly in front of a big furnace with a heavy iron door. Lila stood there, staring at it. She was trembling now. She'd been a fool to come here alone, a fool to do what she was doing. But she had to open the furnace door and see what she knew would be inside. *God, what if the fire was still going? What if—*

But the door was cold. And there was no heat from within the dark, empty recess behind the door. She stooped, peering. No ashes, nothing at all. Unless it had been recently cleaned, the furnace hadn't been used since last spring.

Lila turned away. She saw the old-fashioned laundry tubs, and the table and chair beyond them, next to the wall. There were bottles on the table, and carpentry tools, plus an assortment of knives and needles. Some of the knives were oddly curved, and several of the needles were attached to syringes. Behind them rose a clutter of wooden blocks, heavy wire, and large shapeless blobs of a white substance. One of the bigger fragments looked something like the cast she had worn as a child, that time she'd broken her leg. Lila approached the table, gazing at the knives in puzzled concentration.

Then she heard the sound.

At first she thought it was thunder, but then came the creaking from overhead, and she knew.

Somebody had come into the house. Somebody was tiptoeing along the hall. Was it Sam? Had he come to find her? If so, why didn't he call her name?

And why did he close the cellar door?

The cellar door *had* closed, just now. She could hear the sharp click of the lock, and the footsteps moving away, back along the hall. The intruder must be going upstairs to the second floor.

She was locked in the cellar. And there was no way out, nowhere to hide. The whole basement was visible to anyone descending the cellar stairs. And somebody would be coming down those stairs soon. She knew it.

If she could only keep herself concealed for a moment, then whoever came after her would have to descend all the way into the basement. And she'd have a chance to run for the stairs.

The best place would be under the stairway itself. If she could only cover herself up with some old papers or rags—

Then Lila saw the blanket that hung on the far wall. It was a big Indian blanket, ragged and old. She tugged at it, and the rotted cloth ripped free of the nails which held it in place. It came off the wall, off the door.

The door. The blanket had concealed it completely, but there must be another room here, probably a storage room of some sort. It would be the ideal place to hide and wait.

And she wouldn't have to wait much longer. She could hear the faint, faraway footsteps coming down the hall again, moving along into the kitchen.

Lila tugged at the rusty doorknob, the lock gave way, and the door opened. It was then that she screamed.

She screamed when she saw the old woman lying there, the gaunt, gray-haired old woman whose brown, wrinkled face grinned up at her in an obscene greeting.

"Mrs. Bates!" Lila gasped.

"Yes."

But the voice wasn't coming from those sunken, leathery jaws. It came from behind her, from the top of the cellar stairs, where the figure stood.

Lila turned to stare at the fat, shapeless figure, half concealed by the tight dress which had been pulled down incongruously to cover the garments beneath. She stared up at the shrouding shawl, and at the white, painted, simpering face beneath it. She stared at the garishly reddened lips, watched them part in a convulsive grimace.

"*I am Norma Bates,*" said the high, shrill voice. And then there was the hand coming out, the hand that held the knife, and the feet were mincing down the stairs, and other feet were running, and Lila screamed again as Sam came down the stairs and the knife came up, quick as death. Sam grasped and twisted the hand that held it, twisted it from behind until the knife clattered to the floor.

Lila closed her mouth, but the scream continued. It was the insane scream of a hysterical woman, and it came from the throat of Norman Bates.

Chapter 11

IT TOOK a week to reclaim the cars and the bodies from the swamp. The county highway crew had to come in with a dredge and hoists, but in the end the job was done. They found the money, too, right there in the glove compartment. Funny thing, it didn't even have a speck of mud on it.

Almost the entire front page of the Fairvale *Weekly Herald* was given over to the Bates case. The wire services picked it up, and there was quite a bit about it on television. Some of the write-ups described the "house of horror" and tried their damnedest to make out that Norman Bates had been murdering motel visitors for years. They urged that the entire swamp be drained to see if it would yield more bodies. But then, of course, the newspaper writers didn't have to foot the bill for such a project.

Sheriff Chambers gave out a number of interviews and promised a full investigation of all aspects of the case. The local district attorney called for a speedy trial and did nothing to contradict the rumors that Norman Bates was guilty of cannibalism, satanism, incest, and necrophilia. It was beginning to appear that the entire county had been intimately acquainted with him and that they had all "noticed something funny about the way he acted."

Norman Bates was temporarily confined for observation at the

State Hospital. The motel, of course, was closed, and State Highway Patrol troopers guarded the property against the crowds of morbid curiosity seekers.

Bob Summerfield reported a noticeable increase of business at the hardware store. Everybody wanted to talk to Sam, naturally, but he spent part of the following week in Fort Worth with Lila, then took a run up to the State Hospital, where three psychiatrists were examining Norman Bates.

It wasn't until almost ten days later, however, that Sam was able to get a definite statement from Dr. Nicholas Steiner, who was officially in charge of the medical observation. Sam reported the results of his interview to Lila, at the hotel, when she came in from Fort Worth the following weekend. He was reticent at first, but she insisted on the full details.

"We'll probably never know everything that happened," Sam said. "Dr. Steiner told me they kept Bates under heavy sedation at first, and after he came out of it nobody could get him to talk very much. Steiner says Bates appears to be in a very confused state. A lot of the things Steiner said, about fugue and cathexis and trauma, are way over my head.

"But as near as he can make out, this all started way back in Bates's childhood, long before his mother's death. Norman and his mother were very close, of course, and apparently she dominated him. Whether there was ever anything more to their relationship, Dr. Steiner doesn't know. But he does suspect that Norman was a secret transvestite long before Mrs. Bates died. You know what a transvestite is, don't you?"

"A person who dresses in the clothing of the opposite sex?"

"The way Steiner explained it, there's a lot more to it than that. Transvestites aren't necessarily homosexual, but they identify themselves strongly with members of the other sex. In a way Norman wanted to be like his mother, and in a way he wanted his mother to become a part of himself."

Sam lit a cigarette. "I'm going to skip his school years and his rejection by the army. But it was after that, when he was around nineteen, that his mother must have decided Norman wasn't ever going out into the world on his own. Maybe she deliberately prevented him from growing up; we'll never actually know just how much she was responsible for what he became. It was probably then that he began to develop his interest in occultism, things like that. And it was then that Joe Considine came into the picture.

"Steiner couldn't get Norman to say much about Joe Considine—even today, more than twenty years later, his hatred is so great, he can't talk about the man without flying into a rage. But Steiner talked to the sheriff and he has a pretty fair idea of what really happened.

"Considine was a man in his early forties; when he met Mrs. Bates she was thirty-nine. She was on the skinny side and prematurely gray, but ever since her husband had left her she had owned quite a bit of farm property he'd put in her name, and she was well-off. Considine began to court her. It wasn't too easy—I gather Mrs. Bates hated men ever since her husband deserted her, and this is one of the reasons why she treated Norman the way she did. But Considine finally got her to agree to a marriage. He'd brought up the idea of selling the farm and using the money to build a motel—the old highway ran right alongside the place in those days, and there was a lot of business to be had.

"Apparently, Norman had no objections to the motel. The plan went through, and for the first three months he and his mother ran the new place together. It was only then that his mother told him she and Considine were going to be married."

"And that sent him off?" Lila asked.

"Not exactly," said Sam. "It seems the announcement was made under rather embarrassing circumstances, after Norman had walked in on his mother and Considine together in the upstairs bedroom. We don't know how long it took for the reaction to set in, but we do know what happened as a result. Norman poisoned his mother and Considine with strychnine. Served it to them with their coffee during some sort of private celebration. The coffee was laced with brandy; it must have helped to kill the taste."

"Horrible!" Lila shuddered.

"It *was*. Strychnine poisoning brings on convulsions, but not unconsciousness. The victims usually die from asphyxiation, when the chest muscles stiffen. Norman must have watched it all. And it was too much to bear.

"It was when he was writing the suicide note that Dr. Steiner thinks it happened. He had planned the note, of course, and knew how to imitate his mother's handwriting perfectly. He'd even figured out a reason for the suicide pact—something about a pregnancy, and Considine being unable to marry because he had a wife and family living out on the West Coast, where he'd lived under another name. Nobody noticed what really happened to Norman after he finished the note and phoned the sheriff to come out.

"They knew at the time that he was hysterical from shock and excitement. What they didn't know is that while writing the note he'd changed. Apparently, now that it was all over, he couldn't stand the loss of his mother. He wanted her back. As he wrote the note in her handwriting, addressed to himself, he literally changed his mind. And Norman, or a part of him, *became* his mother.

"Dr. Steiner says these cases are more frequent than you'd think, particularly when the personality is already unstable. And the grief set him off. His reaction was so severe, nobody even thought to question the suicide pact. Considine and his mother were in their graves long before Norman was discharged from the hospital."

"And that's when he dug her up?"

"Apparently, within a few months after his discharge. He had this taxidermy hobby, and knew what he'd have to do."

"But I don't understand. If he thought he *was* his mother—"

"It isn't quite that simple. According to Steiner, Bates was now a multiple personality with at least three facets. There was *Norman*, the little boy who needed his mother and hated anyone who came between him and her. Then, *Norma*, the mother, who could not be allowed to die. The third aspect might be called *Normal*—the adult Norman Bates, who had to go through the daily routine of living and conceal the existence of the other personalities from the world. Of course, the three weren't entirely distinct entities, and each contained elements of the other. Dr. Steiner called it an unholy trinity.

"But the adult Norman Bates kept control well enough so that he was discharged from the hospital. He went back to run the motel. What weighed on him most, as an adult personality, was the guilty knowledge of his mother's death. Preserving her room was not enough. He wanted to preserve her, too; preserve her physically, so that the illusion of her living presence would suppress the guilt feelings.

"So he actually brought her back from the grave and gave her a new life. He put her to bed at night, dressed her and took her down into the house by day. Naturally he concealed all this from outsiders and he did it well. Arbogast must have seen the figure placed in the upstairs window, but there's no proof that anyone else did, in all those years."

"Then the horror wasn't in the house," Lila said. "It was in his head."

"Steiner says the relationship was like that of a ventriloquist and his dummy. Mother and *little* Norman must have carried on regular conversations. And the adult Norman Bates probably rationalized the situation. He was able to pretend sanity, but who knows how much he really knew? He was interested in occultism and metaphysics. He probably believed in spiritualism every bit as much as he believed in the preservative powers of taxidermy. Besides, he couldn't reject or destroy these other parts of his personality without rejecting and destroying himself. He was leading three lives at once and getting away with it, until Mary came along.

"Something happened, and he killed her. *Mother* killed her. There's no way of finding out the actual situation, but Dr. Steiner is sure that whenever a crisis arose, *Norma* became the dominant personality. Bates would start drinking, then black out while *she* took over. During the blackouts, of course, he'd dress up in her clothing. Afterward he'd hide her away, because in his mind she was the real murderer and had to be protected."

"He's insane, of course."

"Psychotic is the word Steiner used. He's going to recommend that Bates be placed in the State Hospital, probably for life."

"Then there won't be any trial?"

"That's what I came here to tell you. I'm sorry. I suppose the way you feel—"

"I'm glad," Lila said slowly. "Right now, I can't even hate him for what he did. He must have suffered more than any of us. In a way I can almost understand. We're all not quite as sane as we pretend to be."

Sam rose, and she walked him to the door. "It's over, and I'm going to try to forget everything that happened."

"Everything?" Sam murmured.

"Well, *almost* everything." She smiled up at him.

And that was the end of it.

Or *almost* the end.

Chapter 12

THE real end came quietly.

It came in the small, barred room where the voices had muttered and mingled for so long a time—the man's voice, the woman's voice, the child's.

The voices had exploded when triggered, but now, almost miraculously, a fusion took place, so that there was only one voice. And that was right, because there was only one person in the room. There always *had* been one person, and *only* one.

She knew it now.

She knew it, and she was glad.

It was so much better to be fully and completely aware of one's self as one *really* was. To be serenely strong, serenely confident, serenely secure.

She could look back upon the past as though it were all a bad dream—a bad dream, peopled with illusions.

There had been a bad boy in the bad dream who had killed her lover and tried to poison her. Somewhere in the dream was the clawing at the throat and the faces that turned blue. Somewhere in the dream was the graveyard at night and the splintering of the coffin lid, and then the moment of discovery, the moment of staring at what lay within. But what lay within wasn't really dead.

Not anymore. The bad boy was dead instead, and that was as it should be.

There had been a bad man in the bad dream, too. He had peeked through the wall, and he drank, and he read filthy books and believed in all sorts of crazy nonsense. But worst of all, he was responsible for the deaths of two innocent people—a young girl with a beautiful body and a man who wore a gray stetson hat. She knew all about it, of course, and that's why she could remember the details. Because she had been there at the time, watching.

The bad man had really committed the murders and then he tried to blame it on her.

Mother killed them. That's what he said, but it was a lie.

How could she kill them when she was only watching, when she couldn't even move, because she had to pretend to be a harmless stuffed figure that couldn't hurt or be hurt but merely exists forever?

She knew that nobody would believe the bad man, and he was dead now, too. The bad man and the bad boy were both dead. She was the only one left, and she was real.

To be the only one, and to know that you are real—that's sanity, isn't it?

But just to be on the safe side, maybe it was best to keep pretending that one was a stuffed figure. Never to move. Just to sit here in the tiny room, forever and ever.

If she sat there without moving, they wouldn't punish her.

If she sat there without moving, they'd know that she was sane.

She sat there for quite a long time, and then a fly came buzzing through the bars.

It lighted right on her hand. If she wanted to, she could reach out and swat the fly.

But she didn't swat it.

She didn't swat it, and she hoped they were watching, because that *proved* what sort of a person she really was.

Why, she wouldn't even harm a fly. . . .

The Hound
of the
Baskervilles

The Hound
of the
Baskervilles

A CONDENSATION OF
THE BOOK BY

**Sir Arthur Conan
Doyle**

ILLUSTRATED BY GUY DEEL

On the grounds of his ancestral estate, near the brooding Devonshire moors, Sir Charles Baskerville is found dead in the night. The cause of death was a heart attack—but at the moment of dying he had been running frantically to escape some terrifying pursuer.

Could it possibly have been the same ghostly hound that had mangled to death Sir Hugo Baskerville two centuries before, and that had ever since stalked as a curse through Baskerville family legend? Recently, mournful bayings and shadowy glimpses of the huge hound had been reported. Was the newly arrived young heir, Sir Henry, in danger of confronting the fiery-fanged monster?

To the mysterious moorland, with its fogs, its ruined Stone Age huts, its quaking bogs, comes the brilliant Mr. Sherlock Holmes of Baker Street to solve the puzzling death and to protect the young heir.

Here is the classic adventure of the world's best-known private investigator, the immortal creation of Sir Arthur Conan Doyle.

Chapter 1

MR. SHERLOCK Holmes, who was usually very late in the mornings, save upon those not infrequent occasions when he was up all night, was seated at the breakfast table. I stood upon the hearthrug and picked up the walking stick which our visitor had left behind him the night before. It was a fine, thick piece of wood, bulbous-headed, of the sort which is known as a penang-lawyer. Just under the head was a broad silver band, nearly an inch across. "To James Mortimer, M.R.C.S., from his friends of the C.C.H." was engraved upon it, with the date "1884." It was just such a stick as the old-fashioned family practitioner used to carry—dignified, solid, and reassuring.

"Well, Watson, what do you make of it?"

Holmes was sitting with his back to me, and I had given him no sign of my occupation.

"How did you know what I was doing? I believe you have eyes in the back of your head."

"I have, at least, a well-polished, silver-plated coffeepot in front of me," said he. "But, tell me, Watson, what do you make of our visitor's stick? Since we have been so unfortunate as to miss him and have no notion of his errand, this accidental souvenir becomes

381

of importance. Let me hear you reconstruct the man by an examination of it."

"I think," said I, following as far as I could the methods of my companion, "that Dr. Mortimer is a successful, elderly medical man, well esteemed, since those who know him give him this mark of their appreciation."

"Good!" said Holmes. "Excellent!"

"I think also that the probability is in favor of his being a country practitioner who does a great deal of his visiting on foot."

"Why so?"

"Because this stick, though originally a very handsome one, has been so knocked about that I can hardly imagine a town practitioner carrying it. The iron tip is worn down, so it is evident that he has done a great amount of walking with it."

"Perfectly sound!" said Holmes.

"And then again, there is the 'friends of the C.C.H.' I should guess that to be the Something Hunt, the local hunt to whose members he has possibly given some surgical assistance and which has made him a small presentation in return."

"Really, Watson, you excel yourself," said Holmes, pushing back his chair and lighting a cigarette. "I am bound to say that you have habitually underrated your own abilities. Without possessing genius, you have a remarkable power of stimulating it. I confess, my dear fellow, that I am very much in your debt."

He had never said as much before, and I must admit that his words gave me keen pleasure, for I had often been piqued by his indifference to my admiration for his methods. I was proud, too, to think that I had so far mastered his system as to apply it in a way which earned his approval. He now took the stick from my hands and examined it for a few minutes with his naked eyes. Then, carrying it to the window, he looked over it again with a convex lens.

"Interesting, though elementary," said he as he returned to his favorite corner of the settee. "One or two indications upon the stick give us the basis for several deductions."

"Has anything escaped me?" I asked with some self-importance.

"I am afraid, my dear Watson, that when I said that you stimulated me I meant, to be frank, that in noting your fallacies I was occasionally guided towards the truth. Not that you are entirely wrong in this instance. The man is certainly a country practitioner. And he walks a good deal. But I would suggest that a presentation to a doctor is more likely to come from a hospital than from a hunt, and that the initials C.C.H. very naturally suggest the words Charing Cross Hospital."

"Well, then, supposing that you are right. What further inferences may we draw?"

"On what occasion would it be most probable that such a presentation would be made? Obviously at the moment when Dr. Mortimer withdrew from the service of the hospital in order to start in practice for himself. We know that he is now a country practitioner. Is it, then, stretching our inference too far to say that the presentation was on the occasion of a change from a town hospital to a country practice?"

"It certainly seems probable."

"Now, you will observe that only a man well established in a London practice could have been on the staff of the hospital, and such a one would not drift into the country. What was his position then? If he was in the hospital and yet not on the staff, he could only have been a house physician—little more than a senior student. And he left five years ago—the date is on the stick. So your middle-aged practitioner vanishes into thin air, my dear Watson, and there emerges a young fellow under thirty, amiable, unambitious, absentminded, and the possessor of a favorite dog, which I should describe roughly as being larger than a terrier and smaller than a mastiff."

I laughed incredulously as Sherlock Holmes leaned back in his settee and blew little wavering rings of smoke up to the ceiling.

"I think that I am fairly justified in my inferences," said Holmes with a mischievous smile. "I said amiable, unambitious, and absentminded; it is my experience that it is only an amiable man in this world who receives testimonials, only an unambitious one who abandons a London career for the country, and only an absentminded one who leaves his stick and not his visiting card after waiting an hour in your room." He had risen and paced the room as he spoke. Now he halted in the recess of the window.

"And the dog?"

"Has been in the habit of carrying this stick behind his master. The marks of his teeth are very plainly visible. His jaw is too broad in my opinion for a terrier and not broad enough for a mastiff. It may have been—yes, by Jove, it *is* a curly-haired spaniel."

There was such a ring of conviction in his voice that I glanced up in surprise. "My dear fellow, how can you possibly be so sure of that?"

"I see the dog himself on our doorstep, and there is the ring of its owner. Don't move, I beg you, Watson. He is a professional brother of yours, and your presence may be of assistance to me. Now is the dramatic moment of fate. What does Dr. James Mortimer, the man of science, ask of Sherlock Holmes, the specialist in crime? Come in!"

Our visitor was a very tall, thin man, with a long nose jutting out between two keen, gray eyes which sparkled brightly from behind a pair of gold-rimmed glasses. Though young, his long back was already bowed, and he walked with a forward thrust of his head and a general air of peering benevolence. As he entered his eyes fell upon the stick in Holmes's hand, and he ran towards it with an exclamation of joy. "I am so very glad," said he. "I was not sure whether I had left it here. I would not lose that stick for the world."

"A presentation, I see," said Holmes.

"From one or two friends at Charing Cross Hospital on the occasion of my marriage."

"Dear, dear, that's bad!" said Holmes, shaking his head.

Dr. Mortimer blinked through his glasses in mild astonishment.

"Why was it bad?"

"Only that you have disarranged our little deductions. Your marriage, you say?"

"Yes, sir. I married, and so left the hospital, and with it all hopes of a consulting practice. It was necessary to make a home of my own, and I settled in Grimpen, a small hamlet on Dartmoor in Devonshire."

"Come, come, we are not so far wrong, after all," said Holmes.

"I presume that it is Mr. Sherlock Holmes who is addressing me and not—" Dr. Mortimer began.

"This is my friend Dr. Watson."

"Glad to meet you, sir. Mr. Holmes, you interest me very much. I had hardly expected so dolichocephalic a skull. Would you have any objection to my running my finger along your parietal fissure? A cast of your skull, sir, until the original is available, would be an ornament to any anthropological museum."

Sherlock Holmes waved our strange visitor into a chair. "You are an enthusiast in your line of thought, I perceive, sir, as I am in mine," said he. "I observe from your forefinger that you make your own cigarettes. Have no hesitation in lighting one."

The man drew out paper and tobacco and twirled the one up in the other with surprising dexterity.

Holmes was silent, but his little darting glances showed me the interest which he took in our curious companion.

"I presume, sir," said he at last, "that it was not merely for the purpose of examining my skull that you have done me the honor to call here last night and again today? I think, Dr. Mortimer, you would do wisely if without more ado you would kindly tell me plainly the exact nature of the problem in which you demand my assistance."

Chapter 2

"I have in my pocket a manuscript," said Dr. James Mortimer.

"I observed it as you entered the room," said Holmes. "Early eighteenth century, unless it is a forgery."

"How can you say that, sir?"

"You have presented an inch or two of it to my examination all the time that you have been talking. It would be a poor expert who could not give the date of a document within a decade or so. I put that at 1730."

"The exact date is 1742." Dr. Mortimer drew it from his breast pocket. "This family paper was committed to my care by Sir Charles Baskerville, whose sudden and tragic death some three months ago created so much excitement in Devonshire. I was his personal friend as well as his medical attendant. He was a strong-minded man, sir, shrewd and practical. Yet he took this document very seriously, and his mind was prepared for just such an end as did eventually overtake him."

Holmes stretched out his hand for the manuscript and flattened it upon his knee. I looked over his shoulder at the yellow paper and the faded script. At the head was written: "Baskerville Hall," and below, in large, scrawling figures: "1742."

"It appears to be a statement of some sort."

"Yes, it is a statement of a legend which runs in the Baskerville family," said Dr. Mortimer. "But it is intimately connected with a most practical, pressing matter, which must be decided within twenty-four hours. With your permission I will read it to you."

Holmes returned the paper to Dr. Mortimer. Then he leaned back in his chair, placed his fingertips together, and closed his eyes with an air of resignation. Dr. Mortimer turned the manuscript to the light and read in a high, cracking voice the following curious narrative:

" 'Of the origin of the Hound of the Baskervilles there have been many statements, yet as I come in a direct line from Hugo Baskerville, and as I had the story from my father, who also had it from his, I have set it down with all belief that it occurred even as is here set forth.

" 'Know then that in the time of the Great Rebellion this Manor of Baskerville was held by Hugo of that name, nor can it be gainsaid that he was a most wild, profane, and godless man. Saints have never flourished in these parts, but there was in him a certain wanton and cruel humor which made his name a byword through the West. It chanced that this Hugo came to love the daughter of a yeoman who held lands near the Baskerville estate. But the young maiden would ever avoid him, for she feared his evil name. So it came to pass that one Michaelmas this Hugo, with five or six of his idle and wicked companions, stole down upon the farm and carried off the maiden, her father and brothers being from home. When they had brought her to the Hall the maiden was placed in an upper chamber, while Hugo and his friends sat down to a long carouse. Now, the poor lass upstairs was like to have her wits turned at the shouting and terrible oaths which came up to her from below. At last in the stress of her fear, by the aid of the growth of ivy which covers the south wall she came down from under the eaves, and so homeward across the moor.

" 'It chanced that some little time later Hugo left his guests to carry food and drink to his captive, and so found the cage empty and the bird escaped. Rushing down the stairs into the dining hall, he sprang upon the great table and cried aloud before all the company that he would that very night render his body and soul to the powers of evil if he might but overtake the wench. And while the revelers stood aghast at the fury of the man, one more wicked or, it may be, more drunken than the rest, cried out that they should put the hounds upon her. Whereat Hugo ran from the house, crying to his grooms that they should saddle his mare and unkennel the pack. Giving the hounds a kerchief of the maid's, he swung them to the line, and so off full cry in the moonlight over the moor.

" 'Now, for some space the revelers stood agape, but anon their bemused wits awoke to the nature of the deed which was like to be done upon the moorlands. Everything was now in an uproar, some calling for their pistols, some for their horses. At length the whole of them, thirteen in number, took horse and started in pursuit.

" 'They had gone a mile or two when they passed one of the night shepherds and cried to him to know if he had seen the hunt. The man, as the story goes, was so crazed with fear that he could scarce speak, but at last he said that he had indeed seen the unhappy maiden, with the hounds upon her track. "But I have seen more than that," said he, "for Hugo Baskerville passed me upon his black mare, and there ran mute behind him such a hound of hell as God forbid should ever be at my heels." So the drunken squires cursed the shepherd and rode onward. But soon their skins turned cold, for there came a galloping across the moor, and Hugo's black mare went past with a trailing bridle and empty saddle. Then the revelers rode close together, for a great fear was on them. Riding slowly over the moor, they came at last upon Hugo's hunting dogs, whimpering in a cluster at the head of a deep dip or goyle, as we call it, some slinking away and some, with starting hackles and staring eyes, gazing down the narrow valley before them.

" 'The company had come to a halt. The most of them would by no means advance, but three of the boldest rode forward down the goyle. There in the center lay the unhappy maid, dead of fear and of fatigue. But it was not the sight of her body, nor yet was it that of the body of Hugo Baskerville lying near her, which raised the hair upon the heads of these three roisterers, but it was that, standing over Hugo and plucking at his throat, there stood a foul thing, a great, black beast shaped like a hound yet larger than any hound that ever mortal eye has rested upon. And even as they looked, the thing tore the throat out of Hugo Baskerville, on which, as it turned its blazing eyes and dripping jaws upon them, the three shrieked with fear and rode for dear life across the moor. One, it is said, died that very night of what he had seen, and the others were but broken men for the rest of their days.

" 'Such is the tale, my sons, of the coming of the hound which is said to have plagued the family so sorely ever since. It cannot be denied that many of the family have been unhappy in their deaths, which have been sudden, bloody, and mysterious, and I counsel you by way of caution to forbear from crossing the moor in those dark hours when the powers of evil are exalted.

" '[This from Hugo Baskerville to his sons Rodger and John.]' "

When Dr. Mortimer had finished reading this singular narrative he pushed his spectacles up on his forehead and stared across at Mr. Sherlock Holmes. The latter yawned and tossed the end of his cigarette into the fire.

"Do you not find it interesting?" Dr. Mortimer asked.

"To a collector of fairy tales."

The doctor drew a folded newspaper out of his pocket. "Now, Mr. Holmes, we will give you something a little more recent. This is the Devon County *Chronicle* of May fourteenth of this year. It is a short account of the death of Sir Charles Baskerville, which occurred a few days before that date."

My friend leaned a little forward and his expression became intent. Our visitor readjusted his glasses and began:

" 'The recent sudden death of Sir Charles Baskerville has cast a gloom over the county. Though he had resided at Baskerville Hall for only two years, his amiability of character and extreme generosity had won the affection and respect of all who had been brought into contact with him. Sir Charles, as is well known, made large sums of money in South African speculation. More wise than those who go on until the wheel turns against them, he realized his gains and returned to England to restore the fallen grandeur of his line. It is common talk how large were those schemes of reconstruction and improvement which have been interrupted by his death. Being himself a childless widower, it was his openly expressed desire that the whole countryside should profit by his good fortune, and many will bewail his untimely end.

" 'The circumstances connected with the death of Sir Charles cannot be said to have been entirely cleared up by the inquest, but at least enough has been done to dispose of those rumors to which local superstition has given rise. There is no reason whatever to suspect that death could be from any but natural causes. In spite of his considerable wealth, Sir Charles was simple in his personal tastes. His indoor servants at Baskerville Hall consisted of a married couple named Barrymore. Their evidence, corroborated by that of Dr. James Mortimer, the friend and medical attendant of the deceased, shows that Sir Charles's health has for some time been impaired, and points especially to some affection of the heart.

" 'Sir Charles was in the habit every night before going to bed of walking down the famous yew alley of Baskerville Hall. On the fourth of May he had declared his intention of starting next day for London, and had ordered Barrymore to prepare his luggage. That night he went out as usual for his nocturnal walk, in the course of which he was in the habit of smoking a cigar. At twelve o'clock Barrymore, finding the hall door still open, became alarmed and went in search of his master. The day had been wet, and Sir Charles's footprints were easily traced down the alley. Halfway down this walk there is a gate which leads out onto the moor. There were indications that Sir Charles had stood for some little time here. He then proceeded down the alley, and it was at the far end of it that his body was discovered. One fact which has not been explained is the statement of Barrymore that his master's footprints altered their character from the time that he passed the moor gate, and that he appeared from thence onward to have been walking upon his toes.

" 'One Murphy, a gypsy horse dealer, who was on the moor at the time, declares that he heard cries, but is unable to state from what direction they came. No signs of violence were to be discovered upon Sir Charles's person, though the doctor's evidence pointed to an almost incredible facial distortion. Dr. Mortimer explained that that is a symptom which is not unusual in cases of death from cardiac exhaustion. The postmortem examination showed long-standing organic disease, and the coroner's jury returned a verdict in accordance with the medical evidence.

" 'It is understood that the next of kin is Mr. Henry Baskerville, the son of Sir Charles's younger brother. The young man when last heard of was in America, and inquiries are being instituted with a view to informing him of his good fortune.' "

Dr. Mortimer refolded his paper and replaced it in his pocket. "Those are the public facts, Mr. Holmes, in connection with the death of Sir Charles Baskerville."

"I must thank you for calling my attention to a case which certainly presents some features of interest. I had observed some newspaper comment at the time, but I was exceedingly preoccupied by other matters, and I lost touch with the case. This article, you say, contains all the public facts?"

"It does."

"Then let me have the private ones," said Sherlock Holmes. He leaned back, put his fingertips together, and assumed his most impassive and judicial expression.

"In doing so," said Dr. Mortimer, "I am telling that which I have not confided to anyone. A man of science shrinks from placing himself in the public position of seeming to endorse a popular superstition. I had the further motive that Baskerville Hall would certainly remain untenanted if anything were to increase its already rather grim reputation. But with you there is no reason why I should not be perfectly frank.

"The moor is very sparsely inhabited, and those who live near each other are thrown very much together. For this reason I saw a good deal of Sir Charles Baskerville. With the exception of Mr. Frankland, of Lafter Hall, and Mr. Stapleton, the naturalist, there are no other men of education within many miles. Sir Charles had brought back much scientific information from South Africa, and many a charming evening we have spent together discussing the comparative anatomy of the Bushman and the Hottentot.

"Within the last few months it became increasingly plain to me that Sir Charles's nervous system was strained to the breaking point. He had taken this legend which I have read you exceedingly to heart—so much so that, although he would walk in his own grounds, he avoided the moor at night. He was honestly convinced that a dreadful fate overhung his family. The idea of some ghastly presence constantly haunted him, and on more than one occasion he has ask ed me whether I had on my medical journeys at night ever seen any strange creature or heard the baying of a hound.

"One evening, some three weeks before the fatal event, he chanced to be at his hall door when I descended from my gig. Standing in front of him, I saw his eyes fix themselves over my shoulder and stare past me with an expression of the most dreadful horror. I whisked round and had just time to catch a glimpse of something which I took to be a large black calf passing at the head of the drive. So alarmed was he that I was compelled to go down to the spot where the animal had been and look around for it. It was gone, however. That evening, to explain the emotion which he had shown, Sir Charles confided to my keeping the narrative which I have read to you. This small episode assumes some importance in view of the tragedy which followed, but I was convinced at the time that his excitement had no justification.

"It was at my advice that Sir Charles was about to go to London. The constant anxiety in which he lived was evidently having a serious effect upon his health. I thought that a few months among the distractions of town would send him back a new man. Mr. Stapleton, a mutual friend, was of the same opinion. At the last instant came this terrible catastrophe.

"On the night of Sir Charles's death Barrymore the butler sent Perkins the groom on horseback to me, and I was able to reach Baskerville Hall within an hour of the event. I checked and corroborated all the facts which were mentioned at the inquest. Finally I carefully examined the body, which had not been touched until my arrival. Sir Charles lay on his face, his arms out, his fingers dug into the ground, and his features convulsed to such an extent that I could hardly have sworn to his identity. There was certainly no physical injury of any kind. But one false statement was made by Barrymore. He said that there were no traces upon the ground round the body. He did not observe any. But I did—some little distance off, but fresh and clear."

"Footprints?"

Dr. Mortimer's voice sank almost to a whisper as he answered, "Mr. Holmes, they were the footprints of a gigantic hound!"

Chapter 3

I confess that at these words a shudder passed through me. Holmes leaned forward in his excitement and his eyes had the hard, dry glitter which shot from them when he was keenly interested.

"You saw this and you said nothing?"

"What was the use?"

"How was it that no one else saw it?"

"The marks were some twenty yards from the body and no one gave them a thought. I don't suppose I should have done so had I not known this legend."

"There are many sheep dogs on the moor?"

"No doubt, but this was no sheep dog. It was enormous."

"But it had not approached the body?"

"No."

"What sort of night was it?"

"Damp and raw."

"What is the alley like?"

"There are two lines of old yew hedge, twelve feet high and impenetrable. The walk in the center is about eight feet across."

"Is there anything between the hedges and the walk?"

"Yes, there is a strip of grass about six feet broad on either side."

"I understand that the yew hedge is penetrated at one point by a gate?"

"Yes, a wicket gate which leads onto the moor."

"To reach the yew alley one either has to come down it from the house or else to enter it by the gate?"

"There is an exit through a summerhouse at the far end. Sir Charles lay about fifty yards from it."

"Now, tell me, Dr. Mortimer—and this is important—the marks which you saw were on the path and not on the grass?"

"No marks could show on the grass."

"Were they on the same side of the path as the gate?"

"Yes, they were on the edge of the path on the same side."

"You interest me exceedingly. Another point. Was the gate closed?"

"Closed and padlocked."

"How high was it?"

"About four feet high."

"Then anyone could have got over it?"

"Yes."

"And what marks did you see by the gate?"

"Sir Charles had evidently stood there for five or ten minutes, because the ash had twice dropped from his cigar."

"Excellent! This is a colleague, Watson, after our own heart. No other marks?"

"Sir Charles had left his own marks all over that patch of gravel. I could discern no others."

Sherlock Holmes struck his hand against his knee. "If I had only been there!" he cried. "Oh, Dr. Mortimer, Dr. Mortimer, to think that you did not call me in!"

"I could not call you in, Mr. Holmes, without disclosing these facts to the world. Besides, there is a realm in which the most acute and most experienced of detectives is helpless."

"You mean that the thing is supernatural?"

"Since the tragedy, Mr. Holmes, there have come to my ears several incidents which are hard to reconcile with the settled order of nature. Before the terrible event occurred several people had seen a creature upon the moor which corresponds with this Baskerville demon, and which could not possibly be any animal known to science. They all agreed that it was a huge creature, luminous, ghastly, and spectral. These men, all of them hardheaded countrymen, tell the same story of this dreadful apparition, the hellhound of the legend. I assure you that it is a hardy man who will cross the moor at night."

"And you, a trained man of science, believe the hound to be supernatural. Yet you must admit that the footprint is material."

"The original hound was material enough to tear a man's throat out, and yet he was diabolical as well."

"Now, Dr. Mortimer, tell me this. If you hold these views, why have you come to consult me at all? How can I assist you?"

"By advising me as to what I should do with Sir Henry Baskerville, who arrives at Waterloo Station"—Dr. Mortimer looked at his watch—"in exactly one hour and a quarter."

"He being the heir?"

"Yes. On the death of Sir Charles we inquired for this young gentleman and found that he had been farming in Canada. From the accounts which have reached us he is an excellent fellow."

"There is no other claimant, I presume?"

"None. Sir Charles was the eldest of three brothers. The second brother, who died young, is the father of this lad Henry. The third, Rodger, was the black sheep of the family. He was the very image, they tell me, of the family picture of old Hugo. He made England too hot to hold him, fled to Central America, and died there in 1876 of yellow fever. Henry is the last of the Baskervilles. Now, Mr. Holmes, what would you advise me to do with him?"

"Why should he not go to the home of his fathers?"

"I feel sure that if Sir Charles could have spoken with me before his death, he would have warned me against bringing the last of the old race to that deadly place. And yet it cannot be denied that the prosperity of the whole poor, bleak countryside depends upon the tenant of the Hall. I fear lest I should be swayed by my own obvious interest in the matter, and that is why I ask for your advice."

Holmes considered for a little time.

"Put into plain words, the matter is this," said he. "In your opinion there is a diabolical agency which makes Dartmoor an unsafe abode for a Baskerville. But surely, if your supernatural theory be correct, it could work the young man evil in London as easily as in Devonshire. A devil with merely local powers like a parish vestry would be inconceivable."

"Your advice, then, is that the young man will be as safe in Devonshire as in London. Is this what you recommend?"

"I recommend, sir, that you call off your spaniel who is scratching at my front door and proceed to Waterloo to meet Sir Henry Baskerville."

"And then?"

"And then you will say nothing to him at all until I have made up my mind about the matter. At ten o'clock tomorrow, Dr. Mortimer, I will be much obliged to you if you will call upon me here and bring Sir Henry Baskerville with you."

"I will do so, Mr. Holmes."

Dr. Mortimer hurried off in his peering, absentminded fashion. Holmes stopped him at the head of the stairs. "Only one more question, Dr. Mortimer. You say that before Sir Charles Baskerville's death several people saw this apparition upon the moor. Did any see it after?"

"I have not heard of any."

"Thank you. Good morning."

Holmes returned to his seat with that quiet look of inward satisfaction which meant that he had a congenial task before him.

"Going out, Watson?"

"Unless I can help you."

"No, my dear fellow, it is at the hour of action that I turn to you for aid. But when you pass Bradley's, would you ask him to send up a pound of the strongest shag tobacco? It would be as well if you could make it convenient not to return before evening. Then I should be very glad to compare impressions as to this most interesting problem which has been submitted to us this morning."

I knew that seclusion and solitude were necessary for those hours of intense concentration during which my friend weighed every particle of evidence and made up his mind as to which points were essential and which immaterial. I therefore spent the day at my club and did not return to Baker Street until evening.

As I entered the sitting room the acrid fumes of strong coarse tobacco took me by the throat and set me coughing. Through the haze I had a vague vision of Holmes coiled up in an armchair with his black clay pipe between his lips. Several rolls of paper lay around him.

"Caught cold, Watson?" said he.

"No, it's this poisonous atmosphere."

"I suppose it *is* pretty thick, now that you mention it. Open the window, then! Where do you think that I have been all day?"

"A fixture here."

"On the contrary, I have been to Devonshire."

"In spirit?"

"Exactly. My body has remained in this armchair. But after you left I sent down to Stamford's for a large-scale ordnance map of this portion of Dartmoor, and my spirit has hovered over it all day. I flatter myself that I could find my way about." He unrolled one section of the map and held it over his knee. "Here you have the particular district which concerns us. That is Baskerville Hall in the middle."

"With a wood round it?"

"Exactly. I fancy the yew alley must stretch along this line, with the moor upon the right of it. This small clump of buildings here is the hamlet of Grimpen. Within a radius of five miles there are, as you see, only a very few scattered dwellings. Here is Lafter Hall, which was mentioned in the narrative, and a house which may be the residence of the naturalist—Stapleton, if I remember right, was his name. Here are two moorland farmhouses, High Tor and Foulmire. Then fourteen miles away the great convict prison of Princetown. Between and around these scattered points extends the desolate, lifeless moor."

"It must be a wild place."

"Yes, the setting is a worthy one. If the devil did desire to have a hand in the affairs of men—"

"Then you are yourself inclining to the supernatural explanation?"

"The devil's agents may be of flesh and blood, may they not? There are two questions waiting for us at the outset. The one is whether any crime has been committed at all; the second is, what is the crime and how was it committed? Of course, if we are dealing with forces outside the ordinary laws of nature, there is an end of our investigation. But we are bound to exhaust all other hypotheses before falling back upon this one. Have you turned the case over in your mind?"

"Yes, I have thought a good deal of it in the course of the day."

"That change in the footprints—what do you make of that?"

"Mortimer said that Sir Charles had walked on tiptoe down that portion of the alley."

"He only repeated what some fool had said at the inquest. The man was running, Watson—running for his life, running until he burst his heart and fell dead upon his face."

"Running from what?"

"There lies our problem. There are indications that he was crazed with fear before ever he began to run."

"How can you say that?"

"I am presuming that the cause of his fears came to him across the moor. If that were so, only a man who had lost his wits would have run *from* the house in the direction where help was least likely to be. Then, again, whom was he waiting for that night, and why was he waiting for him in the yew alley rather than in his own house?"

"You think that he was waiting for someone?"

"The man was elderly and infirm. We can understand his

taking an evening stroll, but the ground was damp and the night inclement. Is it natural that he should stand for five or ten minutes, as Dr. Mortimer deduced from the cigar ash?"

"But he went out every evening."

"I think it unlikely that he waited at the moor gate every evening. On the contrary, the evidence is that he avoided the moor. That night he waited there. It was the night before he made his departure for London. The thing takes shape, Watson. Might I ask you to hand me my violin, and we will postpone all further thought upon this business until we meet Dr. Mortimer and Sir Henry Baskerville in the morning."

Chapter 4

THE clock had just struck ten when Dr. Mortimer was shown up, followed by the young baronet. The latter was a small, alert, dark-eyed man about thirty years of age, very sturdily built, with thick black eyebrows and a strong, pugnacious face. He wore a ruddy-tinted tweed suit and had the weather-beaten appearance of one who has spent most of his time in the open air, and yet there was something in his steady eye and the quiet assurance of his bearing which indicated the gentleman.

"This is Sir Henry Baskerville," said Dr. Mortimer.

"Mr. Sherlock Holmes," said he, "if my friend here had not proposed coming round to you, I should have come on my own account. I understand that you think out little puzzles, and I've had one today which wants more thinking out than I am able to give it."

"Pray take a seat, Sir Henry. Do I understand you to say that you have yourself had some remarkable experience since you arrived in London?"

"Nothing of much importance, Mr. Holmes. Only a joke, as like as not. It was this letter, if you can call it a letter, which reached me this morning."

He laid an ordinary grayish envelope upon the table, and we all bent over it. The address, "Sir Henry Baskerville, Northumberland

Hotel," was printed in rough characters; the postmark "Charing Cross," and the date of posting the preceding evening.

"Who knew that you were going to the Northumberland Hotel?" asked Holmes, glancing keenly at our visitor.

"No one knew. We only decided after I met Dr. Mortimer."

"But Dr. Mortimer was no doubt already stopping there?"

"No, I had been staying with a friend," said the doctor.

Out of the envelope Holmes took a folded half sheet of foolscap paper and spread it flat upon the table. Across the middle of it a single sentence had been formed by pasting printed words upon it. It ran:

As you value your life or your reason keep away from the moor.

The word "moor" only was printed in ink.

"Now," said Sir Henry Baskerville, "perhaps you will tell me, Mr. Holmes, what in thunder is the meaning of that?"

"You shall share our knowledge before you leave this room, Sir Henry. I promise you that. But first let us examine this very interesting document," said Sherlock Holmes. "Have you yesterday's *Times*, Watson?"

"It is here in the corner."

"Might I trouble you for it—the inside page, please, with the leading articles?" He glanced swiftly over it, running his eyes up and down the columns. "Capital article this on free trade. Permit me to give you an extract from it.

"You may be cajoled into imagining that your own special trade or your own industry will be encouraged by a protective tariff, but it stands to reason that such legislation must in the long run keep away wealth from the country, diminish the value of our imports, and lower the general conditions of life in this island.

"What do you think of that, Watson?" cried Holmes in high glee, rubbing his hands together with satisfaction.

Sir Henry Baskerville turned a pair of puzzled eyes upon me.

"I confess that I see no connection with Sir Henry's letter," I said.

"And yet, my dear Watson, there is so very close a connection that the one is extracted out of the other. 'You,' 'your,' 'your,' 'life,' 'reason,' 'value,' 'keep away,' 'from the.' Don't you see now whence these words have been taken?"

"By thunder, you're right!" cried Sir Henry.

"If any possible doubt remained, it is settled by the fact that 'keep away' and 'from the' are cut out in one piece."

"Really, Mr. Holmes, this exceeds anything which I could have imagined," said Dr. Mortimer, gazing at my friend in amazement. "That you should name which newspaper the words were taken from, and add that they came from the leading article, is really one of the most remarkable things which I have ever known. How did you do it?"

"I presume, Doctor, that you could tell the skull of a Negro from that of an Eskimo?"

"Most certainly. The differences are obvious. The supraorbital crest, the facial angle, the—"

"The differences in type are equally obvious. There is as much difference to my eyes between the leaded type style of a *Times* article and the slovenly print of an evening halfpenny paper as there could be between your Negro and your Eskimo, though I confess that once when I was very young I confused the Leeds *Mercury* with the *Western Morning News*. These words could have been taken from nothing but a *Times* leader. As it was done yesterday, the strong probability was that we should find the words in yesterday's issue."

"So far as I can follow you, then, Mr. Holmes," said Sir Henry Baskerville, "someone cut out this message with a scissors—"

"Nail-scissors," said Holmes. "You can see that it was a very short-bladed scissors, since the cutter had to take two snips over 'keep away.'"

"That is so. Someone, then, pasted the words with paste—"

"Gum," said Holmes.

"With gum. But why should the word 'moor' have been written?"

"Because he could not find it in print. 'Moor' is less common than the other words."

"Why, of course, that would explain it. Have you read anything else in this message, Mr. Holmes?"

"The utmost pains have been taken to remove all clues. The address, you observe, is printed in rough characters. But *The Times* is a paper which is seldom found in any hands but those of the highly educated. We may take it, therefore, that the letter was composed by an educated man who wished to pose as an uneducated one. Again, you will observe that the words are not gummed on in an accurate line, but that some are much higher than others. That may point to agitation and hurry upon the part of the cutter. If he were in a hurry, it opens up an interesting question, since any letter posted up to early morning would reach Sir Henry before he would leave his hotel. Did the composer fear an interruption—and from whom?"

"We are coming now rather into the region of guesswork," said Dr. Mortimer.

"Say, rather, into the region of scientific use of the imagination. Now, you would call it a guess, no doubt, but I am almost certain that this address has been written in a hotel."

"How in the world can you say that?"

"Both the pen and the ink have given the writer trouble. The pen has spluttered twice in a single word and has run dry three times in a short address, showing that there was very little ink in the bottle. Now, a private pen or ink bottle is seldom allowed to be in such a state, but in a hotel it is rare to get anything else. Yes, I have very little hesitation in saying that could we examine the wastepaper baskets of the hotels round Charing Cross until we found the remains of the mutilated *Times* leader we could lay our hands straight upon the person who sent this singular message. Halloa! Halloa! What's this?"

He was carefully examining the foolscap upon which the words were pasted, holding it only an inch or two from his eyes.

"Well?"

"Nothing," said he, throwing it down. "It is a blank half sheet of paper, without even a watermark upon it. I think we have drawn as much as we can from this curious letter; and now, Sir Henry, have you observed anyone watching you since you have been in London?"

"I seem to have walked right into the thick of a dime novel," said our visitor. "Why in thunder should anyone watch me?"

"We are coming to that. You have nothing else out of the ordinary routine to report to us before we go into this matter?"

Sir Henry smiled. "I don't know much of British life yet, for I have spent nearly all my time in the States and in Canada. But I hope that to lose one of your boots is not part of the ordinary routine over here."

"You have lost one of your boots?"

"My dear sir," cried Dr. Mortimer, "it is only mislaid. You will find it when you return to the hotel. What is the use of troubling Mr. Holmes with trifles of this kind?"

"Well, he asked me for anything outside the ordinary."

"Exactly," said Holmes, "however foolish the incident may seem. You have lost one of your boots, you say?"

"Mislaid it, anyhow. I put them both outside my door last night, and there was only one in the morning. I could get no sense out of the chap who cleans them. The worst of it is that I only bought the pair last night, and have never had them on."

"If you have never worn them, why did you put them out to be cleaned?"

"They had never been polished."

"Then I understand that on your arrival in London yesterday you went out at once and bought a pair of boots?"

"I did a good deal of shopping. Dr. Mortimer here went round with me. You see, if I am to be squire of Baskerville Hall, I must dress the part, and I have got a little careless in my ways out West. Among other things I bought these brown boots, and had one stolen before ever I had them on my feet."

"It seems a singularly useless thing to steal," said Sherlock Holmes. "I confess that I share Dr. Mortimer's belief that it will not be long before the missing boot is found."

"And now, gentlemen," said the baronet with decision, "it seems to me that it is time you gave me a full account of the business that has brought us here."

"Your request is a very reasonable one," Holmes answered. "Dr. Mortimer, I think you could not do better than to tell your story as you told it to us."

Our scientific friend drew his papers from his pocket and presented the whole case as he had done upon the morning before.

"Well, I seem to have come into an inheritance with a vengeance," said Sir Henry when the long narrative was finished. "Of course, I've heard of the hound ever since I was in the nursery. It's the pet story of the family, though I never thought of taking it seriously before. But as to my uncle's death—I can't get it clear yet. You don't seem quite to have made up your mind whether it's a case for a policeman or a clergyman."

"Precisely."

"And now there's this affair of the letter to me at the hotel. I suppose that fits into its place."

"It seems to show that someone knows more than we do about what goes on upon the moor," said Dr. Mortimer.

"And also," said Holmes, "that someone is not ill-disposed towards you, since they warn you of danger."

"Or it may be that they wish, for their own purposes, to scare me away."

"Well, of course, that is possible also. But the practical point which we now have to decide, Sir Henry, is whether it is or is not advisable for you to go to Baskerville Hall."

Sir Henry's dark brows knitted and his face flushed to a dusky red. "I have hardly had time to think over all that you have told me," he said. "It's a big thing for a man to have to decide at one sitting. I should like to have a quiet hour by myself to make up my mind. Look here, Mr. Holmes, it's half past eleven now and I'm going back to my hotel. Suppose you and Dr. Watson come round and lunch with us at two. I'll be able to tell you more clearly then how this thing strikes me."

"Is that convenient to you, Watson?"

"Perfectly."

"Then you may expect us. Shall I have a cab called?"

"I'd prefer to walk, for this affair has flurried me rather."

"I'll join you in a walk, with pleasure," said Dr. Mortimer.

We heard the steps of our visitors descend the stairs, and t[h]e bang of the front door. In an instant Holmes changed into t[h]e man of action.

"Your hat and boots, Watson, quick! Not a moment to lose[!] He rushed into his room and was back again in a few secon[ds] in a frock coat. We hurried together down the stairs and into t[he] street. Dr. Mortimer and Baskerville were still visible about tw[o] hundred yards ahead of us in the direction of Oxford Street.

Holmes quickened his pace until we had decreased the distan[ce] which divided us by about half. Then, still keeping a hundred yar[ds] behind, we followed into Oxford Street and so down Regent Stre[et.] Once our friends stopped and stared into a shopwindow, upon whi[ch] Holmes did the same. An instant afterwards he gave a little c[ry] of satisfaction, and, following his glance, I saw that a hansom c[ab] with a man inside which had halted on the other side of the stre[et] was now proceeding slowly onward again in the direction of [Sir] Henry and Dr. Mortimer.

"There's our man, Watson! Come along! We'll have a good lo[ok] at him, if we can do no more."

At that instant I was aware of a bushy black beard and a pa[ir] of piercing eyes turned upon us through the side window of t[he] cab. Instantly something was screamed to the driver, and the c[ab] flew madly off down Regent Street. Holmes looked eagerly rou[nd] for another, but no empty one was in sight. Then he dashed [in] wild pursuit amid the stream of the traffic, but already the c[ab] was out of sight.

"There now!" said Holmes bitterly as he emerged panting fr[om] the tide of vehicles. "Was there ever such bad luck and such b[ad] management, too? Watson, Watson, if you are an honest man, y[ou] will record this also and set it against my successes!"

"Who was the man?"

"I have not an idea, but it was evident that Baskerville has be[en] very closely shadowed since he has been in town. When he left with Dr. Mortimer I at once followed them in the hopes of marking down their invisible attendant."

"What a pity we did not get the number of the cab!"

"My dear Watson, clumsy as I have been, you surely do not seriously imagine that I neglected to get the number? Number 2704 is our man."

We had been sauntering slowly down Regent Street during this conversation, and Dr. Mortimer, with his companion, had long vanished in front of us.

"There is no object in our following them," said Holmes. "The shadow has departed and will not return. We must see what further cards we have in our hands and play them with decision."

He turned into one of the district messenger offices, where he was warmly greeted by the manager.

"Ah, Wilson, I see you have not forgotten the little case in which I had the good fortune to help you?"

"No, sir, indeed I have not. You saved my good name, and perhaps my life."

"My dear fellow, you exaggerate. Wilson, you had among your boys a lad named Cartwright, who showed some ability during the investigation."

"Yes, sir, he is still with us."

"Could you ring him up? Thank you! And I should be glad to have change of this five-pound note."

A lad of fourteen, with a bright, keen face, had obeyed the summons of the manager. He stood now gazing with great reverence at the famous detective.

"Let me have the hotel directory," said Holmes. "Thank you! Now, Cartwright, there are the names of twenty-three hotels here, all in the immediate neighborhood of Charing Cross. You will visit each of these in turn."

"Yes, sir."

"You will begin in each case by giving the outside porter one shilling. Here are twenty-three shillings."

"Yes, sir."

"You will tell him that you want to see the wastepaper of yesterday. You will say that an important telegram has miscarried and that you are looking for it. You understand?"

"Yes, sir."

"But what you are really looking for is the center page of *The Times* with some holes cut in it with scissors. Here is a copy of the page. You could easily recognize it, could you not?"

"Yes, sir."

"You will learn in possibly twenty cases out of the twenty-three that the waste of the day before has been burned. In the three other cases you will be shown a heap of paper. The odds are enormously against your finding this page of *The Times* among it. Let me have a report by wire at Baker Street before evening. And now, Watson, it only remains for us to find out by wire the identity of the cabman, number 2704, and then we will drop into one of the Bond Street picture galleries and fill in the time until we are due at the hotel."

Chapter 5

SHERLOCK Holmes had, in a very remarkable degree, the power of detaching his mind at will. For two hours the strange business in which we had been involved appeared to be forgotten, and he would talk of nothing but modern art, of which he had the crudest ideas, until we found ourselves at the Northumberland Hotel.

"Sir Henry Baskerville is upstairs expecting you," said the clerk. "He asked me to show you up at once when you came."

"Have you any objection to my looking at your register?" said Holmes.

"Not in the least."

The book showed that two names had been added after that of Baskerville. One was Theophilus Johnson and family, of Newcastle; the other Mrs. Oldmore and maid, of High Lodge, Alton.

"Surely that must be the same Johnson whom I used to know," said Holmes to the porter. "A lawyer, is he not, gray-headed, and walks with a limp?"

"No, sir, this is Mr. Johnson, the coal owner, a very active gentleman, not older than yourself."

"Surely you are mistaken about his trade?"

"No, sir! He has used this hotel for many years, and he is very well known to us."

"Ah, that settles it. Mrs. Oldmore, too; I seem to remember the name. Excuse my curiosity, but often in calling upon a friend one finds another."

"She is an invalid lady, sir. Her husband was once mayor of Gloucester. She always comes to us when she is in town."

"Thank you; I am afraid I cannot claim her acquaintance. We have established a most important fact by these questions, Watson," he continued in a low voice as we went upstairs together. "We know now that the people who are so interested in our friend have not settled down in his own hotel. That means that while they are very anxious to watch him, they are equally anxious that he should not see them. It suggests—halloa, my dear fellow, what on earth is the matter?"

As we came round the top of the stairs we had run up against Sir Henry Baskerville himself, his face flushed with anger. He held an old black boot in one of his hands.

"Seems to me they are playing me for a sucker in this hotel," he cried in a much broader and more Western dialect than any which we had heard from him in the morning. "They'll find they've started in to monkey with the wrong man unless they are careful. By thunder, if that chap can't find my missing boot, there will be trouble. I can take a joke with the best, Mr. Holmes, but they've got a bit over the mark this time."

"But you said it was a new brown boot that was missing."

"So it was, sir. And now it's an old black one. I only had three pairs in the world—the new brown, the old black, and the patent leathers, which I am wearing. Last night they took one of my brown ones, and today they have sneaked one of the black."

An agitated German waiter appeared upon the scene.

"Well, have you got it?" Sir Henry demanded.

"No, sir," said the waiter. "I have made inquiry all over the hotel, but I can hear no word of it. It shall be found, sir—I promise you that if you have a little patience, it will be found."

"Well, either that boot comes back before sundown, or I'll see the manager and tell him that I go right straight out of this hotel. Well, well, Mr. Holmes, you'll excuse my troubling you about such a trifle—"

"I think it's well worth troubling about, but I don't profess to understand it yet. This case of yours is very complex, Sir Henry. We hold several threads in our hands, and sooner or later one or other of them will guide us to the truth."

We had a pleasant luncheon in which little was said of the business that had brought us together. It was in the private sitting room to which we repaired afterwards that Holmes asked Baskerville what were his intentions.

"To go to Baskerville Hall at the end of the week."

"On the whole," said Holmes, "I think that your decision is a wise one. I have ample evidence that you are being dogged in London, and amid the millions of this great city it is difficult to discover who these people are or what their object can be. You did not know, Dr. Mortimer, that you were followed this morning from my house?"

Dr. Mortimer started violently. "Followed! By whom?"

"That, unfortunately, is what I cannot tell you. Have you among your neighbors any man with a black, full beard?"

"No—or, let me see—why, yes. Barrymore, Sir Charles's butler, is a man with a full, black beard."

"We had best ascertain if he is really at the Hall, or if by any possibility he might be in London."

"How can you do that?"

"Give me a telegraph form. 'Is all ready for Sir Henry?' That will do. Address to Mr. Barrymore, Baskerville Hall. We will send a second wire to the postmaster at Grimpen: 'Telegram to Mr. Barrymore to be delivered into his own hand. If absent, please return wire to Sir Henry Baskerville, Northumberland Hotel.' That should let us know before evening whether Barrymore is at his post or not."

"By the way, Dr. Mortimer, who is this Barrymore, anyhow?" asked Baskerville.

"He is the son of the old caretaker, who is dead. They have looked after the Hall for four generations now. So far as I know, he and his wife are as respectable a couple as any in the county."

"Did Barrymore profit at all by Sir Charles's will?" asked Holmes.

"He and his wife had five hundred pounds each. But I hope that you do not look with suspicious eyes upon everyone who received a legacy from Sir Charles, for I also had a thousand pounds left to me."

"Indeed! And anyone else?"

"There were many insignificant sums to individuals, and a large number of charities. The residue went to Sir Henry."

"And how much was the residue?"

"Seven hundred and forty thousand pounds."

Holmes raised his eyebrows in surprise. "I had no idea that so gigantic a sum was involved," said he.

"We did not know how very rich Sir Charles was until we came to examine his securities. The total value of the estate was close on to a million."

"Dear me! It is a stake for which a man might well play a desperate game. And one more question, Dr. Mortimer. Supposing that anything happened to our young friend here—you will forgive the unpleasant hypothesis!—who would inherit the estate?"

"Since Rodger Baskerville, Sir Charles's younger brother, died unmarried, the estate would descend to a distant cousin, James Desmond, who is an elderly clergyman in Westmorland."

"Have you met Mr. James Desmond?"

"Yes, he once came down to visit Sir Charles. He is a man of venerable appearance and of saintly life. He would be the heir to the estate because that is entailed. He would also be the heir to the money unless it were willed otherwise by the present owner, who can, of course, do what he likes with it."

"And have you made your will, Sir Henry?"

"No, Mr. Holmes. I've had no time. But in any case I feel that the money should go with the title and estate. That was my uncle's idea. How is the owner going to restore the glories of the Baskervilles if he has not money enough to keep up the property?"

"Quite so. Well, Sir Henry, I am of one mind with you as to the advisability of your going down to Devonshire. But you must take with you a trusty man who will be always by your side."

"Is it possible that you could come yourself, Mr. Holmes?"

"If matters came to a crisis, I could, but with my extensive consulting practice, it is impossible for me to be absent from London for an indefinite time. At the present instant one of the most revered names in England is being besmirched by a blackmailer, and only I can stop a disastrous scandal."

"Whom do you recommend, then?"

Holmes laid his hand upon my arm. "If my friend would undertake it, there is no man who is better worth having at your side when you are in a tight place."

The proposition took me completely by surprise, but before I had time to answer, Baskerville seized me by the hand and wrung it heartily. "Well, now, that is real kind of you, Dr. Watson," said he. "If you will see me through, I'll never forget it."

The promise of adventure had always a fascination for me, and I was complimented by the words of Holmes and by the eagerness with which the baronet hailed me as a companion.

"I will come, with pleasure," said I.

"And you will report very carefully to me," said Holmes. "When a crisis comes, as it will do, I will direct how you shall act. I suppose that by Saturday all might be ready?"

"Would that suit Dr. Watson?"

"Perfectly."

"Then on Saturday we shall meet at the ten-thirty train from Paddington."

We had risen to depart when Baskerville gave a cry of triumph, and diving into one of the corners of the room, he drew a brown boot from under a cabinet.

"My missing boot!" he cried.

"That is a very singular thing," Dr. Mortimer remarked. "I searched this room carefully before lunch."

"And so did I," said Baskerville. "Every inch of it."

"In that case the waiter must have placed it there while we were lunching."

The German waiter was sent for but professed to know nothing of the matter, nor could any inquiry clear it up. Another item had been added to that constant and apparently purposeless series of small mysteries which had succeeded each other so rapidly. Holmes sat in silence in the cab as we drove back to Baker Street, and I knew from his drawn brows and keen face that his mind, like my own, was busy in endeavoring to frame some scheme into which all these strange and apparently disconnected episodes could be fitted.

JUST before dinner two telegrams arrived. The first ran: HAVE JUST HEARD THAT BARRYMORE IS AT THE HALL. BASKERVILLE. The second: VISITED TWENTY-THREE HOTELS AS DIRECTED, BUT SORRY TO REPORT UNABLE TO TRACE CUT SHEET OF TIMES. CARTWRIGHT.

"There go two of my threads, Watson. We must cast round for another scent."

"We have still the cabman who drove the spy."

"Exactly. I have wired to get his name and address from the Official Registry. I should not be surprised if this were my answer."

The ring at the bell proved to be something more satisfactory than an answer, for the door opened and a rough-looking fellow entered who was evidently the man himself.

"I got a message from the head office that a gent at this address had been inquiring for number 2704," said he. "I came straight here to ask you to your face what you had against me."

"I have nothing in the world against you, my good man," said Holmes. "On the contrary, I have half a sovereign for you, if you will give me a clear answer to my questions."

"Well, I've had a good day and no mistake," said the cabman with a grin. "What was it you wanted to ask, sir?"

"First of all your name, in case I want you again."

"John Clayton. My cab is out of Shipley's Yard, near Waterloo Station."

"Now, Clayton, tell me about the fare who came and watched this house at ten o'clock this morning and afterwards followed the two gentlemen down Regent Street."

The man looked surprised and a little embarrassed. "The truth is that the gentleman told me that he was a detective and that I was to say nothing about him to anyone," said he.

"My good fellow, this is a very serious business, and you may find yourself in a pretty bad position if you try to hide anything from me. You say that your fare told you that he was a detective? Did he say anything more?"

"He mentioned his name."

Holmes cast a swift glance of triumph at me. "What was the name that he mentioned?"

"His name," said the cabman, "was Mr. Sherlock Holmes."

Never have I seen my friend more completely taken aback. For an instant he sat in silent amazement. Then he burst into a hearty laugh. "A touch, Watson—an undeniable touch!" said he. "I feel a foil as quick and supple as my own. So his name was Sherlock Holmes, was it? Tell me where you picked him up and all that occurred."

"He hailed me at half past nine in Trafalgar Square. He said that he was a detective, and he offered me two guineas if I would do exactly what he wanted all day. I was glad enough to agree. First we drove down to the Northumberland Hotel and waited there until two gentlemen came out and took a cab from the rank. We followed their cab until it pulled up somewhere near here."

"This very door," said Holmes.

"Well, I couldn't be sure of that. We pulled up halfway down the street and waited an hour and a half. Then the two gentlemen passed us, walking, and we followed down Baker Street and along—"

"I know," said Holmes.

"Until we got three-quarters down Regent Street. Then my gentleman threw up the trap, and he cried that I should drive right away to Waterloo Station as hard as I could go. I whipped up the mare and we were there under the ten minutes. Just as he was leaving he turned round and he said, 'It might interest you to know that you have been driving Mr. Sherlock Holmes.' That's how I come to know the name."

"And how would you describe Mr. Sherlock Holmes?"

The cabman scratched his head. "Well, he wasn't altogether such an easy gentleman to describe. I'd put him at forty years of age, and he was of a middle height. He was dressed like a toff, and he had a black beard, cut square at the end, and a pale face."

"Nothing more that you can remember?"

"No, sir, nothing."

"Well, then, here is your half sovereign. There'll be another for you if you can bring any more information. Good night!"

"Good night, sir, and thank you!"

John Clayton departed chuckling, and Holmes turned to me with a shrug of his shoulders and a rueful smile.

"Snap goes our third thread, and we end where we began," said he. "I tell you, Watson, this time we have got a foe who is worthy of our steel. I'm not easy in my mind about sending you to Devonshire. It's an ugly, dangerous business, and the more I see of it the less I like it. Yes, my dear fellow, you may laugh, but I give you my word that I shall be very glad to have you back safe and sound in Baker Street once more."

Chapter 6

SIR Henry Baskerville and Dr. Mortimer were ready upon the appointed day, and we started as arranged for Devonshire. Mr. Sherlock Holmes drove with me to the station and gave me his last parting injunctions and advice.

"I will not bias your mind by suggesting theories or suspicions, Watson," said he; "I wish you simply to report facts in the fullest possible manner to me, and leave me to do the theorizing."

"What sort of facts?" I asked.

"Anything which may seem to have a bearing however indirect upon the case, or any fresh particulars concerning the death of Sir Charles, and especially the relations between young Baskerville and the people who will actually surround him upon the moor.

There are the Barrymore couple. Then there is a groom, if I remember right. There is our friend Dr. Mortimer, whom I believe to be entirely honest, and there is his wife, of whom we know nothing. There is this naturalist, Stapleton, and there is his sister, who is said to be a young lady of attractions. There is Mr. Frankland, of Lafter Hall, who is also an unknown factor, and there are one or two other neighbors. These are the folk who must be your very special study."

"I will do my best."

"Keep your revolver near you night and day, and never relax your precautions."

Our friends had already secured a first-class carriage and were waiting for us upon the platform.

"No, we have no news of any kind," said Dr. Mortimer in answer to my friend's questions. "I can swear to one thing, and that is that we have not been shadowed during the last two days."

"You have always kept together, I presume?"

"Except yesterday afternoon, which I spent at the Museum of the College of Surgeons."

"And I went for a walk in the park," said Baskerville. "But I had no trouble of any kind."

"It was imprudent, all the same," said Holmes. "I beg, Sir Henry, that you will not go about alone. Some great misfortune will befall you if you do. Did you get your other boot?"

"No, sir. It is gone forever."

"Indeed. That is very interesting. Well, good-by," he added as the train began to glide down the platform. "Bear in mind, Sir Henry, one of the phrases in that queer old legend which Dr. Mortimer has read to us and avoid the moor in those hours of darkness when the powers of evil are exalted."

The journey was a swift and pleasant one. In a very few hours the brown earth had become ruddy, the brick had changed to granite, and red cows grazed in well-hedged fields. Young Baskerville stared eagerly out of the window and cried aloud with delight as he recognized the familiar features of the Devon scenery.

"I've been over a good part of the world since I left Devonshire, Dr. Watson," said he; "but I've never seen a place to compare with it."

"But you were very young when you last saw Baskerville Hall, were you not?" Dr. Mortimer asked.

"I was a boy in my teens at the time of my father's death and had never seen the Hall, for he lived in a little cottage on the South Coast. Thence I went straight to a friend in America. I tell you it is all as new to me as it is to Dr. Watson, and I'm as keen as possible to see the moor."

"Then your wish is easily granted, for there is your first sight of the moor," said Dr. Mortimer, pointing out of the window.

Over the green squares of the fields there rose in the distance a gray, melancholy hill with a strange jagged summit, dim and vague in the distance, like some fantastic landscape in a dream. Baskerville sat for a long time, his eyes fixed upon it, and I read upon his eager face how much it meant to him, this first sight of that strange spot where the men of his blood had held sway so long and left their mark so deep.

The train pulled up at a small wayside station and we all descended. Outside, beyond the low, white fence, a wagonette with a pair of horses was waiting. Our coming was evidently a great event, for stationmaster and porters clustered round us to carry out our luggage. It was a sweet, simple country spot, but I was surprised to observe that by the gate there stood two soldierly men in dark uniforms who leaned upon their short rifles and glanced keenly at us as we passed. The groom, a hard-faced, gnarled little fellow, saluted Sir Henry Baskerville, and in a few minutes we were flying swiftly down the broad, white road. Rolling pasturelands curved upward on either side of us, but behind the peaceful and sunlit countryside there rose the long, gloomy curve of the moor, broken by the jagged and sinister hills.

The wagonette swung round into a side road, and we curved upward through deep lanes worn by centuries of wheels, high banks on either side, heavy with dripping moss and fleshy hart's-tongue ferns. Bronzing bracken and mottled bramble gleamed in the light of the sinking sun. At every turn Baskerville gave an exclamation of delight, looking eagerly about him and asking countless questions. To his eyes all seemed beautiful, but to me a tinge of melancholy lay upon the countryside, which bore so clearly the mark of the waning year. Yellow leaves carpeted the lanes and fluttered down upon us as we passed.

"Halloa!" cried Dr. Mortimer. "What is this?"

A steep curve of heath-clad land, an outlying spur of the moor, lay in front of us. On the summit, hard and clear like an equestrian statue upon its pedestal, was a mounted soldier, his rifle poised ready over his forearm. He was watching the road along which we traveled.

"What is this, Perkins?" Dr. Mortimer asked the groom.

Our driver half turned in his seat.

"There's a convict escaped from Princetown, sir. He's been out three days now, and the warders watch every road and every station, but they've had no sight of him yet. The farmers around here don't like it, sir, and that's a fact, for this isn't any ordinary convict. This is a man that would stick at nothing."

"Who is he, then?"

"It is Selden, the Notting Hill murderer."

I remembered the case well, for it was one in which Holmes had taken an interest on account of the peculiar ferocity of the crime. The commutation of the assassin's death sentence had been due to some doubts as to his complete sanity, so wantonly brutal was his conduct. Our wagonette had topped a rise and in front of us rose the huge expanse of the moor, mottled with gnarled and craggy cairns and tors. A cold wind swept down from it and set us shivering. Somewhere there, on that desolate plain, was lurking this fiendish man, hiding in a burrow like a wild beast, his heart full of malignancy against the whole race which had cast him out. It needed but this to complete the grim suggestiveness of the barren waste, the chilling wind, and the darkling sky. Even Baskerville fell silent and pulled his overcoat more closely round him.

We had left the fertile country behind and beneath us. The road ahead grew bleaker and wilder over huge russet and olive slopes. Now and then we passed a moorland cottage, walled and roofed with stone, with no creeper to break its harsh outline. Suddenly we looked down into a cuplike depression, patched with stunted oaks and firs which had been twisted and bent by the fury of years of storm. Two high, narrow towers rose over the trees. The driver pointed with his whip.

"Baskerville Hall," said he.

A few minutes later we had reached the lodge gates, a maze of fantastic tracery in wrought iron, with weather-beaten pillars on either side, surmounted by the boars' heads of the Baskervilles. The lodge was a ruin of black granite and bared ribs of rafters, but facing it was a new building, half constructed, the first fruit of Sir Charles's South African gold.

Through the gateway we passed into the avenue, where the wheels were hushed among the leaves, and the old trees shot their branches in a somber tunnel over our heads. Baskerville shuddered as he looked up the long, dark drive to where the house glimmered like a ghost at the farther end.

"Was it here?" he asked in a low voice.

"No, no, the yew alley is on the other side."

"It's no wonder my uncle felt as if trouble were coming on him in such a place as this," said he, with a gloomy face. "It's enough to scare any man. I'll have a row of electric lamps up here inside of six months, and you won't know it again."

The avenue opened into a broad expanse of turf, and the house lay before us. In the fading light I could see that the center was a heavy block of building from which a porch projected. The whole front was draped in ivy, with here and there a window or a coat of arms breaking through the dark veil. From this central block rose the twin towers, ancient, crenellated, and pierced with many loopholes. To right and left of the turrets were more modern wings of black granite. A dull light shone through heavy mullioned windows, and from the high chimneys which rose from the steep roof there sprang a single black column of smoke.

"Welcome, Sir Henry! Welcome to Baskerville Hall!"

A tall man had stepped from the shadow of the porch to open the door of the wagonette. The figure of a woman was silhouetted

against the yellow light of the hall. She came out and helped the man to hand down our bags.

"You don't mind my driving straight home, Sir Henry?" said Dr. Mortimer. "My wife is expecting me."

"Surely you will stay and have some dinner?"

"No, I must go. I shall probably find some work awaiting me. Good-by, and never hesitate night or day to send for me if I can be of service."

The wheels died away down the drive while Sir Henry and I turned into the hall, and the door clanged heavily behind us. It was a fine apartment in which we found ourselves, large, lofty, and heavily raftered with age-blackened oak. In the great old-fashioned fireplace behind the high iron dogs a log fire crackled and snapped. Sir Henry and I gazed round us at the high, thin windows of old stained glass, the oak paneling, the stags' heads, the coats of arms upon the walls, all dim and somber in the subdued light of the central lamp.

"It's just as I imagined it," said Sir Henry with a boyish enthusiasm. "To think that this should be the same hall in which for five hundred years my people have lived. It strikes me solemn to think of it."

Barrymore had returned from taking our luggage to our rooms. He stood in front of us now with the subdued manner of a well-trained servant. He was a remarkable-looking man, tall, handsome, with a square black beard and pale, distinguished features.

"Would you wish dinner to be served at once, sir?"

"Is it ready?"

"In a very few minutes, sir. You will find hot water in your rooms. My wife and I will be happy, Sir Henry, to stay with you until you have made your fresh arrangements."

"Do you mean that your wife and you wish to leave?"

"Only when it is quite convenient to you, sir." I seemed to discern some signs of emotion upon the butler's white face. "To tell the truth, sir, we were both very much attached to Sir Charles, and his death gave us a shock and made these surroundings very painful to us. I fear that we shall never again be easy in our minds at Baskerville Hall."

"But what do you intend to do?"

"I have no doubt, sir, that we shall succeed in establishing ourselves in some business. Sir Charles's generosity has given us the means to do so. And now, sir, perhaps I had best show you to your rooms."

A square balustraded gallery ran round the top of the old hall, approached by a double stair. From this central point two long corridors extended the whole length of the building, from which all the bedrooms opened. My own was in the same wing as Baskerville's and almost next door to it. These rooms appeared to be much more modern than the central part of the house, and the bright paper and numerous candles did something to remove the somber impression which our arrival had left upon my mind.

But the long dining room which opened out of the hall was a place of shadow and gloom. With rows of flaring torches to light it up, and the color and rude hilarity of an old-time banquet, it might have softened; but now, when two black-clothed gentlemen sat in the little circle of light thrown by a shaded lamp, one's spirit was subdued. A dim line of ancestors stared down upon us and daunted us by their silent company. We talked little, and I for one was glad when the meal was over and we were able to retire into the modern billiard room and smoke a cigarette.

"My word, it isn't a very cheerful place," said Sir Henry. "I don't wonder that my uncle got a little jumpy if he lived all alone in such a house as this. However, if it suits you, we will retire early tonight. Things may seem more cheerful in the morning."

I found myself weary and yet wakeful when I went to bed, and I tossed restlessly from side to side. Far away a chiming clock struck out the quarters of the hours, but otherwise a deathly silence lay upon the old house. And then suddenly, in the very dead of the night, there came a sound to my ears, clear, resonant, and unmistakable. It was the sob of a woman, the muffled, strangling gasp of one who is torn by an uncontrollable sorrow. I sat up in bed and listened intently. The noise was certainly in the house. For half an hour I waited with every nerve on the alert, but there came no other sound save the chiming clock and the rustle of the ivy on the wall.

Chapter 7

THE fresh beauty of the following morning did something to efface from our minds the grim and gray impression which had been left upon both of us by our first experience of Baskerville Hall. As Sir Henry and I sat at breakfast the sunlight flooded in through the high mullioned windows, throwing watery patches of color from the coats of arms which covered them.

"I guess it is ourselves and not the house that we have to blame!" said the baronet. "We were tired with our journey, so we took a gray view of the place. Now we are fresh, so it is all cheerful once more."

"And yet it was not entirely a question of imagination," I answered. "Did you, for example, happen to hear someone, a woman I think, sobbing in the night?"

"That is curious, for I did when I was half asleep fancy that I heard something of the sort."

"I heard it distinctly."

"We must ask about this right away." Sir Henry rang the bell and asked Barrymore whether he could account for our experience. It seemed to me that the pallid features of the butler turned a shade paler still as he listened to his master's question.

"There are only two women in the house, Sir Henry," he answered. "One is the scullery maid, who sleeps in the other wing. The other is my wife, and I can answer for it that the sound could not have come from her."

And yet he lied as he said it, for it chanced that after breakfast I met Mrs. Barrymore in the long corridor with the sun full upon her face. She was a large, impassive, heavy-featured woman with a stern, set expression of mouth. But her telltale eyes were red, and glanced at me from between swollen lids. It was, she, then, who wept in the night, and if she did so, her husband must know it. Yet he had taken the obvious risk of discovery in declaring that it was not so. Why had he done this? And why did she weep so bitterly? Already round this pale-faced, handsome, black-bearded man there was gathering an atmosphere of mystery and of gloom.

Was it possible that it was Barrymore, after all, whom we had seen in the cab in Regent Street? Obviously the first thing to do was to see the Grimpen postmaster and find whether the test telegram had really been placed in Barrymore's own hands.

Sir Henry had numerous papers to examine after breakfast, so that the time was propitious for my excursion. It was a pleasant walk of four miles along the edge of the moor, leading me at last to the small hamlet of Grimpen. Two buildings, which proved to be the inn and the house of Dr. Mortimer, stood high above the rest. The postmaster, who was also the village grocer, had a clear recollection of the telegram.

"Certainly, sir," said he, "I had the telegram delivered to Mr. Barrymore exactly as directed. James, you delivered that telegram to Mr. Barrymore at the Hall last week, did you not?"

"Yes, Father, I delivered it."

"Into his own hands?" I asked.

"Well, he was up in the loft at the time, so I could not put it into his own hands, but I gave it to Mrs. Barrymore, and she promised to deliver it at once."

"Did you see Mr. Barrymore?"

"No, sir. I tell you he was in the loft."

"How do you know he was in the loft?"

"Well, surely his own wife ought to know where he is," said the postmaster testily. "Didn't he get the telegram? If there is any mistake, it is for Mr. Barrymore himself to complain."

It was clear that in spite of Holmes's ruse we had no proof that Barrymore had not been in London all the time. Suppose that the man who had been the last to see Sir Charles alive was also the first to dog the new heir when he returned to England. What interest could he have in persecuting the Baskerville family?

As I walked back along the gray, lonely road my thoughts were suddenly interrupted by the sound of running feet behind me and by a voice which called me by name. I turned, expecting to see Dr. Mortimer, but to my surprise it was a stranger who was pursuing me. He was a small, slim, clean-shaven, prim-faced man, flaxen-haired and lean-jawed, between thirty and forty years of age, dressed in a gray suit and wearing a straw hat. A tin box for botanical specimens hung over his shoulder, and he carried a green butterfly net in one of his hands.

"You will, I am sure, excuse my presumption, Dr. Watson," said he as he came panting up to where I stood. "Here on the moor we do not wait for formal introductions. You may possibly have heard my name from our mutual friend, Mortimer. I am Stapleton, of Merripit House."

"Your net and box would have told me as much," said I, "for I knew that Mr. Stapleton was a naturalist. But how did you know me?"

"I have been calling on Mortimer, and he pointed you out to me as you passed his surgery. As our road lay the same way I thought that I would overtake you and introduce myself. I trust that Sir Henry is none the worse for his journey?"

"He is very well, thank you."

"We were all rather afraid that after the sad death of Sir Charles the new baronet might refuse to live here. Sir Henry has, I suppose, no superstitious fears in the matter?"

"I do not think that it is likely."

"Of course you know the legend of the fiend dog which haunts the family?"

"I have heard it."

"Any number of the peasants about here are ready to swear that they have seen such a creature upon the moor." He spoke with a smile, but I seemed to read in his eyes that he took the matter more seriously. "The story took a great hold upon the imagination of Sir Charles, and I have no doubt that it led to his tragic end."

"But how?"

"His nerves were so worked up that the appearance of any dog might have had a fatal effect upon his diseased heart. I fancy that he really did see something of the kind upon that last night in the yew alley."

"You think, then, that some dog pursued Sir Charles, and that he died of fright in consequence?"

"Have you or Mr. Sherlock Holmes any better explanation?"

The reference to Holmes took away my breath for an instant, but a glance at the placid face and steadfast eyes of my companion showed that no surprise was intended.

"It is useless for us to pretend that we do not know you, Dr. Watson," said he. "Your accounts of your detective have reached us here, and when Mortimer told me your name he could not conceal your identity. If you are here, then it follows that Mr. Sherlock Holmes is interesting himself in the matter. May I ask if he is going to honor us with a visit himself?"

"He cannot leave town at present. He has other cases which engage his attention."

"What a pity! He might throw some light on that which is so dark to us. But as to your own researches, if I had any indication of the nature of your suspicions or how you propose to investigate the case, I might perhaps be of service to you."

"I assure you that I am simply here upon a visit to my friend, Sir Henry, and that I need no help of any kind."

"You are perfectly right to be wary and discreet," said Stapleton. "I am justly reproved for an unjustifiable intrusion, and I promise you that I will not mention the matter again."

We had come to a point where a narrow grassy path struck off from the road and wound away across the moor. A steep, boulder-sprinkled hill lay upon the right. The face which was turned towards us formed a dark cliff, with ferns and brambles growing in its niches. From over a distant rise there floated a gray plume of smoke.

"A moderate walk along this moor path brings us to Merripit House," said he. "Perhaps you will spare an hour that I may have the pleasure of introducing you to my sister?"

My first thought was that I should be by Sir Henry's side. But then I remembered the pile of papers with which his study table was littered. And Holmes had expressly said that I should study the neighbors upon the moor. I accepted Stapleton's invitation, and we turned together down the path.

"It is a wonderful place, the moor," said he, looking round. "You cannot think the wonderful secrets which it contains. It is so vast, and so barren, and so mysterious."

"You know it well, then?"

"I have only been here two years. We came shortly after Sir Charles settled. But my tastes led me to explore every part of the country round, and I should think that there are few men who know it better than I do."

"Is it hard to know?"

"Very hard. You see, for example, this great plain to the north here with the queer hills breaking out of it. Do you notice those bright green spots scattered thickly over it?"

"Yes, they seem more fertile than the rest."

Stapleton laughed. "That is the great Grimpen Mire," said he. "A false step yonder means death to man or beast. Only yesterday I saw one of the moor ponies wander into it. I saw his head for quite a long time craning out of the boghole, but it sucked him down at last. Even in dry seasons it is a danger to cross it, but after these autumn rains it is an awful place. Yet I can find my way to the very heart of it and return alive. By George, there is another of those miserable ponies!"

Something brown was rolling and tossing among the green sedges. Then a long, agonized cry echoed over the moor. It turned me cold with horror, but my companion's nerves seemed to be stronger than mine.

"It's gone!" said he. "Two in two days, and many more, perhaps. It's a bad place, the great Grimpen Mire."

"And you say you can penetrate it?"

"Yes, there are one or two paths which a very active man can take. I have found them out."

"But why should you wish to go into so horrible a place?"

"Well, you see the hills beyond? They are really islands cut off on all sides by the impassable mire. That is where the rare plants and the butterflies are."

"I shall try my luck someday."

He looked at me with a surprised face. "For God's sake put such an idea out of your mind. I assure you that there would not be the least chance of your coming back alive. It is only by remembering certain complex landmarks that I am able to do it."

"Halloa!" I cried. "What is that?"

A long, low moan, indescribably sad, swept over the moor and filled the whole air. From a dull murmur it swelled into a deep roar, and then sank back into a melancholy murmur once again. Stapleton looked at me with a curious expression in his face.

"What is it?" I asked.

"The peasants say it is the Hound of the Baskervilles calling for its prey. I've heard it before, but never quite so loud."

I looked round, with a chill of fear in my heart. Nothing stirred over the vast plain save a pair of ravens, which croaked loudly from a tor behind us.

"You are an educated man. You don't believe such nonsense as that?" said I. "What do you think is the cause of so strange a sound?"

"Bogs make queer noises sometimes. It's the mud settling, or the water rising, or something."

"No, no, that was a living voice."

"Well, perhaps it was. Did you ever hear a bittern booming?"

"No, I never did."

"It's a very rare bird—practically extinct—in England now, but all things are possible upon the moor. I should not be surprised to learn that what we have heard is the cry of the last of the bitterns."

"It's the weirdest, strangest thing that ever I heard in my life."

"Yes, the moor's an uncanny place altogether. Look at the hillside yonder. What do you make of those gray circular rings of stone?"

"Are they sheep pens?"

"No, they are the homes of our worthy ancestors. Prehistoric man lived thickly on the moor. These are his huts with the roofs off. You can even see his hearth and his couch if you have the curiosity to go inside."

"But it is quite a town. When was it inhabited?"

"Neolithic man—no date—grazed his cattle on these slopes, and he learned to dig for tin when the bronze sword began to supersede the stone axe. Look at the great trench in the opposite hill. Oh, excuse me an instant! It is surely a Cyclopides."

A small moth had fluttered across our path, and in an instant Stapleton was rushing with extraordinary energy and speed in pursuit of it. To my dismay the creature flew straight for the great mire, and my acquaintance never paused for an instant, bounding from tuft to tuft, his green net waving in the air. His gray clothes and zigzag progress made him not unlike some huge moth himself. I was standing watching his pursuit with a mixture of admiration and fear lest he should lose his footing in the treacherous mire when I heard the sound of steps and, turning round, found a woman near me upon the path. She had come from the direction in which the plume of smoke indicated the position of Merripit House.

I could not doubt that this was the Miss Stapleton of whom I had been told. The woman who approached me was certainly a beauty, and of a most uncommon type. There could not have been a greater contrast between brother and sister, for Stapleton was neutral tinted, with light hair and gray eyes, while she was darker than any brunette I have seen in England—slim, elegant, and tall. She had a proud, finely cut face, so regular that it might have seemed impassive were it not for the sensitive mouth and the beautiful dark, eager eyes. With her perfect figure and elegant dress she was, indeed, a strange apparition upon a lonely moorland path. Her eyes were on her brother as I turned, and then she quickened her pace towards me.

"Go back!" she said. "Go straight back to London, instantly."

I could only stare at her in stupid surprise.

"Why should I go back?" I asked.

"I cannot explain." She spoke in a low voice, with a curious lisp in her utterance. "But for God's sake do what I ask you."

"But I have only just come."

"Man, man!" she cried. "Can you not tell when a warning is for your own good? Go back to London tonight! Hush, my brother is coming! Not a word of what I have said. Would you mind getting that orchid for me? We are very rich in orchids on the moor, though you are rather late to see the beauties of the place."

Stapleton had abandoned the chase and came back to us breathing hard and flushed with his exertions. "Halloa, Beryl!" said he, and it seemed to me that the tone of his greeting was not altogether a cordial one.

"Well, Jack, you are very hot."

"Yes, I was chasing a Cyclopides. He is seldom found in the late autumn. What a pity that I should have missed him!" He spoke unconcernedly, but his small light eyes glanced incessantly from the girl to me. "You have introduced yourselves, I can see."

"Yes, I was telling Sir Henry that it was rather late for him to see the true beauties of the moor."

"Why, who do you think this is?"

"I imagine that it must be Sir Henry Baskerville."

"No, no," said I. "Only a humble commoner, but his friend. My name is Dr. Watson."

A flush of vexation passed over her expressive face. "We have been talking at cross-purposes," said she.

"Why, you had not very much time for talk," her brother remarked with the same questioning eyes.

"I talked as if Dr. Watson were a resident instead of being merely a visitor," said she. "It cannot much matter to him whether it is early or late for the orchids. But you will come on and see Merripit House?"

A short walk brought us to it, a bleak moorland house, once a farm, but now put into repair and turned into a modern dwelling. An orchard surrounded it, but the trees were stunted and nipped, and the effect of the whole place was mean and melancholy. We were admitted by a rusty-coated old manservant, who seemed in keeping with the house. Inside, however, the rooms were furnished with an elegance in which I seemed to recognize the taste of the lady. As I looked from their windows at the interminable moor I could not but marvel at what could have brought this man and this woman to live in such a place.

"Queer spot to choose, is it not?" said he as if in answer to my thought. "And yet we manage to make ourselves fairly happy, do we not, Beryl?"

"Quite happy," said she, but there was no ring of conviction in her words.

"I had a school in the north country," said Stapleton. "The work to a man of my temperament was mechanical and uninteresting, but the privilege of living with youth, of impressing them with one's own character and ideals was very dear to me. A serious epidemic broke out in the school and three of the boys died. It never recovered from the blow, and much of my capital was swallowed up. And yet, with my strong tastes for botany and zoology, I find an unlimited field of work here, and my sister is as devoted to nature as I am. We have books, we have our studies, and we have interesting neighbors. Poor Sir Charles was an admirable companion. Do you think that I should intrude if I were to call this afternoon and make the acquaintance of Sir Henry?"

"I am sure that he would be delighted."

"Then perhaps you would mention that I propose to do so. Will you come upstairs, Dr. Watson, and inspect my collection of Lepidoptera?"

But I was eager to get back to my charge. I resisted all pressure to stay, and I set off at once upon my return journey, taking the grass-grown path by which we had come. Before I reached the road I was astounded to see Miss Stapleton sitting upon a rock by the side of the track. Her face was beautifully flushed with her exertions, and she held her hand to her side.

"I have run all the way in order to cut you off, Dr. Watson," said she. "I must not stop, or my brother may miss me. I wanted to say to you how sorry I am about the stupid mistake I made in thinking that you were Sir Henry. Please forget the words I said, which have no application whatever to you."

"But I can't forget them, Miss Stapleton," said I. "I am Sir Henry's friend, and his welfare is a very close concern of mine. Tell me why it was that you were so eager that Sir Henry should return to London."

"A woman's whim, Dr. Watson."

"No, no. Be frank with me, Miss Stapleton, for ever since I have been here I have been conscious of shadows all round me. Tell me then what it was that you meant, and I will promise to convey your warning to Sir Henry."

An expression of irresolution passed for an instant over her face, but her eyes had hardened again when she answered me.

"You make too much of it, Dr. Watson," said she. "My brother and I were very much shocked by the death of Sir Charles. We knew him intimately, for his favorite walk was over the moor to our house. He was deeply impressed with the curse which hung over his family, and when this tragedy came I naturally felt that there must be some grounds for the fears which he had expressed. You know the story of the hound?"

"I do not believe in such nonsense."

"But I do. If you have any influence with Sir Henry, take him away from a place which has always been fatal to his family. Why should he wish to live at the place of danger?"

"Because it *is* the place of danger. That is Sir Henry's nature. I fear that unless you can give me some more definite information than this, it would be impossible to get him to move."

"I cannot say anything definite, for I do not know anything definite."

"Miss Stapleton, if you meant no more than this, why should you not wish your brother to overhear what you said?"

"My brother is very anxious to have the Hall inhabited, for he thinks that it is for the good of the poor folk upon the moor. He would be very angry if he knew that I had said anything which might induce Sir Henry to go away. Now, I must get back, or he will miss me and suspect that I have seen you. Good-by!" She turned and disappeared among the scattered boulders, while I, full of vague fears, pursued my way to Baskerville Hall.

Chapter 8

FROM this point onward I will follow the course of events by transcribing my own letters to Mr. Sherlock Holmes. They show my feelings and suspicions of the moment more accurately than my memory can possibly do.

My dear Holmes,

If you have not had any report within the last few days, it is because up to today there was nothing important to relate. Then a surprising circumstance occurred, which I shall tell you in due course. But, first of all, I must keep you in touch with some other factors in the situation.

One of these is the escaped convict upon the moor. A fortnight has passed since his flight, during which he has not been seen and nothing has been heard of him. It is surely inconceivable that he could have held out upon the moor during all that time. Of course, any one of the prehistoric stone huts that are all about us here would give him a hiding place. But there is nothing to eat unless he were to catch and slaughter one of the moor sheep. We think, therefore, that he has gone, and the outlying farmers sleep the better in consequence.

We are four able-bodied men in this household, so that we could take good care of ourselves, but I have had uneasy moments when I have thought of the Stapletons. They live miles from any help. Both Sir Henry and I were concerned at their situation, and it was suggested that Perkins the groom should go over to sleep there, but Stapleton would not hear of it. The fact is that our friend, the baronet, begins to display a considerable interest in our fair neighbor. It is not to be wondered at, for she is a fascinating and beautiful woman. There is something tropical and exotic about her which forms a singular contrast to her cool and unemotional brother. Yet he also gives the idea of hidden fires. I trust that he is kind to her. There is a dry glitter in his eyes and a firm set of his thin lips, which goes with a positive and possibly a harsh nature. You would find him an interesting study.

He came over to call upon Baskerville on that first day, and the very next morning he took us both to show us the spot where the legend of the wicked Hugo is supposed to have had its origin. It was an excursion of some miles across the moor to a place which is so dismal that it might have suggested the story. Sir Henry was much interested and asked Stapleton more than once whether he did really believe in the possibility of the interference of the supernatural in the affairs of men. Stapleton was guarded in his replies, but he told us of similar cases, where families had suffered from some evil influence, and he gave us the impression that he shared the popular view upon the matter.

On our way back we stayed for lunch at Merripit House, and it was there that Sir Henry made the acquaintance of Miss Stapleton. From the first moment that he saw her he appeared to be strongly attracted by her, and I am much mistaken if the feeling was not mutual. Since then hardly a day has passed that we have not seen something of the brother and sister. One would imagine that such a match would be very welcome to Stapleton, and yet I have more than once caught a look of the strongest disapprobation in his face when Sir Henry has been paying some attention to his sister. He is much attached to her, no doubt, and would lead a lonely life without her, but it would seem the height of selfishness if he were to stand in the way of her making so brilliant a marriage. Yet I have several times observed that he has taken pains to prevent them from being tête-à-tête. By the way, your instructions to me never to allow Sir Henry to go out alone will become very much more onerous if a love affair were to be added to our other difficulties.

The other day—Thursday, to be more exact—Dr. Mortimer lunched with us. The Stapletons came in afterwards, and the good doctor took us all to the yew alley, to show us exactly how everything occurred upon that fatal night. It is a long, dismal walk between two high walls of clipped yew, with a narrow band of grass upon either side. Halfway down is the wooden moor gate. Beyond it lies the wide moor. I tried to picture all that had occurred. As the old man stood there he saw something coming across the moor, something which terrified him so that he lost his wits and ran and ran until he died of horror and exhaustion. And from what did he flee? A sheep dog of the moor? Or a spectral hound, black, silent, and monstrous? Was there a human agency in the matter? Did the pale, watchful Barrymore know more than he cared to say? It was all dim and vague, but always there is the dark shadow of crime behind it.

One other neighbor I have met since I wrote last. This is Mr. Frankland, of Lafter Hall, who lives some four miles to the south of us. He is an elderly man, red-faced and choleric. His passion is for British law, and he has spent a large fortune in litigation. He fights for the mere pleasure of fighting. Sometimes he will shut up a right-of-way and defy the parish to make him open it. At others he will with his own hands tear down some other man's gate and declare that a path has existed there from time immemorial, defying the owner to prosecute him for trespass. He is learned in old manorial and communal rights, and he applies his knowledge sometimes in favor of the villagers of Fernworthy and sometimes against them, so that he is periodically either carried in triumph down the village street or else burned in effigy. He is said to have about seven lawsuits upon his hands at present, which will probably swallow up the remainder of his fortune and so draw his sting. Apart from the law he seems a kindly, good-natured person. Being an amateur astronomer, he has an excellent telescope, with which he lies upon the roof of his house and sweeps the moor all day in the hope of catching a glimpse of the escaped convict. There are also rumors that he intends to prosecute Dr. Mortimer for opening a grave without the consent of the next of kin, because he dug up a neolithic skull in the barrow on Long Down. He helps to keep our lives from being monotonous and gives a little comic relief where it is badly needed.

And now let me end on that which is most important and tell you more about the Barrymores, and especially about the surprising development of last night.

First of all about the telegram which you sent from London to make sure that Barrymore was really here. I have already explained that the testimony of the postmaster shows that we have no proof one way or the other. I told Sir Henry how the matter stood, and he at once, in his downright fashion, had Barrymore up and asked him whether he had received the telegram himself. Barrymore said that he had.

"Did the boy deliver it into your own hands?" asked Sir Henry.

Barrymore looked surprised, and considered for a little time.

"No," said he, "I was in the boxroom at the time, and my wife brought it up to me."

"Did you answer it yourself?"

"No, I told my wife what to answer and she went down to write it. I trust that your questions do not mean that I have done anything to forfeit your confidence?"

Sir Henry had to assure him that it was not so and pacify him by giving him a considerable part of his old wardrobe, the London outfit having now all arrived.

Mrs. Barrymore is of interest to me. She is a heavy, solid person, intensely respectable. You could hardly conceive a less emotional subject. Yet I have more than once observed traces of tears upon her face. Some deep sorrow gnaws ever at her heart. Sometimes I suspect Barrymore of being a domestic tyrant. I have always felt that there was something singular and questionable in his character, but the adventure of last night brings all my suspicions to a head.

About two in the morning I was aroused by a stealthy step passing my room. I rose, opened my door, and peeped out. A long black shadow was trailing down the corridor. It was thrown by a man who walked softly down the passage with a candle held in his hand. He was in shirt and trousers, with no covering to his feet. His height told me that it was Barrymore.

I waited until he had passed out of sight and then I followed him. When he had reached the end of the corridor on the opposite side of the gallery, I could see from the glimmer of light through an open door that he had entered one of the rooms. Now, all these rooms are unfurnished and unoccupied, so that his expedition became more mysterious than ever. I crept down the passage as noiselessly as I could and peeped round the corner of the door.

Barrymore was crouching at the window with the candle held against the glass. His profile was half turned towards me, and his face seemed to be rigid with expectation as he stared out into the blackness of the moor. For some minutes he stood watching intently. Then he gave a deep groan and with an impatient gesture he put out the light. Instantly I made my way back to my room,

and very shortly came the stealthy steps passing once more upon their return journey. What it all means I cannot guess, but there is some secret business going on in this house of gloom which sooner or later we shall get to the bottom of.

Chapter 9

Baskerville Hall, October 15

My dear Holmes,

Events are now crowding thick and fast upon us. In some ways things have within the last forty-eight hours become much clearer and in some ways they have become more complicated. But you shall judge for yourself.

On the morning following my adventure I went down the corridor and examined the room in which Barrymore had been on the night before. The western window through which he had stared so intently commands, I noticed, the nearest outlook onto the moor of all the windows in the house. From the others only a distant glimpse can be obtained. It follows, therefore, that Barrymore must have been looking out for something or somebody upon the moor. The night was very dark, so that I can hardly imagine how he could have hoped to see anyone. It had struck me that it was possible that some love intrigue was on foot. That would have accounted for his stealthy movements and also for the uneasiness of his wife. The man is a striking-looking fellow, very well equipped to steal the heart of a country girl.

But whatever the true explanation, I felt that the responsibility of keeping Barrymore's movements to myself was more than I could bear. I had an interview with Sir Henry in his study after breakfast, and I told him all that I had seen. He was less surprised than I had expected.

"I knew that Barrymore walked about nights, and I had a mind to speak to him about it," said he. "Two or three times I have heard his steps in the passage, just about the hour you name."

"Perhaps then he pays a visit every night to that particular window," I suggested.

"Perhaps he does. If so, we should be able to shadow him and see what it is that he is after. We'll sit up in my room tonight and wait until he passes." Sir Henry rubbed his hands with pleasure, and it was evident that he hailed the adventure as a relief to his somewhat quiet life upon the moor.

The baronet has been in communication with the architect who prepared plans for Sir Charles, so that we may expect great changes to begin here soon. It is evident that our friend means to spare no expense to restore the grandeur of his family. When the house is renovated, all that he will need will be a wife to make it complete. Between ourselves, I have seldom seen a man more infatuated with a woman than he is with our beautiful neighbor, Miss Stapleton. And yet the course of true love does not run quite as smoothly as one would under the circumstances expect. Day before yesterday, for example, its surface was broken by a very unexpected ripple.

After our conversation about Barrymore, Sir Henry put on his hat and prepared to go out. As a matter of course I did the same.

"What, are *you* coming, Watson?" he asked, looking at me in a curious way.

"That depends on whether you are going on the moor."

"Yes, I am."

"Well, I am sorry to intrude, but you heard how earnestly Holmes insisted that you should not go alone upon the moor."

Sir Henry put his hand upon my shoulder with a pleasant smile.

"My dear fellow," said he, "I am sure that you are the last man in the world who would wish to be a spoilsport."

I was at a loss what to say, and before I had made up my mind he picked up his cane and was gone. But my conscience reproached me bitterly for having on any pretext allowed him to go out of my sight. I imagined what my feelings would be if I had to return to you and to confess that some misfortune had occurred through my disregard for your instructions. I assure you my cheeks flushed at the very thought. So I set off at once in the direction of Merripit House.

I hurried along the road without seeing anything of Sir Henry, until I came to a hill from which I could command a view. I saw him at once, on the moor path, about a quarter of a mile off, Miss Stapleton by his side. It was clear that they had met by appointment. They were walking slowly along in deep conversation. I stood watching them, very much puzzled as to what I should do next. My clear duty was never for an instant to let him out of my sight. Yet to act the spy was a hateful task. I could see no better course than to observe him from the hill, and to clear my conscience by confessing to him afterwards what I had done.

Sir Henry and the lady had halted on the path, when I was suddenly aware that I was not the only witness of their interview. A wisp of green floating in the air caught my eye, and another glance showed me that it was Stapleton with his butterfly net, moving along the broken ground in their direction. At this instant Sir Henry suddenly drew Miss Stapleton to his side. It seemed to me that she was straining away from him with her face averted. He stooped his head to hers, and she raised one hand as if in protest. Next moment I saw them spring apart and turn hurriedly round. Stapleton was running wildly towards them, his absurd net dangling behind him. He gesticulated and almost danced with excitement in front of the lovers. He seemed to be abusing Sir Henry. The lady stood by in haughty silence. Finally, Stapleton turned upon his heel and beckoned in a peremptory way to his sister, who, after an irresolute glance at Sir Henry, walked off with her brother. The baronet stood for a minute looking after them, and then he walked slowly back the way that he had come, his head hanging, the very picture of dejection.

I was deeply ashamed to have witnessed so intimate a scene without my friend's knowledge. I ran down the hill therefore and met the baronet at the bottom. His face was flushed with anger and his brows were wrinkled, like one who is at his wit's end what to do.

"Halloa, Watson! Where have you dropped from?" said he.

I explained to him how I had found it impossible to remain behind, and how I had witnessed all that had occurred. My frankness disarmed his anger, and he broke at last into a rather rueful laugh.

"By thunder," said he, "the whole countryside seems to have

been out to see me do my wooing—and a mighty poor wooing at that! I always thought her brother sane enough until today, but you can take it from me that either he or I ought to be in a straitjacket. What's the matter with me, anyhow? Is there anything that would prevent me from making a good husband to a woman that I loved?"

"I should say not."

"Yet he would not so much as let me touch the tips of her fingers."

"Did he say so?"

"That, and a deal more. I tell you, Watson, from the first I just felt that she was made for me, and she, too—she was happy when she was with me. But he has never let us get together, and it was only today for the first time that I saw a chance of having a few words with her alone. She was glad to meet me, but when she did it was not love that she would talk about. She kept coming back to it that this was a place of danger, and that she would never be happy until I had left it. I told her that if she really wanted me to go, the only way to work it was for her to arrange to go with me. With that I offered in as many words to marry her, but before she could answer, this brother of hers came running at us with a face like a madman. Those eyes of his were blazing with fury. How dared I offer the lady attentions which were distasteful to her? Did I think that because I was a baronet I could do what I liked? I told him that my feelings towards his sister were such as I was not ashamed of, and that I hoped that she might honor me by becoming my wife. That seemed to make the matter no better, so then I lost my temper, too, and I answered him rather more hotly than I should perhaps. So it ended by his going off with her, as you saw. Just tell me what it all means, Watson, and I'll owe you more than ever I can hope to pay."

I tried one or two explanations, but, indeed, I was completely puzzled myself. Our friend's title, his fortune, his age, his character, and his appearance are all in his favor. However, our conjectures were set at rest by a visit from Stapleton himself that very afternoon. He had come to offer apologies for his rudeness of the morning, and after a long private interview with Sir Henry the upshot of their conversation was that the breach is quite healed, and that we are to dine at Merripit House next Friday.

"I can't forget the look in his eyes when he ran at me this morning, but I must allow that no man could make a more handsome apology than he has done," said Sir Henry.

"Did he give any explanation of his conduct?"

"His sister is everything in his life, he says, so that the thought of losing her was really terrible to him. He had not understood that I was becoming attached to her, but when he saw with his own eyes that she might be taken away from him, it gave him such a shock that he was not responsible for what he said or did. He was very sorry for all that had passed, and he recognized how selfish it would be to hold a beautiful woman like his sister to himself for her whole life. But if she had to leave him, it would take him some time before he could prepare himself to meet the blow. He would withdraw all opposition if I would promise for three months to be content with cultivating the lady's friendship without claiming her love. This I promised, and so the matter rests."

So there is one of our small mysteries cleared up. And now pass on to the mystery of the sobs in the night, of the tearstained face of Mrs. Barrymore, of the secret journey of the butler to the western window. Congratulate me, my dear Holmes, and tell me that I have not disappointed you as an agent. All these things have by one night's work been thoroughly cleared.

I have said "by one night's work," but, in truth, it was by two nights' work, for on the first we drew entirely blank. I sat up with Sir Henry in his room until nearly three o'clock in the morning, but no sound of any sort did we hear except the chiming clock upon the stairs. It was a most melancholy vigil. The next night we lowered the lamp in Sir Henry's room and sat smoking cigarettes without making the least sound. It was incredible how slowly the hours crawled by. One struck, and two, and we had almost given it up in despair when in an instant we both sat bolt upright in our chairs, with all our weary senses keenly on the alert once more. We had heard the creak of a step in the passage.

Very stealthily we heard it pass along until it died away in the distance. Then Sir Henry gently opened his door and we set out in pursuit. Already our man had gone round the gallery, and the corridor was all in darkness. Softly we stole along until we caught a glimpse of the tall, black-bearded figure as he tiptoed down the passage and through the same door as before. We had taken the precaution of leaving our boots behind us, but even so we shuffled cautiously towards the yellow beam of the candle, trying every plank before we put our weight upon it. When at last we reached the door and peeped through we found him crouching at the window, candle in hand, his face pressed against the pane, exactly as I had seen him two nights before.

Sir Henry is a man to whom the most direct way is always the most natural. He walked into the room, and as he did so Barrymore sprang up from the window with a sharp hiss of his breath and stood, livid and trembling, before us.

"What are you doing here, Barrymore?"

"Nothing, sir." His agitation was so great that he could hardly speak, and the shadows sprang up and down from the shaking of his candle. "It was the window, sir. I go round at night to see that they are fastened."

"On the second floor?"

"Yes, sir, all the windows."

"Come, now! No lies! What were you doing at that window?" said Sir Henry sternly.

The fellow looked at us in the last extremity of doubt and misery. "I was doing no harm, sir. I was holding a candle to the window."

"And why were you holding a candle to the window?"

"Don't ask me, Sir Henry—don't ask me! I give you my word, sir, that it is not my secret, and that I cannot tell it."

A sudden idea occurred to me, and I took the candle from the trembling hand of the butler.

"He must have been holding it as a signal," said I. "Let us see if there is any answer." I held it as he had done, and stared out into the darkness of the night. Vaguely I could discern the black bank of the trees and the lighter expanse of the moor. Suddenly

441

a tiny pinpoint of yellow light glowed steadily in the square framed by the window.

"There it is!" I cried.

"No, no, sir, it is nothing—nothing at all!" the butler broke in. "I assure you, sir—"

"Move your light across the window, Watson!" cried the baronet. "See, the other moves also! Now, you rascal, do you deny that it is a signal? Come, speak up! What is this conspiracy that is going on?"

The man's face became openly defiant. "It is my business, and not yours. I will not tell."

"Then you leave my employment right away."

"Very good, sir."

"And you go in disgrace. By thunder, you may well be ashamed of yourself. Your family has lived with mine for over a hundred years, and here I find you deep in some dark plot against me."

"No, no, sir; no, not against you!" It was a woman's voice, and Mrs. Barrymore, paler and more horror-struck than her husband, was standing at the door.

"We have to go, Eliza. This is the end of it. You can pack our things," said the butler.

"Oh, John, John, have I brought you to this? It is my doing, Sir Henry—all mine. He has done nothing except for my sake, and because I asked him."

"Speak out, then! What does it mean?"

"My unhappy brother is hiding on the moor. We cannot let him perish at our very gates. The light is a signal to him that food is ready for him, and his light out yonder is to show the spot to which to bring it."

"Then your brother is—"

"The escaped convict, sir—Selden, the criminal."

Sir Henry and I both stared at Mrs. Barrymore in amazement. Was it possible that this stolidly respectable person was of the same blood as one of the most notorious criminals in the country?

"Yes, sir, my name was Selden, and he is my younger brother. We humored him too much when he was a lad, and then as he grew older he met wicked companions, and the devil entered into him until he broke my mother's heart and dragged our name in the dirt. He sank lower and lower until it is only the mercy of God which has snatched him from the scaffold; but to me, sir, he was always the little curly-headed boy that I had nursed and played with. That was why he broke prison, sir. He knew that we could not refuse to help him. When he dragged himself here one night, with the warders hard at his heels, we took him in and cared for him. Then you returned, sir, and my brother thought he would be safer on the moor until the hue and cry was over. But every second night we made sure he was still there by putting a light in the window, and if there was an answer, my husband took out some bread and meat to him. Every day we hoped that he was gone, but as long as he was there we could not desert him. That is the whole truth, and you will see that if there is blame in the matter it lies with me, for whose sake my husband has done all that he has."

The woman's words came with an intense earnestness which carried conviction with them.

"Well, Barrymore," said Sir Henry, "I cannot blame you for standing by your own wife. Forget what I have said. Go to your room, you two, and we shall talk further in the morning."

When they were gone we looked out of the window again. Far away in the black distance there still glowed that one tiny point of yellow light.

"I wonder he dares," said Sir Henry.

"How far do you think it is?"

"Not more than a mile or two off. By thunder, Watson, I am going out to take that man!"

The same thought had crossed my own mind. It was not as if the Barrymores had taken us into their confidence. Their secret had been forced from them. The man was a danger to the community, an unmitigated scoundrel for whom there was neither pity nor excuse. With his brutal and violent nature, others would have to pay the price if we held our hands.

"I will come," said I.

"Then get your revolver and put on your boots. The sooner we start the better, as the fellow may put out his light and be off."

In five minutes we were outside the door, hurrying through the dark shrubbery, amid the dull moaning of the autumn wind and the rustle of the falling leaves. The night air was heavy with the smell of damp and decay. Clouds were driving over the face of the sky, and just as we came out on the moor a thin rain began to fall. The light still burned steadily in front.

"Are you armed?" I asked.

"I have a hunting crop."

"We must close in on him rapidly, take him by surprise, and have him at our mercy before he can resist."

"I say, Watson," said the baronet, "what would Holmes say to this? How about that hour of darkness in which the power of evil is exalted?"

As if in answer to his words there rose suddenly out of the vast gloom of the moor that strange cry which I had already heard upon the borders of the great Grimpen Mire. It came with the wind through the silence of the night, a long, deep mutter, then a rising howl, and then the sad moan in which it died away. Again and again it sounded, the whole air throbbing with it, strident, wild, and menacing. The baronet caught my sleeve and his face glimmered white through the darkness.

"My God, what's that, Watson?"

"I don't know. I heard it once before. Stapleton said that it might be the calling of a strange bird."

It died away, and an absolute silence closed in upon us.

"Watson," said Sir Henry, "it was the cry of a hound." There was a break in his voice which told of the sudden horror which had seized him. "Tell me, Watson. What do the folk on the countryside say of it?"

I hesitated but could not escape the question. "They say it is the cry of the Hound of the Baskervilles."

He groaned and was silent for a few moments. "A hound it was," he said at last, "but it seemed to come from miles away, over yonder. Isn't that the direction of the great Grimpen Mire?"

"Yes, it is."

"My God, can there be some truth in all these stories? You don't believe that, do you, Watson?"

"No, no."

"And yet it was one thing to laugh about it in London, and it is another to stand out here in the darkness of the moor and to hear such a cry as that. And my uncle! There were footprints of the hound near him. It all fits together. I don't think that I am a coward, Watson, but that sound seemed to freeze my very blood. Feel my hand!"

It was as cold as a block of marble.

"Shall we turn back?"

"No, by thunder; we have come out to get our man, and we will do it. We after the convict, and a hellhound, as likely as not, after us. Come on!"

We stumbled slowly along in the darkness, the yellow speck of light burning steadily in front. Sometimes the glimmer seemed to be far away upon the horizon and sometimes it might have been within a few yards of us. But at last we could see whence it came, and then we knew that we were indeed very close. A guttering candle was stuck in a crevice of the rocks which flanked it on each side so as to keep the wind from it and also to prevent it from being visible, save in the direction of Baskerville Hall. A boulder of granite concealed our approach, and crouching behind it we gazed over it at the signal light.

"What shall we do now?" whispered Sir Henry.

"Wait here. He must be near his light."

The words were hardly out of my mouth when we both saw him. Over the rocks in which the candle burned, there was thrust out an evil yellow face, all seamed and scored with vile passions. Foul with mire, with a bristling beard, and hung with matted hair, it might well have belonged to one of those old savages who dwelt in the burrows on the hillsides. The light beneath him was reflected in his small cunning eyes, which peered fiercely to right and left through the darkness like a crafty animal who has heard the steps of the hunters.

Something had evidently aroused his suspicions. I could read his fears upon his wicked face. Any instant he might dash out the light and vanish in the darkness. I sprang forward therefore, and Sir Henry did the same. At the same moment the convict screamed out a curse at us and hurled a rock, which splintered up against the boulder which had sheltered us. I caught one glimpse of his short, strong figure as he sprang to his feet and turned to run. At the same moment by a lucky chance the moon broke through the clouds. We rushed over the brow of the hill, and there was our man springing over the stones with great speed down the other side. A lucky long shot of my revolver might have crippled him, but I had brought it only to defend myself, not to shoot an unarmed man who was running away.

Sir Henry and I were both in fairly good training, and we ran and ran until we were completely blown, but the space between us and the convict grew ever wider. Finally we stopped and sat panting, while we watched him disappearing in the distance.

And it was at this moment that there occurred a most strange and unexpected thing. The moon was low upon the right, and the jagged pinnacle of a granite tor stood up against the lower curve of its silver disk. There, outlined as black as an ebony statue on that shining background, I saw the figure of a man, a tall, thin man. He stood with his legs a little separated, his arms folded, his head bowed, as if he were brooding over that enormous wilderness of peat and granite which lay before him. He might have been the very spirit of that terrible place. With a cry of surprise I pointed him out to the baronet, but in the instant during which I turned to grab his arm the man was gone.

"A warder, no doubt," said Sir Henry. "The moor has been thick with them since this fellow escaped." Well, perhaps his explanation may be the right one, but I should like to have some further proof of it. Such are the adventures of last night.

We are certainly making progress, my dear Holmes. But the moor with its mysteries and its strange inhabitants remains as inscrutable as ever. Perhaps in my next report I may be able to throw some light upon this also.

Chapter 10

I HAVE now arrived at a point in my narrative where I am compelled to trust once more to my recollections, aided by the diary which I kept at the time. A few extracts from the latter will carry me on to those scenes which are indelibly fixed in my memory.

October 16. A dull and foggy day with a drizzle of rain. The house is banked in with rolling clouds, which rise now and then to show the dreary curves of the moor, and the distant boulders gleaming where the light strikes upon their wet faces. It is melancholy outside and in. The baronet is in a black reaction on this morning following our strange experiences upon the moor. I am conscious myself of a feeling of impending danger, which is the more terrible because I am unable to define it.

Twice I have with my own ears heard the sound which resembled the distant baying of a hound. It is incredible, impossible, that the hound should be outside the ordinary laws of nature. A spectral hound which leaves material footprints and fills the air with its howling is surely not to be thought of. If I have one quality upon earth it is common sense, and nothing will persuade me to believe in such a thing. To do so would be to descend to the level of these poor peasants, who must needs describe a fiend dog with hellfire shooting from his mouth and eyes. But facts are facts, and I have twice heard this crying upon the moor. Suppose that there were really some huge hound loose upon it; where could it lie concealed, where does it get its food, how is it that no one sees it by day? It must be confessed that the natural explanation offers almost as many difficulties as the other.

And always there is the fact of the human agency in London, the man in the cab, and the letter which warned Sir Henry against the moor. Where is that friend or enemy now? Could he—could he be the stranger whom I saw upon the tor? I am ready to swear that he is no one whom I have seen down here, and I have now met all the neighbors. If I could lay my hands upon that man, then at last we might find ourselves at the end of all our difficulties. To this purpose I must now devote all my energies.

We had a small scene this morning after breakfast. Barrymore asked leave to speak with Sir Henry, and they were closeted in his study some little time. Sitting in the billiard room, I more than once heard the sound of voices raised, and I had a pretty good idea what the point was which was under discussion. After a time the baronet opened his door and called for me.

"Barrymore considers that he has a grievance," he said. "He thinks that it was unfair on our part to hunt his brother-in-law down when he, of his own free will, had told us the secret."

The butler was standing very pale but very collected before us. "I may have spoken too warmly, sir," said he, "and if I have, I am sure that I beg your pardon. At the same time, I was very much surprised when I heard you two gentlemen come back this morning and learned that you had been chasing Selden. The poor fellow has enough to fight against without my putting more upon his track."

"The man is a public danger," said the baronet. "There are lonely houses scattered over the moor, and he is a fellow who would stick at nothing. Look at Mr. Stapleton's house, for example, with no one but himself to defend it."

"He'll break into no house, sir. He will never trouble anyone in this country again. I assure you, Sir Henry, that arrangements have been made and in a very few days he will be on his way to South America. I beg of you not to let the police know that he is still on the moor. They have given up the chase there, and he can lie quiet until the ship is ready for him. You can't tell on him without getting my wife and me into trouble."

"But how about the chance of his holding someone up before he goes?"

"He would not do anything so mad, sir. We have provided him with all that he can want. To commit a crime would be to show where he was hiding."

"That is true," said Sir Henry. "Well, Barrymore—"

"God bless you, sir, and thank you from my heart! It would have killed my poor wife had he been taken again."

"I guess we are aiding and abetting a felony, Watson? But, after what we have heard, I don't feel as if I could give the man up. All right, Barrymore, you can go."

With a few broken words of gratitude the man turned, but he hesitated and then came back.

"You've been so kind to us, sir, that I should like to do the best I can for you in return. I know something, Sir Henry, that I found out long after the inquest. Perhaps I should have told you before. It's about poor Sir Charles's death."

The baronet and I were both upon our feet. "What is it?"

"I know why he was at the gate at that hour. It was to meet a woman."

"To meet a woman! He?"

"Yes, sir. I can't give her name, but I can give you the initials. Her initials were L. L."

"How do you know this, Barrymore?"

"Well, Sir Henry, your uncle had a letter that morning. He usually had a great many letters, but the morning before he died, as it chanced, there was only this one, so I took the more notice of it. It was from Coombe Tracey, and it was addressed in a woman's hand."

"Well?"

"Well, sir, only a few weeks ago my wife was cleaning out Sir Charles's study—it had never been touched since his death—and she found the ashes of a burned letter in the back of the grate. The greater part of it was charred to pieces, but on the end of one page the writing could still be read. It seemed to us to be a postscript, and it said, 'Please, please, as you are a gentleman, burn this letter, and be at the gate by ten o'clock.' Beneath it were signed the initials L. L."

"And you have no idea who L. L. is?"

"No, sir. But I expect if we could lay our hands upon that lady, we should know more about Sir Charles's death."

"I cannot understand, Barrymore, how you came to conceal this important information."

"Well, sir, it was immediately after that our own trouble came to us. And then again, sir, we were both of us very fond of Sir

Charles, and it's well to go carefully when there's a lady in the case. Even the best of us—"

"You thought it might injure his reputation?"

"Well, sir, I thought no good could come of it. But now you have been kind to us, and I feel that I should tell you."

"Very good, Barrymore. You can go."

When the butler had left us Sir Henry turned to me. "Well, Watson, what do you think we should do now?"

"Let Holmes know all about it at once."

I went to my room and drew up my report of the morning's conversation for Holmes. It was evident to me that he had been very busy of late, for the notes which I had from Baker Street were few and short, with no comments upon the information which I had supplied. And yet this new factor must surely arrest his attention and renew his interest. I wish that he were here.

October 17. All day today the rain poured down, rustling on the ivy and dripping from the eaves. In the evening I put on my raincoat and I walked far upon the sodden moor, full of dark imaginings. God help those who wander into the great mire now, for even the firm uplands are becoming a morass. I found the black tor upon which I had seen the solitary watcher, and from its craggy summit I looked out myself across the melancholy downs. Nowhere was there any trace of that lonely man whom I had seen on the same spot two nights before.

As I walked back I was overtaken by Dr. Mortimer driving in his gig over a rough moorland track which led from the outlying farmhouse of Foulmire. Hardly a day has passed that he has not called at the Hall to see how we were getting on. He insisted upon my climbing into his gig. I found him much troubled over the disappearance of his little spaniel. It had wandered onto the moor and had never come back. I gave him such consolation as I might, but I thought of the pony on the Grimpen Mire, and I do not fancy that he will see his little dog again.

"By the way, Mortimer," said I as we jolted towards Baskerville Hall, "I suppose there are few people living within driving distance of this whom you do not know?"

"Hardly any, I think."

"Can you, then, tell me the name of any woman whose initials are L. L.?"

He thought for a few minutes, and then said, "There is Laura Lyons, but she lives in Coombe Tracey."

"Who is she?" I asked.

"She is Frankland's daughter."

"What! Old Frankland the crank?"

"Exactly. She married an artist named Lyons, who came sketching on the moor. He proved to be a blackguard and deserted her. Her father refused to have anything to do with her, because she had married without his consent. So, between the old sinner and the young one, the girl has had a pretty bad time."

"How does she live?"

"I fancy old Frankland allows her a pittance, but it cannot be more, for his own affairs are considerably involved. Her story got about, and several of the people here did something to enable her to earn an honest living. Stapleton for one, and Sir Charles for another. I gave a trifle myself. It was to set her up in a typewriting business."

He wanted to know the object of my inquiries, but I am certainly developing the wisdom of the serpent, for when he pressed his questions to an inconvenient extent I asked him casually to what type Frankland's skull belonged, and so heard nothing but craniology for the rest of our drive. I have not lived for years with Sherlock Holmes for nothing.

Mortimer stayed to dinner, and he and the baronet played écarté afterwards. Barrymore brought my coffee into the library, and I took the chance to ask him a few questions.

"Well," said I, "has this relation of yours departed, or is he still lurking out yonder?"

"I don't know, sir. I've not heard of him since I left out food for him last, and that was three days ago."

"Did you see him then?"

"No, sir, but the food was gone when next I went that way."

"Then he was certainly there?"

"So you would think, sir, unless it was the other man who took it."

I sat with my coffee cup halfway to my lips and stared at Barrymore. "You know that there is another man then?"

"Yes, sir, there is another man upon the moor. Selden told me of him, sir, a week ago or more."

"Can you tell me anything more about this stranger? Did Selden find out where he hid, or what he was doing?"

"Selden saw him once or twice, but he is a deep one and gives nothing away. A kind of gentleman he was, as far as Selden could see, but what the man was doing he could not make out."

"And where did Selden say that he lived?"

"Among the stone huts where the old folk used to live."

"But how about his food?"

"Selden found out that he has got a lad who brings all he needs from Coombe Tracey."

When the butler had gone I walked over to the window, and I looked through a blurred pane at the tossing outline of the windswept trees. What deep and earnest purpose can lead a man to lurk upon the moor at such a time! I swear that another day shall not have passed before I have done all that I can to reach the heart of that mystery.

Chapter 11

THE preceding extract from my diary has brought my narrative up to the eighteenth of October, a time when these strange events began to move swiftly towards their terrible conclusion. The incidents of the next few days are so indelibly engraved upon my recollection that I can tell them without reference to notes.

I had no opportunity to tell Sir Henry what I had learned about Mrs. Lyons upon the evening before. At breakfast, however, I informed him about my discovery and asked him whether he would care to accompany me to Coombe Tracey, but on second thoughts it seemed to both of us that if I went alone, the results might be better. The more formal we made the visit, the less information we might obtain. I left Sir Henry behind, therefore, and drove off with Perkins the groom upon my new quest.

When I reached Coombe Tracey I had no difficulty in finding Mrs. Lyons' rooms. A maid showed me in without ceremony, and as I entered the sitting room a lady, who was sitting before a typewriter, sprang up with a pleasant smile of welcome. Her face fell, however, when she saw that I was a stranger, and she sat down again and asked me the object of my visit.

The first impression left by Mrs. Lyons was one of extreme beauty. Her eyes and hair were of the same rich hazel color, and her cheeks were flushed with the exquisite bloom of the brunette, the dainty pink which lurks at the heart of the sulphur rose. But there was something subtly wrong with the face, some coarseness of expression, some hardness, perhaps, of eye which marred its perfect beauty. These, of course, are afterthoughts. At the moment I was simply conscious that I was in the presence of a very handsome woman.

"I have the pleasure," said I, "of knowing your father."

It was a clumsy introduction, and the lady made me feel it.

"There is nothing in common between my father and me," she said. "If it were not for the late Sir Charles Baskerville and some other kind hearts, I might have starved for all that my father cared."

"It was about the late Sir Charles Baskerville that I have come here to see you."

"What can I tell you about him?" she asked, and her fingers played nervously over the keys of her typewriter. "I have already said that I owe a great deal to his kindness. If I am able to support myself, it is largely due to the interest which he took in my unhappy situation."

"Did you correspond with him?"

The lady looked quickly up with an angry gleam in her eyes.

"What is the object of this?" she asked sharply.

"The object is to avoid a public scandal. It is much better that I should ask questions here than that the matter should pass outside our control."

She was silent and her face was very pale. At last she looked up with something reckless and defiant in her manner.

"What are your questions?" she said.

"Did you correspond with Sir Charles?"

"I certainly wrote to him once or twice to acknowledge his delicacy and his generosity."

"Have you the dates of those letters?"

"No."

"Have you ever met him?"

"Yes, once or twice, when he came into Coombe Tracey."

"But if you saw him so seldom and wrote so seldom, how did he know enough about your affairs to be able to help you?"

She met my difficulty with the utmost readiness.

"There were several gentlemen who knew my sad history and united to help me. One was Mr. Stapleton, a neighbor and intimate friend of Sir Charles's. He was exceedingly kind, and it was through him that Sir Charles learned about my affairs."

"Did you ever write to Sir Charles asking him to meet you?"

Mrs. Lyons flushed with anger again. "Really, sir, this is a very extraordinary question."

"I am sorry, madam, but I must repeat it."

"Then I answer, certainly not."

"Not on the very day of Sir Charles's death?"

The flush had faded in an instant, and a deathly face was before me. Her dry lips could not speak the no which I saw rather than heard.

"Surely your memory deceives you," said I. "I could even quote a passage of your letter. It ran, 'Please, please, as you are a gentleman, burn this letter, and be at the gate by ten o'clock.'"

I thought that she had fainted, but she recovered herself by a supreme effort. "Is there no such thing as a gentleman?" she gasped.

"You do Sir Charles an injustice. He *did* burn the letter. But sometimes a letter may be legible even when burned. You acknowledge now that you wrote it?"

"Yes, I did write it," she cried. "Why should I deny it? I have no reason to be ashamed of it. I believed that if I had an interview, I could gain his help."

"But why at such an hour?"

"Because I had only just learned that he was going to London next day."

"But why a rendezvous in the garden instead of a visit to the house?"

"Do you think a woman could go alone at that hour to a bachelor's house?"

"Well, what happened when you did get there?"

"I never went."

"Mrs. Lyons!"

"No, I swear it to you on all I hold sacred. I never went. Something intervened to prevent my going."

"What was that?"

"That is a private matter. I cannot tell it."

Again and again I cross-questioned her, but I could never get past that point.

"Mrs. Lyons," said I as I rose from this long and inconclusive interview, "you are taking a very great responsibility and putting yourself in a very false position by not making an absolutely clean breast of all that you know. Why were you so pressing that Sir Charles should destroy your letter?"

"The matter is a very private one."

"The more reason why you should avoid a public investigation."

"I will tell you, then. If you have heard anything of my unhappy history, you will know that I made a rash marriage and had reason to regret it."

"I have heard as much."

"My life has been one incessant persecution from a husband whom I abhor. The law is upon his side, and every day I am faced by the possibility that he may force me to live with him. At the time that I wrote this letter to Sir Charles I had learned that there was a prospect of my regaining my freedom if certain expenses could be met. It meant everything to me—peace of mind, happiness, self-respect—everything. I thought that if Sir Charles heard the story from my own lips, he would help me."

"Then how is it that you did not go?"

"Because I received help in the interval from another source."

"Why, then, did you not write to Sir Charles and explain this?"

"So I should have done had I not seen his death in the paper next morning."

The woman's story hung together, and all my questions were unable to shake it. I could only check it by finding if she had, indeed, instituted divorce proceedings against her husband at the time of the tragedy. The probability was that she was telling the truth, or at least a part of the truth.

I came away baffled and disheartened. And yet the more I thought of the lady's manner, the more I felt that something was being held back from me. Why should she turn so pale? Why should she fight against every admission until it was forced from her? Why should she have been so reticent at the time of the tragedy? But for the moment I could proceed no farther in her direction. I must turn back to that other clue which was to be sought for among the stone huts upon the moor.

And that was a most vague direction. I realized it as I drove back and noted how hill after hill showed traces of the ancient people. Many hundreds of abandoned huts are scattered throughout the length and breadth of the moor. But I had seen the stranger himself standing upon the summit of the granite tor. That, then, should be the center of my search. From there I should explore every hut upon the moor until I found out from his own lips, at the point of my revolver if necessary, who he was and why he had dogged us so long. He had slipped away from Holmes in London. It would indeed be a triumph for me if I could run him to earth where my master had failed.

Luck had been against us in this inquiry, but now at last it came to my aid. And the messenger of good fortune was none other than Mr. Frankland, who was standing, gray-whiskered and red-faced, outside the gate of his garden, which opened onto the highroad.

"Good day, Dr. Watson," cried he with unwonted good humor. "You must really give your horses a rest and come in to have a glass of wine and to congratulate me."

My feelings towards him were very far from being friendly after what I had heard of his treatment of his daughter, but I was anxious to send Perkins and the wagonette home, and the opportunity was a good one. I alighted and sent a message to Sir Henry that I should walk over in time for dinner. Then I followed Frankland into his dining room.

"It is a great day for me, sir—one of the red-letter days of my life," he cried with many chuckles. "I have brought off a double event. I mean to teach them in these parts that law is law. I have established a right-of-way through the center of old Middleton's park, within a hundred yards of his own front door. What do you think of that? We'll teach these magnates that they cannot ride roughshod over the rights of the commoners, confound them! And I've closed the wood where the Fernworthy folk used to picnic. These infernal people seem to think that they can swarm where they like with their papers and their bottles. Both cases decided, Dr. Watson, and both in my favor."

"Do they do you any good?"

"None, sir, none. I act entirely from a sense of public duty. I have no doubt, for example, that the Fernworthy people will burn me in effigy tonight. I told the police last time they did it that they should stop these disgraceful exhibitions. The county constabulary has not afforded me the protection to which I am entitled. I told them that they would have occasion to regret their treatment of me, and already my words have come true."

"How so?" I asked.

The old man put on a very knowing expression. "Because I could tell them what they are dying to know; but nothing would induce me to help the rascals in any way."

I had seen enough of the contrary nature of the old sinner to understand that any strong sign of interest would be the surest way to stop his confidences. "Some poaching case, no doubt?" said I with an indifferent manner.

"Ha, ha, my boy, a very much more important matter than that! What about the convict on the moor?"

I started. "You don't mean that you know where he is?"

"I may not know exactly where he is, but I am quite sure that I could help the police to lay their hands on him. Has it never

457

struck you that the way to catch that man was to find out where he got his food and so trace it to him?"

He certainly seemed to be getting uncomfortably near the truth. "No doubt," said I; "but how do you know that he is anywhere upon the moor?"

"I know it because I have seen with my own eyes the messenger who takes him his food."

My heart sank for Barrymore. It was a serious thing to be in the power of this spiteful old busybody. But his next remark took a weight from my mind.

"You'll be surprised to hear that his food is taken to him by a child. I see him every day through my telescope upon the roof."

Here was luck indeed! And yet I suppressed all appearance of interest. A child! Barrymore had said that our unknown was supplied by a boy. If I could get Frankland's knowledge, it might save me a long and weary hunt. But incredulity and indifference were evidently my strongest cards.

"I should say it was much more likely that it was the son of one of the moorland shepherds taking out his father's dinner."

The least appearance of opposition struck fire out of the old autocrat. His gray whiskers bristled like those of an angry cat. "Indeed, sir!" said he, pointing out over the wide-stretching moor. "Do you see the low hill beyond Black Tor? It is the stoniest part of the whole moor. Is that a place where a shepherd would be likely to take his station? Your suggestion, sir, is absurd. And you may be sure that I have very good grounds before I come to an opinion. I have seen the boy again and again with his bundle—but wait a moment, Dr. Watson. Is there at the present moment something moving upon that hillside?"

It was several miles off, but I could distinctly see a small dark dot against the dull green and gray.

"Come, sir, come!" cried Frankland, rushing upstairs. "You will see with your own eyes and judge for yourself."

The telescope, a formidable instrument mounted upon a tripod, stood upon the flat roof of the house. Frankland clapped his eye to it and gave a cry of satisfaction.

"Quick, Dr. Watson, quick, before he passes over the hill!"

There he was, sure enough, a small urchin with a little bundle upon his shoulder, toiling slowly up the hill. When he reached the crest he looked round him with a furtive and stealthy air, as one who dreads pursuit. Then he vanished over the hill.

"Certainly, there is a boy who seems to have some secret errand," I said.

"And what the errand is even a county constable could guess. But not one word shall they have from me, and I bind you to secrecy also, Dr. Watson. Not a word! You understand?"

"Just as you wish."

"The police have treated me shamefully—shamefully. For all they cared it might have been me, instead of my effigy, these rascals burned at the stake. Surely you are not going? You will help me to empty the decanter in honor of this great occasion?"

But I resisted all his solicitations and succeeded in dissuading him from his announced intention of walking home with me. I kept the road as long as his eye was on me, and then I struck off across the moor and made for the stony hill over which the boy had disappeared.

The sun was already sinking when I reached the summit, and the long slopes beneath me were all golden green on one side and gray shadow on the other. Over the wide expanse there was no sound and no movement. The barren scene, the sense of loneliness, and the mystery and urgency of my task all struck a chill into my heart. But down beneath me in a cleft of the hills there was a circle of the old stone huts, and in the middle there was one which retained sufficient roof to act as a screen against the weather. My heart leaped within me as I saw it. This must be the burrow where the stranger lurked. At last my foot was on the threshold of his hiding place—his secret was within my grasp.

As I warily approached the hut, all was silent within. Throwing aside my cigarette, I closed my hand upon the butt of my revolver and, walking swiftly up to the door, I looked in. The place was empty, but there were ample signs this was where the man lived. Some blankets rolled in a raincoat lay upon a stone slab. The ashes of a fire were heaped in a rude grate. A litter of empty cans showed that the place had been occupied for some time. In the middle of the hut stood a small cloth bundle—the same, no doubt, which I had seen through the telescope upon the shoulder of the boy. As I set it down after having examined it, my heart leaped to see that beneath it there lay a sheet of paper and that upon it, roughly scrawled in pencil, was written: "Dr. Watson has gone to Coombe Tracey."

For a minute I stood there with the paper in my hands, thinking out the meaning of this curt message. It was I, then, and not Sir Henry, who was being dogged by this secret man. He had not followed me himself, but he had set an agent—the boy, perhaps—upon my track, and this was his report. Possibly I had taken no step since I had been upon the moor which had not been observed and reported. When I thought of the heavy rains and looked at the gaping roof I understood how strong and immutable must be the purpose which had kept the stranger in that inhospitable abode. Was he our malignant enemy, or was he by chance our guardian angel? I swore that I would not leave the hut until I knew.

Outside the sun was sinking low and the west was blazing with scarlet and gold. Its reflection was shot back in ruddy patches by the distant pools which lay amid the great Grimpen Mire. All was sweet and mellow and peaceful in the golden evening light, and yet my soul quivered at the vagueness and the terror of that interview which every instant was bringing nearer. With tingling nerves, I sat in the dark recess of the hut and waited with somber patience for the coming of its tenant.

And then at last I heard the sharp clink of a boot striking upon a stone. Then another and yet another, coming nearer and nearer. I shrank back into the darkest corner and cocked the pistol in my pocket. There was a long pause which showed that the stranger had stopped. Then once more the footsteps approached and a shadow fell across the opening of the hut.

"It is a lovely evening, my dear Watson," said a well-known voice. "I really think that you will be more comfortable outside than in."

Chapter 12

FOR a moment or two I sat breathless, hardly able to believe my ears. Then my senses and my voice came back to me, while a crushing weight of responsibility seemed in an instant to be lifted from my soul.

"Holmes!" I cried. "Holmes!"

"Come out," said he, "and please be careful with the revolver."

I stooped under the rude lintel, and there he sat upon a stone outside, his gray eyes dancing with amusement as they fell upon my astonished features. He was thin and worn, but clear and alert, his keen face bronzed by the sun. In his tweed suit and cloth cap he looked like any other tourist upon the moor, and he had contrived, with his catlike love of personal cleanliness, that his chin should be as smooth and his linen as perfect as if he were in Baker Street.

"I never was more glad to see anyone in my life," said I as I wrung him by the hand.

"Or more astonished, eh?"

"Well, I must confess to it."

"The surprise was not all on one side, I assure you. I had no idea that you had found my occasional retreat, still less that you were inside it, until I was within twenty paces of the door. If you seriously desire to deceive me, you must change your tobacconist; for when I see the stub of a cigarette marked Bradley, Oxford Street, I know that my friend Watson is in the neighborhood. You threw it down, no doubt, at that supreme moment when you charged into the empty hut."

"Exactly."

"So you actually thought that I was the criminal?"

"I did not know who you were, but I was determined to find out."

"Excellent, Watson! You saw me, perhaps, on the night of the convict hunt, when I was so imprudent as to allow the moon to rise behind me?"

"Yes, I saw you then."

"And have no doubt searched all the huts until you came to this one?"

"No, your boy had been observed, and that gave me a guide where to look."

"The old gentleman with the telescope, no doubt. I could not make it out when first I saw the light flashing upon the lens." He rose and peeped into the hut. "Ha, I see that Cartwright has brought up some supplies. What's this paper? So you have been to Coombe Tracey to see Mrs. Laura Lyons, have you?"

"Exactly."

"Well done! Our researches have evidently been running on parallel lines, and when we unite our results I expect we shall have a fairly full knowledge of the case."

"Well, I am glad from my heart that you are here, but how in the name of wonder did you come here, and what have you been doing? I thought that you were in Baker Street working out that case of blackmailing."

"That was what I wished you to think."

"Then you use me, and yet do not trust me!" I cried with some bitterness. "I think that I have deserved better at your hands, Holmes."

"My dear fellow, I beg that you will forgive me if I have seemed to play a trick upon you. In truth, it was partly for your own sake that I did it, and it was my appreciation of the danger which you ran which led me to come down and examine the matter for myself. Had I been with Sir Henry and you, my presence would have warned our very formidable opponents to be on their guard. As it is, I have been able to get about as I could not possibly have done had I been living in the Hall, and I remain an unknown factor in the business, ready to throw in all my weight at a critical moment."

"But why keep me in the dark?"

"You would have wished to tell me something, or in your kindness you would have brought me out some comfort or other, and so an unnecessary risk would be run. I brought Cartwright down with me—you remember the little chap at the express office—and he has seen after my simple wants: a loaf of bread and a clean collar. He has given me an extra pair of eyes upon a very active pair of feet, and both have been invaluable."

"Then my reports have all been wasted!" My voice trembled as I recalled the pains and the pride with which I had composed them.

Holmes took a bundle of papers from his pocket.

"Here are your reports, my dear fellow, and very well thumbed, I assure you. I made excellent arrangements, and they are only delayed one day upon their way. I must compliment you exceedingly upon the zeal and the intelligence which you have shown over an extraordinarily difficult case."

I was still rather raw over the deception which had been practiced upon me, but the warmth of Holmes's praise drove my anger from my mind.

"That's better," said he, seeing the shadow rise from my face. "And now tell me the result of your visit to Mrs. Laura Lyons."

The sun had set and the air had turned chill, and we withdrew into the hut for warmth. There, sitting together in the twilight, I told Holmes of my conversation with the lady.

"This is most important," said he when I had concluded. "You are aware, perhaps, that a close intimacy exists between this lady and the man Stapleton?"

"I did not know of a close intimacy."

"They meet, they write, there is a complete understanding between them. Now, this puts a very powerful weapon into our hands. If I could only use it to detach his wife—"

"His wife?"

"The lady who has passed here as Miss Stapleton is in reality his wife."

"Good heavens, Holmes! Are you sure of what you say? How could he have permitted Sir Henry to fall in love with her?"

"Sir Henry's falling in love could do no harm to anyone except Sir Henry. He took particular care that Sir Henry did not *make* love to her, as you have yourself observed."

"But why this elaborate deception?"

"Because he foresaw that she would be very much more useful to him in the character of a free woman."

All my unspoken instincts, my vague suspicions, suddenly took shape and centered upon the naturalist. In that impassive, colorless man, with his straw hat and his butterfly net, I seemed to see something terrible—a creature of infinite patience and craft, with a smiling face and a murderous heart.

"It is he, then, who is our enemy—it is he who dogged us in London?"

"So I read the riddle."

"And the warning—it must have come from her!"

"Exactly."

The shape of some monstrous villainy, half seen, half guessed, loomed through the darkness which had girt me so long.

"But are you sure of this, Holmes? How do you know that the woman is his wife?"

"Because he so far forgot himself as to tell you a true piece of autobiography when he first met you, and I daresay he has regretted it since. He *was* once a schoolmaster in the north of England. Now, there is no one more easy to trace than a schoolmaster. A little investigation showed me that a school had come to grief under atrocious circumstances, and that the man who had owned it—the name was different—had disappeared with his wife. When I learned that the missing man was devoted to entomology the identification was complete."

"If this woman is in truth his wife, where does Mrs. Laura Lyons come in?" I asked.

"Your interview with the lady has cleared the situation very much. I did not know about her projected divorce. Regarding Stapleton as an unmarried man, she counted no doubt upon becoming his wife. It must be our first duty to undeceive her—both of us—tomorrow. Then we may find the lady of service. But don't you think, Watson, that you are away from Sir Henry rather long? Your place should be at Baskerville Hall."

The last red streaks had faded away in the west and night had settled upon the moor.

"One last question, Holmes," I said as I rose. "What is the meaning of it all? What is he after?"

Holmes's voice sank as he answered, "It is murder, Watson—refined, cold-blooded, deliberate murder. Do not ask me for particulars. With your help he is already almost at my mercy. There is but one danger which can threaten us. It is that he should strike before we are ready to do so. Another day—two at the most—and I have my case complete, but until then guard your charge as closely as ever a fond mother watched her ailing child. Hark!"

A terrible scream—a prolonged yell of horror and anguish burst out of the silence of the moor.

"Oh, my God!" I gasped. "What is it?"

Holmes had sprung to his feet, and I saw his dark, athletic outline at the door of the hut, his face peering into the darkness. "Hush!" he whispered. "Hush!"

The cry had pealed out from somewhere far off on the shadowy plain. Now it burst upon our ears, nearer, louder, more urgent than before.

"Where is it?" Holmes whispered; and I knew from the trill of his voice that he was shaken to the soul. "Where is it, Watson?"

"There, I think." I pointed into the darkness.

Again the agonized cry swept through the silent night, louder and much nearer than ever. And a new sound mingled with it, a deep, muttered rumble, musical and yet menacing, rising and falling like the low, constant murmur of the sea.

"The hound!" cried Holmes. "Come, Watson, come! Great heavens, if we are too late!"

He had started running swiftly over the moor, and I had followed at his heels. But now from somewhere among the broken ground immediately in front of us there came one last despairing yell, and then a dull, heavy thud. We halted and listened. Not another sound broke the heavy silence of the windless night.

I saw Holmes put his hand to his forehead like a man distracted.

"He has beaten us, Watson. We are too late."

Blindly we ran through the gloom, blundering against boulders, forcing our way through gorse bushes, panting up hills, and rushing down slopes, heading always in the direction whence those dreadful sounds had come. The shadows were thick upon the moor, and nothing moved upon its dreary face.

"Can you see anything?" Holmes asked.

"Nothing."

"But, hark, what is that?"

A low moan had fallen upon our ears. There it was again upon our left! On that side a ridge of rocks ended in a sheer cliff which overlooked a stone-strewn slope. On its jagged face was spread-eagled some dark, irregular object. As we ran towards it the vague outline hardened into a definite shape. It was a prostrate man face downward upon the ground, the head doubled under him at a horrible angle, the body hunched together as if in the act of throwing a somersault. So grotesque was the attitude that I could not for the instant realize that that moan had been the passing of his soul. Holmes laid his hand upon the man and held it up again with an exclamation of horror. The gleam of the match which he struck shone upon his clotted fingers and upon the ghastly pool which widened slowly from the crushed skull of the victim. And it shone upon something else which turned our hearts sick and faint within us—the body of Sir Henry Baskerville!

There was no chance of either of us forgetting that peculiar ruddy tweed suit—the very one which he had worn on the first morning that we had seen him in Baker Street. Holmes groaned as the match flickered out, and his face glimmered white through the darkness.

"The brute! The brute!" I cried with clenched hands. "Oh, I shall never forgive myself for having left him to his fate."

"I am more to blame than you, Watson. In order to have my case complete, I have thrown away the life of my client. It is the greatest blow which has befallen me in my career. But how could I know—how *could* I know—that he would risk his life alone upon the moor in the face of all my warnings?"

"That we should have heard his screams—my God, those screams!—and yet have been unable to save him! Where is this brute of a hound which drove him to his death? It may be lurking among these rocks at this instant. And Stapleton, where is he? He shall answer for this deed."

"He shall. I will see to that. Uncle and nephew have been murdered—the one frightened to death by the very sight of a beast which he thought to be supernatural, the other driven to his end in his wild flight to escape from it. But now we have to prove the connection between Stapleton and the hound. We cannot even swear to the existence of the latter, since Sir Henry is dead."

We stood with bitter hearts on either side of the mangled body, overwhelmed by this sudden and irrevocable disaster. Then as the moon rose we climbed to the top of the rocks over which our poor friend had fallen. Far away a single steady yellow light was shining. It could only come from the lonely abode of the Stapletons. With a bitter curse I shook my fist at it as I gazed.

"Why should we not seize him at once?"

"Our case is not complete. It is not what we know, but what we can prove. If we make one false move, the villain may escape us yet. Tonight we can only perform the last offices for our poor friend."

Together we made our way down the precipitous slope and approached the body, black and clear against the silvered stones. The agony of those contorted limbs blurred my eyes with tears.

"We must send for help, Holmes! We cannot carry him all the way to the Hall. Good heavens, are you mad?"

He had uttered a cry and bent over the body. Now he was dancing and laughing and wringing my hand. Could this be my stern, self-contained friend? These were hidden fires, indeed!

"A beard! A beard! The man has a beard!"

"A beard?"

"It is not the baronet—it is—why, it is my neighbor, the convict!"

With feverish haste we turned the body over. There could be no doubt about the beetling forehead, the sunken animal eyes. It was indeed the same face which had glared upon me in the light of the candle—the face of Selden, the criminal.

Then in an instant I remembered how the baronet had told me that he had handed his old wardrobe to Barrymore. Barrymore had passed it on in order to help Selden in his escape. Boots, shirt, cap—it was all Sir Henry's. The tragedy was still black enough, but this man had at least deserved death by the laws of his country. I told Holmes how the matter stood, my heart bubbling over with thankfulness and joy.

"Then the clothes have been the poor devil's death," said he. "It is clear enough that the hound has been laid on from some article of Sir Henry's—the boot which was abstracted in the hotel, in all probability—and so ran this man down. I suppose that it was let loose upon the moor tonight because Stapleton had reason to think that Sir Henry would be there. But the question now is, what shall we do with this poor wretch's body? We cannot leave it here to the foxes and the ravens."

"I suggest that we put it in one of the huts until we can communicate with the police."

"Exactly. I have no doubt that you and I could carry it so far. Halloa, Watson, what's this? It's the man himself, by all that's wonderful and audacious! Not a word to show your suspicions—not a word!"

A figure was approaching us over the moor, and I saw the dull red glow of a cigar. The moon shone upon him, and I could distinguish the dapper shape and jaunty walk of the naturalist. He stopped when he saw us, and then came on again.

"Why, Dr. Watson, that's not you, is it? You are the last man that I should have expected to see out on the moor at this time of night. But, dear me, somebody hurt? Not—don't tell me that it is our friend Sir Henry!" He hurried past me and stooped over the dead man. I heard a sharp intake of his breath and the cigar fell from his fingers.

"Who—who's this?" he stammered.

"It is Selden, the man who escaped from Princetown."

Stapleton turned a ghastly face upon us, but by a supreme effort he had overcome his amazement and his disappointment. He looked sharply from Holmes to me.

"Dear me! What a very shocking affair! How did he die?"

"He appears to have broken his neck by falling over these rocks.

My friend and I were strolling on the moor when we heard a cry."

"I heard a cry also. That was what brought me out. I was uneasy about Sir Henry."

"Why about Sir Henry in particular?" I could not help asking.

"Because I had suggested that he should come over. When he did not come I was surprised, and I naturally became alarmed for his safety when I heard cries upon the moor. By the way"—his eyes darted again from my face to Holmes's—"did you hear anything else besides a cry?"

"No," said Holmes. "What do you mean?"

"Oh, you know the stories that the peasants tell about a phantom hound. It is said to be heard at night upon the moor."

"We heard nothing of the kind," said I.

"And what is your theory of this poor fellow's death?"

"I have no doubt that anxiety and exposure have driven him off his head. He has rushed about the moor in a crazy state and eventually fallen over here and broken his neck."

"That seems the most reasonable theory," said Stapleton, and he gave a sigh which I took to indicate his relief. "What do you think about it, Mr. Sherlock Holmes?"

My friend bowed his compliments. "You are quick at identification," said he.

"We have been expecting you in these parts since Dr. Watson came down. You are in time to see a tragedy."

"Yes, indeed. I will take an unpleasant remembrance back to London with me tomorrow."

"Oh, you return tomorrow?"

"That is my intention."

"I hope your visit has cast some light upon those occurrences which have puzzled us?"

Holmes shrugged his shoulders. "An investigator needs facts and not legends or rumors. It has not been a satisfactory case."

Stapleton still looked hard at him. Then he turned to me. "I think that if we put something over this poor fellow's face, he will be safe until morning."

And so it was arranged. Resisting Stapleton's offer of hospitality, Holmes and I set off to Baskerville Hall, leaving the naturalist to return alone.

Chapter 13

"WHAT a nerve the fellow has!" said Holmes as we walked together across the moor. "How he pulled himself together when he found that the wrong man had fallen a victim to his plot. I told you in London, Watson, that we have never had a foe more worthy of our steel."

"I am sorry that he has seen you."

"And so was I at first. But there was no getting out of it."

"What effect do you think it will have upon his plans?"

"It may cause him to be more cautious, or it may drive him to desperate measures at once. Like most clever criminals, he may be too confident of his own cleverness and imagine that he has completely deceived us."

"Why should we not arrest him at once? Surely we have a case."

"Not a shadow of one—only surmise and conjecture."

"There is Sir Charles's death."

"You and I know that he died of sheer fright, and we know also what frightened him; but how are we to get twelve stolid jurymen to know it?"

"Well, then, tonight?"

"Again, there was no direct connection between the hound and the man's death. We never saw the hound. We heard it, but we could not prove that it was running upon this man's trail. There is a complete absence of motive, and we must reconcile ourselves to the fact that we have no case until we establish one."

I could draw nothing further from him, and he walked, lost in thought, as far as the Baskerville gates.

"Are you coming up?"

"Yes. I see no reason for further concealment. But one last word, Watson. Say nothing of the hound to Sir Henry. Let him think that Selden's death was as Stapleton would have us believe. He will have a better nerve for the ordeal which he will have to undergo tomorrow, when he is engaged, if I remember your report aright, to dine with the Stapletons."

"And so am I."

"Then you must excuse yourself and he must go alone."

Sir Henry was more pleased than surprised to see Sherlock Holmes, for he had for some days been expecting him from London. He did raise his eyebrows, however, when he found that my friend had neither any luggage nor any explanations for its absence. Between us we soon supplied his wants, and then over a belated supper we explained to the baronet as much of our experience as it seemed desirable that he should know. But first I had the unpleasant duty of breaking the news of Selden's death to Barrymore and his wife. To him it may have been a relief, but she wept bitterly in her apron. To her the man of violence always remained the willful little boy of her girlhood, the child who had clung to her hand. Evil indeed is the man who has not one woman to mourn him.

"I've been moping in the house since Watson went off in the morning," said the baronet. "If I hadn't sworn not to go about alone, I might have had a more lively evening, for I had a message from Stapleton asking me over there."

"I have no doubt that you would have had a more lively evening," said Holmes dryly. "By the way, I don't suppose you appreciate that we have been mourning over you as having broken your neck?"

Sir Henry opened his eyes. "How was that?"

"This poor wretch was dressed in your clothes. I fear your servant who gave them to him may get into trouble with the police."

"That is unlikely. There was no mark on any of them, as far as I know."

"That's lucky for him—in fact, it's lucky for all of you, since you are all on the wrong side of the law in this matter."

"But how about the case?" asked the baronet. "As Watson has no doubt told you, we heard the hound on the moor, so I can swear that it is not all empty superstition. If you can muzzle that dog and put him on a chain, you are the greatest detective of all time."

"I will muzzle him and chain him, if you will give me your help and do it blindly, without always asking the reason."

"Whatever you tell me to do I will do."

"Then I think the chances are that our little problem will soon be solved. I have no doubt—" He stopped suddenly and stared fixedly up over my head into the air.

"What is it?" we both cried.

Holmes was repressing some internal emotion. His features were composed, but his eyes shone with amused exultation.

"Excuse the admiration of a connoisseur," said he as he waved his hand towards the line of portraits which covered the opposite wall. "Watson won't allow that I know anything of art, but these are a really very fine series of portraits."

"Well, I'm glad to hear you say so," said Sir Henry, glancing with some surprise at my friend. "I didn't think that you found time for such things."

"I know what is good when I see it, and I see it now. They are all family portraits, I presume?"

"Every one."

"Do you know the names?"

"Barrymore has been coaching me in them."

"Who is the gentleman with the telescope?"

"That is Rear Admiral Baskerville, who served under Rodney in the West Indies. The man with the blue coat and the roll of paper is Sir William Baskerville, who was Chairman of Committees of the House of Commons under Pitt."

"And this Cavalier opposite to me—the one with the black velvet and the lace?"

"Ah, that is the wicked Hugo, who started the Hound of the Baskervilles. We're not likely to forget him."

I gazed with interest and some surprise upon the portrait.

"Dear me!" said Holmes. "He seems a quiet, meek-mannered man enough, but I daresay that there was a lurking devil in his eyes."

Holmes said little more, but his eyes were continually fixed upon the picture of Sir Hugo during supper. Later, when Sir Henry had gone to his room, he led me back into the banqueting hall, his bedroom candle in his hand, and he held it up against the time-stained portrait on the wall.

"Do you see anything there?"

I looked at the broad plumed hat, the curling lovelocks, the white lace collar, and the straight, severe face which was framed between them. It was not a brutal countenance, but it was prim, hard, and stern, with a firm-set, thin-lipped mouth and a coldly intolerant eye.

"Is it like anyone you know? But wait!" Holmes stood upon a chair, and, holding up the light in his left hand, he curved his right arm over the broad hat and round the long ringlets.

"Good heavens!" I cried in amazement.

The face of Stapleton had sprung out of the canvas.

"Ha, you see it now. My eyes have been trained to examine faces and not their trimmings. It is the first quality of a criminal investigator that he should see through a disguise."

"But this is marvelous. It might be his portrait."

"Yes, it is an interesting instance of a throwback, which appears to be both physical and spiritual. The fellow is a Baskerville—that is evident."

"With designs upon the succession."

"Exactly. This chance of the picture has supplied us with one of our most obvious missing links. We have him, Watson, we have him. Before tomorrow night he will be fluttering in our net as helpless as one of his own butterflies. A pin, a cork, and a card, and we add him to the Baker Street collection!" He burst into one of his rare fits of laughter as he turned away. I have not heard him laugh often, and it has always boded ill to somebody.

I was up betimes in the morning, but Holmes was afoot earlier still, for I saw him as I dressed, coming up the drive.

"Yes, we should have a full day today," he remarked, and he rubbed his hands with the joy of action.

"Have you been on the moor already?"

"I have sent a report from Grimpen to Princetown as to the death of Selden. I think I can promise that none of you will be troubled in the matter. And I have also communicated with my faithful Cartwright to set his mind at rest about my safety."

"What is the next move?"

"To see Sir Henry. Ah, here he is!"

"Good morning, Holmes," said the baronet. "You look like a general who is planning a battle with his chief of staff."

"That is the exact situation. Watson was asking for orders."

"And so do I."

"Very good. You are engaged, as I understand, to dine with our friends the Stapletons tonight."

"I hope that you will come also. They are very hospitable people, and I am sure that they would be very glad to see you."

"I fear that Watson and I must go to London."

"To London?" The baronet's face perceptibly lengthened. "I hoped that you were going to see me through this business. The Hall and the moor are not very pleasant places when one is alone."

"My dear fellow, you must trust me implicitly and do exactly what I tell you. You can tell your friends that we should have been happy to have come with you, but that urgent business required us to be in town. We hope very soon to return to Devonshire. Will you give them that message?"

"If you insist upon it."

I saw by the baronet's clouded brow that he was deeply hurt by what he regarded as our desertion.

"When do you desire to go?" he asked coldly.

"Immediately after breakfast. We will drive in to Coombe Tracey, but Watson will leave his things as a pledge that he will come back to you."

"I have a good mind to go to London with you," said the baronet. "Why should I stay here alone?"

"Because you gave me your word that you would do as you were told, and I tell you to stay."

"All right, then, I'll stay."

"One more direction! I wish you to drive to Merripit House this evening. Send back your carriage, however, and let them know that you intend to walk home."

"But crossing the moor is the very thing which you have s
often cautioned me not to do."

"This time you may do it with safety. It is essential that yo
should do it."

"Then I will do it."

"And as you value your life do not go across the moor in an
direction save along the straight path which is your natural wa
home from Merripit House."

"I will do just what you say."

I was much astounded that Holmes would wish me to go wit
him at a moment which he himself declared to be critical. Ther
was nothing for it, however, but implicit obedience; so we bad
good-by to our rueful friend, and a couple of hours afterward
we were at the station of Coombe Tracey and had dispatched th
carriage upon its return journey.

A small boy was waiting upon the platform. "Any orders, sir?"

"You will take this train to town, Cartwright. The moment yo
arrive you will send a wire to Sir Henry Baskerville, in my name
to say that if he finds the pocketbook which I have dropped, h
is to send it by registered post to Baker Street."

"Yes, sir."

"Now, ask at the station office if there is a message for me."

The boy returned with a telegram, which Holmes handed to me
It ran: WIRE RECEIVED. COMING DOWN WITH UNSIGNED WARRANT
ARRIVE FIVE FORTY. LESTRADE.

"That is in answer to mine of this morning. He is the best o
the professionals, I think, and we may need his assistance. Now
Watson, I think that we cannot employ our time better than b
calling upon your acquaintance, Mrs. Laura Lyons."

His plan of campaign was beginning to be evident. He woul
use the baronet in order to convince the Stapletons that we wer
really gone, while we should actually return at the instant whe
we were likely to be needed. That telegram from London, if men
tioned by Sir Henry to the Stapletons, must remove their suspicion
Already I seemed to see our nets drawing closer.

Mrs. Laura Lyons was in her office, and Sherlock Holmes opene his interview with a frankness and directness which considerably amazed her.

"I am investigating the circumstances which attended the death of the late Sir Charles Baskerville," said he. "My friend here, Dr. Watson, has informed me of what you have communicated, and also of what you have withheld in connection with that matter."

"What have I withheld?" she asked defiantly.

"You have confessed that you asked Sir Charles to be at the gate at ten o'clock. We know that that was the place and hour of his death. You have withheld what the connection is between these events."

"There is no connection."

"I think that we shall succeed in establishing a connection. I wish to be perfectly frank with you, Mrs. Lyons. We regard this case as one of murder, and the evidence may implicate not only your friend Mr. Stapleton but his wife as well."

"His wife!" she cried.

"The person who has passed for his sister is really his wife."

"His wife!" Mrs. Lyons said again. "He is not a married man."

Sherlock Holmes shrugged his shoulders.

"Prove it to me! Prove it to me! And if you can do so—" The fierce flash of her eyes said more than any words.

Holmes drew several papers from his pocket. "Here is a photograph of the couple taken in New York four years ago. It is endorsed 'Mr. and Mrs. Vandeleur,' but you will have no difficulty in recognizing him, and her also, if you know her by sight. Here are three written descriptions of Mr. and Mrs. Vandeleur, who at that time kept St. Oliver's private school. Read them and see if you can doubt the identity of these people."

Laura Lyons glanced at them, and then looked up at us with the set, rigid face of a desperate woman.

"Mr. Holmes," she said, "this man had offered me marriage on condition that I could get a divorce from my husband. He has lied to me, the villain, in every conceivable way. I imagined that all was for my own sake. But now I see that I was never anything but a tool in his hands. Why should I try to shield him from the consequences of his own wicked acts? Ask me what you like, and there is nothing which I shall hold back. One thing I swear to you, and that is that when I wrote the letter I never dreamed of any harm to the old gentleman, who had been my kindest friend."

"I entirely believe you, madam," said Sherlock Holmes. "The recital of these events must be very painful to you, and perhaps it will make it easier if I tell you what occurred, and you can check me if I make any mistake. The sending of the letter to Sir Charles was suggested to you by Stapleton?"

"He dictated it."

"And the reason he gave was that you would receive help from Sir Charles for the legal expenses connected with your divorce?"

"Exactly."

"And then after you had sent the letter he dissuaded you from keeping the appointment?"

"He told me that it would hurt his self-respect that any other man should find the money for such an object, and that though he was a poor man himself he would devote his last penny to removing the obstacles which divided us."

"He appears to be a very consistent character. And then you heard nothing until you read the reports of the death in the paper."

"No."

"And he made you swear to say nothing about your appointment with Sir Charles?"

"He did. He said that the death was a very mysterious one, and that I should certainly be suspected if the facts came out."

"Quite so. But you had your suspicions?"

She hesitated and looked down. "I knew him," she said. "But if he had kept faith with me, I should always have done so with him."

"I think that on the whole you have had a fortunate escape," said Holmes. "You have had him in your power and he knew it, and yet you are alive. We must wish you good morning now, Mrs. Lyons, and it is probable that you will very shortly hear from us again."

"Difficulty after difficulty thins away in front of us," said Holmes as we stood waiting for the arrival of the express from town. "I shall soon be in the position of being able to put into a connected narrative one of the most sensational crimes of modern times."

The London express came roaring into the station, and a small, wiry bulldog of a man sprang from a first-class carriage. "Anything good?" Lestrade asked.

"The biggest thing for years," said Holmes. "I think we might get some dinner and then, Lestrade, we will take the London fog out of your throat by giving you a breath of the pure night air of Dartmoor."

Chapter 14

ONE of Sherlock Holmes's defects—if, indeed, one may call it a defect—was that he was exceedingly loath to communicate his full plans to any other person until the instant of their fulfillment. I had often suffered under it, but never more so than during that long drive in the darkness. The great ordeal was in front of us, and yet I could only surmise what Holmes's course of action would be. My nerves thrilled with anticipation when the dark spaces on either side of the narrow road told me that we were back upon the moor once again. Every turn of the wheels was taking us nearer to our supreme adventure.

At last we passed Frankland's house and knew that we were drawing near to the Hall and to the scene of action. At the gate of the avenue we got down, the wagonette was paid off, and we started to walk to Merripit House.

"Are you armed, Lestrade?"

The little detective smiled. "As long as I have a hip pocket, I have something in it. What's the game now?"

"A waiting game."

"My word, it does not seem a very cheerful place," said the detective, glancing round him at the huge lake of fog which lay over the Grimpen Mire. "I see the lights of a house ahead of us."

"That is Merripit House and the end of our journey. I must request you to walk on tiptoe and not to talk above a whisper."

Holmes halted us when we were about two hundred yards from the house. "This will do," said he. "These rocks upon the right make an admirable screen. We shall make our little ambush here. You have been inside the house, have you not, Watson? What are those latticed windows at this end?"

"I think they are the kitchen windows."

"And the one beyond, which shines so brightly?"

"That is certainly the dining room."

"The blinds are up. Creep forward quietly and see what they are doing—but for heaven's sake don't let them know that they are watched!"

I tiptoed down the path and crept behind the low wall which surrounded the stunted orchard until I reached a point whence I could look straight through the uncurtained window.

Sir Henry and Stapleton sat with their profiles towards me on either side of the round table, smoking cigars. Coffee and wine were in front of them. Stapleton was talking with animation, but the baronet looked pale and distracted. The lady was not there.

As I watched them Stapleton rose and left the room, while Sir Henry leaned back in his chair, puffing at his cigar. I heard the creak of a door and the crisp sound of boots upon gravel. Looking along the path, I saw the naturalist pause at the door of an outhouse in the corner of the orchard. A key turned in a lock, and as he passed in there was a curious scuffling noise from within. He was only a minute or so inside, and then I heard him go back along the path and reenter the house. I crept quietly back to where my companions were waiting to tell them what I had seen.

The dense, white fog that hung over the great Grimpen Mire was drifting slowly in our direction and banked itself up like a wall on that side of us. Holmes muttered impatiently as he watched its sluggish drift. "It's moving towards us, Watson."

"Is that serious?"

"Very serious—the one thing upon earth which could have disarranged my plans. Our success and even Sir Henry's life may depend upon his coming out before the fog is over the path."

The stars shone cold and bright, while a half-moon bathed the

whole scene in a soft, uncertain light. Before us lay the dark bulk of the house, outlined against the silver-spangled sky. Broad bars of golden light from the lower windows stretched across the orchard and the moor. One of them was suddenly shut off. The servants had left the kitchen. There only remained the lamp in the dining room where the two men, the murderous host and the unconscious guest, still chatted over their cigars.

Every minute that white woolly plain which covered one-half of the moor was drifting closer and closer to the house. Already the first thin wisps of it were curling across the golden square of the lighted window. The farther wall of the orchard was already invisible, and fog wreaths came crawling round both corners of the house. Holmes struck his hand upon the rock in front of us and stamped his feet in his impatience.

"If he isn't out soon, the path will be covered."

"Shall we move farther back upon higher ground?"

"Yes, I think it would be as well."

So we fell back before the fogbank until we were half a mile from the house, and still that dense white sea swept slowly and inexorably on.

"We are going too far," said Holmes. "We dare not take the chance of his being overtaken before he can reach us." He dropped on his knees and clapped his ear to the ground. "Thank God, I think that I hear him coming."

A sound of quick steps broke the silence of the moor. The steps grew louder, and through the fog, as through a curtain, there stepped the man whom we were awaiting. He came swiftly along the path, passed close to where we lay, and went on up the long slope behind us. As he walked he glanced continually over either shoulder, like a man who is ill at ease.

"*Hist!*" cried Holmes, and I heard the sharp click of a cocking pistol. "Look out! It's coming!"

There was a thin, crisp, continuous patter from somewhere in the heart of that crawling bank. I was at Holmes's elbow, and I glanced for an instant at his face. It was pale and exultant, but suddenly his eyes started forward in a rigid, fixed stare, and his lips parted in amazement. At the same instant Lestrade gave a yell of terror and threw himself face downward upon the ground. I sprang to my feet, my mind paralyzed by the dreadful shape which had sprung out upon us from the shadows of the fog. A hound it was, an enormous coal-black hound, but not such a hound as mortal eyes have ever seen. Fire burst from its open mouth, its eyes glowed with a smoldering glare, its muzzle and hackles and dewlap were outlined in flickering flame. Never in the delirious dream of a disordered brain could anything more savage, more appalling, more hellish be conceived than that dark form and savage face which broke upon us out of the wall of fog.

With long bounds the huge black creature was following hard upon the footsteps of our friend. So paralyzed were we by the apparition that we allowed him to pass before we had recovered our nerve. Then Holmes and I both fired together, and the creature gave a hideous howl, which showed that one at least had hit him. He did not pause, however, but bounded onward. Far away on the path we saw Sir Henry looking back, his face white in the moonlight, his hands raised in horror, glaring helplessly at the frightful thing which was hunting him down.

But that cry of pain from the hound had blown all our fears to the winds. If we could wound him, we could kill him. I am reckoned fleet of foot, but Holmes outpaced me as much as I outpaced Lestrade. In front of us, as we flew up the track, we heard scream after scream from Sir Henry and the deep roar of the hound. I was in time to see the beast spring upon its victim, hurl him to the ground, and worry at his throat. But the next instant Holmes had emptied five barrels of his revolver into the creature's flank. With a last howl of agony and a vicious snap in the air, it rolled upon its back, and then fell limp upon its side. I stooped, panting, and pressed my pistol to the dreadful, shimmering head, but it was useless to press the trigger. The giant hound was dead.

Sir Henry lay insensible where he had fallen. We tore away his collar, and Holmes breathed a prayer of gratitude when we saw that the rescue had been in time. Our friend's eyelids shivered and he made a feeble effort to move. Lestrade thrust his brandy flask between the baronet's teeth, and two frightened eyes were looking up at us.

"My God!" he whispered. "What in heaven's name was it?"

"It's dead, whatever it is," said Holmes. "We've laid away the family ghost once and forever."

In mere size and strength it was a terrible creature which was lying stretched before us. It appeared to be a combination of bloodhound and mastiff—gaunt, savage, and as large as a small lioness. Even now, in the stillness of death, the huge jaws seemed to be dripping with a bluish flame and the small, cruel eyes were ringed with fire. I placed my hand upon the glowing muzzle, and as I held them up my own fingers smoldered and gleamed in the darkness.

"Phosphorous," I said.

"A cunning preparation of it," said Holmes, sniffing at the dead animal. "There is no smell which might have interfered with his power of scent. We owe you a deep apology, Sir Henry, for having exposed you to this fright. I was prepared for a hound, but not for such a creature as this. And the fog gave us little time to receive him."

"You have saved my life."

"Having first endangered it. Are you strong enough to stand?"

"Give me another mouthful of that brandy and I shall be ready for anything. So! Now, what do you propose to do?"

"If you will wait, one of us will go back with you to the Hall."

He tried to stagger to his feet; but he was still ghastly pale and trembling in every limb. We helped him to a rock, where he sat shivering with his face buried in his hands.

"We must leave you now," said Holmes. "The rest of our work must be done, and every moment is of importance.

"It's a thousand to one against finding our man at the house," he continued as we retraced our steps swiftly down the path. "Those shots must have told him that the game was up. He followed the hound to call him off—of that you may be certain. But we'll search the house and make sure."

The front door was open, so we rushed in, to the amazement

of the doddering old manservant. There was no light save in the dining room, but Holmes caught up the lamp and we hurried from room to room. No sign could we see of the man whom we were chasing. On the upper floor, however, one of the bedroom doors was locked.

A faint moaning and rustling came from within. Holmes struck the door just over the lock with the flat of his foot and it flew open. Pistol in hand, we all three rushed into the room. It had been fashioned into a small museum, and the walls were lined by a number of glass-topped cases full of butterflies and moths. In the center of the room an upright beam supported an old roof timber, and to this beam was tied a figure so swathed and muffled in sheets that one could not for the moment tell whether it was that of a man or a woman. One towel passed round the throat and was secured at the back of the pillar. Another covered the lower part of the face, and over it two dark eyes—eyes full of grief and shame and a dreadful questioning—stared back at us. In a minute we had torn off the bonds, and Mrs. Stapleton sank upon the floor in front of us. As her beautiful head fell upon her chest I saw the clear red weal of a whiplash across her neck.

"The brute!" cried Holmes. "Here, Lestrade, your brandy bottle! She has fainted from ill-usage and exhaustion."

She opened her eyes again. "Has he escaped?" she asked.

"He cannot escape us, madam."

"No, no, I did not mean my husband. Sir Henry? Is he safe?"

"Yes."

"And the hound?"

"It is dead."

She gave a long sigh of satisfaction. "Thank God! Oh, this villain! See how he has treated me!" She shot her arms out from her sleeves, and we saw with horror that they were all mottled with bruises. "But this is nothing—nothing! I could endure it all, ill-usage, solitude, a life of deception, everything, as long as I could still cling to the hope that I had his love, but now I know that in this also I have been his dupe and his tool." She broke into passionate sobbing as she spoke.

"You bear him no goodwill, madam," said Holmes. "Tell us then where we shall find him. If you have ever aided him in evil, help us now and so atone."

"There is but one place where he can have fled," she answered. "There is an old tin mine on an island in the heart of the mire. It was there that he kept his hound and there also he had made preparations so that he might have a refuge."

The fogbank lay like white wool against the window. Holmes held the lamp towards it. "No one could find his way into the Grimpen Mire tonight," said he.

She laughed and clapped her hands. Her eyes gleamed with fierce merriment. "He may find his way in, but never out," she cried. "How can he see the guiding wands tonight? We planted them together, he and I, to mark the pathway through the mire."

It was evident to us that all pursuit was in vain until the fog had lifted. Meanwhile we left Lestrade in possession of the house while Holmes and I went back with the baronet to Baskerville Hall. The story of the Stapletons could no longer be withheld from him. He took the blow bravely when he learned the truth about the woman whom he had loved. But the shock of the night's adventures had shattered his nerves, and before morning he lay delirious in a high fever under the care of Dr. Mortimer. The two of them were destined to travel together round the world before Sir Henry had become once more the hale, hearty man that he had been before he became master of that ill-omened estate.

AND now I come rapidly to the conclusion of this singular narrative. On the morning after the death of the hound the fog had lifted, and we were guided by Mrs. Stapleton to the point where they had found a pathway through the bog. It helped us to realize the horror of this woman's life when we saw the eagerness and joy with which she set us on her husband's track. From the end of a thin peninsula of firm, peaty soil a small wand planted here and there showed where the path zigzagged from tuft to tuft of rushes among green-scummed pits and foul quagmires. Rank reeds and lush, slimy water plants sent an odor of decay and a heavy miasmatic vapor onto our faces, while a false step plunged us more than once thigh-deep into the dark, quivering mire. Once only we saw a trace that someone had passed that perilous way before us. From amid a tuft of cotton grass which bore it up out of the slime some dark thing was projecting. Holmes sank to his waist as he stepped from the path to seize it, and had we not been there to drag him out, he could never have set his foot upon firm land again. He held an old black boot in the air. "Meyers, Toronto," was printed on the leather inside.

"It is our friend Sir Henry's missing boot," said he. "Stapleton retained it in his hand after using it to set the hound upon the track. And he hurled it away at this point of his flight. We know at least that he came so far in safety."

But more than that we were never destined to know. As we at last reached firmer ground beyond the morass we all looked eagerly for footsteps. But no slightest sign of them ever met our eyes. If the earth told a true story, then Stapleton never reached that island of refuge towards which he struggled through the fog. Somewhere in the heart of the great Grimpen Mire, down in the foul slime of the huge morass, this cold and cruel-hearted man is forever buried.

Many traces we found of him in the bog-girt island where he had kept the hound. Beside the abandoned mine were the crumbling remains of the cottages of the miners, driven away no doubt by the foul reek of the surrounding swamp. In one of these a staple and chain with a quantity of gnawed bones showed where the animal had been confined. A skeleton with a tangle of brown hair adhering to it lay among the debris.

"A dog!" said Holmes. "By Jove, a curly-haired spaniel. Poor Mortimer will never see his pet again. Well, I do not know that this place contains any secret which we have not already fathomed. Stapleton could hide his hound, but he could not hush its voice, and hence came those cries which even in daylight were not pleasant to hear. It was only on the supreme day that he dared to keep the hound in the outhouse at Merripit. This paste in the can is no doubt the luminous mixture with which the creature was daubed.

It was suggested, of course, by the story of the family hellhound, and by the desire to frighten old Sir Charles to death. I say it again, Watson, that never yet have we helped to hunt down a more dangerous man than he who is lying yonder."

Chapter 15

It was the end of November, and Holmes and I sat, upon a raw and foggy night, on either side of a blazing fire in our sitting room in Baker Street. Since the tragic upshot of our visit to Devonshire he had been engaged in two affairs of the utmost importance, in the first of which he had exposed the atrocious conduct of Colonel Upwood in the famous card scandal of the Nonpareil Club, while in the second he had defended the unfortunate Mme. Montpensier from the charge of murdering her stepdaughter, Mlle. Carère, the young lady who was found six months later alive and married in New York. I had waited patiently to induce him to discuss the details of the Baskerville mystery, for I was aware that his clear and logical mind would not be drawn from its present work to dwell upon memories of the past. Sir Henry and Dr. Mortimer were, however, in London, on their way to that long voyage which had been recommended for the restoration of Sir Henry's shattered nerves. They had called upon us that very afternoon, so that it was natural that the subject should come up for discussion.

"The whole course of events," said Holmes, "from the point of view of the man who called himself Stapleton was simple and direct, although to us it appeared exceedingly complex. I have had the advantage of two conversations with Mrs. Stapleton, and the case has now been entirely cleared up.

"My inquiries show beyond all question that the family portrait did not lie, and that this fellow was a son of that Rodger Baskerville, the younger brother of Sir Charles, who fled with a sinister reputation to South America, where he was said to have died unmarried. He did, as a matter of fact, marry, and had one child, this fellow, whose real name is the same as his father's. He married Beryl Garcia, one of the beauties of Costa Rica, and, having purloined a considerable sum of public money, he changed his name to Vandeleur and fled to England, where he established a school in the east of Yorkshire. His reason for attempting this special line of business was that he had struck up an acquaintance with a consumptive tutor upon the voyage home, and that he had used this man's ability to make the undertaking a success. Fraser, the tutor, died, however, and the school, which had begun well, sank from disrepute into infamy. The Vandeleurs found it convenient to change their name to Stapleton, and he brought the remains of his fortune, his schemes for the future, and his taste for entomology to the south of England. I learn at the British Museum that he was a recognized authority upon the subject, and that the name of Vandeleur has been permanently attached to a certain moth which he had, in his Yorkshire days, been the first to describe.

"We now come to that portion of his life which has proved to be of such intense interest to us. The fellow had evidently made inquiry and found that only two lives intervened between him and a valuable estate. When he went to Devonshire his plans were, I believe, exceedingly hazy, but that he meant mischief from the first is evident from the fact that he took his wife with him as his sister. The idea of using her as a decoy was clearly already in his mind. His first act was to establish himself as near to his ancestral home as he could, and his second was to cultivate a friendship with Sir Charles Baskerville and with the neighbors.

"The baronet himself told him about the family hound, and so prepared the way for his own death. Stapleton, as I will continue to call him, had learned that the old man's heart was weak and that a shock would kill him. He had heard also that Sir Charles was superstitious and had taken this grim legend very seriously. His ingenious mind instantly suggested a way by which the baronet could be done to death, and yet it would be hardly possible to bring home the guilt to the real murderer.

"An ordinary schemer would have been content to work with a savage hound. The use of artificial means to make the creature diabolical was a flash of genius upon his part. The dog he bought in London from Ross and Mangles. It was the strongest and most savage they had. He walked a great distance over the moor so as to get it home without exciting any remarks. He had already on his insect hunts learned to penetrate the Grimpen Mire, and so had found a safe hiding place for the creature. Here he kenneled it and waited his chance.

"But the old gentleman could not be decoyed outside of his grounds at night. Several times Stapleton lurked about with his hound, but without avail. He, or rather his ally, was seen by peasants, and the legend of the demon dog received a new confirmation. He had hoped that his wife might lure Sir Charles to his ruin, but here she proved unexpectedly independent. She would have nothing to do with it, and for a time Stapleton was at a deadlock.

"He found a way out of his difficulties through the chance that Sir Charles, who had conceived a friendship for him, made him the minister of his charity in the case of this unfortunate woman, Mrs. Laura Lyons. He acquired complete influence over her by giving her to understand that in the event of her obtaining a divorce he would marry her. His plans were suddenly brought to a head by his knowledge that Sir Charles was about to leave the Hall on the advice of Dr. Mortimer, with whose opinion he himself pretended to coincide. He therefore put pressure upon Mrs. Lyons to write this letter, imploring the old man to give her an interview before his departure for London. He then, by a specious argument, prevented her from going, and so had his chance.

"Driving back from Coombe Tracey, he was in time to get his hound, to treat it with his infernal paint, and to bring the beast round to the gate at which he expected to find the old gentleman waiting. The dog, incited by its master, sprang over the wicket gate and pursued the unfortunate baronet, who fled screaming down the yew alley. In that gloomy tunnel it must indeed have been a dreadful sight to see that huge black creature, with its flaming jaws and blazing eyes, bounding down the grassy border after its victim. Sir Charles fell dead at the end of the alley from heart disease and terror. On seeing him lying still the creature had probably approached to sniff at him, but finding him dead had turned away again. It was then that it left the prints upon the path which were observed by Dr. Mortimer. The hound was called off to its lair in the Grimpen Mire, and a mystery was left which finally brought the case within the scope of our observation.

"Both of the women concerned in the case, Mrs. Stapleton and Mrs. Laura Lyons, were left with a strong suspicion against Stapleton. Mrs. Stapleton knew that he had designs upon the old man, and also of the existence of the hound. Mrs. Lyons knew neither of these things, but had been impressed by the death occurring at the time of an appointment which was only known to him. However, both of them were under his influence, and he had nothing to fear from them. The first half of his task was successfully accomplished, but the more difficult still remained.

"Stapleton would very soon learn from his friend Dr. Mortimer all details about the arrival of Sir Charles's heir. His first idea was that this young stranger from Canada might possibly be done to death in London without coming down to Devonshire at all. He dared not leave his wife long out of his sight for fear he should lose his influence over her. It was for this reason that he took her to London with him. They lodged, I find, at the Mexborough Private Hotel, which was one of those called upon by young Cartwright in search of evidence. Here he kept his wife imprisoned in her room while he, disguised in a beard, followed Dr. Mortimer to Baker Street and afterwards to the station and to the Northumberland Hotel. His wife had such a fear of her husband—a fear founded upon brutal ill-treatment—that she dared not write to warn the man whom she knew to be in danger. Eventually, as we know, she adopted the expedient of cutting out the words which would form the message and addressing the letter in a disguised hand. It reached the baronet and gave him the first warning of his danger.

"It was essential for Stapleton to get some article of Sir Henry's attire so that, in case he was driven to use the dog, he might have the means of setting him upon his track. We cannot doubt that a servant of the hotel was well bribed to help him in his design. However, the first boot which was procured for him was new and, therefore, useless for his purpose. He then had it returned and obtained another—which proved conclusively that we were dealing with a real hound, as no other supposition could explain this anxiety to obtain an old boot. The more grotesque an incident is, the more carefully it deserves to be examined.

"Then we had the visit from our friends next morning, shadowed always by Stapleton in the cab. From his knowledge of our rooms and of my appearance, as well as from his general conduct, I am inclined to think that Stapleton's career of crime has been by no means limited to this single Baskerville affair. It is suggestive that during the last three years there have been four considerable burglaries in the west country, for none of which was any criminal ever arrested. I cannot doubt that Stapleton recruited his waning resources in this fashion, and that for years he has been a desperate and dangerous man.

"We had an example of his audacity that morning when he sent back my own name to me through the cabman. From that moment he understood that I had taken over the case in London, and that therefore there was no chance for him there. He returned to Dartmoor and awaited the arrival of the baronet."

"One moment!" said I. "What became of the hound when its master was in London?"

"I have given some attention to this matter and it is undoubtedly of importance. There was an old manservant at Merripit House, and I have myself seen him cross the Grimpen Mire by the path which Stapleton had marked out. It is very probable, therefore, that in the absence of his master it was he who cared for the hound, though he may never have known the purpose for which the beast was used.

"One word now as to how I stood myself at that time. It may possibly recur to your memory that when I examined the warning note sent to Sir Henry I held it within a few inches of my eyes, and was conscious of a faint smell of the scent known as white jasmine. The scent suggested the presence of a lady, and already my thoughts began to turn towards the Stapletons. Thus I had made certain of the hound, and had guessed at the criminal before ever we went to the west country.

"It was my game to watch Stapleton. I deceived everybody,

therefore, yourself included, and I came down secretly when I was supposed to be in London. I stayed for the most part at Coombe Tracey, and only used the hut upon the moor when it was necessary to be near the scene of action. When I was watching Stapleton, Cartwright was frequently watching you, so that I was able to keep my hand upon all the strings.

"I have already told you that your reports reached me rapidly, being forwarded instantly from Baker Street to Coombe Tracey. By the time that you discovered me upon the moor I had a complete knowledge of the whole business, but I had not a case which could go to a jury. There seemed to be no alternative but to catch him red-handed, and to do so we had to use Sir Henry as a bait. That Sir Henry should have been exposed to this is, I must confess, a reproach to my management of the case. Only a long journey may enable our friend to recover from his shattered nerves and wounded feelings. His love for the lady was deep and sincere, and to him the saddest part of all this black business was that he should have been deceived by her.

"It only remains to indicate the part which she had played throughout. There can be no doubt that Stapleton exercised an influence over her which may have been love or may have been fear, or very possibly both, since they are by no means incompatible emotions. At his command she consented to pass as his sister, though she was ready to warn Sir Henry so far as she could without implicating her husband. When Stapleton saw the baronet paying court to the lady, even though it was part of his own plan, he could not help revealing the fiery soul which his self-contained manner so cleverly concealed. By encouraging the intimacy he made it certain that Sir Henry would frequently come to Merripit House and that he would sooner or later get the opportunity which he desired. On the day of the crisis, however, his wife turned suddenly against him. She knew that the hound was being kept in the outhouse on the evening that Sir Henry was coming to dinner. She taxed her husband with his intended crime, and a furious scene followed in which he showed her for the first time that she had a rival in his love. Her fidelity turned in an instant to bitter hatred, and he saw that she would betray him. He tied her up, therefore, that she might have no chance of warning Sir Henry, and he hoped, no doubt, that when the whole countryside put down the baronet's death to the curse of his family, as they certainly would do, he could win his wife back to accept an accomplished fact and to keep silent upon what she knew. In this I fancy that he made a miscalculation. A woman of Spanish blood does not condone such an injury so lightly."

"He could not hope to frighten Sir Henry to death as he had done the old uncle," I observed.

"The beast was savage and half starved. If its appearance did not frighten its victim to death, at least it would paralyze the resistance which might be offered."

"No doubt. There only remains one difficulty. If Stapleton came into the succession, how could he explain the fact that he, the heir, had been living unannounced under another name so close to the property? How could he claim it without causing suspicion and inquiry?"

"The past and the present are within the field of my inquiry, but what a man may do in the future is a hard question to answer. Mrs. Stapleton has heard her husband discuss the problem on several occasions. There were three possible courses. He might claim the property from South America, establish his identity before the British authorities there, and so obtain the fortune without ever coming to England at all; or he might adopt an elaborate disguise during the short time that he need be in London; or, again, he might furnish an accomplice with the proofs and papers, putting him in as heir, and retaining a claim upon some proportion of his income. We cannot doubt from what we know of him that he would have found some way out of the difficulty. And now, my dear Watson, I think we may turn our thoughts into more pleasant channels. I have a box for *Les Huguenots*. Might I trouble you then to be ready in half an hour, and we can stop at Marcini's for a little dinner on the way?"

Doctor No

Doctor No

A CONDENSATION OF
THE BOOK BY

Ian
Fleming

ILLUSTRATED BY DAVID PLOURDE

To secret agent James Bond the assignment in sunny Jamaica sounded too soft to be a challenge. But that was before he got there and learned who his adversary was—the nefarious Doctor No of nearby Crab Key. It was also before he met luscious, uninhibited Honeychile Rider. Together she and Bond embarked on a hazardous mission that led them straight into a fiendish trap set for them by Doctor No.

A spine tingler by the late Ian Fleming, himself a former British agent, who knew Jamaica well and whose other action-packed novels include *Goldfinger, From Russia, With Love* and *Casino Royale* (Reader's Digest Great Stories of Mystery and Suspense, Volume I).

Chapter 1

Punctually at six o'clock the sun set with a last yellow flash behind the Blue Mountains, a wave of violet shadow poured down Richmond Road, and the crickets and tree frogs in the fine gardens began to zing and tinkle.

Apart from the background noise of the insects, the wide empty street was quiet. The wealthy owners of the big withdrawn houses— bank managers, company directors and top civil servants—had been home since five o'clock and they would be discussing the day with their wives or taking a shower and changing their clothes. In half an hour the street would come to life again with the cocktail traffic, but now this very superior half mile of "Rich Road," as it was known to the tradesmen of Kingston, held nothing but the suspense of an empty stage and the heavy perfume of night-scented jasmine.

Richmond Road is the "best" road in all Jamaica. It is Jamaica's Park Avenue, its Kensington Palace Gardens. The "best" people live in its big old-fashioned houses, each in an acre or two of beautiful lawn set, too trimly, with the finest trees and flowers. The long, straight road is cool and quiet and apart from the hot, vulgar sprawl of Kingston, where its residents earn their money. At its top are the grounds of King's House, where the governor and

commander in chief of Jamaica lives with his family. In Jamaica
no road could have a finer ending.

On the corner stands number 1 Richmond Road, a substantial
two-story house with broad white-painted verandas running round
both floors. This mansion is the social mecca of Kingston. It
Queen's Club, which for fifty years has boasted the finest cuisine
and cellar in the Caribbean.

At that time of day, on most evenings of the year, you would
find the same four motorcars standing outside the club. They were
the cars belonging to the high bridge game that assembled punctually
at five and played until around midnight. You could almost set
your watch by these cars. They belonged, reading from the order
in which they now stood against the curb, to the brigadier in
command of the Caribbean Defense Force, to Kingston's leading
criminal lawyer and to the mathematics professor from Kingston
University. At the tail of the line stood the black Sunbeam Alpine
of Commander John Strangways, RN (Ret.), regional control officer
for the Caribbean—or, less discreetly, the local representative of
the British Secret Service.

JUST before six fifteen the silence of Richmond Road was softly
broken. Three blind beggars dressed in rags came round the corner
of the intersection and moved slowly down the pavement toward
the four cars. They were Chigroes—Chinese Negroes—bulky men
but bowed as they shuffled along, tapping at the curb with their
white sticks. They walked in file. The first man, who wore blue
glasses and could presumably see better than the others, walked
in front holding a tin cup. The right hand of the second man rested
on his shoulder and the right hand of the third on the shoulder
of the second. The eyes of the second and third men were shut.

The three blind men would not have been incongruous in Kingston
where there are many diseased people on the streets, but in the
quiet rich empty street they made an unpleasant impression. And
it was odd that they should all be Chinese Negroes. This is not
a common mixture of bloods.

In the cardroom, the sunburned hand reached out into the green

502

pool of the center table and gathered up the four cards. There was a quiet snap as the trick went to join the rest. "Hundred honors," said Strangways, "and ninety below." He looked at his watch and stood up. "Back in twenty minutes. Your deal, Bill. Order some drinks. Usual for me."

Bill Templar, the brigadier, pinged the bell by his side. Strangways was already out of the door. The three men sat back resignedly in their chairs. The Jamaican steward came in and they ordered drinks for themselves and Strangways.

There was this maddening interruption every evening at six fifteen. At this time precisely, Strangways had to go to his "office" and "make a call." It was a damned nuisance. But Strangways was a vital part of their four and they put up with it. It was never explained what the call was, and no one asked. Strangways' job was "hush," and that was that. He was rarely away for more than twenty minutes and it was understood that he paid for his absence with a round of drinks.

The drinks came and the three men began to talk racing.

In fact, this was the most important moment in Strangways' day—the time of his duty radio contact with the powerful transmitter on the roof of the building in Regent's Park that is the headquarters of the Secret Service. Every day at six thirty local time, unless he gave warning the day before that he would not be on the air, he would transmit his report and receive his orders. If he failed to come on the air precisely at six thirty, there would be a second call—the blue—at seven, and finally the red call at seven thirty. After this, if his transmitter remained silent, it was an emergency, and Section III, his controlling authority in London, would get on the job of finding out what had happened to him.

Even a blue call means a bad mark for an agent unless his reasons in writing are unanswerable. Strangways had never suffered the ignominy of a blue call, let alone a red. Every evening at precisely six fifteen he left Queen's Club and drove up into the foothills of the Blue Mountains to his neat bungalow. At six twenty-five he walked through the hall to the office at the back. He unlocked the door and locked it again behind him. There Miss Trueblood who passed as his secretary but was in fact his Number Two and a former chief officer, Women's Royal Naval Service, would be sitting in front of the dials inside the dummy filing cabinet. She would have the earphones on and would be making first contact tapping out his call sign, WXN. Strangways would drop into the chair beside her, and at exactly six twenty-eight he would take over from her and wait for WWW in London to acknowledge It was an iron routine.

Strangways, a tall lean man with a black patch over the right eye, walked quickly across the hallway of Queen's Club and through the doors and ran down the three steps to the gravel path.

As he strode down the path and into Richmond Road, there was nothing very much on his mind except the sensual pleasure of the clean fresh evening air. There was, of course, this case he was working on, a curious and complicated affair that M. had nonchalantly tossed over the air at him two weeks ago. But it was going well. A chance lead into the Chinese community had paid off

Automatically part of Strangways' mind took in the three blind men. They were tapping towards him down the sidewalk. He calculated that they would pass him a second or two before he reached his car. Out of shame for his own health and gratitude for it, Strangways felt for a coin. He was parallel with the beggar when his hand went out. The coin clanged in the cup.

"Bless you, master," said the leading man. "Bless you," echoed the other two.

The car key was in Strangways' hand. Vaguely he registered silence as the tapping of the sticks ceased. It was too late.

As Strangways had passed the last man, all three had swiveled Three revolvers with sausage-shaped silencers whipped out of holster concealed among the rags. With precision the three men aimed at different points on Strangways' spine.

The three heavy coughs were almost one. Strangways' body was hurled forward. It lay absolutely still in the small puff of dust from the sidewalk.

It was six seventeen. With a squeal of tires, a motor hearse with black plumes flying from the four corners of its roof took the turn into Richmond Road, shot towards the group and slid to a stop. The doors at the back were opened. So was the plain coffin inside. The three men manhandled the body through the doors and into the coffin. They climbed into the hearse, and the doors were pulled shut. The three Chigroes sat down on three of the four little seats at the corners of the coffin. Roomy black alpaca coats hung over the backs of the seats. They put the coats on over their rags. Then they reached to the floor and picked up black top hats and put them on their heads.

The driver looked nervously over his shoulder. "Go, man. Go!" said the biggest of the killers. He glanced down at the luminous dial of his wristwatch. It said six twenty. Just three minutes for the job. Dead on time.

The hearse made a decorous U-turn and moved away at a sedate speed towards the hills.

"WXN calling WWW.... WXN calling WWW.... WXN..."

The center finger of Mary Trueblood's right hand stabbed softly, elegantly, at the key. She lifted her left wrist. Six twenty-eight. He was a minute late. Mary Trueblood smiled at the thought of the little Sunbeam tearing up the road towards her. Now, in a second, she would hear the quick step, then the key in the lock and he would be sitting beside her. "Sorry, Mary. Damned car wouldn't start."

"WXN calling WWW.... WXN calling WWW." She tuned the dial a hairsbreadth. Her watch said six twenty-nine. She began to worry. In a matter of seconds London would be coming in. Suddenly she thought, God, what could she do if Strangways wasn't on time! It was useless for her to acknowledge London and pretend she was him. Radio Security would be monitoring the call, and those instruments which measured the minute peculiarities in an operator's "fist" would at once detect it wasn't Strangways at the key. The controller had explained it all to her when she had joined the Caribbean station five years before—how a buzzer would sound and the contact be automatically broken if the wrong operator had come on the air. It was the basic protection against a Secret Service transmitter falling into enemy hands.

It had come! Now she was hearing the hollowness in the ether that meant London was coming in. Mary Trueblood glanced at her watch. Six thirty. Panic! But now at last there were the footsteps in the hall. Thank God! In a second he would come in.

"WWW calling WXN. . . . Can you hear me?" London was coming over strong.

The footsteps were at the door.

Coolly and confidently, she tapped back: "Hear you loud and clear. . . . Hear you—"

Behind her there was an explosion. Something hit her on the ankle. It was the lock of the door.

Mary Trueblood swiveled in her chair. A man stood in the doorway. He was a big Chigro with slanting eyes. There was a gun in his hand.

Mary Trueblood opened her mouth to scream. The man smiled broadly. Slowly he lifted the gun and shot her three times in the left breast.

The girl slumped sideways off her chair. For perhaps a second the tiny chirrup of London sounded out into the room. Then it stopped. The buzzer at the controller's desk in Radio Security had signaled that something was wrong on WXN.

The killer walked out of the door. He came back carrying a box labeled PRESTO FIRE and a big sugar sack marked TATE & LYLE. He put the box on the floor and went to the body and forced the sack over it. He dragged the sack out into the hall and came back. In the corner of the room the safe stood open, and the cipher books had been taken out and laid on the desk, ready for work on the London signals. The man threw these and all the papers in the safe into the center of the room. He opened the box of Presto fire lighters, took out a handful, tucked them into the pile and lit them. Then he went out into the hall and lit similar bonfires. Flames began to lick up the paneling.

The man went to the front door and opened it. Through the hibiscus hedge he could see the glint of the hearse. There was

506

no noise except the zing of crickets. Up and down the road there was no other sign of life. The man went back into the smoke-filled hall, shouldered the sack and came out again, walking swiftly down the path. He handed the sack into the hearse and watched the two men force it into the coffin on top of Strangways' body. Then he climbed in and shut the doors and sat down and put on his top hat.

As the first flames showed in the upper windows of the bungalow, the hearse moved quietly from the sidewalk and went up towards the Mona Reservoir. There the weighted coffin would slip down into its fifty-fathom grave, and in just forty-five minutes the personnel and records of the Caribbean station of the Secret Service would be utterly destroyed.

Chapter 2

THREE weeks later, in London, March came in like a rattlesnake. From first light on March 1, hail and icy sleet, with a force eight gale behind them, lashed the city. It was a filthy day and everybody said so—even M., who rarely admitted the existence of weather. When the old black Silver Wraith Rolls stopped outside the building in Regent's Park and he climbed stiffly out onto the pavement, hail hit him in the face like a whiff of small shot.

"Won't be needing the car again today, Smith," he said to the chauffeur. "Take it away and go home. I'll use the tube this evening. No weather for driving a car. Worse than one of those PQ convoys."

Ex-Leading Stoker Smith grinned gratefully. "Aye, aye, sir. And thanks." He watched the erect elderly figure walk round the front of the Rolls and across the pavement and into the building. Just like the old boy. He'd always see the men right first. Smith clicked the gear lever into first and moved off, peering forward through the windscreen. They didn't come like that anymore.

M. went up in the lift to the eighth floor and through the thick-carpeted corridor to his office. He shut the door behind him, took off his overcoat and hung it behind the door. He took out a large silk handkerchief and brusquely wiped it over his face. It was odd, but he wouldn't have done this in front of the porters or the lift man. He went to his desk and sat down and bent towards the intercom. "I'm in, Miss Moneypenny. The signals, please, and anything else you've got. Then get me Sir James Molony. He'll be doing his rounds at St. Mary's about now. Tell the chief of staff I'll see 007 in half an hour. And let me have the Strangways file." M. waited for the metallic "Yes, sir" and released the switch.

He sat back and reached for his pipe and began filling it thoughtfully. He didn't look up when his secretary came in with the stack of papers. A yellow light winked on the intercom. M. picked up one telephone from the row of four. "That you, Sir James? Have you got five minutes?"

"Six, for you." At the other end of the line the famous neurologist chuckled. "Want me to certify one of Her Majesty's ministers?"

"Not today." M. frowned irritably. The old navy had respected governments. "It's about that man of mine you've been handling. We won't bother about the name. This is an open line. I gather you let him out yesterday. Is he fit for duty?"

There was a pause on the other end. Now the voice was professional, judicious. "Physically he's fit as a fiddle. Shouldn't be any aftereffects. Yes, he's all right." There was another pause. "Just one thing, M. There's a lot of tension there, you know. You work these men of yours pretty hard. Can you give him something easy to start with? From what you've told me he's been having a tough time for some years now."

M. said gruffly, "That's what he's paid for. I gather then he's in perfectly good shape. It isn't as if he'd really been damaged like some of the patients I've sent you—men who've been properly put through the mangle."

"Of course, if you put it like that. But pain's an odd thing. We know very little about it. And this man of yours has been in *real* pain, M. Don't think that just because nothing's been broken . . ."

"Quite, quite." Bond had made a mistake and he had suffered for it. In any case M. didn't like being lectured. He said in a milder voice, "Don't let's argue about it. As a matter of fact, I did have it in mind to let him have a bit of a breather. Something's come up in Jamaica." M. glanced at the streaming windows. "It'll be more of a rest cure than anything. Two of my people, a man and a girl, have gone off together. Or that's what it looks like. Our friend can have a spell at being an inquiry agent—in the sunshine too. How's that?"

"Just the ticket. I wouldn't mind the job myself on a day like this." Sir James Molony persisted mildly, "Don't think I wanted to interfere, M., but there are limits to a man's courage. I know you have to treat these men as if they were expendable, but presumably you don't want them to crack at the wrong moment. This one I've had here is tough. I'd say you'll get plenty more work out of him. But you know what Morgan has to say about courage in that book of his."

"Don't recall."

"He says that courage is a capital sum reduced by expenditure. This particular man seems to have been spending pretty hard since before the war. I wouldn't say he's overdrawn—not yet, but there are limits."

"Just so." M. decided that was quite enough of that. Nowadays softness was everywhere. "Don't worry, Sir James. I'll take care of him. By the way, did you ever discover what the stuff was that Russian woman put into him?"

"Got the answer yesterday," said Sir James. "Taken us three months. A bright chap at the School of Tropical Medicine came up with it. The drug was *fugu* poison. It comes from the Japanese globefish. Trust the Russians to use something no one's ever heard of. They might just as well have used curare. It has much the same effect—paralysis of the central nervous system. *Fugu's* scientific name is tetraodontoxin. It's terrible stuff. One shot of it like your man got and in a matter of seconds the motor and respiratory muscles are paralyzed. At first the chap sees double. Next he can't swallow. His head falls and he can't raise it. Dies of respiratory paralysis."

"Lucky he got away with it."

"Miracle. Thanks entirely to that Frenchman who was with him. Gave him artificial respiration until the doctor came. Fortunately the doctor had worked in South America. Diagnosed curare and treated him accordingly. But it was a chance in a million. By the same token, what happened to the Russian woman?"

M. said shortly, "Oh, she died. Well, many thanks, Sir James. And don't worry about your patient. I'll see he has an easy time of it. Good-by."

M. hung up. His face was cold and blank. He pulled over the signal file and went quickly through it. On some of the messages he scribbled a comment. When he had finished he tossed the pile into his out basket and reached again for his pipe and tobacco. Nothing remained in front of him except a buff folder marked with the top secret red star. Across the folder was written in block capitals: CARIBBEAN STATION, and underneath, in italics, *Strangways and Trueblood.*

A light winked on the intercom. M. pressed the switch. "Yes?"

"007's here, sir."

"Send him in. And tell the armorer to come up in five minutes."

M. sat back. His eyes were very bright and watchful.

James Bond came through the door and shut it. He walked to the chair across the desk from M. and sat down.

"Morning, 007."

"Good morning, sir."

There was silence in the room except for the rasping of M.'s pipe. It seemed to be taking a lot of matches to get it going. In the background the sleet slashed against the windows.

It was all just as Bond had remembered it through the months of being shunted from hospital to hospital. To him this represented stepping back into life. Sitting here opposite M. was the symbol of normality he had longed for. He looked across at the shrewd gray eyes. They were watching him. What was coming?

M. threw the box of matches down on the desk. He leaned back.

"How do you feel? Glad to be back?"

"Very glad, sir. And I feel fine."

"Any final thoughts about your last case? You heard I ordered an inquiry. I believe the chief of staff took some evidence from you. Anything to add?"

M.'s voice was businesslike, cold. Bond said, "No, sir. It was a mess. I blame myself for letting that woman get me."

M. leaned forward. "Just so." The voice was velvet, dangerous. "Your gun got stuck, if I recall. This Beretta of yours with the silencer. Something wrong there, 007. Can't afford that sort of mistake if you're to carry a double o number. Would you prefer to drop it and go back to normal duties?"

Bond stiffened. The license to kill for the Secret Service—the double o prefix—was a great honor. It brought Bond the only assignments he enjoyed, the dangerous ones. "No, I wouldn't, sir."

"Then we'll have to change your equipment. That was one of the findings of the court of inquiry. I agree with it."

Bond said obstinately, "I'm used to that gun, sir. I like it. What happened could have happened to anyone. With any kind of gun."

"I don't agree." M. bent to the intercom. "Is the armorer there? Send him in." M. sat back. "You may not know it, 007, but Major Boothroyd's the greatest small-arms expert in the world. We'll hear what he has to say."

The door opened. A short slim man with sandy hair came in and stood beside Bond's chair. Bond hadn't often seen the man before, but he remembered the clear gray eyes that never seemed to flicker. Looking across at M., the man said, "Good morning, sir," in a flat, unemotional voice.

"Morning, Armorer. I want to ask you some questions." M.'s voice was casual. "First of all, what do you think of the Beretta, the .25?"

"Ladies' gun, sir."

M. raised ironic eyebrows at Bond. Bond smiled thinly.

"Really! And why do you say that?"

"No real stopping power, sir. But it's easy to operate. A bit fancy-looking too. Appeals to the ladies."

"How would it be with a silencer?"

"Still less stopping power, sir. And I don't like silencers. They're heavy and get stuck in your clothing."

M. said pleasantly to Bond, "Any comment, 007?"

Bond shrugged. "I don't agree. I've used the .25 Beretta for fifteen years. Never had a stoppage and I haven't missed with it yet. I've used bigger guns—the .45 Colt, for instance. But for close-up work and concealment I like the Beretta." Bond paused. "I'd agree about the silencer, sir. They're a nuisance. But sometimes you have to use them."

"We've seen what happens when you do," said M. dryly. "And as for changing your gun, it's only a question of practice. You'll soon get the feel of a new one." M. allowed a trace of sympathy to enter his voice. "Sorry, 007. But I've decided. Just stand

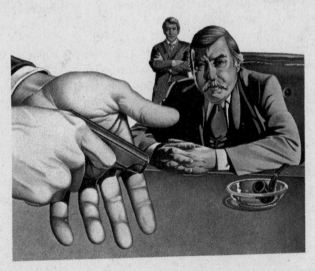

up a moment. I want the armorer to get a look at your build."

Bond stood up and faced the other man. There was no warmth in the two pairs of eyes. Major Boothroyd walked round Bond. He felt Bond's biceps and forearms. He came back in front of him and said, "Might I see your gun?"

Bond's hand went slowly into his coat. He handed over the Beretta. Boothroyd put it down on the desk. "And your holster?"

Bond took off his coat and slipped off the chamois leather holster and harness.

Boothroyd tossed the holster down beside the gun with a motion that sneered. He looked at M. "I think we can do a bit better than this, sir." It was the sort of voice Bond's first expensive tailor had used.

"Well, Armorer, what do you recommend?"

Major Boothroyd put on the expert's voice. "As a matter of fact, sir," he said modestly, "I've just been testing most of the small automatics. Five thousand rounds each at twenty-five yards. Of all of them I'd choose the Walther PPK 7.65 mm. It's a real stopping gun. Of course it's about a .32 caliber as compared with the Beretta's .25, but I wouldn't recommend anything lighter. You can get ammunition for it anywhere in the world."

M. turned to Bond. "Any comments?"

"It's a good gun, sir," Bond admitted. "Bit more bulky than the Beretta. How does the armorer suggest I carry it?"

"Berns-Martin triple-draw holster," said Major Boothroyd succinctly. "Best worn inside the trouser band to the left. But it's all right below the shoulder. Stiff saddle leather. Holds the gun in with a spring. Should make for a quick draw. Three-fifths of a second to hit a man at twenty feet would be about right."

"That's settled then." M.'s voice was final. "And what about something bigger?"

"Of the bigger guns there's only one I'd recommend, sir," said Major Boothroyd stolidly. "Smith and Wesson Centennial Airweight. Revolver—.38 caliber. Hammerless, so it won't catch in clothing. To keep down the weight, the cylinder holds only five cartridges. But by the time they're gone"—Major Boothroyd allowed himself a wintry smile—"somebody's been killed."

"All right," said M. "So it's the Walther and the Smith and Wesson. Send up one of each to 007. And arrange for him to fire them. He's got to be expert in a week. All right then? Thank you, Armorer. I won't detain you."

"Thank you, sir," said Major Boothroyd. He marched stiffly out of the room.

There was a moment's silence. The sleet tore at the windows. M. swiveled his chair and watched the streaming panes. Bond took an opportunity to glance at his watch. Ten o'clock. His eyes slid to the gun on the desk. He thought of his fifteen years' marriage to the ugly bit of metal. He remembered the times its single word had saved his life—and the times when its threat alone had been enough. How many death sentences had it signed? Bond felt unreasonably sad. How could one have such ties with an inanimate object, an ugly one at that? But he had the ties, and M. was going to cut them.

M. swiveled back to face him. "Sorry, James," he said, and there was no sympathy in his voice. "I know how you like that bit of iron. But I'm afraid it's got to go. A gun's more important than a hand or a foot in your job."

Bond smiled thinly. "I know, sir. I shan't argue."

"All right then. We'll say no more about it. Now I've got some more news for you. There's a job come up. In Jamaica. Personnel problem. Routine investigation and report. The sunshine'll do you good and you can practice your new guns on the turtles or whatever they have down there. You can do with a bit of holiday. Like to take it on?"

Bond thought, He's got it in for me over the last job. Feels I let him down. Won't trust me with anything tough. Wants to see. Oh well! He said, "Sounds rather like the soft life, sir. But if it's got to be done . . . If you say so, sir."

"Yes," said M. "I say so."

It was getting dark. Outside, the weather was thickening. M. switched on the green-shaded desk light and pulled the thick file towards him. Bond noticed it for the first time. He read the reversed lettering without difficulty. What had Strangways been up to? Who was Trueblood?

M. pressed a button. "I'll get the chief of staff in on this," he said. "I know the bones of the case, but he can fill in the flesh. It's a drab little story, I'm afraid."

The chief of staff came in. He was a colonel in the Sappers, a man of about Bond's age, but his hair was prematurely gray at the temples from endless work and responsibility. He had physical toughness and a sense of humor. He was Bond's best friend at headquarters. They smiled at each other.

"Bring up a chair, Chief of Staff. I've given 007 the Strangways case. Got to get the mess cleared up before we make a new appointment there; 007 can be acting head of station in the meantime. I want him to leave in a week. And now let's go over the case." He turned to Bond. "I think you knew Strangways, 007. See you worked with him on that treasure business about five years ago. What did you think of him?"

"Good man, sir. Bit highly strung."

"And his Number Two, this girl Mary Trueblood. Ever come across her?"

"No, sir."

"She's got a good record. Chief officer WRNS and then came to us. Good-looker, to judge from her photographs. That probably explains it. Would you say Strangways was a bit of a womanizer?"

"Could have been," said Bond carefully, not wanting to say anything against Strangways. "But what's happened to them, sir?"

"That's what we want to find out," said M. "They simply vanished into thin air about three weeks ago. Left Strangways' bungalow burned to the ground—code books, files. Nothing left. The girl left all her things intact. Must have taken only what she stood up in. Even her passport was in her room. But it would have been easy for Strangways to cook up two passports. He was passport control officer for the island. Any number of planes they could have taken—to Florida or South America, or some other island. Police are still checking the passenger lists. Nothing's come up yet, but airport security doesn't amount to much in that part of the world. Isn't that so, Chief of Staff?"

"Yes, sir." The chief of staff sounded dubious. "But I still can't understand that last radio contact." He turned to Bond. "You see, they began to make their routine contact at six thirty Jamaican time. Someone—Radio Security thinks it was the girl—acknowledged our WWW and then went off the air. We tried to regain contact, but there was something fishy and we broke off. No answer to the blue call, or to the red. So next day Section III sent 258 down from Washington. By that time the police had taken over and the governor had already made up his mind and was trying to get the case hushed up. It all seemed pretty obvious to him. Strangways has had occasional girl trouble. And sex and machete fights are about all the local police understand down there; 258 spent a week scraping around and couldn't turn up a scrap of contrary evidence. He reported accordingly and we sent him back to Washington. Since then the police have gotten nowhere."

The chief of staff looked apologetically at M. "I know you're inclined to agree with the governor, sir, but that radio contact sticks in my throat. I can't see where it fits into the runaway-couple picture. And Strangways' friends at his club say he was perfectly normal. Left in the middle of a rubber of bridge—always did, when it was close to his deadline. Said he'd be back in twenty minutes. Then he vanished into thin air. Even left his car in front of the club. Now why should he set the rest of his bridge four looking for him if he wanted to skip with the girl? It just doesn't make sense to me."

M. grunted noncommittally. "People in—er—in love do stupid things," he said gruffly. "And what other explanation is there? Absolutely no trace of foul play. It's a quiet station. I don't suppose Strangways has had a big case since 007 was there." He turned to Bond. "On what you've heard, what do you think, 007? There's not much else to tell you."

Bond was definite. "I just can't see Strangways flying off the handle like that, sir. The Service was his whole life. He'd never have let it down. I can see him handing in his papers, and the girl doing the same, and then going off with her after you'd sent out reliefs. But I don't believe it was in him to leave us in the air like this."

"Thank you, 007." M.'s voice was controlled. "No one's been jumping to conclusions without weighing all the possibilities. Perhaps you can suggest another solution."

M. sat back and waited. He reached for his pipe and began filling it. The case bored him. It was only to give Bond the pretense of a job, mixed with a rest, that he had decided to send him out to Jamaica to close the case. He put the pipe in his mouth and reached for the matches. "Well?"

Bond wasn't going to be put off his stride. He had liked Strangways and he was impressed by the points the chief of staff had made. He said, "Well, sir. For instance, what was the last case Strangways was working on? Was there anything Section III had asked him to look into? Anything at all in the past few months?"

"Nothing whatsoever." M. was definite. He turned to the chief of staff. "Right?"

"Right, sir," said the chief of staff. "Only that damned business about the birds."

"Oh, that," said M. contemptuously. "Some rot from the zoo or somebody. Wished on us by the Colonial Office. About six weeks ago, wasn't it?"

"That's right, sir. But it wasn't the zoo. It was some people in America called the Audubon Society. They protect rare birds. Got on to our ambassador in Washington, and the Foreign Office passed the buck to the Colonial Office."

Bond persisted. "Could you tell me about it, sir? What did the Audubon people want us to do?"

M. picked up the Strangways file and tossed it in front of the chief of staff. "You tell him, Chief of Staff," he said wearily. "It's all in there."

The chief of staff took the file and riffled through the pages towards the back. He found what he wanted. There was silence in the room while he ran his eyes over some pages of typescript. Then he slapped the file shut. He said, "Well, this is the story as we passed it to Strangways on January twentieth." The chief of staff sat back in his chair. He looked at Bond. "It seems there's a bird called a roseate spoonbill. There's a colored photograph of it in here. Looks like a sort of pink stork with an ugly flat bill. Not many years ago these birds were dying out. Just before the war there were only a few hundred left in the world, mostly in Florida and thereabouts. Then somebody reported a colony of them on an island called Crab Key between Jamaica and Cuba. It's British territory—a dependency of Jamaica. Used to be a guano island,

517

but the quality of the guano was too low for the cost of digging it. When the birds were found there it had been uninhabited for fifty years. The Audubon people went down and ended up by leasing a corner as a sanctuary for these spoonbills. Put two wardens in charge and persuaded the airlines to stop flying over the island and disturbing the birds. The birds flourished, and at the last count there were about five thousand of them on the island.

"Then came the war. The price of guano went up, and some bright chap had the idea of buying the island and starting to work it again. He negotiated with the Jamaican government and bought the place for ten thousand pounds with the condition that he didn't disturb the lease of the sanctuary. That was in 1943. Well, this man imported cheap labor and soon had the place working at a profit, and it's gone on making a profit until recently. Then the price of guano took a dip and it's thought that he must be having a hard time making both ends meet."

"Who is this man?"

"Chinaman, or rather half Chinese, half German. Got a daft name. Calls himself Doctor No—Doctor Julius No."

"No? Spelled like yes?"

"That's right."

"Any facts about him?"

"Nothing except that he keeps very much to himself. Hasn't been seen since he made his deal with the Jamaican government. There's no traffic with the island. It's his and he keeps it private. Well, nothing happened until just before Christmas, when one of the Audubon wardens, a Barbadian, arrived on the north shore of Jamaica in a canoe. He was terribly burned—died in a few days. Before he died he told some crazy story about their camp having been attacked by a dragon with flames coming out of its mouth. This dragon had killed his pal and burned up the camp and gone roaring off into the bird sanctuary, belching fire among the birds and scaring them off. He had been badly burned, but he'd escaped and stolen a canoe and sailed to Jamaica. Poor chap was obviously off his rocker. And that was that, except that a report had to be sent to the Audubon Society. And they weren't satisfied. Sent two of their big brass in a Beechcraft from Miami to investigate. There's an airstrip on the island."

The chief of staff paused. "The Beechcraft crashed on landing and killed the two Audubon men. Well, that aroused these bird people to a fury. They got a U.S. corvette to call on Doctor No. That's how powerful these people are. Seems they've got quite a lobby in Washington. The captain of the ship reported that he was received very civilly by Doctor No. He was taken to the airstrip, where he examined the remains of the plane. Smashed to pieces, but nothing suspicious—came in to land too fast, probably. The bodies of the two men and the pilot had been reverently packed in handsome coffins, which were handed over with quite a ceremony. The captain was very impressed by Doctor No's courtesy. He asked to see the wardens' camp and he was taken there. Doctor No's theory was that the two men had gone mad because of the heat and the loneliness, or that one of them had gone mad and burned down the camp with the other inside it. This seemed possible to the captain when he'd seen what a godforsaken bit of marsh the men had been living in for about ten years. There was nothing else to see and he politely sailed away."

The chief of staff spread his hands. "And that's the lot, except that the captain reported that he saw only a handful of roseate spoonbills. When his report got back to the Audubon Society, apparently the loss of their blasted birds infuriated them, and ever since then they've been nagging at us to have an inquiry into the whole business. Of course nobody at the Colonial Office is in the least interested. So in the end the whole fairy story was dumped in our lap." The chief of staff shrugged. "And that's how this pile of nonsense"—he waved the file—"got landed on Strangways."

M. looked morosely at Bond. "See what I mean, 007? Just the sort of mare's nest these old women's societies are always stirring up." He snorted. "Anyway, you asked about Strangways' last case and that's it. A lot of hullabaloo about a covey of pink storks." M. leaned forward belligerently. "Any questions? I've got a busy day ahead."

Bond grinned. He couldn't help it. M.'s occasional outbursts of rage were so splendid. And nothing set him going so well as any attempt to waste the time and energies and slim funds of the Secret Service. Bond got to his feet. "Perhaps if I could have the file, sir," he said placatingly. "It just strikes me that four people seem to have died more or less because of these birds. Perhaps two more did—Strangways and the Trueblood girl. I agree it sounds ridiculous, but we've got nothing else to go on."

"Take it, take it," said M. impatiently. "And hurry up and get your holiday over."

Bond picked up the file. He also made to pick up his Beretta. "No," said M. sharply. "Leave that. And mind you've got the hang of the other two guns by the time I see you again."

Bond looked across into M.'s eyes. For the first time in his life he hated the man. He knew perfectly well why M. was being mean. It was deferred punishment for his having nearly gotten killed on his last job. Plus getting away from this filthy weather into the sunshine. M. couldn't bear his men to have an easy time. In a way Bond felt sure he was being sent on this cushy assignment to humiliate him. The old bastard.

With the anger balling up inside him like cat's fur, Bond said, "I'll see to it, sir," and turned and walked out of the room.

Chapter 3

THE sixty-eight tons of the Super Constellation hurtled high above the green and brown checkerboard of Cuba and, with only another hundred miles to go, started its slow descent towards Jamaica.

Bond watched the green turtle-backed island grow on the horizon and the water below him turn from the dark blue of the Cuba Deep to the azure of the inshore shoals. Then they were over the north shore and crossing the high mountains of the interior. The setting sun flashed gold on the bright worms of tumbling rivers and streams. Xaymaca, the Arawak Indians had called it—the land of wood and water. Bond's heart lifted with the beauty of one of the most fertile islands in the world.

The other side of the mountains was in deep violet shadow. Lights were already twinkling in the streets of Kingston, but beyond, the far arm of the harbor and the airport were still touched with the sun. Now the Constellation was getting its nose down into a wide sweep. There was a slight thump as the tricycle landing gear extended under the aircraft, and then it was skimming down towards the runway. There was a glimpse of a road and telephone wires. Then the concrete was under the belly of the plane, and there was the soft double thump of a perfect landing and the roar of reversing props as it taxied in towards the low airport buildings.

The sticky fingers of the tropics brushed Bond's face as he left the aircraft and walked over to health and immigration. His passport described him as an import and export merchant.

"Are you here on business or pleasure, sir?"

"Pleasure."

"I hope you enjoy your stay, sir." The immigration officer handed Bond his passport with indifference.

"Thank you."

Bond walked out into the customs hall. At once he saw the tall brown-skinned man against the barrier. He was wearing the same old faded blue shirt and probably the same khaki twill trousers he had been wearing when Bond first met him five years before.

"Quarrel!"

From behind the barrier the Cayman Islander gave a broad grin. He lifted his right forearm across his eyes in the old salute of the West Indians. "How you, cap'n?" he called delightedly.

"I'm fine," said Bond. "Got the car?"

"Sure, cap'n."

The customs officer, who, like most men from the waterfront, knew Quarrel, chalked Bond's bag without opening it, and Bond picked it up and went out through the barrier. Quarrel held out his hand. Bond took the warm dry callused paw and looked into the dark gray eyes that showed descent from a Cromwellian soldier or a pirate of Sir Henry Morgan's time. "You haven't changed, Quarrel," he said affectionately. "How's the turtle fishing?"

"Not so bad, cap'n, an' not so good. Much de same as always."

They were moving towards the exit when there came the sharp

flash of a press camera. A pretty Chinese girl in Jamaican dress lowered her Speed Graphic. "Thank you, gentlemen. I am from the *Daily Gleaner*." She glanced at a list in her hand. "Mr. Bond, isn't it? And how long will you be with us, Mr. Bond?"

Bond was offhand. "In transit," he said shortly. "I think you'll find there were more interesting people on the plane."

"Oh, no, I'm sure not, Mr. Bond. You look very important. And what hotel will you be staying at?"

Damn, thought Bond. He said, "Myrtle Bank," and moved on, vaguely worried. There was no earthly reason why his picture should be wanted by the press. Outside, as they walked towards the parking place, Bond said, "Ever seen that girl before?"

Quarrel reflected. "Reck'n not, cap'n. But de *Gleaner* have plenty camera gals."

They got to the car. It was a black Sunbeam Alpine. Bond looked sharply at it and then at the license plate. Strangways' car. What the hell? "Where did you get this, Quarrel?"

"A.D.C. tell me to take him, cap'n. Why, cap'n? Him no good?"

So the aide-de-camp had told him. "Oh, it's all right," said Bond resignedly. "Come on, let's get going."

Bond got into the passenger seat. It was entirely his fault. He should have guessed at the chance of getting this car, for it would certainly put the finger on him and on what he was doing in Jamaica, if anyone happened to be interested.

THEY moved off down the long cactus-fringed road towards Kingston. Normally, Bond would have sat and enjoyed the beauty of it all—the zing of the crickets, the rush of warm scented air, the ceiling of stars—but now he was cursing his carelessness and knowing what he shouldn't have done.

What he *had* done was to send one signal through the Colonial Office to the governor. In it he had first asked that the A.D.C. should get Quarrel over from the Cayman Islands for an indefinite period on a salary of ten pounds a week. Quarrel had been with Bond on his last adventure in Jamaica. He was a valuable handyman, with all the fine seaman's qualities of the Cayman Islander, and he was a passport into the lower strata of colored life, which would otherwise be closed to Bond. Everybody loved him and he was a splendid companion. Then Bond had asked for a single room and shower at the Blue Hills hotel, for the loan of a car and for Quarrel to meet him with the car at the airport. Most of this had been wrong. In particular, Bond should have taken a taxi to his hotel and made contact with Quarrel later. Then he would have seen the car and had a chance to change it.

As it was, reflected Bond, he might just as well have advertised his visit and its purpose in the *Gleaner*. He sighed. It was the mistakes one made at the beginning of a case that were the worst. They were the ones that got you off on the wrong foot, that gave the enemy the first game. But was there an enemy? Wasn't he being overcautious? On an impulse Bond turned in his seat. A hundred yards behind were two dim sidelights. Most Jamaicans drive with their headlights full on. Bond turned back. He said, "Quarrel. At the end of the Palisadoes, where the left fork goes to Kingston and the right to Port Morant, I want you to turn quickly down the Morant road and stop at once and turn your lights off. Right? And now go like hell."

"Okay, cap'n." Quarrel's voice sounded pleased. He put his foot down to the floorboards. The little car gave a deep growl and tore off down the white road.

Now they were at the end of the straight. The car skidded round the curve where the corner of the harbor bit into the land. Another five hundred yards and they would be at the intersection. Bond looked back. There was no sign of the other car. Here was the signpost. Quarrel did a racing change and hurled the car around on a tight lock. He pulled in to the side and doused his lights. Bond turned and waited. At once he heard the roar of a big car at speed. Lights blazed on, looking for them. Then the car was past and tearing on towards Kingston. Bond had time to notice that it was a big American-type taxicab and that there was no one in it but the driver. Then it was gone.

The dust settled slowly. They sat for ten minutes saying nothing. Then Bond told Quarrel to turn the car and take the Kingston road. He said, "I think that car was interested in us, Quarrel. You don't drive an empty taxi back from the airport. It's an expensive run. Keep a watch out. He may find we've fooled him and be waiting for us."

"Sho ting, cap'n," said Quarrel happily. This was just the sort of life he had hoped for when he got Bond's message.

They came into the stream of Kingston traffic—buses, cars, horse-drawn carts, pannier-laden donkeys. In the crush it was impossible to say if they were being followed. They turned off to the right and up towards the hills. There were many cars behind them. Any one of them could have been the American taxi. They drove for a quarter of an hour up to Half-Way Tree and then onto the Junction Road, the main road across the island. Soon there was a neon sign of a green palm tree, and underneath, BLUE HILLS. THE HOTEL. They drove in and up the drive lined with neatly rounded bushes of bougainvillea.

The Blue Hills was a comfortable old-fashioned hotel with modern trimmings. Bond was welcomed with deference, because his reservation had been made by King's House. He was shown to a fine corner room with a balcony looking out over the distant sweep of Kingston Harbour. Thankfully he took off his London clothes, moist with perspiration, and went into the shower and turned the cold water full on and stood under it for five minutes. Then he pulled on a pair of sea island cotton shorts, unpacked his things and rang for the waiter.

Bond ordered a double gin and tonic with one whole green lime. When the drink came he took it out onto the balcony, and sat and looked out across the spectacular view. He thought how wonderful it was to be away from headquarters and from London and from hospitals and to be here, at this moment, knowing, as all his senses told him, that he was on a good tough case again.

He sat luxuriously, letting the gin relax him until seven fifteen. He had arranged for Quarrel to pick him up at seven thirty. They were going to have dinner together. Bond had asked Quarrel to suggest a place. Quarrel had named a waterfront night spot, The Joy Boat. "Hit no great shakes, cap'n," he had said apologetically, "but de food an' drinks is good and I got a good fren owns de joint. Dey calls him Pus-Feller, seein' how him once fought wit' a big hoctopus."

Bond smiled to himself at the way Quarrel, like most West Indians, added an *h* when it wasn't needed and took it off when it was. He went into his room and dressed in his old dark blue tropical suit, looked in the glass to see that the Walther didn't show under his armpit and went down and out to where the car was waiting.

THEY swooped quietly down through the soft singing dusk into Kingston and turned to the left along the harbor side. At last there was a blaze of golden neon in the shape of a Spanish galleon above green lettering that said THE JOY BOAT. They pulled into a parking place, and Bond followed Quarrel through a gate into a small garden of palm trees growing out of lawn. At the end was the beach and the sea. Tables were dotted about under the palms, and in the center was a small deserted cement dance floor. To one side a calypso trio was improvising on *Take her to Jamaica where the rum come from.*

Only half the tables were filled, mostly by West Indians. There was a sprinkling of British and American sailors with their girls. An immensely fat Negro in a smart white dinner jacket came to meet them.

"Hi, Mr. Q. Long time no see. Nice table for two?"

"That's right, Pus-Feller. Closer to de kitchen dan de music."

The big man chuckled. He led them to a quiet table under a palm tree. "Drinks, gemmun?"

Bond ordered his gin and tonic, and Quarrel a Red Stripe beer. They scanned the menu, and both decided on broiled lobster followed by a rare steak with native vegetables.

The drinks came. A few yards away the sea lisped on the flat sand. Above them the palm fronds clashed softly in the night breeze. Bond thought of the London he had left the day before. He said, "I like this place, Quarrel."

Quarrel was pleased. "Him a good fren of mine, de Pus-Feller. Him knows mostly what goes hon hin Kingston, case you got hany questions, cap'n. Him an' me once share a boat. Then him go hoff one day catching boobies' heggs hat Crab Key. Went swimmin' for heggs an' dis big hoctopus get him. Pus-Feller bust one lung cuttin' hisself free. Dat scare him, an' him sell me his half of de boat an' come to Kingston. Dat were 'fore de war. Now him rich man, whiles I go hon fishin'." Quarrel chuckled.

"Crab Key," said Bond. "What sort of a place is that?"

Quarrel looked at him sharply. "Dat a bad-luck place now, cap'n," he said shortly. "Chinee gemmun buy hit durin' de war and bring in men and dig bird dirt. Don' let nobody land dere and don' let no one get hoff. We gives it a wide bert'."

"Why's that?"

"Him have plenty watchmen. An' guns—machine guns. An' a radar. Frens o' mine have landed dere and never been seen again. Dat Chinee keep him island plenty private. Cap'n"—Quarrel was apologetic—"dat Crab Key scare me plenty."

The food came. While they ate, Bond gave Quarrel an outline of the Strangways case. The West Indian listened carefully, occasionally asking questions. He was particularly interested in the birds on Crab Key and what the watchman had said and how the plane was supposed to have crashed. Finally he pushed his plate away, wiped his mouth and leaned forward. "Cap'n," he said softly, "I no mind if hit was birds or butterflies or bees. If dey was on Crab Key and de commander was stickin' his nose into de business, yo kin bet yo bottom dollar him been mashed. Him and him girl. De Chinee mash dem for sho."

Bond looked into the urgent gray eyes. "What makes you so certain?"

Quarrel spread his hands. "Dat Chinee want be left alone. I know him kill ma frens order keep folk away from de Crab. Him kill hanyone what hinterfere with him."

A glint of light caught the corner of Bond's eye. He turned. The Chinese girl from the airport was in the nearby shadows, dressed now in a sheath of black satin. She had a Leica with a flash attachment in one hand. The other hand held a flashbulb.

"Get that girl," said Bond quickly.

In two strides Quarrel was up with her. He held out his hand. "Evenin', missy," he said softly.

The girl smiled. She let the Leica hang on its strap. She took Quarrel's hand. Quarrel swung her around like a ballet dancer. Now he had her hand behind her back. She looked up at him angrily. "Don't. You're hurting."

Quarrel smiled. "Cap'n like you take a drink wit' we," he said soothingly. He came back to the table, moving the girl along with him. He hooked a chair out with his foot and sat her down beside

him, keeping the grip on her wrist behind her back. They sat bolt upright, like quarreling lovers.

Bond looked into the pretty, angry little face. "Good evening. Why do you want another picture of me?"

"I'm doing the night spots." The Cupid's bow of a mouth parted persuasively. "The first picture of you didn't come out. Tell this man to leave me alone."

"So you work for the *Gleaner*? What's your name?"

"I won't tell you."

Bond cocked an eyebrow at Quarrel.

Quarrel's hand behind the girl's back turned slowly. The girl struggled like an eel. Suddenly she said, "Ow!" sharply and gasped, "Annabel Chung."

Bond said to Quarrel, "Call the Pus-Feller."

Quarrel picked up a fork with his free hand and clanged it against a glass. The Pus-Feller hurried up. "Ever seen this girl before?" Bond asked.

"Yes, boss. She come here sometimes. She bein' a nuisance? Want for me to send her away?"

"No. We like her," said Bond amiably, "but she wants to take a studio portrait of me and I don't know if she's worth the money. Would you call up the *Gleaner* and ask if they've got a photographer called Annabel Chung? If she really is one of their people, she ought to be good enough."

"Sure, boss." The man hurried away.

Bond smiled at the girl. "I'm sorry to exert pressure," he said, "but my export manager in London said that Kingston was full of shady characters. I'm sure you're not one of them, but I really can't understand why you're so anxious to get my picture. Tell me why."

"What I told you," said the girl sulkily. "It's my job."

The Pus-Feller came up. "That's right, boss. Annabel Chung. One of their free-lance girls. They say she takes fine pictures."

"Thanks," said Bond. The man went away. Bond turned back to the girl. "Free lance," he said softly. "That still doesn't explain who wanted my picture." His face went cold. "Now give!"

"No," said the girl sullenly.

"All right, Quarrel. Go ahead." Bond sat back. If he could get the answer out of the girl, he might be saved weeks of legwork.

Quarrel's right shoulder dipped downwards. The girl squirmed to ease the pressure. She hissed out words in Chinese. Sweat beaded on her forehead.

"Tell," said Bond softly. "Tell, and it will stop and we'll be friends and have a drink." He was getting worried. The girl's arm must be on the verge of breaking.

"Damn you." Suddenly the girl's left hand flew up into Quarrel's face. Bond was too slow to stop her. Something glinted and there was a sharp explosion. Blood streamed down Quarrel's cheek. She had smashed the flashbulb on his face. If she had been able to reach an eye, it would have been blinded.

Quarrel's free hand felt his cheek. He put it in front of his eyes and looked at the blood. "Aha!" There was admiration in his voice. He said equably to Bond, "We get nuthen out of dis gal, cap'n. She tough. You want me to break she's arm?"

"Good God, no. Let her go." Bond felt angry with himself for having hurt the girl and still failed. But he had learned something. Whoever was behind her held his people by a steel chain.

Quarrel brought the girl's right arm from behind her back. He still held on to the wrist. Suddenly he let go. The girl shot to her feet and backed away from the table. She hissed furiously, "He'll get you, you bastards!" Then, her Leica dangling, she ran off through the trees.

Quarrel laughed shortly. He took a napkin and wiped it down his cheek and threw it on the ground and took up another. He said to Bond, "Dat a fine piece of woman, you know dat, cap'n? I tink I come back after dat gal sometime."

Appropriately the band started playing "Don' Touch Me Tomato." Bond said, "Quarrel, you leave that girl alone or you'll get a knife between your ribs. Now come on. We'll get the check. It's three o'clock in the morning in London, where I was yesterday. I need sleep. You've got to start getting me into training. I'm not as fit as I ought to be. And it's time you put something on that cheek of yours."

Quarrel grunted reminiscently. He said with quiet pleasure, "Dat were some tough baby." He picked up a fork and clanged it against his glass.

"He'll get you, you bastards." The words were still ringing in Bond's brain the next day as he sat on his balcony and ate breakfast. Now he was sure that Strangways and the girl had been killed. Someone had needed to stop them looking any further into his business, so he had killed them and destroyed the records of what they were investigating. The same person knew that the Secret Service would follow up Strangways' disappearance. Somehow he had known that Bond had been given the job. He had wanted a picture of Bond and he wanted to know where Bond was staying. He would be keeping an eye on Bond to see if Bond picked up any of the leads that had led to Strangways' death. If Bond did so, Bond also would have to be eliminated. And how, Bond wondered, would this person react to their treatment of the Chung girl? If he was as ruthless as Bond supposed, that would be enough. It showed that Bond was on to something. Perhaps someone had leaked. The enemy would be foolish to take chances. If he had any sense, after the Chung incident he would deal with Bond and perhaps also with Quarrel without delay.

Bond lit his first cigarette of the day. Now, who was this enemy? Well, there was only one candidate, and a pretty insubstantial one, Doctor No, Doctor Julius No, the German-Chinese who owned Crab Key. There had been nothing on this man in Records, and a signal to the FBI had been negative. The affair of the roseate spoonbills and the trouble with the Audubon Society meant precisely nothing except, as M. had said, that a lot of old women had got excited about some pink storks. All the same, four people had died, and, most significant to Bond, Quarrel was scared of Doctor No and his island. That was very odd indeed. Cayman Islanders, least of all Quarrel, did not scare easily. And why did Doctor No have this mania for privacy? Why did he go to such trouble to keep people away from his guano island? Guano—bird dung. How valuable was it? Bond was due to call on the governor at ten o'clock. After that he would get hold of the Colonial Secretary and try and find out all about the damned stuff and about Crab Key and, if possible, about Doctor No.

There was a double knock on the door. Bond got up and unlocked it. It was Quarrel, his left cheek decorated with adhesive tape. "Mornin', cap'n. You said eight tirty."

"Yes, come on in, Quarrel. We've got a busy day. Had some breakfast?"

"Yes, tank you, cap'n. Salt fish an' a tot of rum."

"That's tough stuff to start the day on," said Bond.

"Mos' refreshin'," said Quarrel stolidly.

They sat down outside on the balcony. "Now then." Bond offered Quarrel a cigarette and lit one himself. He said, "I'll be spending most of the day at King's House and perhaps at the Institute of Jamaica. I shan't need you till tomorrow, but there are some things for you to do downtown. All right?"

"Okay, cap'n. Jes' yo say."

"First of all, that car of ours. We've got to get rid of it. Go down to one of the hire people and pick up the newest and best little self-drive car you can find. A sedan. Take it for a month. Then hunt around the waterfront and find two men who look as near as possible like us. One must be able to drive a car. Buy them both clothes that look like ours. And the sort of hats we might wear. Say we want a car taken over to Montego tomorrow morning—by the Spanish Town–Ocho Rios road. To be left at Levy's garage there. Right?"

Quarrel grinned. "Yo want fox someone?"

"That's right. They'll get ten pounds each. Say I'm a rich American and I want my car to arrive in Montego Bay driven by a respectable couple of men. Make me out a bit mad. They must be here at six o'clock tomorrow morning. You'll be here with the other car. See they look the part and send them off in the Sunbeam with the roof down. Right?"

"Okay, cap'n."

"What's happened to that house we had on the north shore last time—Beau Desert at Morgan's Harbour? Do you know if it's let?"

"Couldn't say, cap'n. Hit's well away from the tourist places, and dey askin' a big rent for it."

"Well, go to Graham Associates and see if you can rent it for a month, or another bungalow nearby. I don't mind what you pay. Say it's for a rich American, Mr. James. Get the keys and pay the rent." Bond reached into his hip pocket and brought out a wad of notes. "Here's two hundred pounds. Get in touch if you want some more. You know where I'll be."

"Tanks, cap'n," said Quarrel. He stowed the notes away inside his blue shirt. "Anyting helse?"

"No, but take a lot of trouble about not being followed." Bond got up and they went to the door. "See you tomorrow morning at six."

Half an hour later Bond took a taxi to King's House. An A.D.C. took him to the governor's study. It was a large cool room smelling of cigar smoke. The acting governor, in a cream tussah suit and wing collar with spotted bow tie, was sitting at a broad mahogany desk on which there was nothing but the *Daily Gleaner* and a bowl of hibiscus blossoms. He was sixtyish, with a red petulant face and bright, bitter blue eyes. He didn't smile or get up. He said, "Good morning, Mr.—er—Bond. Please sit down."

Bond said, "Good morning, sir," took the chair across the desk from the governor and waited. A friend at the Colonial Office had told him his reception would be frigid. "He's nearly at retiring age. Only an interim appointment. All he wants is to retire and get some directorships in the City. Last thing he wants is any trouble in Jamaica. He keeps on trying to close this Strangways case of yours. Won't like you ferreting about."

The governor cleared his throat. He recognized that Bond wasn't one of the servile ones. "You wanted to see me?"

"Just to make my number, sir," said Bond equably. "I'm here on the Strangways case. I think you had a wire from the Secretary of State."

"I recall the wire. What can I do for you? So far as we're concerned here, the case is closed."

"In what way closed, sir?"

The governor said, "Strangways obviously skipped out with the girl. Some of your—er—colleagues don't seem to be able to leave women alone." The governor clearly included Bond. "Had to bail the chap out of various scandals before now. Doesn't do the colony any good, Mr.—er—Bond. Hope your people will be sending us a rather better type of man to take his place. That is," he added coldly, "if a regional control man is really needed here. Personally I have every confidence in our police."

Bond smiled sympathetically. "I'll report your views, sir. I expect my chief will want to discuss them with the Minister of Defense and the Secretary of State. Naturally, if you would like to take over these extra duties, it will be a saving in manpower so far as my Service is concerned."

The governor looked at Bond suspiciously. Perhaps he had better handle this man a bit more carefully. "This is an informal discussion, Mr. Bond. When I have decided on my views I will communicate them myself to the Secretary of State. In the meantime, is there anyone you wish to see on my staff?"

"I'd like to have a word with the Colonial Secretary, sir."

"Really? And why, pray?"

"There's been some trouble on Crab Key. Something about a bird sanctuary. The case was passed to us by the Colonial Office. My chief asked me to look into it while I'm here."

The governor looked relieved. "Certainly, certainly. I'll see that Mr. Pleydell-Smith receives you straightaway. So you feel we can leave the Strangways case to sort itself out? They'll turn up before long, never fear." He reached over and rang a bell. The A.D.C. came in. "This gentleman would like to see the Colonial Secretary, A.D.C. Take him along to Mr. Pleydell-Smith, would you?" He got up and held out his hand. "Good-by then, Mr. Bond. And I'm so glad we see eye to eye. Crab Key, eh? Never been there myself, but I'm sure it would be worth a visit."

Bond shook hands. "That's what I was thinking. Good-by, sir."

The Colonial Secretary was a youngish shaggy-haired man with bright boyish eyes. He was one of those nervous pipe smokers who are constantly patting their pockets for matches, or knocking ashes out of their pipes.

After pumping Bond's hand and waving vaguely at a chair, Pleydell-Smith walked up and down the room, scratching at his temple. "Bond. Bond! Rings a bell. Yes, by Jove! You were the chap who was mixed up in that treasure business here. By Jove, yes! Four, five years ago. Found the file lying around only the other day. What a lark! I say, wish you'd start another bonfire like that here. Stir the place up a bit. All they think of nowadays is federation and self-determination." Pleydell-Smith sat down opposite Bond and draped a leg over the arm of his chair. "However, I don't want to bore you with all that. What's your problem? Glad to help."

Bond grinned at him. This was more like it. He had found an ally. "Well," he said, "I'm here on the Strangways case. But first of all—how did you come to be looking at that other case of mine? You say you found the file lying about. How was that? Had someone asked for it? I don't want to be indiscreet, I'm just inquisitive."

"I suppose that's your job." Pleydell-Smith reflected, gazing at the ceiling. "Come to think of it, I saw it on my secretary's desk. She's new. Said she was trying to get up to date with the files. Mark you"—the Colonial Secretary hastened to exonerate his girl—"there were plenty of other files on her desk. It was just this one that caught my eye."

"Oh, I see," said Bond. He smiled apologetically. "Sorry, but various people seem to be rather interested in my being here. What I really wanted to talk to you about was Crab Key. Anything you know about the place. And about this Chinaman, Doctor No, who bought it. And anything you can tell me about his guano business. A tall order, I'm afraid, but any scraps will help."

Pleydell-Smith laughed through the stem of his pipe. "Bitten off a bit more than you can chew on guano. Talk to you for hours about it. First job was in the Consular Service, in Peru. Had a lot to do with their people who administer the whole trade." He fished for his matchbox. "As for the rest, it's just a question of getting the file." He rang a bell. The door opened behind Bond. "Miss Taro, the file on Crab Key, please. The one on the sale of the place and the other one on that warden fellow who turned up before Christmas. Miss Longfellow will know where to find them."

A soft voice said, "Yes, sir." Bond heard the door close.

"Now then, guano." Pleydell-Smith tilted his chair back. "As you know, it's bird dung. Comes from two birds, the masked booby and the guanay. So far as Crab Key is concerned, it's only the guanay, otherwise known as the white-breasted cormorant. The guanay is a machine for converting fish into guano. They mostly eat anchovies. They've found up to seventy anchovies inside one bird!"

Bond pursed his lips to show he was impressed. "Really."

"Well, now," continued the Colonial Secretary, "every day each one of these hundreds of thousands of guanays eats a pound or so of fish and deposits an ounce of guano on the *guanera*—that's the guano place."

Bond interrupted. "Why don't they do it in the sea?"

"Don't know." Pleydell-Smith turned the question over in his mind. "Never occurred to me. Anyway, they don't. They do it on the land, and they've been doing it since before Genesis. Around 1850 someone discovered it was the greatest natural fertilizer in the world. And the ships and the men came to the *guaneras* and ravaged them for twenty years or more. It was like the Klondike. People fought over the muck, hijacked each other's ships, shot workers and the like. And people made fortunes out of the stuff."

"Where does Crab Key come in?"

"That was the only *guanera* so far north. But the stuff had a low nitrate content. Water's not as rich round here as it is along the Humboldt Current. So the guano isn't so rich either. Crab Key got worked on and off when the price was high enough, but the whole industry went bust when the Germans invented artificial chemical manure. Then people found that there were snags about the German stuff—it impoverishes the soil, which guano doesn't do—and gradually the price of guano improved and the industry staggered back to its feet. Now it's going fine, except that Peru nationalized her industry and keeps most of the guano to herself, for her own agriculture. And that was where Crab Key came in again."

"Ah."

"Yes," said Pleydell-Smith, patting his pockets for the matches, finding them on the desk, shaking them against his ear and starting his pipe-filling routine. "At the beginning of the war, this Chinaman got the idea that he could make a good thing of the old *guanera* on Crab Key. The price was about fifty dollars a ton this side of the Atlantic, so he bought the island from us, for about ten thousand pounds, as I recall it, and brought in labor. Been working it ever since. Must have made a fortune. He ships direct to Europe—to Antwerp. They send him a ship once a month. He's installed the latest crushers and separators. But God knows what he must pay his labor to make a decent profit at the present price—less than forty dollars a ton in Antwerp. He runs that place like a fortress—sort of forced-labor camp. No one ever gets off it. I've heard some funny rumors, but no one's ever complained. It's his island, of course, and he can do what he likes on it."

Bond hunted for clues. "Would it really be so valuable to him, this place? What do you suppose it's worth?"

Pleydell-Smith said, "The guanay is the most valuable bird in the world. Each pair produces about two dollars' worth of guano in a year, without any expense to the owner. Say they're worth fifteen dollars a pair, and say there are one hundred thousand birds on Crab Key—a reasonable guess. That makes his birds worth a million and a half dollars. Add the value of the installations and you've got a small fortune on that hideous little place. Which reminds me"—Pleydell-Smith pressed the bell—"what the hell has happened to those files? You'll find all the dope you want in them."

The door opened behind Bond. Pleydell-Smith said irritably, "Really, Miss Taro. What about those files?"

"Very sorry, sir," said the soft voice. "But we can't find them."

"What do you mean, can't find them? Who had them last?"

"Commander Strangways, sir."

"Well, I remember distinctly him bringing them back to this room. What happened to them then?"

"Can't say, sir." The voice was unemotional. "The covers are there but there's nothing inside them."

Bond turned in his chair. He glanced at the girl and turned back. He smiled grimly to himself. He knew where the files had gone. He also guessed how the particular significance of "James Bond, import and export merchant," seemed to have leaked out of King's House.

Like Doctor No, like Miss Annabel Chung, the demure little secretary in the horn-rimmed glasses was a Chinese.

Chapter 4

THE Colonial Secretary gave Bond lunch at Queen's Club. They sat in the mahogany-paneled dining room and gossiped about Jamaica. By the time coffee came, Pleydell-Smith was delving well below the surface of the prosperous, peaceful island the world knows.

"It's like this." He began his antics with the pipe. "The Jamaican is a kindly man with the virtues and vices of a child. He lives on a very rich island, but he doesn't get rich from it. He doesn't know how to. The British come and take the easy pickings, then leave. It's the Portuguese who make the most. They came here with the British, but they've stayed. However, they're snobs, and they spend too much of their fortunes on building fine houses and giving dances. Then come the Syrians, very rich, too, but not such good businessmen. They have most of the stores and some of the best hotels. They're not a very good risk. Get overstocked and have to have an occasional fire to get liquid again. Then there are the Indians, with their usual flashy trade in soft goods and the like. Finally there are the Chinese, solid, compact, discreet—the most powerful clique in Jamaica. They've got the bakeries and the laundries and the best food stores. They keep to themselves and keep their strain pure." Pleydell-Smith laughed. "Not that they don't take the black girls when they want them. You can see the result all over Kingston—Chigroes—Chinese Negroes. The Chigroes are a tough, forgotten race. One day they may become a nuisance."

Bond said, "That secretary of yours. Would she be one?"

"That's right. Bright girl and very efficient. Had her for about six months."

"She looks bright," said Bond noncommittally.

Pleydell-Smith glanced at his watch. "That reminds me. Must be getting along. Got to go and read the riot act about those files. Can't think what happened to them—" He broke off. "However, main point is that I haven't been able to give you much dope about Crab Key and this doctor fellow. But I can tell you there wasn't much you'd have found out from the files. He seems to have been a pleasant-spoken chap. Very businesslike. Then there

was that argument with the Audubon Society. I gather you know
all about that. As for the place itself, there was nothing on the
files but one or two prewar reports and a copy of the last ordnance
survey. Godforsaken bloody place, it sounds. Nothing but miles of
mangrove swamps and a huge mountain of bird dung at one end.
But why don't I take you down to the institute and introduce you
to the fellow who runs the map section?"

AN HOUR later Bond was ensconced in a corner of a somber
room at the Institute of Jamaica with the ordnance survey map
of Crab Key, dated 1910, spread out on a table.

The overall area of the island was about fifty square miles.
Three-quarters of this, to the east, was swamp and shallow lake.
From the lake a flat river meandered down to the sea and came
out halfway along the south coast into a small sandy bay. Bond
guessed that somewhere at the headwaters of the river would be
a likely spot for the Audubon wardens to have chosen for their
camp. To the west the island rose steeply to a hill five hundred
feet high and ended abruptly with what appeared to be a sheer
drop to the sea. A dotted line led from this hill to the words GUANO
DEPOSITS. LAST WORKINGS 1880. There was no sign of a road
or even of a track on the island and no sign of a house. The relief
map showed that the island looked rather like a swimming water
rat—a flat spine rising sharply to the head—heading west. It appeared
to be about thirty miles north of Jamaica and about sixty miles
south of Cuba.

Little else could be gleaned from the map. Bond handed it in
to the librarian. Suddenly he felt exhausted. It was only four o'clock,
but it was roasting in Kingston and his shirt was sticking to him.
Bond found a taxi and went back up into the cool hills to his
hotel. Nothing else could be done on this side of the island. He
would spend a quiet evening and be ready to get up early next
morning and be away.

At the reception desk, Bond inquired if there was a message
from Quarrel. "No messages, sir," said the girl. "But a basket of
fruit came from King's House. The messenger took it to your room."

"Thank you." He took his key and went upstairs. It was ridiculously improbable. His hand on his gun, Bond softly approached his door. He turned the key and kicked the door open. The empty room yawned at him. On his dressing table was a large ornate basket of fruit—tangerines, grapefruit, pink bananas and even nectarines. Attached to the handle was a white envelope. Bond opened it. On expensive writing paper was typed: "With the compliments of His Excellency the Governor."

Bond snorted. He stood looking at the fruit. He bent his ear to it and listened. He then took the basket and tipped its contents onto the floor. There was nothing but fruit in the basket. Bond grinned at his precautions. There was a last possibility. He picked up a nectarine and took it into the bathroom. He dropped it in the washbasin and went back to the bedroom and unlocked the wardrobe. Gingerly he lifted out his suitcase and stood it in the middle of the room. He knelt down and looked for the traces of talcum powder he had dusted round the two locks. They were smeared, and there were minute scratches round the keyholes. Bond examined the marks. These people were not as careful as some others he had had to deal with. He unlocked the case. There were four innocent copper studs in the welting at a corner of the lid. Bond pried out one of these studs with his nail. He took hold of it and pulled out three feet of thick steel wire. This wire threaded through small wire loops inside the lid and sewed the case shut. Bond lifted the lid and verified that nothing had been disturbed. From his tool case he took out a jeweler's glass and went back into the bathroom. He screwed the glass into his eye and gingerly picked up the nectarine, revolving it between finger and thumb.

Bond stopped turning the nectarine. He had come to a minute pinhole, its edges faintly discolored. It was in the crevice of the fruit, invisible except under a magnifying glass. Bond put the nectarine down in the basin.

So it *was* war! Well, well. Very interesting. Bond smiled at his reflection in the mirror. So his instincts had been correct. Strangways and the girl had been murdered because they had got too hot on the trail. Then Bond had come on the scene and, thanks to Miss

539

Taro, they had been waiting for him. He had been traced to the Blue Hills hotel. The first shot had been fired. There would be others. And whose finger was on the trigger? Who had him so accurately in his sights? The evidence was nil. But Bond's mind was made up. This was long-range fire from Crab Key. The man behind the gun was Doctor No.

Bond walked back into the bedroom. One by one he picked up the fruit and examined each piece through his glass. The pinprick was always there. Bond rang down and asked for a cardboard box. He packed the fruit in the box and telephoned the Colonial Secretary. "That you, Pleydell-Smith? James Bond speaking. Sorry to bother you. Got a bit of a problem. Is there a chemist's laboratory in Kingston? I see. Well, I've got something I want analyzed. If I sent the box down to you, would you be kind enough to pass it on? I don't want my name to come into this. When you get the report would you send me a telegram telling me the answer? I'll be at Beau Desert, over at Morgan's Harbour. Be glad if you'd keep this to yourself. Many thanks. Lucky I met you this morning. Good-by."

Bond addressed the parcel and went down and paid a taxi to deliver it at once to King's House. It was six o'clock. He went back to his room and had a. shower and ordered a drink. He was about to take it out on the balcony when the telephone rang. It was Quarrel.

"Everyting fixed, cap'n."

"Everything? That's wonderful. That house all right?"

"Everyting okay," Quarrel repeated, his voice careful. "Just as yo done said, cap'n."

"Fine," said Bond.

He put down the telephone and went out onto the balcony. The sun was setting. The wave of violet shadow was creeping down towards the town and the harbor. Bond drank his drink and thought over the details of his plan. Then he went down and had dinner in the half-deserted dining room and read the *Handbook of the West Indies*. By nine o'clock he was nearly asleep. He went back to his room and arranged to be called at five thirty. Then he bolted the door on the inside, and also shut and bolted the slatted jalousies across the windows. It would mean a hot stuffy night. That couldn't be helped. Bond climbed naked under the single sheet and turned over on his left side and slipped his right hand onto the butt of the Walther PPK under the pillow. In five minutes he was asleep.

THE next thing Bond knew was that it was three o'clock in the morning. He knew it was three because the luminous dial of his watch was close to his face. He lay absolutely still. There was not a sound in the room. Outside, too, it was deathly quiet. The moon coming through the slats in the jalousies threw black and white bars across the corner of the room next to his bed. It was as if he were lying in a cage. What had woken him up? Bond moved softly, preparing to slip out of bed.

Bond stopped moving. He stopped as dead as a live man can.

Something had stirred on his right ankle. Now it was moving up the inside of his shin. Bond could feel the hairs on his leg being parted. It was an insect of some sort. A very long one, five or six inches—as long as his hand. He could feel dozens of tiny feet touching his skin. What was it?

The thing on his leg moved again. Suddenly Bond realized that he was afraid, terrified. His instincts, even before they had communicated with his brain, had told his body that he had a centipede on him.

Bond lay frozen. He had once seen a tropical centipede in a bottle of alcohol in a museum. It had been pale brown and flat and five or six inches long. On either side of the blunt head there had been curved poisonous claws. The label on the bottle had said that its poison was mortal if it hit an artery. Bond had looked curiously at it and had moved on.

The centipede had reached his knee. It was starting up his thigh. Whatever happened he mustn't move, mustn't even tremble. Bond's whole consciousness had drained down to the two rows of creeping feet. Now they had reached his flank. God, it was turning down towards his groin! Supposing it liked the warmth there! Could he stand it? Bond could feel it questing among the first hairs. It tickled. The skin on Bond's belly fluttered. There was nothing he could do to control it. But now the thing was turning up and along his stomach. Now it was at his heart. If it bit there, surely it would kill him.

The centipede trampled steadily on, through the thin hairs on Bond's right breast up to his collarbone. It stopped. What was it doing? Bond could feel the blunt head questing blindly to and fro. Then the animal was at the base of his jugular. Perhaps it was intrigued by the pulse. God, if only he could control the pumping of his blood. Damn you! Bond tried to communicate with the centipede. It's nothing. It's not dangerous, that pulse. It means no harm. Get out!

As if the beast had heard, it moved on up the column of the neck and into the stubble on Bond's chin. Now it was at the corner of his mouth, tickling madly. On it went, up along the nose. Softly Bond closed his eyes. Two by two the pairs of feet, moving alternately, trampled across his right eyelid.

Then with incredible deliberation it ambled across Bond's forehead. It stopped below the hair. What the hell was it doing now? Bond could feel it nuzzling at his skin. It was drinking! Drinking the beads of sweat. Bond felt weak with the tension. In a second his limbs would start to tremble. He lay and waited, the breath coming softly through his open, snarling mouth.

The centipede started to move again. It walked into the forest of hair. Bond could feel the roots being pushed aside as it forced its way along. Would it like it there? Would it settle down? How did centipedes sleep? Curled up or at full length? Now it had come to where his head lay against the sheet. Would it walk out onto the pillow or would it stay on in the warm forest? The centipede stopped. Out! OUT! Bond's nerves screamed at it.

The centipede stirred. Slowly it walked out of his hair onto the pillow.

Bond waited a second. Now he could hear the rows of feet picking softly at the cotton.

With a crash that shook the room Bond's body jackknifed out of bed and onto the floor.

At once Bond was on his feet. He turned on the light. He was shaking uncontrollably. He staggered to the bed. There it was, crawling over the edge of the pillow. Bond controlled himself, waiting for his nerves to quiet down. Then, deliberately, he picked up the pillow by one corner and walked into the middle of the room and dropped it. The centipede came out from under the pillow. Bond looked around for something to kill it with. Slowly he picked up a shoe. The danger was past. His mind was now wondering how the centipede had got into his bed. He lifted the shoe and smashed it down. He heard the crack of the hard carapace.

Bond lifted the shoe.

The centipede was whipping from side to side. Bond hit it again. It burst open yellowly.

Bond dropped the shoe and ran for the bathroom and was violently sick.

"BY THE way, Quarrel," Bond said as he drove, "what do you know about centipedes?"

"Centipedes, cap'n?" Quarrel squinted sideways at Bond. "Well, we got some bad ones here in Jamaica. Fo, five inches long. Dey kills folks. Why, cap'n? Yo seen one?"

Bond dodged the question. "Would you expect to find one in a modern house, for instance? In your shoe, or in a drawer, or in your bed?"

"No, sir." Quarrel's voice was definite. "Not hunless dem put dere a purpose. Dey dirty-livin' hinsecks. Mebbe yo find dem in de bush, under logs. But never in de bright places."

"I see." Bond changed the subject. "By the way, did those two men get off all right in the Sunbeam?"

"Sho ting, cap'n. Dey plenty happy wid de job. An' dey look plenty like yo an' me, cap'n." Quarrel chuckled. "I fears dey weren't very good citizens, cap'n. Me, I'm a beggarman, cap'n. An' fo you, cap'n, I get a miserable no-good white man from Betsy's."

"Who's Betsy?"

"She run de lousiest brothel in town."

Bond laughed. "So long as he can drive a car."

They were at the saddleback at Stony Hill where the Junction Road dives down through fifty S-bends towards the north shore. Bond put the Austin A30 into second gear and let it coast. The sun was coming up over the Blue Mountain peak, and shafts of gold lanced into the valley. There were few people on the road—an occasional man going off to his modest acreage on the flank of a steep hill, or a woman sauntering up the road with a covered basket of fruit or vegetables. It was a savage, peaceful scene.

"Cap'n," Quarrel said apologetically, "beggin' yo pardon, but kin yo tell me what yo have in mind for we? I'se bin puzzlin' an' Ah cain't seem to figger hout yo game."

"I've hardly figured it out myself, Quarrel." Bond shifted into high and dawdled through the cool, beautiful glades of Castleton Gardens. "I told you I'm here because Commander Strangways and his secretary have disappeared. I think they've been murdered."

"Dat so?" said Quarrel unemotionally. "Who yo tink done hit?"

"I think Doctor No, that Chinaman on Crab Key, had it done. Strangways was poking his nose into this man's affairs. Doctor No has this mania for privacy. You were telling me so yourself. Mark you, it's not more than a guess about Doctor No. But some funny things happened in the last twenty-four hours. That's why I sent the Sunbeam to Montego, to lay a false scent. And that's why we're going to hide out at Beau Desert for a few days."

"Den what, cap'n?"

"First of all I want you to get me absolutely fit—the way you trained me the last time I was here. Remember?"

"Sho, cap'n. Ah kin do dat ting."

"And then I was thinking you and me might go and take a look at Crab Key."

Quarrel whistled.

"Just sniff around. We needn't get too close to Doctor No's end. I want to take a look at this bird sanctuary. See the wardens' camp. If we find anything wrong, we'll get away again and come back by the front door—with soldiers to help. Have a full-dress inquiry. Can't do that until we've got something to go on. What do you think?"

Quarrel dug into his hip pocket for a cigarette. "Cap'n, Ah tink yo's plumb crazy to trespass hon dat island." He paused. There was no comment. Then, looking sideways at Bond, he said more quietly, in an embarrassed voice, "Jess one ting, cap'n. Ah have some folks back in de Caymans. Would yo consider takin' hout a life hinsurance hon me afore we sail?"

Bond glanced affectionately at the strong brown face. "Of course, Quarrel. I'll fix it at Port Maria. We'll make it big, say five thousand pounds. Now then, how shall we go? Canoe?"

"Dat's right, cap'n." Quarrel's voice was reluctant. "We need a calm sea an' a light wind. Come hin on de noreasterly trades. Mus' be a dark night. By end of de week we git de secon' moon quarter. Where you reckon to land, cap'n?"

"South shore, near the mouth of the river. Then we'll go up the river to the lake. I'm sure that's where the wardens' camp was. So as to have fresh water and be able to get down to the sea to fish."

Quarrel grunted without enthusiasm. "How long we stayin', cap'n? Cain't take a whole lot of food wit' us. Bread, cheese, salt pork. Dat's mighty rough country. Marsh an' mangrove."

Bond said, "Better plan for three days. Weather may break and stop us getting off for a night or two. Couple of good hunting knives. I'll take a gun. You never can tell."

"No, sir," said Quarrel emphatically. He lapsed into a brooding silence which lasted until they got to Port Maria.

They went through the little town and on round the headland to Morgan's Harbour. It was just as Bond remembered—the sugarloaf of the Isle of Surprise rising out of the calm bay, the canoes drawn up, the distant boom of the surf on the reef which had so nearly been his grave. Bond, his mind full of memories, took the car down the little side road and through the cane fields, in the middle of which stood the gaunt ruin of the old great house of Beau Desert plantation.

They came to the gate leading to the bungalow. Quarrel got out and opened the gate, and Bond drove through and pulled up in the yard behind the white single-storied house. It was very quiet.

Bond got out of the car and walked round the house and across the lawn to the edge of the sea. Yes, there it was, the stretch of deep, silent water—the submarine path he had taken to the Isle of Surprise. It sometimes came back to him in nightmares. Bond stood looking at it and thinking of Solitaire, the girl he had brought back, torn and bleeding, from that sea. Then he turned and walked back into the house.

It was eight thirty. Bond changed into sandals and shorts. Soon there was the delicious smell of coffee and frying bacon. They ate breakfast while Bond fixed his training routine—up at seven, swim a quarter of a mile, breakfast, an hour's sunbathing, run a mile, swim again, lunch, sleep, sunbathe, swim a mile, hot bath and massage, dinner and asleep by nine.

After breakfast the routine began.

Nothing interrupted the grinding week except a telegram from Pleydell-Smith and a brief story in the *Daily Gleaner*. The paper said that a Sunbeam Alpine, H 2473, had been involved in a fatal accident on the Devil's Racecourse, a stretch of winding road between Spanish Town and Ocho Rios on the Kingston-Montego route. A runaway lorry, whose driver was being traced, had crashed into the Sunbeam. Both vehicles had hurtled into a ravine. The two occupants of the Sunbeam, Ben Gibbons, of Harbour Street, and Josiah Smith, no address, had been killed. A Mr. Bond, an English visitor who had been lent the car, was asked to contact the police.

Bond burned that copy of the *Gleaner*. He didn't want to upset Quarrel.

The telegram from Pleydell-Smith said:

EACH OBJECT CONTAINED ENOUGH CYANIDE TO KILL A HORSE STOP SUGGEST YOU CHANGE YOUR GROCER STOP GOOD LUCK SMITH

Bond also burned the telegram.

Quarrel hired a canoe and they spent three days sailing it. It was a clumsy shell, with two thwarts, two heavy paddles and a small sail. Quarrel was pleased with it.

"Seven, eight hours, cap'n," he said. "Den we bring down de sail an' use de paddles. Less target for de radar to see."

The weather held. The nights were black as sin. The two men got in their stores. Bond fitted himself out with cheap black canvas jeans, a dark blue shirt and rope-soled shoes.

The last evening came. Bond was glad he was on his way. He admitted to himself that this adventure excited him. It had the right ingredients—physical exertion, mystery and a ruthless enemy. He had a good companion. His cause was just. There might also be the satisfaction of throwing the "bit of holiday" back in M.'s teeth. That had rankled.

The sun blazed beautifully into its grave.

Bond went into his bedroom and took out his two guns. Neither was a part of him as the Beretta had been—an extension of his right hand—but he already knew them as better weapons. Which should he take? Bond picked up each. It had to be the heavier Smith & Wesson. There would be no close shooting, if there was any shooting, on Crab Key. Heavy, long-range stuff—if anything. The brutal, stumpy revolver had an extra twenty-five yards over the Walther. Bond fitted the holster into the waistband of his jeans and clipped in the gun. He put twenty spare rounds in his pocket.

Then he took a pint of Canadian Club Blended Rye and some ice and went and sat in the garden and watched the last light flame and die.

The shadows crept from behind the house and marched across the lawn and enveloped him. The wind that blew at night from the center of the island clattered softly in the tops of the palm trees. For a moment the melancholy of the tropical dusk caught at Bond's heart. He poured a big slug into his glass.

Quarrel came up from the beach. "Time, cap'n."

Bond swallowed his drink and followed the Cayman Islander down to the canoe. It was in the water, its bows on the sand. Quarrel went aft and Bond climbed into the bows. The sail, wrapped round the short mast, was at his back. Bond took up his paddle and pushed off, and they turned and headed out for the break in the creaming waves that was the passage through the reef. They paddled easily, in unison, the paddles turning in their hands so as not to leave the water on the forward stroke. The small waves slapped softly against the bows. Otherwise they made no noise. It was dark. Nobody saw them go.

Bond's only duty was to keep paddling. Quarrel did the steering. At the opening through the reef there was a swirl and suck of conflicting currents. Then they were through, and all around them was the solid oily feel of deep water.

"Okay, cap'n," said Quarrel softly. Bond shipped his paddle. He heard the scratching of Quarrel's nails against canvas as he unwrapped the sail and then the sharp flap as it caught the breeze. The canoe

straightened and began to move. There was a soft hiss under the bows. A handful of spray tossed up into Bond's face. The wind of their movement was cool and would soon get cold. Bond hunched up his knees and put his arms round them. It crossed his mind that it was going to be the hell of a long night.

In the darkness ahead Bond could just make out the rim of the world. Above it the stars began, first sparsely and then merging into a dense bright carpet. Bond looked back. Behind the figure of Quarrel there was a faraway cluster of lights, which would be

Port Maria. Already they were a couple of miles out. Soon they would be a tenth of the way, then a quarter, then half. That would be around midnight, when Bond would take over. Bond sighed and put his head down to his knees and closed his eyes.

He must have slept, because he was awakened by the clonk of a paddle against the boat. He glanced at the luminous blaze of his watch. Twelve fifteen. Stiffly he unbent and turned and scrambled over the thwart.

"Sorry, Quarrel," he said. "You ought to have woken me."

"Hit don' signify, cap'n," said Quarrel with a gray glint of teeth. "Do yo good to sleep."

Gingerly they slipped past each other, and Bond settled in the stern and picked up the paddle. The sail was secured to a bent nail beside him. It was flapping. Bond brought the bows into the wind. For a time this would be fun. There was something to do.

There was no change in the night except that it seemed darker and emptier. The pulse of the sleeping sea seemed slower. The heavy swell was longer. They were running through a patch of phosphorus that dripped jewels when Bond lifted the paddle. How safe it was, slipping through the night in this ridiculous little boat. How kind and soft the sea could be.

One o'clock, two o'clock, three, four. Quarrel awoke and called softly to Bond, "Ah smells land, cap'n." Soon there was a thickening of the darkness ahead. The low shadow slowly took on the shape of a huge swimming rat. A pale moon rose slowly behind them. Now the island showed distinctly, and there was the distant grumble of surf.

They changed places. Quarrel brought down the sail, and they took up the paddles. For at least another mile, thought Bond, they would be invisible in the troughs of the waves. No radar could distinguish them. It was the last mile they would have to hurry over, with the dawn not far off. He could make out the white fringe of surf. The waves became choppier. "Now, cap'n," called Quarrel, and Bond dug deeper and more often. God, it was hard work! Bond's shoulders were aching like fire. The knee he was resting on was beginning to bruise.

It was incredible, but they were coming up with the reef. The surf was a roar. They followed along the edge of the reef, looking for an opening. A hundred yards inside, breaking the sand line, was the shimmer of water running inland. The river! So the landfall had been all right. The wall of surf broke up. There was a patch of black oily current. The nose of the canoe turned towards it and into it. There was a turmoil of water and then a sudden rush forward into peace, and the canoe was moving across a smooth mirror towards the shore.

Quarrel steered the boat towards the lee of a rocky promontory. Bond wondered why the beach didn't shine white under the thin moon. When they grounded and Bond climbed out he understood why. The sand was black, though it was soft to the feet.

They made haste. Quarrel took three short lengths of thick bamboo out of the boat and laid them up the beach. They heaved the nose of the canoe onto the first and pushed the boat up the rollers. Slowly the canoe moved up the sand until at last it was over the back tide line and among rocks and sea-grape bushes. They pushed it another twenty yards inland into the mangrove. There they covered it with dried seaweed and bits of driftwood. Then Quarrel cut screw palm and went back over their tracks, sweeping and tidying.

It was still dark, but the east would soon be turning to pearl. It was five o'clock. They were dead tired. They exchanged a few words and Quarrel went off among the rocks on the promontory. Bond scooped out a depression in the fine dry sand under a bush of sea grape. There he lay down in the sand and rested his head on his arm.

He was at once asleep.

Chapter 5

BOND awoke lazily. The feel of the sand reminded him where he was. He glanced at his watch. Ten o'clock. The sun through the round thick leaves of the sea grape was already hot. A larger shadow moved across the dappled sand in front of his face. Quarrel? Bond peered through the fringe of leaves and grass that concealed

him from the beach. He stiffened, and his heart missed a beat and
then began pounding.

It was a girl, with her back to him. She was almost entirely
naked. She wore only a broad leather belt round her waist, with
a hunting knife in a leather sheath at her right hip. She stood
five yards away on the tide line, looking down at something in
her hand, standing in the classic relaxed pose of the nude, the
weight on the right leg, and the left knee bent slightly inwards.

It was a beautiful back. The skin was a very light uniform café

au lait, with the sheen of dull satin. The legs were straight and
beautiful, with no pinkness showing under the lifted heel.

Her hair was ash blond, and hung below her shoulders and along
the sides of her cheeks in thick wet strands. A green diving mask
was pushed back above her forehead.

The whole scene—the beach, the sea, the girl—reminded Bond
of something. He searched his mind. Yes, she was Botticelli's Venus,
seen from behind.

How had she got there? What was she doing? Bond looked up

and down the beach. It was not black, he now saw, but a deep brown. To the right he could see as far as the river mouth, five hundred yards away. The beach was empty and featureless except for a scattering of small pinkish objects—shells of some sort, Bond supposed. He looked to the left, to where, twenty yards away, the rocks of the small headland began. Yes, there was a yard or two of groove in the sand where a canoe had been drawn up into the shelter of the rocks. It must have been a light one or she couldn't have drawn it up alone. Perhaps the girl wasn't alone. But there was only one set of footprints leading down from the rocks to the sea and another set coming up the beach to where she now stood on the tide line. Did she live here, or had she, too, sailed over from Jamaica that night? What in God's name *was* she doing here?

As if to answer him, the girl made a throwaway gesture of the right hand and scattered a dozen shells on the sand. They were violet pink and seemed to Bond to be the same as he had noticed on the beach. The girl looked down into her left hand and began to whistle happily to herself. She was whistling "Marion," a plaintive little calypso. It went:

> "All day, all night, Marion,
> Sittin' by the seaside siftin' sand—"

The girl broke off to stretch her arms out in a deep yawn. Bond smiled to himself. He wet his lips and took up the refrain:

> "The water from her eyes could sail a boat,
> The hair on her head could tie a goat. . . ."

The hands flew down and the girl whirled about. One hand went to cover her body, and one hand went to her face, covering it below the eyes, wide with fear. "Who's that?" The words came out in a terrified whisper.

Bond got to his feet and stepped out through the sea grape. He held his hands open to show they were empty. He smiled cheerfully. "It's only me. I'm another trespasser. Don't be frightened."

The girl dropped her hand down from her face to the knife at her belt. Bond watched the fingers curl round the hilt. He looked at her face. It was a beautiful face, with a wide mouth and wide-apart, deep blue eyes under lashes paled by the sun. It was a serious face and the jawline was determined—the face of a girl who fends for herself. But once, reflected Bond, she had failed to fend. For the nose was badly broken, smashed crooked like a boxer's. Bond stiffened with revolt at what had happened to this supremely beautiful girl.

The eyes examined him fiercely. "Who are you? What are you doing here?" There was the lilt of a Jamaican accent. The voice was sharp, accustomed to being obeyed.

"I'm an Englishman. I'm interested in birds."

"Oh." The voice was doubtful. "How long have you been watching me? How did you get here?"

"Ten minutes—but no more answers until you tell me who *you* are."

"I'm no one in particular. I come from Jamaica. I collect shells."

"I came in a canoe. Did you?"

"Yes. Where is your canoe?"

"I've got a friend with me. We've hidden it in the mangroves."

"There are no marks of a canoe landing."

"We're careful. We covered them up. Not like you. You ought to take more trouble. Did you use a sail? Right up to the reef?"

"Of course. Why not? I always do."

"Then they'll know you're here. They've got radar."

"They've never caught me yet." The girl took her hand away from her knife. She seemed to think she had the measure of Bond. She said, "What's your name?"

"Bond. James Bond. What's yours?"

She reflected. "Rider."

"What Rider?"

"Honeychile."

Bond smiled.

"What's so funny about it?"

"Nothing. Honeychile Rider. It's a pretty name."

She unbent. "People call me Honey."

"Well, I'm glad to meet you."

The prosaic phrase seemed to remind her of her nakedness. She blushed. She said uncertainly, "I must get dressed." She looked down at the scattered shells round her feet and said sharply, "You're not to touch those while I'm gone."

Bond smiled at the childish challenge. "Don't worry, I'll look after them."

The girl walked over to the rocks and disappeared behind them. Bond bent and picked up one of the shells. It was alive, and the two halves were shut tight. It appeared to be some kind of a cockle, ribbed, and colored a mauve pink. Along both edges of the hinge thin horns stood out. It didn't seem to Bond a very distinguished shell. He replaced it carefully and stood wondering. Was she really collecting shells? But what a risk to take to get them—the voyage over alone in the canoe. And she seemed to realize that this was a dangerous place. "They've never caught me yet." What an extraordinary girl!

Bond's heart warmed and his senses stirred as he thought of her. Already, as he had found so often when people had deformities, he had almost forgotten her broken nose. Where did she live? Who were her parents? There was something uncared for about her—a dog that nobody wants to pet. Who was she?

Bond heard her footsteps. He turned to look. She was dressed almost in rags—a faded brown shirt with torn sleeves and a knee-length patched brown cotton skirt, held in place by the belt with the knife. She had a canvas knapsack slung over one shoulder. She looked like an actress dressed as Robinson Crusoe's man, Friday.

She went down on one knee and began picking up shells and stowing them in the knapsack. Bond said, "Are those rare?"

She sat back and looked up, surveying his face. Apparently she was satisfied. "You promise you won't tell anybody? Swear?"

"I promise," said Bond.

"Well, then, yes, they are rare. Very. You can get five dollars for a perfect specimen. In Miami. That's where I deal. They're called *Venus elegans*—the elegant Venus." Her eyes sparkled with excitement. "This morning I found what I wanted. The bed where they live." She waved towards the sea. "You wouldn't find it though," she added with sudden carefulness. "It's very deep and hidden."

Bond laughed. "I promise I won't steal any. I really don't know anything about shells. Cross my heart."

She stood up. "What about these birds of yours? Are they valuable too? I won't tell either, if you tell me."

"They're called roseate spoonbills," said Bond. "Sort of pink stork with a flat beak. Ever seen any?"

"Oh, *those*," she said scornfully. "There used to be thousands here. But you won't find many now. They scared them all away." She sat down on the sand and put her arms round her knees.

Bond sat down a yard away. He said, "Oh, really? What happened? Who did it?"

She shrugged. "The people here. I don't know who they are. There's a Chinaman. He doesn't like birds or something. He's got a dragon. He sent the dragon after the birds and scared them away. The dragon burned up their nesting places. There used to be two men who looked after the birds. They got scared away too, or killed or something."

It all seemed quite natural to her. She gave the facts indifferently, staring out to sea.

Bond said, "This dragon. What kind is he? Have you seen him?"

"Yes, I've seen him." She made a wry face, as if swallowing bitter medicine. "I've been coming here for about a year, looking for shells. I've found plenty of good ones. Just before Christmas I thought I'd explore the river. I went up it to where the birdmen had their camp. It was all broken up. It was getting late and I decided to spend the night there. In the middle of the night I woke up. The dragon was coming by, only a few yards away from me. It had two great glaring eyes and short wings and a pointed tail. It was all black and gold." She frowned at the expression on Bond's face. "There was a full moon. I could see it clearly. It went by me, making a roaring noise. It went over the marsh and simply climbed over bushes. A whole flock of birds got up in front of it and suddenly a lot of fire came out of its mouth and it burned them up and all the trees they'd been roosting in. It was horrible. The most horrible thing I've ever seen."

The girl peered at Bond's face. "I can see you don't believe me," she said in a furious voice. "You're one of these city people. You don't believe anything. Ugh." She shuddered with dislike.

Bond said, "Honey, there just aren't such things as dragons. You saw something that looked very like a dragon. I'm just wondering what it was."

"How do you know there aren't such things as dragons?" Now he had made her really angry. "Nobody lives on this end of the island. One could easily have survived here. Anyway, what do you think you know about animals and things? I've lived with snakes and things since I was a child. Have you ever seen a praying mantis eat her husband after they've made love? Have you ever seen the mongoose dance? Have you ever had a pet snake that wore a bell round its neck and rang it to wake you? Have you seen a scorpion get sunstroke and kill itself with its own sting?" The girl stopped, out of breath. She said hopelessly, "Oh, you're just city folk like all the rest."

Bond said, "Honey, now look here. You know these things. I can't help it that I live in towns. I'd like to know about your things too. I just haven't had that sort of life. I know other things instead. Like . . ." Bond couldn't think of anything as interesting as hers. He finished lamely, "Like, for instance, that this Chinaman is going to be more interested in your visit this time. This time he's going to try and stop you getting away." He paused, then added, "And me, too, for that matter."

She turned and looked at him with interest. "Oh. Why? But then it doesn't really matter. One just hides during the day and gets away at night. He's sent dogs after me and even a plane. He hasn't got me yet." She examined Bond with a new interest. "Is it you he's after?"

"Well, yes," admitted Bond. "I'm afraid it is. You see we dropped the sail about two miles out so that their radar wouldn't pick us up. I think the Chinaman may have been expecting a visit from me. Your sail will have been reported and I'd bet anything he'll think your canoe was mine. I'd better go wake my friend and we'll talk it over. You'll like him. He's a Cayman Islander, name of Quarrel."

The girl said, "Well, I'm sorry if . . ." The sentence trailed away. "But after all, I couldn't know, could I?"

Bond smiled into the questing blue eyes. He said reassuringly, "Of course you couldn't. It's just bad luck—bad luck for you too. I don't suppose he minds too much about a girl who collects shells. You can be sure they've had a good look at your footprints and found clues like that"—he waved at the scattered shells on the beach. "But I'm afraid he'd take a different view of me. He'll hunt for me with everything he's got. I'm only afraid he may get you in the process. Anyway," Bond said with a grin, "we'll see what Quarrel has to say. You stay here."

Bond walked along the promontory. It took him five minutes to find Quarrel. He was lying between two big rocks, half covered by a board of driftwood. He was still fast asleep, the brown head cradled on his forearm. Bond whistled softly and smiled as the eyes sprang wide open like an animal's. Quarrel scrambled to his feet almost guiltily.

"Mornin', cap'n," he said. "Guess Ah been down deep!"

They sat down and Bond told him about Honeychile Rider and the fix they were in. "And now it's eleven o'clock," Bond added. "And we've got to make a new plan."

Quarrel looked sideways at Bond. "Yo don' plan we jess ditch dis girl?" he asked hopefully. "Ain't nuttin to do wit' we—" Suddenly he stopped. His head pointed like a dog's. He held up a hand for silence, listening intently. In the distance, to the eastwards, there was a faint droning.

Quarrel jumped to his feet. "Quick, cap'n," he said urgently. "Dey's a-comin'."

TEN minutes later the bay was empty and immaculate. Small waves curled lazily in across the water inside the reef and flopped exhausted on the dark sand. There was no longer any trace of footprints. Quarrel had cut branches of mangrove and had walked backwards, sweeping as he went. Where he had swept, the sand was of a different texture, but not so different as to be noticed from outside the reef. The girl's canoe had been pulled deeper among the rocks and covered with driftwood.

Quarrel had gone back to the headland. Bond and the girl lay a few feet apart under the bush of sea grape and gazed silently out across the water to the corner of the headland round which the boat would come.

The boat was perhaps a quarter of a mile away. From the slow pulse of the twin diesels Bond guessed that every cranny of the coastline was being searched. It sounded like a powerful boat. A big cabin cruiser, perhaps.

From the west a wedge of cormorants appeared, flying low over the sea beyond the reef. Bond watched them. They were the first evidence he had seen of the guanay colony at the other end of the island. As he watched they began to go into shallow dives, hitting the water like shrapnel. Almost at once a fresh file appeared from the west, then another and another. For minutes they darkened the skyline, and then they were down on the water, covering several acres, screeching and plunging their heads below the surface, cropping at anchovies.

Bond felt a gentle nudge from the girl. She gestured with her head. "The Chinaman's hens getting their corn."

The iron thud of the diesels was getting louder. The knife of white bows appeared from behind the headland. It was followed by ten yards of empty polished deck, glass windshields, a low-raked cabin with a siren and a radio mast.

Bond's eyes went to the two men standing in the stern. They were pale-skinned Negroes. They wore neat khaki ducks and shirts, broad belts, and visored caps of yellow straw. One of them was holding a black bullhorn with a wire attached. The other was manning a machine gun on a tripod.

The man with the bullhorn let it fall so that it swung on a strap round his neck. He picked up a pair of binoculars and began inching them along the beach. The low murmur of his comment just reached Bond above the flutter of the diesels.

Bond watched the eyes of the binoculars begin with the headland and then sweep the sand. The twin eyes paused among the rocks and moved on. They came back. The murmur of comment rose to a jabber. The man handed the glasses to the machine gunner. The cabin cruiser stopped and backed up. Now she lay outside the reef exactly opposite Bond and the girl. The binoculars were leveled at the rocks where the girl's canoe lay hidden.

Bond thought, Now we've had it. These men know their job.

Bond watched the machine gunner pull the bolt back to load. The scanner lifted his bullhorn and switched it on. The voice roared across the bay. "Okay, folks! Come on out and you won't get hurt." The voice had a trace of an American accent. "We've seen your boat," it thundered. "We ain't fools an' we ain't fooling. Just walk out with your hands up. You'll be okay."

Silence fell. The waves lapped on the beach. Bond could hear the girl breathing. Softly he tugged at her sleeve. "Come close," he whispered. "Smaller target." He felt her warmth nearer to him. He whispered, "Burrow into the sand. Wriggle. Every inch'll help." He felt her do it. He peered out. Now his eyes were only just above the skyline of the top of the beach.

The man was lifting his bullhorn. "Okay, folks! Just so you'll know this thing isn't for show." He lifted his thumb. The machine gunner trained his gun into the tops of the mangroves behind the beach. There came a swift rattling roar. The bullets made the sound of frightened pigeons whistling overhead. Then there was silence. The two men exchanged some words.

"Okay, folks," the scanner said. "You've been warned."

Bond watched the snout of the machine gun swing and depress. The man was going to start with the canoe among the rocks. Bond whispered to the girl, "All right. Keep right down. It won't last long." He felt her hand squeeze his arm. He leaned to the right to cover her head and pushed his face deep into the sand.

This time the crash of noise was terrific. The bullets howled into the headland. Fragments of splintered rock whined over the beach like hornets. Ricochets twanged and buzzed. The bullets came zipping along the tide line towards them. There was a succession of quick close thuds. The bush above them was being torn to shreds. *Zwip. Zwip. Zwip.* It was as if the thong of a steel whip were cutting the bush to pieces. Bits scattered, slowly covering them. Were they hidden by the leaves and debris? The bullets marched away along the shoreline. In a minute the racket stopped.

The silence sang. The girl whimpered softly. Bond hushed her and held her to him. The bullhorn boomed. "Okay, folks. If you still got ears, we'll be along soon to pick up the bits. And we'll be bringing the dogs. 'By for now."

The slow thud of the diesels quickened. The engines accelerated into a roar as the launch made off to the west. Within minutes it was out of earshot.

Bond cautiously raised his head. The bay was serene. All was as before except for the stench of cordite. Bond pulled the girl to her feet. There were tear streaks down her face. She looked at him aghast and said solemnly, "That was horrible. What did they do it for? We might have been killed."

He said, "It's all right, Honey. They're just a lot of bad men who are frightened of us. We can manage them." Bond put his arm round her shoulders. "And you were wonderful. As brave as anything. Come on now, we'll look for Quarrel and make some plans. Anyway, it's time we had something to eat. What do you eat on these expeditions?"

They walked towards the headland. After a minute she said in a controlled voice, "Oh, there's stacks of food about. Sea urchins mostly. Wild bananas. I eat and sleep for two days before I come here. I don't need anything."

Quarrel appeared among the rocks. He stopped, looking down. They came up to him. The girl's canoe was sawed almost in half by the bullets. She gave a cry and looked desperately at Bond. "My boat! How am I to get back?"

"Don' you worry, missy." Quarrel appreciated the loss of a canoe better than Bond. He guessed it might be most of the girl's capital. "Cap'n fix you up wit' anudder. An' you come back wit' we. Us got a fine boat in de mangrove. Hit not get broke. Ah's bin to see him." Quarrel looked at Bond. Now his face was worried. "But cap'n, yo sees what I means about dese folk. Dey means business. Dese dogs dey speak of. Pinschers dey's called. Big bastards. Frens tell me as dere's twenty or moh. We better make plans—an' quick."

"All right, Quarrel. But first we must have something to eat. And I'm damned if I'm going to be scared off the island before I've had a good look. We'll take Honey with us." He turned to the girl. "Is that all right with you? Then we'll sail home together."

The girl looked doubtfully at him. "I guess there's no alternative. I mean, if I won't be in the way. I really don't want anything to eat. But will you take me home as soon as you can? How long are you going to be looking at these birds?"

Bond said evasively, "Not long. I've got to find out what happened to them and why. Then we'll be off." He looked at his watch. "It's twelve now. You wait here. Have a swim or something. Don't walk about leaving footprints. Come on, Quarrel, we'd better get that boat hidden."

It was one o'clock before they were ready. Bond and Quarrel filled the canoe with stones and sand until it sank in a pool among the mangroves. They ate some of their rations avidly—the girl reluctantly—and climbed across the rocks and into the shallow water offshore. Then they trudged along the shallows towards the river mouth down the beach.

It was very hot. A harsh wind had sprung up from the northeast. Quarrel said this wind blew the year round. It dried the guano. The glare from the sea was dazzling. Bond was glad he had taken the trouble to get his skin hardened to the sun.

There was a sandy bar at the river mouth and a long, deep, stagnant pool. They could either get wet or strip. Bond said, "Honey, we can't be shy on this trip. Wear what's sensible and walk behind us." Without waiting for her reply, the two men took off their trousers and packed them in the knapsack. They waded into the pool, Quarrel in front, then Bond, then the girl. The water came up to Bond's waist.

The pool converged into a narrow neck over which the mangroves touched. For a time they waded through a cool tunnel, and then the river broadened into a sluggish channel that meandered ahead among the giant legs of the mangroves. The bottom was muddy, and at each step their feet sank into slime.

Soon, as they got away from the sea, it began to smell bad with a bad-egg, sulfurous smell. The mosquitoes and sand flies began to find them.

Then the mangroves became fewer, the river opened out, and the water grew shallower. They came round a bend and into the open. Honey said, "Better watch out now. We'll be easier to see. It goes on like this for about a mile. Then the river gets narrower until you reach the lake. Then there's the sandspit the birdmen lived on."

They stopped in the shadow of the mangrove tunnel and looked out. The river meandered towards the center of the island. Its banks, fringed with low bamboo and sea grape, would give only half shelter. From its western bank the ground rose slowly up to the sugarloaf about two miles away, which was the *guanera*. Round the base of the mountain there was a scattering of Quonset huts. A zigzag of silver ran down the hillside to the huts—a track, Bond guessed, to bring the guano from the diggings down to the crusher and separator. The summit of the sugarloaf was white, as if with snow. From the peak flew a smoky flag of guano dust. Bond could see the black dots of cormorants against it. They were landing and taking off like bees at a hive.

Bond stood and gazed at the distant glittering mountain of bird dung. So this was the kingdom of Doctor No! Bond thought he had never seen a more godforsaken landscape in his life.

He examined the ground between the river and the mountain. It seemed to be the usual gray dead coral, broken where there was a pocket of earth by low scrub and screw palm.

Bond looked east. There the mangroves in the marshland seemed more hospitable. They marched away in a solid green carpet until they lost their outline in the dancing heat haze on the horizon.

Quarrel's voice broke in on Bond's thoughts. "Dey's a-comin', cap'n."

Bond followed Quarrel's eyes. A big lorry was racing down from the huts, dust streaming from its wheels. Bond followed it until it disappeared among the mangroves at the head of the river. He listened. The baying of dogs came down on the wind.

Quarrel said, "Dey'll come down de ribber, cap'n. Dem'll know we cain't move 'cept up de ribber, assumin' we ain't dead. Dey'll surely come down de ribber to de beach and look for de pieces. Den mos' likely de boat come wit' a dinghy an' take de men and dogs off."

Honey said, "That's what they do when they look for me. It's quite all right. You cut a piece of bamboo, and when they get near, you go under the water and breathe through the bamboo till they've gone."

Bond smiled at Quarrel. He said, "Supposing you get the bamboo while I find a good mangrove clump."

Quarrel nodded dubiously. He started upstream towards a bamboo thicket. Bond turned back into the mangrove tunnel. The girl followed him. Soon he found what he wanted—a crack in the wall of mangrove that seemed to go deeper. He said, "Don't break a branch." He bent his head and waded in.

The channel went in ten yards. The mud under their feet became deeper and softer. Then there was a solid wall of roots, and they could go no farther. The brown water flowed slowly through a wide, quiet pool. Bond stopped. The girl came close to him. "This is real hide-and-seek," she said tremulously.

"Yes, isn't it." Bond was thinking of his gun, wondering how well it would shoot after a bath in the river. He felt a wave of disquiet. It had been a bad break coming across this girl. In combat, like it or not, a girl is your extra heart. The enemy has two targets against your one.

Bond remembered his thirst. He scooped up some water. It was brackish and tasted of earth. He drank some more. The girl put out her hand and stopped him. "Don't drink too much. Wash your mouth and spit. You could get fever." Bond did as she told him.

Quarrel whistled from somewhere in the main stream. Bond answered and waded out towards him. They came back along the channel. Quarrel splashed the mangrove roots with water where their bodies might have brushed. "Kill de smell of us," he explained. He produced his bamboo lengths and began whittling and cutting them. Bond looked to his gun. They stood still in the pool so as not to stir up more mud.

The sunlight dappled down through the thick roof of leaves. Shrimps nibbled softly at their feet. Tension built up in the hot, crouching silence.

It was almost a relief to hear the baying of the dogs.

Chapter 6

THE search party was coming fast down the river. Two men in bathing trunks and waders had to run to keep up with the dogs. They were big Chinese Negroes, wearing shoulder holsters across their naked chests. The pack of Doberman pinschers floundered through the water, baying. They had a scent, and they quested frenziedly, the pointed ears erect on the smooth serpentine heads.

"May be a crocodile," yelled the leading man, who was carrying a short whip.

The other man converged towards him. He shouted excitedly, "For my money it's the limey! Bet ya he's lying up in the mangrove."

They were coming out of the open river into the mangrove tunnel. The first man had a whistle. He blew a blast. When the dogs swept on he laid about him with the whip. The dogs checked, whimpering. The two men took their guns and waded downstream through the straggly legs of the mangroves.

The leading man came to the narrow break that Bond had found. He grasped a dog by the collar and swung it into the channel. The dog snorted eagerly and paddled forward.

The dog and the man came into the small enclosed pool at the end of the channel. The man looked around disgustedly. He caught the dog by the collar and pulled him back. The dog was reluctant to leave. The man lashed down into the water with his whip.

The second man had been waiting at the entrance to the little channel. The first man came out. He shook his head, and they went on downstream, the dogs, now less excited, streaming ahead.

Slowly the noise of the hunt grew less and vanished.

For another five minutes nothing moved in the mangrove pool; then in one corner a thin periscope of bamboo rose slowly out of the water. Bond's face emerged. In his right hand, under the water, the gun was ready. He listened intently. There was silence. Or was there? Was that a soft swish out in the main stream? Was someone wading quietly along in the wake of the hunt? Bond reached out and softly touched the other two bodies that lay in the pool. As the two faces surfaced he put his finger to his lips. It was too late. Quarrel had coughed. Bond nodded urgently towards the

main stream. They all listened. The swishing began again. Whoever it was was coming into the side channel. The tubes of bamboo went back into the three mouths, and the heads submerged again.

Underwater, Bond rested his head in the mud, pinched his nostrils with his left hand and pursed his lips round the tube. He knew the pool had been examined once already. He had felt the disturbance of the swimming dog. That time they had not been found. Would they get away with it again? This time there would have been less chance for the stirred mud to seep away. If this searcher saw the darker brown stain, would he shoot into it? Bond decided that he wouldn't take chances. At the first movement in the water near him he would get to his feet and shoot.

Suddenly Bond cringed. A rubber boot had stepped on his shin and slid off. Would the man think it was a branch? Bond couldn't chance it. With one surge of motion he hurled himself upwards, spitting out the bamboo.

Bond caught a quick impression of a huge body standing almost on top of him and of a swirling rifle butt. His right hand lunged forward, and as the muzzle of his gun touched the glistening right breast he pulled the trigger. The man crashed back like a chopped tree into the water. As he went under, the rubber waders thrashed once. Then there was nothing but muddy froth and a slowly widening red stain.

Bond shook himself. He turned. Quarrel and the girl were standing behind him, water streaming from their bodies. Quarrel was grinning, but the girl's knuckles were at her mouth and her eyes were horror-struck.

Bond said curtly, "I'm sorry, Honey. It had to be done. Come on, let's get going." He took her by the arm and thrust her away from the place, only stopping when they had reached the open river. The landscape was empty again. How much farther had they to go? Bond suddenly felt tired. Now he'd blown his cover. Even if the shot hadn't been heard, the man would be missed. They'd send out another search party, and the dogs would soon get to the body. Then what?

The girl tugged at his sleeve. She said angrily, "It's time you told me what all this is about! Why's everybody trying to kill each other? And who are you? I don't believe all this story about birds. You don't take a revolver after birds."

Bond looked down into the angry, wide-apart eyes. "I'm sorry, Honey. I'm afraid I've got you into a mess. I'll tell you all about it this evening. I've got a bit of a war on with these people. Now I'm only interested in seeing us all off the island without anyone else getting hurt. I've got enough to go on now so that next time I can come back by the front door."

"What do you mean? Are you some sort of a policeman? Are you trying to send this Chinaman to prison?"

"That's about it." Bond smiled down at her. "And now you tell me something. How much farther to the camp?"

"About an hour."

"Is it a good place to hide? Could they find us there easily?"

"They'd have to come across the lake or up the river. It'll be all right so long as they don't send their dragon after us. He can go through the water."

"Oh well," said Bond diplomatically, "let's hope he's got a sore tail or something."

The girl snorted. "All right, Mr. Know-all," she said angrily. "Just you wait."

Quarrel splashed out of the mangroves carrying a rifle. He said apologetically, "No harm 'n havin' anudder gun, cap'n. Looks like us may need hit."

It was a U.S. Army carbine .30. These people certainly had the right equipment. Bond shrugged away his thoughts. "Good," he said. "Now let's get going. Honey says there's another hour to the camp." Bond handed his gun to Quarrel, who stowed it in the sodden knapsack. They moved off again, with Quarrel in the lead and Bond and the girl walking together.

They got some shade from the bamboo and bushes along the western bank, but now they had to face the scorching wind. They splashed water over themselves to cool the burn. Bond was not looking forward to his dinner of soaked bread and cheese and salt pork. How long would they be able to sleep? He hadn't had much last night. He and Quarrel would have to rotate watches. And then tomorrow. Off into the mangrove and work their way to the canoe across the eastern end of the island. And sail the following night. What a prospect! Bond trudged on, thinking of M.'s "sunshine'll do you good" and "bit of holiday." He'd certainly give something for M. to be sharing it with him now.

The river grew narrower until it was only a stream. Then it widened out into a flat marshy estuary beyond which five square miles of shallow lake swept away in a ruffled blue-gray mirror.

Beyond, there was the shimmer of the airstrip. The girl told them to keep to the east, and they worked their way slowly along inside the fringe of bushes.

Suddenly Quarrel stopped, looking at the ground in front of him. Two deep parallel grooves were cut into the mud, with a fainter groove in the center. They were the tracks of something that had come down from the hill and gone across the marsh towards the lake.

The girl said, "That's where the dragon's been."

Quarrel turned his eyes towards her.

Bond walked slowly along the tracks. The outside ones were quite smooth, with an indented curve. They were vast, at least two feet across. The center track was of the same shape, but only three inches across, about the width of a motor tire. The tracks were without a trace of tread. They marched along in a straight line, and the bushes they crossed were squashed flat, as if a tank had gone over them.

Bond couldn't imagine what kind of vehicle had made them. When the girl nudged him and whispered fiercely, "I told you so," he could only say thoughtfully, "Well, Honey, if it isn't a dragon, it's something else I've never seen before."

Farther on, she tugged urgently at his sleeve and pointed forward to a clump of bushes beside the tracks. They were leafless and blackened. In the center were the charred remains of birds' nests. "He breathed on them," she said excitedly. Bond examined the bushes. It was all very odd.

The tracks swerved towards the lake and disappeared into the water. Bond would have liked to follow them, but there was no question of leaving cover. They trudged on.

Slowly the day began to die behind the sugarloaf, and at last the girl pointed ahead through the bushes and Bond could see a long spit of sand running out into the lake. There were thick bushes of sea grape along its spine and, halfway, perhaps a hundred yards from the shore, the remains of a thatched hut. It looked a reasonably attractive place to spend the night. The wind had died and the water was soft and inviting. How heavenly it was going to be to wash in the lake and, after the hours of squelching through the mud, be able to lie down on the hard dry sand!

The sun blazed yellowly and sank behind the mountain. The frogs started up, until the thick dusk was shrill with them. They reached the neck of the sandspit and filed out along a narrow track. They came to the clearing with the smashed remains of the thatched hut.

The big mysterious tracks led out of the water on both sides and through the clearing and over the nearby bushes, as if the thing, whatever it was, had stampeded the place. Many of the bushes were burned. There were the remains of a fireplace and a few scattered cooking pots and empty tins. Quarrel unearthed a couple of unopened tins of pork and beans. The girl found a crumpled sleeping bag.

They left the place and moved farther along to a small sandy clearing. Bond said, "As long as we don't show a light we should be fine here. The first thing is to have a good wash. Honey, you take the rest of the sandspit and we'll have the landward end. See you for dinner in about half an hour."

The girl laughed. "Will you be dressing?"

"Certainly," said Bond. "Trousers."

Quarrel said, "Cap'n, while dere's henough light I'll get dese tins open and get tings fixed for de night." He rummaged in the knapsack. "Here's yo trousers and yo gun. De bread don't feel so good, but hit only wet. Guess we'd better eat de tins tonight an' keep de cheese an' pork. Dose tins is heavy, an' we got plenty footin' tomorrow."

Bond said, "All right, Quarrel. I'll leave the menu to you." He took the gun and the trousers and walked down into the shallow water and back the way they had come. He found a dry stretch of sand and took off his shirt and stepped into the water and lay down. He dug up sand and scrubbed himself with it. Then he lay and luxuriated in the silence and loneliness.

The stars began to shine palely, the stars that had brought them to the island last night. What a trip! But at least it had already paid off. Now he had enough evidence, and witnesses, to go back to the governor and get a full-dress inquiry going into the activities of Doctor No. One didn't use machine guns on people, even on trespassers. And by the same token, what was this thing of Doctor No's that had trespassed on the leasehold of the Audubon Society, smashed their property and possibly killed one of their wardens? That would have to be investigated too. What would he find when he came back to the island through the front door, in a destroyer, perhaps, and with marines? What would be the answer to the riddle of Doctor No? Who *was* Doctor No?

Bond climbed out onto dry land. After pulling on his clammy trousers, he sat down and dismantled his gun. He did it by touch, using his shirt to dry each part. Then he reassembled it. He loaded and tucked the weapon into the holster inside the waistband of his trousers, then walked back to the clearing.

The shadow of Honey reached up and pulled him down beside her. "Come on," she said, "we're starving. There's about two full handfuls each of the beans and a cricket ball of bread. Here, hold out your hand."

Bond smiled at the authority in her voice. He could just make out her silhouette in the dusk. Her head looked sleeker. What would she be like when she was wearing clean clothes? He could see her coming into a room or across the lawn at Beau Desert. She would be a beautiful, ravishing ugly duckling. Why had she never had the broken nose mended? It was an easy operation. Then she would be the most beautiful girl in Jamaica.

Her shoulder brushed against him. Bond reached out and put his open hand down in her lap. She picked up his hand and Bond felt cold beans being poured into it. "There," she said maternally, and carried his laden hand away from her and back to him.

IT WOULD be around eight o'clock, Bond thought. Apart from the background croaking of the frogs it was very quiet. In the far corner of the clearing he could see the dark outline of Quarrel. There was the clink of metal as he dismantled and dried the gun. The food had warmed Bond's stomach. Tomorrow was a long way off. He felt comfortable and drowsy and at peace.

The girl lay beside him in the sleeping bag. She was lying on her back, looking up at the roof of stars. She said, "James. You promised to tell me what this is all about. I shan't go to sleep until you do."

Bond laughed. "I'll tell if you'll tell. I want to know what you're all about."

"I don't mind. I've got no secrets. But you first."

"All right then." Bond pulled his knees up to his chin and put his arms round them. "It's like this. I'm a sort of policeman. They send me out from London when there's something odd going on somewhere. Well, not long ago one of the governor's staff in Kingston, a man called Strangways, friend of mine, disappeared. His secretary did too. Most people thought they'd run away together. I didn't."

Bond told the story in simple terms, with good men and bad men, like an adventure story out of a book. He ended, "So you see, Honey, it's just a question of getting back to Jamaica in the canoe, and then the governor will listen to us and send over soldiers to get this Chinaman to own up. I expect that'll mean he'll go to prison. He'll know that, too, and that's why he's trying to stop us. That's all. Now it's your turn."

The girl said, "You seem to live an exciting life. Your wife can't like you being away so much. Doesn't she worry about you?"

"I'm not married. The only people who worry about me are the ones in my insurance company."

She probed, "But I suppose you have girls."

"Not permanent ones."

"Oh."

There was a pause. Quarrel came over to them. "Cap'n, Ah'll take de fust watch if dat suits. Be out on de point of de sandspit. Ah'll come call you around midnight. Den mebbe at five we all git goin'. Need to get away from dis place afore it's light."

"Suits me," said Bond. "Wake me if you see anything."

Quarrel melted noiselessly away into the shadows.

"I like Quarrel," said the girl. She paused, then said, "Do you really want to know about me? It's not very exciting."

"Of course I do. And don't leave anything out."

"There's nothing to leave out. You could get my whole life on a postcard. To begin with I've never been out of Jamaica. I live at a place called Beau Desert on the north coast."

Bond laughed. "That's odd. So do I. At least for the moment. I didn't notice you about. Do you live up a tree?"

"Oh, I suppose you've taken the beach house. I never go near the place. I live in the great house."

"But that's a ruin in the cane fields."

"I live in the cellars. I've lived there since I was five. It was burned down then, and my parents were killed. I can't remember anything about them. At first I lived there with my black nanny. She died when I was fifteen. For the last five years I've lived there alone."

Bond was appalled. "But wasn't there anyone else to look after you? Didn't your parents leave any money?"

"Not a penny." There was no bitterness in the girl's voice—pride, if anything. "You see the Riders were one of the old Jamaican families. The first one had been given the Beau Desert lands by Cromwell for having been one of the people who signed King Charles's death warrant. He built the great house, and my family lived in it on and off ever since. But then sugar collapsed and I suppose the place was badly run, and by the time my father inherited it there was nothing but debts—mortgages and things. So when my father and mother died the property was sold up. I didn't mind. I was too young. They wanted people to adopt me, the legal people did, but Nanny collected the sticks of furniture that hadn't been burned and we settled down in the ruins and after a bit no one interfered with us. She did a bit of sewing and laundry in the village and grew a few plantains and bananas. It was all right. We had enough. Somehow she taught me to read and write. There was a pile of old books left from the fire. There was an encyclopedia. I started with A when I was about eight. I've got as far as the middle of T." She said defensively, "I bet I know more than you do about a lot of things."

"I bet you do." Bond was lost in the picture of the little flaxen-haired girl pattering about the ruins, with the obstinate old Negress watching over her. "Your nanny must have been a wonderful person."

"She was a darling. I thought I'd die when she did. It wasn't such fun after that. I suddenly had to grow up. And men tried to hurt me. They said they wanted to make love to me." She paused. "I used to be pretty then."

Bond said seriously, "You're one of the most beautiful girls I've ever seen."

"With this nose? Don't be silly."

"You don't understand." Bond tried to find words that she would believe. "Of course anyone can see your nose is broken. But since this morning I've hardly noticed it. When you look at a person you look into their eyes or at their mouth. That's where the expressions are. If you had a beautiful nose as well as the rest of you, you'd be the most beautiful girl in Jamaica."

"Do you mean that?" Her voice was urgent. "When I look in the glass I hardly see anything except my broken nose. I'm sure it's like that with other people who are—well—sort of deformed."

Bond said impatiently, "You're not deformed! Don't talk such nonsense. And anyway, you can have it put right by a simple operation. You've only got to get over to America and it would be done in a week."

She said angrily, "How do you expect me to do that? I've got about fifteen pounds under a stone in my cellar. I've got three skirts and three shirts and a knife and a fish pot. I know all about these operations. The doctor at Port Maria found out for me. He wrote to America. Do you know it would cost me about five hundred pounds, what with the fare to New York and everything?" Her voice became hopeless. "How do you expect me to find that amount of money?"

Bond had already made up his mind what would have to be done about that. Now he said tenderly, "Well, I expect there are ways. But anyway, go on with your story. It's very exciting. You'd got to where your nanny died. What happened then?"

The girl began again reluctantly. "Oh well," she sighed, "I'll have to go back a bit. You see, all the property is in cane and the old house stands in the middle of it. Well, about twice a year they cut the cane and send it to the mill. And when they do that, all the animals and insects and so on that live in the cane fields go into a panic, and most of them have their houses destroyed and get killed. At cutting time some of them took to coming to the ruins of the house and hiding. My nanny was terrified of them to begin with, the mongooses and the snakes and the scorpions and so on, but I made a couple of the cellar rooms into homes for them. They seemed to understand that I was looking after them and they never hurt me. After a bit it was quite natural for them all to come trooping into their rooms and settle down there until the young cane had started to grow again. Then they all filed out and went back to living in the fields.

"They behaved very well except for making a bit of a smell and sometimes fighting. But they all got quite tame with me, and their children did too. Of course the cane cutters found out and saw me walking about with snakes round my neck and so forth, and they got frightened and thought I was obeah. So they left us absolutely alone." She paused. "That's how I found out so much about animals and insects. I used to spend a lot of time in the sea finding out about those people too. It was the same with birds."

"I expect they're much nicer and more interesting than humans," said Bond.

"I don't know about that," said the girl thoughtfully. "I don't know many human people. Most of the ones I have met have been hateful. Except for Nanny, of course. Until—" She broke off with a shy laugh. "Well, anyway, we all lived happily together until I was fifteen and Nanny died, and then things got difficult. There was a man called Mander. A horrible man. He was the white overseer for the people who own the property. He kept coming to see me. He wanted me to move up to his house. I hated him and I used to hide when I heard his horse coming. One night he was drunk and he came into the cellar and fought with me because I wouldn't do what he wanted me to do. You know, the things people in love do."

"Yes, I know."

"I tried to kill him with my knife, but he was very strong and he hit me in the face and broke my nose. He knocked me unconscious and then he did things to me. Next day I wanted to kill myself. I went to the doctor, and he did what he could for my nose and didn't charge me anything. I didn't tell him about the rest. I was too ashamed. The man didn't come back. I waited and did nothing until the next cane cutting. I was waiting for the black widow spiders to come in for shelter. One day they came. I caught the biggest female and shut her in a box. Then I waited for a dark night. I took the box with the spider in it and walked until I came to the man's house. I waited in his garden and watched him go up to bed. Then I climbed onto his balcony. When I heard him snoring I crept through the window. He was lying on the bed, and I shook the spider out onto his stomach. Then I went away and came home."

"God Almighty!" said Bond reverently. "What happened to him?"

She said happily, "He took a week to die. It must have hurt terribly." When Bond made no comment she said anxiously, "You don't think I did wrong, do you?"

"It's not a thing to make a habit of," said Bond. "But I can't say I blame you, the way it was. So what happened then?"

"Well, then I just settled down again. I had to concentrate on getting enough food, and of course all I wanted to do was save up money to get my nose made good again."

"What did you make money at?" asked Bond.

"It was the encyclopedia. It told me that people collect seashells. That one could sell the rare ones. I talked to the local schoolmaster, and he found out that there's an American magazine called *Nautilus* for shell collectors. I had just enough money to subscribe to it, and I began looking for the shells that people said they wanted in the advertisements. I wrote to a dealer in Miami, and he started buying from me. It was thrilling. Of course I made some awful mistakes to begin with. I thought people would like the prettiest shells, but they don't. Very often they want the ugliest. I only got everything right about a year ago, and I've already made fifteen pounds. And then"—she giggled delightedly—"I had a terrific stroke of luck. I went over to Crab Key just before Christmas, and I found these purple shells. They didn't look very exciting, but I sent one or two to Miami and the man wrote back at once and said he could take as many as I could get at five dollars each. He said that I must keep the place where they live a dead secret, as otherwise we'd what he called 'spoil the market' and the price would get cheaper. It's just like having one's private gold mine. Now I may be able to save up enough money in five years to go to America for the operation. That's why I was so suspicious of you when I found you on my beach. I thought you'd come to steal my shells."

"You gave me a bit of a shock. I thought you must be Doctor No's girl friend."

"Thanks very much. I'm nobody's girl friend." She paused. "The trouble is there aren't any men to love at Beau Desert." The voice was getting drowsy. She said, "You're the first Englishman I've ever talked to. I liked you from the beginning. I don't mind telling you these things at all. I suppose there are plenty of other people I should like if I could get away."

"Of course there are. Hundreds. And you're a wonderful girl. I thought so directly I saw you." Bond's body began to stir with the memory of how she had been. He said gruffly, "Now come on, Honey. It's time to go to sleep. There'll be plenty of time to talk when we get back to Jamaica."

"Will there?" she said sleepily. "Promise?"

"Promise."

He heard her stir in the sleeping bag. He looked down. He could just make out the pale profile turned towards him. She gave the deep sigh of a child before it falls asleep.

There was silence in the clearing. Bond put his head down on his knees. He knew it was no good trying to get to sleep. His mind was full of the day and of this extraordinary girl Tarzan. It was as if some beautiful animal had attached itself to him. There would be no dropping the leash until he had solved her problems for her. Of course there would be no difficulty about most of them. He could fix the operation—even, with the help of friends, find a proper job and a home for her. But what about the physical desire he felt for her? One could not make love to a child. But was she a child?

Bond's thoughts were interrupted by a tug at his sleeve. The small voice said, "Why don't you go to sleep? It's nice and warm in the sleeping bag. Would you like to come in?"

"No thank you, Honey. I'll be all right."

There was a pause, then, in a whisper, "If you're thinking . . . I mean—you don't have to make love to me. . . ."

"Honey, darling, you go to sleep. It'd be lovely, but not tonight. I have to take over from Quarrel soon."

"I see." The voice was grudging. "Perhaps when we get back to Jamaica."

"Perhaps."

"Promise. I won't go to sleep until you promise."

Bond said desperately, "Of course I promise. Now go to sleep, Honeychile."

The voice whispered triumphantly, "Now you owe me slave time. You've promised. Good night, darling James."

"Good night, darling Honey."

Chapter 7

THE grip on Bond's shoulder was urgent. Quarrel whispered, "Somepn comin' across de water, cap'n! It de dragon fo sho!"

The girl said anxiously, "What's happened?"

Bond said, "Stay there, Honey! Don't move. I'll be back."

He ran with Quarrel until they came to the tip of the sandspit. They stopped under cover of the final bushes. Bond parted them and looked through.

What was it? Half a mile away, coming across the lake, was a shapeless thing with two glaring orange eyes. From between these, where the mouth might be, fluttered a yard of blue flame. The gray luminescence of the stars showed some kind of a domed head above two batlike wings. The thing was making a low moaning roar that overlaid another noise, a rhythmic thud. It was coming towards them at about ten miles an hour, throwing up a creamy wake.

Quarrel whispered, "Gawd, cap'n! What's dat?"

Bond stood up. "Don't know exactly. Some sort of a tractor dressed up to frighten. It's running on a diesel engine, so you can forget about dragons. Now let's see." Bond spoke half to himself. "No good running away. The thing's too fast for us. Have to fight it here. What'll its weak spots be? The drivers. Of course they'll have protection. We don't know how much. Quarrel, you start firing at that dome on top when it gets to two hundred yards. Aim carefully and keep on firing. When it gets to fifty yards I'll go for its headlights. Must have some kind of giant tires. I'll go for them too. Stay here. I'll go ten yards along. They may start firing back, and we've got to keep the bullets away from the girl. Okay?" Bond reached out and squeezed the big shoulder. "And forget about dragons. It's just some gadget of Doctor No's. Right?"

Quarrel laughed shortly. "Okay, cap'n. Since yo says so."

Bond ran down the sand. He called softly, "Honey!"

"Yes, James." There was relief in the nearby voice.

"Make a hole in the sand like we did on the beach. Behind the thickest roots. There may be some shooting. Don't worry about dragons. This is just a painted-up motorcar with Doctor No's men in it. Don't be frightened. I'm close."

"All right, James." The voice was high with fright.

Bond knelt on one knee in the leaves and peered out. Now the thing was about three hundred yards away, and its yellow headlights were lighting up the sandspit. Blue flame was still fluttering from the mouth. It was coming from a long snout, mocked up with gaping jaws and gold paint to look like a dragon's mouth. Flame-thrower! That would explain the burned bushes.

Bond had to admit that the thing was an awesome sight as it moaned forward through the shallow lake. Against native intruders it would be devastating. But how vulnerable would it be to people with guns, who didn't panic?

He was answered at once. There came the crack of Quarrel's carbine. A spark flew off the domed cabin and there was a dull clang. Quarrel fired another single shot and then a burst. The bullets hammered ineffectually against the cabin. The thing rolled on, swerving slightly to make for the source of the gunfire. Bond cradled the Smith & Wesson on his forearm and took careful aim. The cough of his gun sounded above the rattle of the carbine. One of the headlights shattered and went out. He fired four shots at the other and got it with the fifth. The thing didn't care. It rolled straight on towards Quarrel's hiding place. Bond began firing at the tires. No effect. Solid rubber? The first breath of fear stirred Bond's skin. He reloaded and took a step forward through the bushes. Then he froze, incapable of movement.

Suddenly from the snout a yellow-tipped bolt of blue flame had howled out towards Quarrel's hiding place. There was a single puff of orange and red flame from the bushes and one unearthly scream, immediately choked. Satisfied, the searing tongue of fire licked back into the snout. The thing turned on its axis and stopped dead. Now the blue hole of its mouth aimed straight at Bond.

Bond stood and waited for his unspeakable end. Soon he, too, would flame like a torch. Then it would be Honey's turn. God, what had he led them into! Bond set his teeth. Hurry up, you bastards. Get it over with.

There came the twang of a bullhorn. A voice howled metallically, "Come on out, limey. And the doll. Quick, or you'll fry in hell like your pal."

Bond felt the girl's body against his back. She said hysterically, "I had to come. I had to come."

Bond said, "It's all right, Honey. Keep behind me."

He had made up his mind. Even if death were to come later, it couldn't be worse than this kind of death. Bond drew the girl after him out onto the sand.

The voice howled, "Stop there. Good boy. And drop the pea-shooter. No tricks."

Bond dropped his gun. There was the clang of an iron door being opened. From the back of the dome a man dropped into the water and walked towards them. There was a gun in his hand. The fluttering blue flame lit up his sweating face. He was a Chinese Negro, a big man, clad only in trousers. Handcuffs dangled from his left hand. He stopped and said, "Hold out your hands. Wrists together. Then walk towards me. You first, limey. Slowly or you get an extra navel."

Bond did as he was told. The man snapped the handcuffs on Bond's wrists. "Dumb limey," said the man.

Bond turned his back on the man and walked away. He was going to see Quarrel's body. He had to say good-by. A bullet kicked up sand close to his feet. Bond stopped. "Don't be nervous," he said. "I'm going to take a look at the man you've just murdered. I'll be back."

The man lowered his gun. He laughed harshly. "Okay. Enjoy yourself. Two minutes."

Bond walked on towards the smoking clump of bushes. He got there and looked down, wincing. He said softly, "I'm sorry, Quarrel." He scooped up sand between his manacled hands and poured it over the remains of the eyes. Then he walked back and stood beside the girl.

The man waved them forward with his gun to the back of the machine. There was a small door. A voice from inside said, "Get in and sit on the floor."

They scrambled into the iron box. It stank of sweat and oil. There was just room for them to sit with their knees hunched up. The man with the gun followed them in and switched on a light and sat down on an iron seat beside the driver. He said, "Okay, Sam. Let's get goin'."

The driver pulled down a couple of switches. He put the machine into gear and peered out through a narrow slit in the iron wall in front of him. Bond felt the machine turn. There came a faster beat from the engine and they moved off.

The girl's shoulder pressed against his. "Where are they taking us?" The whisper trembled. She bent her head down to her manacled hands to hide her tears.

Bond turned and looked at her. He shrugged with an indifference he didn't feel. He whispered, "Oh, I expect we're going to see Doctor No. Don't worry too much, Honey. These men are just little gangsters. It'll be different with him. When we get to him don't you say anything. I'll talk for both of us."

Some of the tension went out of her face. She half smiled at him and whispered, "It'll be all right as long as you're there."

Bond shifted so that he was right up against her. He brought his hands close up to his eyes and examined the handcuffs. They were the American police model. He contracted his left hand, the thinner of the two, and tried to pull it through the ring of steel. It was hopeless.

The two men sat on their iron seats with their backs to them, indifferent. They knew they had total command. There wasn't room for Bond to give any trouble. If he somehow managed to open the hatch and drop into the water, where would that get him? They would at once feel the fresh air and stop the machine, and either burn him in the water or pick him up. It annoyed Bond that they didn't worry about him, that they knew he was utterly in their power. These two knew their business. They were professionals. They didn't even talk to each other. There was no nervous chatter about how clever they had been or about their destination. They just drove the machine along, finishing their job.

Bond still had no idea what this contraption was. Under the black and gold paint and the rest of the fancy dress it was some sort of a tractor, but of a kind he had never seen or heard of.

Bond was impressed. He was always impressed by professionalism. Doctor No was obviously a man who took immense pains. Soon Bond would be meeting him. Soon he would be up against the secret of Doctor No. And then what? Bond smiled grimly to himself. He wouldn't be allowed to get away with his knowledge. He would certainly be killed unless he could escape. And what about the girl? Could Bond prove her innocence and have her spared? Conceivably, but she would never be let off the island. She would have to stay there for the rest of her life.

Bond's thoughts were interrupted by rougher going under the wheels. They had crossed the lake and were on the track that led up the mountain to the huts. The cabin tilted and the machine began to climb.

Gray light showed now through the slots in the armor. Dawn was coming up. Outside, another day was beginning. Bond thought of Quarrel, the brave giant who would not be seeing it. He remembered the life insurance. Quarrel had smelled his death. Yet he had followed Bond unquestioningly. His faith in Bond had been stronger than his fear. And Bond had let him down. Would Bond also be the death of the girl?

The driver reached forward to the dashboard. From the front of the machine there sounded the brief howl of a police siren. The machine stopped, idling in neutral. The man took a microphone off a hook beside him. He spoke into it, and Bond could hear the echoing voice of the bullhorn outside. "Okay. Got the limey and the girl. Other man's dead. Open up."

Bond heard a door being pulled on iron rollers. They moved forward a few yards and stopped. The driver switched off the engine. There was a clang as the iron hatch was opened from the outside. Hands took hold of Bond and dragged him roughly out backwards onto a cement floor. Bond stood up. He felt the prod of a gun. A voice said, "Stay where you are. No tricks." Bond looked at the man. He was another Chinese Negro. Another man was prodding the girl with his gun.

Bond looked around him. They were in one of the Quonset huts he had seen from the river. It was a garage and workshop. The "dragon" had been halted over an examination pit in the concrete. The driver and his mate were checking the machine.

One of the guards said, "Passed the message along. The word is to send them through. Everything go okay?"

The co-driver, who seemed to be the senior man present, said, "Sure. Bit of gunfire. Lights gone. Get the boys crackin'—full overhaul. I'll put these two through." He turned to Bond. "Okay, git moving." He gestured down the long hut.

Bond said, "Get moving yourself. Mind your manners. And tell those apes to take their guns off us. They might let one off by mistake. They look dumb enough."

The man came closer. The other three closed up behind him. Hate shone in their eyes. The leading man lifted a clenched fist as big as a small ham and held it under Bond's nose. He said tensely, "Listen, mister. Sometimes us boys is allowed to join in the fun at the end. Once we made it last a whole week. An', jeez, if I get you—" He broke off. His eyes were alight with cruelty. He looked past Bond at the girl. He turned to the other three. "What say, fellers?"

The three men were also looking at the girl. They nodded dumbly, like children in front of a Christmas tree.

Bond longed to run berserk among them, laying into their faces with his manacled wrists. But for the girl he would have done it. He said, "All right, all right. You're four and we're two and we're handcuffed. But just don't push us around too much. Doctor No might not be pleased."

At the name the men's faces changed. Three pairs of eyes looked whitely from Bond to the leader. The leader stared suspiciously at Bond. Then he said lamely, "Okay, okay. This way, mister."

He walked off down the long hut. Close together, Bond and the girl followed.

The man came to a rough wooden door at the end of the hut. There was a bell push beside it. He rang twice and waited. There came a click, and the door opened to reveal ten yards of carpeted rock passage, with another door, cream-painted, at the end.

The man stood aside. "Straight ahead, mister. Knock on the door. The receptionist'll take over." There was no irony in his voice and his eyes were impassive.

Bond led the girl into the passage. The door shut behind them. They walked forward to the cream-painted door and knocked.

The door opened. Bond went through with the girl at his heels. Then he stopped dead in his tracks, staring.

IT WAS the sort of reception room the largest American corporations have on the president's floor in their New York skyscrapers. The floor was carpeted in the thickest wine-red Wilton, and the walls and ceiling were painted a soft dove gray. Color lithographs of Degas ballet sketches were hung in groups on the walls. To Bond's right was a broad desk with a green leather top, handsome matching desk furniture and the most expensive type of intercom. Two tall antique chairs waited for visitors. On the other side of the room was a refectory-type table with shiny magazines and two more chairs. The air held a slight, expensive fragrance.

There were two women in the room. Behind the desk, with pen poised over a printed form, sat an efficient-looking Chinese girl with horn-rimmed spectacles below a bang of black hair cut short. She wore the standard receptionist's smile of welcome—bright, helpful, inquisitive.

Holding the door through which they had come stood an older, rather matronly woman of about forty-five. She also had Chinese

blood. Her appearance—wholesome, bosomy, eager—was almost excessively gracious. Both women were dressed in spotless white, like assistants in an expensive American beauty parlor.

While Bond took in the scene, the woman at the door twittered phrases of welcome, as if they had been caught in a storm and had arrived late at a party.

"You poor dears. We simply didn't know when to expect you. First it was teatime yesterday, then dinner, and only half an hour ago we heard you would be here in time for breakfast. You must be famished. Come help Sister Rose fill in your forms and then I'll pack you both straight off to bed. You must be tired."

Clucking softly, she ushered them to the desk. She got them seated and rattled on, "Now, I'm Sister Lily and this is Sister Rose. She just wants to ask you a few questions. Now, let me see, a cigarette?" She picked up a tooled-leather box. Bond reached out his manacled hands to take a cigarette. Sister Lily gave a squeak of dismay. She sounded genuinely embarrassed. "Oh, but really. Sister Rose, the key, quickly. I've said again and again that patients are never to be brought in like that." There was impatience and distaste in her voice. "Really, that outside staff!"

Sister Rose was just as much put out. She scrabbled in a drawer and handed a key across to Sister Lily, who with much tut-tutting unlocked the two pairs of handcuffs and dropped them, as if they were dirty bandages, into the wastepaper basket.

"Thank you." Bond was unable to think of any way to handle the situation except to fall in with what was happening. He glanced at Honeychile Rider, who sat looking dazed. Bond gave her a reassuring smile.

"Now, if you please." Sister Rose bent over a printed form. "Your name, please, Mr.—er . . ."

"Bryce, John Bryce."

She wrote busily. "Permanent address?"

"Care of the Royal Zoological Society, London."

"Profession."

"Ornithologist."

"Oh dear"—she dimpled at him—"could you please spell that?" Bond did so. "Thank you. Now, let me see, purpose of visit?"

"Birds," said Bond. "I am also a representative of the Audubon Society of New York. They have a lease on part of this island." Bond watched the pen writing down exactly what he had said. After the last word she put a neat query in brackets.

"And"—Sister Rose smiled in the direction of Honeychile—"your wife? Is she also interested in birds?"

"Yes, indeed."

"And her first name?"

"Honeychile."

Sister Rose was delighted. "What a pretty name. And now your next of kin and then we're finished."

Bond gave M.'s real name as next of kin, described him as uncle and gave his address as Managing Director, Universal Export, Regent's Park, London.

Sister Rose finished writing. "There, that's done. Thank you so much, Mr. Bryce."

Bond got up. Honeychile did the same.

Sister Lily said, "Now come along with me, you poor dears." She walked to a door in the far wall. "It's the Cream Suite, isn't it, Sister?"

"That's right. Fourteen and fifteen."

"Thank you, my dear. And now"—she opened the door—"if you'll just follow me. I'm afraid it's a walk."

Bond took the girl's hand, and they followed the motherly bustling figure down a hundred yards of corridor in the same style as the reception room.

Bond answered with polite monosyllables the occasional twittering comments Sister Lily threw over her shoulder. His whole mind was focused on the extraordinary circumstances of their reception. He was quite certain the two women had been genuine. Not a look or a word had been dropped that was out of place. It was obviously a front of some kind, but a solid one, meticulously supported by the decor and the cast. The lack of resonance in the room, and now in the corridor, suggested that they had stepped from the Quonset hut into the side of the mountain and that they were now walking through its base. At a guess, they would be walking towards the west—towards the cliff face with which the island ended. There was no moisture on the walls and the air was cool and pure. A lot of money and good engineering had gone into the job.

They came to a door at the end of the corridor. Sister Lily rang. The door opened at once. An enchanting Chinese girl in a mauve and white flowered kimono stood smiling and bowing. Sister Lily cried, "Here they are at last, May! Mr. and Mrs. John Bryce. And

I know they must be exhausted, so we must take them straight to their rooms for breakfast and a sleep." She turned to Bond. "This is May. Such a dear girl. She will be looking after you both. Anything you want, just ring for May. She's a favorite with all our patients."

Patients, thought Bond. That's the second time she's used the word. He smiled politely at the girl. "How do you do?"

May embraced them both with a warm smile. She said, "I do hope you'll both be comfortable, Mr. Bryce. I took the liberty of ordering breakfast for you. Shall we . . . ?" Corridors branched off to left and right of double lift doors set in the wall. The girl led the way to the right. Bond and Honeychile followed with Sister Lily. Numbered doors led off the corridor on either side. The corridor ended with two doors side by side, 14 and 15. May opened the door of 14 and they followed her in.

It was a charming double bedroom in modern Miami style, with dark green walls, dark polished mahogany floor with occasional thick white rugs, and well-designed bamboo furniture with a chintz of large red roses on a white background. There was a communicating door into a more masculine room, and another that led into an extremely luxurious bathroom with a step-down bath.

It was like being shown into the very latest Florida hotel suite—except that there were no windows and no inside handles to the doors.

May looked hopefully from one to the other.

Bond turned to Honeychile. "It looks very comfortable, don't you think, darling?" She nodded, not looking at him.

There was a timid knock on the door, and another girl, as pretty as May, pattered in with a loaded tray. She put it down on the center table, pulled up two chairs and pattered out of the room. There was a delicious smell of bacon and coffee.

May and Sister Lily backed to the door. The older woman stopped on the threshold. "And now we'll leave you two dear people in peace. If you want anything, just ring. Oh, by the way, you'll find plenty of fresh clothes in the closets. Chinese style, I'm afraid." She twinkled apologetically. "The doctor has given strict orders that you're not to be disturbed. He'd be delighted if you'd join him for dinner this evening. He wants you to have the whole of the rest of the day to yourselves—to get settled, you know." She paused in smiling inquiry. "Shall I say you . . . ?"

"Yes, please," said Bond. "Tell the doctor we shall be delighted to join him for dinner."

"Oh, he'll be so pleased." With a last twitter the two women withdrew and closed the door.

Bond turned towards Honeychile. She still avoided his eyes. It occurred to Bond that she could never have seen such luxury in her life. To her all this must be far more strange and terrifying than what they had gone through outside. She stood and fiddled at the hem of her man-Friday skirt, and her toes gripped nervously into the thick pile carpet. Bond laughed. He took her hands. They were cold. He said, "Honey, we're a couple of scarecrows. There's only one problem. Shall we have breakfast first, while it's hot, or shall we get out of these rags and have a bath and eat the breakfast when it's cold? Don't worry about anything else. We're here in this wonderful little house and that's all that matters. Now then, what shall we do?"

She smiled uncertainly. The blue eyes searched his face. "Don't you think this is all a trap?"

"If it's a trap, we're in it. There's nothing we can do now but eat the cheese. The only question is whether we eat it hot or cold." He pressed her hands. "Really, Honey. Leave the worrying to me. Decide the important things. Bath or breakfast?"

She said reluctantly, "Well, if you think . . . I mean, I'd rather get clean first." She added quickly, "But you've got to help me." She jerked her head towards the bathroom door. "I don't know how to work one of those places. What do you do?"

Bond said seriously, "It's quite easy. I'll set it all up for you. While you're having your bath I'll have my breakfast." Bond went to one of the clothes closets and slid the door back. There were a dozen kimonos. He took out one at random. "Get into this and I'll get the bath ready. Later on you can choose the things you want to wear for bed and dinner."

She said gratefully, "Oh, yes, James."

Bond went into the bathroom and turned on the taps. There was everything—Floris Lime bath essence for men and Guerlain bath cubes for women. He crushed a cube into the water, and at once the room smelled like an orchid house. In a medicine cupboard were toothbrushes and toothpaste, hairbrushes and combs, aspirin and milk of magnesia. There was also an electric razor. Everything was brand-new and untouched.

Bond looked at his filthy unshaved face in the mirror and smiled grimly. The coating on the pill was certainly of the very finest sugar. It would be wise to expect that the medicine inside would be of the bitterest.

He turned back to the bath and felt the water. As he bent over, two arms were thrown round his neck. He stood up. The golden body blazed in the white-tiled bathroom. She kissed him hard and clumsily on the lips. He put his arms round her, his heart pounding. She said breathlessly at his ear, "The Chinese dress felt strange. Anyway, you told that woman we were married."

Bond's hand was on her left shoulder. Her stomach pressed against his. Why not? Why not? Don't be a fool! This is a crazy time for it. You're both in deadly danger. You must stay cold as ice to have any chance of getting out of this mess. Later! Later! Don't be weak.

Bond took his hand from her. He held her at arm's length. He said unsteadily, "Honey, get into that bath before I spank you." Then he went out and into his room and stood in the middle of the floor and waited for his heart to stop pounding.

To clear his mind he went carefully over both rooms, looking for exits, possible weapons, microphones—anything that would add to his knowledge. There were none of these things. In the double bedroom there was an electric clock on the wall, which said eight thirty, and a row of bells beside the bed. They said, ROOM SERVICE, COIFFEUR, MANICURIST, MAID. There was no telephone. High up in a corner of both rooms was a small ventilator grille about two feet square. Useless. The doors appeared to be of metal. Bond threw his body against one of them. It didn't give a millimeter. The place

589

was a prison—an exquisite prison. The trap had shut tight on them.

Bond sat down at the breakfast table. There was a tumbler of pineapple juice in a silver bowl of crushed ice. He swallowed it and lifted the cover off his individual hot plate. Scrambled eggs on toast, bacon, a grilled kidney, two kinds of hot toast, rolls, marmalade and strawberry jam.

From the bathroom came the sound of the girl crooning "Marion." Bond closed his ears to the sound and started on the eggs.

Ten minutes later, Bond heard the bathroom door open and the girl come out. He covered his eyes with his hands. She laughed and said half to herself, "He's a coward. He's frightened of a simple girl." Bond heard her rummaging in the closets. She went on talking. "I wonder why he's frightened. Of course if I wrestled with him, I'd win easily. H'm, now let's see, would he like me in this?" She raised her voice. "Darling James, would you like me in white with pale blue birds flying all over me?"

"Yes, damn you," said Bond. "Now come and have breakfast. I'm getting sleepy."

There was a flurry of feet, and Honey came in and sat down. He took his hands away from his eyes. She was smiling. She looked ravishing. Her pale blond hair was combed and brushed to kill, with one side falling down the side of the cheek and the other slicked back behind her ear. Her skin sparkled with freshness and the big blue eyes were alight with happiness. Now Bond loved the broken nose. It occurred to him that he would be sad when she was just an immaculately beautiful girl like other beautiful girls. But he knew it would be no good trying to persuade her of that. She sat demurely, with her hands in her lap below a cleavage which showed half her breasts and a deep vee of her stomach.

Bond said severely, "Now listen, Honey. You look wonderful, but that isn't the way to wear a kimono. Pull it up right across your body and tie it tight and stop trying to look like a call girl. It just isn't good manners at breakfast."

"Oh, you are stuffy," she said. "Why don't you like playing? I want to play at being married."

"Not at breakfast," said Bond. "Come on and eat up. Anyway,

I'm filthy. I'm going to shave and have a bath." He got up and kissed the top of her head. "And as for playing, as you call it, I'd rather play with you than anyone in the world. But not now." Without waiting for her answer he walked into the bathroom and shut the door.

Bond shaved and had a bath. He felt desperately sleepy. Sleep came to him in waves, so that from time to time he had to stop and bend his head down between his knees. When he came to brush his teeth he could hardly do it. He recognized the signs. He had been drugged. In the coffee or the pineapple juice? It didn't matter. All he wanted to do was lie down. Bond weaved drunkenly to the door. He forgot that he was naked. That didn't matter either. The girl was in bed, fast asleep, naked under a single sheet. The kimono was lying in a pile on the floor.

Bond found the switches and turned out the lights. Now he had to crawl across the floor and into his room to get to his bed. He pulled himself onto it. He reached out and jabbed at the switch on the bed light. He missed it. The lamp crashed to the floor and the bulb burst. With a last effort Bond turned on his side and let the waves sweep over his head.

The luminous figures on the electric clock in the double room said nine thirty.

At ten o'clock the door of the double room opened softly. A very tall thin figure was silhouetted against the lighted corridor. It was a man. He must have been six feet six. He stood with his arms folded, listening. Satisfied, he moved slowly into the room and up to the bed. He knew the way exactly. He bent down and listened to the quiet breathing of the girl. After a moment he reached up to his chest and pressed a switch. A flashlight with a diffused beam came on. The flashlight was attached to him by a belt above the breastbone. He bent forward so that the soft light shone on the girl's face.

The intruder examined the girl's face for several minutes. One of his hands came up and took the sheet at her chin and softly drew it down to the end of the bed. The hand that drew down the sheet was not a hand. It was a pair of articulated steel pincers at the end of a metal stalk that disappeared into a black silk sleeve. It was a mechanical hand.

The man gazed for a long time at the girl's body. Then the claw came out again and drew the sheet back over the girl. The man moved quietly away to the open door of the room where Bond was sleeping.

The man spent longer beside Bond's bed. He scrutinized every line, every shadow on the dark, rather cruel face that lay drowned, almost extinct, on the pillow. He watched the pulse in the neck and counted it. When he had pulled down the sheet he gauged the curve of the muscles on Bond's arms and thighs and in the flat stomach. He even bent over the outflung right hand and examined its life and fate lines.

Finally, with infinite care, the steel claw drew the sheet back up to Bond's neck. For another minute the tall figure stood over the sleeping man. Then it swished softly away and out, and the door closed with a click.

Chapter 8

THE electric clock in the cool dark room showed four thirty.

Outside the mountain, Crab Key had sweltered and stunk its way through another day. At the eastern end of the island the mass of birds—herons, pelicans, sandpipers, flamingos and the few roseate spoonbills—went on with building their nests or fished in the lake. Most of the birds had been disturbed so often that year that they had given up any idea of building. They had been raided at regular intervals by the monster that came at night and burned their roosting places and the beginning of their nests. This year many would not breed. There would be vague movements to migrate, and many would die of the nervous hysteria that seizes bird colonies when they no longer have peace and privacy.

At the other end of the island, on the *guanera* that gave the mountain its snow-covered look, the vast swarm of cormorants had passed their usual day of gorging themselves with fish and paying back the ounce of manure to their owner and protector. Nothing had interfered with *their* nesting season. Now they were noisily fiddling with the untidy piles of sticks that would be their nests.

Below the peak, where the diggings began, the hundred or so Negro men and women who were the labor force were coming to the end of the day's shift. Another fifty cubic yards of guano had been dug out of the mountainside and another twenty yards of terrace had been added to the working level. Here, instead of the stink of the marshes on the rest of the island, there was a strong ammoniac smell, and the ugly hot wind blew the freshly turned whitish brown dust into the eyes and noses of the diggers. But the workers were used to the smell and the dust, and it was easy work. They had no complaints.

The last iron truck of the day started off on the Decauville track that snaked down the mountainside to the crusher and separator. A whistle blew and the workers shouldered their picks and moved down towards the group of Quonset huts that was their compound. Tomorrow, on the other side of the mountain, the monthly ship would be coming into the deep-water quay they had helped to build ten years before, but which, since then, they had never seen. That would mean fresh goods and cheap jewelry at the canteen. It would be a holiday. There would be rum and dancing and a few fights. Life was good.

Life was good, too, for the senior outside staff—all Chinese Negroes, like the men who had hunted Bond and Quarrel and the girl. They stopped work in the garage and machine shops and at the guard posts, and filtered off to the "officers'" quarters. Apart from watch and loading duties, tomorrow would also be a holiday for most of them. They, too, would have their drinking and dancing, and there would be a new monthly batch of girls.

DEEP down in the cool heart of the mountain, far below this well-disciplined surface life, Bond awoke in his comfortable bed. Apart from a slight Nembutal headache he felt fit and rested. Lights were on in the girl's room, and he could hear her moving about. Avoiding the fragments of glass from the broken lamp, he walked over to the clothes closet and put on the first kimono that came to his hand. He went to the door. The girl had a pile of kimonos out on the bed and was trying them on. She had on a very smart one in sky-blue silk. It looked wonderful against the gold of her skin. Bond said, "That's the one."

She whirled around. "Oh, it's you!" She smiled at him. "I thought you'd never wake up. I'd made up my mind to wake you at five. I'm hungry. Can you get us something to eat?"

"Why not?" Bond walked across to the bells. He pressed the one marked ROOM SERVICE. He said, "What about the others? Let's have the full treatment."

She giggled. "But what's a manicurist?"

"Someone who does your nails." At the back of Bond's mind was the urgent necessity to get his hands on some kind of weapon—a pair of scissors would be better than nothing. He pressed two more bells and looked round the room. Someone had come while they were asleep and taken away the breakfast things. There was a drink tray on a sideboard. Propped among the bottles were two menus, huge double-folio pages.

There was a knock on the door and the exquisite May came in. She was followed by two other Chinese girls. Bond brushed aside their amiabilities, ordered tea and toast for Honeychile and told them to look after her hair and nails. Then he went into the bathroom and had a couple of aspirins and a cold shower. He put on his kimono again, reflected that he looked idiotic in it and went back into the room. A beaming May asked if he would be good enough to select what he and Mrs. Bryce would care to have for dinner. Without enthusiasm Bond ordered caviar, lamb cutlets and salad for himself. When Honeychile refused to make any suggestions he chose melon, roast chicken, and vanilla ice cream with hot chocolate sauce for her.

May dimpled her approval. "The doctor asks if seven forty-five would be convenient."

Bond said curtly that it would.

"Thank you, Mr. Bryce. I will call for you at seven forty-four."

Bond walked over to where Honeychile was being ministered to at the dressing table. He watched the busy fingers at work.

So much for his idea of getting hold of a weapon. The scissors and files were attached to the manicurist's waist by a chain. So were the scissors of the hairdresser. Bond sat down on the bed and lost himself in gloomy reflections.

The women left. Bond said perfunctorily, "Honey, you look wonderful." He glanced at the clock on the wall and went to the drink tray and poured himself a stiff bourbon and soda.

In due course there came the soft knock on the door, and the two of them went out of the room and along the corridor. May stopped at the lift. They walked in and the doors shut. Bond observed that it was made by Otis. Everything in the prison was deluxe. He gave a shudder of distaste. The girl noticed. He turned to her. "I'm sorry, Honey. Got a bit of a headache." He didn't want to tell her that all this luxury playacting was getting him down, that he knew it was bad news, but that he hadn't an inkling of a plan of how to get them out of whatever situation they were in.

The girl moved closer to him. She said, "I'm sorry, James. I hope it will go away. You're not angry with me about anything?"

Bond dredged up a smile. He said, "No, darling." He lowered his voice. "Now just leave the talking to me. Be natural and don't be worried by Doctor No. He may be a bit mad."

She nodded solemnly. "I'll do my best."

The lift sighed to a stop. The doors hissed back, and Bond and the girl stepped out into a large room.

It was empty. It was a high-ceilinged room about sixty feet long, lined on three sides with books to the ceiling. At first glance the fourth wall seemed to be made of solid blue-black glass. The room appeared to be a combined study and library. There was a big paper-strewn desk in one corner and a central table with periodicals and newspapers. Comfortable club chairs, upholstered in red leather, were dotted about.

Bond's eye caught a swirl of movement in the dark glass. He walked across the room. A silvery spray of small fish, with a bigger fish in pursuit, fled across the dark blue. What was this? An aquarium? Bond looked upwards. A yard below the ceiling, small waves were lapping at the glass. Above the waves was a strip of grayer blue-black, dotted with sparks of light. This was not an aquarium. This was the sea itself and the night sky. The whole of one side of the room was made of armored glass. They were under the sea, looking straight into its heart.

Bond and the girl stood transfixed. As they watched, there was the glimpse of two great goggling orbs. A golden sheen of head and flank showed for an instant and was gone. A big grouper? A silver swarm of anchovies stopped and hovered and sped away. Bond walked along the wall, fascinated. A big tulip shell was progressing slowly up the window from the floor level. A school of demoiselles and angelfish were nudging against a corner of the glass. A long dark shadow paused in the center of the window and then moved away. If only one could see more!

Obediently two great shafts of light from off the "screen" lanced out into the water. For an instant they searched. Then they converged on the departing shadow, and the dull gray torpedo of a twelve-foot shark showed up in detail. Bond could even see the piglike pink eyes roll inquisitively in the light, and the slow pulse of the slanting gill rakers.

The searchlights went out. Bond turned slowly. He expected to see Doctor No, but still the room was empty. It looked lifeless compared with the pulsing mysteries outside the window. Bond looked back. What must this be like in the colors of day? Or in a storm, when the waves crashed noiselessly against the glass? What an amazing man this must be who had thought of this fantastically beautiful conception, and what an extraordinary engineering feat to have carried it out! How had he done it? How much, God in heaven, could it have cost?

"ONE million dollars."

It was a cavernous, echoing voice, with a trace of American accent. Bond turned away from the window. Doctor No had come through a door behind his desk. He stood looking at them benignly, with a thin smile on his lips.

"I expect you were wondering about the cost. My guests usually think of the material side after about fifteen minutes. Were you?"

"I was."

Still smiling—Bond was to get used to that thin smile—Doctor No came slowly out from behind the desk and moved towards them. He seemed to glide rather than take steps. His knees did not dent the smooth gunmetal sheen of his kimono, and no shoes showed below the sweeping hem.

Bond's first impression was of thinness and height. Doctor No was at least six inches taller than Bond, but the straight immovable poise of his body made him seem still taller. The head also was

elongated and tapered from a round, completely bald skull down to a sharp chin. The skin was of a deep, almost translucent, yellow.

It was impossible to tell Doctor No's age; as far as Bond could see, there were no lines on the face, and the forehead was as smooth as the top of the polished skull. The eyebrows were fine and black and sharply upswept, as if they had been painted on as makeup. Below them, slanting jet-black eyes stared out of the skull. They were without eyelashes. They looked like the mouths of two revolvers, direct and unblinking and totally devoid of expression.

The bizarre gliding figure looked like a giant worm wrapped in gray tinfoil, and Bond would not have been surprised to see the rest of it trailing slimily along the carpet behind.

Doctor No came within three steps of them and stopped. "Forgive me for not shaking hands with you"—the deep voice was flat and even—"I am unable to." Slowly the sleeves parted and opened. "I have no hands."

Two pairs of steel pincers came out on gleaming stalks and were held up for inspection like the hands of a praying mantis. Then the two sleeves joined again.

Bond felt the girl at his side give a start.

The black apertures turned towards her. They slid down to her nose. The voice said flatly, "It is a misfortune." The eyes came back to Bond. "You were admiring my aquarium. Man enjoys the beasts and the birds. I decided to enjoy also the fish. I find them more varied and interesting. I am sure you both share my enthusiasm."

Bond said, "I congratulate you. I shall never forget this room."

"No." It was a statement of fact. "But we have much to talk about. And so little time. Please sit down. You will have a drink? Cigarettes are beside your chairs."

Doctor No moved to a high leather chair and folded himself down onto the seat. Bond took the chair opposite. The girl sat between them.

Bond felt a movement behind him. He looked over his shoulder. A short man in a white jacket, with the build of a wrestler, stood at the drink tray.

Doctor No said, "This is my bodyguard. There is no mystery about his sudden appearance. I carry a walkie-talkie here"—he inclined his chin towards the bosom of his kimono. "Thus I can summon him when he is needed. What will the girl have?"

Not "your wife," Bond thought, and turned to Honeychile. She said quietly, "A Coca-Cola, please."

Bond felt a moment of relief. At least she was not upset by the performance. He said, "And I would like a medium vodka dry martini—with a slice of lemon peel. Shaken and not stirred, please. I would prefer Russian or Polish vodka."

Doctor No gave his thin smile an extra crease. "I see you are a man who knows what he wants. On this occasion your desires will be satisfied. Do you not find that it is generally so? When one wants a thing, one gets it? That is my experience."

"The small things."

"If you fail at the large things, it means you have not large ambitions. Concentration, focus—that is all. The aptitudes come, the tools forge themselves." The thin lips bent minutely downwards in deprecation. "But this is chatter. Instead, let us talk. Both of us, I am sure, prefer talk to conversation. Sam-sam, put the shaker beside the man and the bottle of Coca-Cola beside the girl. It should now be eight ten. We will have dinner at nine precisely."

Doctor No sat slightly more upright in his chair, staring at Bond. Then he said, "And now, Mr. James Bond of the Secret Service, let us tell each other our secrets. First, to show you that I hide nothing, I will tell you mine. Then you will tell me yours." Doctor No's eyes blazed darkly. "But let us tell each other the truth." He drew one steel claw out of the sleeve. "I shall do so. But you must do the same. If you do not, these"—he pointed the claw at his eyes—"will know that you are lying."

Doctor No brought the steel claw delicately in front of each eye and tapped the center of each eyeball. Each eyeball emitted a dull ting. "These," said Doctor No, "see everything."

JAMES Bond picked up his glass and sipped thoughtfully. It seemed pointless to go on bluffing. It was obvious that his cover was in shreds. He must concentrate on protecting the girl. To begin with he must reassure her.

Bond smiled at Doctor No. He said, "I know about your contact in King's House, Miss Taro. She is your agent." Doctor No's expression showed no interest. "But if we are to have a talk, let us have it without any more stage effects. You have lost your hands. You wear mechanical hands. Many men wounded in the war wear them. You wear contact lenses instead of spectacles. You use a walkie-talkie instead of a bell to summon your servant. No doubt you have other tricks. But, Doctor No, you are still a man who sleeps and eats like the rest of us. So no more conjuring tricks, please. I am not one of your guano diggers, and I am not impressed by them."

Doctor No inclined his head a fraction. "Bravely spoken, Mr. Bond. I accept the rebuke. I have no doubt developed annoying mannerisms from living too long in the company of apes. But do not mistake these mannerisms for bluff. However"—Doctor No raised his joined sleeves an inch—"let us proceed with our talk. It is a rare pleasure to have an intelligent listener, and I shall enjoy telling you the story of one of the most remarkable men in the world. I have not told it before. You are the only person I have ever met who will appreciate my story and also keep it to himself." Doctor No paused for the significance of the last word to make itself felt. He continued, "The second of these considerations also applies to the girl."

So that was it. There had been little doubt in Bond's mind ever since the machine gun had opened up on them, and even before then in Jamaica, where the attempts on him had not been halfhearted. Bond had assumed from the first that this man was a killer, that it would be a duel to the death. He had had his usual blind faith that he would win the duel—until the flamethrower had pointed at him. Then he had begun to doubt.

Now he said, "There is no point in the girl hearing this. She has nothing to do with me. I found her yesterday on the beach. She collects shells. Your men destroyed her canoe so I had to bring her with me. Send her away now, and then home. She won't talk."

The girl interrupted fiercely. "I *will* talk! I shall tell everything. And I'm going to stay with you."

Bond looked at her. He said icily, "I don't want you."

Doctor No said softly, "Do not waste your breath on these heroics. Nobody who comes to this island has ever left it. Do you understand? Nobody. It is not my policy. Do not argue with me. It is useless."

Bond examined the face. There was no anger in it—nothing but a supreme indifference. He shrugged. "All right, Honey. And I didn't mean it. I'd hate you to go away. We'll stay together and listen to what the maniac has to say."

The girl nodded happily.

Doctor No said in the same soft resonant voice, "You are right, Mr. Bond. That is just what I am, a maniac. All the greatest men are maniacs. They are possessed by a mania which drives them towards their goal. The great scientists, artists, religious leaders—all maniacs. What else but a blind singleness of purpose could have given focus to their genius? Mania, my dear Mr. Bond, is as priceless as genius." Doctor No sat slightly back in his chair. "I am, as you correctly say, a maniac—a maniac, Mr. Bond, with a mania for power. That"—the black holes glittered blankly at Bond—"is the meaning of my life. That is why I am here. That is why you are here. That is why here exists."

Bond picked up his glass and drained it. He said, "I'm not surprised. It's the old business of thinking you're the King of England, or the President of the United States, or God. The asylums are full of them. The only difference is that instead of being shut up, you've built your own asylum and shut yourself up in it. But why did you do it? Why does sitting shut up in this cell give you the illusion of power?"

Irritation flickered at the corners of the thin mouth. "Mr. Bond, power is sovereignty. Clausewitz's first principle was to have a secure base. From there one proceeds to freedom of action. Together, that is sovereignty. I have secured these things and much besides. No one else in the world possesses them to the same degree. The world is too public. These things can only be secured in privacy. You talk of kings and presidents. How much power do they possess? As much as their people will allow them. Who in the world has the power of life or death over his people? Now that Stalin is dead, can you name any man except myself? And how do I possess that power, that sovereignty? Through privacy. Through the fact that nobody *knows*."

Bond shrugged. "That is only the illusion of power, Doctor No. Any man with a loaded revolver has the power of life and death over his neighbor. Other people besides you have murdered in secret and got away with it. In the end they generally get their deserts. A greater power than they possess is exerted upon them by the community. That will happen to you, Doctor No. I tell you, your

601

search for power is an illusion because power itself is an illusion."

Doctor No said equably, "So is beauty, Mr. Bond. So is art, so is money, so is death. And so, probably, is life. Your play upon words does not shake me. But let us move away from this sterile debate to where I began, with my mania for power, or, if you wish it, for the illusion of power."

"Go ahead." Bond glanced at the girl. She put her hand up to her mouth as if to conceal a yawn. Bond grinned at her.

Doctor No said benignly, "I shall endeavor not to bore you. Facts are much more interesting than theories, don't you agree?" Doctor No was not expecting a reply. He fixed his eye on the tulip shell that had now wandered halfway up the outside of the window. Some small silverfish squirted across the black void.

Doctor No said, "I was the only son of a German Methodist missionary and a Chinese girl of good family. I was born in Peking, but on what is known as the wrong side of the blanket. I was an encumbrance. An aunt of my mother's was paid to bring me up." Doctor No paused. "No love, you see, Mr. Bond. Lack of parental care." He went on, "The seed was sown. I went to work in Shanghai. I became involved with the tongs, with their illicit proceedings. I enjoyed the conspiracies, the burglaries, the murders. They represented revolt against the father figure who had betrayed me. I became adept in the technique of criminality—if you wish to call it that. Then there was trouble. I had to be gotten out of the way. The tongs considered me too valuable to kill. I was smuggled to the United States, to New York. I had been given a letter of introduction to one of the two most powerful tongs in America—the Hip Sings. They took me on as a confidential clerk.

"In due course, at the age of thirty, I was made the equivalent of treasurer. The treasury contained over a million dollars. I coveted this money. Then began the great tong wars of the late 1920s. The two great New York tongs—my own, the Hip Sings, and our rival, the On Lee Ongs—joined in combat. Hundreds on both sides were killed. Then the riot squads came. The police force of New York was mobilized. The two underground armies were pried apart, and the headquarters of the two tongs were raided and the ringleaders sent to jail. I was tipped off about the raid on the Hip Sings. A few hours before it was due, I got to the safe and rifled the million dollars in gold and disappeared into Harlem.

"I was foolish. I should have gone to the farthest corner of the earth. Even from the condemned cells in Sing Sing the heads of my tong reached out for me. They found me. The killers came in the night. They tortured me. I would not say where the gold was, so they cut off my hands to show that the corpse was that of a thief, and they shot me through the heart and went away. But they did not know something. I am the one man in a million who has his heart on the right side of his body. I lived. I survived the months in the hospital. And all the time I planned and planned how to get away with the money—what to do with it."

Doctor No paused. There was a slight flush at his temples. His memories had excited him. For a moment he closed his eyes, composing himself. Bond thought, Now! Shall I leap and kill him? Break off my glass and do it with the jagged stem?

The eyes opened. "I am not boring you? For an instant I felt your attention wandering."

"No." The moment had passed.

The thin lips parted and the story went on. "It was, Mr. Bond, a time for clear, firm decisions. When they let me out of the hospital I went to Silberstein, the greatest stamp dealer in New York. I bought an envelope full of the rarest postage stamps in the world. It took weeks to get them together. But I didn't mind what I paid—in New York, Paris, Zurich. I wanted my gold to be mobile. I invested it in stamps. I had foreseen World War Two. I knew there would be inflation. I knew the best would appreciate, or at least hold their value. And meanwhile I was changing my appearance. I had all my hair taken out by the roots, my thick nose made thin, my mouth widened. I could not get smaller, so I made myself taller. I wore built-up shoes. I had weeks of traction on my spine. I held myself differently. I put away my mechanical hands and wore hands of wax inside gloves. I changed my name to Julius No—the Julius after my father and the No for my rejection of him and of all authority. I threw away my spectacles and wore contact lenses. Then I went to Wisconsin, and got myself enrolled in a medical school. And there, Mr. Bond, I lost myself in the study of the human body and the human mind. Why? Because I wished to know what this clay is capable of. I had to learn what my tools were, before I put them to use on my next goal—total security from physical weaknesses, from material dangers and from the hazards of living. Then from that secure base I would proceed to the achievement of power—the power, Mr. Bond, to do unto others what had been done unto me, the power of life and death."

Bond reached for the shaker and poured himself another drink. He looked at Honeychile. She seemed composed and indifferent—as if her mind were on other things.

Doctor No continued, "In due course I completed my studies, and I left America and went by easy stages round the world. I was looking for my headquarters. It had to be safe from the coming war, it had to be an island, entirely private, and it had to be capable of industrial development. In the end I purchased Crab Key. And here I have remained. They have been secure and fruitful years, without a cloud on the horizon. I was entertained by the idea of amassing a fortune by marketing bird dung, and I attacked the problem with passion. It seemed to me the ideal industry. The birds required no care except to be left in peace. The sole problem was the cost of the labor. The simple Cuban and Jamaican laborer was earning ten shillings a week cutting cane. I tempted a hundred of them over to the island by paying them twelve shillings a week. My men are content with their wages, because they are the highest wages they have ever known. I brought in a dozen Chinese Negroes, with their families, to act as overseers. They receive a pound per week per man. They are tough and reliable. On occasion I had to be ruthless with them, but they soon learned.

"Automatically my people increased in numbers. I added some engineers and builders. We set to work on the mountain. Occasionally I brought in teams of specialists on high wages. They were kept apart from the others. They lived inside the mountain until their work was done, and then left by ship. They put in the ventilation and the elevator. They built this room. Supplies and furnishings

came in from all over the world. It has been hard, Mr. Bond."
The black eyes did not look for sympathy or praise. "But by the
end of last year the work was done. A secure, well-camouflaged
base had been achieved. I was ready to proceed to the next step—an
extension of my power to the outside world."

Doctor No paused. He lifted his arms an inch and dropped them
again resignedly in his lap. "Mr. Bond, I said that there was not
a cloud in the sky during all these years. But there was one—below
the horizon. And do you know what it was? It was a bird, a ridiculous
bird called a roseate spoonbill! You are already aware of some
of the circumstances, Mr. Bond. The two wardens, miles away in
the middle of the lake, were provisioned by launch from Cuba.
Occasionally ornithologists from America came by the launch and
spent days at the camp. I did not mind. The area is out of bounds
to my men. From the first I made it clear to the Audubon Society
that I would not meet their representatives. And then what happens?
One day, out of a clear sky, I get a letter by the monthly boat.
The roseate spoonbills have become one of the bird wonders of
the world. The society gives me formal notification that they intend
to build a hotel on their leasehold, near the river. Bird lovers from
all over the world will come to observe the birds. Films will be
taken. Crab Key, they told me in their flattering, persuasive letter,
would become famous.

"Mr. Bond." Irony gathered at the edges of the smile. "Can you
believe it? This privacy I had achieved! The plans I had for the
future! To be swept aside because of a lot of old women and their
birds! I examined the lease. I wrote, offering a huge sum to buy
it. They refused. So I studied these birds and their habits. And
suddenly the solution was there. Spoonbills are extremely shy. They
frighten easily. I sent to Florida for a marsh buggy—the vehicle
that is used for oil prospecting, that will cover any kind of terrain.
I adapted it to frighten and to burn—not only birds, but humans
as well, for the wardens would have to go too. And one night
in December my marsh buggy howled off across the lake. It smashed
the camp, both wardens were reported killed, it burned the nesting
places, it spread terror among the birds. Complete success! The

spoonbills died in thousands. But then I got a demand for a plane to land on my airstrip. There was to be an investigation. I decide to agree. An accident is arranged. A truck goes out of control on the airstrip. The plane is destroyed. All signs of the truck are removed. The bodies are reverently placed in coffins. As I expected, there is further investigation. A destroyer arrives. I receive the captain courteously. He and his officers are shown the remains of the camp. My men suggest that the wardens went mad with loneliness and fought each other. The survivor set fire to the camp and escaped. The airstrip is examined. My men report that the plane was coming in too fast. The tires must have burst. The bodies are handed over. The officers are satisfied. The ship leaves. Peace reigns again."

Doctor No coughed delicately. He looked from Bond to the girl and back again. "And that, my friends, is my story—or rather the first chapter. Privacy has been reestablished. There are now no roseate spoonbills, so no doubt the Audubon Society will decide to accept my offer for the rest of their lease. No matter. If they start their puny operations again, other misfortunes will befall them."

"Interesting," said Bond. "An interesting case history. So that was why Strangways had to be removed. What did you do with him and his girl?"

"They are at the bottom of the Mona Reservoir. I sent three of my best men. I have a small but efficient machine in Jamaica. I need it. Your Mr. Strangways started ferreting about. Fortunately, by this time the routines of this man were known to me. His death and the girl's were a simple matter of timing. I had hoped to deal with you with similar expedition. I knew what type of a man you were from the files at King's House. I guessed that you would come here, and when the canoe showed up on the radar screen I knew you would not get away."

Bond said, "Your radar is not very efficient. There were two canoes. The one you saw was the girl's. I tell you she had nothing to do with me."

"Then she is unfortunate. I happen to be needing a woman for a small experiment. As we agreed earlier, Mr. Bond, one generally gets what one wants."

Bond looked thoughtfully at Doctor No. He wondered if it was worthwhile even trying to make a dent in this impregnable man. Was it worth wasting breath by threatening or bluffing? Bond had nothing but a miserable two of clubs up his sleeve. The thought of playing it almost bored him. Casually, indifferently, he threw it down.

"Then you're out of luck, Doctor No. You are now a file in London. My thoughts on this case, the evidence of the poisoned fruit, the centipede and the crashed motorcar are on record. So are the names of Miss Chung and Miss Taro. Instructions were left in Jamaica that my report should be opened and acted upon if I failed to return from Crab Key within three days."

Bond paused. The face of Doctor No was impassive. Bond bent forward. "But because of the girl, and only because of her, Doctor No, I will strike a bargain. In exchange for our safe return to Jamaica, you may have a week's start. You may take your packet of stamps and try to get away."

Bond sat back. "Any interest, Doctor No?"

Chapter 9

A VOICE behind Bond said quietly, "Dinner is served."

Bond swung around. It was the bodyguard. Beside him was another man, who might have been his twin.

"Ah, nine o'clock already." Doctor No rose to his feet. "Come. We can continue our conversation in more intimate surroundings."

Double doors stood open in the wall. Bond and the girl followed Doctor No through into a small octagonal mahogany-paneled room lit by a silver chandelier. A round mahogany table was laid for three. Silver and glass twinkled warmly. Doctor No took the center chair and bowed the girl into the chair on his right. They sat down and unfolded napkins of white silk.

At first, Doctor No seemed preoccupied. He slowly ate soup, feeding himself by means of a spoon with a handle that fitted between the pincers. Bond concentrated on hiding his fears from the girl. He ate and talked cheerfully to her about Jamaica—about the birds and the animals and the flowers, which were easy topics for her. She became almost gay. Bond thought they were putting on an excellent imitation of an engaged couple being given dinner by a detested uncle.

Bond had no idea if his thin bluff had worked. He didn't give much for their chances. Doctor No and Doctor No's story exuded impregnability. The incredible biography rang true. Not a word of it was impossible.

Underneath his chatter with the girl, Bond prepared for the worst. There were plenty of weapons beside his plate. When the cutlets came, perfectly cooked, Bond fiddled indecisively with the knives and chose the bread knife to eat them with. While he ate and talked he edged the meat knife towards him. An expansive gesture of his right hand knocked over his glass of champagne, and in the split second of the crash his left hand flicked the knife into the deep sleeve of his kimono. In the midst of Bond's apologies and the confusion as he and the bodyguard mopped up the spilled champagne, Bond raised his left arm and felt the knife slip back to below his armpit and then fall inside the kimono, against his ribs. When he had finished his cutlets he tightened the silk belt round his waist, shifting the knife across his stomach. The knife nestled comfortingly against his skin.

Coffee came and the meal was ended. The two guards came and stood close behind Bond's chair and the girl's, with their arms crossed on their chests, impassive, like executioners. Doctor No put his cup down on its saucer. He sat a fraction more upright and turned his body in Bond's direction. "You have enjoyed your dinner, Mr. Bond?"

Bond took a cigarette from the box in front of him and lit it. He played with the silver table lighter. He smelled bad news coming. He must somehow pocket the lighter. He said easily, "Yes. It was excellent." He looked across at the girl. He leaned forward and rested his forearms on the table, enveloping the lighter. He smiled at her. "I hope I ordered what you like."

"Oh, yes, it was lovely." For her the party was still going on.

Bond turned to Doctor No. He stubbed out his cigarette and

sat back, folding his arms across his chest. The lighter was in his left armpit. "And what happens now, Doctor No?"

"We can proceed to our after-dinner entertainment, Mr. Bond." The thin smile creased. "I have examined your proposition from every angle. I do not accept it."

Bond shrugged his shoulders. "You are unwise."

"No, Mr. Bond. I suspect that your proposition is a goldbrick. People in your trade do not behave as you suggest. They make routine reports to their headquarters. Your little speech reeked of greasepaint and cardboard. No, Mr. Bond, I do not accept your story. If it is true, I am prepared to face the consequences. So the police come, the soldiers. Where are a man and a girl? What man and what girl? I know nothing. Where is your evidence? Your search warrant? The English law is strict, gentlemen. Go home and leave me in peace with my beloved cormorants. You see, Mr. Bond?" The tall pear-shaped head shook gently. "Have you anything else to say? Any questions to ask? You both have a busy night ahead of you. Your time is getting short. And I must get my sleep. The monthly ship is putting in tomorrow and I have the loading to supervise on the quay. Well, Mr. Bond?"

Bond looked across at the girl. She had gone deathly pale. She was gazing at him, waiting for the miracle he would work. He looked down at his hands. He said, playing for time, "And then what? After your busy day with the bird dung, what comes next on your program? What is the next chapter you think you're going to write?"

"Ah, yes." The deep quiet authoritative voice came to Bond as if it were coming down from the night sky. "You must have been wondering, Mr. Bond. You have the habit of inquiry. It persists even to the last, even into the shadows. I admire such qualities in a man with only a few hours to live. So I will tell you. There is more to this place than bird dung. Your instincts did not betray you." Doctor No paused for emphasis. "This island, Mr. Bond, is about to be developed into the most valuable technical intelligence center in the world."

"Really?" Bond focused his eyes on his hands.

"Doubtless you know that Turks Island, about three hundred miles from here through the Windward Passage, is the most important center for testing the guided missiles of the United States?"

"It is an important center, yes."

"Perhaps you have read of rockets that have been going astray recently? The multistage Snark, for instance, that ended its flight in the forests of Brazil instead of the South Atlantic?"

"Yes."

"You recall that it refused to obey the telemetered instructions to change its course, even to destroy itself. It developed a will of its own?"

"I remember."

"There have been other failures from the long list of prototypes—the Zuni, Matador, Petrel, Bomarc—so many names, so many changes, I can't even remember them all. Well, Mr. Bond"—Doctor No could not keep a note of pride out of his voice—"it may interest you to know that the vast majority of those failures have been caused from Crab Key."

"Is that so?"

"You do not believe me? No matter. Others do. Others who have seen the complete abandonment of one series, the Mastodon, because of its recurring navigational errors, its failure to obey the radio directions from Turks Island. Those others are the Russians. The Russians are my partners in this venture. They trained six of my men, Mr. Bond. Two of those men are on watch at this moment, watching the radio frequencies, the beams on which these weapons travel. There is a million dollars' worth of equipment up above us in the rock galleries, Mr. Bond, sending fingers up into the ionosphere, waiting for the signals, jamming them. From time to time a rocket soars up on its way over the Atlantic. And we track it as accurately as they are tracking it in the operations room on Turks Island. Then suddenly our pulses go out to the rocket, its brain is confused, it goes mad, it plunges into the sea, it roars off at a tangent. Another test has failed. The designers are blamed, the manufacturers. There is panic in the Pentagon. Something else must be tried. Of course"—Doctor No was fair—"we, too, have our difficulties. We track many practice shoots without being able to get through to the brain of the new rocket. But then we communicate urgently with Moscow. And the Russians make suggestions. We try them out. And then one day, Mr. Bond, up in the stratosphere the rocket acknowledges our signal. We are recognized, and we can speak to it and change its mind." Doctor No paused. "Do you not find that interesting, Mr. Bond, this little sideline to my business in guano? It is, I assure you, most profitable. It might be still more so. Perhaps Communist China will pay more. Who knows? I already have my feelers out."

Bond lifted his eyes. He looked thoughtfully at Doctor No. So he *had* been right. There *had* been much more in all this than met the eye. This was a big game, a game that explained everything, a game that was certainly, in the international espionage market, well worth the candle. Well, well! Now the pieces in the puzzle fell firmly into place. For this it was certainly worth scaring away a few birds and wiping out a few people. Privacy? Of course Doctor No would have to kill him and the girl. Power? This was it. Doctor No had really got himself into business.

Bond looked into the two black holes with a new respect. He said, "You'll have to kill a lot more people to keep this thing in your hands, Doctor No. It's worth a lot of money. You've got a good property here—a better one than I thought. People are going to want to cut themselves a piece of this cake. I wonder who will get to you first and kill you."

"You cannot play for high stakes without taking risks, Mr. Bond. I accept the dangers, and so far as I can I have equipped myself against them. You see, Mr. Bond"—the deep voice held a hint of greed—"I am on the edge of still greater things. Chapter Two holds the promise of prizes which no one but a fool would throw away because he was afraid. I have told you that I can bend the beams on which these rockets fly. I can make them change course and ignore their radio control. What would you say, Mr. Bond, if I could go further? If I could bring them down into the sea near this island and salvage the secrets of their construction? How much would Russia pay for that to happen, Mr. Bond? And how much for each of the prototypes I captured for them? Shall we say ten million dollars for the whole operation? Twenty million? It would be a priceless victory in the armaments race. I could name my figure. Don't you agree, Mr. Bond? And don't you agree that these considerations make your arguments and threats seem rather puny?"

Bond said nothing. There was nothing to say. Suddenly he was back in the quiet room high up above Regent's Park. He could hear the rain slashing against the window and M.'s voice, impatient, sarcastic, saying, "Oh, that damned business about the birds . . . sunshine'll do you good . . . routine investigation." And he, Bond, had taken a canoe and a fisherman and a picnic lunch and had gone off "to have a look."

Well, he had had his look into Pandora's box. He had found out the answers, been told the secrets—and now? Now he was going to be politely shown the way to his grave, taking the secrets with him and the waif he had picked up and dragged along with him on his lunatic adventure. The bitterness inside Bond came up into his mouth, so that for a moment he thought he was going to retch. He reached for his champagne and emptied the glass. He said harshly, "All right, Doctor No. Now let's get on with the cabaret. What's the program—knife, bullet, poison, rope? But make it quick. I've seen enough of you."

Doctor No's lips compressed into a thin purple line. The eyes were hard as onyx under the billiard-ball forehead. The polite mask had gone. The grand inquisitor sat in the high-backed chair. The hour had struck.

Doctor No spoke a word, and the two guards took a step forward and held the two victims above the elbows, forcing their arms back against the sides of their chairs. Bond concentrated on holding the lighter in his armpit. The hands on his biceps felt like steel bands. He smiled across at the girl. "I'm sorry about this, Honey. I'm afraid we're not going to be able to play together after all."

The girl's eyes were blue-black with fear. Her lips trembled. She said, "Will it hurt?"

"Silence!" Doctor No's voice was the crack of a whip. "Enough of this foolery. Of course it will hurt. I am interested in pain.

I am also interested in finding out how much the human body can endure. From time to time I make experiments on those of my people who have to be punished. And on trespassers like yourselves. You have both put me to a great deal of trouble. In exchange I intend to put you to a great deal of pain. I shall record the length of your endurance. The facts will be noted. One day my findings will be given to the world. Your deaths will have served the purposes of science. It is a year since I put a girl to death in the fashion I have chosen for you, woman. She lasted three hours. I have wanted another girl for comparison. I get what I want." Doctor No's eyes were now fixed on the girl, watching her reactions. She stared back at him, half hypnotized, like a mouse in front of a rattlesnake.

Bond set his teeth.

"You are a Jamaican, so you will know what I am talking about. This island is called Crab Key. It is called by that name because it is infested with crabs, land crabs—what they call in Jamaica black crabs. They weigh about a pound each and are as big as saucers. At this time of year they come up in thousands from the shore and climb up towards the mountain. There, in the coral uplands, they go to ground in holes and spawn. They march up in armies. They march through everything and over everything. They are like the lemmings of Norway. It is a compulsive migration." Doctor No paused. He said softly, "But there is a difference. The crabs devour what they find in their path. And at present, woman, they are running. They are coming up the mountainside in their tens of thousands, great orange and black waves of them, scuttling and scraping against the rock above us at this moment. And tonight in their path they are going to find the body of a woman pegged out—a banquet spread for them—and they will feel the warm body with their pincers, and one will make the first incision with his fighting claws and then . . . and then . . ."

There was a moan from the girl. Her head fell forward onto her chest. She had fainted. Bond's body heaved in his chair. A string of obscenities hissed out between his teeth. The huge hands of the guard were like fire round his arms. He couldn't even move the chair legs on the floor. After a moment he desisted. He waited for his voice to steady, then he said, "You bastard. You'll fry in hell for this."

Doctor No smiled thinly. "Mr. Bond, I do not admit the existence of hell. Console yourself. Perhaps they will start at the throat or the heart. Then it will not be long." He spoke a sentence in Chinese. The guard behind the girl's chair plucked her up and slung the inert body over his shoulder. He went to the door and opened it and went out, closing it noiselessly behind him.

For a moment there was silence in the room. Bond thought of the knife against his skin and of the lighter under his armpit. Could he somehow get within range of Doctor No?

Doctor No said quietly, "Now, Mr. Bond, let us proceed to the method of your departure. That also has its novel aspects. You see, Mr. Bond, I am interested in the anatomy of courage—in the power of the human body to endure. But how to measure human endurance? How to plot a graph of the will to survive? I have given much thought to the problem, and I believe I have solved it. It is, of course, only a rough-and-ready method, and I shall learn by experience as more subjects are put to the test. I have prepared you for the experiment as best I could. I gave you a sedative so that your body should be rested, and I have fed you well so that you may be at full strength. Future—what shall I call them?—patients, will have the same advantages." Doctor No paused, watching Bond's face. "You see, Mr. Bond, I have just finished constructing an obstacle course against death. I will say no more about it, because the element of surprise is one of the constituents of fear. It is the unknown dangers that bear most heavily on the reserves of courage. The gauntlet you will run contains a rich assortment of the unexpected. It will be particularly interesting, Mr. Bond, that a man of your physical qualities is to be my first competitor. It will be most interesting to observe how far you get down the course I have devised. I have high expectations of you. You should go far, but when, as is inevitable, you have finally failed at an obstacle, your body will be recovered, and I shall most meticulously examine the physical state of your remains. The data will be recorded. You will be the first dot on a graph. Something of an honor, is it not, Mr. Bond?"

Bond said nothing. What the hell could this test consist of? Could he conceivably escape from it and get to the girl before it was too late, even if only to kill her and save her from her torture?

Doctor No rose and walked to the door and turned. The menacing black holes looked back at Bond. The purple lips creased. "Run a good race for me, Mr. Bond. My thoughts, as they say, will be with you."

Doctor No turned away, and the door closed softly behind the long thin gunmetal back.

Chapter 10

THERE was a man on the lift. The doors were open, waiting. James Bond, his arms still locked to his sides, was marched in. The doors hissed shut, and they went up. Then the doors opened onto an uncarpeted corridor with gray stone walls. It ran about twenty yards ahead.

"Hold it, Joe," said Bond's guard to the lift man. "I'll be right with you."

Bond was marched down the corridor past doors numbered with letters of the alphabet. There was a faint hum of machinery, and behind one door Bond thought he could catch the crackle of radio static. The end door was marked with a black Q. It was ajar, and the guard pushed Bond into it. Through the door was a stone cell about fifteen feet square. There was nothing in it except a wooden chair, on which lay, neatly folded, Bond's black canvas jeans and blue shirt.

The guard let go of Bond's arms. Bond turned and looked into the broad yellow face below the crinkly hair. There was a hint of curiosity and pleasure in the brown eyes. The man said, "Well, this is it, bud. You're at the starting gate. You can either sit here and rot or find your way out onto the course. Happy landings."

Bond thought it was just worth trying. He glanced past the guard to where the lift man was standing. He said softly, "How would you like to earn ten thousand dollars, guaranteed, and a ticket to anywhere in the world?"

The man's mouth spread in a wide grin to show brownish worn-down teeth.

"Thanks, mister. I'd rather stay alive." And the man shut the door with a solid click.

Bond gave the door a cursory glance. It was made of metal, and there was no handle on the inside. Bond didn't waste his shoulder on it. He went to the chair and sat down on the pile of clothes and looked around. The walls were entirely naked except for a ventilation grille of thick wire in one corner, just below the ceiling. It was wider than his shoulders. It was obviously the way out onto the assault course. The only other break in the walls was a thick glass porthole, no bigger than Bond's head, just above the door. Light from the corridor filtered through it into the cell. There was nothing else. It was no good wasting any more time. It would now be about ten thirty. Outside, somewhere on the mountain, the girl would already be lying, waiting for the rattle of claws on the gray coral. Bond clenched his teeth at the thought. Abruptly he stood up. What the hell was he doing sitting still? Whatever lay on the other side of the wire grille, it was time to go.

Bond took out the knife and the lighter and threw off the kimono. He dressed in the trousers and shirt, and stowed the lighter in his hip pocket. He tried the edge of the knife. It was very sharp. It would be better still if he could get a point on it. He knelt and sharpened the rounded end on the stone floor. After a quarter of an hour he was satisfied. It was no stiletto, but it would serve to stab as well as cut. Bond put the knife between his teeth and set the chair below the grille, then climbed onto it. The grille! If he could tear it off its hinges, the frame of quarter-inch wire might straighten into a spear. That would make a third weapon. Bond reached up with crooked fingers.

The next thing he knew was a searing pain up his arm and the crack of his head hitting the stone floor. He lay stunned, with only the memory of a blue flash and the hiss and crackle of electricity to tell him what had hit him. He lifted his right hand up to his eyes. There was the red smear of an open burn across the inside of his fingers. Seeing it brought on the pain. Bond spat out a four-letter word.

Slowly he got to his feet. He squinted up at the wire grille as if it might strike at him again, like a snake. Grimly he climbed up again onto the chair and looked at the grille. It was intended that he get through it. The shock had been to soften him up—a taste of pain to come. Surely he had blown the fuses with the blasted thing. Surely they would have switched off the current. He looked at it for only an instant; then the fingers of his left hand crooked and went through the wire and gripped.

Nothing! Nothing at all—just wire. Bond grunted. He tugged. The wire gave an inch. He tugged again and it came away in his hand. Bond pulled the grille loose from the two strands of copper wire and got down from the chair. Yes, there was a joint in the frame. He set to work unraveling the mesh. Then, using the chair as a hammer, he straightened the heavy wire.

After ten minutes Bond had a crooked spear about four feet long. One end, where it had originally been cut by pliers, was jagged. Bond turned the blunt end into a clumsy crook. He bent the whole wire double and slipped the spear down a trouser leg. It hung from his waistband to just above the knee. He went back to the chair and climbed up again and reached nervously for the edge of the ventilator shaft. There was no shock. Bond heaved up and through the opening and lay on his stomach, looking along the shaft.

The shaft was about four inches wider than Bond's shoulders. It was circular and of polished metal. Bond reached for the lighter, blessing the inspiration that had made him take it, and flicked it on. Yes, zinc sheeting that looked new. The shaft stretched straight ahead, featureless except for the ridges where the sections of pipe joined. Bond put the lighter back in his pocket and snaked forward.

It was easy going. Cool air from the ventilating system blew strongly in Bond's face. There was a faint luminosity ahead. Bond approached it carefully, his senses questing in front of him like antennae. It was the glint of light against the end of the lateral shaft. He went on until his head touched the metal. Then he twisted over on his back.

Straight above him, at the top of fifty yards or so of vertical shaft, was a steady glimmer. It was like looking up a long gun barrel. Bond inched round the square bend and stood upright. So he was supposed to climb straight up this shining tube of metal! Was it possible? Bond expanded his shoulders. Yes, they gripped the sides. His feet could also get a temporary purchase, though they would slip except where the ridges at the joints gave him an ounce of upward leverage. Bond shrugged and kicked off his shoes. It was no good arguing. He would just have to try.

Six inches at a time, Bond's body began to worm up the metal shaft—expand shoulders to grip the sides, lift feet, lock knees, force the feet outwards against the metal. Contract shoulders and raise them a few inches higher. Do it again, again and again and again. Stop at each tiny bulge and use the millimeter of extra support to get some breath. Don't look up, think only of the inches of metal to be conquered. Don't worry about the glimmer of light that never grows brighter. Don't worry about cramp. Don't worry about your screaming muscles. Don't worry about losing your grip and falling to smash your ankles at the bottom of the shaft.

But then the feet began to sweat and slip. Twice Bond lost a yard before his shoulders could put on the brake. Finally he had to stop altogether to let his sweat dry in the downward draft of air. He waited for a full ten minutes, staring at his faint reflection in the polished metal, the face split in half by the knife between the teeth. At last he began again.

Now half Bond's mind was dreaming while the other half fought the battle. He wasn't even conscious of the strengthening breeze or the slowly brightening light until his head bumped against something. The shock made him slip a yard before his shoulders got a fresh grip. Then he realized. He was at the top! Now he noticed the bright light and the strong wind. Feverishly, but with a more desperate care, he heaved up again until his head touched. The wind was coming into his left ear. Cautiously he turned his head. It was another lateral shaft. Above him, light was shining through a porthole. All he had to do was inch himself around and grip the edge of the new shaft and somehow gather enough strength to heave himself in. Then he would be able to lie down.

With an extra delicacy, born of panic, Bond carried out the maneuver and with his last ounce of strength jackknifed into the opening and crumpled full length on his face.

Later—how much later?—Bond's eyes opened and his body stirred. Painfully he rolled over on his back, his feet and shoulders screaming at him, and lay gathering his wits and summoning more strength.

He lifted his head and looked back at the porthole above the tube out of which he had come. The light was yellowish and the glass looked thick. He remembered the porthole in room Q. There had been nothing breakable about that one, nor, he guessed, would there be here.

Suddenly, behind the glass, he saw movement. As he watched, a pair of eyes materialized from behind a light bulb. They stopped and looked at him. Then they were gone. Bond's lips curled back from his teeth. So his progress was going to be observed, reported to Doctor No!

Bond snarled an obscenity out loud and turned sullenly back on his stomach. He raised his head and looked forward. The tunnel shimmered away into blackness. Come on! No good hanging about. He picked up his knife and put it back between his teeth and winced his way forward.

Soon there was no more light. Bond stopped from time to time and used the lighter, but there was nothing but blackness ahead. The air began to get warmer in the shaft, and, perhaps fifty yards farther, definitely hot. Bond began to sweat. Soon his body was soaked, and he had to pause every few minutes to wipe his eyes. There came a right-hand turn in the shaft. Round it the metal of the big tube was hot against his skin. The smell of heat was very strong. There came another right-angled turn. As soon as Bond's head got around, he lit his lighter and then pulled back and lay panting. His light had flickered on discolored, oyster-hued zinc. The next hazard was to be heat!

Bond groaned aloud. How could he protect his skin from the

metal? But there wasn't anything he could do about it. He could either go back, or stay where he was, or go on. There was no other decision to make. There was one, and only one, grain of consolation. This would not be heat that would kill, only maim. This would not be the final killing ground—only one more test of how much he could take.

Bond thought of the girl and of what she was going through. Oh well. Get on with it.

Bond took his knife and cut the front of his shirt into strips. The only hope was to put wrappings round the parts of his body that would have to bear the brunt—his hands and his feet. Wearily he set to work.

Now he was ready. Bond forged forward.

Keep your naked stomach off the ground! Contract your shoulders! Hands, knees, toes; hands, knees, toes. Faster, faster!

The knees were getting it worst, taking the bulk of Bond's weight. Now the padded hands were beginning to smolder. There was a spark, and another one. His hands shed sparks as he thrust them forward, and the flesh began to burn. Bond lurched and his shoulder hit metal. He screamed. He went on screaming regularly, with each contact of hand or knee or toes. Scream, scream, scream! It helps the pain. Go on! Go on! It can't be much longer. This isn't where you're supposed to die. Don't give up! You can't!

Bond's right hand hit something that gave. There was a stream of ice-cold air. His other hand hit, then his head. Bond felt the edge of an asbestos baffle scrape down his back. He heard the baffle bang shut. He was through. Cool air entered his lungs. Gingerly he laid his fingers down on the metal. It was cold! With a groan Bond fell on his face and lay still.

SOMETIME later the pain revived him. Bond turned sluggishly over on his back. Vaguely he noticed the lighted porthole above him, the eyes gazing down on him. Then he let the black waves take him away again.

Slowly, in the darkness, the blisters formed across the skin, and the bruised feet and shoulders stiffened. The sweat dried on the body, and the cool air in the overheated lungs began its work. The healing sorceries of oxygen and rest pumped life back into the arteries and veins and recharged the nerves.

An eternity later, Bond awoke. He stirred. Agonizingly, he turned over on his stomach and snaked a few yards away from the porthole above him. Then he reached for his lighter and lit it.

Ahead there was only the black full moon, the yawning circular mouth that led into the stomach of death. Bond put back the lighter. He took a deep breath and got to his hands and knees. The pain was no greater, only different. Slowly, stiffly, he winced forward. As he moved he flexed his fingers and toes, testing the pain. This pain is supportable, he argued to himself. If I had been in an airplane crash, they would only diagnose superficial contusions and burns. I would be out of the hospital in a few days. But nagging behind these reflections was the knowledge that he had not yet had the crash—that he was still on his way towards it. When would it come? What shape would it take? How much more was he to be softened up before he reached the real killing ground?

In the darkness the tiny red pinpoints he saw might have been a hallucination, specks before the eyes as a result of exhaustion. Bond stopped and screwed up his eyes. He shook his head. No, the specks were still there. He edged closer. Now they were moving. Bond stopped again. He listened. Above the quiet thumping of his heart there was a soft delicate rustling. The tiny spots had increased in number. Bond reached for his lighter and lit the little yellow flame. The red pinpoints went out. Instead, a yard ahead of him, mesh wire blocked the shaft.

Bond inched forward, the lighter held before him. There was some sort of a cage with small things living in it. He could hear them scuttling back, away from the light. A foot from the mesh he doused the light and waited for his eyes to get used to the dark. As he waited, listening, he could hear the tiny scuttling back towards him, and gradually the forest of red pinpoints gathered again, peering at him through the mesh.

What was it? Bond listened to the pounding of his heart. Snakes? Scorpions? Centipedes?

Carefully he brought his eyes close up to the little glowing forest. He inched the lighter up beside his face and suddenly pressed the lever. He caught a glimpse of tiny claws, of thick furry feet and of furry saclike stomachs.

Bond squinted through the mesh, moving the flame back and forward. Then he doused the light and let the breath come through his teeth in a quiet sigh.

They were spiders—giant tarantulas—three or four inches long. There were twenty of them in the cage. And somehow he had

to get past them. Bond lay and rested and thought while the red eyes gathered again in front of his face.

How deadly were these things? They could certainly kill animals, but how mortal to men were these giant spiders with fur?

But again, would this be Doctor No's killing ground? A bite or two, perhaps—to send one into a delirium of pain. The horror of having to burst through the mesh in the darkness—Doctor No would not have reckoned with Bond's lighter—and squash through the forest of soft, biting bodies!

But Bond had the lighter and the knife and the wire spear. All he needed was the nerve—and infinite, infinite precision.

Bond softly opened the jaws of the lighter and pulled the wick out an inch to give a bigger flame. He lit it, and as the spiders scuttled back he pierced the mesh wire with his knife. He made a hole and seized the flap of wire and wrenched it out of the frame. It tore like stiff calico and came away in one piece. He put the knife back between his teeth and snaked through the opening. The spiders cowered before the flame of the lighter and crowded back on top of one another. Bond slid the wire spear out of his trousers and jabbed the blunt, doubled wire into the middle of them. He jabbed again and again, fiercely pulping the bodies, bashing into the writhing, sickening mess of blood and fur.

Slowly all movement slackened and then ceased. Were they all dead? The flame of the lighter was dying. He would have to chance it. Bond reached forward and slashed open the second curtain of wire, bending it down over the bodies. The light flickered and became a red glow. Bond gathered himself and shot his body over the bloody corpses and through the jagged frame.

All he knew was that he had got through. He heaved himself yards on along the metal shaft and stopped to gather his breath and his nerve.

Above him a light came on. Bond squinted upwards, knowing what he would see. The slanting eyes behind the glass looked keenly down at him. Slowly, behind the bulb, the head moved from side to side. The eyelids dropped in mock pity. A fist, the thumb pointing downwards in farewell, inserted itself between the bulb and the glass. Then it was withdrawn. The light went out. Bond turned his face back to the floor of the shaft. The gesture said that he was coming into the last lap, that the observers had finished with him until they came for his remains. They only wanted him to die, and as miserably as possible.

Bond's teeth ground softly together. He thought of the girl, and the thought gave him strength. He wasn't dead yet. Damn it, he wouldn't die!

Bond tensed his muscles. It was time to go. With extra care

he put his weapons back in their places and painfully dragged himself on into the blackness.

The shaft was beginning to slope gently downwards. It made the going easier. Soon the slope grew steeper, so that Bond could almost slide along. It was a blessed relief not to have to make the effort with his muscles. There was a glimmer of gray light ahead, and the air seemed to have a new, fresh smell to it. What was it? The sea?

Suddenly Bond realized that he was slipping down the shaft. He spread his shoulders and his feet to slow himself. But the shaft was widening. He could no longer get a grip! He was going faster and faster. A bend was just ahead. And it was a bend downwards!

Bond's body crashed into the bend and round it. He was diving head downwards! He was out of control, diving, diving down a gun barrel. Far below there was a circle of gray light. The open air? The sea? The light was tearing up at him. He fought for breath. Stay alive, you fool! Stay alive!

Headfirst, Bond's body shot out of the shaft and fell through the air, slowly, slowly, down towards the gunmetal sea that waited for him a hundred feet below.

Bond's body shattered the dawn sea like a bomb.

As he had hurtled down the shaft towards the widening disk of light, instinct had told him to get his knife from between his teeth, to get his hands forward to break his fall and to keep his head down and his body rigid. So Bond hit the water in the semblance of a dive, and though by the time he had shot twenty feet below the surface he had lost consciousness, the forty-mile-an-hour impact with the water failed to smash him.

Slowly the body rose to the surface and lay, head down, rocking in the ripples. The water-choked lungs somehow contrived to send a last message to the brain. The legs and arms thrashed. The head turned up and, coughing horribly, jerked above the surface and stayed there. The bloodshot eyes saw the lifeline and told the sluggish brain to make for it.

The killing ground was a narrow deep-water inlet at the base of the towering cliff. The lifeline towards which Bond struggled, hampered by the spear in his trouser leg, was a strong wire fence, stretched from the rock walls of the inlet and caging it off from the open sea. The two-foot squares of thick wire were suspended from a cable six feet above the surface and disappeared, algae encrusted, into the depths.

Bond got to the wire and hung, crucified. For fifteen minutes he stayed like that, until he felt strong enough to turn his racked body and see where he was. Blearily his eyes took in the towering cliffs above him and the narrow V of water. The place was in deep gray shadow, cut off from the dawn by the mountain, but out at sea there was the pearly iridescence of first light.

Sluggishly, Bond's mind puzzled over the wire fence. What was its purpose, closing off this dark cleft of sea? Was it to keep things out or keep them in? Bond gazed down. The wire strands vanished into nothingness below his clinging feet. There were small fish round his legs. What were they doing? They seemed to be feeding, darting in towards him and then backing away, catching at black strands. Strands of what? Bond shook his head to clear it. He looked again. They were feeding off his blood.

Bond shivered. Yes, blood was seeping off his body, off the torn shoulders, the knees, into the water. Now for the first time he felt the pain of the seawater on his sores and burns. The pain revived him. If these small fish liked it, what about barracuda and shark? Was that what the wire fence was for, to keep man-eating fish from escaping to sea?

The first thing was to crawl up the wire and get over to the other side. To put the fence between him and whatever lived in this black aquarium.

Weakly, foothold by foothold, Bond climbed up the wire and over the top and down again. Well above the water, he hooked the thick cable under his arms and hung there like a bit of washing on a line.

Now there was nothing much left of Bond, not many reserves. He was on the verge of surrender, of slipping back into the soft arms of the water. How beautiful it would be to give in at last and rest—to feel the sea softly take him to its bed and turn out the light.

It was the explosive flight of the fish from their feeding ground that shook Bond out of his death dreaming. Something had moved far below the surface on the landward side of the fence.

Bond's body tautened. With the electric shock of danger, life flooded back into him, driving out the lethargy.

Bond uncramped the fingers that a long time ago his brain had ordered not to lose his knife. He flexed his fingers and took a fresh grip of the handle. He reached down and touched the crook of the wire spear that still hung inside his trouser leg. He shook his head and focused his eyes. Now what?

The water quivered. Something was stirring in the depths, something huge. A great length of luminescent grayness showed, poised far down in the darkness. Something snaked up from it, a whiplash as thick as Bond's arm. Then two eyes as big as footballs slowly swam up and into Bond's vision. They stopped twenty feet below him and stared up through the quiet water at his face.

Bond's skin crawled on his back. Softly, wearily, his mouth uttered one bitter four-letter word. So this was the last surprise of Doctor No, the end of the race!

Bond stared down half hypnotized into the wavering pools of eye far below. So this was the giant squid, the mythical kraken that could pull ships beneath the waves, the fifty-foot-long monster that battled with whales, that weighed a ton or more. What else did he know about them? That they had two long seizing tentacles and ten holding ones. That they had a huge blunt beak beneath the eyes. That explosive harpoons burst in their jellied mantle without damaging them. That— But the bulging black and white targets of the eyes were rising up towards him. The surface of the water shivered. Now Bond could see the forest of tentacles that flowered out of the face of the thing. They were weaving in front of its eyes like a bunch of thick snakes. Bond could see the dots of the suckers on their undersides. Behind the head the jellied sheen of the body disappeared into the depths. God! The thing was as big as a railway engine!

Softly, discreetly, Bond snaked his feet and then his arms through the squares in the wire, lacing himself into them and anchoring himself. He squinted to right and left. Either way it was twenty yards along the wire to the land. And movement, even if he were capable of it, would be fatal. He must stay dead quiet and pray that the thing would lose interest. If it didn't . . . Softly, Bond's fingers clenched on the puny knife.

The eyes watched him coldly, patiently. Delicately, like the questing trunk of an elephant, one of the long seizing tentacles broke the surface and felt its way up the wire towards his leg. It reached his foot and then walked slowly on up the leg. It got to the bloody kneecap and stopped there, interested. Bond could imagine the message going back down the tentacle to the brain: Yes, it's good to eat! And the brain signaling back: Then get it! Bring it to me!

The suckers walked on up the thigh. A breeze, the first soft breeze of early morning, whispered across the surface of the inlet. A wedge of cormorants took off from the *guanera*. As they swept over, the noise that had disturbed them reached Bond—the triple blast of a ship's siren that means it is ready to take on cargo. It came from Bond's left. The jetty must be beyond that arm of the inlet. The tanker from Antwerp had come in. Antwerp! Part of the world outside—the world that was a million miles away, out of Bond's reach. Just round that corner, men would be in the galley, having breakfast. There would be the sizzle of bacon and eggs, the smell of coffee . . . breakfast cooking. . . .

The suckers were at his hip. Bond could see into the horny cups. A stagnant sea smell reached him. How tough was the mottled gray-brown jelly behind the tentacle? Should he stab? No, it must be a quick hard slash, straight across, like cutting a rope. Never mind about cutting into his own skin.

Now! Bond took a quick glance into the two football eyes. As he did so, the other seizing arm broke the surface and shot straight up at his face. Bond jerked back, and the arm curled round the wire in front of his eyes. In a second it would shift to his thigh or shoulder and he would be finished. Now!

The first tentacle was on his ribs. Without taking aim, Bond's knife hand slashed down and across. He felt the blade bite into the puddingy flesh, and then the knife was almost torn from his grip as the wounded tentacle whipped back into the water. Below him the water boiled and foamed. Now the head of the squid had broken the surface, and the sea was being thrashed by the great heaving mantle round it. The eyes were glaring up at him redly, venomously, and the forest of feeding arms was at his feet and legs, tearing the fabric away and flailing back. Bond was being

pulled down inch by inch. The wire was biting into his armpits. He could even feel his spine being stretched. If he held on, he would be torn in half. Now the eyes and the great triangular beak were right out of the water, and the beak was reaching up for his feet. There was one hope, only one!

Bond thrust his knife between his teeth, and his hand dived for the crook of the wire spear. He tore it out, got it between his two hands and wrenched the doubled wire almost straight.

Now, before he died of the pain! Now, now!

Bond let his body slip down the ladder of wire, and he lunged through and down with all his force.

He caught a glimpse of the tip of his spear lancing into the center of a black eyeball, and then the whole sea erupted up at him in a fountain of blackness and he fell and hung from the wire upside down by the knees, his head an inch from the surface of the water.

What had happened? Had he gone blind? He could see nothing. But he could feel the wire cutting into the tendons behind his knees. So he must be alive! Dazedly, Bond let go the spear from his hand and reached up and felt for the nearest strand of wire. Slowly, agonizingly, he pulled himself up so that he was sitting on the fence. He wiped a hand across his face. Now he could see. He looked down at his body. It was covered with black slime, and blackness stained the sea for twenty yards around. Then Bond realized. The squid had emptied its ink sac at him.

But where was the squid? Bond searched the sea. Nothing, nothing but the spreading stain of black. Not a movement. Not a ripple. Then don't wait! Get away from here! Quick! Wildly, Bond looked to right and left. Left was towards the ship. To build the wire fence the men must have come from the left, from the direction of the jetty. There would be some sort of a path. Bond reached for the top cable and frantically edged along the fence towards the rocky headland twenty yards away.

Bond got to the rock face. Slowly he let himself down to the bottom rung of wire. He gazed vaguely at the water. It was black, impenetrable, as deep as the rest. Should he chance it? He must! He could do nothing until he had washed off the horrible smelly slime. Moodily he took off the rags of his shirt and trousers and hung them on the wire. He looked down at his body, striped and pockmarked with red. On an instinct he felt his pulse. It was slow but regular. The steady thump of life revived his spirits. What the hell was he worrying about? He was alive. Get on. Get moving! Clean yourself and wake up. Count your blessings. Think of the girl. Think of the man you've got to find and kill. Get down into the water and wash!

Ten minutes later, Bond, his wet rags clinging to his scrubbed, stinging body, climbed over the top of the headland.

Yes, it was as he had guessed. A narrow rocky track, made by the feet of the workers, led down the other side and round the bulge of the cliff.

From close by came various sounds. A crane was working. He could hear the changing beat of its engine.

Bond looked up at the sky. It was pale blue. Clouds tinged with golden pink were trailing away towards the horizon. It would be about six o'clock, the dawn of a beautiful day.

Bond, leaving drops of blood behind him, picked his way carefully down the track and along the bottom of the shadowed cliff. Round the bend the track filtered through a maze of giant tumbled boulders. The noises grew louder. Bond crept softly forward. A voice called out, startlingly close, "Okay to go?"

There was a distant answer. "Okay." The crane engine accelerated. A few more yards. One more boulder. Now!

Bond flattened himself against the rock and warily inched his head round the corner.

Chapter 11

BOND took one long comprehensive look and pulled back.

He leaned against the rock and waited for his breathing to get back to normal. He lifted his knife and examined the blade. Satisfied, he slipped it behind him and down the waistband of his trousers. Then Bond meticulously went over the photograph that was in his brain.

Round the corner, not more than ten yards away, was the crane. There was no back to the cabin. Inside it a man sat at the controls. It was the driver of the marsh buggy. In front of him the jetty ran twenty yards out to sea and ended in a T. An aged tanker of around ten thousand tons was secured alongside the top of the T, its decks perhaps twelve feet above the quay. The tanker was called *Blanche*, and the ANT of ANTWERP showed at her stern. There was no sign of life on board except one figure lolling at the wheel in the enclosed bridge. The rest of the crew would be below, battened away from the guano dust. From just to the right of the crane an overhead conveyor belt in a corrugated-iron housing ran out from the cliff face. It was carried on high stanchions above the jetty and stopped just short of the hold of the tanker. Its mouth ended in a huge canvas sock perhaps six feet in diameter. The purpose of the crane was to lift the wire-framed mouth of the sock so that it hung directly over the hold of the tanker, and to move it to right or left to give even distribution. From out of the mouth of the sock, in a solid downward jet, the scrambled-egg-colored guano dust was pouring into the hold of the tanker at a rate of tons a minute.

Below, on the jetty, to the left and to leeward of the drifting smoke of the guano dust, stood the tall, watchful figure of Doctor No, seeing that all went well.

That was all. The morning breeze feathered the deep-water anchorage, still half in shadow beneath the towering cliffs; the conveyor belt thudded quietly on its rollers; the crane's engine chuffed rhythmically. There was no other sound, no other movement, no other life. On the other side of the mountain, men would be working, feeding the guano to the conveyor belt that rumbled away through the bowels of the rock, but on this side no one was allowed and no one was necessary. Apart from aiming the canvas mouth of the conveyor, there was nothing else for anyone to do.

Bond sat and thought, measuring distances, guessing at angles, remembering exactly where the crane driver's hands and feet were on the levers. Slowly a thin, hard smile broke across the haggard face. Yes! It could be done. But softly, gently! The prize was almost intolerably sweet.

Bond reached back and felt the handle of the knife. Shifting it an inch, he took several deep breaths. Then he gave a final flex to his fingers. He was ready.

Bond stepped up to the rock and inched an eye around. Nothing had changed. The crane driver was watchful, absorbed. The neck above the open khaki shirt was naked, waiting. Twenty yards away, Doctor No, also with his back to Bond, stood sentry over the cataract of whitish yellow dust. On the bridge, the man at the wheel was lighting a cigarette.

Bond looked along the ten yards of path that led past the crane. Then he came out from behind the rock and ran.

Bond ran to the right of the crane, to a point he had chosen where the side of the cabin would hide him from the driver and the jetty. He got there and stopped, crouching, listening. The engine hurried on, the conveyor belt rumbled steadily out of the mountain above him. There was no change.

The two iron footholds at the back of the cabin, inches away from Bond's face, looked solid. Anyway, the noise of the engine would drown small sounds. But the single stroke of the knife would have to be mortal. Bond felt along his own collarbone, felt the soft triangle of skin beneath which the jugular pumped, reminded himself to force the blade and hold it in.

For a final second he listened; then he reached behind his back for the knife and went up the iron steps and into the cabin. Standing behind the man's back, he swept the blade downwards and into the square inch of smooth brownish yellow skin.

Bond grabbed him with his left arm as the man's hands and legs splayed away from the controls. Then a strangled noise came from the mouth and the big body crashed to the floor.

Bond's eyes didn't even follow it as far as the ground. He was already in the seat and reaching for the pedals and levers. Everything was out of control. The engine was running in neutral, the wire hawser was tearing off the drum, the canvas mouth of the conveyor belt had wilted and was now pouring its column of dust between the jetty and the ship. Doctor No was staring upwards. His mouth was open. Perhaps he was shouting something.

Coolly, Bond reined the machine in, easing the levers back to the angles at which the driver had been holding them. The engine accelerated, the gears began to work again. The canvas mouth came up and over the ship. The tip of the crane lifted and stopped. The scene was as before. Now!

Bond reached forward for the iron wheel which the driver had been handling when Bond had caught his first glimpse of him.

Which way to turn it? He tried turning it to the left. The tip of the crane veered right. So be it. Bond spun the wheel to the right. Yes, by God, it was answering, moving across the sky, carrying the mouth of the conveyor with it.

Bond's eyes flashed to the jetty. Doctor No had moved a few paces to a stanchion. He had a telephone in his hand. He was trying to get through to the other side of the mountain. Bond could see his hand frantically jiggling the receiver arm.

Bond whirled the director wheel. God, wouldn't it turn any faster?

In seconds Doctor No would get through and it would be too late. Slowly the tip of the crane arced across the sky. Now the mouth of the conveyor was spewing the dust column down over the side of the ship. Now the yellow mound was marching silently across the jetty. Five yards, four, three, two! Don't look around, you bastard! Arrh, got you! Stop the wheel! Now, *you* take it, Doctor No!

At the first brush of the stinking dust column, Doctor No had turned. Bond saw the long arms fling wide as if to embrace the thudding mass. One knee rose to run. The mouth opened, and a thin scream came up to Bond above the noise of the engine. Then there was a brief glimpse of a kind of dancing snowman. And then only a mound of yellow bird dung that grew higher and higher.

"God!" Bond's voice gave back an iron echo from the walls of the cabin.

Now the yellow mountain was twenty feet high. The stuff was spilling off the sides of the jetty. Bond glanced at the ship. As he did so, there came three blasts on its siren and a fourth blast which didn't stop. Bond took his hands off the controls and let them rip. It was time to go. But first he slipped off the iron seat and bent over the dead body and took the revolver out of the holster. He smiled grimly—Smith & Wesson .38. He slipped it down inside his waistband.

He went to the door of the cabin and dropped to the ground.

An iron ladder ran up the cliff behind the crane to where the conveyor housing jutted out. There was a door in the corrugated-iron wall of the housing. Bond scrambled up the ladder. The door opened easily, letting out a puff of guano dust, and he clambered through.

Inside, the clanking of the conveyor belt over its rollers was deafening, but there were dim inspection lights in the ceiling of the tunnel, and a catwalk that stretched away into the mountain alongside the river of dust. Bond moved quickly along it, breathing shallowly against the fishy smell. At all costs he must get to the end before the significance of the ship's siren and of the unanswered telephone overcame the fear of the guards.

Bond ran and stumbled through the echoing, stinking tunnel. How far would it be? Two hundred yards? And then what? Nothing for it but to break out of the tunnel mouth and start shooting—cause a panic and hope for the best. He would get hold of one of the men and wring out of him where the girl was. Then what? When he got to the place on the mountainside, what would he find? What would be left of her?

Bond ran on faster, his head down, watching the narrow breadth of planking beside the rushing river of guano dust. When Bond's head hit into the soft stomach and he felt the hands at his throat, it was too late to think of his revolver. He threw himself down and forward at the legs. The legs gave, and there was a shrill scream as the body crashed down on his back.

Bond had started the heave that would hurl his attacker onto the conveyor belt when the quality of the scream and something light and soft about the body froze his muscles.

It couldn't be!

As if in answer, sharp teeth bit deeply into the calf of his right leg. Bond yelled. Even as he shouted "Honey!" an elbow thudded into his groin.

The breath whistled through Bond's teeth with agony. There was only one way to stop her without throwing her onto the conveyor belt. He took a firm grip of one ankle and stood upright, holding her slung over his shoulder by one leg. The other foot banged against his head, but halfheartedly, as if she, too, realized that something was wrong.

"Stop it, Honey! It's me!"

Through the din of the conveyor belt, Bond's shout got through to her. He heard her cry "James!" from somewhere near the floor. He felt her hands clutch at his legs. "James, James!"

Bond slowly let her down. He turned and knelt and reached for her. "Oh, Honey, Honey. Are you all right?" Desperately, unbelieving, he strained her to him.

"Yes, James! Oh, yes!" He felt her hands at his back and hair. "Oh, James, darling!" She fell against him, sobbing.

"It's all right, Honey." Bond smoothed her hair. "Doctor No's dead. But now we've got to run for it. Come on! How can we get out of the tunnel? How did you get here? We've got to hurry!"

As if in comment, the conveyor belt stopped with a jerk.

Bond pulled the girl to her feet. She was wearing a dirty suit of workmen's blue dungarees, far too big for her. The sleeves and legs were rolled up. She said breathlessly, "Just up there! There's a side tunnel that leads to the machine shops and the garage."

There was no time to talk. Bond said urgently, "Follow me!" and started running. They came to the fork where the side tunnel led off into the rock. Which way would the men come? Down the side tunnel, or along the catwalk in the main tunnel? The sound of voices booming far up the side tunnel answered him. Bond drew the girl a few feet up the main tunnel. He brought her close to him and whispered, "I'm sorry, Honey. I'm afraid I'm going to have to kill them."

"Of course." The answering whisper was matter-of-fact. She pressed his hand and stood back to give him room.

Bond eased the gun out of his waistband. Softly he broke the cylinder and verified with his thumb that all six chambers were loaded. The voices were coming closer. Now he could hear their shoes scuffing the ground.

A first man came out, then a second, then a third. They were carrying their revolvers loosely in their right hands. Bond shot the rear man in the head and the second man in the stomach. The front man's gun was up. A bullet whistled past Bond and away up the main tunnel. Bond's gun crashed. The man clutched at his neck and spun around and fell across the conveyor belt. A puff of fine dust rose in the air and settled.

Bond tucked his hot gun into the waistband of his trousers. He reached for the girl's hand and pulled her after him into the side tunnel. He said, "Sorry about that, Honey," and started running, pulling her after him. There was no sound but the thud of their naked feet on the stone floor.

It was easier going in the side tunnel, but after the tension of the shooting, pain began to crowd in again and take possession of Bond's body. He ran automatically, his whole mind focused on taking the pain and on the problems that waited at the end of the tunnel. His only plan was to shoot anyone who got in his way and somehow get to the garage and the marsh buggy. That was their only hope of getting away from the mountain and down to the coast.

Behind him Honey stumbled. Bond stopped, cursing himself for not having thought of her. She leaned against him, panting. "I'm sorry, James. It's just that . . ."

Bond said anxiously, "Are you hurt, Honey?"

"No. It's just that I'm terribly tired. And my feet got cut on the mountain. If we could walk a bit . . . We're nearly there."

Bond put his arm round her waist and took her weight. He didn't trust himself to look at her feet. He knew they must be bad. They started moving again, Bond's face grim with the extra effort, the girl's feet leaving bloody footsteps on the ground. Almost immediately she whispered urgently, pointing at a wooden door in the wall of the tunnel that was ajar.

Bond took out his gun and gently eased the door open. The long garage was empty. Under the neon lights stood the black and gold painted dragon. It was pointing towards the sliding doors, and the hatch of the armored cabin stood open. Bond prayed that the tank was full.

Suddenly from somewhere outside there was the sound of voices. They came nearer, jabbering urgently.

Bond took the girl by the hand and ran forward. There was only one place to hide—in the marsh buggy. The girl scrambled in. Bond followed, pulling the door shut. They crouched, waiting. Bond thought, Only three rounds left in the gun. Too late he remembered the rack of weapons on the wall of the garage. There came the clang of the door being slid on its runners, and a confusion of talk.

"Better take rifles. Here, Joe! An' some pineapples. Box under de table."

There was the metallic noise of bolts being slid home. More rattling, then, "Okay, let's go! Two abreast till we get to de main tunnel. Shoot at de legs."

Feet echoed on the concrete. Bond held his breath. Would they notice the shut door of the buggy? But they went on into the tunnel and their noise faded away.

Bond touched the girl and put his finger to his lips. Softly he eased open the door and listened again. Nothing. He dropped to the ground and walked to the half-open entrance and edged his head around. There was no one in sight. Dishes and pans clattered in the nearest building, about twenty yards away, and from one of the farther Quonsets came the sound of a guitar and a man's voice singing a calypso. Dogs started to bark halfheartedly and then were silent. The Doberman pinschers.

Bond turned and ran back to the end of the garage. No sound came from the tunnel. Bond closed the tunnel door and bolted it. He went to the arms rack and chose another Smith & Wesson and a U.S. Army carbine. He verified that they were loaded and went to the marsh buggy and handed them in to the girl. Now the entrance door. Bond put his shoulder to it and eased it wide open. Then he ran back and scrambled through the hatch and into the driver's seat. "Shut it, Honey," he whispered urgently, and turned the ignition key.

The needle on the gauge swung to FULL. Pray God the damned thing would start up quickly. Some diesels were slow. Bond stamped his foot on the starter. The engine fluttered and died. And again, but this time the blessed thing fired and the strong iron pulse hammered. Now into gear. Which one? Try this. Yes, it bit. And now they were out and on the track, and Bond rammed his foot down to the floor.

"Anyone after us?" Bond shouted above the noise of the diesel.

"No. Wait! Yes, there's a man come out of the huts! And another! They're shouting at us. Now some more are coming out. One of them's got a rifle. He's lying down. He's firing!"

"Close the slot! Lie down on the floor!" Bond glanced at the speedometer. Twenty. And they were on a slope. There was nothing more to get out of the machine. Bond concentrated on keeping the huge bucking wheels on the track. The cabin bounced and swayed on the springs. It was a job to keep his hands and feet on the controls. An iron fist clanged against the cabin. And another. What was the range? Four hundred? Good shooting! But that would be the lot. He shouted, "Take a look, Honey! Open the slot an inch."

"The man's got up. He's stopped firing. They're all looking after us—a whole crowd of them. Wait, there's something else. The dogs are coming after us! There's no one with them. They're just tearing down the track. Will they catch us?"

"Doesn't matter if they do. Come and sit by me, Honey. Hold tight. Mind your head against the roof." Bond eased up on the throttle. He grinned sideways at her. "Hell, Honey. We've made it. When we get down to the lake I'll stop and shoot up the dogs. If I know those brutes, I've only got to kill one and the whole pack'll stop to eat him."

Bond felt her hand at his neck. She kept it there as they swayed and thundered down the track. At the lake, Bond went on fifty yards into the water and turned the machine around and put it in neutral. Through the oblong slot he could see the pack streaming round the last bend. He reached down for the rifle. Now the dogs were in the water and swimming. Bond sprayed bullets into the middle of them. One floundered, kicking. Then another. He could hear their snarling screams above the engine. A fight had started. He saw one dog leap on one of the wounded ones and sink its teeth into its neck. Now they all seemed to have gone berserk. They were milling around in the frothing bloody water.

Bond dropped the gun. He said, "That's that, Honey," and put the machine into gear and began rolling across the lake towards the mouth of the river.

For five minutes they moved along in silence. Then Bond put a hand on the girl's knee and said, "We should be all right now, Honey. When they find the boss is dead there'll be panic. I guess some of the brighter ones will try and get away to Cuba. They'll worry about their skins, not about us. All the same, we'll not take the canoe out until it's dark. I guess it's about ten by now. We should be at the coast in an hour. Then we'll rest up for the trip. Weather looks all right and there'll be a bit more moon tonight. Think you can make it?"

Her hand squeezed his neck. "Of course I can, James. But what about you? Your poor body! It's nothing but burns and bruises. And what are those red marks across your stomach?"

"Tell you later. I'll be okay. But you tell me what happened to you last night. How in hell did you manage to get away from the crabs? All night long I could only think of you out there being eaten to death."

The girl was actually laughing.

"That man thought he knew everything. Silly old fool. He's much more impressed by the black crabs than I am. To begin with, I don't mind any animal touching me, and anyway, those crabs wouldn't think of even nipping someone if they stay quite still and haven't got an open sore or anything. The whole point is that they don't really like meat. They live mostly on plants and things. If he was right and he did kill a girl that way, either she had an open wound or she must have died of fright. Filthy old man. I only fainted down there at dinner because I knew he'd have something much worse for you."

"Well, I'm damned. I wish to heaven I'd known that. I thought of you being picked to pieces."

The girl snorted. "Of course it wasn't very nice being tied down to pegs. But those men didn't dare touch me. They just made jokes and went away. It was uncomfortable on the rock, but I was thinking of you and of how I could get at Doctor No and kill him. Then I heard the crabs beginning to run, and soon they came rattling along—hundreds. I lay still, and they walked round me and over me. They tickled a bit. But they don't smell or anything, and I just waited for the early morning when they go to sleep. Finally they stopped coming and I could move. I pulled at all the pegs. In the end I got my right hand free, and the rest was easy. I got back to the buildings and began scouting about.

"I went into the machine shop near the garage and found this filthy old suit. Then the conveyor thing started up and I thought about it and I guessed it must be taking the guano through the mountain. I imagined you must be dead by then"—the quiet voice was matter-of-fact—"so I thought I'd get to the conveyor somehow and get through the mountain and kill Doctor No." She giggled. "I took a screwdriver to do it with. When we ran into each other, I'd have stuck it into you, only it was in my pocket and I couldn't get to it! That's all." She caressed the back of his neck again. "Darling, I hope I didn't hurt you too much when we were fighting."

Bond laughed. He reached out and pulled her face to him. Her mouth locked itself against his.

The machine gave a sideways lurch. The kiss ended. They had hit the first mangrove roots at the entrance to the river.

Chapter 12

"You're quite sure of all this?"

The acting governor's eyes were hunted, resentful. How could these things have been going on under his nose, in one of Jamaica's dependencies?

"Yes, sir. Quite sure," said Bond.

"Er—well, we mustn't let any of this get out to the press. You understand that? I'll send my report in to the Secretary of State by the next bag. I'm sure I can rely on your—"

"Excuse me, sir." The brigadier in command of the Caribbean Defense Force was a modern young soldier of thirty-five. He was unimpressed by relics from the Edwardian era of colonial governors, whom he collectively referred to as "feather-hatted fuddy-duddies." "I think we can assume that Commander Bond is unlikely to communicate with anyone except his department. And, sir, I submit that we should take steps to clear up Crab Key without waiting for approval from London. I can provide a platoon ready to embark by this evening. HMS *Narvik* came in yesterday. If the program of receptions and cocktail parties for her could possibly be deferred for forty-eight hours or so . . ." The brigadier let his sarcasm hang in the air.

"I agree with the brigadier, sir." The voice of the police superintendent was edgy. Quick action might save him from a reprimand, but it would have to be quick. "In any case, I shall have to proceed immediately against the various Jamaicans who appear to be implicated. I'll have to get the divers working at Mona. If this is to be cleaned up, we can't afford to wait for London. As Mr.—er—Commander Bond says, most of these gangsters will probably be in Cuba by now. Have to get in touch with my opposite number in Havana and catch up with them before they take to the hills. I think we ought to move at once, sir."

There was silence in the cool shadowy room where the meeting was being held. Far away there was the sound of tennis balls being knocked about. Distantly a young girl's voice called, "Smooth. Your serve, Gladys." The governor's children? Secretaries? From one end

641

of the room, King George VI, from the other end the Queen, looked down the table with grace and good humor.

"What do you think, Colonial Secretary?" The governor's voice was hushed.

Bond listened to the first few words. He soon gathered that Pleydell-Smith agreed with the other two. He stopped listening. His mind drifted into a world of tennis courts and lily ponds and kings and queens, of London, of people being photographed with pigeons on their heads in Trafalgar Square, of the forsythia that would soon be blazing on the bypass roundabouts, of May, the treasured housekeeper in his flat off the King's Road. And then Bond thought of Crab Key, of the hot ugly wind, of the stink of the mangrove swamps, and the jagged gray, dead coral. Up on the *guanera* the cormorants at this hour would be streaming back from their breakfast to deposit their ounce of rent to the landlord who would no longer be collecting. And where would the landlord be? The men from the *Blanche* would have dug him out. The body would have been examined for signs of life and then put somewhere. And where had Doctor No's soul gone to? Had it been a bad soul, or just a mad one?

Bond thought of Quarrel. He remembered the loyalty and even the love that Quarrel had given him—the warmth of the man. Surely he hadn't gone to the same place as Doctor No.

The Colonial Secretary was mentioning Bond's name. Bond pulled himself together.

"... survived is quite extraordinary. I do think, sir, that we should show our gratitude to Commander Bond and to his Service by accepting his recommendations. It does seem, sir, that he has done at least three-quarters of the job. Surely the least we can do is look after the other quarter."

The governor grunted. He squinted down the table at Bond. The chap didn't seem to be paying much attention. There was something to be said for sending the *Narvik*. News would leak, of course. Then suddenly the governor saw the headlines: GOVERNOR TAKES SWIFT ACTION ... THE NAVY'S THERE! Perhaps, after all, it would be better to do it that way. Even go down and see the troops off himself. Yes, that was it, by Jove. That was the way to play the hand. The governor embraced the conference with a wry smile of surrender.

"So I am overruled, gentlemen. Well, then"—the voice was avuncular, telling the children that just this once—"I accept your verdict. Colonial Secretary, will you call upon the commanding officer of HMS *Narvik* and explain the position. Brigadier, I leave the military arrangements in your hands." The governor rose. He inclined his head regally in the direction of Bond. "And it only remains to express my appreciation to Commander—er—Bond for his part in this affair."

OUTSIDE, the sun blazed down on the gravel sweep. The interior of the Austin A30 was a Turkish bath. Bond's bruised hands cringed as they took the wheel. Pleydell-Smith leaned through the window. "Is there anything else I can do for you? You really think you ought to go back to Beau Desert? They were quite definite at the hospital that they want to have you for a week."

"Thanks," said Bond shortly, "but I've got to get back. See the girl's all right. You got off that signal to my chief?"

"Urgent rates."

"Well, then"—Bond pressed the starter—"I guess that's the lot. You'll see the people at the Institute of Jamaica about the girl, won't you? She really knows a hell of a lot about natural history. If they've got the right sort of job ... Like to see her settled. I'll take her up to New York myself and see her through the operation. She'd be ready to start in a couple of weeks after that. Incidentally"—Bond looked embarrassed—"she's really a hell of a fine girl. When she comes back ... if you and your wife ... You know. Just so there's someone to keep an eye on her."

Pleydell-Smith smiled. "Don't worry about that. I'll see to it. Betty's rather a hand at that sort of thing. She'll like taking the girl under her wing."

"Thanks. And thanks for everything else." Bond put the car in gear and went off down the avenue lined with tropical shrubbery. He went fast, scattering gravel. He wanted to get the hell away from King's House, and the tennis, and the kings and queens. He even wanted to get the hell away from kindly Pleydell-Smith. All he wanted now was to get back across the Junction Road to Beau Desert. He swung out onto the main road and put his foot down.

The night voyage under the stars had been without incident. No one had come after them. The girl had done most of the sailing. Bond had not argued with her. He had lain in the bottom of the boat, totally collapsed, like a dead man. When they reached Morgan's Harbour she had had to help him out of the boat and across the lawn and into the house. He had clung to her and cursed her softly as she cut his clothes off him and took him into the shower. She had said nothing when she saw his battered body under the lights. She had turned the water full on and washed him down. Then there had been a wonderful breakfast as the dawn flared up across the bay, and then the ghastly drive over to Kingston to the emergency ward. Pleydell-Smith had been summoned. The doctor had written busily in his duty report. What? Probably just "multiple burns and contusions." Then, with promises that he would come into the private ward on the next day, Bond had gone off with Pleydell-Smith to King's House. He had enciphered a short message to M. via the Colonial Office, which he had coolly concluded with:

REGRET MUST AGAIN REQUEST SICK LEAVE STOP SURGEONS REPORT FOLLOWS STOP KINDLY INFORM ARMORER SMITH AND WESSON INEFFECTIVE AGAINST FLAMETHROWER

Now, as Bond swung the little car down the S-bends towards the north shore, he regretted the gibe. M. wouldn't like it. It was cheap. It wasted cipher groups. Oh well. Bond swerved to avoid a thundering red bus. He had just wanted M. to know that it hadn't quite been a holiday in the sun. He would apologize when he sent in his written report.

Bond's bedroom was cool and dark. There were a plate of sandwiches and a thermos of coffee beside the turned-down bed. On the pillow was a sheet of paper with big childish writing. It said, "You are staying with me tonight. I can't leave my animals. They were fussing. And I can't leave you. And you owe me slave time. I will come at seven. Your H."

In the dusk she came across the lawn to where Bond was sitting, finishing a bourbon on the rocks. She was wearing a black and white striped cotton skirt and a tight sugar-pink blouse. The golden hair smelled of cheap shampoo. She looked incredibly fresh and beautiful. She reached out her hand, and Bond took it and followed her up the drive and along a narrow well-trodden path through the sugarcane. Then there was a patch of tidy lawn up against thick broken stone walls, and steps that led down to a heavy door whose edges glinted with light.

She looked up at him from the door. "Don't be frightened. The cane's high and they're most of them out."

Bond didn't know what he had expected. He had vaguely thought of a flat earthen floor and damp walls. There would be a few sticks of furniture, a broken bedstead and a strong zoo smell.

Instead, it was rather like being inside a very large tidy cigar box. The floor and ceiling were of highly polished cedar, and the walls were paneled with split bamboo. The light came from a dozen candles in a fine silver chandelier. High up in the walls there were three square windows, through which Bond could see the stars. Under the chandelier a table was laid for two with expensive old-fashioned silver and glass.

Bond said, "Honey, what a lovely room. From what you said I thought you lived in a sort of zoo."

She laughed. "I got out the old silver and things. I've never had it out before. It does look rather nice, doesn't it?" She paused. "My bedroom's in there." She gestured at a door. "It's very small, but there's room for both of us. Now come on. I'm afraid it's cold dinner—just lobsters and fruit."

Bond walked over to her. He took her in his arms and held her and looked down into the shining blue eyes. "Honey, you're a wonderful girl. You're one of the most wonderful girls I've ever known. I hope the world's not going to change you too much. D'you really want to have that operation? I love your face—just as it is. It's part of you."

645

She frowned and freed herself. "You're not to be serious tonight. Don't talk about these things. This is my night with you. Please talk about love. Promise? Now come on. You sit there."

Bond sat down. He smiled up at her. He said, "I promise."

She said, "Here's the mayonnaise. I made it myself. And take some bread and butter." She sat down opposite him and began to eat, watching him. When she saw that he seemed satisfied she said, "Now you can start telling me about love. Everything about it. Everything you know."

Bond looked across into the flushed, golden face. The eyes were bright and soft in the candlelight, but with the same imperious glint they had held when he had first seen her on the beach and she had thought he had come to steal her shells.

"Well . . ." Bond found he couldn't eat any more. He said, "Honey, I can either eat or talk love to you. I can't do both."

"You're going to Kingston tomorrow. You'll get plenty to eat there. Talk love."

Bond's eyes were fierce blue slits. He got up and went down on one knee beside her. Their mouths met and clung, exploring.

Above them the candles began to dance. A big hawkmoth had come in. It whirred round the chandelier. The girl's eyes opened, looked at the moth. She got up, and without saying anything took down the candles one by one and blew them out. The moth whirred away through one of the windows.

The girl stood away from the table. She undid her blouse. Then she came to Bond and took him by the hand and lifted him up. She led him away from the table and through a door. The filtering moonlight shone down on a bed. On the bed was a sleeping bag, its mouth laid open.

The girl looked up at him. She said, practically, "I bought this sleeping bag today. It's a double one. It cost a lot of money. Take those off and get in. You promised. You owe me slave time."

"But . . ."

"Do as you're told."